# 29 SHORT STORIES
## an introductory anthology

Alfred A. Knopf            New York

edited by
**MICHAEL TIMKO**
Queens College of the
City University of New York

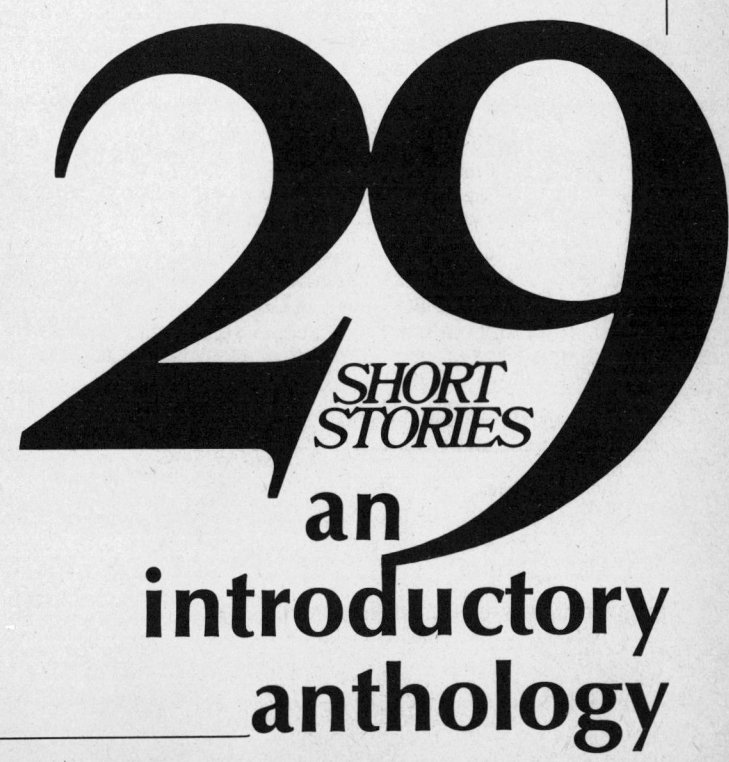

29 SHORT STORIES

an introductory anthology

For Hester Marie Peltier

Copyright © 1975 by Alfred A. Knopf, Inc.

All rights reserved under International and Pan-American Copyright Conventions. No part of this book may be reproduced in any form or by any means, electronic or mechanical, including photocopying, without permission in writing from the publisher. All inquiries should be addressed to Alfred A. Knopf, Inc., 201 East 50th Street, New York, N.Y. 10022. Published in the United States by Alfred A. Knopf, Inc., New York, and simultaneously in Canada by Random House of Canada Limited, Toronto. Distributed by Random House, Inc., New York.

Library of Congress Cataloging in Publication Data

Timko, Michael, 1925–   comp.
   Twenty-nine short stories.

   Includes index.
   1. Short stories.  2. Short story.  I. Title.
PZ1.T55Tw   [PN6014]         823'.01         74-31093
ISBN 0-394-31910-9

Manufactured in the United States of America.

First Edition
98765432

"Big Boy Leaves Home" by Richard Wright from *Uncle Tom's Cabin*. Copyright 1936 by Richard Wright; renewed 1964 by Ellen Wright. Reprinted by permission of Harper & Row, Publishers, Inc.

"The Blue Hotel" by Stephen Crane. Reprinted from *Twenty Stories* by Stephen Crane, by permission of Alfred A. Knopf, Inc. Copyright by Alfred A. Knopf, Inc., 1899, 1926.

"Christmas Song" by Langston Hughes from *The Best of Simple*, 1961. Copyright 1961 by Langston Hughes. Reprinted by permission of Farrar, Straus & Giroux, Inc.

"Clay" by James Joyce from *Dubliners*. Originally published in 1916 by B. W. Huebsch, Inc. Copyright 1967 by the Estate of James Joyce. All rights reserved. Reprinted by permission of The Viking Press, Inc.

"A Clean, Well-Lighted Place" (copyright 1933 Charles Scribner's Sons) reprinted by permission of Charles Scribner's Sons from *Winner Take Nothing* by Ernest Hemingway.

"A Completion of Personality" by Ralph Ellison from John Hersey, ed., *Ralph Ellison: A Collection of Critical Essays*. Copyright 1974, pp. 1–19. Reprinted by permission of Prentice-Hall, Inc., Englewood Cliffs, New Jersey.

"Cosmic Irony in Hardy's 'The Three Strangers'" by William Van O'Connor from *The English Journal*, May 1958. Copyright 1958 by the National Council of Teachers of English. Reprinted by permission of the publisher.

"Flying Home" by Ralph Ellison from Edwin Seaver, ed., *Cross Section*, 1944. Copyright renewed 1944 by Ralph Ellison. Reprinted by permission of William Morris Agency, Inc., on behalf of the author.

"The Forks" by J. F. Powers from *The Prince of Darkness and Other Stories* by J. F. Powers. Copyright 1947 by J. F. Powers. Reprinted by permission of Doubleday & Company, Inc.

"Gladius Dei" by Thomas Mann. Copyright 1936; renewed 1964 by Alfred A. Knopf, Inc. Reprinted from *Stories of Three Decades* by Thomas Mann, translated by H. T. Lowe-Porter, by permission of the publisher.

"A Good Man Is Hard to Find" by Flannery O'Connor. Copyright 1953 by Flannery O'Connor. Reprinted from her volume *A Good Man Is Hard to Find and Other Stories* by permission of Harcourt Brace Jovanovich, Inc.

"Gym Period" by Rainer Maria Rilke from *Primal Sound and Other Prose Pieces* by Rainer Maria Rilke. Reprinted by permission of the translator, Carl Niemeyer, and of Insel Verlag. Copyright 1961 by Insel Verlag, Frankfurt am Main. All rights reserved.

"He" by Katherine Anne Porter. Copyright 1930, 1958 by Katherine Anne Porter. Reprinted from her volume *Flowering Judas and Other Stories* by permission of Harcourt Brace Jovanovich, Inc.

"Hue and Cry" by James Alan McPherson. Copyright 1968, 1969 by James Alan McPherson. Reprinted by permission of Little, Brown and Company in association with *The Atlantic Monthly Press*.

"Legend and Symbol in Hardy's 'The Three Strangers'" by James L. Roberts. Copyright 1962 by The Regents of the University of California. Reprinted from *Nineteenth-Century Fiction* 17, No. 2, by permission of The Regents.

"Life for Phoenix" by Neil D. Isaacs from Sewanee Review 71, 1963, pp. 75–81. Copyright 1963 by the University of the South. Reprinted by permission of the editor.

# acknowledgments

"The Loves of Franklin Ambrose" by Joyce Carol Oates from *Playboy*, January 1972. Copyright 1972 by Joyce Carol Oates. Reprinted by permission of the author and her agent, Blanche C. Gregory, Inc.

"The Magic Barrel" by Bernard Malamud. Copyright 1954, 1958 by Bernard Malamud. Reprinted by permission of Farrar, Straus & Giroux, Inc.

"The Man With the Knives" by Heinrich Böll from *Children Are Civilians Too* by Heinrich Böll, translated by Leila Vennewitz. Copyright 1970 by Heinrich Böll. Reprinted by permission of McGraw-Hill Book Company.

"Margins" by Donald Barthelme from *Come Back, Dr. Caligari* by Donald Barthelme. Copyright 1964 by Donald Barthelme. Reprinted by permission of Little, Brown and Company in association with *The Atlantic Monthly Press*.

"Next Door" by Kurt Vonnegut, Jr. Copyright 1955 by Kurt Vonnegut, Jr. Originally published in *Cosmopolitan*. Reprinted from *Welcome to the Monkey House* by Kurt Vonnegut, Jr., with the permission of Seymour Lawrence, Delacorte Press.

"Richard Wright in a Moment of Truth" by Blyden Jackson from *The Southern Literary Journal* 2, June 1972. Copyright 1972 by *The Southern Literary Journal*.

"The Rocking-Horse Winner" by D. H. Lawrence from *The Complete Short Stories of D. H. Lawrence*. Copyright 1933 by the Estate of D. H. Lawrence; renewed 1961 by Angelo Ravagli and C. M. Weekley, Executors of the Estate of Frieds Lawrence Ravagli. All rights reserved. Reprinted by permission of The Viking Press, Inc.

"The Shape of the Sword" by Jorge Luis Borges, translated by Donald A. Yates. Reprinted from *Labyrinths, Selected Stories and Other Writings*, edited by Donald A. Yates and James E. Irby. Copyright 1962 by New Directions Publishing, Inc. Reprinted by permission of New Directions Publishing, Inc.

"The Soujourner" by Carson McCullers from *The Ballad of the Sad Café*, 1951. Copyright 1955 by Carson McCullers. Reprinted by permission of the publisher, Houghton Mifflin Company.

"Sonny's Blues" by James Baldwin from *Going to Meet the Man* by James Baldwin. Copyright 1957 by James Baldwin. Originally published in *Partisan Review*. Reprinted by permission of the publisher, The Dial Press.

"The Story of a Panic" by E. M. Forster from *The Collected Tales of E. M. Forster*. Published 1947 by Alfred A. Knopf, Inc. Reprinted by permission of the publisher.

"The Three Strangers" by Thomas Hardy from *Wessex Tales* by Thomas Hardy. Reprinted by permission of the trustees of the Hardy Estate and The Macmillan Company of Canada, Ltd.

"The Tree of Knowledge" by Henry James from *The Soft Side* by Henry James. Reprinted by permission of Alexander R. James, Literary Executor.

"Types of Narration" by Wayne Booth from *The Rhetoric of Fiction* by Wayne Booth, 1961. Reprinted by permission of The University of Chicago Press.

"Uncle T" by Brian Moore. Copyright 1960 by Brian Moore. Reprinted by permission of Collins Knowlton Wing, Inc.

"A Wagner Matinee" by Willa Cather. Reprinted from *Youth and the Bright Medusa* by Willa Cather, courtesy of Alfred A. Knopf, Inc.

"Wilhelm" by Gabrielle Roy from her volume *Streets of Riches*. Copyright 1957 by Gabrielle Roy. Reprinted by permission of Harcourt Brace Jovanovich, Inc.

"A Worn Path" by Eudora Welty from her volume *A Curtain of Green and Other Stories*. Copyright 1941, 1969 by Eudora Welty. Reprinted by permission of Harcourt Brace Jovanovich.

introduction ix

an anthology of short stories
## ISOLATION AND INVOLVEMENT 3

**Willa Cather** A Wagner Matinee 3
**James Baldwin** Sonny's Blues 10
**Katherine Anne Porter** He 36
**Kurt Vonnegut, Jr.** Next Door 44
**Ernest Hemingway** A Clean, Well-Lighted Place 51

## COWARDICE AND COURAGE 56

**Richard Wright** Big Boy Leaves Home 56
**Heinrich Boll** The Man with the Knives 87
**Jorge Luis Borges** The Shape of the Sword 95
**Stephen Crane** The Blue Hotel 99
**Brian Moore** Uncle T 122

## LOVE AND DESIRE 138

**Bernard Malamud** The Magic Barrel 138
**James Alan McPherson** Hue and Cry 152
**James Joyce** Clay 185
**Henry James** The Tree of Knowledge 191

## FAITH AND FATE 203

**Thomas Hardy** The Three Strangers 203
**Thomas Mann** Gladius Dei 221
**E. M. Forster** The Story of a Panic 232
**J. F. Powers** The Forks 250

## PREJUDICE AND PERCEPTION 262

**Gabrielle Roy** Wilhelm 262
**Flannery O'Connor** A Good Man Is Hard to Find 267
**Ralph Ellison** Flying Home 280
**Joyce Carol Oates** The Loves of Franklin Ambrose 296

# contents

## PARABLE AND ALLEGORY 307

    **Nathaniel Hawthorne**    The Minister's Black Veil    307
    **D. H. Lawrence**    The Rocking-Horse Winner    318
    **Donald Barthelme**    Margins    330

## THE HUMAN CONDITION 335

    **Rainer Maria Rilke**    Gym Period    335
    **Langston Hughes**    Christmas Song    339
    **Carson McCullers**    The Sojourner    342
    **Eudora Welty**    A Worn Path    350

## comments and criticism 359
Introduction    361

## CRITIC AND WRITER: TWO VIEWS 362

    **Wayne Booth**    Types of Narration    362
    **Ralph Ellison**    A Completion of Personality    375

## CRITICAL ESSAYS AND APPRAISALS 382

    **Blyden Jackson**    Richard Wright in a Moment of Truth    382
    **Neil Isaacs**    Life for Phoenix    393
    **W. Van O'Connor**    Cosmic Irony in Hardy's "The Three Strangers"    398
    **James L. Roberts**    Legend and Symbol in Hardy's "The Three Strangers"    407

## A GLOSSARY OF USEFUL TERMS 410

## AN INDEX OF AUTHORS AND TITLES 417

Reading fiction should be exciting and exhilarating. It should also be stimulating and rewarding. Above all, it should be a humanistic enterprise, one that increases the reader's awareness of human qualities and concerns. Years ago Matthew Arnold summarized what he felt to be the primary values of a classical education, and his words apply equally well to the reading of fiction. When we receive the results of science, Arnold said, we are still in "the sphere of intellect and knowledge." For him, these spheres were not enough: "There will be found to arise an invincible desire to relate [these results] to the sense in us for conduct, and to the sense in us for beauty." Fiction should indeed put us into relation with our sense for conduct, our sense for beauty; otherwise it may become for us, as did unrelated facts for Arnold, "unsatisfying" and "wearying."

If the selections in this anthology are not, in Arnold's words, "the best of what has been thought and said in the world," they do represent the best work of some of the acknowledged masters of the genre, and they illustrate a tremendous range of subject matter, technique, and theme. The grouping of the stories under headings such as "Isolation and Involvement" and "Cowardice and Courage" is by no means an attempt to narrow the reader's responses; on the contrary, it can enrich or broaden responses. A story by Willa Cather placed next to one by Kurt Vonnegut or James Baldwin offers the benefits of comparison and contrast, the advantage of seeing various narrative approaches and thematic concerns in juxtaposition. Surely there is something to be gained from having one of the early practitioners of the short story, Nathaniel Hawthorne, in the same group with one of England's greatest short story writers, D. H. Lawrence, and one of America's most exciting contemporary writers, Donald Barthelme.

Another point should be made, which is that the best of what has been written cannot really be categorized; it knows no bounds. Each of these stories could fit as well into another grouping, for each has the depth and richness that characterize the best fiction. Ralph Ellison, who, like Arnold, has always been concerned with humanistic values, expresses this transcendent quality in his comments on what he calls the "morality of fiction": "If the writer starts with anger," Ellison says, "then if he is truly writing he immediately translates it through his craft into consciousness, and thus into understanding, into in-

# introduction

sight, perception. Perhaps that's where the morality of fiction lies. You see a situation which outrages you, but as you write about the characters who embody that which outrages, your sense of craft and the moral role of your craft demands that you depict those characters in the breadth of their humanity. You try to give them the density of the human rather than the narrow intensity of the demonic." Herein, I think, lies the appeal and the ultimate triumph of these stories. The writers represented in the following pages are concerned not with the "narrow intensity of the demonic," but with "the density of the human." They are also concerned with the "moral role" of their craft.

Two of our most prominent contemporary critics have echoed this humanistic concern. "A piece of fiction," Cleanth Brooks and Robert Penn Warren have written, "is a tissue of significances, some great and some small, but all of them aspects, finally, of the total significance of the piece. And one must remember that this total significance is not merely some idea which can be abstracted from the 'story' and stated in general terms. It is the fact of the idea's living in action, in the 'story,' which makes the idea significant, for the underlying significance of all fiction may be the faith of the writer that experience itself is significant and not a mere flux of unrelated items. That is, in other terms, he has a faith that man is a responsible being, and he tries to validate this faith by the responsible and vital organization of his art."

To aid readers in their pursuit of both pleasure and reward, I have provided several complementary sections. The glossary of basic critical terms will seem superfluous to some, but there may be those who will find it helpful. Two other sections, "Critic and Writer: Two Views" and "Critical Essays and Appraisals," should prove valuable. The juxtaposition of a critic's comments on a technical aspect of fiction with a writer's own view of his craft provides one possible approach to the fiction. The analyses give clues to the stories under discussion and hint of ways to respond that are not simply emotional reactions but mature and responsible examinations of works that demand such responses.

The justification of *Twenty-Nine Short Stories* rests on the hope that readers will gain not only pleasure but also that perception, emphasized by Arnold, Ellison, and Brooks and Warren, which derives from the "density of the human"—the perception that is based, ultimately, on humanistic concerns and ideals. If *Twenty-Nine Short Stories* fulfills this hope, it will enable readers to approach that moment when they perceive "the underlying significance of all fiction."

# an anthology
## of short stories

# Isolation and Involvement

## A WAGNER MATINEE

**Willa Cather**

*Born in 1876 in Winchester, Virginia, Willa Cather spent her formative years in Nebraska, where she attended Red Cloud High School and then the University of Nebraska, from which she was graduated in 1895. She taught English in high school in Pittsburgh and worked for a time on the Pittsburgh* Daily Leader. *Her first volume of short stories,* The Troll Garden, *was published in 1905; in 1906 she moved to New York and became managing editor of McClure's Magazine. Six years later she resigned to devote full time to her writing, and in 1922 she was awarded the Pulitzer Prize for the novel* One of Ours. *Perhaps her best-known novels are* O Pioneers! *(1913),* My Antonia *(1918), and* Death Comes for the Archbishop *(1927). Her other works include the short story collections* Youth and the Bright Medusa *(1920), from which "A Wagner Matinee" is taken, and* The Old Beauty and Others, *published posthumously in 1948, a year after her death. Katherine Anne Porter, in her Afterword to* The Troll Garden, *summarized the qualities that distinguish "A Wagner Matinee" and the other writings of Willa Cather: "They still live with morning freshness in my memory," Miss Porter wrote, "their clearness, warmth of feeling, calmness of in-*

telligence, an ample human view of things; in short the sense of an artist at work in whom one could have complete confidence."

I received one morning a letter, written in pale ink on glassy, blue-lined notepaper, and bearing the postmark of a little Nebraska village. This communication, worn and rubbed, looking as though it had been carried for some days in a coat pocket that was none too clean, was from my Uncle Howard and informed me that his wife had been left a small legacy by a bachelor relative who had recently died, and that it would be necessary for her to go to Boston to attend to the settling of the estate. He requested me to meet her at the station and render her whatever services might be necessary. On examining the date indicated as that of her arrival I found it no later than tomorrow. He had characteristically delayed writing until, had I been away from home for a day, I must have missed the good woman altogether.

The name of my Aunt Georgiana called up not alone her own figure, at once pathetic and grotesque, but opened before my feet a gulf of recollection so wide and deep that, as the letter dropped from my hand, I felt suddenly a stranger to all the present conditions of my existence, wholly ill at ease and out of place amid the familiar surroundings of my study. I became, in short, the gangling farm boy my aunt had known, scourged with chilblains and bashfulness, my hands cracked and sore from the corn husking. I felt the knuckles of my thumb tentatively, as though they were raw again. I sat again before her parlor organ, fumbling the scales with my stiff, red hands, while she, beside me, made canvas mittens for the huskers.

The next morning, after preparing my landlady somewhat, I set out for the station. When the train arrived I had some difficulty in finding my aunt. She was the last of the passengers to alight, and it was not until I got her into the carriage that she seemed really to recognize me. She had come all the way in a day coach; her linen duster had become black with soot, and her black bonnet gray with dust, during the journey. When we arrived at my boardinghouse the landlady put her to bed at once and I did not see her again until the next morning.

Whatever shock Mrs. Springer experienced at my aunt's appearance she considerately concealed. As for myself, I saw my aunt's misshapen figure with that feeling of awe and respect with which we behold explorers who have left their ears and fingers north of Franz Josef Land, or their health somewhere along the Upper Congo. My Aunt Georgiana had been a music teacher at the Boston Conservatory, somewhere back in the latter sixties. One summer, while visiting in the little village among the Green Mountains where her ancestors had dwelt for generations, she had kindled the callow fancy of the most idle and shiftless of all the village lads, and had conceived for this Howard Carpenter one of those extravagant passions which a handsome country boy of twenty-one sometimes inspires in an angular, spectacled woman of thirty. When she returned to her duties in Boston Howard followed her, and the upshot of this inexplicable infatuation was that she eloped with him, eluding the reproaches of her family and the criticisms of her friends by going with him to the Nebraska frontier. Carpenter, who, of course, had no money, had taken a homestead in Red Willow County, fifty miles from the railroad. There they had measured off their quarter section themselves by driving across the prairie in a wagon, to the wheel of which they had tied a red cotton handkerchief, and counting off its revolutions. They built a dugout in the red hillside, one of those cave dwellings whose inmates so often reverted to primitive conditions. Their water they got from the lagoons where the buffalo drank, and their slender stock of provisions was always at the mercy of bands of roving Indians. For thirty years my aunt had not been further than fifty miles from the homestead.

But Mrs. Springer knew nothing of all this, and must have been considerably shocked at what was left of my kinswoman. Beneath the soiled linen duster which, on her arrival, was the most conspicuous feature of her costume, she wore a black stuff dress, whose ornamentation showed that she had surrendered herself unquestioningly into the hands of a country dressmaker. My poor aunt's figure, however, would have presented astonishing difficulties to any dressmaker. Originally stooped, her shoulders were now almost bent together over her sunken chest. She wore no stays, and her gown, which trailed unevenly behind, rose in a sort of peak over her abdomen. She wore ill-fitting false teeth, and her skin was as yellow as a Mongolian's from constant exposure to a pitiless wind and to the alkaline water which hardens the most transparent cuticle into a sort of flexible leather.

I owed to this woman most of the good that ever came my way in my boyhood, and had a reverential affection for her. During the years when I was riding herd for my uncle, my aunt, after cooking the three meals—the first of which was ready at six o'clock in the morning—and putting the six children to bed, would often stand until midnight at her ironing board, with me at the kitchen table beside her, hearing me recite Latin declensions and conjugations, gently shaking me when my drowsy head sank down over a page of irregular verbs. It was to her, at her ironing or mending, that I read my first Shakespeare, and her old textbook on mythology was the first that ever came into my empty hands. She taught me my scales and exercises, too—on the little parlor organ, which her husband had bought her after fifteen years, during which she had not so much as seen any instrument, but an accordion that belonged to one of the Norwegian farmhands. She would sit beside me by the hour, darning and counting while I struggled with the "Joyous Farmer," but she seldom talked to me about music, and I understood why. She was a pious woman; she had the consolations of religion and, to her at least, her martyrdom was not wholly sordid. Once when I had been doggedly beating out some easy passages from an old score of *Euryanthe* I had found among her music books, she came up to me and, putting her hands over my eyes, gently drew my head back upon her shoulder, saying tremulously, "Don't love it so well, Clark, or it may be taken from you. Oh, dear boy, pray that whatever your sacrifice may be, it be not that."

When my aunt appeared on the morning after her arrival she was still in a semisomnambulant state. She seemed not to realize that she was in the city where she had spent her youth, the place longed for hungrily half a lifetime. She had been so wretchedly train-sick throughout the journey that she had no recollection of anything but her discomfort, and, to all intents and purposes, there were but a few hours of nightmare between the farm in Red Willow County and my study on Newbury Street. I had planned a little pleasure for her that afternoon, to repay her for some of the glorious moments she had given me when we used to milk together in the straw-thatched cowshed and she, because I was more than usually tired, or because her husband had spoken sharply to me, would tell me of the splendid performance of the *Huguenots* she had seen in Paris, in her youth. At two o'clock the Symphony Orchestra was to give a Wagner program, and I intended to take my aunt; though, as I conversed with her I grew doubtful about her enjoyment of it. Indeed, for her own sake, I could only wish her taste for such things quite dead, and the long struggle mercifully ended at last. I suggested our visiting the Conservatory and the Common before lunch, but she seemed altogether too timid to wish to venture out. She questioned me absently about various changes in the city, but she was chiefly concerned that she had forgotten to leave instructions about feeding half-skimmed milk to a certain weakling calf, "old Maggie's calf, you know, Clark," she explained, evidently having forgotten how long I had been away. She was further troubled because she had neglected to tell her daughter about the freshly opened kit of mackerel in the cellar, which would spoil if it were not used directly.

I asked her whether she had ever heard any of the Wagnerian operas and found that she had not, though she was perfectly familiar with their respective situations, and had once possessed the piano score of *The Flying Dutchman*. I began to think it would have been best to get her back to Red Willow County without waking her, and regretted having suggested the concert.

From the time we entered the concert hall, however, she was a trifle less passive and inert, and for the first time seemed to perceive her surroundings. I had felt some trepidation lest she might become aware of the absurdities of her attire, or might experience some painful embarrassment at stepping suddenly into the world to which she had been dead for a quarter of a century. But, again, I found how superficially I had judged her. She sat looking about her with eyes as impersonal, almost as stony, as those with which the granite Rameses in a museum watches the froth and fret that ebbs and flows about his pedestal—separated from it by the lonely stretch of centuries. I have seen this same aloofness in old miners who drift into the Brown Hotel at Denver, their pockets full of bullion, their linen soiled, their haggard faces unshaven; standing in the thronged corridors as solitary as though they were still in a frozen camp on the Yukon, conscious that certain experiences have isolated them from their fellows by a gulf no haberdasher could bridge.

We sat at the extreme left of the first balcony, facing the arc of our own and the balcony above us, veritable hanging gardens, brilliant as tulip beds. The matinee audience was made up chiefly of women. One lost the contour of faces and figures—indeed, any effect of line whatever—and there was only the color of bodices past counting, the shimmer of fabrics soft and firm, silky and sheer: red, mauve, pink, blue, lilac, purple, ecru, rose, yellow, cream, and white, all the colors that an impressionist finds in a sunlit landscape, with here and there the dead shadow of a frock coat. My Aunt Georgiana regarded them as though they had been so many daubs of tube-paint on a palette.

When the musicians came out and took their places, she gave a little stir of anticipation and looked with quickening interest down over the rail at that invariable grouping, perhaps the first wholly familiar thing that had greeted her eye since she had left old Maggie and her weakling calf. I could feel how all those details sank into her soul, for I had not forgotten how they had sunk into mine when I came fresh from plowing forever and forever between green aisles of corn, where, as in a treadmill, one might walk from daybreak to dusk without perceiving a shadow of change. The clean profiles of the musicians, the gloss of their linen, the dull black of their coats, the beloved shapes of the instruments, the patches of yellow light thrown by the green-shaded lamps on the smooth, varnished bellies of the cellos and the bass viols in the rear, the restless, wind-tossed forest of fiddle necks and bows—I recalled how, in the first orchestra I had ever heard, those long bow strokes seemed to draw the heart out of me, as a conjurer's stick reels out yards of paper ribbon from a hat.

The first number was the *Tannhauser* overture. When the horns drew out the first strain of the Pilgrim's chorus my Aunt Georgiana clutched my coat sleeve. Then it was I first realized that for her this broke a silence of thirty years; the inconceivable silence of the plains. With the battle between the two motives, with the frenzy of the Venusberg theme and its ripping of strings, there came to me an overwhelming sense of the waste and wear we are so powerless to combat; and I saw again the tall, naked house on the prairie, black and grim as a wooden fortress; the black pond where I had learned to swim, its margin pitted with sun-dried cattle tracks; the rain-gullied clay banks about the naked house, the four dwarf ash seedlings where the dishcloths were always hung to dry before the kitchen door. The world there was the flat world of the ancients; to the east, a cornfield that stretched to daybreak; to the west, a corral that reached to sunset; between, the conquests of peace, dearer bought than those of war.

The overture closed; my aunt released my coat sleeve, but she said nothing. She sat staring at the orchestra through a dullness of thirty years, through the films made little by little by each of the three hundred and sixty-five days in every one of them. What, I wondered, did she get from it? She had been a good pianist in her day I knew, and her musical education had been broader than that of most music teachers of a quarter of a century ago. She had often told me of Mozart's operas and Meyerbeer's, and I could remember hearing her sing, years ago, certain melodies of Verdi's. When I had fallen ill with a fever in her house she used to sit by my cot in the evening—when the cool, night wind blew in through the faded mosquito netting tacked over the window, and I lay watching a certain bright star that burned red above the cornfield—and sing "Home to our mountains, O, let us return!" in a way fit to break the heart of a Vermont boy near dead of homesickness already.

I watched her closely through the prelude to *Tristan and Isolde,* trying vainly to conjecture what that seething turmoil of strings and winds might mean to her, but she sat mutely staring at the violin bows that drove obliquely downward, like the pelting streaks of rain in a summer shower. Had this music any message for her? Had she enough left to at all comprehend this power which had kindled the world since she had left it? I was in a fever of curiosity, but Aunt Georgiana sat silent upon her peak in Darien. She preserved this utter immobility throughout the number from *The Flying Dutchman,* though her fingers worked mechanically upon her black dress, as though, of themselves, they were recalling the piano score they had once played. Poor old hands! They had been stretched and twisted into mere tentacles to hold and lift and knead with; the palms unduly swollen, the fingers bent and knotted—on one of them a thin, worn band that had once been a wedding ring. As I pressed and gently quieted one of those groping hands I remembered with quivering eyelids their services for me in other days.

Soon after the tenor began the "Prize Song," I heard a quick drawn breath and turned to my aunt. Her eyes were closed, but the tears were glistening on her cheeks, and I think, in a moment more, they were in my eyes as well. It never really died, then—the soul that can suffer so excruciatingly and so interminably; it withers to the outward eye only; like that strange moss which can lie on a dusty shelf half a century and yet, if placed in water, grows green again. She wept so throughout the development and elaboration of the melody.

During the intermission before the second half of the concert, I questioned my aunt and found that the "Prize Song" was not new to her. Some years before there had drifted to the farm in Red Willow County a young German, a tramp cowpuncher, who had sung the chorus at Bayreuth, when he was a boy, along with the other peasant boys and girls. Of a Sunday morning he used to sit on his gingham-sheeted bed in the hands' bedroom which opened off the kitchen, cleaning the leather of his boots and saddle, singing the "Prize Song," while my aunt went about her work in the kitchen. She had hovered about him until she had prevailed upon him to join the country church, though his sole fitness for this step, insofar as I could gather, lay in his boyish face and his possession of this divine melody. Shortly afterward he had gone to town on the Fourth of July, been drunk for several days, lost his money at a faro table, ridden a saddled Texan steer on a bet, and disappeared with a fractured collarbone. All this my aunt told me huskily, wanderingly, as though she were talking in the weak lapses of illness.

"Well, we have come to better things than the old *Trovatore* at any rate, Aunt Georgie?" I queried, with a well-meant effort at jocularity.

Her lip quivered and she hastily put her handkerchief up to her mouth. From behind it she murmured, "And you have been hearing this ever since you left me, Clark?" Her question was the gentlest and saddest of reproaches.

The second half of the program consisted of four numbers from the *Ring*, and closed with Siegfried's funeral march. My aunt wept quietly, but almost continuously, as a shallow vessel overflows in a rainstorm. From time to time her dim eyes looked up at the lights which studded the ceiling, burning softly under their dull glass globes; doubtless they were stars in truth to her. I was still perplexed as to what measure of musical comprehension was left to her, she who had heard nothing but the singing of gospel hymns at Methodist services in the square frame schoolhouse on Section Thirteen for so many years. I was wholly unable to gauge how much of it had been dissolved in soapsuds, or worked into bread, or milked into the bottom of a pail.

The deluge of sound poured on and on; I never knew what she found in the shining current of it; I never knew how far it bore her, or past what happy islands. From the trembling of her face I could well believe that before the last numbers she had been carried out where the myriad graves are, into the gray, nameless burying grounds of the sea; or into some world of death vaster yet, where, from the beginning of the world, hope has lain down with hope and dream with dream and, renouncing, slept.

The concert was over; the people filed out of the hall chattering and laughing, glad to relax and find the living level again, but my kinswoman made no effort to rise. The harpist slipped its green felt cover over his instrument; the flute players shook the water from their mouthpieces; the men of the orchestra went out one by one, leaving the stage to the chairs and music stands, empty as a winter cornfield.

I spoke to my aunt. She burst into tears and sobbed pleadingly. "I don't want to go, Clark, I don't want to go!"

I understood. For her, just outside the door of the concert hall, lay the black pond with the cattle-tracked bluffs; the tall, unpainted house, with weather-curled boards; naked as a tower, the crook-backed ash seedlings where the dishcloths hung to dry; the gaunt, molting turkeys picking up refuse about the kitchen door.

---

# SONNY'S BLUES

## James Baldwin

*Playwright, essayist, lecturer, poet, and writer of fiction, James Baldwin became one of the most influential voices of the black literary community during the sixties. Born in 1924 in New York's Harlem, Baldwin had a notoriously unhappy childhood. He himself has written that his early life can be dismissed "with the restrained observation that I certainly would not consider living it again." Much of his early suffering he owed to his cruel stepfather, David Baldwin, a storefront preacher. Baldwin himself was a preacher (from the age of fourteen to seventeen), but he had always had a strong desire to be a writer. "I began plotting novels at about the time I learned to read," he has written. He left Harlem and lived for a number of years in Greenwich Village, working during the day and writing at night. A turning point came when, with the help of Richard Wright, he was granted the Eugene F. Saxton Memorial Trust Award in 1945, which enabled him to devote his time to writing. He left for France in 1948, telling friends he would never return; there he completed* Go Tell It on the Mountain *(1953). Many of his writings reflect his commitment to the civil rights movement in the sixties in America. These include* Notes of a Native Son *(1955) and* Nobody Knows My Name *(1961),* The Fire Next Time *(1963), the novel* Another Country *(1962), and the play* Blues for Mister Charlie *(1964). Other works are* Giovanni's Room *(1956);* Going to Meet the Man *(1965), a collection of short stories; and* A Rap on Race *(1971), from tape recordings of conversations with Margaret Mead. His latest novel,* If Beale Street Could Talk *(1974), deals with the struggles and sorrows of Tish, a nineteen-year-old black girl. In reviewing this novel for* The New York Times, *Joyce Carol Oates concluded with words that apply to much of Baldwin's work, and certainly to "Sonny's Blues": "If Beale Street Could Talk is a moving, painful story. It is so vividly human and so obviously based upon reality, that it strikes us as timeless—an art that has not the slightest need of esthetic trick, and even less need of fashionable apocalyptic excesses."*

I read about it in the paper, in the subway, on my way to work. I read it, and I couldn't believe it, and I read it again. Then perhaps I just stared at it, at the newsprint spelling out his name, spelling out the story. I stared at it in the swinging lights of the subway car, and in the faces and bodies of the people, and in my own face, trapped in the darkness which roared outside.

It was not to be believed and I kept telling myself that, as I walked from the subway station to the high school. And at the same time I couldn't doubt it. I was scared, scared for Sonny. He became real to me again. A great block of ice got settled in my belly and kept melting there slowly all day long, while I taught my classes algebra. It was a special kind of ice. It kept melting, sending trickles of ice water all up and down my veins, but it never got less. Sometimes it hardened and seemed to expand until I felt my guts were going to come spilling out or that I was going to choke or scream. This would always be at a moment when I was remembering some specific thing Sonny had once said or done.

When he was about as old as the boys in my classes his face had been bright and open, there was a lot of copper in it; and he'd had wonderfully direct brown eyes, and great gentleness and privacy. I wondered what he looked like now. He had been picked up, the evening before, in a raid on an apartment downtown, for peddling and using heroin.

I couldn't believe it: but what I mean by that is that I couldn't find any room for it anywhere inside me. I had kept it outside me for a long time. I hadn't wanted to know. I had had suspicions, but I didn't name them. I kept putting them away. I told myself that Sonny was wild, but he wasn't crazy. And he'd always been a good boy, he hadn't ever turned hard or evil or disrespectful, the way kids can, so quick, so quick, especially in Harlem. I didn't want to believe that I'd ever see my brother going down, coming to nothing, all that light in his face gone out, in the condition I'd already seen so many others. Yet it had happened and here I was, talking about algebra to a lot of boys who might, every one of them for all I knew, be popping off needles every time they went to the head. Maybe it did more for them than algebra could.

I was sure that the first time Sonny had ever had horse, he couldn't have been much older than these boys were now. These boys, now, were living as we'd been living then, they were growing up with a rush and their heads bumped abruptly against the low ceiling of their actual possibilities. They were filled with rage. All they really knew were two darknesses, the darkness of their lives, which was now closing in on them, and the darkness of the movies, which had blinded them to that other darkness, and in which they now, vindictively, dreamed, at once more together than they were at any other time and more alone.

When the last bell rang, the last class ended, I let out my breath. It seemed I'd been holding it for all that time. My clothes were wet—I may have looked as though I'd been sitting in a steam bath, all dressed up, all afternoon. I sat alone in the classroom a long time. I listened to the boys outside, downstairs, shouting and cursing and laughing. Their laughter struck me for perhaps the first time. It was not the joyous laughter which —God knows why—one associates with children. It was mocking and insular, its intent was to denigrate. It was disenchanted, and in this, also, lay the authority of their curses. Perhaps I was listening to them because I was thinking about my brother and in them I heard my brother. And myself.

One boy was whistling a tune, at once very complicated and very simple, it seemed to be pouring out of him as though he were a bird, and it sounded very cool and moving through all that harsh, bright air, only just holding its own through all those other sounds.

I stood up and walked over to the window and looked down into the courtyard. It was the beginning of the spring and the sap was rising in the boys. A teacher passed through them every now and again, quickly, as though he or she couldn't wait to get out of that courtyard, to get those boys out of their sight and off their minds. I started collecting my stuff. I thought I'd better get home and talk to Isabel.

The courtyard was almost deserted by the time I got downstairs. I saw this boy standing in the shadow of a doorway, looking just like Sonny. I almost called his name. Then I saw that it wasn't Sonny, but somebody we used to know, a boy from around our block. He'd been Sonny's friend. He'd never been mine, having been too young for me, and, anyway, I'd never liked him. And now, even though he was a grown-up man, he still hung around that block, still spent hours on the street corners, was always high and raggy. I used to run into him from time to time and he'd often work around to asking me for a quarter or fifty cents. He always had some real good excuse, too, and I always gave it to him, I don't know why.

But now, abruptly, I hated him. I couldn't stand the way he looked at me, partly like a dog, partly like a cunning child. I wanted to ask him what the hell he was doing in the school courtyard.

He sort of shuffled over to me, and he said, "I see you got the papers. So you already know about it."

"You mean about Sonny? Yes, I already know about it. How come they didn't get you?"

He grinned. It made him repulsive and it also brought to mind what he'd looked like as a kid. "I wasn't there. I stay away from them people."

"Good for you." I offered him a cigarette and I watched him through the smoke. "You come all the way down here just to tell me about Sonny?"

"That's right." He was sort of shaking his head and his eyes looked strange, as though they were about to cross. The bright sun deadened his damp dark brown skin and it made his eyes look yellow and showed up the dirt in his kinked hair. He smelled funky. I moved a little away from him and I said, "Well, thanks. But I already know about it and I got to get home."

"I'll walk you a little ways," he said. We started walking. There were a couple of kids still loitering in the courtyard and one of them said goodnight to me and looked strangely at the boy beside me.

"What're you going to do?" he asked me. "I mean, about Sonny?"

"Look. I haven't seen Sonny for over a year, I'm not sure I'm going to do anything. Anyway, what the hell *can* I do?"

"That's right," he said quickly, "ain't nothing you can do. Can't much help old Sonny no more, I guess."

It was what I was thinking and so it seemed to me he had no right to say it.

"I'm surprised at Sonny, though," he went on—he had a funny way of talking, he looked straight ahead as though he were talking to himself— "I thought Sonny was a smart boy, I thought he was too smart to get hung."

"I guess he thought so too," I said sharply, "and that's how he got hung. And how about you? You're pretty goddam smart, I bet."

Then he looked directly at me, just for a minute. "I ain't smart," he said. "If I was smart, I'd have reached for a pistol a long time ago."

"Look. Don't tell *me* your sad story, if it was up to me, I'd give you one." Then I felt guilty—guilty, probably, for never having supposed that the poor bastard *had* a story of his own, much less a sad one, and I asked, quickly, "What's going to happen to him now?"

He didn't answer this. He was off by himself some place. "Funny thing," he said, and from his tone we might have been discussing the quickest way to get to Brooklyn, "when I saw the papers this morning, the first thing I asked myself was if I had anything to do with it. I felt sort of responsible."

I began to listen more carefully. The subway station was on the corner, just before us, and I stopped. He stopped, too. We were in front of a bar and he ducked slightly, peering in, but whoever he was looking for didn't seem to be there. The juke box was blasting away with something black and bouncy and I half watched the barmaid as she danced her way from the juke box to her place behind the bar. And I watched her face as she laughingly responded to something someone said to her, still keeping time to the music. When she smiled one saw the little girl, one sensed the doomed, still-struggling woman beneath the battered face of the semi-whore.

"I never *give* Sonny nothing," the boy said finally, "but a long time ago I come to school high and Sonny asked me how it felt." He paused, I couldn't bear to watch him, I watched the barmaid, and I listened to the music which seemed to be causing the pavement to shake. "I told him it felt great." The music stopped, the barmaid paused and watched the juke box until the music began again. "It did."

All this was carrying me some place I didn't want to go. I certainly didn't want to know how it felt. It filled everything, the people, the houses, the music, the dark, quicksilver barmaid, with menace; and this menace was their reality.

"What's going to happen to him now?" I asked again.

"They'll send him away some place and they'll try to cure him." He shook his head. "Maybe he'll even think he's kicked the habit. Then they'll let him loose"—he gestured, throwing his cigarette into the gutter. "That's all."

"What do you mean, that's *all?*"

But I knew what he meant.

"I *mean*, that's *all*." He turned his head and looked at me, pulling down the corners of his mouth. "Don't you know what I mean?" he asked, softly.

"How the hell *would* I know what you mean?" I almost whispered it, I don't know why.

"That's right," he said to the air, "how would *he* know what I mean?" He turned toward me again, patient and calm, and yet I somehow felt him shaking, shaking as though he were going to fall apart. I felt that ice in my guts again, the dread I'd felt all afternoon; and again I watched the barmaid, moving about the bar, washing glasses, and singing. "Listen. They'll let him out and then it'll just start all over again. That's what I mean."

"You mean—they'll let him out. And then he'll just start working his way back in again. You mean he'll never kick the habit. Is that what you mean?"

"That's right," he said, cheerfully. "*You* see what I mean."

"Tell me," I said at last, "why does he want to die? He must want to die, he's killing himself, why does he want to die?"

He looked at me in surprise. He licked his lips. "He don't want to die. He wants to live. Don't nobody want to die, ever."

Then I wanted to ask him—too many things. He could not have answered, or if he had, I could not have borne the answers. I started walking. "Well, I guess it's none of my business."

"It's going to be rough on old Sonny," he said. We reached the subway station. "This is your station?" he asked. I nodded. I took one step down. "Damn!" he said, suddenly. I looked up at him. He grinned again. "Damn it if I didn't leave all my money home. You ain't got a dollar on you, have you? Just for a couple of days, is all."

All at once something inside gave and threatened to come pouring out of me. I didn't hate him any more. I felt that in another moment I'd start crying like a child.

"Sure," I said. "Don't sweat." I looked in my wallet and didn't have a dollar, I only had a five. "Here," I said. "That hold you?"

He didn't look at it—he didn't want to look at it. A terrible, closed look came over his face, as though he were keeping the number on the bill a secret from him and me. "Thanks," he said, and now he was dying to see me go. "Don't worry about Sonny. Maybe I'll write him or something."

"Sure," I said. "You do that. So long."

"Be seeing you," he said. I went on down the steps.

And I didn't write Sonny or send him anything for a long time. When I finally did, it was just after my little girl died, he wrote me back a letter which made me feel like a bastard.

Here's what he said:

> Dear brother,
>
> You don't know how much I needed to hear from you. I wanted to write you many a time but I dug how much I must have hurt you and so I didn't write. But now I feel like a man who's been trying to climb up out of some deep, real deep and funky hole and just saw the sun up there, outside. I got to get outside.
>
> I can't tell you much about how I got here. I mean I don't know how to tell you. I guess I was afraid of something or I was trying to escape from something and you know I have never been very strong in the head (smile). I'm glad Mama and Daddy are dead and can't see what's happened to their son and I swear if I'd known what I was doing I would never have hurt you so, you and a lot of other fine people who were nice to me and who believed in me.
>
> I don't want you to think it had anything to do with me being a musician. It's more than that. Or maybe less than that. I can't get anything straight in my head down here and I try not to think about what's going to happen to me when I get outside again. Sometime I think I'm going to flip and *never* get outside and sometime I think I'll come straight back. I tell you one thing, though, I'd rather blow my brains out than go through this again. But that's what they all say, so they tell me. If I tell you when I'm coming to New York and if you could meet me, I sure would appreciate it. Give my love to Isabel and the kids and I was sure sorry to hear about little Gracie. I wish I could be like Mama and say the Lord's will be done, but I don't know it seems to me that trouble is the one thing that never does get stopped and I don't know what good it does to blame it on the Lord. But may be it does some good if you believe it.
>
> Your brother,
> Sonny

Then I kept in constant touch with him and I sent him whatever I could and I went to meet him when he came back to New York. When I saw him many things I thought I had forgotten came flooding back to me. This was because I had begun, finally, to wonder about Sonny, about the life that Sonny lived inside. This life, whatever it was, had made him older and thinner and it had deepened the distant stillness in which he had always moved. He looked very unlike my baby brother. Yet, when he smiled, when we shook hands, the baby brother I'd never known looked out from the depths of his private life, like an animal waiting to be coaxed into the light.

"How you been keeping?" he asked me.

"All right. And you?"

"Just fine." He was smiling all over his face. "It's good to see you again."

"It's good to see you."

The seven years' difference in our ages lay between us like a chasm: I wondered if these years would ever operate between us as a bridge. I was remembering, and it made it hard to catch my breath, that I had been there when he was born; and I had heard the first words he had ever spoken. When he started to walk, he walked from our mother straight to me. I caught him just before he fell when he took the first steps he ever took in this world.

"How's Isabel?"

"Just fine. She's dying to see you."

"And the boys?"

"They're fine, too. They're anxious to see their uncle."

"Oh, come on. You know they don't remember me."

"Are you kidding? Of course they remember you."

He grinned again. We got into a taxi. We had a lot to say to each other, far too much to know how to begin.

As the taxi began to move, I asked, "You still want to go to India?"

He laughed. "You still remember that. Hell, no. This place is Indian enough for me."

"It used to belong to them," I said.

And he laughed again. "They damn sure knew what they were doing when they got rid of it."

Years ago, when he was around fourteen, he'd been all hipped on the idea of going to India. He read books about people sitting on rocks, naked, in all kinds of weather, but mostly bad, naturally, and walking barefoot through hot coals and arriving at wisdom. I used to say that it sounded to me as though they were getting away from wisdom as fast as they could. I think he sort of looked down on me for that.

"Do you mind," he asked, "if we have the driver drive alongside the park? On the west side—I haven't seen the city in so long."

"Of course not," I said. I was afraid that I might sound as though I were humoring him, but I hoped he wouldn't take it that way.

So we drove along, between the green of the park and the stony, lifeless elegance of hotels and apartment buildings, toward the vivid, killing streets of our childhood. These streets hadn't changed, though housing projects jutted up out of them now like rocks in the middle of a boiling sea. Most of the houses in which we had grown up had vanished, as had the stores from which we had stolen, the basements in which we had first tried sex, the rooftops from which we had hurled tin cans and bricks. But houses exactly like the houses of our past yet dominated the landscape, boys exactly like the boys we once had been found themselves smothering in these houses, came down into the streets for light and air and found themselves encircled by disaster. Some escaped the trap, most didn't. Those who got out always left something of themselves behind, as some animals amputate a leg and leave it in the trap. It might be said, perhaps, that I had escaped, after all, I was a school teacher; or that Sonny had, he hadn't lived in Harlem for years. Yet, as the cab moved uptown through streets which seemed, with a rush, to darken with dark people, and as I covertly studied Sonny's face, it came to me that what we both were seeking through our separate cab windows was that part of ourselves which had been left behind. It's always at the hour of trouble and confrontation that the missing member aches.

We hit 110th Street and started rolling up Lenox Avenue. And I'd known this avenue all my life, but it seemed to me again, as it had seemed on the day I'd first heard about Sonny's trouble, filled with a hidden menace which was its very breath of life.

"We almost there," said Sonny.

"Almost." We were both too nervous to say anything more.

We lived in a housing project. It hasn't been up long. A few days after it was up it seemed uninhabitably new, now, of course, it's already run-down. It looks like a parody of the good, clean, faceless life—God knows the people who live in it do their best to make it a parody. The beat-looking grass lying around isn't enough to make their lives green, the hedges will never hold out the streets, and they know it. The big windows fool no one, they aren't big enough to make space out of no space. They don't bother with the windows, they watch the TV screen instead. The playground is most popular with the children who don't play at jacks, or skip rope, or roller skate, or swing, and they can be found in it after dark. We moved in partly because it's not too far from where I teach, and partly for the kids; but it's really just like the houses in which Sonny and I grew up. The same things happen, they'll have the same things to remember. The moment Sonny and I started into the house I had the feeling that I was simply bringing him back into the danger he had almost died trying to escape.

Sonny has never been talkative. So I don't know why I was sure he'd be dying to talk to me when supper was over the first night. Everything went fine, the oldest boy remembered him, and the youngest boy liked him, and Sonny had remembered to bring something for each of them; and Isabel, who is really much nicer than I am, more open and giving, had gone to a lot of trouble about dinner and was genuinely glad to see him. And she's always been able to tease Sonny in a way that I haven't. It was nice to see her face so vivid again and to hear her laugh and watch her make Sonny laugh. She wasn't or, anyway, she didn't seem to be, at all uneasy or embarrassed. She chatted as though there were no subject which had to be avoided and she got Sonny past his first, faint stiffness. And thank God she was there, for I was filled with that icy dread again. Everything I did seemed awkward to me, and everything I said sounded freighted with hidden meaning. I was trying to remember everything I'd heard about dope addiction and I couldn't help watching Sonny for signs. I wasn't doing it out of malice. I was trying to find out something about my brother. I was dying to hear him tell me he was safe.

"Safe!" my father grunted, whenever Mama suggested trying to move to a neighborhood which might be safer for children. "Safe, hell! Ain't no place safe for kids, nor nobody."

He always went on like this, but he wasn't, ever, really as bad as he sounded, not even on weekends, when he got drunk. As a matter of fact, he was always on the lookout for "something a little better," but he died before he found it. He died suddenly, during a drunken weekend in the middle of the war, when Sonny was fifteen. He and Sonny hadn't ever got on too well. And this was partly because Sonny was the apple of his father's eye. It was because he loved Sonny so much and was frightened for him, that he was always fighting with him. It doesn't do any good to fight with Sonny. Sonny just moves back, inside himself, where he can't be reached. But the principal reason that they never hit it off is that they were so much alike. Daddy was big and rough and loud-talking, just the opposite of Sonny, but they both had—that same privacy.

Mama tried to tell me something about this, just after Daddy died. I was home on leave from the army.

This was the last time I ever saw my mother alive. Just the same, this picture gets all mixed up in my mind with pictures I had of her when she was younger. The way I always see her is the way she used to be on a Sunday afternoon, say, when the old folks were talking after the big Sunday dinner. I always see her wearing pale blue. She'd be sitting on the sofa. And my father would be sitting in the easy chair, not far from her. And the living room would be full of church folks and relatives. There they sit, in chairs all around the living room, and the night is creeping up outside, but nobody knows it yet. You can see the darkness growing against the windowpanes and you hear the street noises every now and again, or maybe the jangling beat of a tambourine from one of the churches close by, but it's real quiet in the room. For a moment nobody's talking, but every face looks darkening, like the sky outside. And my mother rocks a little from the waist, and my father's eyes are closed. Everyone is looking at something a child can't see. For a minute they've forgotten the children. Maybe a kid is lying on the rug, half asleep. Maybe somebody's got a kid in his lap and is absent-mindedly stroking the kid's head. Maybe there's a kid, quiet and big-eyed, curled up in a big chair in the corner. The silence, the darkness coming, and the darkness in the faces frighten the child obscurely. He hopes that the hand which strokes his forehead will never stop—will never die. He hopes that there will never come a time when the old folks won't be sitting around the living room, talking about where they've come from, and what they've seen, and what's happened to them and their kinfolk.

But something deep and watchful in the child knows that this is bound to end, is already ending. In a moment someone will get up and turn on the light. Then the old folks will remember the children and they won't talk any more that day. And when light fills the room, the child is filled with darkness. He knows that every time this happens he's moved just a little closer to that darkness outside. The darkness outside is what the old folks have been talking about. It's what they've come from. It's what they endure. The child knows that they won't talk any more because if he knows too much about what's happened to *them*, he'll know too much too soon, about what's going to happen to *him*.

The last time I talked to my mother, I remember I was restless. I wanted to get out and see Isabel. We weren't married then and we had a lot to straighten out between us.

There Mama sat, in black, by the window. She was humming an old church song, *Lord, you brought me from a long ways off*. Sonny was out somewhere. Mama kept watching the streets.

"I don't know," she said, "if I'll ever see you again, after you go off from here. But I hope you'll remember the things I tried to teach you."

"Don't talk like that," I said, and smiled. "You'll be here a long time yet."

She smiled, too, but she said nothing. She was quiet for a long time. And I said, "Mama, don't you worry about nothing. I'll be writing all the time, and you be getting the checks. . . ."

"I want to talk to you about your brother," she said, suddenly. "If anything happens to me he ain't going to have nobody to look out for him."

"Mama," I said, "ain't nothing going to happen to you *or* Sonny. Sonny's all right. He's a good boy and he's got good sense."

"It ain't a question of his being a good boy," Mama said, "nor of his having good sense. It ain't only the bad ones, nor yet the dumb ones that gets sucked under." She stopped, looking at me. "Your Daddy once had a brother," she said, and she smiled in a way that made me feel she was in pain. "You didn't never know that, did you?"

"No," I said, "I never knew that," and I watched her face.

"Oh, yes," she said, "your Daddy had a brother." She looked out of the window again. "I know you never saw your Daddy cry. But *I* did—many a time, through all these years."

I asked her, "What happened to his brother? How come nobody's ever talked about him?"

This was the first time I ever saw my mother look old.

"His brother got killed," she said, "when he was just a little younger than you are now. I knew him. He was a fine boy. He was maybe a little full of the devil, but he didn't mean nobody no harm."

Then she stopped and the room was silent, exactly as it had sometimes been on those Sunday afternoons. Mama kept looking out into the streets.

"He used to have a job in the mill," she said, "and, like all young folks, he just liked to perform on Saturday nights. Saturday nights, him and your father would drift around to different places, go to dances and things like that, or just sit around with people they knew, and your father's brother would sing, he had a fine voice, and play along with himself on his guitar. Well, this particular Saturday night, him and your father was coming home from some place, and they were both a little drunk and there was a moon that night, it was bright like day. Your father's brother was feeling kind of good, and he was whistling to himself, and he had his guitar slung over his shoulder. They was coming down a hill and beneath them was a road that turned off from the highway. Well, your father's brother, being always kind of frisky, decided to run down this hill, and he did, with that guitar banging and clanging behind him, and he ran across the road, and he was making water behind a tree. And your father was sort of amused at him and he was still coming down the hill, kind of slow. Then he heard a car motor and that same minute his brother stepped from behind the tree, into the road, in the moonlight. And he started to cross the road. And your father started to run down the hill, he says he don't know why. This car was full of white men. They was all drunk, and when they seen your father's brother they let out a great whoop and holler and they aimed the car straight at him. They was having fun, they just wanted to scare him, the way they do sometimes, you know. But they was drunk. And I guess the boy, being drunk, too, and scared, kind of lost his head. By the time he jumped it was too late. Your father says he heard his brother scream when the car rolled over him, and he heard the wood of that guitar when it give, and he heard them strings go flying, and he heard them white men shouting, and the car kept on a-going and it ain't stopped till this day. And, time your father got down the hill, his brother weren't nothing but blood and pulp."

Tears were gleaming on my mother's face. There wasn't anything I could say.

"He never mentioned it," she said, "because I never let him mention it before you children. Your Daddy was like a crazy man that night and for many a night thereafter. He says he never in his life seen anything as dark as that road after the lights of that car had gone away. Weren't nothing, weren't nobody on that road, just your Daddy and his brother and that busted guitar. Oh, yes. Your Daddy never did really get right again. Till the day he died he weren't sure but that every white man he saw was the man that killed his brother."

She stopped and took out her handkerchief and dried her eyes and looked at me.

"I ain't telling you all this," she said, "to make you scared or bitter or to make you hate nobody. I'm telling you this because you got a brother. And the world ain't changed."

I guess I didn't want to believe this. I guess she saw this in my face. She turned away from me, toward the window again, searching those streets.

"But I praise my Redeemer," she said at last, "that He called your Daddy home before me. I ain't saying it to throw no flowers at myself, but, I declare, it keeps me from feeling too cast down to know I helped your father get safely through this world. Your father always acted like he was the roughest, strongest man on earth. And everybody took him to be like that. But if he hadn't had *me* there—to see his tears!"

She was crying again. Still, I couldn't move. I said, "Lord, Lord, Mama, I didn't know it was like that."

"Oh, honey," she said, "there's a lot that you don't know. But you are going to find out." She stood up from the window and came over to me. "You got to hold on to your brother," she said, "and don't let him fall, no matter what it looks like is happening to him and no matter how evil you gets with him. You going to be evil with him many a time. But don't you forget what I told you, you hear?"

"I won't forget," I said. "Don't you worry, I won't forget. I won't let nothing happen to Sonny."

My mother smiled as though she were amused at something she saw in my face. Then, "You may not be able to stop nothing from happening. But you got to let him know you's *there*."

Two days later I was married, and then I was gone. And I had a lot of things on my mind and I pretty well forgot my promise to Mama until I got shipped home on a special furlough for her funeral.

And, after the funeral, with just Sonny and me alone in the empty kitchen, I tried to find out something about him.

"What do you want to do?" I asked him.

"I'm going to be a musician," he said.

For he had graduated, in the time I had been away, from dancing to the juke box to finding out who was playing what, and what they were doing with it, and he had bought himself a set of drums.

"You mean, you want to be a drummer?" I somehow had the feeling that being a drummer might be all right for other people but not for my brother Sonny.

"I don't think," he said, looking at me very gravely, "that I'll ever be a good drummer. But I think I can play a piano."

I frowned. I'd never played the role of the older brother quite so seriously before, had scarcely ever, in fact, *asked* Sonny a damn thing. I sensed myself in the presence of something I didn't really know how to handle, didn't understand. So I made my frown a little deeper as I asked: "What kind of musician do you want to be?"

He grinned. "How many kinds do you think there are?"

"Be *serious*," I said.

He laughed, throwing his head back, and then looked at me. "I *am* serious."

"Well, then, for Christ's sake, stop kidding around and answer a serious question. I mean, do you want to be a concert pianist, you want to play classical music and all that, or—or what?" Long before I finished he was laughing again. "For Christ's *sake*, Sonny!"

He sobered, but with difficulty. "I'm sorry. But you sound so—*scared!*" and he was off again.

"Well, you may think it's funny now, baby, but it's not going to be so funny when you have to make your living at it, let me tell you *that*." I was furious because I knew he was laughing at me and I didn't know why.

"No," he said, very sober now, and afraid, perhaps, that he'd hurt me, "I don't want to be a classical pianist. That isn't what interests me. I mean"—he paused, looking hard at me, as though his eyes would help me to understand, and then gestured helplessly, as though perhaps his hand would help— "I mean, I'll have a lot of studying to do, and I'll have to study *everything*, but, I mean, I want to play *with*—jazz musicians." He stopped. "I want to play jazz," he said.

Well, the word had never before sounded as heavy, as real, as it sounded that afternoon in Sonny's mouth. I just looked at him and I was probably frowning a real frown by this time. I simply couldn't see why on earth he'd want to spend his time hanging around nightclubs, clowning around on bandstands, while people pushed each other around a dance floor. It seemed—beneath him, somehow. I had never thought about it before, had never been forced to, but I suppose I had always put jazz musicians in a class with what Daddy called "good-time people."

"Are you *serious?*"

"Hell, *yes*, I'm serious."

He looked more helpless than ever, and annoyed, and deeply hurt.

I suggested, helpfully: "You mean—like Louis Armstrong?"

His face closed as though I'd struck him. "No. I'm not talking about none of that old-time, down home crap."

"Well, look, Sonny, I'm sorry, don't get mad. I just don't altogether get it, that's all. Name somebody—you know, a jazz musician you admire."

"Bird."

"Who?"

"Bird! Charlie Parker! Don't they teach you nothing in the goddamn army?"

I lit a cigarette. I was surprised and then a little amused to discover that I was trembling. "I've been out of touch," I said. "You'll have to be patient with me. Now. Who's this Parker character?"

"He's just one of the greatest jazz musicians alive," said Sonny, sullenly, his hands in his pockets, his back to me. "Maybe *the* greatest," he added, bitterly, "that's probably why *you* never heard of him."

"All right," I said, "I'm ignorant. I'm sorry. I'll go out and buy all the cat's records right away, all right?"

"It don't," said Sonny, with dignity, "make any difference to me. I don't care what you listen to. Don't do me no favors."

I was beginning to realize that I'd never seen him so upset before. With another part of my mind I was thinking that this would probably turn out to be one of those things kids go through and that I shouldn't make it seem important by pushing it too hard. Still, I didn't think it would do any harm to ask: "Doesn't all this take a lot of time? Can you make a living at it?"

He turned back to me and half leaned, half sat, on the kitchen table. "Everything takes time," he said, "and—well, yes, sure, I can make a living at it. But what I don't seem to be able to make you understand is that it's the only thing I want to do."

"Well, Sonny," I said, gently, "you know people can't always do exactly what they *want* to do—"

"*No,* I don't know that," said Sonny, surprising me. "I think people *ought* to do what they want to do, what else are they alive for?"

"You getting to be a big boy," I said desperately, "it's time you started thinking about your future."

"I'm thinking about my future," said Sonny, grimly. "I think about it all the time."

I gave up. I decided, if he didn't change his mind, that we could always talk about it later. "In the meantime," I said, "you got to finish school." We already decided that he'd have to move in with Isabel and her folks. I knew this wasn't the ideal arrangement because Isabel's folks are inclined to be dicty and they hadn't especially wanted Isabel to marry me. But I didn't know what else to do. "And we have to get you fixed up at Isabel's."

There was a long silence. He moved from the kitchen table to the window. "That's a terrible idea. You know it yourself."

"Do you have a *better* idea?"

He just walked up and down the kitchen for a minute. He was as tall as I was. He had started to shave. I suddenly had the feeling that I didn't know him at all.

He stopped at the kitchen table and picked up my cigarettes. Looking at me with a kind of mocking, amused defiance, he put one between his lips. "You mind?"

"You smoking already?"

He lit the cigarette and nodded, watching me through the smoke. "I just wanted to see if I'd have the courage to smoke in front of you." He grinned and blew a great cloud of smoke to the ceiling. "It was easy." He looked at my face. "Come on, now. I bet you was smoking at my age, tell the truth."

I didn't say anything but the truth was on my face, and he laughed. But now there was something very strained in his laugh. "Sure. And I bet that ain't all you was doing."

He was frightening me a little. "Cut the crap," I said. "We already decided that you was going to go and live at Isabel's. Now what's got into you all of a sudden?"

"*You* decided it," he pointed out. "I didn't decide nothing." He stopped in front of me, leaning against the stove, arms loosely folded. "Look, brother. I don't want to stay in Harlem no more, I really don't." He was very earnest. He looked at me, then over toward the kitchen window. There was something in his eyes I'd never seen before, some thoughtfulness, some worry all his own. He rubbed the muscle of one arm. "It's time I was getting out of here."

"Where do you want to *go*, Sonny?"

"I want to join the army. Or the navy, I don't care. If I say I'm old enough, they'll believe me."

Then I got mad. It was because I was so scared. "You must be crazy. You goddamn fool, what the hell do you want to go and join the *army* for?"

"I just told you. To get out of Harlem."

"Sonny, you haven't even finished *school*. And if you really want to be a musician, how do you expect to study if you're in the *army?*"

He looked at me, trapped, and in anguish. "There's ways. I might be able to work out some kind of deal. Anyway, I'll have the G.I. Bill when I come out."

"*If* you come out." We stared at each other. "Sonny, please. Be reasonable. I know the setup is far from perfect. But we got to do the best we can."

"I ain't learning nothing in school," he said. "Even when I go." He turned away from me and opened the window and threw his cigarette out into the narrow alley. I watched his back. "At least, I ain't learning nothing you'd want me to learn." He slammed the window so hard I thought the glass would fly out, and turned back to me. "And I'm sick of the stink of these garbage cans!"

"Sonny," I said, "I know how you feel. But if you don't finish school now, you're going to be sorry later that you didn't." I grabbed him by the shoulders. "And you only got another year. It ain't so bad. And I'll come back and I swear I'll help you do *whatever* you want to do. Just try to put up with it till I come back. Will you please do that? For me?"

He didn't answer and he wouldn't look at me.

"Sonny. You hear me?"

He pulled away. "I hear you. But you never hear anything *I* say."

I didn't know what to say to that. He looked out of the window and then back at me. "OK," he said, and sighed. "I'll try."

Then I said, trying to cheer him up a little, "They got a piano at Isabel's. You can practice on it."

And as a matter of fact, it did cheer him up for a minute. "That's right," he said to himself. "I forgot that." His face relaxed a little. But the worry, the thoughtfulness, played on it still, the way shadows play on a face which is staring into the fire.

But I thought I'd never hear the end of that piano. At first, Isabel would write me, saying how nice it was that Sonny was so serious about his music and how, as soon as he came in from school, or wherever he had been when he was supposed to be at school, he went straight to that piano and stayed there until suppertime. And, after supper, he went back to that piano and stayed there until everybody went to bed. He was at the piano all day Saturday and all day Sunday. Then he bought a record player and started playing records. He'd play one record over and over again, all day long sometimes, and he'd improvise along with it on the piano. Or he'd play one section of the record, one chord, one change, one progression, then he'd do it on the piano. Then back to the record. Then back to the piano.

Well, I really don't know how they stood it. Isabel finally confessed that it wasn't like living with a person at all, it was like living with sound. And the sound didn't make any sense to her, didn't make any sense to any of them—naturally. They began, in a way, to be afflicted by this presence that was living in their home. It was as though Sonny were some sort of god, or monster. He moved in an atmosphere which wasn't like theirs at all. They fed him and he ate, he washed himself, he walked in and out of their door; he certainly wasn't nasty or unpleasant or rude, Sonny isn't any of those things; but it was as though he were all wrapped up in some cloud, some fire, some vision all his own; and there wasn't any way to reach him.

At the same time, he wasn't really a man yet, he was still a child, and they had to watch out for him in all kinds of ways. They certainly couldn't throw him out. Neither did they dare to make a great scene about that piano because even they dimly sensed, as I sensed, from so many thousands of miles away, that Sonny was at that piano playing for his life.

But he hadn't been going to school. One day a letter came from the school board and Isabel's mother got it—there had, apparently, been other letters but Sonny had torn them up. This day, when Sonny came in, Isabel's mother showed him the letter and asked where he'd been spending his time. And she finally got it out of him that he'd been down in Greenwich Village, with musicians and other characters, in a white girl's apartment. And this scared her and she started to scream at him and what came up, once she began—though she denies it to this day—was what sacrifices they were making to give Sonny a decent home and how little he appreciated it.

Sonny didn't play the piano that day. By evening, Isabel's mother had calmed down but then there was the old man to deal with, and Isabel herself. Isabel says she did her best to be calm but she broke down and started crying. She says she just watched Sonny's face. She could tell, by watching him, what was happening with him. And what was happening was that they penetrated his cloud, they had reached him. Even if their fingers had been a thousand times more gentle than human fingers ever are, he could hardly help feeling they had stripped him naked and were spitting on that nakedness. For he also had to see that his presence, that music, which was life or death to him, had been torture for them and that they had endured it, not at all for his sake, but only for mine. And Sonny couldn't take that. He can take it a little better today than he could then but he's still not very good at it and, frankly, I don't know anybody who is.

The silence of the next few days must have been louder than the sound of all the music ever played since time began. One morning, before she went to work, Isabel was in his room for something and she suddenly realized that all of his records were gone. And she knew for certain that he was gone. And he was. He went as far as the navy would carry him. He finally sent me a postcard from some place in Greece and that was the first I knew that Sonny was still alive. I didn't see him any more until we were both back in New York and the war had long been over.

He was a man by then, of course, but I wasn't willing to see it. He came by the house from time to time, but we fought almost every time we met. I didn't like the way he carried himself, loose and dreamlike all the time, and I didn't like his friends, and his music seemed to be merely an excuse for the life he led. It sounded just that weird and disordered.

Then we had a fight, a pretty awful fight, and I didn't see him for months. By and by I looked him up, where he was living, in a furnished room in the Village, and I tried to make it up. But there were lots of other people in the room and Sonny just lay on his bed, and he wouldn't come downstairs with me, and he treated these other people as though they were his family and I weren't. So I got mad and then he got mad, and then I told him that he might just as well be dead as live the way he was living. Then he stood up and he told me not to worry about him any more in life, that he *was* dead as far as I was concerned. Then he pushed me to the door and the other people looked on as though nothing were happening, and he slammed the door behind me. I stood in the hallway, staring at the door. I heard somebody laugh in the room and then the tears came to my eyes. I started down the steps, whistling to keep from crying, I kept whistling to myself, *You going to need me, baby, one of these cold, rainy days.*

I read about Sonny's trouble in the spring. Little Grace died in the fall. She was a beautiful little girl. But she only lived a little over two years. She died of polio and she suffered. She had a slight fever for a couple of days, but it didn't seem like anything and we just kept her in bed. And we would certainly have called the doctor, but the fever dropped, she seemed to be all right. So we thought it had just been a cold. Then, one day, she was up, playing, Isabel was in the kitchen fixing lunch for the two boys when they'd come in from school, and she heard Grace fall down in the living room. When you have a lot of children you don't always start running when one of them falls, unless they start screaming or something. And, this time, Grace was quiet. Yet, Isabel says that when she heard that *thump* and then that silence, something happened in her to make her afraid. And she ran to the living room and there was little Grace on the floor, all twisted up, and the reason she hadn't screamed was that she couldn't get her breath. And when she did scream, it was the worst sound, Isabel says, that she'd ever heard in all her life, and she still hears it sometimes in her dreams. Isabel will sometimes wake me up with a low, moaning, strangled sound and I have to be quick to awaken her and hold her to me and where Isabel is weeping against me seems a mortal wound.

I think I may have written Sonny the very day that little Grace was buried. I was sitting in the living room in the dark, by myself, and I suddenly thought of Sonny. My trouble made his real.

One Saturday afternoon, when Sonny had been living with us, or, anyway, been in our house, for nearly two weeks, I found myself wandering aimlessly about the living room, drinking from a can of beer, and trying to work up the courage to search Sonny's room. He was out, he was usually out whenever I was home, and Isabel had taken the children to see their grandparents. Suddenly I was standing still in front of the living room window, watching Seventh Avenue. The idea of searching Sonny's room made me still. I scarcely dared to admit to myself what I'd be searching for. I didn't know what I'd do if I found it. Or if I didn't.

On the sidewalk across from me, near the entrance to a barbecue joint, some people were holding an old-fashioned revival meeting. The barbecue cook, wearing a dirty white apron, his conked hair reddish and metallic in the pale sun, and a cigarette between his lips, stood in the doorway, watching them. Kids and older people paused in their errands and stood there, along with some older men and a couple of very toughlooking women who watched everything that happened on the avenue, as though they owned it, or were maybe owned by it. Well, they were watching this, too. The revival was being carried on by three sisters in black, and a brother. All they had were their voices and their Bibles and a tambourine. The brother was testifying and while he testified two of the sisters stood together, seeming to say, amen, and the third sister walked around with the tambourine outstretched and a couple of people dropped coins into it. Then the brother's testimony ended and the sister who had been taking up the collection dumped the coins into her palm and transferred them to the pocket of her long black robe. Then she raised both hands, striking the tambourine against the air, and then against one hand, and she started to sing. And the two other sisters and the brother joined in.

It was strange, suddenly, to watch, though I had been seeing these street meetings all my life. So, of course, had everybody else down there. Yet, they paused and watched and listened and I stood still at the window. *"Tis the old ship of Zion,"* they sang, and the sister with the tambourine kept a steady, jangling beat, *"it has rescued many a thousand!"* Not a soul under the sound of their voices was hearing this song for the first time, not one of them had been rescued. Nor had they seen much in the way of rescue work being done around them. Neither did they especially believe in the holiness of the three sisters and the brother, they knew too much about them, knew where they lived, and how. The woman with the tambourine, whose voice dominated the air, whose face was bright with joy, was divided by very little from the woman who stood watching her, a cigarette between her heavy, chapped lips, her hair a cuckoo's nest, her face scarred and swollen from many beatings, and her black eyes glittering like coal. Perhaps they both knew this, which was why, when, as rarely, they addressed each other, they addressed each other as Sister. As the singing filled the air the watching, listening faces underwent a change, the eyes focusing on something within; the music seemed to soothe a poison out of them; and time seemed, nearly, to fall away from the sullen, belligerent, battered faces, as though they were fleeing back to their first condition, while dreaming of their last. The barbecue cook half shook his head and smiled, and dropped his cigarette and disappeared into his joint. A man fumbled in his pockets for change and stood holding it in his hand impatiently, as though he had just remembered a pressing appointment further up the avenue. He looked furious. Then I saw Sonny, standing on the edge of the crowd. He was carrying a wide, flat notebook with a green cover, and it made him look, from where I was standing, almost like a schoolboy. The coppery sun brought out the copper in his skin, he was very faintly smiling, standing very still. Then the singing stopped, the tambourine turned into a collection plate again. The furious man dropped in his coins and vanished, so did a couple of the women, and Sonny dropped some change in the plate, looking directly at the woman with a little smile. He started across the avenue, toward the house. He has a slow, loping walk, something like the way Harlem hipsters walk, only he's imposed on this his own half-beat. I had never really noticed it before.

I stayed at the window, both relieved and apprehensive. As Sonny disappeared from my sight, they began singing again. And they were still singing when his key turned in the lock.

"Hey," he said.

"Hey, yourself. You want some beer?"

"No. Well, maybe." But he came up to the window and stood beside me, looking out. "What a warm voice," he said.

They were singing *If I could only hear my mother pray again!*

"Yes," I said, "and she can sure beat that tambourine."

"But what a terrible song," he said, and laughed. He dropped his notebook on the sofa and disappeared into the kitchen. "Where's Isabel and the kids?"

"I think they went to see their grandparents. You hungry?"

"No." He came back into the living room with his can of beer. "You want to come some place with me tonight?"

I sensed, I don't know how, that I couldn't possibly say no. "Sure. Where?"

He sat down on the sofa and picked up his notebook and started leafing through it. "I'm going to sit in with some fellows in a joint in the Village."

"You mean, you're going to play, tonight?"

"That's right." He took a swallow of his beer and moved back to the window. He gave me a sidelong look. "If you can stand it."

"I'll try," I said.

He smiled to himself and we both watched as the meeting across the way broke up. The three sisters and the brother, heads bowed, were singing *God be with you till we meet again.* The faces around them were very quiet. Then the song ended. The small crowd dispersed. We watched the three women and the lone man walk slowly up the avenue.

"When she was singing before," said Sonny, abruptly, "her voice reminded me for a minute of what heroin feels like sometimes—when it's in your veins. It makes you feel sort of warm and cool at the same time. And distant. And—and sure." He sipped his beer, very deliberately not looking at me. I watched his face. "It makes you feel—in control. Sometimes you've got to have that feeling."

"Do you?" I sat down slowly in the easy chair.

"Sometimes." He went to the sofa and picked up his notebook again. "Some people do."

"In order," I asked, "to play?" And my voice was very ugly, full of contempt and anger.

"Well"—he looked at me with great, troubled eyes, as though, in fact, he hoped his eyes would tell me things he could never otherwise say—"they *think* so. And *if* they think so—!"

"And what do *you* think?" I asked.

He sat on the sofa and put his can of beer on the floor. "I don't know," he said, and I couldn't be sure if he were answering my question or pursuing his thoughts. His face didn't tell me. "It's not so much to *play*. It's to *stand* it, to be able to make it at all. On any level." He frowned and smiled: "In order to keep from shaking to pieces."

"But these friends of yours," I said, "they seem to shake themselves to pieces pretty goddamn fast."

"Maybe." He played with the notebook. And something told me that I should curb my tongue, that Sonny was doing his best to talk, that I should listen. "But of course you only know the ones that've gone to pieces. Some don't—or at least they haven't *yet* and that's just about all *any* of us can say." He paused. "And then there are some who just live, really, in hell, and they know it and they see what's happening and they go right on. I don't know." He sighed, dropped the notebook, folded his arms. "Some guys, you can tell from the way they play, they on something *all* the time. And you can see that, well, it makes something real for them. But of course," he picked up his beer from the floor and sipped it and put the can down again, "they *want* to, too, you've got to see that. Even some of them that say they don't—*some*, not all."

"And what about you?" I asked—I couldn't help it. "What about you? Do *you* want to?"

He stood up and walked to the window and remained silent for a long time. Then he sighed. "Me," he said. Then: "While I was downstairs before, on my way here, listening to that woman sing, it struck me all of a sudden how much suffering she must have had to go through—to sing like that. It's *repulsive* to think you have to suffer that much."

I said: "But there's no way not to suffer—is there, Sonny?"

"I believe not," he said and smiled, "but that's never stopped anyone from trying." He looked at me. "Has it?" I realized, with this mocking look, that there stood between us, forever, beyond the power of time or forgiveness, the fact that I had held silence—so long!—when he had needed human speech to help him. He turned back to the window. "No, there's no way not to suffer. But you try all kinds of ways to keep from drowning in it, to keep on top of it, and to make it seem—well, like *you*. Like you did something, all right, and now you're suffering for it. You know?" I said nothing. "Well you know," he said, impatiently, "why *do* people suffer? Maybe it's better to do something to give it a reason, *any* reason."

"But we just agreed," I said, "that there's no way not to suffer. Isn't it better, then, just to—take it?"

"But nobody just takes it," Sonny cried, "that's what I'm telling you! *Everybody* tries not to. You're just hung up on the *way* some people try—it's not *your* way!"

The hair on my face began to itch, my face felt wet. "That's not true," I said, "that's not true. I don't give a damn what other people do. I don't even care how they suffer. I just care how *you* suffer." And he looked at me. "Please believe me," I said, "I don't want to see you—die—trying not to suffer."

"I won't," he said, flatly, "die trying not to suffer. At least, not any faster than anybody else."

"But there's no need," I said, trying to laugh, "is there? in killing yourself."

I wanted to say more, but I couldn't. I wanted to talk about will power and how life could be—well, beautiful. I wanted to say that it was all within; but was it? or, rather, wasn't that exactly the trouble? And I wanted to promise that I would never fail him again. But it would all have sounded—empty words and lies.

So I made the promise to myself and prayed that I would keep it.

"It's terrible sometimes, inside," he said, "that's what's the trouble. You walk these streets, black and funky and cold, and there's not really a living ass to talk to, and there's nothing shaking, and there's no way of getting it out—that storm inside. You can't talk it and you can't make love with it, and when you finally try to get with it and play it, you realize *nobody's* listening. So *you've* got to listen. You got to find a way to listen."

And then he walked away from the window and sat on the sofa again, as though all the wind had suddenly been knocked out of him. "Sometimes you'll do *anything* to play, even cut your mother's throat." He laughed and looked at me. "Or your brother's." Then he sobered. "Or your own." Then: "Don't worry. I'm all right now and I think I'll *be* all right. But I can't forget—where I've been. I don't mean just the physical place I've been, I mean where I've *been*. And *what* I've been."

"What have you been, Sonny?" I asked.

He smiled—but sat sideways on the sofa, his elbow resting on the back, his fingers playing with his mouth and chin, not looking at me. "I've been something I didn't recognize, didn't know I could be. Didn't know anybody could be." He stopped, looking inward, looking helplessly young, looking old. "I'm not talking about it now because I feel *guilty* or anything like that—maybe it would be better if I did, I don't know. Anyway, I can't really talk about it. Not to you, not to anybody," and now he turned and faced me. "Sometimes, you know, and it was actually when I was most *out* of the world, I felt that I was in it, that I was *with* it, really, and I could play or I didn't really have to *play*, it just came out of me, it was there. And I don't know how I played, thinking about it now, but I know I did awful things, those times, sometimes, to people. Or it wasn't that I *did* anything to them—it was that they weren't real." He picked up the beer can; it was empty; he rolled it between his palms: "And other times—well, I needed a fix, I needed to find a place to lean, I needed to clear a space to *listen*—and I couldn't find it, and I—went crazy, I did terrible things to *me*, I was terrible *for* me." He began pressing the beer can between his hands, I watched the metal begin to give. It glittered, as he played with it, like a knife, and I was afraid he would cut himself, but I said nothing. "Oh well. I can never tell you. I was all by myself at the bottom of something, stinking and sweating and crying and shaking, and I smelled it, you know? *my* stink, and I thought I'd die if I couldn't get away from it and yet, all the same, I knew that everything I was doing was just locking me in with it. And I didn't know," he paused, still flattening the beer can, "I didn't know, I still *don't* know, something kept telling me that maybe it was good to smell your own stink, but I didn't think that *that* was what I'd been trying to do—and—who can stand it?" and he abruptly dropped the ruined beer can, looking at me with a small, still smile, and then rose, walking to the window as though it were the lodestone rock. I watched his face, he watched the avenue. "I couldn't tell you when Mama died—but the reason I wanted to leave Harlem so bad was to get away from drugs. And then, when I ran away, that's what I was running from—really. When I came back, nothing had changed, *I* hadn't changed, I was just—older." And he stopped, drumming with his fingers on the windowpane. The sun had vanished, soon darkness would fall. I watched his face. "It can come again," he said, almost as though speaking to himself. Then he turned to me. "It can come again," he repeated. "I just want you to know that."

"All right," I said, at last. "So it can come again. All right."

He smiled, but the smile was sorrowful. "I had to try to tell you," he said.

"Yes," I said. "I understand that."

"You're my brother," he said, looking straight at me, and not smiling at all.

"Yes," I repeated, "yes. I understand that."

He turned back to the window, looking out. "All that hatred down there," he said, "all that hatred and misery and love. It's a wonder it doesn't blow the avenue apart."

We went to the only nightclub on a short, dark street, downtown. We squeezed through the narrow, chattering, jampacked bar to the entrance of the big room, where the bandstand was. And we stood there for a moment, for the lights were very dim in this room and we couldn't see. Then, "Hello, boy," said a voice and an enormous black man, much older than Sonny or myself, erupted out of all that atmospheric lighting and put an arm around Sonny's shoulder. "I been sitting right here," he said, "waiting for you."

He had a big voice, too, and heads in the darkness turned toward us.

Sonny grinned and pulled a little away, and said, "Creole, this is my brother. I told you about him."

Creole shook my hand. "I'm glad to meet you, son," he said, and it was clear that he was glad to meet me *there*, for Sonny's sake. And he smiled, "You got a real musician in *your* family," and he took his arm from

Sonny's shoulder and slapped him, lightly, affectionately, with the back of his hand.

"Well. Now I've heard it all," said a voice behind us. This was another musician, and a friend of Sonny's, a coal-black, cheerful-looking man, built close to the ground. He immediately began confiding to me, at the top of his lungs, the most terrible things about Sonny, his teeth gleaming like a lighthouse and his laugh coming up out of him like the beginning of an earthquake. And it turned out that everyone at the bar knew Sonny, or almost everyone; some were musicians, working there, or nearby, or not working, some were simply hangers-on, and some were there to hear Sonny play. I was introduced to all of them and they were all very polite to me. Yet, it was clear that, for them, I was only Sonny's brother. Here, I was in Sonny's world. Or, rather: his kingdom. Here, it was not even a question that his veins bore royal blood.

They were going to play soon and Creole installed me, by myself, at a table in a dark corner. Then I watched them, Creole, and the little black man, and Sonny, and the others, while they horsed around, standing just below the bandstand. The light from the bandstand spilled just a little short of them and, watching them laughing and gesturing and moving about, I had the feeling that they, nevertheless, were being most careful not to step into that circle of light too suddenly: that if they moved into the light too suddenly, without thinking, they would perish in flame. Then, while I watched, one of them, the small, black man, moved into the light and crossed the bandstand and started fooling around with his drums. Then—being funny and being, also, extremely ceremonious—Creole took Sonny by the arm and led him to the piano. A woman's voice called Sonny's name and a few hands started clapping. And Sonny, also being funny and being ceremonious, and so touched, I think, that he could have cried, but neither hiding it nor showing it, riding it like a man, grinned, and put both hands to his heart and bowed from the waist.

Creole then went to the bass fiddle and a lean, very bright-skinned brown man jumped up on the bandstand and picked up his horn. So there they were, and the atmosphere on the bandstand and in the room began to change and tighten. Someone stepped up to the microphone and announced them. Then there were all kinds of murmurs. Some people at the bar shushed others. The waitress ran around, frantically getting in the last orders, guys and chicks got closer to each other, and the lights on the bandstand, on the quartet, turned to a kind of indigo. Then they all looked different there. Creole looked about him for the last time, as though he were making certain that all his chickens were in the coop, and then he—jumped and struck the fiddle. And there they were.

All I know about music is that not many people ever really hear it. And even then, on the rare occasions when something opens within, and the music enters, what we mainly hear, or hear corroborated, are personal, private, vanishing evocations. But the man who creates the music is hearing something else, is dealing with the roar rising from the void and imposing order on it as it hits the air. What is evoked in him, then, is of another order, more terrible because it has no words, and triumphant, too, for that same reason. And his triumph, when he triumphs, is ours. I just watched Sonny's face. His face was troubled, he was working hard, but he wasn't with it. And I had the feeling that, in a way, everyone on the bandstand was waiting for him, both waiting for him and pushing him along. But as I began to watch Creole, I realized that it was Creole who held them all back. He had them on a short rein. Up there, keeping the beat with his whole body, wailing on the fiddle, with his eyes half closed, he was listening to everything, but he was listening to Sonny. He was having a dialogue with Sonny. He wanted Sonny to leave the shoreline and strike out for the deep water. He was Sonny's witness that deep water and drowning were not the same thing—he had been there, and he knew. And he wanted Sonny to know. He was waiting for Sonny to do the things on the keys which would let Creole know that Sonny was in the water.

And, while Creole listened, Sonny moved, deep within, exactly like someone in torment. I had never before thought of how awful the relationship must be between the musician and his instrument. He has to fill it, this instrument, with the breath of life, his own. He has to make it do what he wants it to do. And a piano is just a piano. It's made out of so much wood and wires and little hammers and big ones, and ivory. While there's only so much you can do with it, the only way to find this out is to try; to try and make it do everything.

And Sonny hadn't been near a piano for over a year. And he wasn't on much better terms with his life, not the life that stretched before him now. He and the piano stammered, started one way, got scared, stopped; started another way, panicked, marked time, started again; then seemed to have found a direction, panicked again, got stuck. And the face I saw on Sonny I'd never seen before. Everything had been burned out of it, and, at the same time, things usually hidden were being burned in, by the fire and fury of the battle which was occurring in him up there.

Yet, watching Creole's face as they neared the end of the first set, I had the feeling that something had happened, something I hadn't heard. Then they finished, there was scattered applause, and then, without an instant's warning, Creole started into something else, it was almost sardonic, it was *Am I Blue*. And, as though he commanded, Sonny began to play. Something began to happen. And Creole let out the reins. The dry, low, black man said something awful on the drums, Creole answered, and the drums talked back. Then the horn insisted, sweet and high, slightly detached perhaps, and Creole listened, commenting now and then, dry, and driving, beautiful and calm and old. Then they all came together again, and Sonny was part of the family again. I could tell this from his face. He seemed to have found, right there beneath his fingers, a damn brand-new piano. It seemed that he couldn't get over it. Then, for awhile, just being happy with Sonny, they seemed to be agreeing with him that brand-new pianos certainly were a gas.

Then Creole stepped forward to remind them that what they were playing was the blues. He hit something in all of them, he hit something in me, myself, and the music tightened and deepened, apprehension began to beat the air. Creole began to tell us what the blues were all about. They were not about anything very new. He and his boys up there were keeping it new, at the risk of ruin, destruction, madness, and death, in order to find new ways to make us listen. For, while the tale of how we suffer, and how we are delighted, and how we may triumph is never new, it always must be heard. There isn't any other tale to tell, it's the only light we've got in all this darkness.

And this tale, according to that face, that body, those strong hands on those strings, has another aspect in every country, and a new depth in every generation. Listen, Creole seemed to be saying, listen. Now these are Sonny's blues. He made the little black man on the drums know it, and the bright, brown man on the horn. Creole wasn't trying any longer to get Sonny in the water. He was wishing him Godspeed. Then he stepped back, very slowly, filling the air with the immense suggestion that Sonny speak for himself.

Then they all gathered around Sonny and Sonny played. Every now and again one of them seemed to say, amen. Sonny's fingers filled the air with life, his life. But that life contained so many others. And Sonny went all the way back, he really began with the spare, flat statement of the opening phrase of the song. Then he began to make it his. It was very beautiful because it wasn't hurried and it was no longer a lament. I seemed to hear with what burning he had made it his, with what burning we had yet to make it ours, how we could cease lamenting. Freedom lurked around us and I understood, at last, that he could help us to be free if we would listen, that he would never be free until we did. Yet, there was no battle in his face now. I heard what he had gone through, and would continue to go through until he came to rest in earth. He had made it his: that long line, of which we knew only Mama and Daddy. And he was giving it back, as everything must be given back, so that, passing through death, it can live forever. I saw my mother's face again, and felt, for the first time, how the stones of the road she had walked on must have bruised her feet. I saw the moonlit road where my father's brother died. And it brought something else back to me, and carried me past it, I saw my little girl again and felt Isabel's tears again, and I felt my own tears begin to rise. And I was yet aware that this was only a moment, that the world waited outside as hungry as a tiger, and that trouble stretched above us, longer than the sky.

Then it was over. Creole and Sonny let out their breath, both soaking wet, and grinning. There was a lot of applause and some of it was real. In the dark, the girl came by and I asked her to take drinks to the bandstand.

There was a long pause, while they talked up there in the indigo light and after awhile I saw the girl put a Scotch and milk on top of the piano for Sonny. He didn't seem to notice it, but just before they started playing again, he sipped from it and looked toward me, and nodded. Then he put it back on top of the piano. For me, then, as they began to play again, it glowed and shook above my brother's head like the very cup of trembling.

---

# HE

## Katherine Anne Porter

*Born in 1894 in Indian Creek, Texas, Katherine Anne Porter spent her early years in that state and Louisiana. Her first fiction was published in* The Century Magazine *and other little magazines, and in 1930 her first collection,* Flowering Judas and Other Stories, *in which "He" first appeared, was an immediate literary success. This was followed by other collections of stories and essays, the best known of which are* Pale Horse, Pale Rider (*three novelettes, 1939*), The Leaning Tower and Other Stories (*1944*), *and* The Days Before (*1952*). *Her only novel,* Ship of Fools, *was published in 1962, but, typically, she had worked on it for many years. Among her other honors are an honorary Doctor of Letters degree from the Women's College of the University of North Carolina, an appointment as Fellow in Regional American Literature of the Library of Congress, and Guggenheim Fellowships in 1931 and 1938. Known as a meticulous craftsman and stylist, Katherine Anne Porter stands today as one of the most distinguished writers in modern American letters.*

Life was very hard for the Whipples. It was hard to feed all the hungry mouths, it was hard to keep the children in flannels during the winter, short as it was: "God knows what would become of us if we lived North," they would say: keeping them decently clean was hard. "It looks like our luck won't never let up on us," said Mr. Whipple, but Mrs. Whipple was all for taking what was sent and calling it good, anyhow when the neighbors were in earshot. "Don't ever let a soul hear us complain," she kept saying to her husband. She couldn't stand to be pitied. "No, not if it comes to it that we have to live in a wagon and pick cotton around the country," she said, "nobody's going to get a chance to look down on us."

Mrs. Whipple loved her second son, the simple-minded one, better than she loved the other two children put together. She was forever saying so, and when she talked with certain of her neighbors she would even throw in her husband and her mother for good measure.

"You needn't keep on saying it around," said Mr. Whipple; "you'll make people think nobody else has any feeling about Him but you."

"It's natural for a mother," Mrs. Whipple would remind him. "You know yourself it's more natural for a mother to be that way. People don't expect so much of fathers, some way."

This didn't keep the neighbors from talking plainly among themselves. "A Lord's pure mercy if He should die," they said. "It's the sins of the fathers," they agreed among themselves. "There's bad blood and bad doings somewhere, you can bet on that." This behind the Whipples' backs. To their faces everybody said, "He's not so bad off. He'll be all right yet. Look how He grows!"

Mrs. Whipple hated to talk about it, she tried to keep her mind off it, but every time anybody set foot in the house, the subject always came up, and she had to talk about Him first, before she could get on to anything else. It seemed to ease her mind. "I wouldn't have anything happen to Him for all the world, but it just looks like I can't keep Him out of mischief. He's so strong and active, He's always into everything; He was like that since He could walk. It's actually funny sometimes, the way He can do anything; it's laughable to see Him up to His tricks. Emly has more accidents; I'm forever tying up her bruises, and Adna can't fall a foot without cracking a bone. But He can do anything and not get a scratch. The preacher said such a nice thing once when he was here. He said, and I'll remember it to my dying day, 'The innocent walk with God —that's why He don't get hurt.'" Whenever Mrs. Whipple repeated these words, she always felt a warm pool spread in her breast, and the tears would fill her eyes, and then she could talk about something else.

He did grow and He never got hurt. A plank blew off the chicken house and struck Him on the head and He never seemed to know it. He had learned a few words, and after this He forgot them. He didn't whine for food as the other children did, but waited until it was given Him; He ate squatting in the corner, smacking and mumbling. Rolls of fat covered Him like an overcoat, and He could carry twice as much wood and water as Adna. Emly had a cold in the head most of the time—"She takes after me," said Mrs. Whipple—so in bad weather they gave her the extra blanket off His cot. He never seemed to mind the cold.

Just the same, Mrs. Whipple's life was a torment for fear something might happen to Him. He climbed the peach trees much better than Adna and went skittering along the branches like a monkey, just a regular monkey. "Oh, Mrs. Whipple, you hadn't ought to let Him do that. He'll lose His balance sometime. He can't rightly know what He's doing."

Mrs. Whipple almost screamed out at the neighbor. "He *does* know what He's doing! He's as able as any other child! Come down out of there, you!" When He finally reached the ground she could hardly keep her hands off Him for acting like that before people, a grin all over His face and her worried sick about Him all the time.

"It's the neighbors," said Mrs. Whipple to her husband. "Oh, I do mortally wish they would keep out of our business. I can't afford to let Him do anything for fear they'll come nosing around about it. Look at the bees, now. Adna can't handle them, they sting him up so; I haven't got time to do everything, and now I don't dare let Him. But if He gets a sting He don't really mind."

"It's just because He ain't got sense enough to be scared of anything," said Mr. Whipple.

"You ought to be ashamed of yourself," said Mrs. Whipple, "talking that way about your own child. Who's to take up for Him if we don't, I'd like to know? He sees a lot that goes on, He listens to things all the time. And anything I tell Him to do He does it. Don't never let anybody hear you say such things. They'd think you favored the other children over Him."

"Well, now, I don't, and you know it, and what's the use of getting all worked up about it? You always think the worst of everything. Just let Him alone, He'll get along somehow. He gets plenty to eat and wear, don't He?" Mr. Whipple suddenly felt tired out. "Anyhow, it can't be helped now."

Mrs. Whipple felt tired too, she complained in a tired voice. "What's done can't never be undone, I know that good as anybody; but He's my child, and I'm not going to have people say anything. I'm sick of people coming around saying things all the time."

In the early fall Mrs. Whipple got a letter from her brother saying he and his wife and two children were coming over for a little visit next Sunday week. "Put the big pot in the little one," he wrote at the end. Mrs. Whipple read this part out loud twice, she was so pleased. Her brother was a great one for saying funny things. "We'll just show him that's no joke," she said; "we'll just butcher one of the suckling pigs."

"It's a waste, and I don't hold with waste the way we are now," said Mr. Whipple. "That pig'll be worth money by Christmas."

"It's a shame and a pity we can't have a decent meal's vittles once in a while when my own family comes to see us," said Mrs. Whipple. "I'd hate for his wife to go back and say there wasn't a thing in the house to eat. My God, it's better than buying up a great chance of meat in town. There's where you'd spend the money!"

"All right, do it yourself then," said Mr. Whipple. "Christamighty, no wonder we can't get ahead!"

The question was how to get the little pig away from his ma, a great fighter, worse than a Jersey cow. Adna wouldn't try it; "That sow'd rip my insides out all over the pen." "All right, old fraidy," said Mrs. Whipple, "*He's* not scared. Watch *Him* do it." And she laughed as though it was all a good joke and gave Him a little push towards the pen. He sneaked up and snatched the pig right away from the teat and galloped back and was over the fence with the sow raging at His heels. The little black squirming thing was screeching like a baby in a tantrum, stiffening its back and stretching its mouth to the ears. Mrs. Whipple took the pig with her face stiff and sliced its throat with one stroke. When He saw the blood He gave a great jolting breath and ran away. "But He'll forget and eat plenty, just the same," thought Mrs. Whipple. Whenever she was thinking, her lips moved making words. "He'd eat it all if I didn't stop Him. He'd eat up every mouthful from the other two if I'd let Him."

She felt badly about it. He was ten years old now and a third again as large as Adna, who was going on fourteen. "It's a shame, a shame," she kept saying under her breath, "and Adna with so much brains!"

She kept on feeling badly about all sorts of things. In the first place it was the man's work to butcher; the sight of the pig scraped pink and naked made her sick. He was too fat and soft and pitiful-looking. It was simply a shame the way things had to happen. By the time she had finished it up, she almost wished her brother would stay at home.

Early Sunday morning Mrs. Whipple dropped everything to get Him all cleaned up. In an hour He was dirty again, with crawling under fences after a possum, and straddling along the rafters of the barn looking for eggs in the hayloft. "My Lord, look at you now after all my trying! And here's Adna and Emly staying so quiet. I get tired trying to keep you decent. Get off that shirt and put on another, people will say I don't half dress you!" And she boxed Him on the ears, hard. He blinked and blinked and rubbed His head, and His face hurt Mrs. Whipple's feelings. Her knees began to tremble, she had to sit down while she buttoned His shirt. "I'm just all gone before the day starts."

The brother came with his plump healthy wife and two great roaring hungry boys. They had a grand dinner, with the pig roasted to a crackling in the middle of the table, full of dressing, a pickled peach in his mouth and plenty of gravy for the sweet potatoes.

"This looks like prosperity all right," said the brother; "you're going to have to roll me home like I was a barrel when I'm done."

Everybody laughed out loud; it was fine to hear them laughing all at once around the table. Mrs. Whipple felt warm and good about it. "Oh, we've got six more of these; I say it's as little as we can do when you come to see us so seldom."

He wouldn't come into the dining room, and Mrs. Whipple passed it off very well. "He's timider than my other two," she said, "He'll just have to get used to you. There isn't everybody He'll make up with; you know how it is with some children, even cousins." Nobody said anything out of the way.

"Just like my Alfy here," said the brother's wife. "I sometimes got to lick him to make him shake hands with his own grandmammy."

So that was over, and Mrs. Whipple loaded up a big plate for Him first, before everybody. "I always say He ain't to be slighted, no matter who else goes without," she said, and carried it to Him herself.

"He can chin Himself on the top of the door," said Emly, helping along.

"That's fine, He's getting along fine," said the brother.

They went away after supper. Mrs. Whipple rounded up the dishes, and sent the children to bed and sat down and unlaced her shoes. "You see?" she said to Mr. Whipple. "That's the way my whole family is. Nice and considerate about everything. No out-of-the-way remarks—they *have* got refinement. I get awfully sick of people's remarks. Wasn't that pig good?"

Mr. Whipple said, "Yes, we're out three hundred pounds of pork, that's all. It's easy to be polite when you come to eat. Who knows what they had in their minds all along?"

"Yes, that's like you," said Mrs. Whipple. "I don't expect anything else from you. You'll be telling me next that my own brother will be saying around that we made Him eat in the kitchen! Oh, my God!" she rocked her head in her hands, a hard pain started in the very middle of her forehead. "Now it's all spoiled, and everything was so nice and easy. All right, you don't like them and you never did—all right, they'll not come here again soon, never you mind! But they *can't* say He wasn't dressed every lick as good as Adna—oh, honest, sometimes I wish I was dead!"

"I wish you'd let up," said Mr. Whipple. "It's bad enough as it is."

It was a hard winter. It seemed to Mrs. Whipple that they hadn't ever known anything but hard times, and now to cap it all a winter like this. The crops were about half of what they had a right to expect; after the cotton was in it didn't do much more than cover the grocery bill. They swapped off one of the plow horses, and got cheated, for the new one died of the heaves. Mrs. Whipple kept thinking all the time it was terrible to have a man you couldn't depend on not to get cheated. They cut down on everything, but Mrs. Whipple kept saying there are things you can't cut down on, and they cost money. It took a lot of warm clothes for Adna and Emly, who walked four miles to school during the three-months session. "He sets around the fire a lot, He won't need so much," said Mr. Whipple. "That's so," said Mrs. Whipple, "and when He does the outdoor chores He can wear your tarpaullion coat. I can't do no better, that's all."

In February He was taken sick, and lay curled up under His blanket looking very blue in the face and acting as if He would choke. Mr. and Mrs. Whipple did everything they could for Him for two days, and then they were scared and sent for the doctor. The doctor told them they must keep Him warm and give Him plenty of milk and eggs. "He isn't as stout as He looks, I'm afraid," said the doctor. "You've got to watch them when they're like that. You must put more cover onto Him, too."

"I just took off His big blanket to wash," said Mrs. Whipple, ashamed. "I can't stand dirt."

"Well, you'd better put it back on the minute it's dry," said the doctor, "or He'll have pneumonia."

Mr. and Mrs. Whipple took a blanket off their own bed and put His cot in by the fire. "They can't say we didn't do everything for Him," she said, "even to sleeping cold ourselves on His account."

When the winter broke He seemed to be well again, but He walked as if His feet hurt Him. He was able to run a cotton planter during the season.

"I got it all fixed up with Jim Ferguson about breeding the cow next time," said Mr. Whipple. "I'll pasture the bull this summer and give Jim some fodder in the fall. That's better than paying out money when you haven't got it."

"I hope you didn't say such a thing before Jim Ferguson," said Mrs. Whipple. "You oughtn't to let him know we're so down as all that."

"Godamighty, that ain't saying we're down. A man is got to look ahead sometimes. He can lead the bull over today. I need Adna on the place."

At first Mrs. Whipple felt easy in her mind about sending Him for the bull. Adna was too jumpy and couldn't be trusted. You've got to be steady around animals. After He was gone she started thinking, and after a while she could hardly bear it any longer. She stood in the lane and watched for Him. It was nearly three miles to go and a hot day, but He oughtn't to be so long about it. She shaded her eyes and stared until colored bubbles floated in her eyeballs. It was just like everything else in life, she must always worry and never know a moment's peace about anything. After a long time she saw Him turn into the side lane, limping. He came on very slowly, leading the big hulk of an animal by a ring in the nose, twirling a little stick in His hand, never looking back or sideways, but coming on like a sleepwalker with His eyes half shut.

Mrs. Whipple was scared sick of bulls; she had heard awful stories about how they followed on quietly enough, and then suddenly pitched on with a bellow and pawed and gored a body to pieces. Any second now that black monster would come down on Him; my God, He'd never have sense enough to run.

She mustn't make a sound nor a move; she mustn't get the bull started. The bull heaved his head aside and horned the air at a fly. Her voice burst out of her in a shriek, and she screamed at Him to come on, for God's sake. He didn't seem to hear her clamor, but kept on twirling His switch and limping on, and the bull lumbered along behind him as gently as a calf. Mrs. Whipple stopped calling and ran towards the house, praying under her breath: "Lord, don't let anything happen to Him. Lord, you *know* people will say we oughtn't to have sent Him. You *know* they'll say we didn't take care of Him. Oh, get Him home, safe home, safe home, and I'll look out for Him better! Amen."

She watched from the window while He led the beast in, and tied him up in the barn. It was no use trying to keep up, Mrs. Whipple couldn't bear another thing. She sat down and rocked and cried with her apron over her head.

From year to year the Whipples were growing poorer. The place just seemed to run down of itself, no matter how hard they worked. "We're losing our hold," said Mrs. Whipple. "Why can't we do like other people and watch for our best chances? They'll be calling us poor white trash next."

"When I get to be sixteen I'm going to leave," said Adna. "I'm going to get a job in Powell's grocery store. There's money in that. No more farm for me."

"I'm going to be a school-teacher," said Emly. "But I've got to finish the eighth grade, anyhow. Then I can live in town. I don't see any chances here."

"Emly takes after my family," said Mrs. Whipple. "Ambitious every last one of them, and they don't take second place for anybody."

When fall came Emly got a chance to wait on table in the railroad eating-house in the town near-by, and it seemed such a shame not to take it when the wages were good and she could get her food too, that Mrs. Whipple decided to let her take it, and not bother with school until the next session. "You've got plenty of time," she said. "You're young and smart as a whip."

With Adna gone too, Mr. Whipple tried to run the farm with just Him to help. He seemed to get along fine, doing His work and part of Adna's without noticing it. They did well enough until Christmas time, when one morning He slipped on the ice coming up from the barn. Instead of getting up He thrashed round and round, and when Mr. Whipple got to Him, He was having some sort of fit.

They brought Him inside and tried to make Him sit up, but He blubbered and rolled, so they put Him to bed and Mr. Whipple rode to town for the doctor. All the way there and back he worried about where the money was to come from: it sure did look like he had about all the troubles he could carry.

From then on He stayed in bed. His legs swelled up double their size, and the fits kept coming back. After four months, the doctor said, "It's no use, I think you'd better put Him in the County Home for treatment right away. I'll see about it for you. He'll have good care there and be off your hands."

"We don't begrudge Him any care, and I won't let Him out of my sight," said Mrs. Whipple. "I won't have it said I sent my sick child off among strangers."

"I know how you feel," said the doctor. "You can't tell me anything about that, Mrs. Whipple. I've got a boy of my own. But you'd better listen to me. I can't do anything more for Him, that's the truth."

Mr. and Mrs. Whipple talked it over a long time that night after they went to bed. "It's just charity," said Mrs. Whipple, "that's what we've come to, charity! I certainly never looked for this."

"We pay taxes to help support the place just like everybody else," said Mr. Whipple, "and I don't call that taking charity. I think it would be fine to have Him where He'd get the best of everything . . . and besides, I can't keep up with these doctor bills any longer."

"Maybe that's why the doctor wants us to send Him—he's scared he won't get his money," said Mrs. Whipple.

"Don't talk like that," said Mr. Whipple, feeling pretty sick, "or we won't be able to send Him."

"Oh, but we won't keep Him there long," said Mrs. Whipple. "Soon's He's better, we'll bring Him right back home."

"The doctor has told you and told you time and again He can't ever get better, and you might as well stop talking," said Mr. Whipple.

"Doctors don't know everything," said Mrs. Whipple, feeling almost happy. "But anyhow, in the summer Emly can come home for a vacation and Adna can get down for Sundays: we'll all work together and get on our feet again, and the children will feel they've got a place to come to."

All at once she saw it full summer again, with the garden going fine, and new white roller shades up all over the house, and Adna and Emly home, so full of life, all of them happy together. Oh, it could happen, things would ease up on them.

They didn't talk before Him much, but they never knew just how much He understood. Finally the doctor set the day, and a neighbor who owned a double-seated carryall offered to drive them over. The hospital would have sent an ambulance, but Mrs. Whipple couldn't stand to see Him going away looking so sick as all that. They wrapped Him in blankets, and the neighbor and Mr. Whipple lifted Him into the back seat of the carryall beside Mrs. Whipple, who had on her black shirtwaist. She couldn't stand to go looking like charity.

"You'll be all right, I guess I'll stay behind," said Mr. Whipple. "It don't look like everybody ought to leave the place at once."

"Besides, it ain't as if He was going to stay forever," said Mrs. Whipple to the neighbor. "This is only for a little while."

They started away, Mrs. Whipple holding to the edges of the blankets to keep Him from sagging sideways. He sat there blinking and blinking. He worked His hands out and began rubbing His nose with His knuckles, and then with the end of the blanket. Mrs. Whipple couldn't believe what she saw; He was scrubbing away big tears that rolled out of the corners of His eyes. He sniveled and made a gulping noise. Mrs. Whipple kept saying, "Oh, honey, you don't feel so bad, do you? You don't feel so bad, do you?" for He seemed to be accusing her of something. Maybe He remembered that time she boxed His ears, maybe He had been scared that day with the bull, maybe He had slept cold and couldn't tell her about it; maybe He knew they were sending Him away for good and all because they were too poor to keep Him. Whatever it was, Mrs. Whipple couldn't bear to think of it. She began to cry, frightfully, and wrapped her arms tight around Him. His head rolled on her shoulder: she had loved Him as much as she possibly could, there were Adna and Emly who had to be thought of too, there was nothing she could do to make up to Him for His life. Oh, what a mortal pity He was ever born.

They came in sight of the hospital, with the neighbor driving very fast, not daring to look behind him.

---

# NEXT DOOR

## Kurt Vonnegut, Jr.

*Born in Indianapolis, Indiana, in 1922, Kurt Vonnegut attended Cornell University, Carnegie Institute of Technology, and the University of Chicago. He has worked as a police reporter and in public relations; he has also lectured a good deal and has taught in various colleges and universities. He was awarded the Purple Heart for his service in World War II. In addition to his novels and short stories, he has written for television and the theater. Among his works are* Player Piano *(1951),* The Sirens of Titan *(1959),* Cat's Cradle *(1963),* God Bless You, Mr. Rosewater *(1965),* Slaughterhouse Five *(1969), all novels; and* Welcome to the Monkey House *(1970), a collection of short stories in which "Next Door" appears. He has also written two plays,* Happy Birthday, Wanda June *and* Between Time and Timbuktu. *His latest novel is* Breakfast of Champions *(1973), and he has just recently published* Wampeters, Foma & Gramfallons *(1974), a collection of essays, lectures, and reviews. Known for a time simply as a science fiction writer, Vonnegut has now become firmly established as a writer of black comedy. What distinguishes Vonnegut from other black-comedy writers, perhaps, and the most noticeable characteristic of "Next Door," is his ability to be humorous and yet perceptively objective at the same time. "There is no self-pity at the core of Vonnegut's work," Richard Schickel has written, "only the purifying laughter of a man who has survived that stage. It is this maturity which, in the last analysis, separates him from most black comedians." Vonnegut himself has written: "I have been a writer since 1949. I am self-taught. I have no theories about writing that might help others. When I write I simply become what I seemingly must become. I am six feet two and weigh nearly two hundred pounds and am badly coordinated, except when I swim. All that borrowed meat does the writing. In the water I am beautiful."*

The old house was divided into two dwellings by a thin wall that passed on, with high fidelity, sounds on either side. On the north side were the Leonards. On the south side were the Hargers.

The Leonards—husband, wife, and eight-year-old son—had just moved in. And, aware of the wall, they kept their voices down as they argued in a friendly way as to whether or not the boy, Paul, was old enough to be left alone for the evening.

"Shhhhh!" said Paul's father.

"Was I shouting?" said his mother. "I was talking in a perfectly normal tone."

"If I could hear Harger pulling a cork, he can certainly hear you," said his father.

"I didn't say anything I'd be ashamed to have anybody hear," said Mrs. Leonard.

"You called Paul a baby," said Mr. Leonard. "That certainly embarrasses Paul—and it embarrasses me."

"It's just a way of talking," she said.

"It's a way we've got to stop," he said. "And we can stop treating him like a baby, too—*tonight*. We simply shake his hand, walk out, and go to the movie." He turned to Paul. "You're not afraid—are you boy?"

"I'll be all right," said Paul. He was very tall for his age, and thin, and had a soft, sleepy, radiant sweetness engendered by his mother. "I'm fine."

"Damn right!" said his father, clouting him on the back. "It'll be an adventure."

"I'd feel better about this adventure, if we could get a sitter," said his mother.

"If it's going to spoil the picture for you," said the father, "let's take him with us."

Mrs. Leonard was shocked. "Oh—it isn't for children."

"I don't care," said Paul amiably. The why of their not wanting him to see certain movies, certain magazines, certain books, certain television shows was a mystery he respected—even relished a little.

"It wouldn't kill him to see it," said his father.

"You *know* what it's about," she said.

"What *is* it about?" said Paul innocently.

Mrs. Leonard looked to her husband for help, and got none. "It's about a girl who chooses her friends unwisely," she said.

"Oh," said Paul. "That doesn't sound very interesting."

"Are we going, or aren't we?" said Mr. Leonard impatiently. "The show starts in ten minutes."

Mrs. Leonard bit her lip. "All right!" she said bravely. "You lock the windows and the back door, and I'll write down the telephone numbers for the police and the fire department and the theater and Dr. Failey." She turned to Paul. "You *can* dial, can't you, dear?"

"He's been dialing for years!" cried Mr. Leonard.

"Ssssssh!" said Mrs. Leonard.

"Sorry," Mr. Leonard bowed to the wall. "My apologies."

"Paul, dear," said Mrs. Leonard, "what are you going to do while we're gone?"

"Oh—look through my microscope, I guess," said Paul.

"You're not going to be looking at germs, are you?" she said.

"Nope—just hair, sugar, pepper, stuff like that," said Paul.

His mother frowned judiciously. "I think that would be all right, don't you?" she said to Mr. Leonard.

"Fine!" said Mr. Leonard. "Just as long as the pepper doesn't make him sneeze!"

"I'll be careful," said Paul.

Mr. Leonard winced. "Shhhhh!" he said.

Soon after Paul's parents left, the radio in the Harger apartment went on. It was on softly at first—so softly that Paul, looking through his microscope on the living room coffee table, couldn't make out the announcer's words. The music was frail and dissonant—unidentifiable.

Gamely, Paul tried to listen to the music rather than to the man and woman who were fighting.

Paul squinted through the eyepiece of his microscope at a bit of his hair far below, and he turned a knob to bring the hair into focus. It looked like a glistening brown eel, flecked here and there with tiny spectra where the light struck the hair just so.

There—the voices of the man and woman were getting louder again, drowning out the radio. Paul twisted the microscope knob nervously, and the objective lens ground into the glass slide on which the hair rested.

The woman was shouting now.

Paul unscrewed the lens, and examined it for damage.

Now the man shouted back—shouted something awful, unbelievable.

Paul got a sheet of lens tissue from his bedroom, and dusted at the frosted dot on the lens, where the lens had bitten into the slide. He screwed the lens back in place.

All was quiet again next door—except for the radio.

Paul looked down into the microscope, down into the milky mist of the damaged lens.

Now the fight was beginning again—louder and louder, cruel and crazy.

Trembling, Paul sprinkled grains of salt on a fresh slide, and put it under the microscope.

The woman shouted again, a high, ragged, poisonous shout.

Paul turned the knob too hard, and the fresh slide cracked and fell in triangles to the floor. Paul stood, shaking, wanting to shout, too—to shout in terror and bewilderment. It had to stop. Whatever it was, it *had* to stop!

"If you're going to yell, turn up the radio!" the man cried.

Paul heard the clicking of the woman's heels across the floor. The radio volume swelled until the boom of the bass made Paul feel like he was trapped in a drum.

"And now!" bellowed the radio, "for Katy from Fred! For Nancy from Bob, who thinks she's swell! For Arthur, from one who's worshipped him from afar for six weeks! Here's the old Glenn Miller Band and that all-time favorite, *Stardust!* Remember! If you have a dedication, call Milton nine-three-thousand! Ask for All-Night Sam, the record man!"

The music picked up the house and shook it.

A door slammed next door. Now someone hammered on a door.

Paul looked down into his microscope once more, looked at nothing—while a prickling sensation spread over his skin. He faced the truth: The man and woman would kill each other, if he didn't stop them.

He beat on the wall with his fist, "Mr. Harger! Stop it!" he cried. "Mrs. Harger! Stop it!"

"For Ollie from Lavinia!" All-Night Sam cried back at him. "For Ruth from Carl, who'll never forget last Tuesday! For Wilber from Mary, who's lonesome tonight! Here's the Sauter-Finnegan Band asking, *Love, What Are You Doing to My Heart?*"

Next door, crockery smashed, filling a split second of radio silence. And then the tidal wave of music drowned everything again.

Paul stood by the wall, trembling in his helplessness. "Mr. Harger! Mrs. Harger! Please!"

"Remember the number!" said All-Night Sam. "Milton nine-three-thousand!"

Dazed, Paul went to the phone and dialed the number.

"WJCD," said the switchboard operator.

"Would you kindly connect me with All-Night Sam?" said Paul.

"Hello!" said All-Night Sam. He was eating, talking with a full mouth. In the background, Paul could hear sweet, bleating music, the original of what was rending the radio next door.

"I wonder if I might make a dedication," said Paul.

"Dunno why not," said Sam. "Ever belong to any organization listed as subversive by the Attorney General's office?"

Paul thought a moment. "Nossir—I don't think so, sir," he said.

"Shoot," said Sam.

"From Mr. Lemuel K. Harger to Mrs. Harger," said Paul.

"What's the message?" said Sam.

"I love you," said Paul. "Let's make up and start all over again."

The woman's voice was so shrill with passion that it cut through the din of the radio, and even Sam heard it.

"Kid—are you in trouble?" said Sam. "Your folks fighting?"

Paul was afraid that Sam would hang up on him if he found out that Paul wasn't a blood relative of the Hargers. "Yessir," he said.

"And you're trying to pull 'em back together again with this dedication?" said Sam.

"Yessir," said Paul.

Sam became very emotional. "O.K., kid," he said hoarsely, "I'll give it everything I've got. Maybe it'll work. I once saved a guy from shooting himself the same way."

"How did you do that?" said Paul, fascinated.

"He called up and said he was gonna blow his brains out," said Sam, "and I played *The Bluebird of Happiness*." He hung up.

Paul dropped the telephone into its cradle. The music stopped, and Paul's hair stood on end. For the first time, the fantastic speed of modern communications was real to him, and he was appalled.

"Folks!" said Sam, "I guess everybody stops and wonders sometimes what the heck he thinks he's doin' with the life the good Lord gave him! It may seem funny to you folks, because I always keep a cheerful front, no matter how I feel inside, that I wonder sometimes, too! And then, just like some angel was trying to tell me, 'Keep going, Sam, keep going,' something like this comes along."

"Folks!" said Sam, "I've been asked to bring a man and his wife back together again through the miracle of radio! I guess there's no sense in kidding ourselves about marriage! It isn't any bowl of cherries! There's ups and downs, and sometimes folks don't see how they can go on!"

Paul was impressed with the wisdom and authority of Sam. Having the radio turned up high made sense now, for Sam was speaking like the right-hand man of God.

When Sam paused for effect, all was still next door. Already the miracle was working.

"Now," said Sam, "a guy in my business has to be half musician, half philosopher, half psychiatrist, and half electrical engineer! And! If I've learned one thing from working with all you wonderful people out there, it's this: if folks would swallow their self-respect and pride, there wouldn't be any more divorces!"

There were affectionate cooings from next door. A lump grew in Paul's throat as he thought about the beautiful thing he and Sam were bringing to pass.

"Folks!" said Sam, "that's all I'm gonna say about love and marriage! That's all anybody needs to know! And now, for Mrs. Lemuel K. Harger, from Mr. Harger—I love you! Let's make up and start all over again!" Sam choked up. "Here's Eartha Kitt, and *Somebody Bad Stole De Wedding Bell!*"

The radio next door went off.

The world lay still.

A purple emotion flooded Paul's being. Childhood dropped away, and he hung, dizzy, on the brink of life, rich, violent, rewarding.

There was movement next door—slow, foot-dragging movement.

"So," said the woman.

"Charlotte—" said the man uneasily. "Honey—I swear."

"'I love you,'" she said bitterly, "'let's make up and start all over again.'"

"Baby," said the man desperately, "it's another Lemuel K. Harger. It's got to be!"

"You want your wife back?" she said. "All right—I won't get in her way. She can have you, Lemuel—you jewel beyond price, you."

"*She* must have called the station," said the man.

"She can have you, you philandering, two-timing, two-bit Lochinvar," she said. "But you won't be in very good condition."

"Charlotte—put down that gun," said the man. "Don't do anything you'll be sorry for."

"That's all behind me, you worm," she said.

There were three shots.

Paul ran out into the hall, and bumped into the woman as she burst from the Harger apartment. She was a big, blonde woman, all soft and awry, like an unmade bed.

She and Paul screamed at the same time, and then she grabbed him as he started to run.

"You want candy?" she said wildly. "Bicycle?"

"No, thank you," said Paul shrilly. "Not at this time."

"You haven't seen or heard a thing!" she said. "You know what happens to squealers?"

"Yes!" cried Paul.

She dug into her purse, and brought out a perfumed mulch of face tissues, bobbypins and cash. "Here!" she panted. "It's yours! And there's more where that came from, if you keep your mouth shut." She stuffed it into his trousers pocket.

She looked at him fiercely, then fled into the street.

Paul ran back into his apartment, jumped into bed, and pulled the covers up over his head. In the hot, dark cave of the bed, he cried because he and All-Night Sam had helped to kill a man.

A policeman came clumping into the house very soon, and he knocked on both apartment doors with his billyclub.

Numb, Paul crept out of the hot, dark cave, and answered the door. Just as he did, the door across the hall opened, and there stood Mr. Harger, haggard but whole.

"Yes, sir?" said Harger. He was a small, balding man, with a hairline mustache. "Can I help you?"

"The neighbors heard some shots," said the policeman.

"Really?" said Harger urbanely. He dampened his mustache with the tip of his little finger. "How bizarre. I heard nothing." He looked at Paul sharply. "Have you been playing with your father's guns again, young man?"

"Oh, nossir!" said Paul, horrified.

"Where are your folks?" said the policeman to Paul.

"At the movies," said Paul.

"You're all alone?" said the policeman.

"Yessir," said Paul. "It's an adventure."

"I'm sorry I said that about the guns," said Harger. "I certainly would have heard any shots in this house. The walls are thin as paper, and I heard nothing."

Paul looked at him gratefully.

"And you didn't hear any shots, either, kid?" said the policeman.

Before Paul could find an answer, there was a disturbance out on the street. A big, motherly woman was getting out of a taxicab and wailing at the top of her lungs. "Lem! Lem, baby."

She barged into the foyer, a suitcase bumping against her leg and tearing her stocking to shreds. She dropped the suitcase, and ran to Harger, throwing her arms around him.

"I got your message, darling," she said, "and I did just what All-Night Sam told me to do. I swallowed my self-respect, and here I am!"

"Rose, Rose, Rose—my little Rose," said Harger. "Don't ever leave me again." They grappled with each other affectionately, and staggered into their apartment.

"Just look at this apartment!" said Mrs. Harger. "Men are just lost without women!" As she closed the door, Paul could see that she was awfully pleased with the mess.

"You *sure* you didn't hear any shots?" said the policeman to Paul.

The ball of money in Paul's pocket seemed to swell to the size of a watermelon. "Yessir," he croaked.

The policeman left.

Paul shut his apartment door, shuffled into his bedroom, and collapsed on the bed.

The next voices Paul heard came from his own side of the wall. The voices were sunny—the voices of his mother and father. His mother was singing a nursery rhyme and his father was undressing him.

"Diddle-diddle-dumpling, my son John," piped his mother, "Went to bed with his stockings on. One shoe off, and one shoe on—diddle-diddle-dumpling, my son John."

Paul opened his eyes.

"Hi, big boy," said his father, "you went to sleep with all your clothes on."

"How's my little adventurer?" said his mother.

"O.K.," said Paul sleepily. "How was the show?"

"It wasn't for children, honey," said his mother. "You would have liked the short subject, though. It was all about bears—cunning little cubs."

Paul's father handed her Paul's trousers, and she shook them out, and hung them neatly on the back of a chair by the bed. She patted them smooth, and felt the ball of money in the pocket. "Little boys' pockets!" she said, delighted. "Full of childhood's mysteries. An enchanted frog? A magic pocketknife from a fairy princess?" She caressed the lump.

"He's not a little boy—he's a big boy," said Paul's father. "And he's too old to be thinking about fairy princesses."

Paul's mother held up her hands. "Don't rush it, don't rush it. When I saw him asleep there, I realized all over again how dreadfully short childhood is." She reached into the pocket and sighed wistfully. "Little boys are so hard on clothes—especially pockets."

She brought out the ball and held it under Paul's nose. "Now, would you mind telling Mommy what we have here?" she said gaily.

The ball bloomed like a frowzy chrysanthemum, with ones, fives, tens, twenties, and lipstick-stained Kleenx for petals. And rising from it, befuddling Paul's young mind, was the pungent musk of perfume.

Paul's father sniffed the air. "What's that smell?" he said.

Paul's mother rolled her eyes. *"Tabu,"* she said.

---

# A CLEAN, WELL-LIGHTED PLACE

## Ernest Hemingway

*Born in Oak Park, Illinois, on July 21, 1898, Ernest Hemingway, novelist, playwright, short story writer, and war correspondent, spent most of his childhood and youth in Michigan, attending local schools and winning fame as a boxer and football player. During World War I he served as a volunteer in France and Italy, was wounded, and sent home. He also served as a war correspondent at various times, a continuation of a career in journalism begun as a reporter on the Kansas City Star. He gained fame as one of the writers of the "lost generation" that settled in Paris right after World War I, and was identified with such figures as Ezra Pound, Gertrude Stein, and F. Scott Fitzgerald. Perhaps his best-known novels are* The Sun Also Rises *(1926),* A Farewell to Arms *(1929),* For Whom the Bell Tolls *(1940), and* The Old Man and the Sea *(1952), the last cited when he was awarded the Nobel Prize for Literature in 1954. After World War II, he lived in Cuba until the revolution; he died on July 2, 1961, in Ketchum, Idaho, of a gunshot wound, probably self-inflicted. Among his other works are* Death in the Afternoon *(1932), a book dealing with bullfighting, and several collections of short stories, including* In Our Time *(1924) and* Winner Take Nothing *(1933), in which "A Clean, Well-Lighted Place" appears. Hemingway's characteristic style and tone—the deceptive simplicity, the authentic rhythms of speech, the ironic undertone—are all found in "A Clean, Well-Lighted Place," which also reflects his characteristic sense of disillusionment and nihilism. It also reveals, in E. M. Halli-*

day's words, "Hemingway's preoccupation with the human predicament and a moral code that might satisfactorily control it." In reading Hemingway, Halliday rightly concludes, it is "impossible to avoid the impression that this writer was dealing with something of final importance to us all."

It was late and every one had left the café except an old man who sat in the shadow the leaves of the tree made against the electric light. In the day time the street was dusty, but at night the dew settled the dust and the old man liked to sit late because he was deaf and now at night it was quiet and he felt the difference. The two waiters inside the café knew that the old man was a little drunk, and while he was a good client they knew that if he became too drunk he would leave without paying, so they kept watch on him.

"Last week he tried to commit suicide," one waiter said.

"Why?"

"He was in despair."

"What about?"

"Nothing."

"How do you know it was nothing?"

"He has plenty of money."

They sat together at a table that was close against the wall near the door of the café and looked at the terrace where the tables were all empty except where the old man sat in the shadow of the leaves of the tree that moved slightly in the wind. A girl and a soldier went by in the street. The street light shone on the brass number on his collar. The girl wore no head covering and hurried beside him.

"The guard will pick him up," one waiter said.

"What does it matter if he gets what he's after?"

"He had better get off the street now. The guard will get him. They went by five minutes ago."

The old man sitting in the shadow rapped on his saucer with his glass. The younger waiter went over to him.

"What do you want?"

The old man looked at him. "Another brandy," he said.

"You'll be drunk," the waiter said. The old man looked at him. The waiter went away.

"He'll stay all night," he said to his colleague. "I'm sleepy now. I never get into bed before three o'clock. He should have killed himself last week."

The waiter took the brandy bottle and another saucer from the counter inside the café and marched out to the old man's table. He put down the saucer and poured the glass full of brandy.

"You should have killed yourself last week," he said to the deaf man.

The old man motioned with his finger. "A little more," he said. The waiter poured on into the glass so that the brandy slopped over and ran down the stem into the top saucer of the pile. "Thank you," the old man said. The waiter took the bottle back inside the café. He sat down at the table with his colleague again.

"He's drunk now," he said.

"He's drunk every night."

"What did he want to kill himself for?"

"How should I know."

"How did he do it?"

"He hung himself with a rope."

"Who cut him down?"

"His niece."

"Why did they do it?"

"Fear for his soul."

"How much money has he got?"

"He's got plenty."

"He must be eighty years old."

"Anyway I should say he was eighty."

"I wish he would go home. I never get to bed before three o'clock. What kind of hour is that to go to bed?"

"He stays up because he likes it."

"He's lonely. I'm not lonely. I have a wife waiting in bed for me."

"He had a wife once too."

"A wife would be no good to him now."

"You can't tell. He might be better with a wife."

"His niece looks after him."

"I know. You said she cut him down."

"I wouldn't want to be that old. An old man is a nasty thing."

"Not always. This old man is clean. He drinks without spilling. Even now, drunk. Look at him."

"I don't want to look at him. I wish he would go home. He has no regard for those who must work."

The old man looked from his glass across the square, then over at the waiters.

"Another brandy," he said, pointing to his glass. The waiter who was in a hurry came over.

"Finished," he said, speaking with that omission of syntax stupid people employ when talking to drunken people or foreigners. "No more tonight. Close now."

"Another," said the old man.

"No. Finished." The waiter wiped the edge of the table with a towel and shook his head.

The old man stood up, slowly counted the saucers, took a leather coin purse from his pocket and paid for the drinks, leaving half a peseta tip.

The waiter watched him go down the street, a very old man walking unsteadily but with dignity.

"Why didn't you let him stay and drink?" the unhurried waiter asked. They were putting up the shutters. "It is not half-past two."

"I want to go home to bed."

"What is an hour?"

"More to me than to him."

"An hour is the same."

"You talk like an old man yourself. He can buy a bottle and drink at home."

"It's not the same."

"No, it is not," agreed the waiter with a wife. He did not wish to be unjust. He was only in a hurry.

"And you? You have no fear of going home before your usual hour?"

"Are you trying to insult me?"

"No, hombre, only to make a joke."

"No," the waiter who was in a hurry said, rising from pulling down the metal shutters. "I have confidence. I am all confidence."

"You have youth, confidence, and a job," the older waiter said. "You have everything."

"And what do you lack?"

"Everything but work."

"You have everything I have."

"No. I have never had confidence and I am not young."

"Come on. Stop talking nonsense and lock up."

"I am of those who like to stay late at the café," the older waiter said. "With all those who do not want to go to bed. With all those who need a light for the night."

"I want to go home and into bed."

"We are of two different kinds," the older waiter said. He was now dressed to go home. "It is not only a question of youth and confidence although those things are very beautiful. Each night I am reluctant to close up because there may be some one who needs the café."

"Hombre, there are bodegas open all night long."

"You do not understand. This is a clean and pleasant café. It is well lighted. The light is very good and also, now, there are shadows of the leaves."

"Good night," said the younger waiter.

"Good night," the other said. Turning off the electric light he continued the conversation with himself. It is the light of course but it is necessary that the place be clean and pleasant. You do not want music. Certainly you do not want music. Nor can you stand before a bar with dignity although that is all that is provided for these hours. What did he fear? It was not fear or dread. It was a nothing that he knew too well. It was all a nothing and a man was nothing too. It was only that and light was all it needed and a certain cleanness and order. Some lived in it and never felt it but he knew it all was nada y pues nada y pues nada. Our nada who art in nada, nada be thy name thy kingdom nada thy will be nada in nada as it is in nada. Give us this nada our daily nada and nada us our nada as we nada our nadas and nada us not into nada but deliver us from nada; pues nada. Hail nothing full of nothing, nothing is with thee. He smiled and stood before a bar with a shining steam pressure coffee machine.

"What's yours?" asked the barman.

"Nada."

"Otro loco mas," said the barman and turned away.

"A little cup," said the waiter.

The barman poured it for him.

"The light is very bright and pleasant but the bar is unpolished," the waiter said.

The barman looked at him but did not answer. It was too late at night for conversation.

"You want another copita?" the barman asked.

"No, thank you," said the waiter and went out. He disliked bars and bodegas. A clean, well-lighted café was a very different thing. Now, without thinking further, he would go home to his room. He would lie in the bed and finally, with daylight, he would go to sleep. After all, he said to himself, it is probably only insomnia. Many must have it.

# Cowardice and Courage

## BIG BOY LEAVES HOME

**Richard Wright**

*Born in Mississippi in 1908, Richard Wright suffered much during his early years from poverty, prejudice, and a poor education. Leaving Mississippi, he went first to Memphis and then to Chicago, where he became associated with the Communist movement and began writing for such leftist journals as* New Masses *and* International Literature. *In 1937 Wright moved to New York and served for a time as Harlem correspondent for the* Daily Worker. *He had begun to write fiction while he was in Chicago, and in 1938 he published his first work,* Uncle Tom's Cabin, *a collection of short stories that includes "Big Boy Leaves Home." With the reception accorded that book and his first novel* Native Son *(1940), Wright achieved both financial and literary success. He broke with the Communist Party in 1944 and in 1947 went to France, where he lived until his death in 1960. Perhaps the best known among his other works are* Black Boy *(1945), an autobiographical account of his early years in the South;* The Outsider *(1953); and* Eight Men, *a posthumous collection of short stories, plays, and an essay. A recent biography by John A. Williams,* The Most Native of Sons *(1970), is a good introduction to Wright's life, and Kenneth Kinnamon's* The Emergence of Richard

Wright: A Study in Literature and Society (1972) *is an excellent critical study. Perhaps the ending of Wright's own essay on* Native Son, *"How Bigger Was Born," is a fitting comment on his place in American writing, for it reveals Wright's own view of his craft and his heritage:* "Early American writers, Henry James and Nathaniel Hawthorne, complained bitterly about the bleakness and flatness of the American scene. But I think that if they were alive, they'd feel at home in modern America. True, we have no great church in America; our national traditions are still of such a sort that we are not wont to brag of them. . . . But we do have in the Negro the embodiment of a past tragic enough to appease the spiritual hunger of even a James; and we have in the oppression of the Negro a shadow athwart our national life dense and heavy enough to satisfy even the gloomy broodings of a Hawthorne. And if Poe were alive, he would not have to invent horror; horror would invent him."

## I

Y*o mama don wear no drawers . . .*

Clearly, the voice rose out of the woods, and died away. Like an echo another voice caught it up:

*Ah seena when she pulled em off . . .*

Another, shrill, cracking, adolescent:

*N she washed 'em in alcohol . . .*

Then a quartet of voices, blending in harmony, floated high above the tree tops:

*N she hung 'em out in the hall . . .*

Laughing easily, four black boys came out of the woods into cleared pasture. They walked lollingly in bare feet, beating tangled vines and bushes with long sticks.

"Ah wished Ah knowed some mo lines t tha song."

"Me too."

"Yeah, when yuh gits t where she hangs em out in the hall yuh has t stop."

"Shucks, whut goes wid *hall?*"

"*Call.*"

"*Fall.*"

"*Wall.*"

"*Quall.*"

They threw themselves on the grass, laughing.

"Big Boy?"

"Huh?"

"Yuh know one thing?"

"Whut?"

"Yuh sho is crazy!"

"Crazy?"

"Yeah, yuh crazys a bed-bug!"

"Crazy bout whut?"
"Man, whoever hearda *quall*?"
"Yuh said yuh wanted something t go wid *hall*, didnt yuh?"
"Yeah, but whuts a *quall*?"
"Nigger, a *qualls* a *quall*."
They laughed easily, catching and pulling long green blades of grass with their toes.
"Waal, ef a *qualls* a *quall*, whut IS a *quall*?"
"Oh, Ah know."
"Whut?"
"Tha ol song goes something like this:

>Yo mama don wear no drawers,
>   Ah seena when she pulled em off,
>N she washed em in alcohol,
>   N she hung em out in the hall,
>N then she put em back on her QUALL!"

They laughed again. Their shoulders were flat to the earth, their knees propped up, and their faces square to the sun.
"Big Boy, yuhs CRAZY!"
"Don ax me nothin else."
"Nigger, yuhs CRAZY!"
They fell silent, smiling, drooping the lids of their eyes softly against the sunlight.
"Man, don the groun feel warm?"
"Jus lika bed."
"Jeeesus, Ah could stay here ferever."
"Me too."
"Ah kin feel tha ol sun goin all thu me."
"Feels like mah bones is warm."
In the distance a train whistled mournfully.
"There goes number fo!"
"Hittin on all six!"
"Highballin it down the line!"
"Boun fer up Noth, Lawd, boun fer up Noth!"
They began to chant, pounding bare heels in the grass.

>Dis train boun fo Glory
>Dis train, Oh Hallelujah
>Dis train boun fo Glory
>Dis train, Oh Hallelujah
>Dis train boun fo Glory
> Ef yuh ride no need fer fret er worry
>Dis train, Oh Hallelujah
>Dis train . . .

Dis train don carry no gambler
Dis train, Oh Hallelujah
Dis train don carry no gambler
Dis train, Oh Hallelujah
Dis train don carry no gambler
No fo day creeper er midnight rambler
Dis train, Oh Hallelujah
Dis train . . .

When the song ended they burst out laughing, thinking of a train bound for Glory.

"Gee, thas a good ol song!"

"Huuuuummmmmmmmman . . ."

"Whut?"

"Geeee whiiiiiiz . . ."

"Whut?"

"Somebody don let win! Das whut!"

Buck, Bobo, and Lester jumped up. Big Boy stayed on the ground, feigning sleep.

"Jeeesus, tha sho stinks!"

"Big Boy!"

Big Boy feigned to snore.

"Big Boy!"

Big Boy stirred as though in sleep.

"Big Boy!"

"Hunh?"

"Yuh rotten inside!"

"Rotten?"

"Lawd, cant yuh smell it?"

"Smell whut?"

"Nigger, yuh mus gotta bad col!"

"*Smell whut?*"

"NIGGER, YUH BROKE WIN!"

Big Boy laughed and fell back on the grass, closing his eyes.

"The hen whut cackles is the hen whut laid the egg."

"We ain no hens."

"Yuh cackled, didnt yuh?"

The three moved off with noses turned up.

"C mon!"

"Where yuh-all goin?"

"T the creek fer a swim."

"Yeah, les swim."

"Naw buddy naw!" said Big Boy, slapping the air with a scornful palm.

"Aw, c mon! Don be a heel!"

"N git *lynched?* Hell naw!"

"He ain gonna see us."

"How yuh know?"

"Cause he ain."

"Yuh-all go on. Ahma stay right here," said Big Boy.

"Hell, let im stay! C mon, les go," said Buck.

The three walked off, swishing at grass and bushes with sticks. Big Boy looked lazily at their backs.

"Hey!"

Walking on, they glanced over their shoulders.

"Hey, niggers!"

"C mon!"

Big Boy grunted, picked up his stick, pulled to his feet, and stumbled off.

"Wait!"

"C mon!"

He ran, caught up with them, leaped upon their backs, bearing them to the ground.

"Quit, Big Boy!"

"Gawddam, nigger!"

"Git t hell offa me!"

Big Boy sprawled in the grass beside them, laughing and pounding his heels in the ground.

"Nigger, what yuh think we is, hosses?"

"How come yuh awways hoppin on us?"

"Lissen, wes gonna double-team on yuh one of these days n beat yo ol ass good."

Big Boy smiled.

"Sho nough?"

"Yeah, don yuh like it?"

"We gonna beat yuh sos yuh cant walk!"

"N dare yuh to do nothin erbout it!"

Big Boy bared his teeth.

"C mon! Try it now!"

The three circled around him.

"Say, Buck, yuh grab his feets!"

"N yuh git his head, Lester!"

"N Bobo, yuh git berhin n grab his arms!"

Keeping more than arm's length, they circled round and round Big Boy.

"C mon!" said Big Boy, feinting at one and then the other.

Round and round they circled, but could not seem to get any closer. Big Boy stopped and braced his hands on his hips.

"Is all three of yuh-all scareda me?"

"Les git im some other time," said Bobo, grinning.

"Yeah, we kin ketch yuh when yuh ain thinkin," said Lester.

"We kin trick yuh," said Buck.

They laughed and walked together.
Big Boy belched.
"Ahm hongry," he said.
"Me too."
"Ah wished Ah hada big hot pota belly-busters!"
"Cooked wid some good ol salty ribs . . ."
"N some good ol egg cornbread . . ."
"N some buttermilk . . ."
"N some hot peach cobbler swimmin in juice . . ."
"Nigger, hush!"
They began to chant, emphasizing the rhythm by cutting at grass with sticks.

>  Bye n bye
>  Ah wanna piece of pie
>  Pies too sweet
>  Ah wanna piece of meat
>  Meats too red
>  Ah wanna piece of bread
>  Breads too brown
>  Ah wanna go t town
>  Towns too far
>  Ah wanna ketch a car
>  Cars too fas
>  Ah fall n break mah ass
>  Ahll understan it better bye n bye . . .

They climbed over a barbed-wire fence and entered a stretch of thick woods. Big Boy was whistling softly, his eyes half-closed.
"LES GIT IM!"
Buck, Lester, and Bobo whirled, grabbed Big Boy about the neck, arms, and legs, bearing him to the ground. He grunted and kicked wildly as he went back into weeds.
"Hol im tight!"
"Git his arms! Git his arms!"
"Set on his legs so he cant kick!"
Big Boy puffed heavily, trying to get loose.
"WE GOT YUH NOW, GAWDDAMMIT, WE GOT YUH NOW!"
"Thas a Gawddam lie!" said Big Boy. He kicked, twisted, and clutched for a hold on one and then the other.
"Say, yuh-all hep me hol his arms!" said Bobo.
"Aw, we got this bastard now!" said Lester.
"Thas a Gawddam lie!" said Big Boy again.
"Say, yuh-all hep me hol his arms!" called Bobo.
Big Boy managed to encircle the neck of Bobo with his left arm. He tightened his elbow scissors-like and hissed through his teeth:

"Yuh got me, ain yuh?"

"Hol im!"

"Les beat this bastard's ass!"

"Say, hep me hol his *arms!* Hes got aholda mah *neck!*" cried Bobo.

Big Boy squeezed Bobo's neck and twisted his head to the ground.

"Yuh got me, ain yuh?"

"Quit, Big Boy, yuh chokin me; yuh hurtin mah neck!" cried Bobo.

"Turn me loose!" said Big Boy.

"Ah ain got yuh! Its the others whut got yuh!" pleaded Bobo.

"Tell them others t git t hell offa me or Ahma break yo neck," said Big Boy.

"Ssssay, yyyuh-all gggit ooooffa Bbig Boy. Hhhes got me," gurgled Bobo.

"Cant yuh hol im?"

"Nnaw, hhes ggot mmah nneck . . ."

Big Boy squeezed tighter.

"N Ahma break it too less yuh tell em t git t hell offa me!"

"Ttturn mmmeee llloose," panted Bobo, tears gushing.

"Cant yuh hol im, Bobo?" asked Buck.

"Nnaw, yuh-all tturn im lloose; hhhes got mah nnneck . . ."

"Grab his neck, Bobo . . ."

"Ah cant; yugurgur . . ."

To save Bobo, Lester and Buck got up and ran to a safe distance. Big Boy released Bobo, who staggered to his feet, slobbering and trying to stretch a crick out of his neck.

"Shucks, nigger, yuh almos broke mah neck," whimpered Bobo.

"Ahm gonna break yo ass nex time," said Big Boy.

"Ef Bobo coulda hel yuh we woulda had yuh," yelled Lester.

"Ah wuznt gonna let im do that," said Big Boy.

They walked together again, swishing sticks.

"Yuh see," began Big Boy, "when a ganga guys jump on yuh, all yuh gotta do is jus put the heat on one of them n make im tell the others t let up, see?"

"Gee, thas a good idee!"

"Yeah, thas a good idee!"

"But yuh almos broke mah neck, man," said Bobo.

"Ahma smart nigger," said Big Boy, thrusting out his chest.

## II

They came to the swimming hole.

"Ah ain goin in," said Bobo.

"Done got scared?" asked Big Boy.

"Naw, Ah ain scared . . ."

"How come yuh ain goin in?"

"Yuh know ol man Harvey don erllow no niggers t swim in this hole."

"N jus las year he took a shot at Bob fer swimmin in here," said Lester.
"Shucks, ol man Harvey ain studyin bout us niggers," said Big Boy.
"Hes at home thinkin about his jelly-roll," said Buck.
They laughed.
"Buck, yo mins lowern a snakes belly," said Lester.
"Ol man Harveys too doggone ol t think erbout jelly-roll," said Big Boy.
"Hes dried up; all the saps done lef im," said Bobo.
"C mon, les go!" said Big Boy.
Bobo pointed.
"See tha sign over yonder?"
"Yeah."
"Whut it say?"
"NO TRESPASSIN," read Lester.
"Know whut tha mean?"
"Mean ain no dogs n niggers erllowed," said Buck.
"Waal, wes here now," said Big Boy. "Ef he ketched us even like this thered be trouble, so we just as waal go on in . . ."
"Ahm wid the nex one!"
"Ahll go ef anybody else goes!"
Big Boy looked carefully in all directions. Seeing nobody, he began jerking off his overalls.
"LAS ONE INS A OL DEAD DOG!"
"THAS YO MA!"
"THAS YO PA!"
"THAS BOTH YO MA N YO PA!"
They jerked off their clothes and threw them in a pile under a tree. Thirty seconds later they stood, black and naked, on the edge of the hole under a sloping embankment. Gingerly Big Boy touched the water with his foot.
"Man, this waters col," he said.
"Ahm gonna put mah cloes back on," said Bobo, withdrawing his foot.
Big Boy grabbed him about the waist.
"Like hell yuh is!"
"Git outta the way, nigger!" Bobo yelled.
"Throw im in!" said Lester.
"Duck im!"
Bobo crouched, spread his legs, and braced himself against Big Boy's body. Locked in each other's arms, they tussled on the edge of the hole, neither able to throw the other.
"C mon, les me n yuh push em in."
"O.K."
Laughing, Lester and Buck gave the two locked bodies a running push. Big Boy and Bobo splashed, sending up silver spray in the sunlight. When Big Boy's head came up he yelled:
"Yuh bastard!"

"Tha wuz yo ma yuh pushed!" said Bobo, shaking his head to clear the water from his eyes.

They did a surface dive, came up and struck out across the creek. The muddy water foamed. They swam back, waded into shallow water, breathing heavily and blinking eyes.

"C mon in!"

"Man, the waters fine!"

Lester and Buck hesitated.

"Les wet em," Big Boy whispered to Bobo.

Before Lester and Buck could back away, they were dripping wet from handsful of scooped water.

"Hey, quit!"

"Gawddam, nigger! Tha waters col!"

"C mon in!" called Big Boy.

"We jus as waal go on in now," said Buck.

"Look n see ef anybodys comin."

Kneeling, they squinted among the trees.

"Ain nobody."

"C mon, les go."

They waded in slowly, pausing each few steps to catch their breath. A desperate water battle began. Closing eyes and backing away, they shunted water into one another's faces with the flat palms of hands.

"Hey, cut it out!"

"Yeah, Ahm bout drownin!"

They came together in water up to their navels, blowing and blinking. Big Boy ducked, upsetting Bobo.

"Look out, nigger!"

"Don holler so loud!"

"Yeah, they kin hear yo ol big mouth a mile erway."

"This waters too col fer me."

"Thas cause it rained yistiddy."

They swam across and back again.

"Ah wish we hada bigger place t swim in."

"The white folks got plenty swimmin pools n we ain got none."

"Ah useta swim in the ol Missippi when we lived in Vicksburg."

Big Boy put his head under the water and blew his breath. A sound came like that of a hippopotamus.

"C mon, les be hippos."

Each went to a corner of the creek and put his mouth just below the surface and blew like a hippopotamus. Tiring, they came and sat under the embankment.

"Look like Ah gotta chill."

"Me too."

"Les stay here n dry off."

"Jeeesus, Ahm col!"

They kept still in the sun, suppressing shivers. After some of the water had dried off their bodies they began to talk through clattering teeth.

"Whut would yuh do ef ol man Harveyd come erlong right now?"

"Run like hell!"

"Man, Ahd run so fas hed thinka black streaka lightnin shot pass im."

"But spose he hada gun?"

"Aw, nigger, shut up!"

They were silent. They ran their hands over wet, trembling legs, brushing water away. Then their eyes watched the sun sparkling on the restless creek.

Far away a train whistled.

"There goes number seven!"

"Headin fer up Noth!"

"Blazin it down the line!"

"Lawd, Ahm goin Noth some day."

"Me too, man."

"They say colored folks up Noth is got ekual rights."

They grew pensive. A black winged butterfly hovered at the water's edge. A bee droned. From somewhere came the sweet scent of honeysuckles. Dimly they could hear sparrows twittering in the woods. They rolled from side to side, letting sunshine dry their skins and warm their blood. They plucked blades of grass and chewed them.

"Oh!"

They looked up, their lips parting.

"Oh!"

A white woman, poised on the edge of the opposite embankment, stood directly in front of them, her hat in her hand and her hair lit by the sun.

"It's a woman!" whispered Big Boy in an underbreath. "A *white* woman!"

They stared, their hands instinctively covering their groins. Then they scrambled to their feet. The white woman backed slowly out of sight. They stood for a moment, looking at one another.

"Les git outta here!" Big Boy whispered.

"Wait till she goes erway."

"Les run, theyll ketch us here naked like this!"

"Mabbe theres a man wid her."

"C mon, les git our cloes," said Big Boy.

They waited a moment longer, listening.

"Whut t hell! Ahma git mah cloes," said Big Boy.

Grabbing at short tufts of grass, he climbed the embankment.

"Don run out there now!"

"C mon back, fool!"

Bobo hesitated. He looked at Big Boy, and then at Buck and Lester.

"Ahm goin wid Big Boy n git mah cloes," he said.

"Don run out there naked like tha, fool!" said Buck. "Yuh don know whos out there!"

Big Boy was climbing over the edge of the embankment.

"C mon," he whispered.

Bobo climbed after. Twenty-five feet away the woman stood. She had one hand over her mouth. Hanging by fingers, Buck and Lester peeped over the edge.

"C mon back; that womans scared," said Lester.

Big Boy stopped, puzzled. He looked at the woman. He looked at the bundle of clothes. Then he looked at Buck and Lester.

"C mon, les git our cloes!"

He made a step.

"Jim!" the woman screamed.

Big Boy stopped and looked around. His hands hung loosely at his sides. The woman, her eyes wide, her hand over her mouth, backed away to the tree where their clothes lay in a heap.

"Big Boy, come back n wait till shes gone!"

Bobo ran to Big Boy's side.

"Les go home! Theyll ketch us here," he urged.

Big Boy's throat felt tight.

"Lady, we wanna git our cloes," he said.

Buck and Lester climbed the embankment and stood indecisively. Big Boy ran toward the tree.

"Jim!" the woman screamed. "Jim! Jim!"

Black and naked, Big Boy stopped three feet from her.

"We wanna git our cloes," he said again, his words coming mechanically.

He made a motion.

"You go away! You go away! I tell you, you go away!"

Big Boy stopped again, afraid. Bobo ran and snatched the clothes. Buck and Lester tried to grab theirs out of his hands.

"You go away! You go away! You go away!" the woman screamed.

"Les go!" said Bobo, running toward the woods.

CRACK!

Lester grunted, stiffened, and pitched forward. His forehead struck a toe of the woman's shoes.

Bobo stopped, clutching the clothes. Buck whirled. Big Boy stared at Lester, his lips moving.

"Hes gotta gun; hes gotta gun!" yelled Buck, running wildly.

CRACK!

Buck stopped at the edge of the embankment, his head jerked backward, his body arched stiffly to one side; he toppled headlong, sending up a shower of bright spray to the sunlight. The creek bubbled.

Big Boy and Bobo backed away, their eyes fastened fearfully on a white man who was running toward them. He had a rifle and wore an army officer's uniform. He ran to the woman's side and grabbed her hand.

"You hurt, Bertha, you hurt?"

She stared at him and did not answer.

The man turned quickly. His face was red. He raised the rifle and pointed it at Bobo. Bobo ran back, holding the clothes in front of his chest.

"Don shoot me, Mistah, don shoot me . . ."

Big Boy lunged for the rifle, grabbing the barrel.

"You black sonofabitch!"

Big Boy clung desperately.

"Let go, you black bastard!"

The barrel pointed skyward.

CRACK!

The white man, taller and heavier, flung Big Boy to the ground. Bobo dropped the clothes, ran up, and jumped onto the white man's back.

"You black sonsofbitches!"

The white man released the rifle, jerked Bobo to the ground, and began to batter the naked boy with his fists. Then Big Boy swung, striking the man in the mouth with the barrel. His teeth caved in, and he fell, dazed. Bobo was on his feet.

"C mon, Big Boy, les go!"

Breathing hard, the white man got up and faced Big Boy. His lips were trembling, his neck and chin wet with blood. He spoke quietly.

"Give me that gun, boy!"

Big Boy leveled the rifle and backed away.

The white man advanced.

"Boy, I say give me that gun!"

Bobo had the clothes in his arms.

"Run, Big Boy, run!"

The man came at Big Boy.

"Ahll kill yuh; Ahll kill yuh!" said Big Boy.

His fingers fumbled for the trigger.

The man stopped, blinked, spat blood. His eyes were bewildered. His face whitened. Suddenly, he lunged for the rifle, his hands outstretched.

CRACK!

He fell forward on his face.

"Jim!"

Big Boy and Bobo turned in surprise to look at the woman.

"Jim!" she screamed again, and fell weakly at the foot of the tree.

Big Boy dropped the rifle, his eyes wide. He looked around. Bobo was crying and clutching the clothes.

"Big Boy, Big Boy . . ."

Big Boy looked at the rifle, started to pick it up, but didn't. He seemed at a loss. He looked at Lester, then at the white man; his eyes followed a thin stream of blood that seeped to the ground.

"Yuh done killed im," mumbled Bobo.

"Les go home!"

Naked, they turned and ran toward the woods. When they reached the barbed-wire fence they stopped.

"Les git our cloes on," said Big Boy.

They slipped quickly into overalls. Bobo held Lester's and Buck's clothes.

"Whut we gonna do wid these?"

Big Boy stared. His hands twitched.

"Leave em."

They climbed the fence and ran through the woods. Vines and leaves switched their faces. Once Bobo tripped and fell.

"C mon!" said Big Boy.

Bobo started crying, blood streaming from his scratches.

"Ahm scared!"

"C mon! Don cry! We wanna git home fo they ketches us!"

"Ahm scared!" said Bobo again, his eyes full of tears.

Big Boy grabbed his hand and dragged him along.

"C mon!"

### III

They stopped when they got to the end of the woods. They could see the open road leading home, home to ma and pa. But they hung back, afraid. The thick shadows cast from the trees were friendly and sheltering. But the wide glare of sun stretching out over the fields was pitiless. They crouched behind an old log.

"We gotta git home," said Big Boy.

"Theys gonna lynch us," said Bobo, half-questioningly.

Big Boy did not answer.

"Theys gonna lynch us," said Bobo again.

Big Boy shuddered.

"Hush!" he said. He did not want to think of it. He could not think of it; there was but one thought, and he clung to that one blindly. He had to get home, home to ma and pa.

Their heads jerked up. Their ears had caught the rhythmic jingle of a wagon. They fell to the ground and clung flat to the side of a log. Over the crest of the hill came the top of a hat. A white face. Then shoulders in a blue shirt. A wagon drawn by two horses pulled into full view.

Big Boy and Bobo held their breath, waiting. Their eyes followed the wagon till it was lost in dust around a bend of the road.

"We gotta git home," said Big Boy.

"Ahm scared," said Bobo.

"C mon! Les keep t the fields."

They ran till they came to the cornfields. Then they went slower, for last year's corn stubbles bruised their feet.

They came in sight of a brickyard.

"Wait a minute," gasped Big Boy.

They stopped.

"Ahm goin on t mah home n yuh better go on t yos."

Bobo's eyes grew round.

"Ahm scared!"

"Yuh better go on!"

"Lemme go wid yuh; theyll ketch me . . ."

"Ef yuh kin git home mabbe yo folks kin hep yuh t git erway."

Big Boy started off. Bobo grabbed him.

"Lemme go wid yuh!"

Big Boy shook free.

"Ef yuh stay here theys gonna lynch yuh!" he yelled, running.

After he had gone about twenty-five yards he turned and looked; Bobo was flying through the woods like the wind.

Big Boy slowed when he came to the railroad. He wondered if he ought to go through the streets or down the track. He decided on the tracks. He could dodge a train better than a mob.

He trotted along the ties, looking ahead and back. His cheek itched, and he felt it. His hand came away smeared with blood. He wiped it nervously on his overalls.

When he came to his back fence he heaved himself over. He landed among a flock of startled chickens. A bantam rooster tried to spur him. He slipped and fell in front of the kitchen steps, grunting heavily. The ground was slick with greasy dishwater.

Panting, he stumbled through the doorway.

"Lawd, Big Boy, whuts wrong wid yuh?"

His mother stood gaping in the middle of the floor. Big Boy flopped wordlessly onto a stool, almost toppling over. Pots simmered on the stove. The kitchen smelled of food cooking.

"Whuts the matter, Big Boy?"

Mutely, he looked at her. Then he burst into tears. She came and felt the scratches on his face.

"Whut happened t yuh, Big Boy? Somebody been botherin yuh?"

"They after me, Ma! They after me . . ."

"Who!"

"Ah . . . Ah . . . We . . ."

"Big Boy, whuts wrong wid yuh?"

"He killed Lester n Buck," he muttered simply.

"Killed!"

"Yessum."

"Lester n Buck!"

"Yessum, Ma!"
"How killed?"
"He shot em, Ma!"
"Lawd Gawd in Heaven, have mercy on us all! This is mo trouble, mo trouble," she moaned, wringing her hands.
"N Ah killed im, Ma . . ."
She stared, trying to understand.
"Whut happened, Big Boy?"
"We tried t git our cloes from the tree . . ."
"Whut tree?"
"We wuz swimmin, Ma. N the white woman . . ."
"*White* woman? . . ."
"Yessum. She wuz at the swimmin hole . . ."
"Lawd have mercy! Ah knowed yuh boys wuz gonna keep on till yuh got into somethin like this!"
She ran into the hall.
"Lucy!"
"Mam?"
"C mere!"
"Mam?"
"C mere, Ah say!"
"Whutcha wan, Ma? Ahm sewin."
"Chile, will yuh c mere like Ah ast yuh?"
Lucy came to the door holding an unfinished apron in her hands. When she saw Big Boy's face she looked wildly at her mother.
"Whuts the matter?"
"Wheres Pa?"
"Hes out front, Ah reckon."
"Git im, quick!"
"Whuts the matter, Ma?"
"Go git you Pa, Ah say!"
Lucy ran out. The mother sank into a chair, holding a dish rag. Suddenly, she sat up.
"Big Boy, Ah thought yuh wuz at school?"
Big Boy looked at the floor.
"How come yuh didnt go t school?"
"We went t the woods."
She sighed.
"Ah done done all Ah kin fer yuh, Big Boy. Only Gawd kin hep yuh now."
"Ma, don let em git me; don let em git me . . ."
His father came into the doorway. He stared at Big Boy, then at his wife.
"Whuts Big Boy inter now?" he asked sternly.
"Saul, Big Boy's done gone n got inter trouble wid the white folks."

The old man's mouth dropped, and he looked from one to the other.
"Saul, we gotta git im erway from here."
"Open yo mouth n talk! Whut yuh been doin?" The old man gripped Big Boy's shoulders and peered at the scratches on his face.
"Me n Lester n Buck n Bobo wuz out on old man Harveys place swimmin . . ."
"Saul, its a *white* woman!"
Big Boy winced. The old man compressed his lips and stared at his wife. Lucy gaped at her brother as though she had never seen him before.
"What happened? Cant yuh-all talk?" the old man thundered, with a certain helplessness in his voice.
"We wuz swimmin," Big Boy began, "n then a white woman comes up t the hole. We got up right erway t git our cloes sos we could git erway, n she started screamin. Our cloes wuz right by the tree where she wuz standin, n when we started t git em she jus screamed. We tol her we wanted our cloes . . . Yuh see, Pa, she wuz standing right *by* our cloes; n when we went t git em she jus screamed . . . Bobo got the cloes, n then he shot Lester . . ."
"*Who* shot Lester?"
"The white man."
"Whut white man?"
"Ah dunno, Pa. He wuz a soljer, n he had a rifle."
"A soljer?"
"Yessuh."
"A *soljer?*"
"Yessuh, Pa. A soljer."
The old man frowned.
"N then what yuh-all do?"
"Waal, Buck said, 'Hes gotta gun!' N we started runnin. N then he shot Buck, n he fell in the swimmin hole. We didnt see im no mo . . . He wuz close on us then. He looked at the white woman n then he started t shoot Bobo. Ah grabbed the gun, n we started fightin. Bobo jumped on his back. He started beatin Bobo. Then Ah hit im wid the gun. Then he started at me n Ah shot im. Then we run . . ."
"Who seen?"
"Nobody."
"Wheres Bobo?"
"He went home."
"Anybody run after yuh-all?"
"Nawsuh."
"Yuh see anybody?"
"Nawsuh. Nobody but a white man. But he didn't see us."
"How long fo yuh-all lef the swimmin hole?"
"Little while ergo."

The old man nervously brushed his hand across his eyes and walked to the door. His lips moved, but no words came.

"Saul, whut we gonna do?"

"Lucy," began the old man, "go t Brother Sanders n tell im Ah said c mere; n go t Brother Jenkins n tell im Ah said c mere; n go to Elder Peters n tell im Ah said c mere. N don say nothin t nobody but whut Ah tol yuh. N when yuh git thu come straight back. Now go!"

Lucy dropped her apron across the back of a chair and ran down the steps. The mother bent over, crying and praying. The old man walked slowly over to Big Boy.

"Big Boy?"

Big Boy swallowed.

"Ahm talkin t yuh!"

"Yessuh."

"How come yuh didnt go t school this mawnin?"

"We went t the woods."

"Didnt yo ma send yuh t school?"

"Yessuh."

"How come yuh didnt go?"

"We went t the woods."

"Don yuh know thas wrong?"

"Yessuh."

"How come yuh go?"

Big Boy looked at his fingers, knotted them, and squirmed in his seat.

"AHM TALKIN T YUH!"

His wife straightened up and said reprovingly:

"Saul!"

The old man desisted, yanking nervously at the shoulder straps of his overalls.

"How long wuz the woman there?"

"Not long."

"Wuz she young?"

"Yessuh. Lika gal."

"Did yuh-all say anythin t her?"

"Nawsuh. We jus said we wanted our cloes."

"N whut she say?"

"Nothin, Pa. She jus backed erway t the tree n screamed."

The old man stared, his lips trying to form a question.

"Big Boy, did yuh-all bother her?"

"Nawsuh, Pa. We didnt *touch* her."

"How long fo the white man come up?"

"Right erway."

"Whut he say?"

"Nothin. He jus cussed us."

Abruptly the old man left the kitchen.

"Ma, cant Ah go fo they ketches me?"

"Sauls doin whut he kin."

"Ma, Ma, Ah don wan em t ketch me . . ."

"Sauls doin whut he kin. Nobody but the good Lawd kin hep us now."

The old man came back with a shotgun and leaned it in a corner. Fascinatedly, Big Boy looked at it.

There was a knock at the front door.

"Liza, see whos there."

She went. They were silent, listening. They could hear her talking.

"Whos there?"

"Me."

"Who?"

"Me, Brother Sanders."

"C mon in. Sauls waitin fer yuh."

Sanders paused in the doorway, smiling.

"Yuh sent fer me, Brother Morrison?"

"Brother Sanders, wes in deep trouble here."

Sanders came all the way into the kitchen.

"Yeah?"

"Big Boy done gone n killed a white man."

Sanders stopped short, then came forward, his face thrust out, his mouth open. His lips moved several times before he could speak.

"A *white* man?"

"They gonna kill me; they gonna kill me!" Big Boy cried, running to the old man.

"Saul, cant we git im erway somewhere?"

"Here now, take it easy; take it easy," said Sanders, holding Big Boy's wrists.

"They gonna kill me; they gonna lynch me!"

Big Boy slipped to the floor. They lifted him to a stool. His mother held him closely, pressing his head to her bosom.

"Whut we gonna do?" asked Sanders.

"Ah done sent fer Brother Jenkins n Elder Peters."

Sanders leaned his shoulders against the wall. Then, as the full meaning of it all came to him, he exclaimed:

"Theys gonna git a mob! . . ." His voice broke off and his eyes fell on the shotgun.

Feet came pounding on the steps. They turned toward the door. Lucy ran in crying. Jenkins followed. The old man met him in the middle of the room, taking his hand.

"Wes in bad trouble here, Brother Jenkins. Big Boy's done gone n killed a white man. Yuh-alls gotta hep me . . ."

Jenkins looked hard at Big Boy.

"Elder Peters says hes comin," said Lucy.

"When all this happen?" asked Jenkins.

"Near bout a hour ergo, now," said the old man.
"Whut we gonna do?" asked Jenkins.
"Ah wanna wait till Elder Peters come," said the old man helplessly.
"But we gotta work fas ef we gonna do anythin," said Sanders. "Well git in trouble just standin here like this."
Big Boy pulled away from his mother.
"Pa, lemme go now! Lemme go now!"
"Be still, Big Boy!"
"Where kin yuh go?"
"Ah could ketch a freight!"
"Thas *sho* death!" said Jenkins. "They'll be watchin em all!"
"Kin yuh-all hep me wid some money?" the old man asked.
They shook their heads.
"Saul, whut kin we do? Big Boy cant stay here."
There was another knock at the door.
The old man backed stealthily to the shotgun.
"Lucy go!"
Lucy looked at him, hesitating.
"Ah better go," said Jenkins.
It was Elder Peters. He came in hurriedly.
"Good evenin, everbody!"
"How yuh, Elder?"
"Good evenin."
"How yuh today?"
Peters looked around the crowded kitchen.
"Whuts the matter?"
"Elder, wes in deep trouble," began the old man. "Big Boy n some mo boys . . ."
". . . Lester n Buck n Bobo . . ."
". . . wuz over on ol man Harveys place swimmin."
"N he don like us niggers *none*," said Peters emphatically. He widened his legs and put his thumbs in the armholes of his vest.
". . . n some white woman . . ."
"Yeah?" said Peters, coming closer.
". . . comes erlong n the boys tries t git their cloes where they done lef em under a tree. Waal, she started screamin n all, see? Reckon she thought the boys wuz after her. Then a white man in a soljers suit shoots two of em . . ."
". . . Lester n Buck . . ."
"Huummm," said Peters. "Tha wuz ol man Harveys son."
"Harveys son?"
"Yuh mean the one tha wuz in the Army?"
"Yuh mean Jim?"
"Yeah," said Peters. "The papers said he wuz here fer a vacation from his regiment. N tha woman the boys saw wuz jus erbout his wife . . ."

They stared at Peters. Now that they knew what white person had been killed, their fears became definite.

"N whut else happened?"

"Big Boy shot the man . . ."

"Harveys *son*?"

"He had t, Elder. He wuz gonna shoot im ef he didnt . . ."

"Lawd!" said Peters. He looked around and put his hat back on.

"How long ergo wuz this?"

"Mighty near an hour, now, Ah reckon."

"Do the white folks know yit?"

"Don know, Elder."

"Yuh-all better git this boy outta here right now," said Peters. "Cause ef yuh don theres gonna be a lynchin . . ."

"Where kin Ah go, Elder?" Big Boy ran up to him.

They crowded around Peters. He stood with his legs wide apart, looking up at the ceiling.

"Mabbe we kin hide im in the church till he kin git erway," said Jenkins.

Peters' lips flexed.

"Naw, Brother, thall never do! Theyll git im there sho. N anyhow, ef they ketch im there itll ruin us all. We gotta git the boy outta town . . ."

Sanders went up to the old man.

"Lissen," he said in a whisper. "Mah son, Will, the one whut drives fer the Magnolia Express Comny, is taking a truck o goods t Chicawgo in the mawnin. If we kin hide Big Boy somewhere till then, we kin put im on the truck . . ."

"Pa, please, lemme go wid Will when he goes in the mawnin," Big Boy begged.

The old man stared at Sanders.

"Yuh reckon thas safe?"

"Its the only thing yuh *kin* do," said Peters.

"But where we gonna hide im till then?"

"Whut time yo boy leavin out in the mawnin?"

"At six."

They were quiet, thinking. The water kettle on the stove sang.

"Pa, Ah knows where Will passes erlong wid the truck out on Bullards Road. Ah kin hide in one of them ol kilns . . ."

"Where?"

"In one of them kilns we built . . ."

"But theyll git yuh there," wailed the mother.

"But there ain no place else fer im t go."

"Theres some holes big ernough fer me t git in n stay till Will comes erlong," said Big Boy. "Please, Pa, lemme go fo they ketches me . . ."

"Let im go!"

"Please, Pa . . ."

The old man breathed heavily.

"Lucy, git his things!"

"Saul, theyll git im out there!" wailed the mother, grabbing Big Boy. Peters pulled her away.

"Sister Morrison, ef yuh don let im go n git erway from here hes gonna be caught shos theres a Gawd in Heaven!"

Lucy came running with Big Boy's shoes and pulled them on his feet. The old man thrust a battered hat on his head. The mother went to the stove and dumped the skillet of corn pone into her apron. She wrapped it, and unbuttoning Big Boy's overalls, pushed it into his bosom.

"Heres somethin fer yuh t eat; n pray, Big Boy, cause thas all anybody kin do now . . ."

Big Boy pulled to the door, his mother clinging to him.

"Let im go, Sister Morrison!"

"Run fas, Big Boy!"

Big Boy raced across the yard, scattering the chickens. He paused at the fence and hollered back:

"Tell Bobo where Ahm hidin n tell im t c mon!"

## IV

He made for the railroad, running straight toward the sunset. He held his left hand tightly over his heart, holding the hot pone of corn bread there. At times he stumbled over the ties, for his shoes were tight and hurt his feet. His throat burned from thirst; he had had no water since noon.

He veered off the track and trotted over the crest of a hill, following Bullard's Road. His feet slipped and slid in the dust. He kept his eyes straight ahead, fearing every clump of shrubbery, every tree. He wished it were night. If he could only get to the kilns without meeting anyone. Suddenly a thought came to him like a blow. He recalled hearing the old folks tell tales of blood-hounds, and fear made him run slower. None of them had thought of that. Spose blood-houns wuz put on his trail? Lawd! Spose a whole pack of em, foamin n howlin, tore im t pieces? He went limp and his feet dragged. Yeah, thas whut they wuz gonna send after im, blood-houns! N then thered be no way fer im t dodge! Why hadnt Pa let im take tha shotgun? He stopped. He oughta go back n git tha shotgun. And then when the mob came he would take some with him.

In the distance he heard the approach of a train. It jarred him back to a sharp sense of danger. He ran again, his big shoes sopping up and down in the dust. He was tired and his lungs were bursting from running. He wet his lips, wanting water. As he turned from the road across a plowed field he heard the train roaring at his heels. He ran faster, gripped in terror.

He was nearly there now. He could see the black clay on the sloping hillside. Once inside a kiln he would be safe. For a little while, at least. He thought of the shotgun again. If he only had something! Someone to talk to . . . Thas right! Bobo! Bobod be wid im. Hed almost fergot Bobo. Bobod bringa gun; he knowed he would. N tergether they could kill the whole mob. Then in the mawning theyd git inter Will's truck n go far erway, t Chicawgo . . .

He slowed to a walk, looking back and ahead. A light wind skipped over the grass. A beetle lit on his cheek and he brushed it off. Behind the dark pines hung a red sun. Two bats flapped against that sun. He shivered, for he was growing cold; the sweat on his body was drying.

He stopped at the foot of the hill, trying to choose between two patches of black kilns high above him. He went to the left, for there lay the ones he, Bobo, Lester, and Buck had dug only last week. He looked around again; the landscape was bare. He climbed the embankment and stood before a row of black pits sinking four and five feet deep into the earth. He went to the largest and peered in. He stiffened when his ears caught the sound of a whir. He ran back a few steps and poised on his toes. Six foot of snake slid out of the pit and went into coil. Big Boy looked around wildly for a stick. He ran down the slope, peering into the grass. He stumbled over a tree limb. He picked it up and tested it by striking it against the ground.

Warily, he crept back up the slope, his stick poised. When about seven feet from the snake he stopped and waved the stick. The coil grew tighter, the whir sounded louder, and a flat head reared to strike. He went to the right, and the flat head followed him, the blue-black tongue darting forth; he went to the left, and the flat head followed him there too.

He stopped, teeth clenched. He had to kill this snake. Jus had t kill im! This wuz the safest pit on the hillside. He waved the stick again, looking at the snake before, thinking of a mob behind. The flat head reared higher. With stick over shoulder, he jumped in, swinging. The stick sang through the air, catching the snake on the side of the head, sweeping him out of coil. There was a brown writhing mass. Then Big Boy was upon him, pounding blows home, one on top of the other. He fought viciously, his eyes red, his teeth bared in a snarl. He beat till the snake lay still; then he stomped it with his heel, grinding its head into the dirt.

He stopped, limp, wet. The corners of his lips were white with spittle. He spat and shuddered.

Cautiously, he went to the hole and peered. He longed for a match. He imagined whole nests of them in there waiting. He put the stick into the hole and waved it around. Stooping, he peered again. It mus be awright. He looked over the hillside, his eyes coming back to the dead snake. Then he got to his knees and backed slowly into the hole.

When inside he felt there must be snakes all about him, ready to strike. It seemed he could see and feel them there, waiting tensely in coil. In the dark he imagined long white fangs ready to sink into his neck, his side, his legs. He wanted to come out, but kept still. Shucks, he told himself, ef there wuz any snakes in here they sho woulda done bit me by now. Some of his fear left, and he relaxed.

With elbows on ground and chin on palms, he settled. The clay was cold to his knees and thighs, but his bosom was kept warm by the hot pone of corn bread. His thirst returned and he longed for a drink. He was hungry, too. But he did not want to eat the corn pone. Naw, not now. Mabbe after erwhile, after Bobod came. Then theyd both eat the corn pone.

The view from his hole was fringed by the long tufts of grass. He could see all the way to Bullard's Road, and even beyond. The wind was blowing, and in the east the first touch of dusk was rising. Every now and then a bird floated past, a spot of wheeling black printed against the sky. Big Boy sighed, shifted his weight, and chewed at a blade of grass. A wasp droned. He heard number nine, far away and mournful.

The train made him remember how they had dug these kilns on long hot summer days, how they had made boilers out of big tin cans, filled them with water, fixed stoppers for steam, cemented them in holes with wet clay, and built fires under them. He recalled how they had danced and yelled when a stopper blew out of a boiler, letting out a big spout of steam and a shrill whistle. There were times when they had the whole hillside blazing and smoking. Yeah, yuh see, Big Boy wuz Casey Jones n wuz speedin it down the gleamin rails of the Southern Pacific. Bobo had number two on the Santa Fe. Buck wuz on the Illinoy Central. Lester the Nickel Plate. Lawd, how they shelved the wood in! The boiling water would almost jar the cans loose from the clay. More and more pine-knots and dry leaves would be piled under the cans. Flames would grow so tall they would have to shield their eyes. Sweat would pour off their faces. Then, suddenly, a peg would shoot high into the air, and

Pssseeeezzzzzzzzzzzzzzzzzzz . . .

Big Boy sighed and stretched out his arm, quenching the flames and scattering the smoke. Why didnt Bobo c mon? He looked over the fields; there was nothing but dying sunlight. His mind drifted back to the kilns. He remembered the day when Buck, jealous of his winning, had tried to smash his kiln. Yeah, that ol sonofabitch! Naw, Lawd! He didnt go t say tha! What wuz he thinkin erbout? Cussin the dead! Yeah, po ol Buck wuz dead now. N Lester too. Yeah, it wuz awright fer Buck t smash his kiln. Sho. N he wished he hadnt socked ol Buck so hard tha day. He wuz sorry fer Buck now. N he sho wished he hadnt cussed po ol Bucks ma, neither. Tha wuz sinful! Mabbe Gawd would git im fer tha? But he didnt go t do it! Po Buck! Po Lester! Hed never treat anybody like tha ergin, never . . .

Dusk was slowly deepening. Somewhere, he could not tell exactly where, a cricket took up a fitful song. The air was growing soft and heavy. He looked over the fields, longing for Bobo . . .

He shifted his body to ease the cold damp of the ground, and thought back over the day. Yeah, hed been dam right erbout not wantin t go swimmin. N ef hed followed his right min hed neverve gone n got inter all this trouble. At first hed said naw. But shucks, somehow hed just went on wid the res. Yeah, he shoulda went on t school tha mawnin, like Ma told im t do. But, hell, who wouldnt git tireda awways drivin a guy t school! Tha wuz the big trouble awways drivin a guy t school. He wouldnt be in all this trouble now ef it wuznt fer that Gawddam school! Impatiently, he took the grass out of his mouth and threw it away, demolishing the little red school house . . .

Yeah, ef they had all kept still n quiet when tha ol white woman showed-up, mabbe shedve went on off. But yuh never kin tell erbout these white folks. Mabbe she wouldntve went. Mabbe tha white man woulda killed all of em! All *fo* of em! Yeah, yuh never kin tell erbout white folks. Then, ergin, mabbe tha white woman woulda went on off n laffed. Yeah, mabbe tha white man woulda said: *Yuh nigger bastards git t hell outta here! Yuh know Gawddam well yuh don berlong here!* N then they woulda grabbed their cloes n run like all hell . . . He blinked the white man away. Where wuz Bobo? Why didnt he hurry up n c mon?

He jerked another blade and chewed. Yeah, ef pa had only let im have tha shotgun! He could stan off a whole mob wid a shotgun. He looked at the ground as he turned a shotgun over in his hands. Then he leveled it at an advancing white man. *Boooom!* The man curled up. Another came. He reloaded quickly, and let him have what the other had got. He too curled up. Then another came. He got the same medicine. Then the whole mob swirled around him, and he blazed away, getting as many as he could. They closed in; but, by Gawd, he had done his part, hadnt he? N the newspapersd say: NIGGER KILLS DOZEN OF MOB BEFO LYNCHED! Er mabbe theyd say: TRAPPED NIGGER SLAYS TWENTY BEFO KILLED! He smiled a little. Tha wouldnt be so bad, would it? Blinking the newspaper away, he looked over the fields. Where wuz Bobo? Why didnt he hurry up n c mon?

He shifted, trying to get a crick out of his legs. Shucks, he wuz gittin tireda this. N it wuz almos dark now. Yeah, there wuz a little bittie star way over yonder in the eas. Mabbe tha white man wuznt dead? Mabbe they wuznt even lookin fer im? Mabbe he could go back home now? Naw, better wait erwhile. Thad be bes. But, Lawd, ef he only had some water! He could hardly swallow, his throat was so dry. Gawddam them white folks! Thas all they wuz good fer, t run a nigger down lika rabbit! Yeah, they git yuh in a corner n then they let yuh have it. A thousan of em! He shivered, for the cold of the clay was chilling his bones. Lawd, spose they foun im here in this hole? N wid nobody t hep im? . . . But ain no use in thinkin erbout tha; wait till trouble come fo yuh start fightin it. But ef tha mob came one by one hed wipe em all out. Clean up the whole bunch. He caught one by the neck and choked him long and hard, choked him till his tongue and eyes popped out. Then he jumped upon his chest and stomped him like he had stomped that snake. When he had finished with one, another came. He choked him too. Choked till he sank slowly to the ground, gasping . . .

"Hoalo!"

Big Boy snatched his fingers from the white man's neck and looked over the fields. He saw nobody. Had someone spied him? He was sure that somebody had hollered. His heart pounded. But, shucks, nobody couldnt see im here in this hole . . . But mabbe theyd seen im when he wuz comin n had laid low n wuz now closin in on im! Praps they wuz signalin fer the others? Yeah, they wuz creepin up on im! Mabbe he oughta git up n run . . . Oh! Mabbe tha wuz Bobo! Yeah, Bobo! He oughta clim out n see ef Bobo wuz lookin fer im . . . He stiffened.

"Hoalo!"

"Hoalo!"

"Wheres yuh?"

"Over here on Bullards Road!"

"C mon over!"

"Awright!"

He heard footsteps. Then voices came again, low and far away this time.

"Seen anybody?"

"Naw. Yuh?"

"Naw."

"Yuh reckon they got erway?"

"Ah dunno. Its hard t tell."

"Gawddam them sonofabitchin niggers!"

"We oughta kill ever black bastard in this country!"

"Waal, Jim got two of em, anyhow."

"But Bertha said there wuz *fo!*"

"Where in hell they hidin?"

"She said one of em wuz named Big Boy, or somethin like tha."

"We went t his shack lookin fer im."

"Yeah?"

"But we didnt fin im."

"These niggers stick tergether; they don never tell on each other."

"We looked all thu the shack n couldnt fin hide ner hair of im. Then we drove the ol woman n man out n set the shack on fire . . ."

"Jeesus! Ah wished Ah coulda been there!"

"Yuh shoulda heard the ol nigger woman howl . . ."

"Hoalo!"

"C mon over!"

Big Boy eased to the edge and peeped. He saw a white man with a gun slung over his shoulder running down the slope. Wuz they gonna search the hill? Lawd, there wuz no way fer im t git erway now; he wuz caught! He shoulda knowed theyd git im here. N he didnt hava thing, notta thing t fight wid. Yeah, soon as the blood-houns came theyd fin im. Lawd, have mercy! Theyd lynch im right here on the hill . . . Theyd git im n tie im t a stake n burn im erlive! Lawd! Nobody but the good Lawd could hep im now, nobody . . .

He heard more feet running. He nestled deeper. His chest ached. Nobody but the good Lawd could hep now. They wuz crowdin all round im n when they hada big crowd theyd close in on im. Then itd be over . . . The good Lawd would have t hep im, cause nobody could hep im now, nobody . . .

And then he went numb when he remembered Bobo. Spose Bobod come now? Hed be caught sho! Both of em would be caught! Theyd make Bobo tell where he wuz! Bobo oughta not try to come now. Somebody oughta tell im . . . But there wuz nobody; there wuz no way . . .

He eased slowly back to the opening. There was a large group of men. More were coming. Many had guns. Some had coils of rope slung over shoulders.

"Ah tell yuh they still here, somewhere . . ."

"But we looked all over!"

"What t hell! Wouldnt do t let em git erway!"

"Naw. Ef they git erway notta woman in this town would be safe."

"Say, whuts tha yuh got?"

"Er pillar."

"Fer whut?"

"Feathers, fool!"

"Chris! Thisll be hot ef we kin ketch them niggers!"

"Ol Anderson said he wuz gonna bringa barrela tar!"

"Ah got some gasoline in mah car ef yuh need it."

Big Boy had no feelings now. He was waiting. He did not wonder if they were coming after him. He just waited. He did not wonder about Bobo. He rested his cheek against the cold clay, waiting.

A dog barked. He stiffened. It barked again. He balled himself into a knot at the bottom of the hole, waiting. Then he heard the patter of dog feet.

"Look!"

"Whuts he got?"

"Its a snake!"

"Yeah, the dogs foun a snake!"

"Gee, its a big one!"

"Shucks, Ah wish he could fin one of them sonofabitchin niggers!"

The voices sank to low murmurs. Then he heard number twelve, its bell tolling and whistle crying as it slid along the rails. He flattened himself against the clay. Someone was singing:

>We'll hang ever nigger t a sour apple tree . . .

When the song ended there was hard laughter. From the other side of the hill he heard the dog barking furiously. He listened. There was more than one dog now. There were many and they were barking their throats out.

"Hush, Ah hear them dogs!"

"When theys barkin like tha theys foun somethin!"

"Here they come over the hill!"

"WE GOT IM! WE GOT IM!"

There came a roar. Tha mus be Bobo; tha mus be Bobo . . . In spite of his fear, Big Boy looked. The road, and half of the hillside across the road, were covered with men. A few were at the top of the hill, stenciled against the sky. He could see dark forms moving up the slopes. They were yelling.

"By Gawd, we got im!"

"C mon!"

"Where is he?"

"Theyre bringin im over the hill!"

"Ah got a rope fer im!"

"Say, somebody go n git the others!"

"Where is he? Cant we see im, Mister?"

"They say Berthas comin, too."

"Jack! Jack! Don leave me! Ah wanna see im!"

"Theyre bringin im over the hill, sweetheart!"

"AH WANNA BE THE FIRS T PUT A ROPE ON THA BLACK BASTARDS NECK!"

"Les start the fire!"

"Heat the tar!"

"Ah got some chains t chain im."

"Bring im over this way!"

"Chris, Ah wished Ah hada drink . . ."

Big Boy saw men moving over the hill. Among them was a long dark spot. Tha mus be Bobo; tha mus be Bobo theys carryin . . . They'll git im here. He oughta git up n run. He clamped his teeth and ran his hand across his forehead, bringing it away wet. He tried to swallow, but could not; his throat was dry.

They had started the song again:

>We'll hang ever nigger t a sour apple tree . . .

There were women singing now. Their voices made the song round and full. Song waves rolled over the top of pine trees. The sky sagged low, heavy with clouds. Wind was rising. Sometimes cricket cries cut surprisingly across the mob song. A dog had gone to the utmost top of the hill. At each lull of the song his howl floated full into the night.

Big Boy shrank when he saw the first tall flame light the hillside. Would they see im here? Then he remembered you could not see into the dark if you were standing in the light. As flames leaped higher he saw two men rolling a barrel up the slope.

"Say, gimme a han here, will yuh?"

"Awright, heave!"

"C mon! Straight up! Git t the other end!"

"Ah got the feathers here in this pillar!"

"BRING SOME MO WOOD!"

Big Boy could see the barrel surrounded by flames. The mob fell back, forming a dark circle. Theyd fin im here! He had a wild impulse to climb out and fly across the hills. But his legs would not move. He stared hard, trying to find Bobo. His eyes played over a long dark spot near the fire. Fanned by wind, flames leaped higher. He jumped. That dark spot had moved. Lawd, thas Bobo; thas Bobo . . .

He smelt the scent of tar, faint at first, then stronger. The wind brought it full into his face, then blew it away. His eyes burned and he rubbed them with his knuckles. He sneezed.

"LES GIT SOURVINEERS!"

He saw the mob close in around the fire. Their faces were hard and sharp in the light of the flames. More men and women were coming over the hill. The long dark spot was smudged out.

"Everbody git back!"

"Look! Hes gotta finger!"

"C MON! GIT THE GALS BACK FROM THE FIRE!"

"Hes got one of his ears, see?"

"Whuts the matter!"

"A woman fell out! Fainted, Ah reckon . . ."

The stench of tar permeated the hillside. The sky was black and the wind was blowing hard.

"HURRY UP N BURN THE NIGGER FO IT RAINS!"

Big Boy saw the mob fall back, leaving a small knot of men about the fire. Then, for the first time, he had a full glimpse of Bobo. A black body flashed in the light. Bobo was struggling, twisting; they were binding his arms and legs.

When he saw them tilt the barrel he stiffened. A scream quivered. He knew the tar was on Bobo. The mob fell back. He saw a tar-drenched body glistening and turning.

"THE BASTARDS GOT IT!"

There was a sudden quiet. Then he shrank violently as the wind carried, like a flurry of snow, a widening spiral of white feathers into the night. The flames leaped tall as the trees. The scream came again. Big Boy trembled and looked. The mob was running down the slopes, leaving the fire clear. Then he saw a writhing white mass cradled in yellow flame, and heard screams, one on top of the other, each shriller and shorter than the last. The mob was quiet now, standing still, looking up the slopes at the writhing white mass gradually growing black, growing black in a cradle of yellow flame.

"PO ON MO GAS!"

"Gimme a lif, will yuh!"

Two men were struggling, carrying between them a heavy can. They set it down, tilted it, leaving it so that the gas would trickle down to the hollowed earth around the fire.

Big Boy slid back into the hole, his face buried in clay. He had no feelings now, no fears. He was numb, empty, as though all blood had been drawn from him. Then his muscles flexed taut when he heard a faint patter. A tiny stream of cold water seeped to his knees, making him push back to a drier spot. He looked up; rain was beating in the grass.

"Its rainin!"

"C mon, les git t town!"

". . . don worry, when the fire git thu wid im hell be gone . . ."

"Wait, Charles! Don leave me; its slippery here . . ."

"Ahll take some of yuh ladies back in mah car . . ."

Big Boy heard the dogs barking again, this time closer. Running feet pounded past. Cold water chilled his ankles. He could hear raindrops steadily hissing.

Now a dog was barking at the mouth of the hole, barking furiously, sensing a presence there. He balled himself into a knot and clung to the bottom, his knees and shins buried in water. The bark came louder. He heard paws scraping and felt the hot scent of dog breath on his face. Green eyes glowed and drew nearer as the barking, muffled by the closeness of the hole, beat upon his eardrums. Backing till his shoulders pressed against the clay, he held his breath. He pushed out his hands, his fingers stiff. The dog yawped louder, advancing, his bark rising sharp and thin. Big Boy rose to his knees, his hands before him. Then he flattened out still more against the bottom, breathing lungsful of hot dog scent, breathing it slowly, hard, but evenly. The dog came closer, bringing hotter dog scent. Big Boy could go back no more. His knees were slipping and slopping in the water. He braced himself, ready. Then, he never exactly knew how—he never knew whether he had lunged or the dog had lunged—they were together, rolling in the water. The green eyes were beneath him, between his legs. Dognails bit into his arms. His knees slipped backward and he landed full on the dog; the dog's breath left in a heavy gasp. Instinctively, he fumbled for the throat as he felt the dog twisting between his knees. The dog snarled, long and low, as though gathering strength. Big Boy's hands traveled swiftly over the dog's back, groping for the throat. He felt dognails again and saw green eyes, but his fingers had found the throat. He choked, feeling his fingers sink; he choked, throwing back his head and stiffening his arms. He felt the dog's body heave, felt dognails digging into his loins. With strength flowing from fear, he closed his fingers, pushing his full weight on the dog's throat. The dog heaved again, and lay still . . . Big Boy heard the sound of his own breathing filling the hole, and heard shouts and footsteps above him going past.

For a long, long time he held the dog, held it long after the last footstep had died out, long after the rain had stopped.

## V

Morning found him still on his knees in a puddle of rainwater, staring at the stiff body of a dog. As the air brightened he came to himself slowly. He held still for a long time, as though waking from a dream, as though trying to remember.

The chug of a truck came over the hill. He tried to crawl to the opening. His knees were stiff and a thousand needle-like pains shot from the bottom of his feet to the calves of his legs. Giddiness made his eyes blur. He pulled up and looked. Through brackish light he saw Will's truck standing some twenty-five yards away, the engine running. Will stood on the runningboard, looking over the slopes of the hill.

Big Boy scuffled out, falling weakly in the wet grass. He tried to call to Will, but his dry throat would make no sound. He tried again.

"Will!"

Will heard, answering:

"Big Boy, c mon!"

He tried to run, and fell. Will came, meeting him in the tall grass.

"C mon," Will said, catching his arm.

They struggled to the truck.

"Hurry up!" said Will, pushing him onto the runningboard.

Will pushed back a square trapdoor which swung above the back of the driver's seat. Big Boy pulled through, landing with a thud on the bottom. On hands and knees he looked around in the semi-darkness.

"Wheres Bobo?"

Big Boy stared.

"Wheres Bobo?"

"They got im."

"When?"

"Las night."

"The mob?"

Big Boy pointed in the direction of a charred sapling on the slope of the opposite hill. Will looked. The trapdoor fell. The engine purred, the gears whined, and the truck lurched forward over the muddy road, sending Big Boy on his side.

For a while he lay as he had fallen, on his side, too weak to move. As he felt the truck swing around a curve he straightened up and rested his back against a stack of wooden boxes. Slowly, he began to make out objects in the darkness. Through two long cracks fell thin blades of daylight. The floor was of smooth steel, and cold to his thighs. Splinters and bits of sawdust danced with the rumble of the truck. Each time they swung around a curve he was pulled over the floor; he grabbed at corners of boxes to steady himself. Once he heard the crow of a rooster. It made him think of home, of ma and pa. He thought he remembered hearing somewhere that the house had burned, but could not remember where . . . It all seemed unreal now.

He was tired. He dozed, swaying with the lurch. Then he jumped awake. The truck was running smoothly, on gravel. Far away he heard two short blasts from the Buckeye Lumber Mill. Unconsciously, the thought sang through his mind: Its six erclock . . .

The trapdoor swung in. Will spoke through a corner of his mouth.

"How yuh comin?"

"Awright."

"How they git Bobo?"

"He wuz comin over the hill."

"Whut they do?"

"They burnt im . . . Will, Ah wan some water; mah throats like fire . . ."

"Well git some when we pass a fillin station."

Big Boy leaned back and dozed. He jerked awake when the truck stopped. He heard Will get out. He wanted to peep through the trapdoor, but was afraid. For a moment, the wild fear he had known in the hole came back. Spose theyd search n fin im? He quieted when he heard Will's footstep on the runningboard. The trapdoor pushed in. Will's hat came through, dripping.

"Take it, quick!"

Big Boy grabbed, spilling water into his face. The truck lurched. He drank. Hard cold lumps of brick rolled into his hot stomach. A dull pain made him bend over. His intestines seemed to be drawing into a tight knot. After a bit it eased, and he sat up, breathing softly.

The truck swerved. He blinked his eyes. The blades of daylight had turned brightly golden. The sun had risen.

The truck sped over the asphalt miles, sped northward, jolting him, shaking out of his bosom the crumbs of corn bread, making them dance with the splinters and sawdust in the golden blades of sunshine.

He turned on his side and slept.

# THE MAN WITH THE KNIVES

## Heinrich Boll

*Born in Cologne, Germany, in 1917, Heinrich Boll, essayist and playwright as well as fiction writer, remains less known in America than his fellow writers Uwe Johnson and Gunter Grass, whose fictional techniques at times make Boll's work seem almost old-fashioned. It should be remembered, however, that Boll, who has been writing actively for over twenty-five years, was one of the famous "Group 47," whose aim was to revitalize the German language after the Nazi regime. This purpose is clearly achieved in his first novel,* The Train Was on Time *(1949), and in the stories in his collection* Traveller, If You Came to Spa *(1956). Certainly "The Man with the Knives," even in translation, illustrates what Anthony Burgess calls Boll's "clean, spare, workmanlike" language, "altogether purged of Nazi debasements." Perhaps the award to Boll in 1972 of the Nobel Prize for Literature for his "contribution to the renewal of German literature"—and more particularly for his latest novel,* Group Portrait with Lady—*will bring his work the acclaim it richly deserves here in America. In the present situation, it would seem appropriate to recognize a writer who, in the words of Richard Locke, is "an ironic realist" who is "unashamed to talk of good and evil, love and hate."*

TRANSLATOR: Richard Graves

Jupp was holding the knife by the point of the blade and letting it swing idly from side to side. It was a long breadknife with a thin blade and one could see that it was sharp. With a sudden movement he threw it up into the air. It went up, humming like a boat's propeller, cut through a patch of fading sunlight looking like a golden fish, struck the ceiling, lost its momentum and fell sharply down, point foremost, straight for Jupp's head, on which Jupp had, with the speed of lightning, placed a thick square of wood. The point of the blade went plunk into the wood and the knife stuck fast with its handle swinging in the air. Jupp took the piece of wood from his head, freed the knife and flung it angrily at the door, where it stuck trembling in a panel till at last it swung itself out of its notch and fell on the floor.

"It's sickening," said Jupp softly, "my act is based on the self-evident principle that the public, when they pay their money at the door, prefer to see turns in which there is danger to life or limb, just as it was in the Roman circus—they want at least to know that blood *could* flow, do you follow me? But there's no danger in what I actually do." He lifted up the knife and with a flick of the wrist sent it into the woodwork at the top of the window with such violence that the panes rattled and looked as though they might fall out of their brittle frames.

This throw, sure and masterly, reminded me of the dreary war days when he used to send his pocketknife climbing up and down the wooden supports in the air-raid shelter. "There's nothing I wouldn't do," he went on, "to give the public a thrill. I'd cut my ears off to please them, if only I could find someone to stick them on again. I couldn't live without ears: I'd sooner spend the rest of my life in prison. Now, come along with me." He pulled the door open, pushed me in front of him and we walked out on to the staircase, on the walls of which rags of wallpaper were only to be seen in places where the paper was so tightly stuck to the wall that it was impossible to tear it off. The rest had gone to light stoves. Then we crossed a disused bathroom and came out on to a sort of terrace with a floor of broken concrete and patches of moss growing here and there. Jupp pointed upward and said, "Of course, the more headroom I've got for my knife, the better the performance goes, but I must have a ceiling for the knife to strike against so that it will lose its impetus and come straight down point foremost on my useless head. Look." He pointed upward where the iron framework of a broken down balcony projected into the air and said, "This is where I practiced—all day for a whole year. Watch me now." He sent the knife whizzing up. Its flight was marvelously steady and regular, as tireless as a bird's, then it struck the base of the balcony and shot down with breath-taking speed into the block of wood on Jupp's head. It must have given him a considerable shock but Jupp didn't bat an eyelid. The knife point was at least an inch deep in the wood.

"Bravo," I cried, "that's a masterpiece. Your people must admit that that's an act worth seeing."

Jupp pulled the knife casually out of the wood, and held it up. "Yes," he said, "I suppose they do. They give me twelve marks a night for playing about with my knife in between two longer numbers. But my act is too simple. A man, a knife, a block of wood—you follow me—there's no variety, no tension. I ought to have a half-naked woman on the stage with me and to sling my knife a hair's breadth past her nose. That would get them! But where can I find such a woman?"

We went back into the room and he laid the knife carefully on the table, with the square of wood beside it, and rubbed his hands. Then we sat down in silence on a chest by the stove. I took a hunk of bread out of my pocket and said, "Have some."

"Gladly," he said, "and I'll make some coffee and afterward you will come with me to the show and see my act."

He stuck some wood in the stove and put a saucepan over the opening. "I'm in despair," he said. "I think I look too serious. Perhaps I do look a bit like a sergeant, what do you think?"

"Oh, nonsense. You've never been a sergeant and aren't in the least like one. Do you smile when they clap?"

"Obviously—and I bow too."

"I couldn't do that. I couldn't smile at a cemetery."

"You are quite wrong. That's just where you ought to smile."

"I don't understand you."

"I mean because they aren't really dead. No one is dead. Do you understand?"

"I understand what you say but I don't believe it."

"You've still got something of the lieutenant about you. Yes, of course, they're asleep for longer in a cemetery. But as for my public, I'm happy if I can amuse them. They are lifeless, so I tickle them a little and get paid for doing it. Perhaps one of them when he goes home after the show will not forget me. Maybe he will say to himself, 'Damn it, the man with the knives—he wasn't afraid and I'm always afraid, damn it. . . .' For you know they are all afraid all the time. They drag their fear behind them like a leaden shadow and I am happy if I can make them forget it and laugh a bit. You see I have good reason to smile at them."

I said nothing and watched the water boiling. Jupp poured coffee into the brown enamel pot and we drank out of it in turn as we munched my bread. Outside it was slowly growing dark and the twilight flowed into the room like a flood of soft gray milk.

"What do you do for a living?" Jupp asked me.

"Nothing . . . I live from hand to mouth."

"That's a hard calling."

"Yes, to earn the bread we're eating, I've had to break a hundred stones . . . casual labor they call it."

"Hm . . . would you like to see another of my tricks?"

I nodded and he got up, switched on the light and went to the wall where he pushed a hanging on one side revealing the outline of a man roughly drawn in charcoal on the reddish distemper. A curious eminence rising above the head of the figure seemed to represent a hat. When I came near I could see that the figure was drawn on a cleverly camouflaged door.

I began to be interested when Jupp pulled out from under his wretched bed a pretty brown box and placed it on the table. Before opening it he came to me and put four cigarette papers on the table saying, "Roll a couple of fags with these."

I changed my place so that I could see him better and get more benefit from the warmth of the stove. While I was carefully laying out the cigarette papers, Jupp pressed a spring which opened the box and pulled out a curious sort of case. It was one of those roll-up cloth contraptions with a lot of pockets in which our mothers used to keep the knives and forks and spoons belonging to their trousseaus. He unfastened the catch and rolled it out on the table. It contained a dozen knives with horn handles of the kind which, in the days when our young mothers used to dance La Valse, were called hunting cutlery. I spread out the tobacco carefully on two of the slips and rolled a couple of cigarettes.

"Here you are," I said, handing them to Jupp, who handed one back to me, saying, "Thanks." Then he showed me the whole of the case and said, "This is the only thing that I was able to save from my parents' belongings. Everything else was burnt, blown to pieces or stolen. When I came out of prison, ragged and wretched, I possessed nothing, absolutely nothing, till one day a distinguished old lady who had known my mother sought me out and gave me this pretty little box. A few days before she was killed by the bombs, mother had given her this little thing to look after and so it was saved. Funny, isn't it? But then of course one knows that when people are threatened with destruction they try to save the most peculiar things—never the most necessary ones. So I became the possessor of this box and its contents which originally consisted of the brown coffeepot, twelve forks, twelve knives and twelve spoons—oh, and the big breadknife as well. I sold the spoons and forks and lived on the proceeds for a year, while I was learning to use the knives, the whole thirteen of them. Watch me!"

I passed him the spill with which I had lit my cigarette. Jupp lit his own and stuck it on to his lower lip. Then he fastened the loop of the case to a button high up on the shoulder of his jacket and let the case unroll itself along his arm, looking like some fancy war decoration. Then, with incredible rapidity, he picked the knives out of their case and before I could properly follow the motion of his hands, he had flung all twelve of them at the shadowy figure on the door, which reminded me of those ghastly swinging figures, the precursors of final defeat, which we used to see hanging from every advertisement pillar and at the corner of every street. I looked and saw that there were two knives in the man's hat, two over each shoulder and three neatly outlining each of his arms.

"Crazy," I said. "Absolutely crazy! What an act that would make with a little building up!"

"Yes, but it wants a man—a live man—or better still a woman, and that," he said, as he pulled the knives out of the door and put them carefully back in the case, "that is what I shall never find. The women are too frightened and the men too dear. I can quite understand that. It's a dangerous job."

Jupp took another pull at his flimsy cigarette and threw the scanty remnant behind the stove.

"Come," he said, "I think we ought to be going." He put his head out of the window, murmured, "It's raining, damn it," and said, "It's a few minutes before eight and I come on at half-past."

As he was packing the knives in the little leather box I put my face to the window and looked out. I heard the gentle murmur of the rain as it fell on the ruined villas, and behind a line of swaying poplars I heard the screech of passing trams. But I couldn't see a clock anywhere.

"How do you know what time it is?" I asked.

"By instinct. That's part of my training." I looked at him uncomprehendingly. He helped me on with my overcoat and then put on his own wind-jacket. I have a damaged shoulder and can only move my arm within a limited range: just enough for breaking stones. We put on our caps and went out into the dim passage. It was a comfort to hear the quiet sound of voices and laughter from somewhere in this lonely house.

As we went down the stairs Jupp said, "I have taken a lot of trouble to get on the track of certain cosmic laws." As he spoke, he put down his box on a step and stretched out his arms on either side of him, looking like Icarus as we see him in the old pictures taking off for a flight. On his sober face there was a strange expression, at once cool and dreamy, half-possessed and half-calculating—a magical look which filled me with fear. "So," he said quietly, "I stretch out my hands into the air and I see them growing longer and longer till they penetrate into a region where other laws apply; they pass through a veil behind which lie strange enchanting thrills which I grasp—just grasp—and then I clutch the laws which govern them, like a happy thief, clasp them to myself and carry them away with me!" He clenched his hands and pressed them to his body. "Come along," he said and his face resumed its old prosaic expression. I followed him in a dream.

Outside the rain was falling steadily. The air struck cold and we turned up our collars and shrank shivering into ourselves. An evening mist streamed through the streets already tinted with the blue-black darkness of night. In the basements of many of the blitzed villas one could see a faint and pitiful candlelight showing beneath the black ruins that overlay them. The street turned imperceptibly into a muddy track with dim wooden shanties barely visible in the darkness to right and left which seemed to be floating in the uncared-for gardens like threatening junks in a shallow backwater. Then we crossed the tramway and walked down a narrow lane leading to the suburbs where a few houses were still standing in the midst of heaps of rubble and debris, till we suddenly came out into a lively, populous street. We moved along with the stream of people on the pavement for a while and then turned off down a dark lane, where the brightly illuminated sign of the Seven Mills was reflected on the wet asphalt.

The entrance to the variety theater was empty. The show had started some time ago, and we heard the buzz of voices from the inside coming to us through the shabby red curtains.

Jupp laughed as he showed me a photo of himself in cowboy dress hanging between the pictures of two smirking dancing girls with spangles all over their chests. Below it stood the words: *The Man with the Knives.*

"Come along," said Jupp, and before I realized what I was doing I found myself walking down an unsuspected passage and climbing a narrow, winding, ill-lit staircase in which the smell of sweat and make-up betrayed the nearness of the stage. Jupp, who was leading the way, suddenly stopped at a bend in the staircase; he set down his box and putting his hands on my shoulders asked me in a low voice, "Have you got the nerve?"

I had long been expecting this question, but its suddenness frightened me. I expect I didn't look very brave when I answered, "The courage of despair!"

"That's the right kind," he said, suppressing a laugh. "Are you game?"

I was silent, and then suddenly we heard a storm of wild laughter from inside the house. It was so loud and violent that I started and found myself trembling.

"I'm afraid," I said softly.

"So am I," he answered. "Have you no confidence in me?"

"Yes, of course I have but . . . come on," I said hoarsely, pushing him forward and adding, "It's all one to me."

We came up into a narrow corridor with a number of plywood compartments on either side. A few gaily clad figures were moving about and, through a gap in the wings, I saw a clown on the stage opening his cavernous mouth. We heard once more a wild burst of laughter from the public, but then Jupp pulled me into a compartment and shut the door behind us. I looked round me. The compartment was very small and almost unfurnished. There was a mirror on the wall, and Jupp's cowboy kit was hanging on a solitary nail, while an old pack of cards lay on a rickety chair. Jupp was in a hurry; he was likewise nervous. He helped me off with my wet overcoat, slapped down his cowboy suit on the chair and hung up my coat and his wind-jacket on the nail. Over the partition wall of our cabin I could see a red-painted Doric column with an electric clock on it which pointed to twenty-five minutes past eight.

"Five minutes more," murmured Jupp, as he pulled on his costume. "Shall we have a rehearsal?"

At that moment there was a knock on the door and someone called, "Get ready."

Jupp buttoned up his jacket and put on his wild west hat. I said with a hysterical laugh, "Do you want to hang the condemned man experimentally before you finally execute him?"

Jupp took hold of his box and drew me out of the compartment. In the passage we found a bald-pated man watching the end of the clown's turn. Jupp whispered something in his ear, which I didn't catch. The man looked up with a frightened expression. Then he stared at me and looked at Jupp again and shook his head emphatically. Jupp whispered to him again.

For my part I didn't care what happened to me. They could make a pincushion of me if they wanted to. I had a trick shoulder; I had just smoked a reefer and next morning I had to break seventy-five stones for which I should get three-quarters of a loaf of bread. But tomorrow . . .

The act was over and the applause flooded into the wings. The clown reeled out through the opening with a weary, drawn face and came up to us. He stood waiting for a few seconds with a morose expression and then went back on to the stage and bowed to the audience with a friendly smile. The orchestra played a flourish and Jupp went on whispering to the man with the bald head. The clown went back three times to bow and smile at the applauding public. Then the band began to play a march and Jupp, carrying his box, walked on to the stage with firm steps. He was greeted with a few perfunctory claps. Then I watched with weary eyes while Jupp fixed up the cards on a row of nails and pierced each one of them with his knives exactly through the center. The applause became livelier, but was still half-hearted. Then to the soft accompaniment of gently tapping drums, he went through his performance with the bread-knife and the wooden block and, in spite of my indifference, I noticed that it was a bit thin. On the other side of the stage I caught sight of a few scantily dressed girls staring at the show from the wings . . . and then the man with the bald head caught hold of me and dragged me on to the stage, saluted Jupp with a flourish and said with a stage policeman's voice, "Good evening, Mr. Borgalewski."

"Good evening, Mr. Clodpuncher," said Jupp in duly solemn tones.

"I have brought you here a horse-thief, an out-and-out rascal, Mr. Borgalewski. We want you to tickle him a bit with those smart looking knives of yours, before we hang him . . . a real rascal. . . ." His voice seemed to me ridiculous, mean and artificial at the same time—like paper flowers and cheap face-paint. I threw a glance at the audience and saw in front of me a dim, dully gleaming, tense, thousand-headed monster sitting in the darkness ready to spring. From that moment I simply switched off. Nothing mattered a damn any more. The glare of the spotlights dazzled me and in my shabby suit and wretched gaping shoes, I might well have passed for a horse-thief.

"Leave him to me, Mr. Clodpuncher," said Jupp, "I'll soon settle his hash."

"Good, I'll leave you to take care of him. Don't spare the knives."

Jupp grabbed me by the collar while Mr. Clodpuncher shambled off the stage with a grin on his face. A piece of cord flew on to the stage from somewhere and then Jupp tied me to a Doric pillar in front of one of the blue-painted doors that led into the wings. I had a strange delirious feeling in which indifference was uppermost. On my right I heard the curious, many-voiced murmuring of the excited audience and perceived that Jupp had been quite right when he spoke of their blood-lust, which hovered trembling in the sweet, stale atmosphere, while the tense drumming of the band, keyed to a kind of voluptuous cruelty, enhanced the impression of a terrible tragi-comedy in which real blood would flow—blood that the management had paid for. I looked straight ahead of me and let myself slump, but the tightly fastened cord held me upright. The drumbeats grew softer and softer as Jupp, with professional neatness, picked the knives out of the playing cards and placed them in his case, looking at me the while with an expression of melodramatic contempt. Then, when he had put all his knives away, he turned to the audience and said in an affected voice, "Ladies and gentlemen, I am now going to crown this gentleman with knives, but I want you to see that my knives are by no means blunt," and as he spoke he fished a piece of string out of his pocket and, with uncanny calm, took the knives one after the other out of the case and, touching the string with each, cut it into twelve pieces. Then he replaced each knife carefully in its pocket.

All this while I was looking over his head, past the half-naked girls in the wings, and, as it seemed to me, into a new life.

The air was electrified by the excitement of the public. Jupp came up to me and pretended to tighten up the cords that bound me and as he did so he whispered, "Keep absolutely still—not a move—and don't be afraid, my dear fellow."

His delay in getting to work had relieved the tension, which looked as if it might fizzle out, but then he suddenly clutched the air, and waved his hands like softly whirring birds. Over his face came that expression of magical repose which had so overwhelmed me on the staircase.

At the same time his face and his gestures seemed to hypnotize the audience. I thought I heard him give a strange, alarming groan and realized that it was a warning signal to me.

I called back my eyes from the infinite distance in which they had been swimming and focused them on Jupp, who was now standing straight in front of me. Then he raised his hand and slowly grasped the case. The moment had come. I stood still, absolutely still, and closed my eyes.

It was a wonderful feeling—lasting a few seconds only, I don't know how many. As I heard the soft hissing of the knives and felt their wind as they whizzed past me into the door, I seemed to be walking on a narrow plank over a bottomless abyss, walking safely and surely, but fully conscious of the danger. I was afraid, but knew full well that I would not fall. I did not count the knives but found myself opening my eyes, just as the last knife pierced the door a hair's breadth from my right hand.

A storm of applause roused me from my trance. I opened my eyes wide and looked into Jupp's pale face. He ran up to me and unfastened me with nervous hands. Then he dragged me into the middle of the stage, right up to the footlights. He bowed and I bowed and, in the midst of the swelling applause, he pointed to me and I to him. Then we smiled at one another and bowed, smiling, to the public.

Back in the dressing room, we didn't say a word. Jupp threw the perforated pack of cards on to the chair, took my coat from its nail and helped me on with it. Then he hung up his cowboy costume and put on his wind-jacket. We both put on our caps and as I opened the door the man with the bald head hurried up to us saying, "Salary raised to forty marks!" He handed Jupp a few notes. At that moment I understood that Jupp was now my boss and we looked at one another and smiled.

Jupp took my arm and we walked side by side down the narrow, ill-lit stairs smelling of stale grease-paint. When we had reached the exit Jupp laughed and said, "Now we'll buy cigarettes and some bread. . . ."

It was at least an hour before I realized that I now had a regular profession—a job in which I had nothing to do but to submit myself and dream a bit—for twelve seconds, or twenty, maybe. I was now the man the knives were thrown at.

---

# THE SHAPE OF THE SWORD

## Jorge Luis Borges

*Poet, essayist, and author, Borges was born on August 24, 1899, in Buenos Aires and, because of World War I, was educated in Geneva. After three years in Spain, during which he wrote poetry and was influenced by the avant-garde Ultraista movement, he returned in 1921 to Buenos Aires. His early writings were almost exclusively poetry and essays, but in the thirties he turned to fiction, devoting most of his effort to what have been characterized as "metaphysical fictions." El jardín de senderos que se bifurcan, his first important collection of stories, was published in 1941. This was followed in 1944 by Ficciones and in 1949 by El Aleph, two of his finest collections of short stories. The best of these are translated in Labyrinths, edited by Donald A. Yates and James E. Irby (New Directions, 1962). In the fifties, suffering from near blindness, Borges began dictating "parables," which were published in El Hacedor in 1960. Among his major awards have been the "Prize of Honor" from the Sociedad Argentina de Escritores (1944), the National Prize for Literature (1956), and the International Publisher's Prize (Prix Formentor, 1961). He has traveled and taught in the United States. Although the influence of Kafka, Poe, Chesterton, and H. G. Wells is evident in his fiction, there is nothing derivative about it. His stories continue to impress and enlighten, even in translation, because, as James Irby has written in the introduction to Labyrinths, "they grow out of the deep confrontation of literature and life which is not only the central problem of all literature but also that of all human experience: the problem of illusion and reality."*

TRANSLATOR: Donald A. Yates

A spiteful scar crossed his face: an ash-colored and nearly perfect arc that creased his temple at one tip and his cheek at the other. His real name is of no importance; everyone in Tacuarembó called him the "Englishman from La Colorada." Cardoso, the owner of those fields, refused to sell them: I understand that the Englishman resorted to an unexpected argument: he confided to Cardoso the secret of the scar. The Englishman came from the border, from Río Grande del Sur; there are many who say that in Brazil he had been a smuggler. The fields were overgrown with grass, the waterholes brackish; the Englishman, in order to correct those deficiencies, worked fully as hard as his laborers. They say that he was severe to the point of cruelty, but scrupulously just. They say also that he drank: a few times a year he locked himself into an upper room, not to emerge until two or three days later as if from a battle or from vertigo, pale, trembling, confused and as authoritarian as ever. I remember the glacial eyes, the energetic leanness, the gray mustache. He had no dealings with anyone; it is a fact that his Spanish was rudimentary and cluttered with Brazilian. Aside from a business letter or some pamphlet, he received no mail.

The last time I passed through the northern provinces, a sudden overflowing of the Caraguatá stream compelled me to spend the night at La Colorada. Within a few moments, I seemed to sense that my appearance was inopportune; I tried to ingratiate myself with the Englishman; I resorted to the least discerning of passions: patriotism. I claimed as invincible a country with such spirit as England's. My companion agreed, but added with a smile that he was not English. He was Irish, from Dungarvan. Having said this, he stopped short, as if he had revealed a secret.

After dinner we went outside to look at the sky. It had cleared up, but beyond the low hills the southern sky, streaked and gashed by lightning, was conceiving another storm. Into the cleared up dining room the boy who had served dinner brought a bottle of rum. We drank for some time, in silence.

I don't know what time it must have been when I observed that I was drunk; I don't know what inspiration or what exultation or tedium made me mention the scar. The Englishman's face changed its expression; for a few seconds I thought he was going to throw me out of the house. At length he said in his normal voice:

"I'll tell you the history of my scar under one condition: that of not mitigating one bit of the opprobrium, of the infamous circumstances."

I agreed. This is the story that he told me, mixing his English with Spanish, and even with Portuguese:

"Around 1922, in one of the cities of Connaught, I was one of the many who were conspiring for the independence of Ireland. Of my comrades, some are still living, dedicated to peaceful pursuits; others, paradoxically, are fighting on desert and sea under the English flag; another, the most worthy, died in the courtyard of a barracks, at dawn, shot by men filled with sleep; still others (not the most unfortunate) met their destiny in the anonymous and almost secret battles of the civil war. We were Republicans, Catholics; we were, I suspect, Romantics. Ireland was for us not only the utopian future and the intolerable present; it was a bitter and cherished mythology, it was the circular towers and the red marshes, it was the repudiation of Parnell and the enormous epic poems which sang of the robbing of bulls which in another incarnation were heroes and in others fish and mountains . . . One afternoon I will never forget, an affiliate from Munster joined us: one John Vincent Moon.

"He was scarcely twenty years old. He was slender and flaccid at the same time; he gave the uncomfortable impression of being invertebrate. He had studied with fervor and with vanity nearly every page of Lord knows what Communist manual; he made use of dialectical materialism to put an end to any discussion whatever. The reasons one can have for hating another man, or for loving him, are infinite: Moon reduced the history of the universe to a sordid economic conflict. He affirmed that the revolution was predestined to succeed. I told him that for a gentleman only lost causes should be attractive . . . Night had already fallen; we continued our disagreement in the hall, on the stairs, then along the vague streets. The judgments Moon emitted impressed me less than his irrefutable, apodictic note. The new comrade did not discuss: he dictated opinions with scorn and with a certain anger.

"As we were arriving at the outlying houses, a sudden burst of gunfire stunned us. (Either before or afterwards we skirted the blank wall of a factory or barracks.) We moved into an unpaved street; a soldier, huge in the firelight, came out of a burning hut. Crying out, he ordered us to stop. I quickened my pace; my companion did not follow. I turned around: John Vincent Moon was motionless, fascinated, as if eternized by fear. I then ran back and knocked the soldier to the ground with one blow, shook Vincent Moon, insulted him and ordered him to follow. I had to take him by the arm; the passion of fear had rendered him helpless. We fled, into the night pierced by flames. A rifle volley reached out for us, and a bullet nicked Moon's right shoulder; as we were fleeing amid pines, he broke out in weak sobbing.

"In that fall of 1923 I had taken shelter in General Berkeley's country house. The general (whom I had never seen) was carrying out some administrative assignment or other in Bengal; the house was less than a century old, but it was decayed and shadowy and flourished in puzzling corridors and in pointless antechambers. The museum and the huge library usurped the first floor: controversial and uncongenial books which in some manner are the history of the nineteenth century; scimitars from Nishapur, along whose captured arcs there seemed to persist still the wind and violence of battle. We entered (I seem to recall) through the rear. Moon, trembling, his mouth parched, murmured that the events of the night were interesting; I dressed his wound and brought him a cup of tea; I was able to determine that his 'wound' was superficial. Suddenly he stammered in bewilderment:

" 'You know, you ran a terrible risk.'

"I told him not to worry about it. (The habit of the civil war had incited me to act as I did; besides, the capture of a single member could endanger our cause.)

"By the following day Moon had recovered his poise. He accepted a cigarette and subjected me to a severe interrogation on the 'economic resources of our revolutionary party.' His questions were very lucid; I told him (truthfully) that the situation was serious. Deep bursts of rifle fire agitated the south. I told Moon our comrades were waiting for us. My overcoat and my revolver were in my room; when I returned I found Moon stretched out on the sofa, his eyes closed. He imagined he had a fever; he invoked a painful spasm in his shoulder.

"At that moment I understood that his cowardice was irreparable. I clumsily entreated him to take care of himself and went out. This frightened man mortified me, as if I were the coward, not Vincent Moon. Whatever one man does, it is as if all men did it. For that reason it is not unfair that one disobedience in a garden should contaminate all humanity; for that reason it is not unjust that the crucifixion of a single Jew should be sufficient to save it. Perhaps Schopenhauer was right: I am all other men, any man is all men, Shakespeare is in some manner the miserable John Vincent Moon.

"Nine days we spent in the general's enormous house. Of the agonies and the successes of the war I shall not speak: I propose to relate the history of the scar that insults me. In my memory, those nine days form only a single day, save for the next to the last, when our men broke into a barracks and we were able to avenge precisely the sixteen comrades who had been machine-gunned in Elphin. I slipped out of the house towards dawn, in the confusion of daybreak. At nightfall I was back. My companion was waiting for me upstairs: his wound did not permit him to descend to the ground floor. I recall him having some volume of strategy in his hand, F. N. Maude or Clausewitz. 'The weapon I prefer is the artillery,' he confessed to me one night. He inquired into our plans; he liked to censure them or revise them. He also was accustomed to denouncing 'our deplorable economic basis'; dogmatic and gloomy, he predicted the disastrous end. *'C'est une affaire flambée,'* he murmured. In order to show that he was indifferent to being a physical coward, he magnified his mental arrogance. In this way, for good or for bad, nine days elapsed.

"On the tenth day the city fell definitely to the Black and Tans. Tall, silent horsemen patrolled the roads; ashes and smoke rode on the wind; on the corner I saw a corpse thrown to the ground, an impression less firm in my memory than that of a dummy on which the soldiers endlessly practiced their marksmanship, in the middle of the square . . . I had left when dawn was in the sky; before noon I returned. Moon, in the library, was speaking with someone; the tone of his voice told me he was talking on the telephone. Then I heard my name; then, that I would return at seven; then, the suggestion that they should arrest me as I was crossing the garden. My reasonable friend was reasonably selling me out. I heard him demand guarantees of personal safety.

"Here my story is confused and becomes lost. I know that I pursued the informer along the black, nightmarish halls and along deep stairways of dizzyness. Moon knew the house very well, much better than I. One or two times I lost him. I cornered him before the soldiers stopped me. From one of the general's collections of arms I tore a cutlass: with that half moon I carved into his face forever a half moon of blood. Borges, to you, a stranger, I have made this confession. Your contempt does not grieve me so much."

Here the narrator stopped. I noticed that his hands were shaking.

"And Moon?" I asked him.

"He collected his Judas money and fled to Brazil. That afternoon, in the square, he saw a dummy shot up by some drunken men."

I waited in vain for the rest of the story. Finally I told him to go on.

Then a sob went through his body; and with a weak gentleness he pointed to the whitish curved scar.

"You don't believe me?" he stammered. "Don't you see that I carry written on my face the mark of my infamy? I have told you the story thus so that you would hear me to the end. I denounced the man who protected me: I am Vincent Moon. Now despise me."

---

# THE BLUE HOTEL

## Stephen Crane

*Born in Newark, New Jersey, on November 1, 1871, Stephen Crane was the fourteenth and last child of the Reverend Jonathan Townley Crane, a Methodist minister, and Helen Peck Crane. After a year each at Lafayette College and Syracuse University, helping to pay his way by writing for the New York* Tribune, *he moved to New York and worked as a reporter. His first novel,* Maggie: A Girl of the Streets, *regarded by critics as the first naturalistic or deterministic American novel, was published at his own expense in 1893. It was his next book,* The Red Badge of Courage, *published in 1895, that brought him fame. Crane served as a war correspondent during the Greco-*

*Turkish and the Spanish-American wars, but he continued to write the poetry and fiction for which he is famous today. Married in 1898, he settled in England and died of tuberculosis in 1900, at twenty-eight. His other works include* The Open Boat and Other Tales of Adventure *(1898),* The Black Riders and Other Lines *(1895), a book of poems, and* The Monster and Other Stories *(1899), in which "The Blue Hotel" appears. "The Blue Hotel" is a classic example of Crane's deterministic view, his belief that humans are moved by circumstances and events beyond their control; it is also an outstanding example of his characteristic ironic tone. Robert Spiller has written that Crane's fiction bears "the imprint of genius" and provides "much of the direction and method of such writers as Hemingway, Faulkner, and others who were not to appear for at least another quarter-century."*

# I

The Palace Hotel at Fort Romper was painted a light blue, a shade that is on the legs of a kind of heron, causing the bird to declare its position against any background. The Palace Hotel, then, was always screaming and howling in a way that made the dazzling winter landscape of Nebraska seem only a gray swampish hush. It stood alone on the prairie, and when the snow was falling the town two hundred yards away was not visible. But when the traveller alighted at the railway station he was obliged to pass the Palace Hotel before he could come upon the company of low clapboard houses which composed Fort Romper, and it was not to be thought that any traveller could pass the Palace Hotel without looking at it. Pat Scully, the proprietor, had proved himself a master of strategy when he chose his paints. It is true that on clear days, when the great transcontinental expresses, long lines of swaying Pullmans, swept through Fort Romper, passengers were overcome at the sight, and the cult that knows the brown-reds and the subdivisions of the dark greens of the East expressed shame, pity, horror, in a laugh. But to the citizens of this prairie town and to the people who would naturally stop there, Pat Scully had performed a feat. With this opulence and splendor, these creeds, classes, egotisms, that streamed through Romper on the rails day after day, they had no color in common.

As if the displayed delights of such a blue hotel were not sufficiently enticing, it was Scully's habit to go every morning and evening to meet the leisurely trains that stopped at Romper and work his seductions upon any man that he might see wavering, gripsack in hand.

One morning, when a snow-crusted engine dragged its long string of freight cars and its one passenger coach to the station, Scully performed the marvel of catching three men. One was a shaky and quick-eyed Swede, with a great shining cheap valise; one was a tall bronzed cowboy, who was on his way to a ranch near the Dakota line; one was a little silent man from the East, who didn't look it, and didn't announce it. Scully

**Fri** Connections pp 73-77
Write a few paragraphs comparing the 2 prints.

**Mon.** 12-5, 12-6

**Fri** Rd 61-70 in Connections Using the suggestions on p. 71 write outline for "Personal Experience" paper.

practically made them prisoners. He was so nimble and merry and kindly that each probably felt it would be the height of brutality to try to escape. They trudged off over the creaking board sidewalks in the wake of the eager little Irishman. He wore a heavy fur cap squeezed tightly down on his head. It caused his two red ears to stick out stiffly, as if they were made of tin.

At last, Scully, elaborately, with boisterous hospitality, conducted them through the portals of the blue hotel. The room which they entered was small. It seemed to be merely a proper temple for an enormous stove, which, in the center, was humming with godlike violence. At various points on its surface the iron had become luminous and glowed yellow from the heat. Beside the stove Scully's son Johnnie was playing High-Five with an old farmer who had whiskers both gray and sandy. They were quarrelling. Frequently the old farmer turned his face toward a box of sawdust—colored brown from tobacco juice—that was behind the stove, and spat with an air of great impatience and irritation. With a loud flourish of words Scully destroyed the game of cards, and bustled his son up-stairs with part of the baggage of the new guests. He himself conducted them to three basins of the coldest water in the world. The cowboy and the Easterner burnished themselves fiery red with this water, until it seemed to be some kind of metal polish. The Swede, however, merely dipped his fingers gingerly and with trepidation. It was notable that throughout this series of small ceremonies the three travellers were made to feel that Scully was very benevolent. He was conferring great favors upon them. He handed the towel from one to another with an air of philanthropic impulse.

Afterward they went to the first room, and, sitting about the stove, listened to Scully's officious clamor at his daughters, who were preparing the midday meal. They reflected in the silence of experienced men who tread carefully amid new people. Nevertheless, the old farmer, stationary, invincible in his chair near the warmest part of the stove, turned his face from the sawdust-box frequently and addressed a glowing commonplace to the strangers. Usually he was answered in short but adequate sentences by either the cowboy or the Easterner. The Swede said nothing. He seemed to be occupied in making furtive estimates of each man in the room. One might have thought that he had the sense of silly suspicion which comes to guilt. He resembled a badly frightened man.

Later, at dinner, he spoke a little, addressing his conversation entirely to Scully. He volunteered that he had come from New York, where for ten years he had worked as a tailor. These facts seemed to strike Scully as fascinating, and afterward he volunteered that he had lived at Romper for fourteen years. The Swede asked about the crops and the price of labor. He seemed barely to listen to Scully's extended replies. His eyes continued to rove from man to man.

Finally, with a laugh and a wink, he said that some of these Western communities were very dangerous; and after his statement he straightened his legs under the table, tilted his head, and laughed again, loudly. It was plain that the demonstration had no meaning to the others. They looked at him wondering and in silence.

## II

As the men trooped heavily back into the front room, the two little windows presented views of a turmoiling sea of snow. The huge arms of the wind were making attempts—mighty, circular, futile—to embrace the flakes as they sped. A gate-post like a still man with a blanched face stood aghast amid this profligate fury. In a hearty voice Scully announced the presence of a blizzard. The guests of the blue hotel, lighting their pipes, assented with grunts of lazy masculine contentment. No island of the sea could be exempt in the degree of this little room with its humming stove. Johnnie, son of Scully, in a tone which defined his opinion of his ability as a card-player, challenged the old farmer of both gray and sandy whiskers to a game of High-Five. The farmer agreed with a contemptuous and bitter scoff. They sat close to the stove, and squared their knees under a wide board. The cowboy and the Easterner watched the game with interest. The Swede remained near the window, aloof, but with a countenance that showed signs of an inexplicable excitement.

The play of Johnnie and the gray-beard was suddenly ended by another quarrel. The old man arose while casting a look of heated scorn at his adversary. He slowly buttoned his coat, and then stalked with fabulous dignity from the room. In the discreet silence of all the other men the Swede laughed. His laughter rang somehow childish. Men by this time had begun to look at him askance, as if they wished to inquire what ailed him.

A new game was formed jocosely. The cowboy volunteered to become the partner of Johnnie, and they all then turned to ask the Swede to throw in his lot with the little Easterner. He asked some questions about the game, and, learning that it wore many names, and that he had played it when it was under an alias, he accepted the invitation. He strode toward the men nervously, as if he expected to be assaulted. Finally, seated, he gazed from face to face and laughed shrilly. This laugh was so strange that the Easterner looked up quickly, the cowboy sat intent and with his mouth open, and Johnnie paused, holding the cards with still fingers.

Afterward there was a short silence. Then Johnnie said, "Well, let's get at it. Come on now!" They pulled their chairs forward until their knees were hunched under the board. They began to play, and their interest in the game caused the others to forget the manner of the Swede.

The cowboy was a board-whacker. Each time that he held superior cards he whanged them, one by one, with exceeding force, down upon the improvised table, and took the tricks with a glowing air of prowess and pride that sent thrills of indignation into the hearts of his opponents. A game with a board-whacker in it is sure to become intense. The countenances of the Easterner and the Swede were miserable whenever the cowboy thundered down his aces and kings, while Johnnie, his eyes gleaming with joy, chuckled and chuckled.

Because of the absorbing play none considered the strange ways of the Swede. They paid strict heed to the game. Finally, during a lull caused by a new deal, the Swede suddenly addressed Johnnie: "I suppose there have been a good many men killed in this room." The jaws of the others dropped and they looked at him.

"What in hell are you talking about?" said Johnnie.

The Swede laughed again his blatant laugh, full of a kind of false courage and defiance. "Oh, you know what I mean all right," he answered.

"I'm a liar if I do!" Johnnie protested. The card was halted, and the men stared at the Swede. Johnnie evidently felt that as the son of the proprietor he should make a direct inquiry. "Now, what might you be drivin' at, mister?" he asked. The Swede winked at him. It was a wink full of cunning. His fingers shook on the edge of the board. "Oh, maybe you think I have been to nowheres. Maybe you think I'm a tenderfoot?"

"I don't know nothin' about you," answered Johnnie, "and I don't give a damn where you've been. All I got to say is that I don't know what you're driving at. There hain't never been nobody killed in this room."

The cowboy, who had been steadily gazing at the Swede, then spoke: "What's wrong with you, mister?"

Apparently it seemed to the Swede that he was formidably menaced. He shivered and turned white near the corners of his mouth. He sent an appealing glance in the direction of the little Easterner. During these moments he did not forget to wear his air of advanced pot-valor. "They say they don't know what I mean," he remarked mockingly to the Easterner.

The latter answered after prolonged and cautious reflection. "I don't understand you," he said, impassively.

The Swede made a movement then which announced that he thought he had encountered treachery from the only quarter where he had expected sympathy, if not help. "Oh, I see you are all against me. I see—"

The cowboy was in a state of deep stupefaction. "Say," he cried, as he tumbled the deck violently down upon the board, "say, what are you gettin' at, hey?"

The Swede sprang up with the celerity of a man escaping from a snake on the floor. "I don't want to fight!" he shouted. "I don't want to fight!"

The cowboy stretched his long legs indolently and deliberately. His hands were in his pockets. He spat into the sawdust-box. "Well, who the hell thought you did?" he inquired.

The Swede backed rapidly toward a corner of the room. His hands were out protectingly in front of his chest, but he was making an obvious struggle to control his fright. "Gentlemen," he quavered, "I suppose I am going to be killed before I can leave this house! I suppose I am going to be killed before I can leave this house!" In his eyes was the dying-swan look. Through the windows could be seen the snow turning blue in the shadow of dusk. The wind tore at the house, and some loose thing beat regularly against the clapboards like a spirit tapping.

A door opened, and Scully himself entered. He paused in surprise as he noted the tragic attitude of the Swede. Then he said, "What's the matter here?"

The Swede answered him swiftly and eagerly: "These men are going to kill me."

"Kill you!" ejaculated Scully. "Kill you! What are you talkin'?"

The Swede made the gesture of a martyr.

Scully wheeled sternly upon his son, "What is this, Johnnie?"

The lad had grown sullen. "Damned if I know," he answered. "I can't make no sense to it." He began to shuffle the cards, fluttering them together with an angry snap. "He says a good many men have been killed in this room, or something like that. And he says he's goin' to be killed here too. I don't know what ails him. He's crazy, I shouldn't wonder."

Scully then looked for explanation to the cowboy, but the cowboy simply shrugged his shoulders.

"Kill you?" said Scully again to the Swede. "Kill you? Man, you're off your nut."

"Oh, I know," burst out the Swede. "I know what will happen. Yes, I'm crazy—yes. Yes, of course, I'm crazy—yes. But I know one thing—" There was a sort of sweat of misery and terror upon his face. "I know I won't get out of here alive."

The cowboy drew a deep breath, as if his mind was passing into the last stages of dissolution. "Well, I'm doggoned," he whispered to himself.

Scully wheeled suddenly and faced his son. "You've been troublin' this man!"

Johnnie's voice was loud with its burden of grievance. "Why, good Gawd, I ain't done nothin' to 'im."

The Swede broke in. "Gentlemen, do not disturb yourselves. I will leave this house. I will go away, because"—he accused them dramatically with his glance—"because I do not want to be killed."

Scully was furious with his son. "Will you tell me what is the matter, you young divil? What's the matter, anyhow? Speak out!"

"Blame it!" cried Johnnie in despair, "don't I tell you I don't know? He—he says we want to kill him, and that's all I know. I can't tell what ails him."

The Swede continued to repeat: "Never mind, Mr. Scully; never mind. I will leave this house. I will go away, because I do not wish to be killed. Yes, of course, I am crazy—yes. But I know one thing! I will go away. I will leave this house. Never mind, Mr. Scully; never mind. I will go away."

"You will not go 'way," said Scully. "You will not go 'way until I hear the reason of this business. If anybody has troubled you I will take care of him. This is my house. You are under my roof, and I will not allow any peaceable man to be troubled here." He cast a terrible eye upon Johnnie, the cowboy, and the Easterner.

"Never mind, Mr. Scully; never mind. I will go away. I do not wish to be killed." The Swede moved toward the door which opened upon the stairs. It was evidently his intention to go at once for his baggage.

"No, no," shouted Scully peremptorily; but the white-faced man slid by him and disappeared. "Now," said Scully severely, "what does this mane?"

Johnnie and the cowboy cried together: "Why, we didn't do nothin' to 'im!"

Scully's eyes were cold. "No," he said, "you didn't?"

Johnnie swore a deep oath. "Why, this is the wildest loon I ever see. We didn't do nothin' at all. We were jest sittin' here playin' cards, and he—"

The father suddenly spoke to the Easterner. "Mr. Blanc," he asked, "what has these boys been doin'?"

The Easterner reflected again. "I didn't see anything wrong at all," he said at last, slowly.

Scully began to howl. "But what does it mane?" He stared ferociously at his son. "I have a mind to lather you for this, my boy."

Johnnie was frantic. "Well, what have I done?" he bawled at his father.

### III

"I think you are tongue-tied," said Scully finally to his son, the cowboy, and the Easterner; and at the end of this scornful sentence he left the room.

Upstairs the Swede was swiftly fastening the straps of his great valise. Once his back happened to be half turned toward the door, and, hearing a noise there, he wheeled and sprang up, uttering a loud cry. Scully's wrinkled visage showed grimly in the light of the small lamp he carried. This yellow effulgence, streaming upward, colored only his prominent features, and left his eyes, for instance, in mysterious shadow. He resembled a murderer.

"Man! man!" he exclaimed, "have you gone daffy?"

"Oh, no! Oh, no!" rejoined the other. "There are people in this world who know pretty nearly as much as you do—understand?"

For a moment they stood gazing at each other. Upon the Swede's deathly pale cheeks were two spots brightly crimson and sharply edged, as if they had been carefully painted. Scully placed the light on the table and sat himself on the edge of the bed. He spoke ruminatively. "By cracky, I never heard of such a thing in my life. It's a complete muddle. I can't, for the soul of me, think how you ever got this idea into your head." Presently he lifted his eyes and asked: "And did you sure think they were going to kill you?"

The Swede scanned the old man as if he wished to see into his mind. "I did," he said at last. He obviously suspected that this answer might precipitate an outbreak. As he pulled on a strap his whole arm shook, the elbow wavering like a bit of paper.

Scully banged his hand impressively on the footboard of the bed. "Why, man, we're goin' to have a line of ilictric street-cars in this town next spring."

" 'A line of electric street-cars,' " repeated the Swede, stupidly.

"And," said Scully, "there's a new railroad goin' to be built down from Broken Arm to here. Not to mention the four churches and the smashin' big brick schoolhouse. Then there's the big factory, too. Why, in two years Romper'll be a met-tro-*pol*-is."

Having finished the preparation of his baggage, the Swede straightened himself. "Mr. Scully," he said, with sudden hardihood, "how much do I owe you?"

"You don't owe me anythin'," said the old man, angrily.

"Yes, I do," retorted the Swede. He took seventy-five cents from his pocket and tendered it to Scully; but the latter snapped his fingers in disdainful refusal. However, it happened that they both stood gazing in a strange fashion at three silver pieces on the Swede's open palm.

"I'll not take your money," said Scully at last. "Not after what's been goin' on here." Then a plan seemed to strike him. "Here," he cried, picking up his lamp and moving toward the door. "Here! Come with me a minute."

"No," said the Swede, in overwhelming alarm.

"Yes," urged the old man. "Come on! I want you to come and see a picter—just across the hall—in my room."

The Swede must have concluded that his hour was come. His jaw dropped and his teeth showed like a dead man's. He ultimately followed Scully across the corridor, but he had the step of one hung in chains.

Scully flashed the light high on the wall of his own chamber. There was revealed a ridiculous photograph of a little girl. She was leaning against a balustrade of gorgeous decoration, and the formidable bang to her hair was prominent. The figure was as graceful as an upright sledstake, and, withal, it was of the hue of lead. "There," said Scully, tenderly, "that's the picter of my little girl that died. Her name was Carrie. She had the purtiest hair you ever saw! I was that fond of her, she—"

Turning then, he saw that the Swede was not contemplating the picture at all, but, instead, was keeping keen watch on the gloom in the rear.

"Look, man!" cried Scully, heartily. "That's the picter of my little gal that died. Her name was Carrie. And then here's the picter of my oldest boy, Michael. He's a lawyer in Lincoln, an' doin' well. I gave that boy a grand eddication, and I'm glad for it now. He's a fine boy. Look at 'im now. Ain't he bold as blazes, him there in Lincoln, an honored an' respicted gintleman! An honored and respicted gintleman," concluded Scully with a flourish. And, so saying, he smote the Swede jovially on the back.

The Swede faintly smiled.

"Now," said the old man, "there's only one more thing." He dropped suddenly to the floor and thrust his head beneath the bed. The Swede could hear his muffled voice. "I'd keep it under me piller if it wasn't for that boy Johnnie. Then there's the old woman—Where is it now? I never put it twice in the same place. Ah, now come out with you!"

Presently he backed clumsily from under the bed, dragging with him an old coat rolled into a bundle. "I've fetched him," he muttered. Kneeling on the floor, he unrolled the coat and extracted from its heart a large yellow-brown whiskey-bottle.

His first maneuver was to hold the bottle up to the light. Reassured, apparently, that nobody had been tampering with it, he thrust it with a generous movement toward the Swede.

The weak-kneed Swede was about to eagerly clutch this element of strength, but he suddenly jerked his hand away and cast a look of horror upon Scully.

"Drink," said the old man affectionately. He had risen to his feet, and now stood facing the Swede.

There was a silence. Then again Scully said: "Drink!"

The Swede laughed wildly. He grabbed the bottle, put it to his mouth; and as his lips curled absurdly around the opening and his throat worked, he kept his glance, burning with hatred, upon the old man's face.

## IV

After the departure of Scully the three men, with the cardboard still upon their knees, preserved for a long time an astounded silence. Then Johnnie said: "That's the doddangedest Swede I ever see."

"He ain't no Swede," said the cowboy, scornfully.

"Well, what is he then?" cried Johnnie. "What is he then?"

"It's my opinion," replied the cowboy deliberately, "he's some kind of a Dutchman." It was a venerable custom of the country to entitle as Swedes all light-haired men who spoke with a heavy tongue. In consequence the idea of the cowboy was not without its daring. "Yes, sir," he repeated. "It's my opinion this feller is some kind of a Dutchman."

"Well, he says he's a Swede, anyhow," muttered Johnnie, sulkily. He turned to the Easterner: "What do you think, Mr. Blanc?"

"Oh, I don't know," replied the Easterner.

"Well, what do you think makes him act that way?" asked the cowboy.

"Why, he's frightened." The Easterner knocked his pipe against a rim of the stove. "He's clear frightened out of his boots."

"What at?" cried Johnnie and the cowboy together.

The Easterner reflected over his answer.

"What at?" cried the others again.

"Oh, I don't know, but it seems to me this man has been reading dime novels, and he thinks he's right out in the middle of it—the shootin' and stabbin' and all."

"But," said the cowboy, deeply scandalized, "this ain't Wyoming, ner none of them places. This is Nebrasker."

"Yes," added Johnnie, "an' why don't he wait till he gits *out West?*"

The travelled Easterner laughed. "It isn't different there even—not in these days. But he thinks he's right in the middle of hell."

Johnnie and the cowboy mused long.

"It's awful funny," remarked Johnnie at last.

"Yes," said the cowboy. "This is a queer game. I hope we don't git snowed in, because then we'd have to stand this here man bein' around with us all the time. That wouldn't be no good."

"I wish pop would throw him out," said Johnnie.

Presently they heard a loud stamping on the stairs, accompanied by ringing jokes in the voice of old Scully, and laughter, evidently from the Swede. The men around the stove stared vacantly at each other. "Gosh!" said the cowboy. The door flew open, and old Scully, flushed and anecdotal, came into the room. He was jabbering at the Swede, who followed him, laughing bravely. It was the entry of two roisterers from a banquet hall.

"Come now," said Scully sharply to the three seated men, "move up and give us a chance at the stove." The cowboy and the Easterner obediently sidled their chairs to make room for the newcomers. Johnnie, however, simply arranged himself in a more indolent attitude, and then remained motionless.

"Come! Git over, there," said Scully.

"Plenty of room on the other side of the stove," said Johnnie.

"Do you think we want to sit in the draught?" roared the father.

But the Swede here interposed with a grandeur of confidence. "No, no. Let the boy sit where he likes," he cried in a bullying voice to the father.

"All right! All right!" said Scully, deferentially. The cowboy and the Easterner exchanged glances of wonder.

The five chairs were formed in a crescent about one side of the stove. The Swede began to talk; he talked arrogantly, profanely, angrily. Johnnie, the cowboy, and the Easterner maintained a morose silence, while old Scully appeared to be receptive and eager, breaking in constantly with sympathetic ejaculations.

Finally the Swede announced that he was thirsty. He moved in his chair, and said that he would go for a drink of water.

"I'll git it for you," cried Scully at once.

"No," said the Swede, contemptuously. "I'll get it for myself." He arose and stalked with the air of an owner off into the executive parts of the hotel.

As soon as the Swede was out of hearing Scully sprang to his feet and whispered intensely to the others: "Up-stairs he thought I was tryin' to poison 'im."

"Say," said Johnnie, "this makes me sick. Why don't you throw 'im out in the snow?"

"Why, he's all right now," declared Scully. "It was only that he was from the East, and he thought this was a tough place. That's all. He's all right now."

The cowboy looked with admiration upon the Easterner. "You were straight," he said. "You were on to that there Dutchman."

"Well," said Johnnie to his father, "he may be all right now, but I don't see it. Other time he was scared, but now he's too fresh."

Scully's speech was always a combination of Irish brogue and idiom, Western twang and idiom, and scraps of curiously formal diction taken from the story-books and newspapers. He now hurled a strange mass of language at the head of his son. "What do I keep? What do I keep? What do I keep?" he demanded, in a voice of thunder. He slapped his knee impressively, to indicate that he himself was going to make reply, and that all should heed. "I keep a hotel," he shouted. "A hotel, do you mind? A guest under my roof has sacred privileges. He is to be intimidated by none. Not one word shall he hear that would prijudice him in favor of goin' away. I'll not have it. There's no place in this here town where they can say they iver took in a guest of mine because he was afraid to stay here." He wheeled suddenly upon the cowboy and the Easterner. "Am I right?"

"Yes, Mr. Scully," said the cowboy, "I think you're right."

"Yes, Mr. Scully," said the Easterner, "I think you're right."

## V

At six-o'clock supper, the Swede fizzed like a fire-wheel. He sometimes seemed on the point of bursting into riotous song, and in all his madness he was encouraged by old Scully. The Easterner was encased in reserve; the cowboy sat in wide-mouthed amazement, forgetting to eat, while Johnnie wrathily demolished great plates of food. The daughters of the house, when they were obliged to replenish the biscuits, approached as warily as Indians, and, having succeeded in their purpose, fled with ill-concealed trepidation. The Swede domineered the whole feast, and he gave it the appearance of a cruel bacchanal. He seemed to have grown suddenly taller; he gazed, brutally disdainful, into every face. His voice rang through the room. Once when he jabbed out harpoon-fashion with his fork to pinion a biscuit, the weapon nearly impaled the hand of the Easterner, which had been stretched quietly out for the same biscuit.

After supper, as the men filed toward the other room, the Swede smote Scully ruthlessly on the shoulder. "Well, old boy, that was a good, square meal." Johnnie looked hopefully at his father; he knew that shoulder was tender from an old fall; and, indeed, it appeared for a moment as if Scully was going to flame out over the matter, but in the end he smiled a sickly smile and remained silent. The others understood from his manner that he was admitting his responsibility for the Swede's new viewpoint.

Johnnie, however, addressed his parent in an aside. "Why don't you license somebody to kick you downstairs?" Scully scowled darkly by way of reply.

When they were gathered about the stove, the Swede insisted on another game of High-Five. Scully gently deprecated the plan at first, but the Swede turned a wolfish glare upon him. The old man subsided, and the Swede canvassed the others. In his tone there was always a great threat. The cowboy and the Easterner both remarked indifferently that they would play. Scully said that he would presently have to go to meet the 6.58 train, and so the Swede turned menacingly upon Johnnie. For a moment their glances crossed like blades, and then Johnnie smiled and said, "Yes, I'll play."

They formed a square, with the little board on their knees. The Easterner and the Swede were again partners. As the play went on, it was noticeable that the cowboy was not board-whacking as usual. Meanwhile, Scully, near the lamp, had put on his spectacles and, with an appearance curiously like an old priest, was reading a newspaper. In time he went out to meet the 6.58 train, and, despite his precautions, a gust of polar wind whirled into the room as he opened the door. Besides scattering the cards, it chilled the players to the marrow. The Swede cursed frightfully. When Scully returned, his entrance disturbed a cosy and friendly scene. The Swede again cursed. But presently they were once more intent, their heads bent forward and their hands moving swiftly. The Swede had adopted the fashion of board-whacking.

Scully took up his paper and for a long time remained immersed in matters which were extraordinarily remote from him. The lamp burned badly, and once he stopped to adjust the wick. The newspaper, as he turned from page to page, rustled with a slow and comfortable sound. Then suddenly he heard three terrible words: "You are cheatin'!"

Such scenes often prove that there can be little of dramatic import in environment. Any room can present a tragic front; any room can be comic. This little den was now hideous as a torture-chamber. The new faces of the men themselves had changed it upon the instant. The Swede held a huge fist in front of Johnnie's face, while the latter looked steadily over it into the blazing orbs of his accuser. The Easterner had grown pallid; the cowboy's jaw had dropped in that expression of bovine amazement which was one of his important mannerisms. After the three words, the first sound in the room was made by Scully's paper as it floated forgotten to his feet. His spectacles had also fallen from his nose, but by a clutch he had saved them in air. His hand, grasping the spectacles, now remained poised awkwardly and near his shoulder. He stared at the card-players.

Probably the silence was while a second elapsed. Then, if the floor had been suddenly twitched out from under the men they could not have moved quicker. The five had projected themselves headlong toward a common point. It happened that Johnnie, in rising to hurl himself upon the Swede, had stumbled slightly because of his curiously instinctive care for the cards and the board. The loss of the moment allowed time for the arrival of Scully, and also allowed the cowboy time to give the Swede a great push which sent him staggering back. The men found tongue together, and hoarse shouts of rage, appeal, or fear burst from every throat. The cowboy pushed and jostled feverishly at the Swede, and the Easterner and Scully clung wildly to Johnnie; but through the smoky air, above the swaying bodies of the peace-compellers, the eyes of the two warriors ever sought each other in glances of challenge that were at once hot and steely.

Of course the board had been overturned, and now the whole company of cards was scattered over the floor, where the boots of the men trampled the fat and painted kings and queens as they gazed with their silly eyes at the war that was waging above them.

Scully's voice was dominating the yells. "Stop now! Stop, I say! Stop, now—"

Johnnie, as he struggled to burst through the rank formed by Scully and the Easterner, was crying, "Well, he says I cheated! He says I cheated! I won't allow no man to say I cheated! If he says I cheated, he's a ——— ———!"

The cowboy was telling the Swede, "Quit, now! Quit, d'ye hear—"

The screams of the Swede never ceased: "He did cheat! I saw him! I saw him—"

As for the Easterner, he was importuning in a voice that was not heeded: "Wait a moment, can't you? Oh, wait a moment. What's the good of a fight over a game of cards? Wait a moment—"

In this tumult no complete sentences were clear. "Cheat"—"Quit"—"He says"—these fragments pierced the uproar and rang out sharply. It was remarkable that, whereas Scully undoubtedly made the most noise, he was the least heard of any of the riotous band.

Then suddenly there was a great cessation. It was as if each man had paused for breath; and although the room was still lighted with the anger of men, it could be seen that there was no danger of immediate conflict, and at once Johnnie, shouldering his way forward, almost succeeded in confronting the Swede. "What did you say I cheated for? What did you say I cheated for? I don't cheat, and I won't let no man say I do!"

The Swede said, "I saw you! I saw you!"

"Well," cried Johnnie, "I'll fight any man what says I cheat!"

"No, you won't," said the cowboy. "Not here."

"Ah, be still, can't you?" said Scully, coming between them.

The quiet was sufficient to allow the Easterner's voice to be heard. He was repeating, "Oh, wait a moment, can't you? What's the good of a fight over a game of cards? Wait a moment!"

Johnnie, his red face appearing above his father's shoulder, hailed the Swede again. "Did you say I cheated?"

The Swede showed his teeth. "Yes."

"Then," said Johnnie, "we must fight."

"Yes, fight," roared the Swede. He was like a demoniac. "Yes, fight! I'll show you what kind of a man I am! I'll show you who you want to fight! Maybe you think I can't fight! Maybe you think I can't! I'll show you, you skin, you cardsharp! Yes, you cheated! You cheated! You cheated!"

"Well, let's go at it, then, mister," said Johnnie, coolly.

The cowboy's brow was beaded with sweat from his efforts in intercepting all sorts of raids. He turned in despair to Scully. "What are you goin' to do now?"

A change had come over the Celtic visage of the old man. He now seemed all eagerness; his eyes glowed.

"We'll let them fight," he answered, stalwartly. "I can't put up with it any longer. I've stood this damned Swede till I'm sick. We'll let them fight."

## VI

The men prepared to go out-of-doors. The Easterner was so nervous that he had great difficulty in getting his arms into the sleeves of his new leather coat. As the cowboy drew his fur cap down over his ears his hands trembled. In fact, Johnnie and old Scully were the only ones who displayed no agitation. These preliminaries were conducted without words.

Scully threw open the door. "Well, come on," he said. Instantly a terrific wind caused the flame of the lamp to struggle at its wick, while a puff of black smoke sprang from the chimney-top. The stove was in mid-current of the blast, and its voice swelled to equal the roar of the storm. Some of the scarred and bedabbled cards were caught up from the floor and dashed helplessly against the farther wall. The men lowered their heads and plunged into the tempest as into a sea.

No snow was falling, but great whirls and clouds of flakes, swept up from the ground by the frantic winds, were streaming southward with the speed of bullets. The covered land was blue with the sheen of an unearthly satin, and there was no other hue save where, at the low, black railway station—which seemed incredibly distant—one light gleamed like a tiny jewel. As the men floundered into a thigh-deep drift, it was known that the Swede was bawling out something. Scully went to him, put a hand on his shoulder, and projected an ear. "What's that you say?" he shouted.

"I say," bawled the Swede again, "I won't stand much show against this gang. I know you'll all pitch on me."

Scully smote him reproachfully on the arm. "Tut, man!" he yelled. The wind tore the words from Scully's lips and scattered them far alee.

"You are all a gang of—" boomed the Swede, but the storm also seized the remainder of this sentence.

Immediately turning their backs upon the wind, the men had swung around a corner to the sheltered side of the hotel. It was the function of the little house to preserve here, amid this great devastation of snow, an irregular V-shape of heavily encrusted grass, which crackled beneath the feet. One could imagine the great drifts piled against the windward side. When the party reached the comparative peace of this spot it was found that the Swede was still bellowing.

"Oh, I know what kind of a thing this is! I know you'll all pitch on me. I can't lick you all!"

Scully turned upon him panther-fashion. "You'll not have to whip all of us. You'll have to whip my son Johnnie. An' the man what troubles you durin' that time will have me to dale with."

The arrangements were swiftly made. The two men faced each other, obedient to the harsh commands of Scully, whose face, in the subtly luminous gloom, could be seen set in the austere impersonal lines that are pictured on the countenances of the Roman veterans. The Easterner's teeth were chattering, and he was hopping up and down like a mechanical toy. The cowboy stood rock-like.

The contestants had not stripped off any clothing. Each was in his ordinary attire. Their fists were up, and they eyed each other in a calm that had the elements of leonine cruelty in it.

During this pause, the Easterner's mind, like a film, took lasting impressions of three men—the iron-nerved master of the ceremony; the Swede, pale, motionless, terrible; and Johnnie, serene yet ferocious, brutish yet heroic. The entire prelude had in it a tragedy greater than the tragedy of action, and this aspect was accentuated by the long, mellow cry of the blizzard, as it sped the tumbling and wailing flakes into the black abyss of the south.

"Now!" said Scully.

The two combatants leaped forward and crashed together like bullocks. There was heard the cushioned sound of blows, and of a curse squeezing out from between the tight teeth of one.

As for the spectators, the Easterner's pent-up breath exploded from him with a pop of relief, absolute relief from the tension of the preliminaries. The cowboy bounded into the air with a yowl. Scully was immovable as from supreme amazement and fear at the fury of the fight which he himself had permitted and arranged.

For a time the encounter in the darkness was such a perplexity of flying arms that it presented no more detail than would a swiftly revolving wheel. Occasionally a face, as if illumined by a flash of light, would shine out, ghastly and marked with pink spots. A moment later, the men might have been known as shadows, if it were not for the involuntary utterance of oaths that came from them in whispers.

Suddenly a holocaust of warlike desire caught the cowboy, and he bolted forward with the speed of a broncho. "Go it, Johnnie! go it! Kill him! Kill him!"

Scully confronted him. "Kape back," he said; and by his glance the cowboy could tell that this man was Johnnie's father.

To the Easterner there was a monotony of unchangeable fighting that was an abomination. This confused mingling was eternal to his sense, which was concentrated in a longing for the end, the priceless end. Once the fighters lurched near him, and as he scrambled hastily backward he heard them breathe like men on the rack.

"Kill him, Johnnie! Kill him! Kill him! Kill him!" The cowboy's face was contorted like one of those agony masks in museums.

"Keep still," said Scully, icily.

Then there was a sudden loud grunt, incomplete, cut short, and Johnnie's body swung away from the Swede and fell with sickening heaviness to the grass. The cowboy was barely in time to prevent the mad Swede from flinging himself upon his prone adversary. "No, you don't," said the cowboy, interposing an arm. "Wait a second."

Scully was at his son's side. "Johnnie! Johnnie, me boy!" His voice had a quality of melancholy tenderness. "Johnnie! Can you go on with it?" He looked anxiously down into the bloody, pulpy face of his son.

There was a moment of silence, and then Johnnie answered in his ordinary voice, "Yes, I—it—yes."

Assisted by his father he struggled to his feet. "Wait a bit now till you git your wind," said the old man.

A few paces away the cowboy was lecturing the Swede. "No, you don't! Wait a second!"

The Easterner was plucking at Scully's sleeve. "Oh, this is enough," he pleaded. "This is enough! Let it go as it stands. This is enough!"

"Bill," said Scully, "git out of the road." The cowboy stepped aside. "Now." The combatants were actuated by a new caution as they advanced toward collision. They glared at each other, and then the Swede aimed a lightning blow that carried with it his entire weight. Johnnie was evidently half stupid from weakness, but he miraculously dodged, and his fist sent the overbalanced Swede sprawling.

The cowboy, Scully, and the Easterner burst into a cheer that was like a chorus of triumphant soldiery, but before its conclusion the Swede had scuffled agilely to his feet and come in berserk abandon at his foe. There was another perplexity of flying arms, and Johnnie's body again swung away and fell, even as a bundle might fall from a roof. The Swede instantly staggered to a little wind-waved tree and leaned upon it, breathing like an engine, while his savage and flame-lit eyes roamed from face to face as the men bent over Johnnie. There was a splendor of isolation in his situation at this time which the Easterner felt once when, lifting his eyes from the man on the ground, he beheld that mysterious and lonely figure, waiting.

"Are you any good yet, Johnnie?" asked Scully in a broken voice.

The son gasped and opened his eyes languidly. After a moment he answered, "No—I ain't—any good—any—more." Then, from shame and bodily ill, he began to weep, the tears furrowing down through the blood-stains on his face. "He was too—too—too heavy for me."

Scully straightened and addressed the waiting figure. "Stranger," he said, evenly, "it's all up with our side." Then his voice changed into that vibrant huskiness which is commonly the tone of the most simple and deadly announcements. "Johnnie is whipped."

Without replying, the victor moved off on the route to the front door of the hotel.

The cowboy was formulating new and unspellable blasphemies. The Easterner was startled to find that they were out in a wind that seemed to come direct from the shadowed arctic floes. He heard again the wail of the snow as it was flung to its grave in the south. He knew now that all this time the cold had been sinking into him deeper and deeper, and he wondered that he had not perished. He felt indifferent to the condition of the vanquished man.

"Johnnie, can you walk?" asked Scully.

"Did I hurt—hurt him any?" asked the son.

"Can you walk, boy? Can you walk?"

Johnnie's voice was suddenly strong. There was a robust impatience in it. "I asked you whether I hurt him any!"

"Yes, yes, Johnnie," answered the cowboy, consolingly; "he's hurt a good deal."

They raised him from the ground, and as soon as he was on his feet he went tottering off, rebuffing all attempts at assistance. When the party rounded the corner they were fairly blinded by the pelting of the snow. It burned their faces like fire. The cowboy carried Johnnie through the drift to the door. As they entered, some cards again rose from the floor and beat against the wall.

The Easterner rushed to the stove. He was so profoundly chilled that he almost dared to embrace the glowing iron. The Swede was not in the room. Johnnie sank into a chair and, folding his arms on his knees, buried his face in them. Scully, warming one foot and then the other at a rim of the stove, muttered to himself with Celtic mournfulness. The cowboy had removed his fur cap, and with a dazed and rueful air he was running one hand through his tousled locks. From overhead they could hear the creaking of boards, as the Swede tramped here and there in his room.

The sad quiet was broken by the sudden flinging open of a door that led toward the kitchen. It was instantly followed by an inrush of women. They precipitated themselves upon Johnnie amid a chorus of lamentation. Before they carried their prey off to the kitchen, there to be bathed and harangued with that mixture of sympathy and abuse which is a feat of their sex, the mother straightened herself and fixed old Scully with an eye of stern reproach. "Shame be upon you, Patrick Scully!" she cried. "Your own son, too. Shame be upon you!"

"There, now! Be quiet, now!" said the old man, weakly.

"Shame be upon you, Patrick Scully!" the girls, rallying to this slogan, sniffed disdainfully in the direction of those trembling accomplices, the cowboy and the Easterner. Presently they bore Johnnie away, and left the three men to dismal reflection.

## VII

"I'd like to fight this here Dutchman myself," said the cowboy, breaking a long silence.

Scully wagged his head sadly. "No, that wouldn't do. It wouldn't be right. It wouldn't be right."

"Well, why wouldn't it?" argued the cowboy. "I don't see no harm in it."

"No," answered Scully, with mournful heroism. "It wouldn't be right. It was Johnnie's fight, and now we mustn't whip the man just because he whipped Johnnie."

"Yes, that's true enough," said the cowboy; "but—he better not get fresh with me, because I couldn't stand no more of it."

"You'll not say a word to him," commanded Scully, and even then they heard the tread of the Swede on the stairs. His entrance was made theatric. He swept the door back with a bang and swaggered to the middle of the room. No one looked at him. "Well," he cried, insolently, at Scully, "I s'pose you'll tell me now how much I owe you?"

The old man remained stolid. "You don't owe me nothin'."

"Huh!" said the Swede, "huh! Don't owe 'im nothin'."

The cowboy addressed the Swede. "Stranger, I don't see how you come to be so gay around here."

Old Scully was instantly alert. "Stop!" he shouted, holding his hand forth, fingers upward. "Bill, you shut up!"

The cowboy spat carelessly into the sawdust-box. "I didn't say a word, did I?" he asked.

"Mr. Scully," called the Swede, "how much do I owe you?" It was seen that he was attired for departure, and that he had his valise in his hand.

"You don't owe me nothin'," repeated Scully in the same imperturbable way.

"Huh!" said the Swede. "I guess you're right. I guess if it was any way at all, you'd owe me somethin'. That's what I guess." He turned to the cowboy. " 'Kill him! Kill him! Kill him!' " he mimicked, and then guffawed victoriously. " 'Kill him!' " He was convulsed with ironical humor.

But he might have been jeering the dead. The three men were immovable and silent, staring with glassy eyes at the stove.

The Swede opened the door and passed into the storm, giving one derisive glance backward at the still group.

As soon as the door was closed, Scully and the cowboy leaped to their feet and began to curse. They trampled to and fro, waving their arms and smashing into the air with their fists. "Oh, but that was a hard minute!" wailed Scully. "That was a hard minute! Him there leerin' and scoffin'! One bang at his nose was worth forty dollars to me that minute! How did you stand it, Bill?"

"How did I stand it?" cried the cowboy in a quivering voice. "How did I stand it? Oh!"

The old man burst into sudden brogue. "I'd loike to take that Swade," he wailed, "and hould 'im down on a shtone flure and bate 'im to a jelly wid a shtick!"

The cowboy groaned in sympathy. "I'd like to git him by the neck and ha-ammer him"—he brought his hand down on a chair with a noise like a pistol-shot—"hammer that there Dutchman until he couldn't tell himself from a dead coyote!"

"I'd bate 'im until he—"

"I'd show him some things—"

And then together they raised a yearning, fanatic cry—"Oh-o-oh! if we only could—"

"Yes!"

"Yes!"

"And then I'd—"

"Oh-o-oh!"

## VIII

The Swede, tightly gripping his valise, tacked across the face of the storm as if he carried sails. He was following a line of little naked, gasping trees which, he knew, must mark the way of the road. His face, fresh from the pounding of Johnnie's fists, felt more pleasure than pain in the wind and the driving snow. A number of square shapes loomed upon him finally, and he knew them as the houses of the main body of the town. He found a street and made travel along it, leaning heavily upon the wind whenever, at a corner, a terrific blast caught him.

He might have been in a deserted village. We picture the world as thick with conquering and elate humanity, but here, with the bugles of the tempest pealing, it was hard to imagine a peopled earth. One viewed the existence of man then as a marvel, and conceded a glamor of wonder to these lice which were caused to cling to a whirling, fire-smitten, ice-locked, disease-stricken, space-lost bulb. The conceit of man was explained by this storm to be the very engine of life. One was a coxcomb not to die in it. However, the Swede found a saloon.

In front of it an indomitable red light was burning, and the snowflakes were made blood-color as they flew through the circumscribed territory of the lamp's shining. The Swede pushed open the door of the saloon and entered. A sanded expanse was before him, and at the end of it four men sat about a table drinking. Down one side of the room extended a radiant bar, and its guardian was leaning upon his elbows listening to the talk of the men at the table. The Swede dropped his valise upon the floor and, smiling fraternally upon the barkeeper, said "Gimme some whiskey, will you?" The man placed a bottle, a whiskey-glass, and a glass of ice-thick water upon the bar. The Swede poured himself an abnormal portion of whiskey and drank it in three gulps. "Pretty bad night," remarked the bartender, indifferently. He was making the pretension of blindness which is usually a distinction of his class; but it could have been seen that he was furtively studying the half-erased blood-stains on the face of the Swede. "Bad night," he said again.

"Oh, it's good enough for me," replied the Swede, hardily as he poured himself some more whiskey. The barkeeper took his coin and manoevered it through its reception by the highly nickeled cash-machine. A bell rang; a card labelled "20 cts." had appeared.

"No," continued the Swede, "this isn't too bad weather. It's good enough for me."

"So?" murmured the barkeeper, languidly.

The copious drams made the Swede's eyes swim, and he breathed a trifle heavier. "Yes, I like this weather. I like it. It suits me." It was apparently his design to impart a deep significance to these words.

"So?" murmured the bartender again. He turned to gaze dreamily at the scroll-like birds and bird-like scrolls which had been drawn with soap upon the mirrors in back of the bar.

"Well, I guess I'll take another drink," said the Swede, presently. "Have something?"

"No, thanks; I'm not drinkin'," answered the bartender. Afterward he asked, "How did you hurt your face?"

The Swede immediately began to boast loudly. "Why, in a fight. I thumped the soul out of a man down here at Scully's hotel."

The interest of the four men at the table was at last aroused.

"Who was it?" said one.

"Johnnie Scully," blustered the Swede. "Son of the man what runs it.

He will be pretty near dead for some weeks, I can tell you. I made a nice thing of him, I did. He couldn't get up. They carried him in the house. Have a drink?"

Instantly the men in some subtle way encased themselves in reserve. "No, thanks," said one. The group was of curious formation. Two were prominent local business men; one was the district attorney; and one was a professional gambler of the kind known as "square." But a scrutiny of the group would not have enabled an observer to pick the gambler from the men of more reputable pursuits. He was, in fact, a man so delicate in manner, when among people of fair class, and so judicious in his choice of victims, that in the strictly masculine part of the town's life he had come to be explicitly trusted and admired. People called him a thoroughbred. The fear and contempt with which his craft was regarded were undoubtedly the reason why his quiet dignity shone conspicuous above the quiet dignity of men who might be merely hatters, billiard-markers, or grocery-clerks. Beyond an occasional unwary traveller who came by rail, this gambler was supposed to prey solely upon reckless and senile farmers, who, when flush with good crops, drove into town in all the pride and confidence of an absolutely invulnerable stupidity. Hearing at times in circuitous fashion of the despoilment of such a farmer, the important men of Romper invariably laughed in contempt of the victim, and if they thought of the wolf at all, it was with a kind of pride at the knowledge that he would never dare think of attacking their wisdom and courage. Besides, it was popular that this gambler had a real wife and two real children in a neat cottage in a suburb, where he led an exemplary home life; and when any one even suggested a discrepancy in his character, the crowd immediately vociferated descriptions of this virtuous family circle. Then men who led exemplary home lives, and men who did not lead exemplary home lives, all subsided in a bunch, remarking that there was nothing more to be said.

However, when a restriction was placed upon him—as, for instance, when a strong clique of members of the new Pollywog Club refused to permit him, even as a spectator, to appear in the room of the organization —the candor and gentleness with which he accepted the judgment disarmed many of his foes and made his friends more desperately partisan. He invariably distinguished between himself and a respectable Romper man so quickly and frankly that his manner actually appeared to be a continual broadcast compliment.

And one must not forget to declare the fundamental fact of his entire position in Romper. It is irrefutable that in all affairs outside his business, in all matters that occur eternally and commonly between man and man, this thieving card-player was so generous, so just, so moral, that, in a contest, he could have put to flight the consciences of nine tenths of the citizens of Romper.

And so it happened that he was seated in this saloon with the two prominent local merchants and the district attorney.

The Swede continued to drink raw whiskey, meanwhile babbling at the barkeeper and trying to induce him to indulge in potations. "Come on. Have a drink. Come on. What—no? Well, have a little one, then. By gawd, I've whipped a man to-night, and I want to celebrate. I whipped him good, too. Gentlemen," the Swede cried to the men at the table, "have a drink?"

"Ssh!" said the barkeeper.

The group at the table, although furtively attentive, had been pretending to be deep in talk, but now a man lifted his eyes toward the Swede and said, shortly, "Thanks. We don't want any more."

At this reply the Swede ruffled out his chest like a rooster. "Well," he exploded, "it seems I can't get anybody to drink with me in this town. Seems so, don't it? Well!"

"Ssh!" said the barkeeper.

"Say," snarled the Swede, "don't you try to shut me up. I won't have it. I'm a gentleman, and I want people to drink with me. And I want 'em to drink with me now. Now—do you understand?" He rapped the bar with his knuckles.

Years of experience had calloused the bartender. He merely grew sulky. "I hear you," he answered.

"Well," cried the Swede, "listen hard then. See those men over there? Well, they're going to drink with me, and don't you forget it. Now you watch."

"Hi!" yelled the barkeeper, "this won't do!"

"Why won't it?" demanded the Swede. He stalked over to the table, and by chance laid his hand upon the shoulder of the gambler. "How about this?" he asked wrathfully. "I asked you to drink with me."

The gambler simply twisted his head and spoke over his shoulder. "My friend, I don't know you."

"Oh, hell!" answered the Swede, "come and have a drink."

"Now, my boy," advised the gambler, kindly, "take your hand off my shoulder and go 'way and mind your own business." He was a little, slim man, and it seemed strange to hear him use this tone of heroic patronage to the burly Swede. The other men at the table said nothing.

"What! You won't drink with me, you little dude? I'll make you then! I'll make you!" The Swede had grasped the gambler frenziedly at the throat, and was dragging him from his chair. The other men sprang up. The barkeeper dashed around the corner of his bar. There was a great tumult, and then was seen a long blade in the hand of the gambler. It shot forward, and a human body, this citadel of virtue, wisdom, power, was pierced as easily as if it had been a melon. The Swede fell with a cry of supreme astonishment.

The prominent merchants and the district attorney must have at once tumbled out of the place backward. The bartender found himself hanging limply to the arm of a chair and gazing into the eyes of a murderer.

"Henry," said the latter, as he wiped his knife on one of the towels that hung beneath the bar rail, "you tell 'em where to find me. I'll be home, waiting for 'em." Then he vanished. A moment afterward the barkeeper was in the street dinning through the storm for help and, moreover, companionship.

The corpse of the Swede, alone in the saloon, had its eyes fixed upon a dreadful legend that dwelt atop of the cash-machine: "This registers the amount of your purchase."

## IX

Months later, the cowboy was frying pork over the stove of a little ranch near the Dakota line, when there was a quick thud of hoofs outside, and presently the Easterner entered with the letters and the papers.

"Well," said the Easterner at once, "the chap that killed the Swede has got three years. Wasn't much, was it?"

"He has? Three years?" The cowboy poised his pan of pork, while he ruminated upon the news. "Three years. That ain't much."

"No. It was a light sentence," replied the Easterner as he unbuckled his spurs. "Seems there was a good deal of sympathy for him in Romper."

"If the bartender had been any good," observed the cowboy, thoughtfully, "he would have gone in and cracked that there Dutchman on the head with a bottle in the beginnin' of it and stopped all this here murderin'."

"Yes, a thousand things might have happened," said the Easterner, tartly.

The cowboy returned his pan of pork to the fire, but his philosophy continued. "It's funny, ain't it? If he hadn't said Johnnie was cheatin' he'd be alive this minute. He was an awful fool. Game played for fun, too. Not for money. I believe he was crazy."

"I feel sorry for that gambler," said the Easterner.

"Oh, so do I," said the cowboy. "He don't deserve none of it for killin' who he did."

"The Swede might not have been killed if everything had been square."

"Might not have been killed?" exclaimed the cowboy. "Everythin' square? Why, when he said that Johnnie was cheatin' and acted like such a jackass? And then in the saloon he fairly walked up to git hurt?" With these arguments the cowboy browbeat the Easterner and reduced him to rage.

"You're a fool!" cried the Easterner, viciously. "You're a bigger jackass than the Swede by a million majority. Now let me tell you one thing. Let me tell you something. Listen! Johnnie *was* cheating!"

" 'Johnnie,' " said the cowboy, blankly. There was a minute of silence, and then he said, robustly, "Why, no. The game was only for fun."

"Fun or not," said the Easterner, "Johnnie was cheating. I saw him. I know it. I saw him. And I refused to stand up and be a man. I let the Swede fight it out alone. And you—you were simply puffing around the place and wanting to fight. And then old Scully himself! We are all in it! This poor gambler isn't even a noun. He is kind of an adverb. Every sin is the result of a collaboration. We, five of us, have collaborated in the murder of this Swede. Usually there are from a dozen to forty women really involved in every murder, but in this case it seems to be only five men—you, I, Johnnie, old Scully; and that fool of an unfortunate gambler came merely as a culmination, the apex of a human movement, and gets all the punishment."

The cowboy, injured and rebellious, cried out blindly into this fog of mysterious theory: "Well, I didn't do anythin', did I?"

---

# UNCLE T

## Brian Moore

*Born in Belfast, Northern Ireland, in 1921, Moore attended Mt. Malachi's College, but left before graduating because of the war. He saw service in the British Ministry of War Transport in North Africa, Italy, and France, then emigrated to Canada in 1948 and lived there until 1959. A Canadian citizen, he now resides in California, where he writes film scripts. For his novel* The Luck of Ginger Coffey (1960), *he was awarded a Governor-General's Award; other honors include a Guggenheim Fellowship (1959) and the Quebec Literary Prize (1958). Among his works are the following:* The Lonely Passion of Judith Hearne (1956), The Feast of Lupercal (1957), The Emperor of Ice Cream (1965), I Am Mary Dunne (1968), *and* Catholics (1973). *Moore has often been compared to James Joyce, and there is much in his work to justify this comparison. Jack Ludwig, for instance, has stated that Moore has "Joyce's compassion, Joyce's ability to see past hierarchies." The difference for Ludwig, however, is that Moore has "none of Joyce's anger." Moore, Ludwig concludes, "does not blame. His focus is on suffering itself. . . . His insignificant characters suffer much from contemplating their own insignificance." The reader may surely see in Uncle T one of Moore's "typical" characters, one of those insignificant characters who "suffer much" from this self-contemplation.*

Vincent Bishop, standing at his hotel room window saw in momentary reflection from the windowpane a nervous young man with dark eyes and undisciplined black hair. Above Times Square the sky hemorrhaged in an advertising glare. His reflection dissolved. He turned away.

"Are you nearly ready, Barbara?" he called.

She was in the bathroom putting polish on her nails. His uncle was due any minute. Maybe he should have bought a bottle to offer his uncle a drink before they started off? The half-dozen roses he had chosen for his aunt—maybe he should have taken them out of the box and let them stand in water for a while? Were half a dozen roses enough?

"Barbara, do you think I should run down to the lobby and get a box of chocolates?"

She did not hear him. Her and her nails. If this was the way she kept him waiting on the second day of their honeymoon, what faced him in the years to come? What would his uncle think of her? Or of him? How could he tell? He had never met his uncle. This morning, as soon as he and his bride checked into the hotel after the flight from Toronto, his uncle had been on the phone to invite them to dinner at his apartment. He was coming now to pick them up. He sounded very kind, but what could you tell from a voice on the phone?

Of course there was his letter. That was the important thing.

Grenville Press
182 West 15th St.
New York, N.Y. 10011

Dear Vincent,

    I am delighted to hear that you are planning to get married and that you are contemplating a honeymoon trip to New York. Both Bernadette and I offer our heartiest congratulations to you and our best wishes to your fiancée. Needless to say, we are looking forward to meeting you at last, but unfortunately, I cannot offer to put you up, as ours is a very small apartment. However, don't worry, I will find you a hotel room.

    I was most interested to read that you do not want to return to Ireland when your exchange teaching year in Canada is completed. I can well see the problems of going home with a new bride who is neither Irish nor Catholic and not likely to enjoy the atmosphere there at all. Now, as you also mention that you are fed up with teaching and would like to find something else, let me make you a proposal. How would you consider joining me here at Grenville Press? I'm sure that a young man with your background would be ideal for the editorial side of the business. As you know, Bernadette and I have no children and we consider you very much a member of our family. I might add that since I bought out old Grenville's widow last year, I am now the proprietor of this firm.

    Anyway, since you are coming to visit us in New York, we can talk about this in more detail. In the meantime, let me say that although we know each other only from letters, I have long thought that you—a rebel, a wanderer and a lover of literature—must be very much like me when I was your age. I look forward to our meeting. Till then,

Affectionately,
Uncle T

Uncle T. Three years ago, in Ireland, Vincent sat in his bedroom sending letters over all the world's oceans, messages in bottles, appeals for rescue. *I am twenty-two years old and have just completed an Honors English Language and Literature degree at the Queen's University of Belfast. I am anxious to live abroad.* Resident clerk in the Shan States, shipping aide in Takoradi, plantation overseer in British Guiana—any job, anywhere, which would exorcise the future then facing him: a secondary school in an Ulster town, forty lumps of boys waiting at forty desks, rain on the windowpanes, two local cinemas, a dance on Saturday nights.

Back with the foreign postmarks, the form replies, the we-regret-to-inform-you's came a letter signed "Uncle T." A letter in answer to Vincent's veiled appeal to a never-seen uncle who was now, Vincent's mother said, a partner in a New York publishing firm. The letter contained a fifty-dollar money order. The writer regretted that he could not suggest any job at that time, but hoped that, relations established, he and Vincent would keep in touch.

They kept in touch. Even for a young iconoclast there was comfort in a precedent. And what better precedent than Uncle Turlough Carnahan, who, like himself, had published poems in undergraduate magazines, who had once formed a university socialist club, and who (again, like Vincent) had left his parents' house forever after a bitter anticlerical dispute? Vincent wanted to escape from Ireland. Uncle Turlough lived in America. Vincent dreamed of some sort of literary career. Uncle Turlough, by all accounts, had achieved it. Was it any wonder then that this relative was the one Vincent boasted of to his bride?

"Well, will I pass muster for the great man?" Barbara asked, coming from the bathroom, her nail polish still wet, her hands extended before her like a temple dancer's. She was small and fair and neat; her girlish dresses drew attention to her breasts and legs. They had met three months ago when she began to teach modern dance at the Toronto high school where Vincent was spending his exchange year. Since then, she and he had rarely been separated; yet they were strangers still, unsure of each other, too anxious to please.

"Pass muster?" he said. "You'll do more than that." He bent to kiss her ear as the room telephone growled twice.

"That must be him, Vincent."

"Hello," said the telephone voice. "Are you decent? Can I come up for a moment?"

"Of course."

The phone went dead. "He's on his way up," Vincent told her.

"Oh Vincent, I'm so nervous."

How could she be? What was Uncle Turlough to her, who three months ago had never even heard his name? Whereas he, for how many years had he dreamed that one day his uncle might beckon him into his literary world he dreamed of? How would she understand his panic now as he waited at the door of their room, remembering the slight, dark youth he had seen so often in his mother's photograph album, wondering how the person who knocked lightly on the door would differ from that youth. Of course, those photographs would be thirty-five years old. Uncle Turlough must be almost sixty.

He opened the door.

"Vincent, how are you? Welcome to New York." The stranger shook hands, then moved past Vincent. "And this must be Barbara. How are you, my dear? Why, you're even more lovely than he said you were. Welcome, welcome."

On the telephone Vincent had noticed it but had not been sure. Now, he was. The stranger's voice had no trace of his own harsh Ulster burr, but was soft, broguey, nasal, like the voice of an American imitating an Irish accent. Confidential and cozy, it told Barbara, "Do you know, it's an extraordinary thing, my dear, but this husband of yours is the spitting image of me when I was his age. Look at us together. Don't you still see a resemblance?"

What resemblance? Vincent thought, but hoped Barbara would have the sense to pretend.

"Oh, yes," she said, "of course, I see it."

The stranger bobbed his head in acknowledgment, and as he did Vincent noticed his hair, black and shiny as a crow's wing, unexpected as the chocolate-brown overcoat and blood-colored shoes. Resemblance?

"Do you have a couple of glasses, by any chance?" the stranger said, unbuttoning his overcoat to reveal a rumpled gray suit, too tight at the middle button. From his jacket pocket he took a pint bottle of whiskey and broke the seal. "Bernadette won't be expecting us for a while," he said. "I left the office early. I thought we might have one for the road here, before we start."

Obediently, Barbara went into the bathroom, returning with two water glasses. "I'd better phone for ice," she said.

"Don't bother," the stranger said. "Just run the cold tap awhile. There's no sense letting them rob you blind with their room service."

He poured two large whiskies and presented them to his guests. "I don't need a glass," he said, raising the pint to his lips. "It's bottles up for me." Silent, they watched, their own drinks untasted. Then Barbara took the two glasses of neat whiskey and went to run the cold tap, as ordered. If it were one of her relatives, Vincent thought, there'd be no surprise, the uncle would be just as advertised, solid, Canadian, safe; he would be the man he said he was and not—what? Oh, Uncle, what uneasy eyes you have! What ruddy cheeks you have, Uncle dear!

"And how's your mother keeping?" the stranger asked.

"She's well."

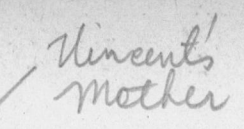

"Dear little Eileen. Many is the time I've wanted to go home and see her and my other brothers and sisters and all the rest of the Carnahan clan. Maybe I will, some day. Maybe I will."

He recorked the pint and put it on their dressing table. "I'll just leave this here in case you youngsters need a little refreshment when you get home tonight. After all, it's your honeymoon." He winked at Barbara, who was coming out of the bathroom, a wink at once collusive and apologetic. "Although you know, Barbara, my old mother used to say you should never give an Irishman the choice between a girl and the bottle. Because it's a proven fact that most of them will prefer the bottle. Am I right, Vince?" He punched Vincent's shoulder in uncertain good-fellowship. "Now, finish up that sup of drink and we'll be on our way."

Obediently, they drank their whiskies. Obediently they got their coats and followed him to the elevator. At the lobby entrance the hotel doorman approached, asking if they wanted a cab. The stranger shook his head. "You two wait here," he said, and ran a block down the street to find a cab himself.

"*Well,*" Barbara said.

"Well, what?"

She made a face. "I do not like thee, Uncle T, the reason why is plain to see."

"What are you talking about?"

"Just look at him, Vincent. His hair, for one thing."

"What about it?"

"Lovely head of hair," she said. "It's dyed."

"Oh, come off it."

"It's d-y-e-d," she said. "And I'll bet that's not the only phony thing about him."

"Now wait a minute. What do you mean?"

"Darling," she said, "if he's a publisher, I'm Mrs. Roosevelt."

"Now give the man a chance, will you? Why jump to conclusions?"

She did not answer, for at that moment, a cab drew up in full view of the doorman and the stranger leaned out, beckoning them to come. In shame, they passed the doorman's contempt. *Give the man a chance.* . . . But as the taxi rushed them onto the bright carnival rink of Times Square, Vincent heard his father's dry, diagnostic voice: "If your mother's family have a weakness, it's that never in my life have I known any of them to spoil a good story for the sake of the truth." Upgrading their relations, exaggerating their triumphs, hiding their shortcomings under a bluster of palaver—wasn't that what his father thought of the Carnahan clan? Even his mother, hadn't she a touch of it? When twenty-five exchange teachers had been picked to go out to Canada, hadn't she told all her friends the story as though her son were the only one chosen? And this stranger was his mother's brother. Could those letters about Grenville Press be Carnahan exaggeration? No, of course no. *Give the man a chance.*

"Your wife's an American, isn't she, Mr. Carnahan?" Barbara asked.

"Yes, Bernadette was born right here in New York City, although she's of good Irish stock. Where do your people come from, my dear?"

"My grandparents came from England," Barbara said.

"Both sides?"

"Both sides."

And wasn't there a certain Anglo-Saxon attitude in the way she said that? But the stranger did not seem to notice. On and on he went, telling about the Tenderloin district, pointing out the Flatiron building, keeping the small talk afloat as though to distract his listeners from the true facts of the journey. For their taxi was moving from bad to worse, entering streets that Vincent would not have dreamed of in his afternoon of sightseeing along the elegance of Fifth Avenue, streets of houses whose front entrances looked like rear exits, of stale little basement shops left over from an older New York, of signs which proposed *Keys Made, Rooms to Let, Shoes Repaired.* A group of sallow-skinned men played pitchpenny on the pavement. The taxi stopped.

"Here we are," the broguey voice said. "It's very convenient, you know, because it's right downtown."

They skirted the pitchpenny players, entered the apartment building, and climbed two narrow flights of stairs, their guide hurrying ahead of them to press a buzzer outside one of the corridor doors. He rang twice, and as on a signal, a woman opened the door, drawing a mauve woolen stole tight about her bosom as she met the corridor draft. To Vincent's surprise, she was in her late thirties, a brassy blonde, blown stout, wearing a gray sateen dress one size too small for her, moving her weight uncomfortably on tiny ankles and feet. "Bernadette," the stranger said. And kissed her cheek.

Those heads together, kissing, made Vincent think of their mutual hairdressing problems. Did they dye each other's? Awkwardly, he offered his gift of flowers.

"Oh, roses! Aren't they lovely! Thank you, Vincent. Aren't you the perfect gentleman! Barbara, dear, do you want to come with me and freshen up a little? Turlough, take their coats, will you?"

The sight of their overcoats disappearing into a closet reminded Vincent that the evening was a sentence still to be served. If only he had come alone to New York, if only he hadn't told Barbara that this job would be the end of their worries about what to do when his exchange year was over. If only—he thought of his father's remark—yes, if only he hadn't behaved like a Carnahan. And now, in confirmation of his mother's blood, the first thing he noticed in the living room was a familiar face in a familiar oval frame. Dyed hair or not, publisher or not, this stranger was his kinsman. The photograph was of Vincent's maternal grandmother.

The living room was strangely bare, its furniture worn and discolored, as though his uncle and aunt had several small children and had long ago given up the struggle with appearances. Yet the letter said there were no children. He looked at the bookcase near what must be his uncle's easy chair. Shakespeare, and some poetry, secondhand copies of Goethe, Swift, Dante, Dickens, Flaubert. All were dusty as though they had not been disturbed since the flat was first moved into. By a small table near the reading lamp were several well-used copies of *The Saturday Evening Post*.

"Glass of sherry?" his uncle said, coming in with a tray on which were four glasses, none of them used. But the newly broken tinfoil seal of the sherry bottle lay beside them and the sherry bottle had already been depleted. Dark, uneasy eyes saw Vincent notice the diminished bottle level, skittered nervously toward the door as Aunt Bernadette reappeared with Barbara. Everyone sat down. Sherry was poured. The verbal gropings began. Aunt Bernadette brought out her wedding present (an ugly salad bowl) and was duly thanked for it. She asked about the wedding. Had they had a big reception? Had they sent photographs to Vincent's mother? How was his mother keeping, by the way?

"She's in great form, from the letters she sends," Vincent said.

"And your Dad, how is he? Turlough tells me you and your Dad didn't always hit it off too well. I hope you made it up with him before you came out here?"

Made it up? He had gone back to Drumconer Avenue the week before he sailed as an exchange teacher. His mother received him, talked to him for a long while, then asked him to wait. He sat alone in the drawing room, listening for his father's step. He heard his father leave the surgery and go along the hall. His father did not come up. He went out of the drawing room and looked over the banister. His father was at the front door, putting on his hat and coat. "Father?" he said. "Father? . . ."

His father did not look up. "I have to go out on a sick call," his father said.

"But couldn't you spare a minute? Or could I come with you?"

His father did not answer. His father reached down into the monk's bench for his consulting bag. His father's attitude had not changed since that day two years before when he looked up from the breakfast table, the newspaper shaking in his fingers. "So this is your damn socialism, is it? Have you seen the paper? My son up on a platform at the university, helping a couple of Protestants to run down his religion and his country. My son! Oh, haven't I reared a right pup. You're going to apologize, do you hear? You're going to sit down this minute and write a public apology and send it out to this newspaper. Do you hear me? This minute!"

Vincent refused. His sister wept: she said his conduct had broken their mother's heart. His mother packed a suitcase and went on a pilgrimage to Lough Derg, walking in her bare feet over the stones of that penitential island, praying God to give her son back the gift of faith. But despite his father's rage, his sister's tears, his mother's penance, he could not recant. Oh, yes, he loved them, he loved them all. But fourteen and eight made twenty-two, eight years of hypocrisy, of going to Mass and the sacraments for their sake. He tried to tell the truth in that university debate. The truth troubled him. But his father belonged to a generation who had had their troubles; they had no time for any others. And so after a month of his father's silent anger, Vincent left home to become a schoolmaster in a provincial town. And two years later when he returned, hoping to see his father, his father reached down into the monk's bench in the hall, picked up his consulting bag and opened the front door, leaving his plea unanswered. What answer had he wanted, he wondered? Forgiveness? Or merely some sign that they still were kin? They knew, both he and his father, that if he crossed the Atlantic he might never return. But his father had to go out on a sick call. His father walked down the path, opened the garden gate, did not look back. Went down the avenue, turned the corner, no look back.

And now, remembering this, what should he say to his uncle's wife? What should he answer this strange woman who asked if he had "made it up"?

"Ah, your father always was stubborn," Uncle Turlough said, seeing his hesitation. "I remember well. He and I were schoolmates. . . ."

"Stubborn?" Aunt Bernadette said. "But isn't it children that are stubborn when they go against their own parents? Don't be putting excuses into the boy's head, Turlough. You've no right. Look what happened with your own father. When you heard he was dead you sat in this room and wept." She turned to Vincent. "Too late to make it up then," she said. "Too late."

Her face was very close. Her flabby, powdered cheeks were pitted and spongy as angel food cake. Yet a few years ago she must have been pretty enough to make an old fool dye his hair. A few years ago, before the fat, before the coarseness, before the skin began to sag as though the body had sprung a slow leak. An old man marries a pretty face and ends up in a room with a monster. Strange monster, what right have you to reproach me with my father? He turned from her, determined to ignore her.

She would not be ignored. "Oh, I know you think it's none of my business," she said. "But Turlough tells me you're just like he was when he first came out here. So, I'm warning you, Vincent. Don't make his mistake."

"Now Bernadette, now dear," Uncle Turlough said. "You're confusing two different cases entirely."

"Am I? You never went home because you were too stubborn to go back on all your boasting. You were even ashamed of me."

"Now, that's not true, sweetheart. . . ."

"It is true." She turned to Barbara. "He's always complaining that I don't have his education. Well, I don't, but is that my fault? Oh, let me tell you, dear, your troubles are only starting when you marry into this Carnahan clan."

"I can't believe I'll have any trouble," Barbara said, smiling.

"Do you mean because you're better educated than me?"

"I didn't mean that at all, Mrs. Carnahan."

"Oh yes, you did. But don't forget you're a Protestant. Show me the mixed marriage that doesn't have its troubles. You'll have your share of tears."

"Drinks? Drinks, anyone?" Uncle Turlough said in a hoarse voice. "Barbara, a little more? Vincent, can I top that up for you? Bernadette? Anyone? . . ."

No one answered him. Barbara sat stiff in her chair, her eyes fixed on the lamp across the room. Aunt Bernadette, her neck red beneath the powder line, looked at Barbara in open dislike.

"Charity," Uncle Turlough said, pouring himself the drink that no one else wanted. "Charity for the other person's point of view, that's what counts. Don't try to make everyone else the same as you, that's the thing I've learned as I get older. . . . Vincent, maybe you'd like to switch to a shot of whiskey?"

Maybe he would. Getting drunk might be the only way to survive this evening. So Vincent said yes, aware of Barbara's sudden disapproval, watching her gather up her handbag as though she were preparing to walk out on him. In that moment he felt her Protestant prejudice against all the things which the words "Irish Catholic" must bring into her mind: vulgarity, backwardness, bigotry, drunkenness. But the litanies of love he had recited to her these past three months, didn't they count for anything? Didn't she know very well that he was no longer a Catholic, that it was not his fault that he had been born Irish, that he could hardly be held responsible for relatives he had never laid eyes on? If her lovemaking last night meant anything more than animal desire, wouldn't she be suffering with him now, not sitting in judgment on him as though he had tricked her?

Still, he had tricked her, hadn't he? Tricked her by boasting of his publisher uncle, tricked her by holding out New York as bait, knowing how bored she was with Toronto. Yes, he had. She knew it and she would make him pay for it. She stirred in her chair, turned toward his uncle, and in a disarmingly innocent voice, asked the question Vincent had feared all evening. "By the way, Mr. Carnahan, we've been wondering what sort of books you publish. Is it mostly fiction, or nonfiction?"

Aunt Bernadette looked at her husband. "Fiction?"

"What about the dinner, dear?" Uncle Turlough asked. "Isn't it nearly ready?"

"I'll go and see."

In the silence which followed Aunt Bernadette's departure, Uncle Turlough poured himself another sherry. "Well . . ." he said. "Well, I thought Vincent and I would talk business tomorrow at the office. Tonight, let's just enjoy ourselves, eh?"

"Oh, I wasn't thinking of it in that sense," Barbara said. "I was just wondering if perhaps I've read some of your authors?"

"Authors?" Dark, uneasy eyes appealed to Vincent, found no support, fixed their gaze on a neutral corner. "We—ah—we don't do any fiction, my dear. Not that I wouldn't be happy to, mind you. But you see—perhaps I've never explained this properly in my letters—we're in a more specialized field."

"Oh, really?"

Vincent stared at her, willing her to look at him. Drop it, can't you? But she had no mercy. "Well," she said, "what sort of books do you do, then?"

"Books? Not too many books, I'm afraid. You see we're not what you might call book publishers. We do a few directories. And we do brochures and booklets and pamphlets—that sort of work."

*"Directories?"*

"Well, for instance, we do a dental directory that's a very profitable line. We try to get out a new edition every five years. You'd be surprised how many dentists can afford to shell out five dollars for a nicely got-up book that has their name in it."

"Dinner's ready," said Aunt Bernadette.

Dinner. The fusty dining room was crowded with heavy walnut furniture which, by the awkwardness of its presence, announced that their hosts did not often eat there. There was, however, a bottle of wine, and the main dish of roast beef and baked potatoes was good and plentiful. A plated silver candlestick with three candles lit. An Irish linen tablecloth still glistening new, its folds heavily creased from years of lying in a gift box, proclaimed that in honor of Vincent and his bride Aunt Bernadette had set out her best. But Barbara did not relent; the questions continued. Behind his uncle's apologetic smiles, behind the evasions, the unwillingness to be specific, Barbara laid the imposture bare; Grenville Press, those boastful letters notwithstanding, was in reality a hole-and-corner print shop whose main activity consisted in cooking up lists of names in the manner of a spurious *Who's Who*. There was, Uncle Turlough admitted, a great deal of work in canvassing people to get them to buy the books and brochures in which their names would be included, a great deal of "sounding out groups in specialized fields to see if the response merits publication."

"And what exactly did you have in mind for Vincent in all this?" Barbara asked.

"Well. . . ." His uncle's dark eyes sought out Aunt Bernadette, who sat silent, eating with a concentration which showed plainly how she had come to lose her looks. "Well, I thought he might take Miss Henshaw's place. Eh, Bernadette?"

Aunt Bernadette nodded, still chewing.

"As a matter of fact, Vincent, the week you wrote to me saying you wanted to stay, that was the week we found out Miss Henshaw had cancer of the bowel. She was our editor, my right arm, and old Grenville's before me. Wonderful woman, she could turn out anything you wanted, from a seed catalogue to a school prospectus. She was a great loss, but"—he smiled painfully at Vincent—"if it had to happen, then what better time than now, which it gives me a chance to offer you a good job with the firm. Which you'll accept, I hope."

Barbara was waiting. He must speak. "Well," he said, "of course my teaching year isn't over yet. I haven't really made up my mind."

"But you're fed up with teaching, your letter said."

"Yes."

"And you have to find some sort of job here, don't you?"

"Yes."

"And you wrote that you'd like to live in New York, didn't you?"

"Yes."

"Well, then?"

Vincent did not answer. "I think Vincent was under the impression that you were a book publisher," Barbara said.

"Book publisher? Book publisher. I see. So you thought we were something on the order of Scribner's, did you? Something in that class. Ah, I'm afraid that's not the case, although who knows, great trees from little acorns, as the saying goes. Well, maybe it's my fault. Maybe I made the firm sound a little more important than it really is. But that's only human, isn't it? Isn't it, Vincent?"

Vincent nodded, his eyes on the tablecloth. Aunt Bernadette, speaking for the first time since she had started eating, announced that she would serve coffee in the front room.

"Coffee, yes," Uncle Turlough said, lurching to his feet, tossing his napkin on the table. "Coffee it is. And we'll have a spot of brandy in your honor, children. Come along, Barbara, let me take you in."

Coffee was poured. Aunt Bernadette took her cup and retired to the kitchen, refusing Barbara's halfhearted offer to help with the dishes. Uncle Turlough handed brandies around, then moved uncertainly into the center of the room, his own glass held aloft.

"A toast," he said. "I mean, I want to tell you both how happy I am that you're here at last. I want to tell you how much tonight means to me. You see, Vincent, you're the first relative I've laid eyes on since the day I left Ireland. Yes, this is a great occasion. As you know, I've no children of my own and reading Vincent's letters was like living my own life over again. Funny, isn't it, how you and I have done so many of the same things? Yes. . . . So, *Cead Mile Failte* to you and to this lovely bride of yours, and may this night be the beginning of your long and happy memories of New York."

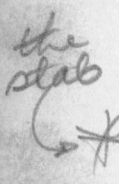

Vincent raised his glass but Barbara put hers down. "I'm superstitious,"

she said, smiling. "I never like to drink to something before we've really made our minds up."

"Well then, let's say, here's hoping," his uncle said. "Here's hoping you'll like it enough to stay. Eh, Vincent?"

"Here's hoping," Vincent said, smiling in embarrassment. He and his uncle drank, Barbara did not pick up her glass. His uncle noticed that.

"As for the money," his uncle said. "I think I'll be able to start you on more than you're earning as a schoolmaster." He turned to Barbara, empty glass in his hand, in an attitude which reminded Vincent of a beggar asking alms. "And you know, Barbara," he said, "if it's moving to a new place that worries you, Bernadette and I will do all we can to help you get settled."

"It's not the moving that worries me," she said.

"Then what is it, my dear?"

"Well, if you must know," she said, "I'm worried about the job and whether it's what Vincent wants."

Said, her sentence hung in the air like smoke after a bullet. His uncle turned toward Vincent, waiting, his puffy face curiously immobile, his dark eyes stilled at last. In the kitchen Aunt Bernadette could be heard turning on taps, stacking dinner dishes. No one spoke, and after a few moments his uncle pulled out his handkerchief and coughed into it. Coughed and coughed, bending almost double while Vincent watched, heartsick, waiting for the paroxysm to wear itself out, watching as his uncle straightened up again, handkerchief still shielding his mouth, eyes staring at them in bloodshot, watery contrition. "Yes . . . well, of course, that's for you and Vincent to decide," his uncle said. "Excuse me—this cough. Sorry. Anyway, it's my fault, talking business to a young couple on their honeymoon. *Mea culpa*. Now, let's talk about something else. How was your trip?"

"Very tiring," Barbara said. "I don't know about Vincent, but I feel quite exhausted."

"Sorry to hear that," his uncle said. "If you're tired we mustn't keep you too late. But it's still the shank of the evening, after all. Would you like another cup of coffee?"

"No, thank you."

Again there was silence. "Vincent tells me you teach modern dance," his uncle began. "I'm a great admirer of Katherine Dunham. Have you ever seen her troupe?"

"Yes."

"And Martha Graham's 'Letter to the World,'" his uncle continued. "Yes, I used to go to a lot of ballet once upon a time." He smiled at her as he spoke, smiled as though pleading for her friendship. But Barbara did not return his smile and so, rejected, he reached unsteadily for the bottle and poured himself another brandy. Vincent tried to speak; in that moment he felt embarrassed for this man who had written a letter, booked a hotel room, bought a festive meal, made a speech of welcome, and who, his illusion of family feeling destroyed, sat silent, half drunk, his smile rejected. Vincent talked. He talked of the Abbey Theatre, of the plays he had seen in Toronto. For a few minutes, he and his uncle stumbled over broken rocks of conversation, recalling the sights and spectacles of former days. But a conversation with no dark corners could no longer be sustained. The talk died. Aunt Bernadette came back into the room to collect the coffee cups. Barbara gathered up her handbag.

"It's been a lovely evening, Mrs. Carnahan," she said, "and a wonderful dinner. But I'm afraid you must excuse me. I'm awfully tired from the plane trip. We had to be up so early this morning."

Aunt Bernadette bent down, put the coffee pot on her tray, stacked the saucers, heaped the cups on top.

"Leave those dishes, won't you dear?" Uncle Turlough said. "What's it matter?"

"I just want to put them in the sink."

"But Barbara's leaving, dear."

"I won't be a minute." She picked up the tray, went out of the room, and again they heard the rush of water taps in the kitchen.

"Bernadette won't be a minute," Uncle Turlough said. "She . . . she likes to get the dishes done in one washing. I'll just go and hurry her up. Sit down for a second, Barbara, I'll be back in a moment."

He went out.

"My God, Barbara, it's not ten o'clock yet. You could have been a bit more polite to them."

"I didn't feel like it," she said. "I'm sick. Why didn't you have the guts to tell him? You'd be insane to take that job. *Insane*. Why didn't you speak up?"

"Shh! They'll hear you."

"Well, what do I care? Do you think I want to spend our honeymoon being shown around by him and that floozy of his? My God, Vincent—"

But at that moment the sound of unmistakably quarrelsome voices reached them from the kitchen. "I don't care," Aunt Bernadette's voice said. "Let them go."

"Ah now, wait a minute, sweetheart—"

"Oh, shut up! I know you. It's your own fault. It's an old story, making yourself out to be something you never were."

"Shh!" his uncle's voice pleaded. Mumbling, indistinct, the argument died to whispers. A door shut. Uncle Turlough came from the kitchen, his face again fixed in its apologetic smile.

"We really must go," Barbara said, standing up.

"Oh? Well then, I'll just run down and find a taxi for you. Just a minute, I won't be long. Bernadette? . . . Bernadette, will you get the children's coats?"

In answer the water taps roared again in the kitchen.

"Won't be long," Uncle Turlough said, opening the apartment door. "Vincent, get yourself a drink."

The front door shut. Vincent stood up and walked toward the brandy bottle. He had drunk too much. He felt slow, uncoordinated, dull.

"Vincent, you're not going to have another drink!"

"I am."

"I'm getting my coat then. Where is it?"

"In the closet in the hall."

He heard her leave the room. He picked up the bottle. Perhaps in twenty years his face would bloat and blotch as his uncle's had. Drink, that was an Irish weakness. Self-deceit, that was an Irish weakness. He drank the brandy. He stared at the bookshelves with their dusty, unused books. Drunkenly, he turned to face his Carnahan grandmother on the mantelpiece. Never give an Irishman the choice between a girl and the bottle, she had said. Most of them will prefer the bottle.

The front door opened and he heard his uncle call, "Barbara, let me help you with that coat. And is this Vincent's coat? I have a cab waiting downstairs. Where's Vincent?"

His uncle came in, his step unsteady, his face still fixed in that apologetic smile which was, wasn't it, the very mirror of the man? "Here's your coat, Vincent lad. And wait till I get your aunt. Bernadette? Bernadette?"

He went out again and Vincent heard him go into the kitchen. A moment later, the front door shut. Vincent ran out to the hall. She was gone. Furious at her, he opened the front door to call her back, but as he did, his uncle returned from the kitchen. "Oh, there you are," his uncle said. "Bernadette asked me to say goodnight for her, she has a touch of migraine." He held out a clumsy parcel. "Your wedding present," he said. "I wrapped it up for you. Now, what about a nightcap? One for the road. Where's Barbara?"

"I asked her to go down and hold the cab."

His lie, complementing his uncle's, their mutual shame as they stood face to face, each seeking to atone for his wife's rudeness, each hoping to preserve the fiction of family unity . . . Oh God, Vincent thought, we are alike. Quickly, he opened the front door. "No thanks," he said. "Goodnight, and thank you for a very nice evening. Don't bother to come down, please."

"No bother at all. But are you sure now, you wouldn't stay a wee while? You could send Barbara home if she's tired and then we could sit down over a glass, just the two of us."

"I'm afraid I'd better go. Barbara is waiting, you see."

"I see," his uncle said. "Yes, of course. All right, I'll come down and say goodnight to her."

"Please, it's not necessary."

"No bother," his uncle said, following him out, pursuing him down two flights of stairs, coming with him into the street. The taxi waited, its bright ceiling light showing Barbara huddled in the far corner of the back seat. She did not appear to see them, and Vincent, afraid that she would refuse to say good-bye, hurried ahead of his uncle and pulled open the taxi door. "Say good-bye to him, will you?" he whispered.

"Where is he?" She looked past him, peering into the darkness of the shabby street. But his uncle had stopped about twelve feet from the taxi. She waved to him and he raised his hand and waved back. "Goodnight, my dear," he called. "Have a good rest."

"Goodnight, Mr. Carnahan. And thank you." She smiled at him and leaned back in her seat. For her it was over; she wanted to go back to the hotel, to escape forever from these people she despised. "Come on," she said. "Get in."

But as she spoke, Vincent heard a low voice behind him. "Vincent? Vincent?"

*Father?* he had called. *Father?* But his father had not looked back. His father had walked down the path, opened the gate, no look back. Went down the avenue, turned the corner, no look back.

He turned back. There, half drunk on the pavement stood a fat old man with dyed hair. Where was the boy who once wrote poems, the young iconoclast who once spoke out against the priests? What had done this to him? Was it drink, or exile, or this marriage to a woman twenty years his junior? Or had that boy never been? What did this old man want of him now, Vincent wondered? Forgiveness? Or merely some sign that they still were kin?

"Vincent," his uncle said. "I'll see you tomorrow, won't I?"

"Yes."

"And Vincent? It's a good job, on my word of honor it is. I hope you'll take it, Vincent."

"Well, I must think about it, Uncle Turlough."

"Of course, of course. And Vincent? Bernadette, ah, you shouldn't mind her. Some days she's not herself. I'm sorry you didn't enjoy yourself this evening."

"But we did. We had a very good time."

"Thanks, Vince, thanks for saying that. Now, I don't want to keep you but I wish we'd had more time to talk. I know you don't like the looks of the job. I think you don't like the looks of me, either. Well, I can't say I blame you, no, I can't say I blame you one bit. But, Vincent?"

"Yes, Uncle Turlough?"

"I was counting on your coming in with me. I had great hopes of passing on the business—but, never mind, if you don't want the job you don't want it and there's no use talking. Go on back now. You're on your honeymoon, you have better things to do than sit around at night with the likes of me. So off with you, lad, and good luck to you."

"Goodnight, Uncle Turlough."

As he shook hands with his uncle, Vincent looked at the taxi. There she sat, her pretty face averted in contempt. Was that all last night's lovemaking had meant to her? Didn't she know it was for both their sakes that he had come here this evening, that unless he could find something to do on this side of the water, she would be condemned to a life of drizzling boredom as a schoolteacher's wife in an Irish country town?

He leaned into the taxi. "Barbara, let's not go just yet."

"I'm tired," she said. "I'm leaving."

He fumbled in his trouser pocket. "Here's your fare then." He pushed the money at her and shut the taxi door. The taxi moved away from the curb. He watched; she did not look back.

"What's the matter, Vincent?"

He turned, his face forming an apologetic smile, his dark, uneasy eyes searching his kinsman's face. "I've changed my mind," he said. "Maybe I'll have one for the road, after all."

"I knew it, I knew it," said his spitting image.

# Love and Desire

## THE MAGIC BARREL

**Bernard Malamud**

Born in Brooklyn in 1914, Malamud attended Erasmus Hall High School in Brooklyn, City College of New York, receiving his B.A. in 1936, and Columbia University, from which he was awarded an M.A. in 1942. He taught for a time at Oregon State College, the experience there serving as material for his novel A New Life (1961); since 1961 he has been writer-in-residence at Bennington College in Vermont. His other works include The Magic Barrel (1958), Idiots First (1963), Pictures of Fidelman (1969), and Rembrandt's Hat (1973), collections of short stories; and the novels The Natural (1952), The Assistant (1957), considered by many to be his finest, The Fixer (1966), and The Tenants (1971). Malamud is one of the group of Jewish-American writers that emerged after World War II, and he has found much of the material for his fiction in what is called the Jewish experience. The strength of his writing, as can be seen in "The Magic Barrel," lies in his ability to merge realism and fantasy and to write about his characters with great sympathy and understanding. In his best stories Malamud demonstrates what Anthony Burgess has described as "disinterested responsibility," by which is meant "the true spiritual love one human being ought to feel for another." In them are also found Malamud's masterful use of language. "One cannot sit on language," Malamud himself has written; "it moves beyond the presence of things into the absence of things, the illusion of things. Art must interpret, or it is mindless."

Not long ago there lived in uptown New York, in a small, almost meager room, though crowded with books, Leo Finkle, a rabbinical student in the Yeshivah University. Finkle, after six years of study, was to be ordained in June and had been advised by an acquaintance that he might find it easier to win himself a congregation if he were married. Since he had no present prospects of marriage, after two tormented days of turning it over in his mind, he called in Pinye Salzman, a marriage broker whose two-line advertisement he had read in the *Forward*.

The matchmaker appeared one night out of the dark fourth-floor hallway of the graystone rooming house where Finkle lived, grasping a black, strapped portfolio that had been worn thin with use. Salzman, who had been long in the business, was of slight but dignified build, wearing an old hat, and an overcoat too short and tight for him. He smelled frankly of fish, which he loved to eat, and although he was missing a few teeth, his presence was not displeasing, because of an amiable manner curiously contrasted with mournful eyes. His voice, his lips, his wisp of beard, his bony fingers were animated, but give him a moment of repose and his mild blue eyes revealed a depth of sadness, a characteristic that put Leo a little at ease although the situation, for him, was inherently tense.

He at once informed Salzman why he had asked him to come, explaining that his home was in Cleveland, and that but for his parents, who had married comparatively late in life, he was alone in the world. He had for six years devoted himself almost entirely to his studies, as a result of which, understandably, he had found himself without time for a social life and the company of young women. Therefore he thought it the better part of trial and error—of embarrassing fumbling—to call in an experienced person to advise him on these matters. He remarked in passing that the function of the marriage broker was ancient and honorable, highly approved in the Jewish community, because it made practical the necessary without hindering joy. Moreover, his own parents had been brought together by a matchmaker. They had made, if not a financially profitable marriage—since neither had possessed any worldly goods to speak of—at least a successful one in the sense of their everlasting devotion to each other. Salzman listened in embarrassed surprise, sensing a sort of apology. Later, however, he experienced a glow of pride in his work, an emotion that had left him years ago, and he heartily approved of Finkle.

The two went to their business. Leo had led Salzman to the only clear place in the room, a table near a window that overlooked the lamp-lit city. He seated himself at the matchmaker's side but facing him, attempting by an act of will to suppress the unpleasant tickle in his throat. Salzman eagerly unstrapped his portfolio and removed a loose rubber band from a thin packet of much-handled cards. As he flipped through them, a gesture and sound that physically hurt Leo, the student pretended not to see and gazed steadfastly out the window. Although it was still February, winter was on its last legs, signs of which he had for the first time in years begun to notice. He now observed the round white moon, moving high in the sky through a cloud menagerie, and watched with half-open mouth as it penetrated a huge hen, and dropped out of her like an egg laying itself. Salzman, though pretending through eyeglasses he had just slipped on, to be engaged in scanning the writing on the cards, stole occasional glances at the young man's distinguished face, noting with pleasure the long, severe scholar's nose, brown eyes heavy with learning, sensitive yet ascetic lips, and a certain, almost hollow quality of the dark cheeks. He gazed around at shelves upon shelves of books and let out a soft, contented sigh.

When Leo's eyes fell upon the cards, he counted six spread out in Salzman's hand.

"So few?" he asked in disappointment.

"You wouldn't believe me how much cards I got in my office," Salzman replied. "The drawers are already filled to the top, so I keep them now in a barrel, but is every girl good for a new rabbi?"

Leo blushed at this, regretting all he had revealed of himself in a curriculum vitae he had sent to Salzman. He had thought it best to acquaint him with his strict standards and specifications, but in having done so, felt he had told the marriage broker more than was absolutely necessary.

He hesitantly inquired, "Do you keep photographs of your clients on file?"

"First comes family, amount of dowry, also what kind promises," Salzman replied, unbuttoning his tight coat and settling himself in the chair. "After comes pictures, rabbi."

"Call me Mr. Finkle. I'm not yet a rabbi."

Salzman said he would, but instead called him doctor, which he changed to rabbi when Leo was not listening too attentively.

Salzman adjusted his horn-rimmed spectacles, gently cleared his throat and read in an eager voice the contents of the top card:

"Sophie P. Twenty-four years. Widow one year. No children. Educated high school and two years college. Father promises eight thousand dollars. Has wonderful wholesale business. Also real estate. On the mother's side comes teachers, also one actor. Well known on Second Avenue."

Leo gazed up in surprise. "Did you say a widow?"

"A widow don't mean spoiled, rabbi. She lived with her husband maybe four months. He was a sick boy she made a mistake to marry him."

"Marrying a widow has never entered my mind."

"This is because you have no experience. A widow, especially if she is young and healthy like this girl, is a wonderful person to marry. She will be thankful to you the rest of her life. Believe me, if I was looking now for a bride, I would marry a widow."

Leo reflected, then shook his head.

Salzman hunched his shoulders in an almost imperceptible gesture of disappointment. He placed the card down on the wooden table and began to read another:

"Lily H. High school teacher. Regular. Not a substitute. Has savings and new Dodge car. Lived in Paris one year. Father is successful dentist thirty-five years. Interested in professional man. Well Americanized family. Wonderful opportunity.

"I knew her personally," said Salzman. "I wish you could see this girl. She is a doll. Also very intelligent. All day you could talk to her about books and theyater and what not. She also knows current events."

"I don't believe you mentioned her age?"

"Her age?" Salzman said, raising his brows. "Her age is thirty-two years."

Leo said after a while, "I'm afraid that seems a little too old."

Salzman let out a laugh. "So how old are you, rabbi?"

"Twenty-seven."

"So what is the difference, tell me, between twenty-seven and thirty-two? My own wife is seven years older than me. So what did I suffer?—Nothing. If Rothschild's a daughter wants to marry you, would you say on account her age, no?"

"Yes," Leo said dryly.

Salzman shook off the no in the yes. "Five years don't mean a thing. I give you my word that when you will live with her for one week you will forget her age. What does it mean five years—that she lived more and knows more than somebody who is younger? On this girl, God bless her, years are not wasted. Each one that it comes makes better the bargain."

"What subject does she teach in high school?"

"Languages. If you heard the way she speaks French, you will think it is music. I am in the business twenty-five years, and I recommend her with my whole heart. Believe me, I know what I'm talking, rabbi."

"What's on the next card?" Leo said abruptly.

Salzman reluctantly turned up the third card:

"Ruth K. Nineteen years. Honor student. Father offers thirteen thousand cash to the right bridegroom. He is a medical doctor. Stomach specialist with marvelous practice. Brother in law owns own garment business. Particular people."

Salzman looked as if he had read his trump card.

"Did you say nineteen?" Leo asked with interest.

"On the dot."

"Is she attractive?" He blushed. "Pretty?"

Salzman kissed his finger tips. "A little doll. On this I give you my word. Let me call the father tonight and you will see what means pretty."

But Leo was troubled. "You're sure she's that young?"

"This I am positive. The father will show you the birth certificate."

"Are you positive there isn't something wrong with her?" Leo insisted.

"Who says there is wrong?"

"I don't understand why an American girl her age should go to a marriage broker."

A smile spread over Salzman's face.

"So for the same reason you went, she comes."

Leo flushed. "I am pressed for time."

Salzman, realizing he had been tactless, quickly explained. "The father came, not her. He wants she should have the best, so he looks around himself. When we will locate the right boy he will introduce him and encourage. This makes a better marriage than if a young girl without experience takes for herself. I don't have to tell you this."

"But don't you think this young girl believes in love?" Leo spoke uneasily.

Salzman was about to guffaw but caught himself and said soberly, "Love comes with the right person, not before."

Leo parted dry lips but did not speak. Noticing that Salzman had snatched a glance at the next card, he cleverly asked, "How is her health?"

"Perfect," Salzman said, breathing with difficulty. "Of course, she is a little lame on her right foot from an auto accident that it happened to her when she was twelve years, but nobody notices on account she is so brilliant and also beautiful."

Leo got up heavily and went to the window. He felt curiously bitter and upbraided himself for having called in the marriage broker. Finally, he shook his head.

"Why not?" Salzman persisted, the pitch of his voice rising.

"Because I detest stomach specialists."

"So what do you care what is his business? After you marry her do you need him? Who says he must come every Friday night in your house?"

Ashamed of the way the talk was going, Leo dismissed Salzman, who went home with heavy, melancholy eyes.

Though he had felt only relief at the marriage broker's departure, Leo was in low spirits the next day. He explained it as arising from Salzman's failure to produce a suitable bride for him. He did not care for his type of clientele. But when Leo found himself hesitating whether to seek out another matchmaker, one more polished than Pinye, he wondered if it could be—his protestations to the contrary, and although he honored his father and mother—that he did not, in essence, care for the matchmaking institution? This thought he quickly put out of his mind yet found himself still upset. All day he ran around in the woods—missed an important appointment, forgot to give out his laundry, walked out of a Broadway cafeteria without paying and had to run back with the ticket in his hand; had even not recognized his landlady in the street when she passed with a friend and courteously called out, "A good evening to you,

Doctor Finkle." By nightfall, however, he had regained sufficient calm to sink his nose into a book and there found peace from his thoughts.

Almost at once there came a knock on the door. Before Leo could say enter, Salzman, commercial cupid, was standing in the room. His face was gray and meager, his expression hungry, and he looked as if he would expire on his feet. Yet the marriage broker managed, by some trick of the muscles, to display a broad smile.

"So good evening. I am invited?"

Leo nodded, disturbed to see him again, yet unwilling to ask the man to leave.

Beaming still, Salzman laid his portfolio on the table. "Rabbi, I got for you tonight good news."

"I've asked you not to call me rabbi. I'm still a student."

"Your worries are finished. I have for you a first-class bride."

"Leave me in peace concerning this subject." Leo pretended lack of interest.

"The world will dance at your wedding."

"Please, Mr. Salzman, no more."

"But first must come back my strength," Salzman said weakly. He fumbled with the portfolio straps and took out of the leather case an oily paper bag, from which he extracted a hard, seeded roll and a small, smoked white fish. With a quick motion of his hand he stripped the fish out of its skin and began ravenously to chew. "All day in a rush," he muttered.

Leo watched him eat.

"A sliced tomato you have maybe?" Salzman hesitantly inquired.

"No."

The marriage broker shut his eyes and ate. When he had finished he carefully cleaned up the crumbs and rolled up the remains of the fish, in the paper bag. His spectacled eyes roamed the room until he discovered, amid some piles of books, a one-burner gas stove. Lifting his hat he humbly asked, "A glass tea you got, rabbi?"

Conscience-stricken, Leo rose and brewed the tea. He served it with a chunk of lemon and two cubes of lump sugar, delighting Salzman.

After he had drunk his tea, Salzman's strength and good spirits were restored.

"So tell me, rabbi," he said amiably, "you considered some more the three clients I mentioned yesterday?"

"There was no need to consider."

"Why not?"

"None of them suits me."

"What then suits you?"

Leo let it pass because he could give only a confused answer.

Without waiting for a reply, Salzman asked, "You remember this girl I talked to you—the high school teacher?"

"Age thirty-two?"

But, surprisingly, Salzman's face lit in a smile. "Age twenty-nine."

Leo shot him a look. "Reduced from thirty-two?"

"A mistake," Salzman avowed. "I talked today with the dentist. He took me to his safety deposit box and showed me the birth certificate. She was twenty-nine years last August. They made her a party in the mountains where she went for her vacation. When her father spoke to me the first time I forgot to write the age and I told you thirty-two, but now I remember this was a different client, a widow."

"The same one you told me about? I thought she was twenty-four?"

"A different. Am I responsible that the world is filled with widows?"

"No, but I'm not interested in them, nor for that matter, in school teachers."

Salzman pulled his clasped hands to his breast. Looking at the ceiling he devoutly exclaimed. "Yiddishe kinder, what can I say to somebody that he is not interested in high school teachers? So what then you are interested?"

Leo flushed but controlled himself.

"In what else will you be interested," Salzman went on, "if you not interested in this fine girl that she speaks four languages and has personally in the bank ten thousand dollars? Also her father guarantees further twelve thousand. Also she has a new car, wonderful clothes, talks on all subjects, and she will give you a first-class home and children. How near do we come in our life to paradise?"

"If she's so wonderful, why wasn't she married ten years ago?"

"Why?" said Salzman with a heavy laugh. "—Why? Because she is *partikiler*. This is why. She wants the *best*."

Leo was silent, amused at how he had entangled himself. But Salzman had aroused his interest in Lily H., and he began seriously to consider calling on her. When the marriage broker observed how intently Leo's mind was at work on the facts he had supplied, he felt certain they would soon come to an agreement.

Late Saturday afternoon, conscious of Salzman, Leo Finkle walked with Lily Hirschorn along Riverside Drive. He walked briskly and erectly, wearing with distinction the black fedora he had that morning taken with trepidation out of the dusty hat box on his closet shelf, and the heavy black Saturday coat he had thoroughly whisked clean. Leo also owned a walking stick, a present from a distant relative, but quickly put temptation aside and did not use it. Lily, petite and not unpretty, had on something signifying the approach of spring. She was au courant, animatedly, with all sorts of subjects, and he weighed her words and found her surprisingly sound—score another for Salzman, whom he uneasily sensed to be somewhere around hiding perhaps high in a tree along the street, flashing the lady signals with a pocket mirror; or perhaps a cloven-hoofed

Pan, piping nuptial ditties as he danced his invisible way before them, strewing wild buds on the walk and purple grapes in their paths, symbolizing fruit of a union, though there was of course still none.

Lily startled Leo by remarking, "I was thinking of Mr. Salzman, a curious figure, wouldn't you say?"

Not certain what to answer, he nodded.

She bravely went on, blushing, "I for one am grateful for his introducing us. Aren't you?"

He courteously replied, "I am."

"I mean," she said with a little laugh—and it was all in good taste, or at least gave the effect of being not in bad—"do you mind that we came together so?"

He was not displeased with her honesty, recognizing that she meant to set the relationship aright, and understanding that it took a certain amount of experience in life, and courage, to want to do it quite that way. One had to have some sort of past to make that kind of beginning.

He said that he did not mind. Salzman's function was traditional and honorable—valuable for what it might achieve, which, he pointed out, was frequently nothing.

Lily agreed with a sigh. They walked on for a while and she said after a long silence, again with a nervous laugh, "Would you mind if I asked you something a little bit personal? Frankly, I find the subject fascinating." Although Leo shrugged, she went on half embarrassedly, "How was it that you came to your calling? I mean was it a sudden passionate inspiration?"

Leo, after a time, slowly replied, "I was always interested in the Law."

"You saw revealed in it the presence of the Highest?"

He nodded and changed the subject. "I understand that you spent a little time in Paris, Miss Hirschorn?"

"Oh, did Mr. Salzman tell you, Rabbi Finkle?" Leo winced but she went on, "It was ages ago and almost forgotten. I remember I had to return for my sister's wedding."

And Lily would not be put off. "When," she asked in a trembly voice, "did you become enamored of God?"

He stared at her. Then it came to him that she was talking not about Leo Finkle, but of a total stranger, some mystical figure, perhaps even passionate prophet that Salzman had dreamed up for her—no relation to the living or dead. Leo trembled with rage and weakness. The trickster had obviously sold her a bill of goods, just as he had him, who'd expected to become acquainted with a young lady of twenty-nine, only to behold, the moment he laid eyes upon her strained and anxious face, a woman past thirty-five and aging rapidly. Only his self control had kept him this long in her presence.

"I am not," he said gravely, "a talented religious person," and in seeking words to go on, found himself possessed by shame and fear. "I think," he said in a strained manner, "that I came to God not because I loved Him, but because I did not."

This confession he spoke harshly because its unexpectedness shook him.

Leo wilted. Leo saw a profusion of loaves of bread go flying like ducks high over his head, not unlike the winged loaves by which he had counted himself to sleep last night. Mercifully, then, it snowed, which he would not put past Salzman's machinations.

He was infuriated with the marriage broker and swore he would throw him out of the room the minute he reappeared. But Salzman did not come that night, and when Leo's anger had subsided, an unaccountable despair grew in its place. At first he thought this was caused by his disappointment in Lily, but before long it became evident that he had involved himself with Salzman without a true knowledge of his own intent. He gradually realized—with an emptiness that seized him with six hands—that he had called in the broker to find him a bride because he was incapable of doing it himself. This terrifying insight he had derived as a result of his meeting and conversation with Lily Hirschorn. Her probing questions had somehow irritated him into revealing—to himself more than her—the true nature of his relationship to God, and from that it had come upon him, with shocking force, that apart from his parents, he had never loved anyone. Or perhaps it went the other way, that he did not love God so well as he might, because he had not loved man. It seemed to Leo that his whole life stood starkly revealed and he saw himself for the first time as he truly was—unloved and loveless. This bitter but somehow not fully unexpected revelation brought him to a point of panic, controlled only by extraordinary effort. He covered his face with his hands and cried.

The week that followed was the worst of his life. He did not eat and lost weight. His beard darkened and grew ragged. He stopped attending seminars and almost never opened a book. He seriously considered leaving the Yeshivah, although he was deeply troubled at the thought of the loss of all his years of study—saw them like pages torn from a book, strewn over the city—and at the devastating effect of this decision upon his parents. But he had lived without knowledge of himself, and never in the Five Books and all the Commentaries—mea culpa—had the truth been revealed to him. He did not know where to turn, and in all this desolating loneliness there was no *to whom,* although he often thought of Lily but not once could bring himself to go downstairs and make the call. He became touchy and irritable, especially with his landlady, who asked him all manner of personal questions; on the other hand, sensing his own disagreeableness, he waylaid her on the stairs and apologized abjectly, until mortified, she ran from him. Out of this, however, he drew the consolation that he was a Jew and that a Jew suffered. But gradually, as the long and terrible week drew to a close, he regained his composure and some idea of purpose in life: to go on as planned. Although he was imperfect, the ideal was not. As for his quest of a bride, the thought of continuing afflicted him with anxiety and heartburn, yet perhaps with this new knowledge of himself he would be more successful than in the past. Perhaps love would now come to him and a bride to that love. And for this sanctified seeking who needed a Salzman?

The marriage broker, a skeleton with haunted eyes, returned that very night. He looked, withal, the picture of frustrated expectancy—as if he had steadfastly waited the week at Miss Lily Hirschorn's side for a telephone call that never came.

Casually coughing, Salzman came immediately to the point: "So how did you like her?"

Leo's anger rose and he could not refrain from chiding the matchmaker: "Why did you lie to me, Salzman?"

Salzman's pale face went dead white, the world had snowed on him.

"Did you not state that she was twenty-nine?" Leo insisted.

"I give you my word—"

"She was thirty-five, if a day. *At least* thirty-five."

"Of this don't be too sure. Her father told me—"

"Never mind. The worst of it was that you lied to her."

"How did I lie to her, tell me?"

"You told her things about me that weren't true. You made me out to be more, consequently less than I am. She had in mind a totally different person, a sort of semi-mystical Wonder Rabbi."

"All I said, you was a religious man."

"I can imagine."

Salzman sighed. "This is my weakness that I have," he confessed. "My wife says to me I shouldn't be a salesman, but when I have two fine people that they would be wonderful to be married, I am so happy that I talk too much." He smiled wanly. "This is why Salzman is a poor man."

Leo's anger left him. "Well, Salzman, I'm afraid that's all."

The marriage broker fastened hungry eyes on him.

"You don't want any more a bride?"

"I do," said Leo, "but I have decided to seek her in a different way. I am no longer interested in an arranged marriage. To be frank, I now admit the necessity of premarital love. That is, I want to be in love with the one I marry."

"Love?" said Salzman, astounded. After a moment he remarked, "For us, our love is our life, not for the ladies. In the ghetto they—"

"I know, I know," said Leo. "I've thought of it often. Love, I have said to myself, should be a by-product of living and worship rather than its own end. Yet for myself I find it necessary to establish the level of my need and fulfill it."

Salzman shrugged but answered, "Listen, rabbi, if you want love, this I can find for you also. I have such beautiful clients that you will love them the minute your eyes will see them."

Leo smiled unhappily. "I'm afraid you don't understand."

But Salzman hastily unstrapped his portfolio and withdrew a manila packet from it.

"Pictures," he said, quickly laying the envelope on the table.

Leo called after him to take the pictures away, but as if on wings of the wind, Salzman had disappeared.

March came. Leo had returned to his regular routine. Although he felt not quite himself yet—lacked energy—he was making plans for a more active social life. Of course it would cost something, but he was an expert in cutting corners; and when there were no corners left he would make circles rounder. All the while Salzman's pictures had lain on the table, gathering dust. Occasionally as Leo sat studying, or enjoying a cup of tea, his eyes fell on the manila envelope, but he never opened it.

The days went by and no social life to speak of developed with a member of the opposite sex—it was difficult, given the circumstances of his situation. One morning Leo toiled up the stairs to his room and stared out the window at the city. Although the day was bright his view of it was dark. For some time he watched the people in the street below hurrying along and then turned with a heavy heart to his little room. On the table was the packet. With a sudden relentless gesture he tore it open. For a half-hour he stood by the table in a state of excitement, examining the photographs of the ladies Salzman had included. Finally, with a deep sigh he put them down. There were six, of varying degrees of attractiveness, but look at them long enough and they all became Lily Hirschorn: all past their prime, all starved behind bright smiles, not a true personality in the lot. Life, despite their frantic yoohooings, had passed them by; they were pictures in a brief case that stank of fish. After a while, however, as Leo attempted to return the photographs into the envelope, he found in it another, a snapshot of the type taken by a machine for a quarter. He gazed at it a moment and let out a cry.

Her face deeply moved him. Why, he could at first not say. It gave him the impression of youth—spring flowers, yet age—a sense of having been used to the bone, wasted; this came from the eyes, which were hauntingly familiar, yet absolutely strange. He had a vivid impression that he had met her before, but try as he might he could not place her although he could almost recall her name, as if he had read it in her own handwriting. No, this couldn't be; he would have remembered her. It was not, he affirmed, that she had an extraordinary beauty—no, though her face was attractive enough; it was that *something* about her moved him. Feature for feature, even some of the ladies of the photographs could do better; but she leaped forth to his heart—had *lived,* or wanted to—more than just wanted, perhaps regretted how she had lived—had somehow deeply suffered: it could be seen in the depths of those reluctant eyes, and from the way the light enclosed and shone from her, and within her, opening realms of possibility: this was her own. Her he desired. His head ached and eyes narrowed with the intensity of his gazing, then as if an obscure fog had blown up in the mind, he experienced fear of her and was aware that he had received an impression, somehow, of evil. He shuddered, saying softly, it is thus with us all. Leo brewed some tea in a small pot and sat sipping it without sugar, to calm himself. But before he had finished drinking, again with excitement he examined the face and found it good: good for Leo Finkle. Only such a one could understand him and help him seek whatever he was seeking. She might, perhaps, love him. How she had happened to be among the discards in Salzman's barrel he could never guess, but he knew he must urgently go find her.

Leo rushed downstairs, grabbed up the Bronx telephone book, and searched for Salzman's home address. He was not listed, nor was his office. Neither was he in the Manhattan book. But Leo remembered having written down the address on a slip of paper after he had read Salzman's advertisement in the "personals" column of the *Forward*. He ran up to his room and tore through his papers, without luck. It was exasperating. Just when he needed the matchmaker he was nowhere to be found. Fortunately Leo remembered to look in his wallet. There on a card he found his name written and a Bronx address. No phone number was listed, the reason—Leo now recalled—he had originally communicated with Salzman by letter. He got on his coat, put a hat on over his skull cap and hurried to the subway station. All the way to the far end of the Bronx he sat on the edge of his seat. He was more than once tempted to take out the picture and see if the girl's face was as he remembered it, but he refrained, allowing the snapshot to remain in his inside coat pocket, content to have her so close. When the train pulled into the station he was waiting at the door and bolted out. He quickly located the street Salzman had advertised.

The building he sought was less than a block from the subway, but it was not an office building, nor even a loft, nor a store in which one could rent office space. It was a very old tenement house. Leo found Salzman's name in pencil on a soiled tag under the bell and climbed three dark flights to his apartment. When he knocked, the door was opened by a thin, asthmatic, gray-haired woman, in felt slippers.

"Yes?" she said, expecting nothing. She listened without listening. He could have sworn he had seen her, too, before but knew it was an illusion.

"Salzman—does he live here? Pinye Salzman," he said, "the matchmaker?"

She stared at him a long minute. "Of course."

He felt embarrassed. "Is he in?"

"No." Her mouth, though left open, offered nothing more.

"The matter is urgent. Can you tell me where his office is?"

"In the air." She pointed upward.
"You mean he has no office?" Leo asked.
"In his socks."

He peered into the apartment. It was sunless and dingy, one large room divided by a half-open curtain, beyond which he could see a sagging metal bed. The near side of the room was crowded with rickety chairs, old bureaus, a three-legged table, racks of cooking utensils, and all the apparatus of a kitchen. But there was no sign of Salzman or his magic barrel, probably also a figment of the imagination. An odor of frying fish made Leo weak to the knees.

"Where is he?" he insisted. "I've got to see your husband."

At length she answered, "So who knows where he is? Every time he thinks a new thought he runs to a different place. Go home, he will find you."

"Tell him Leo Finkle."

She gave no sign she had heard.

He walked downstairs, depressed.

But Salzman, breathless, stood waiting at his door.

Leo was astounded and overjoyed. "How did you get here before me?"

"I rushed."

"Come inside."

They entered. Leo fixed tea, and a sardine sandwich for Salzman. As they were drinking he reached behind him for the packet of pictures and handed them to the marriage broker.

Salzman put down his glass and said expectantly, "You found somebody you like?"

"Not among these."

The marriage broker turned away.

"Here is the one I want." Leo held forth the snapshot.

Salzman slipped on his glasses and took the picture into his trembling hand. He turned ghastly and let out a groan.

"What's the matter?" cried Leo.

"Excuse me. Was an accident this picture. She isn't for you."

Salzman frantically shoved the manila packet into his portfolio. He thrust the snapshot into his pocket and fled down the stairs.

Leo, after momentary paralysis, gave chase and cornered the marriage broker in the vestibule. The landlady made hysterical outcries but neither of them listened.

"Give me back the picture, Salzman."

"No." The pain in his eyes was terrible.

"Tell me who she is then."

"This I can't tell you. Excuse me."

He made to depart, but Leo, forgetting himself, seized the matchmaker by his tight coat and shook him frenziedly.

"Please," sighed Salzman. *"Please."*

Leo ashamedly let him go. "Tell me who she is," he begged. "It's very important for me to know."

"She is not for you. She is a wild one—wild, without shame. This is not a bride for a rabbi."

"What do you mean wild?"

"Like an animal. Like a dog. For her to be poor was a sin. This is why to me she is dead now."

"In God's name, what do you mean?"

"Her I can't introduce to you," Salzman cried.

"Why are you so excited?"

"Why, he asks," Salzman said, bursting into tears. "This is my baby, my Stella, she should burn in hell."

Leo hurried up to bed and hid under the covers. Under the covers he thought his life through. Although he soon fell asleep he could not sleep her out of his mind. He woke, beating his breast. Though he prayed to be rid of her, his prayers went unanswered. Through days of torment he endlessly struggled not to love her; fearing success, he escaped it. He then concluded to convert her to goodness, himself to God. The idea alternately nauseated and exalted him.

He perhaps did not know he had come to a final decision until he encountered Salzman in a Broadway cafeteria. He was sitting alone at a rear table, sucking the bony remains of a fish. The marriage broker appeared haggard, and transparent to the point of vanishing.

Salzman looked up at first without recognizing him. Leo had grown a pointed beard and his eyes were weighted with wisdom.

"Salzman," he said, "love has at last come to my heart."

"Who can love from a picture?" mocked the marriage broker.

"It is not impossible."

"If you can love her, then you can love anybody. Let me show you some new clients that they just sent me their photographs. One is a little doll."

"Just her I want," Leo murmured.

"Don't be a fool, doctor. Don't bother with her."

"Put me in touch with her, Salzman," Leo said humbly. "Perhaps I can be of service."

Salzman had stopped eating and Leo understood with emotion that it was now arranged.

Leaving the cafeteria, he was, however, afflicted by a tormenting suspicion that Salzman had planned it all to happen this way.

Leo was informed by letter that she would meet him on a certain corner, and she was there one spring night, waiting under a street lamp. He appeared, carrying a small bouquet of violets and rosebuds. Stella stood by the lamp post, smoking. She wore white with red shoes, which fitted his expectations, although in a troubled moment he had imagined the dress red, and only the shoes white. She waited uneasily and shyly. From afar he saw that her eyes—clearly her father's—were filled with desperate innocence. He pictured, in her, his own redemption. Violins and lit candles revolved in the sky. Leo ran forward with flowers outthrust.

Around the corner, Salzman, leaning against a wall, chanted prayers for the dead.

---

# HUE AND CRY

## James Alan McPherson

*Born in Savannah, Georgia, in 1943, and educated at Morris Brown College, Morgan State College, Harvard University, and the University of Iowa, James Alan McPherson teaches at the University of Iowa and is a contributing editor for the* Atlantic. *His first book of short stories,* Hue and Cry *(1969), won high praise, and he is currently at work on a novel. McPherson is considered to be one of the most promising writers of this generation, winning praise from, among others, Ralph Ellison, who has called him a "writer of insight, sympathy, and humor and one of the most gifted young Americans I've had the privilege to read."*

A joke is an epigram on the death of a feeling.<br>—Friedrich Nietzsche

But if that is all there is, what is left of life and why are we alive?"
"Because we know no better way to be."
"And are these our only options?"
"These few should be sufficient."
"But what of those who look for more?"
"One must either hate or pity them."
"Why hate?"
"Because they make us uncomfortable in their lack of loyalties to these options."
"Why pity?"
"Because we know that they must pay for our discomfort."
"But is it necessary that they should pay?"
"Always."

"On what authority?"

"For all of those who took the easy options; for all of those who are unhappy in their choices."

"And are there many of these unhappy?"

"Look around you."

"And what of those who look for more? Are they just as plentiful and just as unhappy?"

"Look around you. They live in dark and secret places, but one can see they are many and unhappy. And one can see how they pay."

"How do they pay?"

And then there was the getting to sleep. It would start with his moving across the double bed, slowly, for a position; and it would continue that way until he had moved to the edge of the bed, with the sheets still holding to his body, slippery and clinging at the same time. The sleep would come on him in the same slow way, like a very hot bath beginning to feel good and then getting cold too soon. Eric could not maintain the necessary consistency and would find himself still trying to reach sleep with his mind because his body had long before gone away. Then there was the telephone. Eric wanted it to ring, and he lay waiting for it. And then he did not want it to ring, and he waited for it not to. Besides these two things was his mind, which did not want anything but not being able to think. But he thought, in his double bed, in the night, in the dark. His thoughts were red behind his eyes, if he closed them, and if he held his eyes open in the room, his thoughts were black. Trying to keep his eyes closed was very hard, because then his mind was free to consider the old thoughts and the telephone. He willed that sleep should come, had to come, if only he were patient and disciplined with his mind; and if he willed that the thoughts should not come down on him. He shifted on the sheet into a new position and prepared himself to fight his mind. But the preparation was very hard. And he began thinking again.

Eric got up and went into the bathroom for the bottle of Librium. He found it in the dark and then put on the light and looked at the bottle. It was almost empty. He held it in his hand and thought about the cigarettes and the other bottles and the expense, and he knew it would be no good. The bathroom light was very bright and it hurt Eric's eyes when he looked into the mirror over the washbowl and saw his own naked body reflected much whiter than it actually was. Then he thought about the alternative to taking the Librium and, still looking into the mirror, he felt ashamed of his body. He was not pleased with darkness but he did not want to see himself or feel himself or be aware of what he was, and the darkness helped some with these things.

"It's no damn good," he said aloud in the dark and put the unopened bottle on the washbowl. Then he wanted to cry.

Going back into the bedroom, he picked up the telephone and brought it close to his bed, sat on the scattered sheets, and dialed the number in the dark. The red glow around the numbers on his clock showed it was almost 2:30 in the morning. After two rings he wanted to hang up, but something—perhaps the idea of sleeplessness, he thought—would not let him and seemed to dictate that he let the telephone ring a third, a fourth, and then a fifth time.

"Hello." He could tell that she had not been sleeping.

"Were you sleeping?" he asked anyway.

There was a little pause and some audible breathing. Eric knew she would not lie. "No," she said at last.

"I don't know why I called. I honestly don't know why."

"You couldn't sleep," she said.

"I was just thinking," he said. "Are you tired?"

"Yes."

"Are you alone?"

"Yes." Her voice was much heavier.

"Can I just talk to you?"

"What about? We've said all we have to."

"I'm sorry, truly I am."

"For what?" she said sharply. "What have *you* got to be sorry about?"

"For the way things are. Everything's just so messed up."

"And I'm black," she said. "That makes it messier." Her voice was not angry, just heavy, and Eric knew that if they talked longer she would be crying and he would have to go out walking all through the night. But he had called her, and he played with what he would say in his mind because he knew that if he was not careful he would begin to repeat himself.

"I'm sorry about everything. I'm sorry for the whole world and everybody in it. I'm sorry I'm alive." He had made his voice softer.

"Please don't do that, Eric," she said. "Oh, please, please don't start that. I just want to sleep."

He knew that he had said that too many times and now she did not believe him. "Can I see you?" he asked, his voice very close to pleading.

She was silent for a moment and Eric thought about where he would go if he had to walk. "When?" she finally said.

"Tonight. Now."

"Why now? Because it's dark? Because *you* can't sleep and want to make love?"

"That's not it at all," Eric said quickly. "You know that's not it."

"But it's what we've come to, isn't it?"

Now Eric was silent. He could say nothing more without repeating himself and he did not want to do that.

"Is this all we have left, the night, and calling whenever one of us gets horny?"

"Don't," he said. "It was so beautiful. Don't dirty it. I know I deserve it but please don't say it now."

"When *will* I say it?" she said.

"I love you," Eric said. He said it soft in the telephone and he knew that he was repeating himself, but now it did not matter. "You know I love you and I love you so much it hurts to say it the way things are. I can't sleep. I can't take any more pills. I haven't even talked to another girl since last week and I don't know if I can ever talk to another girl."

"I hate you, Eric," she said.

Now there was nothing more to repeat. "I won't call again," he said. "It was rotten of me to do this anyway."

"Eric?"

"What?"

"You can come for tonight. I don't want anything beyond tonight."

"I don't want to use you. I swear to God I don't want to just use you."

"I know," she said. "It's just that I can't sleep."

## II

Margot Payne had been very bright in school and had never learned to dance. As a child, the brightness and the sense of superiority which she began to feel over the other, less intelligent, black children in her Cleveland school had not lost her many friends, but neither had it gained her any. And the dancing, which was never really important to her, had not mattered until she was much older, and until the other children became aware of her intellectual superiority and began to resent her because of it. Then the dancing became all at once very important to her. Margot's parents were very proud of her because of the reports, but secretly they worried over her integration in the community. They urged her to dance. And her mother, a cautious, sharp woman, counseled her in little nighttime bedroom sessions about black men and how important it was for a black woman of high intelligence to make it as imperceptible as possible, because they would resent it and her for having it.

She had tried very hard to feel accepted. And although she made great efforts to laugh and mix and dance, she still grew resentful and somewhat introverted because she found that she could not talk to anyone she knew about the things that really mattered to her. She loved to discover new ideas. She loved to think, and she loved to argue. But she did very little of this. In her early teens she began to date Ray, a fellow who loved his motorcycle better than anything else in the world and who had quit school to prove it. She rode through most of Cleveland with him on the cycle, clinging to his back, and her friends saw her and the rugged, green-shirted Ray, and she was sad because she knew they had developed some respect for her only because she was on the cycle, clinging to a boy who would always be intellectually dead. And when she had tried to talk to Ray about ambition and the dividing line, represented by the cycle, between pastime and purpose, he would put her off and begin to polish the chrome on his bike. Once, when she had suggested that he get a steady job so that he could afford a car, he had looked at her from under his helmet, considered tremendously the suggestion, and said at last: "You know, you *right*, baby! You stick with me and I bet you can learn me a lot." Then she had known that it would not work and she had stopped seeing him. Afterwards, she was hurt when she saw other girls in her place on the cycle, clinging to Ray's green back, and when she realized that it was not the chrome cycle or Ray's reputation as a mover or the new girl's attractiveness to Ray that had put her there; it was Margot's own property value that had caused it, the secret, never admitted reverence and respect which the other girls had for her intelligence and her ability to choose a man of distinction. She was aware that *she* had made Ray's reputation for him merely by allowing her body and mind, and all they secretly represented to the others, to pause in idle proximity to his own native dullness as a kind of foil. And at first she thought it kind of funny, a sort of happy-sad commentary on the crass stupidity of people; but later, when she had to date boys who had no cars or cycles or even dimes for the buses, she did not think it so funny. She began to think harder about learning the dance.

She dated Hank, a big, self-assured fellow with a reputation for being mean to girls. She began to date him because in those late teenage years she had become more aware of her mind and its powers much superior to those of the people around her. She believed that she could control Hank, and in order to do it she had to be herself, smart, confident, superior, and she had to constantly remind Hank of it. In conversation she began to convince him of his own intellectual inferiority and she began to manipulate him in small ways. At first she was hesitant but then, when she observed her successes, she began to rather enjoy dictating to him where they should go, what they should do and how he should address her at certain times, and how to regard her in the company of other teenagers. In the latter part of the relationship, she took immense pleasure in constantly reminding him how much of an honor it should be for him to have a girl of her mind. The dull Hank complied, not because he was easy or grateful or a truly simple-minded person, but because he had only one motive in mind, one purpose in the total relationship for which he was firmly enduring these manipulations. Margot was a virgin, and the slow but crudely clever Hank had it in his mind that she should not be that way very much longer. And so he accepted, with a little pretense of fight, her spurts of self-assured mental superiority, her directions and daily increasing manipulations; and when the time was right for him to become conveniently angry, he did it with relish, beat her just enough to put her in her place, and then made love to her. As a final and absolute assertion of his manliness, he made her crawl naked on the floor of his room, crying and sobbing, placed one huge foot on her neck, pressing her face down, and compelled her to kiss the other. She did it. And in doing so, she forced from her mind all that she had known and all that she had ever expected to know about the dance.

### III

Eric came in the door and she stood by in her nightgown, the short pink one he had bought her, waiting, her arm raised to the door frame, her breasts obviously firm and growing under the gown. They embraced and there was the sound of sobbing between them, and Eric did not know whether it was Margot's sound or his own. It did not matter. They clung and swayed together in the dark room and pulled away from each other, from time to time, to kiss, to breathe, to exchange deep, truthful looks into eyes that could scarcely be seen in the little light coming from the bedroom. They did not talk. And at the right moment Eric lifted her up and carried her into the other room.

In the middle of it she began to cry and he had to fight himself and the animal in him to stop his hungry thrusts, and he put his hand to her face to touch the tears. He did not try to stop them with his hand; she was crying for both of them and he knew it and was grateful.

"If there was any other way," he said very carefully, "I'd take it. I do want you to be happy."

She said nothing.

"I'm sorry I came," he said. "But I *had* to."

"For this?" Her eyes were closed.

Eric thought about the truth and how, when he was younger, he had always tried to use it to ennoble himself. "Yes," he said, "for this." And now he did not feel so noble.

Margot opened her eyes and looked at Eric. He was now holding his head down, touching her breasts with his hair without meaning to. He wanted very badly to move his body again, but he did not want to be the first to start it because he knew that he would not think much of himself afterwards.

"What are we going to do?" Margot said.

"I don't know," he said.

"I don't want to marry you now," she said. "I did, I really did once but I don't want it now."

"I wish we had done it before," he said. "Before everything got all mixed up."

"I want your baby," Margot said.

Eric pulled his head up and looked at her. "What baby?"

"The one we could have now."

"How could we?"

"I haven't taken anything for a week."

Eric caught himself pulling away. Then he said: "Why didn't you tell me?"

"I want it," she said. "I don't want you but I want it. Please don't move. Please don't. Just stay here with me."

"But I don't want you to do this, not for me."

Margot began to move slowly on the bed and Eric could not help himself. "When you think about it," she was saying, "nothing in the world matters at all."

Eric did not say anything. He was caught in his hunger and it increased. He felt thirst and heat and cold, and the melting and hard feel of himself far deep inside, close, and then far away, now above him, now down there and up again. He wanted to drink, he wanted to feel himself flow all over the bed, he wanted to cry, he wanted to moan, and he felt hunger. He knew, as she did, the right moment to press closer and deeper and where to put his arms and hands and lips, and where to expect hers, and how to receive them and all there was to know about the very last delicious moments before there would be an afterwards.

"Why do people make love?"

"Because for some things they do not know how to talk."

"What does it do for a man?"

"It makes him feel very big and then it makes him feel very small."

"Why does he feel small?"

"Because sometimes he does not know what to say afterwards."

"Is it really necessary to say anything?"

"For some men it is necessary."

"Why should a man talk when he has gained everything a few minutes before?"

"Some men do not see it as a gain."

"Are there such men?"

"Many. But you will never know them in public."

"How is it that some people make such bad matches that they can only talk at night?"

"It is because they chose inconvenient options and will not admit it at least part of the time."

"Are such people crazy?"

"No. They are only people."

"What can be done for them?"

"Nothing."

"Is that really enough to have?"

"No. But see what they have in the night."

## IV

Eric Carney was a Quaker, and had been taught all his life to look for causes. His father, in their little New Hampshire town, had called it "having a sense of purpose," and Eric had looked for this sense all through his life, and had taken the search with him to college. The tremendous social sensitivity he had inherited from the ideas of his people caused him to have a great number of false starts and a great deal of hurt during his first days. But he had learned, through trial and error, to be less a do-gooder and more a genuine person. And he had learned to live with being a genuine person and to this extent he was a social pacifist. He had gone to a good college in the East, a rather conservative college, and at first there had been few causes or few opportunities for him to feel and exercise his own sense of stewardship. But he contented himself with committee work, which he found dull, unproductive and routine.

Then the Southern marches began. Eric went down with the very first car to leave the campus. It was a very small, very backward, very grievously sick Mississippi backwater town, and Eric walked in the dangerous parts of it for a semester and a summer, becoming very busy and very purposeful. Even after going into that town became a badge for people from other schools, much like himself, and even after he sensed the dissatisfaction of the local blacks with the many people of his maudlin sensitivity and perpetually understanding nature, he had tried to keep up his voter registration, community organization and other works. He was proud that he had come early, before the rush, and he was especially glad that he had not in all his time there grown a beard or used anything stronger than pot. But, for all his care, he still sensed that the locals, after having surveyed the novelty of the mass migration of innocents and the heavy smell of absolute goodness in the thick, hot air, had slowly and subconsciously rejected the bounty of spiritual munificence and did not really want him, or any of the people like him, in their primitive places. It was, he thought, not because he lacked sincerity, but because he had too much of it. When he realized this he had got angry at first; but then he also realized that there was an inverse relationship, in that town and perceptible to the natives in all their sublime innocence, between the quality of goodness and the number of people contributing to it. Then he had known that staying longer would be no good.

He returned to school in the fall, his sense of purpose shaken but just as strong. He took a black roommate in an apartment, and was extraordinarily nice when he brought in girls who were not like him. The black fellow hated him for this, but Eric never knew this or understood why.

These were the autumn days when the dialogue over making a revolution and a truly democratic society flowed loosely and desperately in the air, and hung over nighttime bull sessions with heavy cigarette smoke, and when everyone felt he had to make some movement, however slight or inconsequential, toward the attainment of goals not yet defined. Everyone was seeking something better, but there was no piper, no steady drumbeat or distant shield to lead them on to that better thing. There was only dialogue, and pamphlets of many colors to hand out, and more dialogue, albeit much more heated, and an occasional break for coffee or sex or pot, and then the words continued. There was a sense of quiet, a very heavy sound, and then there was a sense of motion, rapid and yet subtle, and slow: there were long heated talks over beer mugs late into the night when young men would rise to their feet and shake their fists in the air while girls watched them, in squatting positions, cross-legged, their eyes excited. In secret places, very well publicized, there was talk of the Party and the essentials of making a revolution, and the first Che books (abridged) were coming off the presses. And then there were martyrs in the country, many more than were needed to truly make something rapid and reforming come, the thought of which drove students to near madness and frantic conversation. But nothing happened; and nothing came except the weekends, when they relaxed, left off the dialogue and the books, and sought quieter places, away, in the country.

## V

Eric and Margot met at a small party of people resting from the week's dialogue. At first Eric thought her extremely plain; for, unlike many of his socially conscious friends, his sense of social purpose did not warp his perception or his sense of aesthetics. He had the only possible sense of beauty, having all his life been conditioned to revere a certain standard. He knew there were valid discriminations a man must make between fat girls and girls of better builds, and he also knew that color did not make any less valid these discriminations. The girl was not really beautiful. She was a very smooth near-black, with short hair, not *au naturel,* and large glasses which shielded huge, arrogantly staring eyes that moved over him and the people in the noisy room with a quickness that, to Eric looking at her, seemed almost defensive. There was a kind of stoop in her shoulders which did not make her unattractive, but Eric was most of all aware of a powerful intelligence behind those eyes which made him uneasy, and the shape of her breasts under the white blouse she wore. Much later, thinking about that night in his bed, alone, he confessed to himself that it had not really been her eyes at all that first attracted him. It had been the determined lips below them.

"Will you introduce me to him?" the girl had said directly to Eric, indicating with her bold eyes Jerry, his roommate, a very well built, very handsome and confident mulatto who had, a minute before, been conversing with Eric and who had just turned away to laugh with well-kept white teeth at something funny that someone in a small group next to Eric had said.

"His name is Jerry," Eric had said.

"Will you introduce me?" she said.

"What's your name?"

"Margot."

He had turned to his roommate. "Jerry," he said. "Jerry, I want you to meet a friend of mine."

Jerry turned away from the group and looked at Margot. "Hi," he said.

"Her name is Margot," said Eric.

"Hi, Margot," said Jerry. "Glad to know you." Then, because she did not say anything but only stared at him, making him uncomfortable because he had been laughing with three white girls, Jerry turned away again.

Eric shrugged his shoulders, as if to bear responsibility for and to dismiss the discourtesy.

"It really doesn't matter anyway," she said before he could say anything. "He wouldn't be a nice person to know."

Hearing this served to reinforce Eric's initial impression of the girl's perception, for he suddenly realized that, truthfully, Jerry was not a nice person to know. But he had never let himself admit it to his mind. He got her a drink and they talked and Eric was impressed by her very excellent command of the language. Unlike many of the blacks he knew, she did not slur her words or singsong them, or talk rapidly, or self-consciously give crisp, overdone enunciations to prove her command; she pronounced each word with a cool precision that was natural and unpracticed. She was well read in contemporary literature, and was a science major at an all-girl school which, she said, was very fine and proper but which reeked with decadence. She had a number of good ideas, all her own, so that at no point in the evening was there ever the need to retreat into the inevitable racial or revolutionary dialogue. Eric was a good listener, especially with blacks, and the evening passed without his ever having to interject into the conversation any fuel to keep it going. And then he found himself responding, talking about himself, his school, his family, his Southern mission, and the things that made up his life and the things that really mattered to him. He noticed that the girl had a peculiar method of listening: she never nodded in agreement or shook her head in disagreement, but looked severe, as if she were instantaneously evaluating in her mind all that was being said and placing him in a category. Eric felt uncomfortable, defensive, slightly agitated, and he had a sense of lacking something, for in all his previous dealings with blacks it had always been he who had felt the confidence and who communicated, in silence, the necessary understanding which made the other person feel comfortable. But now the old situation was reversed. He wished that she would smile; he wished that she would not. He did not want her to look that directly into his eyes; and then he did want it. Her expression carried an air of superiority, of absolute belonging, of something nicely like condescension about it; and alternatively, through the first part of the evening, Eric liked her very much and was afraid of her. Perhaps, he thought, it was because she really regarded him as an equal. Perhaps she thought of him as her inferior. This was a new feeling for Eric. And he liked it. Then, after their third drink, and after she had told him some funny things about the housemothers at her school and their monthly uses of *Playboy*, she smiled and there were two dimples in her face and her chin stood out, and her lips parted and Eric was not afraid any more. And then it came on him that all along she had been very beautiful and had waited, testingly, until now to show it to him.

## VI

Eric had never had a steady girl during his three and a half years at college, although he had had his own share of the total sexual experience. Now he found himself fighting longings for something steady, something certain, something in opposition to the uncertainty of the times. He thought about Margot a lot during the week, and then he put her out of his mind and got back to the dialogue. But on Thursday night she called him and the decision, which he later justified as his own, was made.

They began to date on weekends. At first he would go to pick her up at school and bring her to town on Friday nights. He tried to be very proper about it because he was aware, as he was sure she was, of the expectations which inevitably cloud this special kind of relationship. He wanted very much for it to be different. On the first three weekends he got a room for her with friends, and he kissed her only three times during all of this. At the beginning of the fourth weekend, however, he very cautiously and matter-of-factly invited her to spend the time in his apartment. She was very direct about her acceptance and it had surprised him, and even frightened him a little. The early part of the evening they spent talking to Jerry, the handsome roommate, who slyly glared at Margot whenever Eric was not looking. Jerry was that unhappy kind of person who wanted everything in the world without having to deserve it. He made certain comments involving witless sexual innuendo and laughed considerably before he went off on his own date, leaving them alone in the room. Eric was very uncomfortable and embarrassed. He sat away from her, on the floor.

"Don't feel you have to stay," he said. "If you don't want to stay, I'll understand."

"I want to stay," she said.

"Jerry is really a well-meaning person."

"You don't have to apologize for him. I know his type."

Eric had been aware for a long time, perhaps even since that slight hint at their meeting, that she did have the ability to perceive and categorize people. This confirmation, now, gave him considerable discomfort and very little to say.

"At first I thought I liked Jerry," Margot went on, "but I don't. I can't respect him."

"Why not?"

"He doesn't seem to have a purpose or anything to care about."

Eric leaned towards her on the floor. "What do *you* care about?" he asked.

"You," she said quite frankly. She was being honest because she could be no other way with him.

"Why?"

"Because you love me."

Eric thought very carefully and then found that he too could be no other way but honest. "I do," he said. "Margot, I really do."

Then she was close to him on the floor and they were kissing.

Much later that night, in the close, warm darkness of his bed, they talked. They exchanged childhoods, truthfully. Margot spoke of Ray and Hank and all the people like him who had made her very afraid to love anyone or to feel anything. Eric talked of his sense of social purpose, of stewardship, of right, and of too much wrong in the wrong, of what he had tried to do in life and what was still before him. He spoke of inequalities, racial and intellectual, of making a revolution, and of the responsibilities of his generation and the changes they must make. Margot did not care for causes: she had had a single one all her life, and she knew in her mind, in the single bed pressed very close to Eric with her breasts against his body and feeling his breathing inside herself as he talked on and on, that, unlike him, she had come closer to her singular goal in the last five hours than Eric would ever get to all of his during his life. She was happy. And she cared no more for talk of causes, even as Eric's voice went on beside her. To bring the talk closer to herself, she told him how she disliked school and how his coming had saved her from becoming an academic animal. Eric was sympathetic. He stopped his monologue and allowed her to talk. He found that her talking, her carrying the conversation, made him feel at ease and he knew that he would try very hard to keep the racial thing from touching them. Then he touched her in the dark, ever so gently, in a neutral place with his hand, and knew that the same thought was with her when she covered his hand with her own.

Going to the bathroom late that next morning, Margot passed through the living room where Jerry was sitting, apparently waiting for just this opportunity. He smiled knowingly and she pulled Eric's blue cloth robe close about her throat.

"Sleep good?" Jerry said. He smiled.

"Fine," she said.

"How was it?"

She thought of ignoring him and the comment. But then she could not because she quite suddenly had the thought that now should be the time to put Jerry in his place for the duration. "Very good," she told him.

Jerry smiled confidently. He was handsome and he had always known it. "I can do better," he said. He maintained the smile so that she could see his very white teeth shine beneath his black moustache.

"Shall I tell Eric that?" she said. "Or will you?"

"What the hell," Jerry said. "He knows it." He smiled some more. Then he added, almost an intentional afterthought: "I'll call you sometime this week."

Now she looked at him and smiled, indicating with her eyes not flattery but amusement. "Don't bother."

"You can't be serious about *him*. He's a crazy liberal. He doesn't even know what he's doing yet."

Margot remembered the evening she had first seen Jerry from across a room and how she thought he was very striking. She remembered how he had snubbed her, and the three white girls with him, and how they had smiled at her in amusement, confident that their handsome plaything could not be taken from all three of them by her. She disliked Jerry for allowing them to smile at her that way. Now she wanted to hurt him.

"How was your Anglo-Saxon last night?" she asked.

"Very good." Jerry's teeth flashed white again as he smiled.

"Do you think she'll call *you* again next weekend, or somebody else?"

"What the hell do you mean? I got her in my *bag!*"

"And she comes whenever you call?"

"Yeah."

"Why?"

"*She's in my bag!*" Jerry said. He was not smiling. He was getting very irritated.

Margot knew that she was winning. "Next time she calls," she told Jerry, "before you go running over, ask her to describe your face."

"What the hell is *that* supposed to mean?" said Jerry.

But she had gone into the bathroom and locked the door. And Jerry sat on the chair in the living room, thinking, not quite sure whether or not he had been cut. Then he laughed aloud, with an unnatural enthusiasm calculated to carry the sound into the bathroom and above the noise of the running shower. He had decided that the thing was not a cut. The idea of its being so was silly. His girl was the liberated daughter of one of the oldest and wealthiest families in the East, and a sufficient amount of its three generations of money was firmly invested in his car, his clothes and his pockets.

"Silly bitch," Jerry said aloud. "What a silly bitch this is."

## VII

Margot found that she could not bring herself to study even a little during the week. She found that she did not want to do anything. She found that she loved to spend the week thinking about the weekends. She liked to lie on her bed during the day and play with ideas, both his and her own, carefully held over and salvaged from the last weekend. She liked to glance up at the framed picture of him on her dresser and discover new ways of seeing his face. She liked to have other girls come in the room and watch them become uneasy when they saw the picture. She especially liked it when they felt they had to say something nice about his looks: the sharpness of his nose and how well it sat on his sensitive face, the thrust and determination and sensitivity of his chin, the warm eyes, the way his mouth was sad but almost smiling. She liked the way they would inevitably ask if they were going to get married, and the way some of the girls made little impromptu social observations, almost in apology, when she said that they were very seriously considering it. And she tried not to see the way some of them would smile, secretly, and look at other girls in a knowing way.

She waited for weekends and did nothing else. And when they came they were very beautiful, and she always brought new ideas away from them back to the campus and her room, to be selectively considered and tested against her own until the next weekend. She failed two final examinations, but did not care because she knew that she did not want to pass them. And when, in June, there were no more weekends, they went away together to a California town, very small and colorful and very close to the beaches, for the summer. They did Eric's community work by day, and walked the warm-sanded beaches by night. Eric wrote small poems for her in the wet, white sand and she learned to memorize them very quickly, in the moonlight, before the white foam, pushed in by the inevitable sea, came up the beach to wash them away. Sometimes they lay in the quiet of the warm night, the waves coming up to their naked feet, and talked and kissed and looked up at the stars and out to where they met the distant waterline. Again he spoke of his societal obligations, and again she listened selectively to what was said. She did not want to think of society or community, at night in the dark warm wet sand, or anything beyond herself and that part of him which gave her happiness.

"We ought to get married," he had said close to her ear one night. "We ought to do it while it's still summer."

She thought of the girls and their social commentaries, and had said: "Everybody thinks we're in for it."

"I don't care," Eric said. "I know what I want."

"I wouldn't want you to hate me later, when it hurts."

"I can't hate," he said. "It's not in me."

"But people can put it there."

He kissed her ear. "Everything's changing now. In a few years nobody'll give it a second thought."

"It's nice to think that."

"But it's true," he said. "You'll see. As soon as everybody over thirty-five dies, it'll be a new society."

"I don't want to trap you through an idea, Eric. You could be wrong, and then you'll hate me for it."

Eric had never thought about being wrong himself. Only fighting what he believed to be wrong was in his conception of stewardship. "You'll see," he assured her. "Only people over thirty-five have this thing. If we can't change them, we'll just wait them out."

"Listen," Margot said, "please don't make me a crusade. I just couldn't stand being that."

"How can you say that. I love you."

"Just don't."

He had kissed her again and then they lay very still and quiet in the night and waited for the bigger waves to drive them further up onto the beach.

## VIII

That fall she had left school for good, telling her parents that she could not bear its isolation any longer and that she could learn more on her own, reading, meeting intellectual people, and working for a time in the city. She found a secretarial job, very close to where Eric lived, and together, armed with a list of fair housing subscribers, they found a small apartment for her. At first they had considered living together, but she had rejected the idea because of her parents, two extremely class-conscious, fatally middle-class people, and the grief she had caused them by quitting school. They both agreed that living apart for a while would be better, and that they could always move into her apartment if they found separate living quarters too inconvenient.

The domesticity began. Eric went to classes and she went to work, and they met every day for lunch. Then Eric went back to study and she went back to work, and they met again, in the evening, at her apartment, for dinner and the afterwards. She taught herself to cook and she learned to invent new things in her kitchen, just to surprise him. He would always be very happy when he came in to something new she had done, and sometimes they would cling to each other in that happiness for so long that they did not eat until late into the night.

One weekend he drove her to New Hampshire to meet his parents. They were Quakers and had known that their son was bringing a special girl home, but when they arrived the father was away in the woods, hunting, and the mother, a slim, well-preserved woman of fifty with brown hair like Eric's, had given them tea and then sat across the room in a single cushioned chair and looked at Margot, politely, but very close to tears.

"We'll get married tonight," Eric had told her driving home in the car. "We've got to do it now if we're going to."

"No. Not now," she said. She had been cut, and knew that whatever dignity she had managed to bring away from that house would not let her take advantage of Eric's embarrassment. "We'll wait."

"They're over thirty-five," he said. "They can't understand."

She was thinking very rapidly now. "Half the world is over thirty-five," she said. "What are we trying to prove?"

"Nothing. It's just that we've got a right to live."

She was silent as he speeded along the turnpike. She wanted him to go much faster. She wanted to get out of the car and run much, much faster than it was moving. She wanted to cry. "Let's drop it for a while," she said abruptly. "It might be good if we both started seeing other people."

"Why?"

"It might just be good."

"I don't want you to see anybody else."

"It's no good this way."

"Then let's just get married."

"No."

"You don't love me."

"That's not it," she said. "I'm just scared of your ideas."

He looked over at her, next to the window. She was looking out at the blur of black and dark green trees in the forests along the road.

"What's wrong with my ideas?" he said.

"I don't know. I don't know if I'm a person to you or an idea. Right now, back there, I felt like a damn cause."

"That's silly," he said. But he said it very slowly. "You know that's silly."

Margot made no reply. And they drove the rest of the way into the city in almost total silence. Leaving her at the door to her apartment, Eric held his head down and put his hand on her arm.

"We'll wait," he told her. But he held his head so that she could not see his eyes.

## IX

The students had got a fresh dialogue going because there was a war being fought somewhere, for no reason at all. The unabridged Che books had now come into the stores and many people were making a living printing anti posters of different colors. People were fasting now who had never known hunger in their lives, and they did these things in groups and wore badges so that they would be known. This was a great inclusive dialogue and it had room for the words of many people. Everyone had to contribute, everyone could contribute, there was a solid front of words. The same people who had been very good in the South a few years before and who had faded with the exodus and with the coming of black awareness, now came back, more colorful, more determined, more aggressive in their new goal. In college communities up and down the East Coast, people shunned parties where there was no dialogue. There were great migrations of these people across the country, displaced by a hard depression that was not economic; rootless, searching people, coming and going in the night, sleeping in basements and grouped in parks, cross-legged, long-haired, talking, always talking and plotting openly the fall of something secret. Everyone had hair, everyone grew it long, as if in this there could be some statement of self-assertion, an affirmative break with tradition. But everyone began to look alike, and for some, it, and the dialogue, became no good.

Eric did not grow his hair long. He was too much of a thinker. He saw insincerity and infidelity to the cause in the crowd, and he kept clear of certain of its elements. It had always been his philosophy that deeds should be the proper advertisement of a man, and so he kept his hair brown and short and his chin clean, and said very little. He was also selective about groups and certain people who espoused impossibilities. But the dialogue he loved, and he kept close to it, because it helped him to forget other things, things it would do him no good to remember. He was waiting. But he did not know or bring himself to understand just what he was waiting for. Sometimes he thought it was Margot; and sometimes he knew it was not. Sometimes he thought it was a vigil, his self-created wake for everyone over thirty-five. And then he sometimes thought it might be that he was waiting for everything and everyone about him, and not just those people over thirty-five, to end.

But waiting for something, waiting for everything to end, was very hard; especially at night. Eric had to take pills in order to wait. And still nothing happened. Going, always going, to the antiwar dialogue was not enough; something was still missing. He began to have truthful talks with himself, in his mind, at night, in bed, alone. And he recognized that he loved and needed Margot, not because she was black and married by nature to a cause that had once been very close to him, but because for over a year he had been making room for her inside himself through a slow and secret process of which he had not, until now, been aware; and now there was all that room, reserved and waiting, and he had nothing to fill it. Talk of the Revolution and the War was not enough; the words had no substance at night, when there was no group, when all those who talked went away in couples, boys and girls, enchanted with the ideas that had flowed and determined to carry the discussion further when they were alone, again in couples, again boys and girls. Eric had a void in his mind, an empty space in his bed, and a nothingness in that special place he had made that ate at him, especially in the night. He had the capacity; but nowhere was there a girl who could fill all the space inside him. It would take at least two, or perhaps three girls to do it, if it could be done at all. But he wanted only one, and he could not call her, he thought, because of the profound dilemma with which he found himself confronted. Both horns of it touched on marriage. If he asked her again, he knew that she would think it was for the same old reasons that frightened her: the cause, his slightly paternalistic attitudes, his reaction against his family and his crusade against people over thirty-five. She would refuse and he knew that he could never convince her that it was any other way with him because he did not know himself what his real motives were. On the other hand, if he saw her again without ever proposing marriage, it would intimate to her that she had been right all along, and that he thought of her only as a cause, an idea, a purpose, and that when the time came for an affirmation of his motives, his silence would make him seem guilty of a recognition in himself of these, the very suspicions she held against his motives. He could not call her and yet he could not get her out of his mind.

And then one night he had called her after a week of rationalizing in his mind that he could no longer sleep until he did it. And later, in her bed, she had wanted his baby and he could not give it to her because he was afraid of the dilemma and how it could get to be very complicated if that should come about. He had left the next morning, very early, before she came awake. But before he left the room he paused over the bed and looked down at her, asleep and, in her own secret way, very beautiful. He wanted to touch her or do something, leave something there in the bed, in the room, to show her when she woke that he remembered all the good that had been and still existed, however far away it went at times, and that he still had the capacity with him, waiting. But if he touched her he knew that she would wake up and talk, and there was only that one thing he could leave, the complicating thing, and so he could only look down at her, and then walk away.

## X

"Eric? *Eric.*"

It was morning and he had gone. Margot did not move from the bed. She knew that he had gone and she did not want more hurt by looking in the kitchen or the bathroom. She also knew that he would not be back; if he came at all, ever again, it would never again be the way he had come in the night, just before dawn, five hours before.

She did not want to go to work, although she was very late; and so she remained in bed. She was empty and she could not bear being empty and covering the space she felt with clothes and walking streets crowded with fuller people, people going someplace important to them and doing things essential to them in these places, and then returning, much later in the evening, to better places to meet the valued persons who were the very reason for their coming and going and living each day just for the end of it. She had none of these things and did not want to be near people who felt something more than the nullity she knew was within her.

She fell asleep. And when she opened her eyes again it was late afternoon by the sound of the homeward traffic outside her bedroom window. She looked up, in the bed, and watched the white ceiling getting to be darker shades of white, and she was trying in her mind to draw some philosophical lesson and relevance to her own situation out of the way the ceiling was getting when she fell asleep again. When she awoke this time the room was quite dark and it was late night outside. Voices were calling other voices, and someone, a girl, was laughing from far away down the street. Then she started to cry. Being in the darkness made her sob even harder and soon she could not control her movements on the bed and fell out of it, slowly, uncaring, onto the floor, where she continued sobbing. Such was the heavy sound of her own voice in the totally dark room, that she scarcely heard the banging on the door and the loud voice behind it.

"How long will this girl cry?"
"Until she is quite sure she can feel nothing else."
"For whom does she cry?"
"For herself, and all those like her who come into the better options."
"But see her now. Is this a better thing?"
"At least she is suffering. Cowardly people never suffer."
"How can practicality be cowardly?"
"It stifles growth."
"Can one say that she is growing?"
"Yes. She is building something."
"What?"
"Something inside herself."
"But will it help her?"
"Come and see what it will hold out. And note also what it will hold in. Come and see how she will grow."

## XI

Margot Payne began to do volunteer community work in a ghetto Housing Office three nights a week and all day on Saturday. She was very efficient with the poor who had dealings with her; but no one of them could say that he had ever seen her smile. The Revolution talk had drained the ghetto of its once plentiful store of volunteer workers and her coming to the inefficiently run Housing Office had a double advantage: first of all it provided her with as much work as she wanted for as much time as she needed to give, and it gave the office the benefit of her desire to accomplish as many things of a material, substantive nature as she could handle. Secondly, it allowed her to come into her blackness again.

She was intelligent, alert, and far more efficient than most of the paid employees in the office. But the high school graduates, the girls, did not envy her because she never said anything of a personal nature or smiled at any of the men in the office. This made her somewhat mysterious and extremely interesting to many of the men who worked there. One of those, who was very interested in her and her reasons for working so long and hard in a place where most people merely pretended to work and found excuses to get out of the office most of the time, was Charles Wright.

Wright was a plodder, a fellow of average intellect and even less perception. He had taken a rather dubious degree in history and political science at a very small, very unknown college somewhere in the South, which qualified him to do nothing at all. But having this small badge, and being black besides, *was* more than adequate credentials to qualify him for a job in one of the many federally sponsored ghetto projects, where he was paid rather handsomely to administrate promises and frustrate the lives of poor people. This was not intentional on his part; he saw it rather as his taking advantage of an unchangeable system full of cynical blunderers, incompetents and do-gooders before someone else took advantage of it. To him it was a matter of trying to make the best possible life for himself in an organization which would retaliate against anyone who genuinely tried to make things work.

Because he was a plodder, very few girls had ever been nice to him, and his primary purpose in taking such a job had been to earn the necessary capital to purchase a car, prestige whiskey, a good apartment, and well-tailored clothes; all of which he expected to use in luring a wife. It had not worked; and now he was seven years out of school and wifeless. Although he wore a full beard and stylish clothes and tried to maintain the image of a rather reserved swinger, inwardly he was desperate and searching and still a plodder. He was almost twenty-eight. And the girls to whom he was nice, and from whom he patiently expected eventual reciprocation, saw that he was an old plodder and knew that they did not have to be nice to him. He was persistent in being good when dealing with reluctance and was persistently used by girls of even very slight social significance. He got very little sex because most of the girls with whom he shared an evening in his apartment could sense, in his eagerness to please, that he was the nondemanding kind of fellow who, if put down on the first or second or even the third date, would nevertheless call again, always once more, for another evening.

Margot had refused his first invitations. But then, on weekends and sometimes late at night, the loneliness got into her and she knew that she needed something. She had perceived all there was to know about Charles Wright during her first few weeks in the office and knew that it was only necessary to be nice to him, with certain reservations set out beforehand, and he would be all right. In her misery and in her recreation of something solid within her, she recognized that she needed someone to be very interested in her; someone always close at hand over whom she could exercise some control. She had called Charles Wright at first, some six or so weeks after his last invitation to dinner in his apartment had been extended. He was in the exact state as when they last talked and was very, very eager to cook dinner for her.

And it began that way. They began to date very frequently, and being nice to Charles and knowing that she was giving him her company out of charity rather than any genuine interest in him as a man, made her feel a little good. She tried very hard to lose what was still left of her old self in him. And he was grateful for her company, and for that alone. Of course he tried from time to time to seduce her, but each attempt, and they were relatively few, ended with his pathetically begging her for something she knew she could not give. She pitied him, she did not love him, and she could not make herself give anything to him, although she pitied his pleadings. They went out, they sat and talked, they kissed, they smiled and held off and then kissed some more. But all of it made her feel nothing.

"I don't want to take advantage of you," Charles told her once in his bedroom after being put off again. "I won't take advantage of you."

"I know that."

"I really like you a lot, you know that?"

She was silent.

"In fact," Charles said, "I love you."

"You shouldn't," she had said. "You shouldn't love anybody."

"All I want is to get married," said Charles. "To be honest, that's all I really want."

Again she said nothing.

"Do you want to marry me?"

She thought about it for a minute, how it would be to see his face for year after year and to know his mind before he even knew it himself. "I can't marry anybody," she said at last.

"Is it because of Eric?" Of course she had told him about Eric.

"No. That's really all over now." She made her face very firm. "I think I hate him now."

"You ought to get married or something. Go back to school. If you don't, you're bound to get used by other guys."

"I don't think so."

"You know I wouldn't use you, don't you?"

"I know." She put her hand on his knee and thought about Eric and their last night and the eternity of a day afterwards. And then she thought about how she was crying in the dark and the banging and voices from her apartment door that made her stop crying. She had gone to the door with a sheet wrapped around her body. It was Jerry, Eric's roommate, drunk, loud, insistent that she sleep with him now that it was all over between Eric and herself. Jerry had even brought a friend along. Both of them knew that it was all over. Both of them insisted that she sleep with them. She had slammed the door and fallen to the rug on the living-room floor. And then she had really cried.

"I can't marry anybody," she said to Charles. "I can't love anybody."

He kissed her on the forehead, very tentatively and with the greatest tenderness, lest she should misconstrue his meaning.

"I do like you," she said. And then she kissed him back, and in her mind decided that she should be nice to him in the only way possible to prove the little affection she was holding out to him.

It was not very hard to like Charles Wright. He had in him a store of affection and tenderness, possibly saved from all the girls who had never been nice to him, which he poured over her. He was a very violent and very satisfying lovemaker, as though she represented to him all the women he had never had and would ever have in this life. He was satisfying and he was kind.

Sometimes, in the night, when a nervous spasm went through her body and caused her to wake, she would look up and see him, eyes white and genuinely concerned in the dark, his hand stroking her body, not sensually, but paternally and soothing.

"What's the matter?" he would ask.

"Nothing."

"Do you want to take something?"

"No."

"Was it a bad dream?"

"It wasn't a dream. I get that way sometimes."

"Do you really love me?" he would ask.

Now she would feel good toward him because he was there and so desperate in his eyes for some certain affirmation of even the slightest affection. "I really do," she would tell him. And then sometimes they would make love, or just lie close together and sleep in his bed, because he did not want her to be away, for a single night, in her own bed.

"I really do love you," she would say again, and make it the last thing said before sleep came. And when it did come, in her thoughts all night, she believed it and came close to the border territories of happiness.

## XII

Few women had ever been nice to Charles Wright. It was not because of his lack of looks or status: he had both these things. His many failures before, during and even after college when he had arrived at a comfortable station in life might have come because, like so many other plain people, there was very little about him that was exciting. He represented stability at its very worst. And while this condition might have worked well to his advantage with older women, it did him very little good among the girls to whom his appetites went; girls much younger than himself. In his thoughts was a sad obsession, a kind of deadly flirtation with capturing all the youthful pleasures he had missed while he had been making his way up in life. He poured his feelings freely onto girls who, because of their age and the excitement of the times and environment, had very little use for men of stability. He could have had many younger girls, if that was all he wanted. But he craved more; he wanted very desperately to marry one and pull her out of the crowd. And marriage, to the girls who represented the most excitement for him, was something to be put off for years, or until they could do no better. Charles still had all his hair, and a beard, but he no longer liked to dance or experience new things. He was older and almost set in his ways and had created a life-style that, while not totally unpleasant, was extremely ritualized. And Charles found it very difficult to make the slightest variances in it. He went to work and ate at set times, he went to bed before 1:00 A.M. and he preferred to date only on weekends. Although he had a relatively new convertible, he would never drive it with the roof down. He watched certain dubious shows on television, preferred classical music to jazz or folk-rock, and liked to talk, in open conversation, about his personal problems rather than those of the times. As a husband he would have been a very good find for some girl in her late twenties, but as a companion for a girl barely into her twenties, he had very little property value.

Then, quite rapidly, he began to undergo a sort of metamorphosis that came about primarily through his relationship with Margot. She made him go to places where, a few months earlier, he would have felt quite inadequate. They frequented discothèques, secret parties where pipefuls of marijuana and stronger drugs were passed about; they walked in the woods on weekends and mingled with people who eagerly talked of riots and the making of a revolution. In going along with Margot in her desperate sallies to forget and to live her life to the fullest, Charles Wright began to alter his life-style, and his property value increased tremendously. He grew his beard fuller, which made him look younger. He dressed less conservatively, and he talked less of himself and more of the problems of a generation that was no longer his own.

Quite suddenly, he was no longer the same dullard that he had been. His property value was up and he began to notice it. He began to think more about enjoying himself for the moment and less about entertaining with the idea of possible marriage always in his mind, quite close to his present plans. And what was even more remarkable was the happy knowledge that other girls, younger girls, seeing him in this blissful state with Margot, began to take an interest in him. Very soon, younger, permissive, exciting girls, the ones he had always wanted, became available for dates; for by pure chance, he had fallen thankful victim to that peculiar desire of uncertain, searching young girls to want only what other not-so-searching young girls have. Charles Wright now received flirtations and invitations from girls who only three months before would not have looked at him once. And typically, like so many of those who have been denied all the things they think they have always wanted and then fall over facsimiles of what the old ideas had been, Charles began to take advantage of as many accessibilities as he could touch. This newly blown popularity bubble went quite to his head and he began to make some radical changes in his style. While he had always been a weekend dater, even confining most of his outings with Margot to weekends, he now began to sneak out during the week, after work. He suddenly discovered why coffeehouses were made dark, and he joined those who frequented the coffee circuit and the luncheon-date route; and he also found that he too had a touch of a certain form of wit which some girls found exciting and pleasing and entertaining. Now he began to bring girls into his bed on nights when he had very carefully arranged for Margot to be sleeping in her own.

He was nervous about this at first; he had been really moral and was new to rationalizations. The first girl's name was Marsha, a girl not black, but who was looking to drown herself in blackness. She was from a very rich family and was, predictably, in revolt against its money and status and traditions. She was seeing a psychiatrist, like many, many girls caught up in the nebulous ideas of the times, and she catered exclusively to black men because, she told him, they were just beautiful.

On the first summer night in his apartment he had played for her a very old, scratched album of an obscure black jazz pianist from his youth. The picture on the cover of the album showed him a very old, toothless, dissipated man.

"Oh he's *so* beautiful," Marsha had said. "Look at his color. See how his face changes colors when you look at it from different angles."

"Yeah, he is," Charles agreed.

"*You're* beautiful," she said.

"Thank you," said the uncertain Charles.

"Everyone in your race is beautiful. Everybody but me. I'm not at all pretty."

"But you are," he protested.

"No, I'm not," she said sadly. "I don't tan well."

"But you don't *need* a tan. You look good the way you are."

"I'm pale and ugly. All of us are too pale. Everybody in the world ought to be black or at least brown."

This was a notion never before touched upon in Charles's mind and he gave it good consideration. "I don't know," he finally said. "Being brown never did *me* much good."

"I know," Marsha said. "It's a dirty shame. Don't you hate us for it?"

"No."

"Well, *goddamn!* You should!"

Suddenly the idea registered in Charles's mind and he knew the vocabulary he should use to make the evening go all right.

"I guess I do," he said slowly and seriously.

"I know you do and I'm sorry. Truly I am."

"That's all right."

"Do you hate me?"

Charles looked at her: hair long and brown, eyes very green, lips nice and pulled down at the corners, sadly, in anticipation of his answer.

"I'll try real hard not to," he said.

She was very grateful. So much so that she was very nice to him that night in his bed.

"Is it a bad thing to feed on sickness?"

"If everything grows from it, feeding becomes necessary in order to live."

"Does it make one feel bad?"

"Only if one spends time thinking about it."

"Are we all as ill as we pretend to be?"

"No. But it is still better for the mind if one does pretend."

"Why?"

"In order to rationalize appetites."

"Are appetites everything in life?"

"Almost."

"Then what is left of fidelity?"

"Very much. But only when it is convenient."

"Then this is not the first moral man to fall?"

"No. But he will flatter himself by thinking that."

"Is he *really* a good man?"

"A long time ago he was not. But now he is about to be. He is coming into his morality."

After that it was not very hard for other girls to get to be nice to Charles. He began to rather enjoy letting them. He began to enjoy the ways he was learning of lying to Margot. He began to enjoy the way she seemed to worry when he was late and unnervous meeting her after work in the evening. And when he was with her at parties or in groups of their friends, his private ones among them, he began to enjoy the secret looks he could exchange with certain people without her ever knowing who, and why it was being done.

One night Margot found something unfortunate in his bed and sat thinking for a few minutes. She looked at him, wrapped in a towel, just out of the shower and regarding himself in a mirror. He took a long time before the mirror combing his hair and picking at his thick beard. He took a long time just looking at himself. Then, after she had picked up the thing in the bed and looked at it closely, she quite suddenly began to reconsider the advantages of having Charles, even as he reconsidered his own advantages in the mirror. She brushed another brown hair off the pillow and behind the bed.

"We ought to get married," she said. "I've been thinking it over and you're right. I guess I'm ready for it now."

Charles turned from the mirror but did not rush over to the bed and embrace her thankfully, as she had expected. He just looked at her. She waited for him to speak. He said nothing.

"Don't you want to marry me?"

"Sure," he said. "Sure I do. And we'll do it too. In a few years."

"But just two months ago you were *begging* me to marry you."

"I still am. But I've been thinking about it. We don't really know each other yet."

"It's been ten months already. How long does it take to be sure, anyway?"

Charles came over from the dresser and sat beside her on the bed. He touched her face. "Look," he said. "I tell you the truth. I need a better job before we can do it. I want to give you everything I can when we do it."

"That's not the real reason and you know it," she said.

"What other reason *would* I have?"

She thought about the brown hair and about Eric and the girls at school, and she felt about to explode. But she had made something solid inside herself from all her sufferings, something that took complete control just before emotion came; and so it allowed her to sit there while he talked on and on about the guilt he felt over his job, about how he wanted them to live in style, about how hard it was for an almost confirmed bachelor to change his habits quickly, about the summer riots and the possibility of concentration camps for blacks and his daily musing about leaving the country. But he said not one word about the brown hair.

"What does that leave for us?" she had said after Charles had run quite out of excuses.

"We'll do it for sure in a little while," he said. "When everything's settled."

"Maybe I won't be around then," she said flatly.

Charles smiled, his newly acquired confidence shining through his teeth. "You'll be around," he said.

And she was always around after that. Margot made it a point to always be around, unexpectedly, after work or late at night when she knew he expected her to be at home. She made a very special point of telling all their friends that they were planning to be married, and was especially decisive in announcing to a fellow who called her at home when Charles was there, that she was now engaged and expected to be married within a month, or two at the most. Charles, sitting at her table and pensively eating the dinner she had cooked for him, was very nervous and said nothing after she had hung up. That night he went home early and when she called him later, at 1:30 A.M., she could tell by his breathing and carefully worded sentences that he had been drinking and that he was not alone.

Seeing Eric when she was with Charles was the hardest part. He would always be alone, and looked always sad. And she would know that, had it not been for the hard, careful thing that was growing inside her, she would not have slighted him or refused to smile the many times they met by chance at a party or a lecture or in the street, when she had done just that. He and Charles always spoke and were extremely polite to each other, and she did not think it fair that they should be so resigned and without any indications of rivalry. But they were always friendly, and though they said very little, she knew that they respected each other; although that respect was uncomfortable and maintained, she liked to think, for her benefit. That irritated her. But what irritated her most was Eric's never offering congratulations to them, as if he did not know they were to be married. She wanted him to say something, to call her aside and plead with her not to do it, to offer threats against the marriage, against Charles. But, in the streets or at parties or wherever the three of them met, he only waved or made polite small talk, his eyes only suggesting to her own what she knew, what she expected, what she found herself wanting him to say.

Now she became obsessed with the idea of marriage. She pounded at it in bedtime talks with him; she repeated the announcement to her friends, his friends, to all the people he respected, that their ceremony was imminent and just a matter of months away. On three occasions she took him to her home in Cleveland to meet her family, and they liked him. They seemed to like him more after each visit. And she reminded him of this, constantly, persistently, encouragingly, along with promptings that he should set a date as soon as possible. She found herself driven to having a date, set and certain, waiting for her to meet it, waiting for it to meet her, and save her from something hard and cold and lonely, something around which she could not form words. It was something beyond love now, or something below it, or something that had nothing at all to do with love. She did not know.

"I don't care about you having other girls," she told him one hot August evening in his bedroom. "It really doesn't matter to me if you have all the girls you think you need until we get married. I really don't mind at all. Just tell me *when*."

"We'll do it one day," he had told her, thinking about a new girl he had met, a friend of Margot's, who had made certain intimations that, if given the opportunity, she would be very nice to him. "We'll do it one day, soon too."

"September? October? *When?*"

Charles thought about it. About all of it. "Maybe I better get a new job first. I'm not making enough at the Housing Office."

"That's stupid," she said. "You don't even *work* at the Housing Office. You get paid twelve thousand dollars a year for doing nothing." She looked into his eyes. They were moving away from hers in the dark room. "That's plenty for two people to live on."

"What do you know?" he said. "I do my part. What are you trying to do, run my life?" He sat up in the bed and reached over to the table, feeling for a cigarette.

She knew that he was trying to get the start of an argument out of her. And she knew why he was doing it. "No," she said resignedly. "I'm sorry."

"Don't think you can walk into my life and run it. I got along good before I met you. I can still do it too."

"I'm sorry," she said again.

"You're not the *only* girl in the world that wants to get married."

She did not answer.

"I'm about the best thing that ever happened to you. And I know it."

Now she was looking up at the darkness on the white ceiling. It was in gray and black patterns, and the gray was hard to distinguish from the black. Charles puffed on his cigarette. He was not angry and he knew it. He was just safe.

"Charles?" she said, still lying back and looking up at the patterns on the ceiling.

"Yeah."

"*Please* marry me."

Charles could feel himself getting angry. He tried not to be but it seemed no good to try. He felt like he had just run over a rabbit or a squirrel or a bird in the dark with his car and he was angry because he could not stop at once to see if it was still alive. He felt bad.

"We'll talk about it," he said.

The new girl's name was Karen. She was chubby and aggressive but she had a certain laugh and a mind quite a lot sharper than Charles's, and he was very interested in her, although he did not want to be seen with her in public places because she was chubby and because she was a friend of Margot's. After the first time she came up she had suggested that they live together. She had already been quite nice to Charles and, with the suggestion of cohabitation, promised to be even nicer. This suggestion had frightened Charles at first because he did not know how to accept anyone beyond Margot in his bed in the morning. None of the other girls had ever stayed over because Margot had a key and sometimes stopped at his apartment for coffee on her way to work; and he tried to be cautious enough to remove all evidence of the previous night's visitor and to always wake up alone, just in case Margot came in before he left for work or after he had gone. But the thought of having someone permanent, albeit chubby, in his bed in the morning without matrimonial ties or the threat of them was a new one for Charles, one that merited some consideration.

"Think about it," said Karen. "Just don't think too long. I can always go someplace else."

"I'm thinking about it now," he told her.

Karen leaned closer to him on the sofa. "Of course you could have other girls just like I would see other fellows. But neither of us should have any regulars."

"Why do you want to move in?" Charles asked.

"I like you," she said. "I like men who know what they're doing. There're too many boys around. You can't grow with them."

"But you don't want to marry me?" said Charles. He was thinking very fast, almost faster than his capacity to think.

She looked him full in the face and then went all sad around the mouth. "Not now," she said. "You know how bad the times are. My parents might bitch about it. They aren't bad people, but they honestly aren't ready for it yet. I really want to do it. I really might do it someday, but just think about the times and all the trouble I'd be inviting."

"It was just a thought," said Charles.

The girl was relieved. She put her hand on his knee and looked directly into his eyes with some sad indications of passion in her own. "One day it'll all be different," she said. She patted his knee, reassuringly.

"Yeah," said Charles. "It was just a thought."

"But we could still live together."

"Yeah," Charles said. "We could still do that."

"And no regulars for me and no regulars for you."

The thoughts were very hard for him to face now and he wanted to stop thinking about the rabbits and birds he might crush and never see for the speed of his car. He wondered if birds had an awful lot of blood in them. He wondered if birds bled after they had been crushed and were dead. He wondered if Karen cared or whether she would stop her car if she should ever crush something. And he wondered if after being with her, he would care. But he was tired of thinking.

"We'll talk some more about it later," he told her.

Karen smiled at him and then moved very close to Charles on the sofa.

Margot Payne did not sleep well at night. She did not want to lie on her back because then she would have to look up at the ceiling. And if she lay on her belly her face would be pressed down into the pillow, and before she knew it there would be a wet spot on the pillow. She was losing control over her crying and now seemed to do it whenever she was in bed alone, or whenever something not human pressed close against her breast and body. Now she found that the bed was responsible for the tears and there was no way open in her mind to rationalize their coming when they did. Earlier, before Charles had undergone his metamorphosis, she had been quick to assign the cause of them to Eric. But now, with this thing happening to Charles and with the growth of her dependency on him, she was able to make other assignments for the crying. It was Charles's fault, and it was the fault of many of her friends, girls who, unsuspecting of the consequences to her, took him to their breasts for a while because he seemed to them, for the moment, an exciting thing to have, and taking him for the moment seemed like an exciting thing to do. And while she understood this and the way they were, it gave her small comfort knowing the causes, and it did not help sleep come any easier. She found it very difficult to approach sleep.

She was thinking about Charles Wright all the time now. She could not help herself. He was very little like Eric, but, like Eric, she could sense him slipping away from her. And like Eric, there was nothing she could do to hold him. This was especially hard to understand because she knew that, having a mind that was by far superior to his, she should have had very little difficulty. But she did. The marriage bothered her too. She did not know if she really wanted the thing itself or just the comfort which she expected to draw from the mere idea of a date, a point, something on which her mind could be fixed and something that promised an afterwards and at the same time an end to the uncertainty she was feeling. She did not know exactly why she wanted it; but she wanted it.

Sometimes in the night when she could not sleep she would watch the late show or listen to the radio or read textbooks from school which she should have read two years before. And sometimes she would walk, not with direction, but aimlessly, wherever her mood carried her body. She did not walk to be picked up by boys on the street or men in passing cars; she was faithful, she told herself, to what she was; and she was, she told herself, a girl about to be married or about to know when it was that she was going to be married. She walked because she could not sleep.

And walking one night the idea suddenly came to her that a certain airline offered special honeymoon flights to Bermuda for hesitant people who chose to wait until September to get married. It was still late August and there was still time to get married and make the special rates for September honeymooners. She thought that she should tell Charles about this immediately and not stop over for coffee the next morning with the news, when it would not be as fresh and exciting and inspirational. She went to his apartment, content with the idea that more than justified her coming to wake him after twelve, and only a little apprehensive over what she might find there. Charles was a long time coming to the door, arriving at least five minutes after her third knock. She did not want to use her key.

"What do you want?" he had opened the door only a little way and stood behind it in his robe looking out at her, with something in his face quite a long way from sleep. "What do you want?" he said again.

"Let's have a cup of coffee. I have something good to tell you."

Charles held the door firm, opened only as much as would allow his face to show. But that was enough to tell her everything.

"Aren't you going to invite me in?"

"It's late. If I drink coffee I won't be able to get to sleep and I have to work tomorrow."

"We can just talk, then. Can't I come in?"

Charles made his words very precise now. It took a great deal of control because there were hundreds of words in his mouth all trying to say different things about the different feelings that were going through him. "I really wish you wouldn't," he said, selectively. "I really wish you would just go home and come back tomorrow morning for the coffee."

She stood in the hall and understood what was in the house and why his head had to be held against the edge of the door. And she also understood now just why she had come. The special rates for honeymooners was no new thought; her mind had just made it convenient.

"You have company?"

"No. Of course not. No."

"Can't I spend the night here?"

"I really wish you wouldn't."

Then there was the sound of someone's yawn from the bedroom; a sound, it seemed to Margot, that was deliberate and domestic and possessive at the same time. It was a bored sound and it made her go all tight inside when he, in some play at slyness, shifted his eyes momentarily from her face to the direction of the sound.

And now something went out of her, away, distant, ghostlike in its passage from her as she stood there. But Charles did not see it go and for a moment she felt sorry for him, almost as sorry for him as she was feeling for herself.

"I just came by to tell you," she began. Then she made her voice louder. "I just came by to say that you're right. There's no sense in playing marriage. If we're not going to do it we might as well stop playing house."

Charles just looked at her.

"I just wanted to tell you," she went on, "there wasn't much left in me. But what there was, you could have had."

"What are you trying to say?" Charles was afraid now of losing the peg that was solely responsible for holding his new self together. He was afraid of looking at the bird just after it had been crushed. And he was afraid that Karen, in the bedroom, would hear the sound of fear in his voice and not think him a man from whom she could learn things.

"What are you trying to say?"

"Nothing."

"Why don't you just go on home. We can talk tomorrow."

"No."

"We could have breakfast. I don't really have to go to work if I don't want to."

"No."

"Anyway," he said very rapidly, "we'll talk about it later."

"Sure."

He stood, embarrassed, expectant, waiting for her to look away or turn away so that he could feel justified in closing the door. She looked at him, in a way very much like pity, for an entire minute and he saw that something very important had gone out of the way she looked. It made him uneasy.

Then she turned her back, walked a few steps, and heard the door close and the lock turn and the chain push into place behind her. And she stood there, in the hall outside his door, waiting for the inevitable voices, just to give him every benefit. And when they came, it was as she had perceived they would be: his voice beginning, low and nervous and very fast, talking, soothing, perhaps apologizing. Then a second voice, which did not say very much, but which brought on a hurried response, unintelligible to her in the hall, just after its every few words. Margot pulled the last loose part of herself together and walked heavily down the hall, the sound of her shoes like a steady drumbeat on the floor, and out into the night.

Jerry Howard fancied himself a man about town, although that was far from what he actually was. He liked to think of himself as one of the very rich, that very special kind of self-possessed rich person who would be welcomed at any door among those of his acquaintances, at any time in the night. This night he was drunk. He had been drinking all week, in fact, because he had very little else to do until his friend returned from her European holiday. Earlier that evening he had decided that he did not want a girl; for he had made the very disconcerting discovery that girls, most girls, were beginning to bore him. He was only twenty-two and sometimes he worried about what would happen to him when he got older and found that girls still bored him. Secretly, he had certain fears of becoming a homosexual in later life, and this is what brought him away from his drinking sometimes late at night when he felt the fleeting need for having a girl. He wanted to exercise the need before it passed because he was very much afraid of what would happen to him after he lost all contact with it. And this is what brought him, once again, to Margot Payne's door at three in the morning. And this is what caused him to pound on the door and call her name and laugh aloud at what he was doing, and hope that she would not be in. Margot opened the door.

"What do you want?"

"I want to come in." Jerry smiled his old white smile.

She held the door open for him and he paused for a moment in disbelief, and then passed into the room. Then she closed the door and turned, and looked at Jerry; her face hard, her eyes staring as always, her arms locked behind her back as she leaned against the door.

"What do you want?"

"I thought you'd be glad to see me."

"I'm not," Margot said.

"My former roommate Eric sends his love." He smiled some more.

She made no reply.

Jerry walked about the small living room. He was very nervous under her eyes. He tried always to look away from her. "Why aren't you in bed?" he asked, brushing his fingers lightly across the table top.

"I was walking," she said.

"You horny?"

"No."

"Can't sleep, huh?"

"Yes."

"I guess you want to go to bed, huh?"

"Yes," Margot said.

Jerry walked over to the door where she was still leaning.

"With me?"

She looked him in the face and he lowered his eyes to her breasts not because he wanted to look at them at that moment, but because he was afraid that she would see in his face the fear he had of the thing possibly waiting for him on the other side of twenty-two. "Want to go to bed with me?"

"Why not," Margot said.

Jerry stepped back, away from her for a moment and brought his eyes up to a neutral part of her face, below her eyes. In her face there was nothing: not the slightest movement of her lips, not the barest hint of breathing about her nose, not the least movement of her chin. Jerry was not accustomed to this; there was no passion and it frightened him. He considered her and he considered the absence of passion in her face. He also considered what possibly waited for him on the other side of twenty-two. Then he smiled, still uncomfortable but confident that he had won something. "What a silly bitch you are," he said. "What a real silly bitch *you* are."

Then he touched her and she did not resist.

"Between my eyes I see three people and they are all unhappy. Why?"

"Perhaps it is because they are alive. Perhaps it is because they once were. Perhaps it is because they have to be. I do not know."

"But all around them is the smell of something dead and yet each of them is with someone. Why then are they unhappy?"

"Perhaps they have found a better way to be."

"But *is* this way better?"

"I do not know."

"Then what have we gained from seeing all this?"

"Nothing."

"Then what have *they* gained from doing all this?"

"Nothing."

"Then what will they feel tomorrow and the next day?"

"Nothing."

"But if this is all there is, what is left of life and why are we alive?"

---

# CLAY

## James Joyce

*Born in Dublin in 1882, educated in Jesuit schools, Joyce left Ireland in 1902 and spent most of his mature life in exile on the Continent, chiefly in Paris. His autobiographical novel,* Portrait of the Artist as a Young Man (1916), *traces his gradual shift from devout Catholicism to determined anti-Catholicism. His fascination with language and his interest in experimentation are evident in* Ulysses (1922) *and* Finnegan's Wake (1939). *His other works include* Chamber Music (1907), *a book of poems;* Exiles (1914), *a play; and* Dubliners (1914), *the collection of short stories from which "Clay" is taken. He died in Zurich on January 13, 1914, a recognized master of fiction, a writer whose influence, acknowledged and unacknowledged, has had its effect on many. "Clay" is a story that illustrates especially well Joyce's attitude toward his native country; "Maria," writes Robert Adams in his study of Joyce, "is an image of death settling over Ireland, a snug little ghost celebrating in sentimentality and pretense the successful burial of every cruel, vital truth."*

The matron had given her leave to go out as soon as the women's tea was over and Maria looked forward to her evening out. The kitchen was spick and span: the cook said you could see yourself in the big copper boilers. The fire was nice and bright and on one of the side-tables were four very big barmbracks. These barmbracks seemed uncut; but if you went closer you would see that they had been cut into long thick even slices and were ready to be handed round at tea. Maria had cut them herself.

Maria was a very, very small person indeed but she had a very long nose and a very long chin. She talked a little through her nose, always soothingly: "*Yes, my dear,*" and "*No, my dear.*" She was always sent for when the women quarreled over their tubs and always succeeded in making peace. One day the matron had said to her:

"Maria, you are a veritable peace-maker!"

And the sub-matron and two of the Board ladies had heard the compliment. And Ginger Mooney was always saying what she wouldn't do to the dummy who had charge of the irons if it wasn't for Maria. Everyone was so fond of Maria.

The women would have their tea at six o'clock and she would be able to get away before seven. From Ballsbridge to the Pillar, twenty minutes; from the Pillar to Drumcondra, twenty minutes; and twenty minutes to buy the things. She would be there before eight. She took out her purse with the silver clasps and read again the words *A Present from Belfast.* She was very fond of that purse because Joe had brought it to her five years before when he and Alphy had gone to Belfast on a Whit-Monday trip. In the purse were two half-crowns and some coppers. She would have five shillings clear after paying tram fare. What a nice evening they would have, all the children singing! Only she hoped that Joe wouldn't come in drunk. He was so different when he took any drink.

Often he had wanted her to go and live with them; but she would have felt herself in the way (though Joe's wife was ever so nice with her) and she had become accustomed to the life of the laundry. Joe was a good fellow. She had nursed him and Alphy too; and Joe used often say:

"Mamma is mamma but Maria is my proper mother."

After the break-up at home the boys had got her that position in the *Dublin by Lamplight* laundry, and she liked it. She used to have such a bad opinion of Protestants but now she thought they were very nice people, a little quiet and serious, but still very nice people to live with. Then she had her plants in the conservatory and she liked looking after them. She had lovely ferns and wax-plants and, whenever anyone came to visit her, she always gave the visitor one or two slips from her conservatory. There was one thing she didn't like and that was the tracts on the walls; but the matron was such a nice person to deal with, so genteel.

When the cook told her everything was ready she went into the women's room and began to pull the big bell. In a few minutes the women began to come in by twos and threes, wiping their steaming hands on their petticoats and pulling down the sleeves of their blouses over their red steaming arms. They settled down before their huge mugs which the cook and the dummy filled up with hot tea, already mixed with milk and sugar in huge tin cans. Maria superintended the distribution of the barmbrack and saw that every woman got her four slices. There was a great deal of laughing and joking during the meal. Lizzie Fleming said Maria was sure to get the ring and, though Fleming had said that for so many Hallow Eves, Maria had to laugh and say she didn't want any ring or man either; and when she laughed her gray-green eyes sparkled with disappointed shyness and the tip of her nose nearly met the tip of her chin. Then Ginger Mooney lifted up her mug of tea and proposed Maria's health while all the other women clattered with their mugs on the table, and said she was sorry she hadn't a sup of porter to drink it in. And Maria laughed again till the tip of her nose nearly met the tip of her chin and till her minute body nearly shook itself asunder because she knew that Mooney meant well though, of course, she had the notions of a common woman.

But wasn't Maria glad when the women had finished their tea and the cook and the dummy had begun to clear away the tea-things! She went into her little bedroom and, remembering that the next morning was a mass morning, changed the hand of the alarm from seven to six. Then she took off her working skirt and her house-boots and laid her best skirt out on the bed and her tiny dress-boots beside the foot of the bed. She changed her blouse too and, as she stood before the mirror, she thought of how she used to dress for mass on Sunday morning when she was a young girl; and she looked with quaint affection at the diminutive body which she had so often adorned. In spite of its years she found it a nice tidy little body.

When she got outside the streets were shining with rain and she was glad of her old brown waterproof. The tram was full and she had to sit on the little stool at the end of the car, facing all the people, with her toes barely touching the floor. She arranged in her mind all she was going to do and thought how much better it was to be independent and to have your own money in your pocket. She hoped they would have a nice evening. She was sure they would but she could not help thinking what a pity it was Alphy and Joe were not speaking. They were always falling out now but when they were boys together they used to be the best of friends: but such was life.

She got out of her tram at the Pillar and ferreted her way quickly among the crowds. She went into Downes's cake-shop but the shop was so full of people that it was a long time before she could get herself attended to. She bought a dozen of mixed penny cakes, and at last came out of the shop laden with a big bag. Then she thought what else would she buy: she wanted to buy something really nice. They would be sure to have plenty of apples and nuts. It was hard to know what to buy and all she could think of was cake. She decided to buy some plumcake but Downes's plumcake had not enough almond icing on top of it so she went over to a shop in Henry Street. Here she was a long time in suiting herself and the stylish young lady behind the counter, who was evidently a little annoyed by her, asked her was it wedding-cake she wanted to buy. That made Maria blush and smile at the young lady; but the young lady took it all very seriously and finally cut a thick slice of plumcake, parceled it up and said:

"Two-and-four, please."

She thought she would have to stand in the Drumcondra tram because none of the young men seemed to notice her but an elderly gentleman made room for her. He was a stout gentleman and he wore a brown hard hat; he had a square red face and a grayish mustache. Maria thought he was a colonel-looking gentleman and she reflected how much more polite he was than the young men who simply stared straight before them. The gentleman began to chat with her about Hallow Eve and the rainy weather. He supposed the bag was full of good things for the little ones and said it was only right that the youngsters should enjoy themselves while they were young. Maria agreed with him and favored him with demure nods and hems. He was very nice with her, and when she was getting out at the Canal Bridge she thanked him and bowed, and he bowed to her and raised his hat and smiled agreeably; and while she was going up along the terrace, bending her tiny head under the rain, she thought how easy it was to know a gentleman even when he has a drop taken.

Everybody said: *"O, here's Maria!"* when she came to Joe's house. Joe was there, having come home from business, and all the children had their Sunday dresses on. There were two big girls in from next door and games were going on. Maria gave the bag of cakes to the eldest boy, Alphy, to divide and Mrs. Donnelly said it was too good of her to bring such a big bag of cakes and made all the children say:

"Thanks, Maria."

But Maria said she had brought something special for papa and mamma, something they would be sure to like, and she began to look for her plumcake. She tried in Downes's bag and then in the pockets of her waterproof and then on the hallstand but nowhere could she find it. Then she asked all the children had any of them eaten it—by mistake, of course—but the children all said no and looked as if they did not like to eat cakes if they were to be accused of stealing. Everybody had a solution for the mystery and Mrs. Donnelly said it was plain that Maria had left it behind her in the tram. Maria, remembering how confused the gentleman with the grayish mustache had made her, colored with shame and vexation and disappointment. At the thought of the failure of her little surprise and of the two and four-pence she had thrown away for nothing she nearly cried outright.

But Joe said it didn't matter and made her sit down by the fire. He was very nice with her. He told her all that went on in his office, repeating for her a smart answer which he had made to the manager. Maria did not understand why Joe laughed so much over the answer he had made but she said that the manager must have been a very overbearing person to deal with. Joe said he wasn't so bad when you knew how to take him, that he was a decent sort so long as you didn't rub him the wrong way. Mrs. Donnelly played the piano for the children and they danced and sang. Then the two next-door girls handed round the nuts. Nobody could find the nutcrackers and Joe was nearly getting cross over it and asked how did they expect Maria to crack nuts without a nutcracker. But Maria said she didn't like nuts and that they weren't to bother about her. Then Joe asked would she take a bottle of stout and Mrs. Donnelly said there was port wine too in the house if she would prefer that. Maria said she would rather they didn't ask her to take anything: but Joe insisted.

So Maria let him have his way and they sat by the fire talking over old times and Maria thought she would put in a good word for Alphy. But Joe cried that God might strike him stone dead if ever he spoke a word to his brother again and Maria said she was sorry she had mentioned the matter. Mrs. Donnelly told her husband it was a great shame for him to speak that way of his own flesh and blood but Joe said that Alphy was no brother of his and there was nearly being a row on the head of it. But Joe said he would not lose his temper on account of the night it was and asked his wife to open some more stout. The two next-door girls had arranged some Hallow Eve games and soon everything was merry again. Maria was delighted to see the children so merry and Joe and his wife in such good spirits. The next-door girls put some saucers on the table and then led the children up to the table, blindfold. One got the prayer-book and the other three got the water; and when one of the next-door girls got the ring Mrs. Donnelly shook her finger at the blushing girl as much as to say: *O, I know all about it!* They insisted then on blindfolding Maria and leading her up to the table to see what she would get; and, while they were putting on the bandage, Maria laughed and laughed again till the tip of her nose nearly met the tip of her chin.

They led her up to the table amid laughing and joking and she put her hand out in the air as she was told to do. She moved her hand about here and there in the air and descended on one of the saucers. She felt a soft wet substance with her fingers and was surprised that nobody spoke or took off her bandage. There was a pause for a few seconds; and then a great deal of scuffling and whispering. Somebody said something about the garden, and at last Mrs. Donnelly said something very cross to one of the next-door girls and told her to throw it out at once: that was no play. Maria understood that it was wrong that time and so she had to do it over again: and this time she got the prayer-book.

After that Mrs. Donnelly played Miss McCloud's Reel for the children and Joe made Maria take a glass of wine. Soon they were all quite merry again and Mrs. Donnelly said Maria would enter a convent before the year was out because she had got the prayer-book. Maria had never seen Joe so nice to her as he was that night, so full of pleasant talk and reminiscences. She said they were all very good to her.

At last the children grew tired and sleepy and Joe asked Maria would she not sing some little song before she went, one of the old songs. Mrs. Donnelly said: *"Do, please, Maria!"* and so Maria had to get up and stand beside the piano. Mrs. Donnelly bade the children be quiet and listen to Maria's song. Then she played the prelude and said *"Now, Maria!"* and Maria, blushing very much, began to sing in a tiny quavering voice. She sang *I Dreamt that I Dwelt,* and when she came to the second verse she sang again:

> I dreamt that I dwelt in marble halls
>   With vassals and serfs at my side
> And of all who assembled within those walls
>   That I was the hope and the pride.
>
> I had riches too great to count, could boast
>   Of a high ancestral name,
> But I also dreamt, which pleased me most,
>   That you loved me still the same.

But no one tried to show her her mistake; and when she had ended her song Joe was very much moved. He said that there was no time like the long ago and no music for him like poor old Balfe, whatever other people might say; and his eyes filled up so much with tears that he could not find what he was looking for and in the end he had to ask his wife to tell him where the corkscrew was.

---

# THE TREE OF KNOWLEDGE

## Henry James

*Born in New York City in 1843, Henry James was educated in private schools and spent one year at Harvard Law School. The family's wealth enabled James to travel extensively, especially to Europe, and the international scene became one of the chief interests of his fiction, particularly the juxtaposition of European and American cultures. He became a British subject in 1915 and died in England in 1916. His literary career covered a period of some forty years, and his novels, short stories, essays, and drama represent the work of a dedicated artist whose chief interest lay always in his craft. His novels include* Roderick Hudson (*1875*), The American (*1877*), Daisy Miller (*1878*), Washington Square (*1881*), The Portrait of a Lady (*1881*), The Princess Casamassima (*1886*), The Spoils of Poynton (*1897*), What Maisie Knew (*1897*), The Wings of the Dove (*1902*), The Ambassadors (*1903*), *and* The Golden Bowl (*1904*). *The last three, often regarded as his best works, reflect most accurately his thematic interests and stylistic qualities. In his later years he wrote two autobiographical works,* A Small Boy and Others (*1913*) *and* Notes of a Son and Brother (*1914*). *A complete listing of James's writings is found in* A Bibliography of Henry James, *edited by Leon Edel and Dan H. Laurence (*1957*; rev. ed., *1961*). In talking of James's short stories or "tales," of which he wrote over a hundred, Leon Edel has written of the fascination in watching James "go about his business: he is always precise, always master of his materials, always ready to clear the way and confront his audience." Edel concludes: "And whether he wears the mask of comedy or of tragedy, we are aware that he is summarizing life, capturing some fragment of it, seeking its essence."*

It was one of the secret opinions, such as we all have, of Peter Brench that his main success in life would have consisted in his never having committed himself about the work, as it was called, of his friend Morgan Mallow. This was a subject on which it was, to the best of his belief, impossible with veracity to quote him, and it was nowhere on record that he had, in the connexion, on any occasion and in any embarrassment, either lied or spoken the truth. Such a triumph had its honour even for a man of other triumphs—a man who had reached fifty, who had escaped marriage, who had lived within his means, who had been in love with Mrs. Mallow for years without breathing it, and who, last but not least, had judged himself once for all. He had so judged himself in fact that he felt an extreme and general humility to be his proper portion; yet there was nothing that made him think so well of his parts as the course he had steered so often through the shallows just mentioned. It became thus a real wonder that the friends in whom he had most confidence were just those with whom he had most reserves. He couldn't tell Mrs. Mallow—or at least he supposed, excellent man, he couldn't—that she was the one beautiful reason he had never married; any more than he could tell her husband that the sight of the multiplied marbles in that gentleman's studio was an affliction of which even time had never blunted the edge. His victory, however, as I have intimated, in regard to these productions, was not simply in his not having let it out that he deplored them; it was, remarkably, in his not having kept it in by anything else.

The whole situation, among these good people, was verily a marvel, and there was probably not such another for a long way from the spot that engages us—the point at which the soft declivity of Hampstead began at that time to confess in broken accents to Saint John's Wood. He despised Mallow's statues and adored Mallow's wife, and yet was distinctly fond of Mallow, to whom, in turn, he was equally dear. Mrs. Mallow rejoiced in the statues—though she preferred, when pressed, the busts; and if she was visibly attached to Peter Brench it was because of his affection for Morgan. Each loved the other moreover for the love borne in each case to Lancelot, whom the Mallows respectively cherished as their only child and whom the friend of their fireside identified as the third—but decidedly the handsomest—of his godsons. Already in the old years it had come to that—that no one, for such a relation, could possibly have occurred to any of them, even to the baby itself, but Peter. There was luckily a certain independence, of the pecuniary sort, all round: the Master could never otherwise have spent his solemn *Wanderjahre* in Florence and Rome, and continued by the Thames as well as by the Arno and the Tiber to add unpurchased group to group and model, for what was too apt to prove in the event mere love, fancy-heads of celebrities either too busy or too buried—too much of the age or too little of it—to sit. Neither could Peter, lounging in almost daily, have found time to keep the whole complicated tradition so alive by his presence. He was massive but mild, the depositary of these mysteries—large and loose and ruddy and curly, with deep tones, deep eyes, deep pockets, to say nothing of the habit of long pipes, soft hats and brownish greyish weather-faded clothes, apparently always the same.

He had "written," it was known, but had never spoken, never spoken in particular of that; and he had the air (since, as was believed, he continued to write) of keeping it up in order to have something more—as if he hadn't at the worst enough—to be silent about. Whatever his air, at any rate, Peter's occasional unmentioned prose and verse were quite truly the result of an impulse to maintain the purity of his taste by establishing still more firmly the right relation of fame to feebleness. The little green door of his domain was in a garden-wall on which the discoloured stucco made patches, and in the small detached villa behind it everything was old, the furniture, the servants, the books, the prints, the immemorial habits and the new improvements. The Mallows, at Carrara Lodge, were within ten minutes, and the studio there was on their little land, to which they had added, in their happy faith, for building it. This was the good fortune, if it was not the ill, of her having brought him in marriage a portion that put them in a manner at their ease and enabled them thus, on their side, to keep it up. And they did keep it up—they always had—the infatuated sculptor and his wife, for whom nature had refined on the impossible by relieving them of the sense of the difficult. Morgan had at all events everything of the sculptor but the spirit of Phidias—the brown velvet, the becoming *beretto*, the "plastic" presence, the fine fingers, the beautiful accent in Italian and the old Italian factotum. He seemed to make up for everything when he addressed Egidio with the "tu" and waved him to turn one of the rotary pedestals of which the place was full. They were tremendous Italians at Carrara Lodge, and the secret of the part played by this fact in Peter's life was in a large degree that it gave him, sturdy Briton as he was, just the amount of "going abroad" he could bear. The Mallows were all his Italy, but it was in a measure for Italy he liked them. His one worry was that Lance—to which they had shortened his godson—was, in spite of a public school, perhaps a shade too Italian. Morgan meanwhile looked like somebody's flattering idea of somebody's own person as expressed in the great room provided at the Uffizi Museum for the general illustration of that idea by eminent hands. The Master's sole regret that he hadn't been born rather to the brush than to the chisel sprang from his wish that he might have contributed to that collection.

It appeared with time at any rate to be to the brush that Lance had been born; for Mrs. Mallow, one day when the boy was turning twenty, broke it to their friend, who shared, to the last delicate morsel, their problems and pains, that it seemed as if nothing would really do but that he should embrace the career. It had been impossible longer to remain blind to the fact that he was gaining no glory at Cambridge, where Brench's own college had for a year tempered its tone to him as for Brench's own sake. Therefore why renew the vain form of preparing him for the impossible? The impossible—it had become clear—was that he should be anything but an artist.

"Oh dear, dear!" said poor Peter.

"Don't you believe in it?" asked Mrs. Mallow, who still, at more than forty, had her violet velvet eyes, her creamy satin skin and her silken chestnut hair.

"Believe in what?"

"Why in Lance's passion."

"I don't know what you mean by 'believing in it.' I've never been unaware, certainly, of his disposition, from his earliest time, to daub and draw; but I confess I've hoped it would burn out."

"But why should it," she sweetly smiled, "with his wonderful heredity? Passion is passion—though of course indeed *you*, dear Peter, know nothing of that. Has the Master's ever burned out?"

Peter looked off a little and, in his familiar formless way, kept up for a moment, a sound between a smothered whistle and a subdued hum. "Do you think he's going to be another Master?"

She seemed scarce prepared to go that length, yet she had on the whole a marvellous trust. "I know what you mean by that. Will it be a career to incur the jealousies and provoke the machinations that have been at times almost too much for his father? Well—say it may be, since nothing but clap-trap, in these dreadful days, *can*, it would seem, make its way, and since, with the curse of refinement and distinction, one may easily find one's self begging one's bread. Put it at the worst—say he *has* the misfortune to wing his flight further than the vulgar taste of his stupid countrymen can follow. Think, all the same, of the happiness—the same the Master has had. He'll *know*."

Peter looked rueful. "Ah but *what* will he know?"

"Quiet joy!" cried Mrs. Mallow, quite impatient and turning away.

## II

He had of course before long to meet the boy himself on it and to hear that practically everything was settled. Lance was not to go up again, but to go instead to Paris where, since the die was cast, he would find the best advantages. Peter had always felt he must be taken as he was, but had never perhaps found him so much of that pattern as on this occasion. "You chuck Cambridge then altogether? Doesn't that seem rather a pity?"

Lance would have been like his father, to his friend's sense, had he had less humour, and like his mother had he had more beauty. Yet it was a good middle way for Peter that, in the modern manner, he was, to the eye, rather the young stockbroker than the young artist. The youth reasoned that it was a question of time—there was such a mill to go through, such an awful lot to learn. He had talked with fellows and had judged. "One has got, today," he said, "don't you see? to know."

His interlocutor, at this, gave a groan. "Oh hang it, *don't* know!"

Lance wondered. " 'Don't'? Then what's the use—?"

"The use of what?"

"Why of anything. Don't you think I've talent?"

Peter smoked away for a little in silence; then went on: "It isn't knowledge, it's ignorance that—as we've been beautifully told—is bliss."

"Don't you think I've talent?" Lance repeated.

Peter, with his trick of queer kind demonstrations, passed his arm round his godson and held him a moment. "How do I know?"

"Oh," said the boy, "if it's your own ignorance you're defending—!"

Again, for a pause, on the sofa, his godfather smoked. "It isn't. I've the misfortune to be omniscient."

"Oh well," Lance laughed again, "if you know *too* much—!"

"That's what I do, and it's why I'm so wretched."

Lance's gaiety grew. "Wretched? Come, I say!"

"But I forgot," his companion went on—"you're not to know about that. It would indeed for you too make the too much. Only I'll tell you what I'll do." And Peter got up from the sofa. "If you'll go up again I'll pay your way at Cambridge."

Lance stared, a little rueful in spite of being still more amused. "Oh Peter! You disapprove so of Paris?"

"Well, I'm afraid of it."

"Ah I see!"

"No, you don't see—yet. But you will—that is you would. And you mustn't."

The young man thought more gravely. "But one's innocence, already—!"

"Is considerably damaged? Ah that won't matter," Peter persisted—"we'll patch it up here."

"Here? Then you want me to stay at home?"

Peter almost confessed to it. "Well, we're so right—we four together—just as we are. We're so safe. Come, don't spoil it."

The boy, who had turned to gravity, turned from this, on the real pressure in his friend's tone, to consternation. "Then what's a fellow to be?"

"My particular care. Come, old man"—and Peter now fairly pleaded—"*I'll* look out for you."

Lance, who had remained on the sofa with his legs out and his hands in his pockets, watched him with eyes that showed suspicion. Then he got up. "You think there's something the matter with me—that I can't make a success."

"Well, what do you call a success?"

Lance thought again. "Why the best sort, I suppose, is to please one's self. Isn't that the sort that, in spite of cabals and things, is—in his own peculiar line—the Master's?"

There were so much too many things in this question to be answered at once that they practically checked the discussion, which became particularly difficult in the light of such renewed proof that, though the young man's innocence might, in the course of his studies, as he contended, somewhat have shrunken, the finer essence of it still remained. That was indeed exactly what Peter had assumed and what above all he desired; yet perversely enough it gave him a chill. The boy believed in the cabals and things, believed in the peculiar line, believed, to be brief, in the Master. What happened a month or two later wasn't that he went up again at the expense of his godfather, but that a fortnight after he had got settled in Paris this personage sent him fifty pounds.

He had meanwhile at home, this personage, made up his mind to the worst; and what that might be had never yet grown quite so vivid to him as when, on his presenting himself one Sunday night, as he never failed to do, for supper, the mistress of Carrara Lodge met him with an appeal as to—of all things in the world—the wealth of the Canadians. She was earnest, she was even excited. "Are many of them *really* rich?"

He had to confess he knew nothing about them, but he often thought afterwards of that evening. The room in which they sat was adorned with sundry specimens of the Master's genius, which had the merit of being, as Mrs. Mallow herself frequently suggested, of an unusually convenient size. They were indeed of dimensions not customary in the products of the chisel, and they had the singularity that, if the objects and features intended to be small looked too large, the objects and features intended to be large looked too small. The Master's idea, either in respect to this matter or to any other, had in almost any case, even after years, remained undiscoverable to Peter Brench. The creations that so failed to reveal it stood about on pedestals and brackets, on tables and shelves, a little staring white population, heroic, idyllic, allegoric, mythic, symbolic, in which "scale" had so strayed and lost itself that the public square and the chimney-piece seemed to have changed places, the monumental being all diminutive and the diminutive all monumental; branches at any rate, markedly, of a family in which stature was rather oddly irrespective of function, age and sex. They formed, like the Mallows themselves, poor Brench's own family—having at least to such a degree the note of familiarity. The occasion was one of those he had long ago learnt to know and to name—short flickers of the faint flame, soft gusts of a kinder air. Twice a year regularly the Master believed in his fortune, in addition to believing all the year round in his genius. This time it was to be made by a bereaved couple from Toronto, who had given him the handsomest order for a tomb to three lost children, each of whom they desired to see, in the composition, emblematically and characteristically represented.

Such was naturally the moral of Mrs. Mallow's question: if their wealth was to be assumed, it was clear, from the nature of their admiration, as well as from mysterious hints thrown out (they were a little odd!) as to other possibilities of the same mortuary sort, that their further patronage might be; and not less evident that should the Master become at all known in those climes nothing would be more inevitable than a run of Canadian custom. Peter had been present before at runs of custom, colonial and domestic—present at each of those of which the aggregation had left so few gaps in the marble company round him; but it was his habit never at these junctures to prick the bubble in advance. The fond illusion, while it lasted, eased the wound of elections never won, the long ache of medals and diplomas carried off, on every chance, by every one but the Master; it moreover lighted the lamp that would glimmer through the next eclipse. They lived, however, after all—as it was always beautiful to see—at a height scarce susceptible of ups and downs. They strained a point at times charmingly, strained it to admit that the public was here and there not too bad to buy; but they would have been nowhere without their attitude that the Master was always too good to sell. They were at all events deliciously formed, Peter often said to himself, for their fate; the Master had a vanity, his wife had a loyalty, of which success, depriving these things of innocence, would have diminished the merit and the grace. Any one could be charming under a charm, and as he looked about him at a world of prosperity more void of proportion even than the Master's museum he wondered if he knew another pair that so completely escaped vulgarity.

"What a pity Lance isn't with us to rejoice!" Mrs. Mallow on this occasion sighed at supper.

"We'll drink to the health of the absent," her husband replied, filling his friend's glass and his own and giving a drop to their companion; "but we must hope he's preparing himself for a happiness much less like this of ours this evening—excusable as I grant it to be!—than like the comfort we have always (whatever has happened or has not happened) been able to trust ourselves to enjoy. The comfort," the Master explained, leaning back in the pleasant lamplight and firelight, holding up his glass and looking round at his marble family, quartered more or less, a monstrous brood, in every room—"the comfort of art in itself!"

Peter looked a little shyly at his wine. "Well—I don't care what you may call it when a fellow doesn't—but Lance must learn to *sell*, you know. I drink to his acquisition of the secret of a base popularity!"

"Oh, yes, *he* must sell," the boy's mother, who was still more, however, this seemed to give out, the Master's wife, rather artlessly allowed.

"Ah," the sculptor after a moment confidently pronounced, "Lance *will*. Don't be afraid. He'll have learnt."

"Which is exactly what Peter," Mrs. Mallow gaily returned—"why in the world were you so perverse, Peter?—wouldn't when he told him hear of."

Peter, when this lady looked at him with accusatory affection—a grace on her part not infrequent—could never find a word; but the Master, who was always all amenity and tact, helped him out now as he had often helped him before. "That's his old idea, you know—on which we've so often differed: his theory that the artist should be all impulse and instinct. *I* go in of course for a certain amount of school. Not too much —but a due proportion. There's where his protest came in," he continued to explain to his wife, "as against what *might*, don't you see? be in question for Lance."

"Ah well"—and Mrs. Mallow turned the violet eyes across the table at the subject of this discourse—"he's sure to have meant of course nothing but good. Only that wouldn't have prevented him, if Lance *had* taken his advice, from being in effect horribly cruel."

They had a sociable way of talking of him to his face as if he had been in the clay or—at most—in the plaster, and the Master was unfailingly generous. He might have been waving Egidio to make him revolve. "Ah but poor Peter wasn't so wrong as to what it may after all come to that he *will* learn."

"Oh but nothing artistically bad," she urged—still, for poor Peter, arch and dewy.

"Why just the little French tricks," said the Master: on which their friend had to pretend to admit, when pressed by Mrs. Mallow, that these aesthetic vices had been the objects of his dread.

## III

"I know now," Lance said to him the next year, "why you were so much against it." He had come back supposedly for a mere interval and was looking about him at Carrara Lodge, where indeed he had already on two or three occasions since his expatriation briefly reappeared. This had the air of a longer holiday. "Something rather awful has happened to me. It *isn't* so very good to know."

"I'm bound to say high spirits don't show in your face," Peter was rather ruefully forced to confess. "Still, are you very sure you do know?"

"Well, I at least know about as much as I can bear." These remarks were exchanged in Peter's den, and the young man, smoking cigarettes, stood before the fire with his back against the mantel. Something of his bloom seemed really to have left him.

Poor Peter wondered. "You're clear then as to what in particular I wanted you not to go for?"

"In particular?" Lance thought. "It seems to me that in particular there can have been only one thing."

They stood for a little sounding each other. "Are you quite sure?"

"Quite sure I'm a beastly duffer? Quite—by this time."

"Oh!"—and Peter turned away as if almost with relief.

"It's *that* that isn't pleasant to find out."

"Oh I don't care for 'that,'" said Peter, presently coming round again. "I mean I personally don't."

"Yet I hope you can understand a little that I myself should!"

"Well, what do you mean by it?" Peter sceptically asked.

And on this Lance had to explain—how the upshot of his studies in Paris had inexorably proved a mere deep doubt of his means. These studies had so waked him up that a new light was in his eyes; but what the new light did was really to show him too much. "Do you know what's the matter with me? I'm too horribly intelligent. Paris was really the last place for me. I've learnt what I can't do."

Poor Peter stared—it was a staggerer; but even after they had had, on the subject, a longish talk in which the boy brought out to the full the hard truth of his lesson, his friend betrayed less pleasure than usually breaks into a face to the happy tune of "I told you so!" Poor Peter himself made now indeed so little a point of having told him so that Lance broke ground in a different place a day or two after. "What was it then that—before I went—you were afraid I should find out?" This, however, Peter refused to tell him—on the ground that if he hadn't yet guessed perhaps he never would, and that in any case nothing at all for either of them was to be gained by giving the thing a name: Lance eyed him on this an instant with the bold curiosity of youth—with the air indeed of having in his mind two or three names, of which one or other would be right. Peter nevertheless, turning his back again, offered no encouragement, and when they parted afresh it was with some show of impatience on the side of the boy. Accordingly on their next encounter Peter saw at a glance that he had now, in the interval, divined and that, to sound his note, he was only waiting till they should find themselves alone. This he had soon arranged and he then broke straight out. "Do you know your conundrum has been keeping me awake? But in the watches of the night the answer came over me—so that, upon my honour, I quite laughed out. Had you been supposing I had to go to Paris to learn *that?*" Even now, to see him still so sublimely on his guard, Peter's young friend had to laugh afresh. "You won't give a sign till you're sure? Beautiful old Peter!" But Lance at last produced it. "Why, hang it, the truth about the Master."

It made between them for some minutes a lively passage, full of wonder for each at the wonder of the other. "Then how long have you understood—"

"The true value of his work? I understood it," Lance recalled, "as soon as I began to understand anything. But I didn't begin fully to do that, I admit, till I got *là-bas.*"

"Dear, dear!"—Peter gasped with retrospective dread.

"But for what have you taken me? I'm a hopeless muff—that I *had* to have rubbed in. But I'm not such a muff as the Master!" Lance declared.

"Then why did you never tell me—?"

"That I hadn't, after all"—the boy took him up—"remained such an idiot? Just because I never dreamed *you* knew. But I beg your pardon. I only wanted to spare you. And what I don't now understand is how the deuce then for so long you've managed to keep bottled."

Peter produced his explanation, but only after some delay and with a gravity not void of embarrassment. "It was for your mother."

"Oh!" said Lance.

"And that's the great thing now—since the murder *is* out. I want a promise from you. I mean"—and Peter almost feverishly followed it up—"a vow from you, solemn and such as you owe me here on the spot, that you'll sacrifice anything rather than let her ever guess—"

"That *I've* guessed?"—Lance took it in. "I see." He evidently after a moment had taken in much. "But what is it you've in mind that I may have a chance to sacrifice?"

"Oh one has always something."

Lance looked at him hard. "Do you mean that *you've* had—?" The look he received back, however, so put the question by that he found soon enough another. "Are you really sure my mother doesn't know?"

Peter, after renewed reflexion, was really sure. "If she does she's too wonderful."

"But aren't we all too wonderful?"

"Yes," Peter granted—"but in different ways. The thing's so desperately important because your father's little public consists only, as you know then," Peter developed—"well, of how many?"

"First of all," the Master's son risked, "of himself. And last of all too. I don't quite see of whom else."

Peter had an approach to impatience. "Of your mother, I say—*always*."

Lance cast it all up. "You absolutely feel that?"

"Absolutely."

"Well then with yourself that makes three."

"Oh *me*."—and Peter, with a wag of his kind old head, modestly excused himself. "The number's at any rate small enough for any individual dropping out to be too dreadfully missed. Therefore, to put it in a nutshell, take care, my boy—that's all—that *you're* not!"

"I've got to keep on humbugging?" Lance wailed.

"It's just to warn you of the danger of your failing of that that I've seized this opportunity."

"And what do you regard in particular," the young man asked, "as the danger?"

"Why this certainty: that the moment your mother, who feels so strongly, should suspect your secret—well," said Peter desperately, "the fat would be on the fire."

Lance for a moment seemed to stare at the blaze. "She'd throw me over?"

"She'd throw *him* over."

"And come round to us?"

Peter, before he answered, turned away. "Come round to *you*." But he had said enough to indicate—and, as he evidently trusted, to avert—the horrid contingency.

## IV

Within six months again, none the less, his fear was on more occasions than one all before him. Lance had returned to Paris for another trial; then had reappeared at home and had had, with his father, for the first time in his life, one of the scenes that strike sparks. He described it with much expression to Peter, touching whom (since they had never done so before) it was the sign of a new reserve on the part of the pair at Carrara Lodge that they at present failed, on a matter of intimate interest, to open themselves—if not in joy then in sorrow—to their good friend. This produced perhaps practically between the parties a shade of alienation and a slight intermission of commerce—marked mainly indeed by the fact that to talk at his ease with his old playmate Lance had in general to come to see him. The closest if not quite the gayest relation they had yet known together was thus ushered in. The difficulty for poor Lance was a tension at home—begotten by the fact that his father wished him to be at least the sort of success he himself had been. He hadn't "chucked" Paris—though nothing appeared more vivid to him than that Paris had chucked him: he would go back again because of the fascination in trying, in seeing, in sounding the depths—in learning one's lesson, briefly, even if the lesson were simply that of one's impotence in the presence of one's larger vision. But what did the Master, all aloft in his senseless fluency, know of impotence, and what vision—to be called such—had he in all his blind life ever had? Lance, heated and indignant, frankly appealed to his godparent on this score.

His father, it appeared, had come down on him for having, after so long, nothing to show, and hoped that on his next return this deficiency would be repaired. *The* thing, the Master complacently set forth was—for any artist, however inferior to himself—at least to "do" something. "What can you do? That's all I ask!" *He* had certainly done enough, and there was no mistake about what he had to show. Lance had tears in his eyes when it came thus to letting his old friend know how great the strain might be on the "sacrifice" asked of him. It wasn't so easy to continue humbugging—as from son to parent—after feeling one's self despised for not grovelling in mediocrity. Yet a noble duplicity was what, as they intimately faced the situation, Peter went on requiring; and it was still for a time what his young friend, bitter and sore, managed loyally to comfort him with. Fifty pounds more than once again, it was true, rewarded both in London and in Paris the young friend's loyalty; none the less sensibly, doubtless, at the moment, that the money was a direct advance on a decent sum for which Peter had long since privately prearranged an ultimate function. Whether by these arts or others, at all events, Lance's just resentment was kept for a season—but only for a season—at bay. The day arrived when he warned his companion that he could hold out—or hold in—no longer. Carrara Lodge had had to listen to another lecture delivered from a great height—an infliction really heavier at last than, without striking back or in some way letting the Master have the truth, flesh and blood could bear.

"And what I don't see is," Lance observed with a certain irritated eye for what was after all, if it came to that, owing to himself too; "what I don't see is, upon my honour, how *you*, as things are going, can keep the game up."

"Oh the game for me is only to hold my tongue," said placid Peter. "And I have my reason."

"Still my mother?"

Peter showed a queer face as he had often shown it before—that is by turning it straight away. "What will you have? I haven't ceased to like her."

"She's beautiful—she's a dear of course," Lance allowed; "but what is she to you, after all, and what is it to you that, as to anything whatever, she should or she shouldn't?"

Peter, who had turned red, hung fire a little. "Well—it's all simply what I make of it."

There was now, however, in his young friend a strange, an adopted insistence. "What are you after all to *her?*"

"Oh nothing. But that's another matter."

"She cares only for my father," said Lance the Parisian.

"Naturally—and that's just why."

"Why you've wished to spare her?"

"Because she cares so tremendously much."

Lance took a turn about the room, but with his eyes still on his host. "How awfully—always—you must have liked her!"

"Awfully. Always," said Peter Brench.

The young man continued for a moment to muse—then stopped again in front of him. "Do you know how much she cares?" Their eyes met on it, but Peter, as if his own found something new in Lance's, appeared to hesitate, for the first time in an age, to say he did know. "*I've* only just found out," said Lance. "She came to my room last night, after being present, in silence and only with her eyes on me, at what I had had to take from him; she came—and she was with me an extraordinary hour."

He had paused again and they had again for a while sounded each other. Then something—and it made him suddenly turn pale—came to Peter. "She *does* know?"

"She does know. She let it all out to me—so as to demand of me no more than 'that,' as she said, of which she herself had been capable. She has always, always known," said Lance without pity.

Peter was silent a long time; during which his companion might have heard him gently breathe, and on touching him might have felt within him the vibration of a long low sound suppressed. By the time he spoke at last he had taken everything in. "Then I do see how tremendously much."

"Isn't it wonderful?" Lance asked.

"Wonderful," Peter mused.

"So that if your original effort to keep me from Paris was to keep me from knowledge—!" Lance exclaimed as if with a sufficient indication of this futility.

It might have been at the futility. Peter appeared for a little to gaze. "I think it must have been—without my quite at the time knowing it—to keep *me!*" he replied at last as he turned away.

# Faith and Fate

## THE THREE STRANGERS

**Thomas Hardy**

Born in 1840 in Dorsetshire, the southern county of England that serves as the setting for much of his fiction and poetry, Hardy was first apprenticed to a local architect and for a time was himself a successful architect, winning a prize offered by the Royal Institute in 1863. He had always, however, been interested in writing and had attended evening classes at the University of London. Receiving no encouragement for his early poetry, financial or critical, he turned to the writing of fiction. His first novel, Desperate Remedies, was published in 1871, and then for a period of some twenty-five years he wrote a long series of novels, the best known, perhaps, being Far from the Madding Crowd (1874), The Return of the Native (1878), The Mayor of Casterbridge (1885–1886), Tess of the D'Urbervilles (1891), and Jude the Obscure (1895), regarded by much of the public as "immoral." By this time he could afford to return to poetry, to which he devoted most of his remaining years. When he died in 1928, he was an acknowledged giant of English literature. An excellent introduction to Hardy's work, both fiction and poetry, is Irving Howe's Thomas Hardy (1968). "The Three Strangers" contains the same themes found in many of Hardy's novels and poems—that is, the dominance of chance in the world and the basic irony underlying life. It also illustrates his use of Dorsetshire for background, setting, and characters. "Anyone who has become familiar with the timbre of Hardy's voice," writes Howe, "both in an *early work like* Under the Greenwood Tree *and a late one like* Tess of the D'Urbervilles, *could not fail immediately to recognize a tale like 'The Withered Arm' or 'The Three Strangers' as uniquely his."*

Among the few features of agricultural England which retain an appearance but little modified by the lapse of centuries, may be reckoned the long, grassy and furzy downs, coombs, or ewe-leases, as they are called according to their kind, that fill a large area of certain counties in the south and southwest. If any mark of human occupation is met with hereon, it usually takes the form of the solitary cottage of some shepherd.

Fifty years ago such a lonely cottage stood on such a down, and may possibly be standing there now. In spite of its loneliness, however, the spot, by actual measurement, was not three miles from a county-town. Yet that affected it little. Three miles of irregular upland, during the long inimical seasons, with their sleets, snows, rains, and mists, afford withdrawing space enough to isolate a Timon or a Nebuchadnezzar; much less, in fair weather, to please that less repellent tribe, the poets, philosophers, artists, and others who "conceive and meditate of pleasant things."

Some old earthen camp or barrow, some clump of trees, at least some starved fragment of ancient hedge is usually taken advantage of in the erection of these forlorn dwellings. But, in the present case, such a kind of shelter had been disregarded. Higher Crowstairs, as the house was called, stood quite detached and undefended. The only reason for its precise situation seemed to be the crossing of two footpaths at right angles hard by, which may have crossed there and thus for a good five hundred years. Hence the house was exposed to the elements on all sides. But, though the wind up here blew unmistakably when it did blow, and the rain hit hard whenever it fell, the various weathers of the winter season were not quite so formidable on the down as they were imagined to be by dwellers on low ground. The raw rimes were not so pernicious as in the hollows, and the frosts were scarcely so severe. When the shepherd and his family who tenanted the house were pitied for their sufferings from the exposure, they said that upon the whole they were less inconvenienced by "wuzzes and flames" (hoarses and phlegms) than when they had lived by the stream of a snug neighbouring valley.

The night of March 28, 182–, was precisely one of the nights that were wont to call forth these expressions of commiseration. The level rainstorm smote walls, slopes, and hedges like the clothyard shafts of Senlac and Crecy. Such sheep and outdoor animals as had no shelter stood with their buttocks to the winds; while the tails of little birds trying to roost on some scraggy thorn were blown inside-out like umbrellas. The gable-end of the cottage was stained with wet, and the eavesdroppings flapped against the wall. Yet never was commiseration for the shepherd more misplaced.

For that cheerful rustic was entertaining a large party in glorification of the christening of his second girl.

The guests had arrived before the rain began to fall, and they were all now assembled in the chief or living room of the dwelling. A glance into the apartment at eight o'clock on this eventful evening would have resulted in the opinion that it was as cosy and comfortable a nook as could be wished for in boisterous weather. The calling of its inhabitant was proclaimed by a number of highly-polished sheep-crooks without stems that were hung ornamentally over the fireplace, the curl of each shining crook varying from the antiquated type engraved in the patriarchal pictures of old family Bibles to the most approved fashion of the last local sheep-fair. The room was lighted by half-a-dozen candles, having wicks only a trifle smaller than the grease which enveloped them, in candlesticks that were never used but at high-days, holy-days, and family feasts. The lights were scattered about the room, two of them standing on the chimney-piece. This position of candles was in itself significant. Candles on the chimney-piece always meant a party.

On the hearth, in front of a back-brand to give substance, blazed a fire of thorns, that crackled "like the laughter of the fool."

Nineteen persons were gathered here. Of these, five women, wearing gowns of various bright hues, sat in chairs along the wall; girls shy and not shy filled the window-bench; four men, including Charley Jake the hedge-carpenter, Elijah New the parish-clerk, and John Pitcher, a neighbouring dairyman, the shepherd's father-in-law, lolled in the settle; a young man and maid, who were blushing over tentative *pourparlers* on a life-companionship, sat beneath the corner-cupboard; and an elderly engaged man of fifty or upward moved restlessly about from spots where his betrothed was not to the spot where she was. Enjoyment was pretty general, and so much the more prevailed in being unhampered by conventional restrictions. Absolute confidence in each other's good opinion begat perfect ease, while the finishing stroke of manner, amounting to a truly princely serenity, was lent to the majority by the absence of any expression or trait denoting that they wished to get on in the world, enlarge their minds, or do any eclipsing thing whatever—which nowadays so generally nips the bloom and *bonhomie* of all except the two extremes of the social scale.

Shepherd Fennel had married well, his wife being a dairyman's daughter from a vale at a distance, who brought fifty guineas in her pocket—and kept them there, till they should be required for ministering to the needs of a coming family. This frugal woman had been somewhat exercised as to the character that should be given to the gathering. A sit-still party had its advantages; but an undisturbed position of ease in chairs and settles was apt to lead on the men to such an unconscionable deal of toping that they would sometimes fairly drink the house dry. A dancing-party was the alternative; but this, while avoiding the foregoing objection on the score of good drink, had a counter-balancing disadvantage in the matter of good victuals, the ravenous appetites engendered by the exercise causing immense havoc in the buttery. Shepherdess Fennel fell back upon the intermediate plan of mingling short dances with short periods of talk and singing, so as to hinder any ungovernable rage in either. But this scheme was entirely confined to her own gentle mind: the shepherd himself was in the mood to exhibit the most reckless phases of hospitality.

The fiddler was a boy of those parts, about twelve years of age, who had a wonderful dexterity in jigs and reels, though his fingers were so small and short as to necessitate a constant shifting for the high notes, from which he scrambled back to the first position with sounds not of unmixed purity of tone. At seven the shrill tweedle-dee of this youngster had begun, accompanied by a booming ground-bass from Elijah New, the parish-clerk, who had thoughtfully brought with him his favourite musical instrument, the serpent. Dancing was instantaneous, Mrs. Fennel privately enjoining the players on no account to let the dance exceed the length of a quarter of an hour.

But Elijah and the boy in the excitement of their position quite forgot the injunction. Moreover, Oliver Giles, a man of seventeen, one of the dancers, who was enamoured of his partner, a fair girl of thirty-three rolling years, had recklessly handed a new crown-piece to the musicians, as a bribe to keep going as long as they had muscle and wind. Mrs. Fennel, seeing the steam begin to generate on the countenances of her guests, crossed over and touched the fiddler's elbow and put her hand on the serpent's mouth. But they took no notice, and fearing she might lose her character of genial hostess if she were to interfere too markedly, she retired and sat down helpless. And so the dance whizzed on with cumulative fury, the performers moving in their planet-like courses, direct and retrograde, from apogee to perigee, till the hand of the well-kicked clock at the bottom of the room had travelled over the circumference of an hour.

While these cheerful events were in course of enactment within Fennel's pastoral dwelling an incident having considerable bearing on the party had occurred in the gloomy night without. Mrs. Fennel's concern about the growing fierceness of the dance corresponded in point of time with the ascent of a human figure to the solitary hill of Higher Crowstairs from the direction of the distant town. This personage strode on through the rain without a pause, following the little-worn path which, further on in its course, skirted the shepherd's cottage.

It was nearly the time of full moon, and on this account, though the sky was lined with a uniform sheet of dripping cloud, ordinary objects out of doors were readily visible. The sad wan light revealed the lonely pedestrian to be a man of supple frame; his gait suggested that he had somewhat passed the period of perfect and instinctive agility, though not so far as to be otherwise than rapid of motion when occasion required.

At a rough guess, he might have been about forty years of age. He appeared tall, but a recruiting sergeant, or other person accustomed to the judging of men's heights by the eye, would have discerned that this was chiefly owing to his gauntness, and that he was not more than five-feet-eight or nine.

Notwithstanding the regularity of his tread there was caution in it, as in that of one who mentally feels his way; and despite the fact that it was not a black coat nor a dark garment of any sort that he wore, there was something about him which suggested that he naturally belonged to the black-coated tribes of men. His clothes were of fustian, and his boots hobnailed, yet in his progress he showed not the mud-accustomed bearing of hobnailed and fustianed peasantry.

By the time that he had arrived abreast of the shepherd's premises the rain came down, or rather came along, with yet more determined violence. The outskirts of the little settlement partially broke the force of wind and rain, and this induced him to stand still. The most salient of the shepherd's domestic erections was an empty sty at the forward corner of his hedgeless garden, for in these latitudes the principle of masking the homelier features of your establishment by a conventional frontage was unknown. The traveller's eye was attracted to this small building by the pallid shine of the wet slates that covered it. He turned aside, and, finding it empty, stood under the pent-roof for shelter.

While he stood the boom of the serpent within the adjacent house, and the lesser strains of the fiddler, reached the spot as an accompaniment to the surging hiss of the flying rain on the sod, its louder beating on the cabbage-leaves of the garden, on the straw hackles of eight or ten beehives just discernible by the path, and its dripping from the eaves into a row of buckets and pans that had been placed under the walls of the cottage. For at Higher Crowstairs, as at all such elevated domiciles, the grand difficulty of housekeeping was an insufficiency of water; and a casual rainfall was utilized by turning out, as catchers, every utensil that the house contained. Some queer stories might be told of the contrivances for economy in suds and dish-waters that are absolutely necessitated in upland habitations during the droughts of summer. But at this season there were no such exigencies; a mere acceptance of what the skies bestowed was sufficient for an abundant store.

At last the notes of the serpent ceased and the house was silent. This cessation of activity aroused the solitary pedestrian from the reverie into which he had lapsed, and, emerging from the shed, with an apparently new intention, he walked up the path to the house-door. Arrived here, his first act was to kneel down on a large stone beside the row of vessels, and to drink a copious draught from one of them. Having quenched his thirst he rose and lifted his hand to knock, but paused with his eye upon the panel. Since the dark surface of the wood revealed absolutely nothing, it was evident that he must be mentally looking through the door, as if he wished to measure thereby all the possibilities that a house of this sort might include, and how they might bear upon the question of his entry.

In his indecision he turned and surveyed the scene around. Not a soul was anywhere visible. The garden-path stretched downward from his feet, gleaming like the track of a snail; the roof of the little well (mostly dry), the well-cover, the top rail of the garden-gate, were varnished with the same dull liquid glaze; while, far away in the vale, a faint whiteness of more than usual extent showed that the rivers were high in the meads. Beyond all this winked a few bleared lamplights through the beating drops—lights that denoted the situation of the county-town from which he had appeared to come. The absence of all notes of life in that direction seemed to clinch his intentions, and he knocked at the door.

Within, a desultory chat had taken the place of movement and musical sound. The hedge-carpenter was suggesting a song to the company, which nobody just then was inclined to undertake, so that the knock afforded a not unwelcome diversion.

"Walk in!" said the shepherd promptly.

The latch clicked upward, and out of the night our pedestrian appeared upon the door-mat. The shepherd arose, snuffed two of the nearest candles, and turned to look at him.

Their light disclosed that the stranger was dark in complexion and not unprepossessing as to feature. His hat, which for a moment he did not remove, hung low over his eyes, without concealing that they were large, open, and determined, moving with a flash rather than a glance round the room. He seemed pleased with his survey, and, baring his shaggy head, said, in a rich deep voice, "The rain is so heavy, friends, that I ask leave to come in and rest awhile."

"To be sure, stranger," said the shepherd. "And faith, you've been lucky in choosing your time, for we are having a bit of a fling for a glad cause—though, to be sure, a man could hardly wish that glad cause to happen more than once a year."

"Nor less," spoke up a woman. "For 'tis best to get your family over and done with, as soon as you can, so as to be all the earlier out of the fag o't."

"And what may be this glad cause?" asked the stranger.

"A birth and christening," said the shepherd.

The stranger hoped his host might not be made unhappy either by too many or too few of such episodes, and being invited by a gesture to a pull at the mug, he readily acquiesced. His manner, which, before entering, had been so dubious, was now altogether that of a careless and candid man.

"Late to be traipsing athwart this coomb—hey?" said the engaged man of fifty.

"Late it is, master, as you say.—I'll take a seat in the chimney-corner, if you have nothing to urge against it, ma'am; for I am a little moist on the side that was next the rain."

Mrs. Shepherd Fennel assented, and made room for the self-invited comer, who, having got completely inside the chimney-corner, stretched out his legs and his arms with the expansiveness of a person quite at home.

"Yes, I am rather cracked in the vamp," he said freely, seeing that the eyes of the shepherd's wife fell upon his boots, "and I am not well fitted either. I have had some rough times lately, and have been forced to pick up what I can get in the way of wearing, but I must find a suit better fit for working-days when I reach home."

"One of hereabouts?" she inquired.

"Not quite that—further up the country."

"I thought so. And so be I; and by your tongue you come from my neighbourhood."

"But you would hardly have heard of me," he said quickly. "My time would be long before yours, ma'am, you see."

This testimony to the youthfulness of his hostess had the effect of stopping her cross-examination.

"There is only one thing more wanted to make me happy," continued the new-comer. "And that is a little baccy, which I am sorry to say I am out of."

"I'll fill your pipe," said the shepherd.

"I must ask you to lend me a pipe likewise."

"A smoker, and no pipe about 'ee?"

"I have dropped it somewhere on the road."

The shepherd filled and handed him a new clay pipe, saying, as he did so, "Hand me your baccy-box—I'll fill that too, now I am about it."

The man went through the movement of searching his pockets.

"Lost that too?" said his entertainer, with some surprise.

"I am afraid so," said the man with some confusion. "Give it to me in a screw of paper." Lighting his pipe at the candle with a suction that drew the whole flame into the bowl, he resettled himself in the corner and bent his looks upon the faint steam from his damp legs, as if he wished to say no more.

Meanwhile the general body of guests had been taking little notice of this visitor by reason of an absorbing discussion in which they were engaged with the band about a tune for the next dance. The matter being settled, they were about to stand up when an interruption came in the shape of another knock at the door.

At sound of the same the man in the chimney-corner took up the poker and began stirring the brands as if doing it thoroughly were the one aim of his existence; and a second time the shepherd said, "Walk in!" In a moment another man stood upon the straw-woven door-mat. He too was a stranger.

This individual was one of a type radically different from the first. There was more of the commonplace in his manner, and a certain jovial cosmopolitanism sat upon his features. He was several years older than the first arrival, his hair being slightly frosted, his eyebrows bristly, and his whiskers cut back from his cheeks. His face was rather full and flabby, and yet it was not altogether a face without power. A few grog-blossoms marked the neighbourhood of his nose. He flung back his long drab greatcoat, revealing that beneath it he wore a suit of cinder-gray shade throughout, large heavy seals, of some metal or other that would take a polish, dangling from his fob as his only personal ornament. Shaking the water-drops from his low-crowned glazed hat, he said, "I must ask for a few minutes' shelter, comrades, or I shall be wetted to my skin before I get to Casterbridge."

"Make yourself at home, master," said the shepherd, perhaps a trifle less heartily than on the first occasion. Not that Fennel had the least tinge of niggardliness in his composition; but the room was far from large, spare chairs were not numerous, and damp companions were not altogether desirable at close quarters for the women and girls in their bright-coloured gowns.

However, the second comer, after taking off his greatcoat, and hanging his hat on a nail in one of the ceiling-beams as if he had been specially invited to put it there, advanced and sat down at the table. This had been pushed so closely into the chimney-corner, to give all available room to the dancers, that its inner edge grazed the elbow of the man who had ensconced himself by the fire; and thus the two strangers were brought into close companionship. They nodded to each other by way of breaking the ice of unacquaintance, and the first stranger handed his neighbour the family mug—a huge vessel of brown ware, having its upper edge worn away like a threshold by the rub of whole generations of thirsty lips that had gone the way of all flesh, and bearing the following inscription burnt upon its rotund side in yellow letters:

THERE IS NO FUN<br>
UNTiLL i CUM.

The other man, nothing loth, raised the mug to his lips, and drank on, and on, and on—till a curious blueness overspread the countenance of the shepherd's wife, who had regarded with no little surprise the first stranger's free offer to the second of what did not belong to him to dispense.

"I knew it!" said the toper to the shepherd with much satisfaction. "When I walked up your garden before coming in, and saw the hives all of a row, I said to myself, 'Where there's bees there's honey, and where there's honey there's mead.' But mead of such a truly comfortable sort as this I really didn't expect to meet in my older days." He took yet another pull at the mug, till it assumed an ominous elevation.

"Glad you enjoy it!" said the shepherd warmly.

"It is a goodish mead," assented Mrs. Fennel, with an absence of enthusiasm which seemed to say that it was possible to buy praise for one's cellar at too heavy a price. "It is trouble enough to make—and really I hardly think we shall make any more. For honey sells well, and we ourselves can make shift with a drop o' small mead and metheglin for common use from the comb-washings."

"O, but you'll never have the heart!" reproachfully cried the stranger in cinder-gray, after taking up the mug a third time and setting it down empty. "I love mead, when 'tis old like this, as I love to go to church o' Sundays, or to relieve the needy any day of the week."

"Ha, ha, ha!" said the man in the chimney-corner, who, in spite of the taciturnity induced by the pipe of tobacco, could not or would not refrain from this slight testimony to his comrade's humour.

Now the old mead of those days, brewed of the purest first-year or maiden honey, four pounds to the gallon—with its due complement of white of eggs, cinnamon, ginger, cloves, mace, rosemary, yeast, and processes of working, bottling, and cellaring—tasted remarkably strong; but it did not taste so strong as it actually was. Hence, presently, the stranger in cinder-gray at the table, moved by its creeping influence, unbuttoned his waistcoat, threw himself back in his chair, spread his legs, and made his presence felt in various ways.

"Well, well, as I say," he resumed, "I am going to Casterbridge, and to Casterbridge I must go. I should have been almost there by this time; but the rain drove me into your dwelling, and I'm not sorry for it."

"You don't live in Casterbridge?" said the shepherd.

"Not as yet; though I shortly mean to move there."

"Going to set up in trade, perhaps?"

"No, no," said the shepherd's wife. "It is easy to see that the gentleman is rich, and don't want to work at anything."

The cinder-gray stranger paused, as if to consider whether he would accept that definition of himself. He presently rejected it by answering, "Rich is not quite the word for me, dame. I do work, and I must work. And even if I only get to Casterbridge by midnight I must begin work there at eight tomorrow morning. Yes, het or wet, blow or snow, famine or sword, my day's work tomorrow must be done."

"Poor man! Then, in spite o' seeming, you be worse off than we?" replied the shepherd's wife.

"'Tis the nature of my trade, men and maidens. 'Tis the nature of my trade more than my poverty. . . . But really and truly I must up and off, or I shan't get a lodging in the town." However, the speaker did not move, and directly added, "There's time for one more draught of friendship before I go; and I'd perform it at once if the mug were not dry."

"Here's a mug o' small," said Mrs. Fennel. "Small, we call it, though to be sure 'tis only the first wash o' the combs."

"No," said the stranger disdainfully. "I won't spoil your first kindness by partaking o' your second."

"Certainly not," broke in Fennel. "We don't increase and multiply every day, and I'll fill the mug again." He went away to the dark place under the stairs where the barrel stood. The shepherdess followed him.

"Why should you do this?" she said reproachfully, as soon as they were alone. "He's emptied it once, though it held enough for ten people; and now he's not contented wi' the small, but must needs call for more o' the strong! And a stranger unbeknown to any of us. For my part, I don't like the look o' the man at all."

"But he's in the house, my honey; and 'tis a wet night, and a christening. Daze it, what's a cup of mead more or less? There'll be plenty more next bee-burning."

"Very well—this time, then," she answered, looking wistfully at the barrel. "But what is the man's calling, and where is he one of, that he should come in and join us like this?"

"I don't know. I'll ask him again."

The catastrophe of having the mug drained dry at one pull by the stranger in cinder-gray was effectually guarded against this time by Mrs. Fennel. She poured out his allowance in a small cup, keeping the large one at a discreet distance from him. When he had tossed off his portion the shepherd renewed his inquiry about the stranger's occupation.

The latter did not immediately reply, and the man in the chimney-corner, with sudden demonstrativeness, said, "Anybody may know my trade—I'm a wheelwright."

"A very good trade for these parts," said the shepherd.

"And anybody may know mine—if they've the sense to find it out," said the stranger in cinder-gray.

"You may generally tell what a man is by his claws," observed the hedge-carpenter, looking at his own hands, "My fingers be as full of thorns as an old pin-cushion is of pins."

The hands of the man in the chimney-corner instinctively sought the shade, and he gazed into the fire as he resumed his pipe. The man at the table took up the hedge-carpenter's remark, and added smartly, "True; but the oddity of my trade is that, instead of setting a mark upon me, it sets a mark upon my customers."

No observation being offered by anybody in elucidation of this enigma the shepherd's wife once more called for a song. The same obstacles presented themselves as at the former time—one had no voice, another had forgotten the first verse. The stranger at the table, whose soul had now risen to a good working temperature, relieved the difficulty by exclaiming that, to start the company, he would sing himself. Thrusting one thumb into the arm-hole of his waistcoat, he waved the other hand in the air, and, with an extemporizing gaze at the shining sheep-crooks above the mantelpiece, began:

>"O my trade it is the rarest one,
>   Simple shepherds all—
> My trade is a sight to see;
> For my customers I tie, and take them up on high,
>   And waft 'em to a far countree!"

The room was silent when he had finished the verse—with one exception, that of the man in the chimney-corner, who, at the singer's word, "Chorus!" joined him in a deep bass voice of musical relish:

>"And waft 'em to a far countree!"

Oliver Giles, John Pitcher the dairyman, the parish-clerk, the engaged man of fifty, the row of young women against the wall, seemed lost in thought not of the gayest kind. The shepherd looked meditatively on the ground, the shepherdess gazed keenly at the singer, and with some suspicion; she was doubting whether this stranger were merely singing an old song from recollection, or was composing one there and then for the occasion. All were as perplexed at the obscure revelation as the guests at Belshazzar's Feast, except the man in the chimney-corner, who quietly said, "Second verse, stranger," and smoked on.

The singer thoroughly moistened himself from his lips inwards, and went on with the next stanza as requested:

>"My tools are but common ones,
>   Simple shepherds all—
> My tools are no sight to see:
> A little hempen string, and a post whereon to swing,
>   Are implements enough for me!"

Shepherd Fennel glanced round. There was no longer any doubt that the stranger was answering his question rhythmically. The guests one and all started back with suppressed exclamations. The young woman engaged to the man of fifty fainted half-way, and would have proceeded, but finding him wanting in alacrity for catching her she sat down trembling.

"O, he's the—!" whispered the people in the background, mentioning the name of an ominous public officer. "He's come to do it! 'Tis to be at Casterbridge jail tomorrow—the man for sheep-stealing—the poor clockmaker we heard of, who used to live away at Shottsford and had no work to do—Timothy Summers, whose family were a-starving, and so he went out of Shottsford by the high-road, and took a sheep in open daylight, defying the farmer and the farmer's wife and the farmer's lad, and every man jack among 'em. He" (and they nodded towards the stranger of the deadly trade) "is come from up the country to do it because there's not enough to do in his own county-town, and he's got the place here now our own county man's dead; he's going to live in the same cottage under the prison wall."

The stranger in cinder-gray took no notice of this whispered string of observations, but again wetted his lips. Seeing that his friend in the chimney-corner was the only one who reciprocated his joviality in any way, he held out his cup towards that appreciative comrade, who also held out his own. They clinked together, the eyes of the rest of the room hanging upon the singer's actions. He parted his lips for the third verse but at that moment another knock was audible upon the door. This time the knock was faint and hesitating.

The company seemed scared; the shepherd looked with consternation towards the entrance, and it was with some effort that he resisted his alarmed wife's deprecatory glance, and uttered for the third time the welcoming words, "Walk in!"

The door was gently opened, and another man stood upon the mat. He, like those who had preceded him, was a stranger. This time it was a short, small personage, of fair complexion, and dressed in a decent suit of dark clothes.

"Can you tell me the way to—?" he began: when, gazing round the room to observe the nature of the company amongst whom he had fallen, his eyes lighted on the stranger in cinder-gray. It was just at the instant when the latter, who had thrown his mind into his song with such a will that he scarcely heeded the interruption, silenced all whispers and inquiries by bursting into his third verse:

> "Tomorrow is my working day,
>     Simple shepherds all—
> Tomorrow is a working day for me:
> For the farmer's sheep is slain, and the lad who did it ta'en,
>     And on his soul may God ha' merc-y!"

The stranger in the chimney-corner, waving cups with the singer so heartily that his mead splashed over on the hearth, repeated in his bass voice as before:

> "And on his soul may God ha' merc-y!"

All this time the third stranger had been standing in the doorway. Finding now that he did not come forward or go on speaking, the guests particularly regarded him. They noticed to their surprise that he stood before them the picture of abject terror—his knees trembling, his hand shaking so violently that the door-latch by which he supported himself rattled audibly: his white lips were parted, and his eyes fixed on the merry officer of justice in the middle of the room. A moment more and he had turned, closed the door, and fled.

"What a man can it be?" said the shepherd.

The rest, between the awfulness of their late discovery and the odd conduct of this third visitor, looked as if they knew not what to think, and said nothing. Instinctively they withdrew further and further from the grim gentleman in their midst, whom some of them seemed to take for the Prince of Darkness himself, till they formed a remote circle, an empty space of floor being left between them and him—

. . . circulus, cujus centrum diabolus.

The room was so silent—though there were more than twenty people in it—that nothing could be heard but the patter of the rain against the window-shutters, accompanied by the occasional hiss of a stray drop that fell down the chimney into the fire, and the steady puffing of the man in the corner, who had now resumed his pipe of long clay.

The stillness was unexpectedly broken. The distant sound of a gun reverberated through the air—apparently from the direction of the county-town.

"Be jiggered!" cried the stranger who had sung the song, jumping up.

"What does that mean?" asked several.

"A prisoner escaped from the jail—that's what it means."

All listened. The sound was repeated, and none of them spoke but the man in the chimney-corner, who said quietly, "I've often been told that in this county they fire a gun at such times; but I never heard it till now."

"I wonder if it is *my* man?" murmured the personage in cinder-gray.

"Surely it is!" said the shepherd involuntarily. "And surely we've zeed him! That little man who looked in at the door by now, and quivered like a leaf when he zeed ye and heard your song!"

"His teeth chattered, and the breath went out of his body," said the dairyman.

"And his heart seemed to sink within him like a stone," said Oliver Giles.

"And he bolted as if he'd been shot at," said the hedge-carpenter.

"True—his teeth chattered, and his heart seemed to sink; and he bolted as if he'd been shot at," slowly summed up the man in the chimney-corner.

"I didn't notice it," remarked the hangman.

"We were all a-wondering what made him run off in such a fright," faltered one of the women against the wall, "and now 'tis explained!"

The firing of the alarm gun went on at intervals, low and sullenly, and their suspicions became a certainty. The sinister gentleman in cinder-gray roused himself. "Is there a constable here?" he asked, in thick tones. "If so, let him step forward."

The engaged man of fifty stepped quavering out from the wall, his betrothed beginning to sob on the back of the chair.

"You are a sworn constable?"

"I be, sir."

"Then pursue the criminal at once, with assistance, and bring him back here. He can't have gone far."

"I will, sir, I will—when I've got my staff. I'll go home and get it, and come sharp here, and start in a body."

"Staff!—never mind your staff; the man'll be gone!"

"But I can't do nothing without my staff—can I, William, and John, and Charles Jake? No; for there's the king's royal crown a painted on en in yaller and gold, and the lion and the unicorn, so as when I raise en up and hit my prisoner, 'tis made a lawful blow thereby. I wouldn't 'tempt to take up a man without my staff—no, not I. If I hadn't the law to gie me courage, why, instead o' my taking up him he might take up me!"

"Now, I'm a king's man myself, and can give you authority enough for this," said the formidable officer in gray. "Now then, all of ye, be ready. Have ye any lanterns?"

"Yes—have ye any lanterns?—I demand it!" said the constable.

"And the rest of you able-bodied—"

"Able-bodied men—yes—the rest of ye!" said the constable.

"Have you some good stout staves and pitchforks—"

"Staves and pitchforks—in the name o' the law! And take 'em in yer hands and go in quest, and do as we in authority tell ye!"

Thus aroused, the men prepared to give chase. The evidence was, indeed, though circumstantial, so convincing, that but little argument was needed to show the shepherd's guests that after what they had seen it would look very much like connivance if they did not instantly pursue the unhappy third stranger, who could not as yet have gone more than a few hundred yards over such uneven country.

A shepherd is always well provided with lanterns; and, lighting these hastily, and with hurdle-staves in their hands, they poured out of the door, taking a direction along the crest of the hill, away from the town, the rain having fortunately a little abated.

Disturbed by the noise, or possibly by unpleasant dreams of her baptism, the child who had been christened began to cry heart-brokenly in the room overhead. These notes of grief came down through the chinks of the floor to the ears of the women below, who jumped up one by one, and seemed glad of the excuse to ascend and comfort the baby, for the incidents of the last half-hour greatly oppressed them. Thus in the space of two or three minutes the room on the ground-floor was deserted quite.

But it was not for long. Hardly had the sound of footsteps died away when a man returned round the corner of the house from the direction the pursuers had taken. Peeping in at the door, and seeing nobody there, he entered leisurely. It was the stranger of the chimney-corner, who had gone out with the rest. The motive of his return was shown by his helping himself to a cut piece of skimmer-cake that lay on a ledge beside where he had sat, and which he had apparently forgotten to take with him. He also poured out half a cup more mead from the quantity that remained, ravenously eating and drinking these as he stood. He had not finished when another figure came in just as quietly—his friend in cinder-gray.

"O—you here?" said the latter, smiling. "I thought you had gone to help in the capture." And this speaker also revealed the object of his return by looking solicitously round for the fascinating mug of old mead.

"And I thought you had gone," said the other, continuing his skimmer-cake with some effort.

"Well, on second thoughts, I felt there were enough without me," said the first confidentially, "and such a night as it is, too. Besides, 'tis the business o' the Government to take care of its criminals—not mine."

"True; so it is. And I felt as you did, that there were enough without me."

"I don't want to break my limbs running over the humps and hollows of this wild country."

"Nor I neither, between you and me."

"These shepherd-people are used to it—simple-minded souls, you know, stirred up to anything in a moment. They'll have him ready for me before the morning, and no trouble to me at all."

"They'll have him, and we shall have saved ourselves all labour in the matter."

"True, true. Well, my way is to Casterbridge; and 'tis as much as my legs will do to take me that far. Going the same way?"

"No, I am sorry to say! I have to get home over there" (he nodded indefinitely to the right), "and I feel as you do, that it is quite enough for my legs to do before bedtime."

The other had by this time finished the mead in the mug, after which, shaking hands heartily at the door, and wishing each other well, they went their several ways.

In the meantime the company of pursuers had reached the end of the hog's-back elevation which dominated this part of the down. They had decided on no particular plan of action; and, finding that the man of the baleful trade was no longer in their company, they seemed quite unable to form any such plan now. They descended in all directions down the hill, and straightway several of the party fell into the snare set by Nature for all misguided midnight ramblers over this part of the cretaceous formation. The "lanchets," or flint slopes, which belted the escarpment at intervals of a dozen yards, took the less cautious ones unawares, and losing their footing on the rubbly steep they slid sharply downwards, the lanterns rolling from their hands to the bottom, and there lying on their sides till the horn was scorched through.

When they had again gathered themselves together the shepherd, as the man who knew the country best, took the lead, and guided them round these treacherous inclines. The lanterns, which seemed rather to dazzle their eyes and warn the fugitive than to assist them in the exploration, were extinguished, due silence was observed; and in this more rational order they plunged into the vale. It was a grassy, briery, moist defile, affording some shelter to any person who had sought it; but the party perambulated it in vain, and ascended on the other side. Here they wandered apart, and after an interval closed together again to report progress. At the second time of closing in they found themselves near a lonely ash, the single tree on this part of the coomb, probably sown there by a passing bird some fifty years before. And here, standing a little to one side of the trunk, as motionless as the trunk itself, appeared the man they were in quest of, his outline being well defined against the sky beyond. The band noiselessly drew up and faced him.

"Your money or your life!" said the constable sternly to the still figure.

"No, no," whispered John Pitcher. " 'Tisn't our side ought to say that. That's the doctrine of vagabonds like him, and we be on the side of the law."

"Well, well," replied the constable impatiently; "I must say something, mustn't I? and if you had all the weight o' this undertaking upon your mind, perhaps you'd say the wrong thing too!—Prisoner at the bar, surrender, in the name of the Father—the Crown, I mane!"

The man under the tree seemed now to notice them for the first time, and, giving them no opportunity whatever for exhibiting their courage, he strolled slowly towards them. He was, indeed, the little man, the third stranger; but his trepidation had in a great measure gone.

"Well, travellers," he said, "did I hear ye speak to me?"

"You did: you've got to come and be our prisoner at once!" said the constable. "We arrest 'ee on the charge of not biding in Casterbridge jail in a decent proper manner to be hung tomorrow morning. Neighbours, do your duty, and seize the culpet!"

On hearing the charge the man seemed enlightened, and, saying not another word, resigned himself with preternatural civility to the search-party, who, with their staves in their hands, surrounded him on all sides, and marched him back towards the shepherd's cottage.

It was eleven o'clock by the time they arrived. The light shining from the open door, a sound of men's voices within, proclaimed to them as they approached the house that some new events had arisen in their absence. On entering they discovered the shepherd's living room to be invaded by two officers from Casterbridge jail, and a well-known magistrate who lived at the nearest county-seat, intelligence of the escape having become generally circulated.

"Gentlemen," said the constable, "I have brought back your man—not without risk and danger; but every one must do his duty! He is inside this circle of able-bodied persons, who have lent me useful aid, considering their ignorance of Crown work. Men, bring forward your prisoner!" And the third stranger was led to the light.

"Who is this?" said one of the officials.

"The man," said the constable.

"Certainly not," said the turnkey; and the first corroborated his statement.

"But how can it be otherwise?" asked the constable. "Or why was he so terrified at sight o' the singing instrument of the law who sat there?" Here he related the strange behaviour of the third stranger on entering the house during the hangman's song.

"Can't understand it," said the officer coolly. "All I know is that it is not the condemned man. He's quite a different character from this one; a gauntish fellow, with dark hair and eyes, rather good-looking, and with a musical bass voice that if you heard it once you'd never mistake as long as you lived."

"Why souls—'twas the man in the chimney-corner!"

"Hey—what?" said the magistrate, coming forward after inquiring particulars from the shepherd in the background. "Haven't you got the man after all?"

"Well, sir," said the constable, "he's the man we were in search of, that's true; and yet he's not the man we were in search of. For the man we were in search of was not the man we wanted, sir, if you understand my every-day way; for 'twas the man in the chimney-corner!"

"A pretty kettle of fish altogether!" said the magistrate. "You had better start for the other man at once."

The prisoner now spoke for the first time. The mention of the man in the chimney-corner seemed to have moved him as nothing else could do. "Sir," he said, stepping forward to the magistrate, "take no more trouble about me. The time is come when I may as well speak. I have done nothing; my crime is that the condemned man is my brother. Early this afternoon I left home at Shottsford to tramp it all the way to Casterbridge jail to bid him farewell. I was benighted, and called here to rest and ask the way. When I opened the door I saw before me the very man, my brother, that I thought to see in the condemned cell at Casterbridge. He was in this chimney-corner; and jammed close to him, so that he could not have got out if he had tried, was the executioner who'd come to take his life, singing a song about it and not knowing that it was his victim who was close by, joining in to save appearances. My brother threw a glance of agony at me, and I knew he meant, 'Don't reveal what you see; my life depends on it.' I was so terror-struck that I could hardly stand, and, not knowing what I did, I turned and hurried away."

The narrator's manner and tone had the stamp of truth, and his story made a great impression on all around. "And do you know where your brother is at the present time?" asked the magistrate.

"I do not. I have never seen him since I closed this door."

"I can testify to that, for we've been between ye ever since," said the constable.

"Where does he think to fly to?—what is his occupation?"

"He's a watch-and-clock-maker, sir."

" 'A said 'a was a wheelwright—a wicked rogue," said the constable.

"The wheels of clocks and watches he meant, no doubt," said Shepherd Fennel. "I thought his hands were palish for's trade."

"Well, it appears to me that nothing can be gained by retaining this poor man in custody," said the magistrate; "your business lies with the other, unquestionably."

And so the little man was released off-hand; but he looked nothing the less sad on that account, it being beyond the power of magistrate or constable to raze out the written troubles in his brain, for they concerned another whom he regarded with more solicitude than himself. When this was done, and the man had gone his way, the night was found to be so far advanced that it was deemed useless to renew the search before the next morning.

Next day, accordingly, the quest for the clever sheep-stealer became general and keen, to all appearance at least. But the intended punishment was cruelly disproportioned to the transgression, and the sympathy of a great many country-folk in that district was strongly on the side of the fugitive. Moreover, his marvellous coolness and daring in hob-and-nobbing with the hangman, under the unprecedented circumstances of the shepherd's party, won their admiration. So that it may be questioned if all those who ostensibly made themselves so busy in exploring woods and fields and lanes were quite so thorough when it came to the private examination of their own lofts and outhouses. Stories were afloat of a mysterious figure being occasionally seen in some old overgrown trackway or other, remote from turnpike roads; but when a search was instituted in any of these suspected quarters nobody was found. Thus the days and weeks passed without tidings.

In brief, the bass-voiced man of the chimney-corner was never recaptured. Some said that he went across the sea, others that he did not, but buried himself in the depths of a populous city. At any rate, the gentleman in cinder-gray never did his morning's work at Casterbridge, nor met anywhere at all, for business purposes, the genial comrade with whom he had passed an hour of relaxation in the lonely house on the slope of the coomb.

The grass has long been green on the graves of Shepherd Fennel and his frugal wife; the guests who made up the christening party have mainly followed their entertainers to the tomb; the baby in whose honour they all had met is a matron in the sere and yellow leaf. But the arrival of the three strangers at the shepherd's that night, and the details connected therewith, is a story as well known as ever in the country about Higher Crowstairs.

# GLADIUS DEI

## Thomas Mann

*Born in Lübeck, Germany, in 1875, Thomas Mann, one of the most famous writers of the twentieth century, spent his childhood and youth in that famous seaport city. His first important novel,* Buddenbrooks, *published in 1901, is set in Lübeck and is largely autobiographical. Mann became an exile during the Nazi regime; his books were banned, and in 1936 he was deprived of his citizenship. His years of exile were spent in Switzerland, Palestine, Egypt, and the United States, where he lectured at Princeton University for a time. He became an American citizen in 1944. In 1953 he returned to Switzerland and died in Zurich in 1955 while working on his last novel,* The Confessions of Felix Krull, *published posthumously that year. Among Mann's best known works are* The Magic Mountain *(1924), considered by many his masterpiece, the* Joseph and His Brothers *tetralogy (1933–1944), and* Dr. Faustus *(1948). Mann's legacy is clearly seen in "Gladius Dei," particularly that quality Kenneth Douglas has called his "desire to comprehend." "Without relinquishing the German burgher's virtues," Douglas states, "Mann grew to be a citizen of the world. Rooted in his milieu and origins, he is yet, somewhat like Joyce, outside them. The literatures of Germany and the rest of Europe, philosophy, history, music, psychology, all contributed to make of Mann a mirror of his age."*

Munich was radiant. Above the gay squares and white columned temples, the classicistic monuments and the baroque churches, the leaping fountains, the palaces and parks of the Residence there stretched a sky of luminous blue silk. Well-arranged leafy vistas laced with sun and shade lay basking in the sunshine of a beautiful day in early June.

There was a twittering of birds and a blithe holiday spirit in all the little streets. And in the squares and past the rows of villas there swelled, rolled, and hummed the leisurely, entertaining traffic of that easy-going, charming town. Travelers of all nationalities drove about in the slow little droshkies, looking right and left in aimless curiosity at the housefronts; they mounted and descended museum stairs. Many windows stood open and music was heard from within: practicing on piano, cello, or violin—earnest and well-meant amateur efforts; while from the Odeon came the sound of serious work on several grand pianos.

Young people, the kind that can whistle the Nothung motif, who fill the pit of the Schauspielhaus every evening, wandered in and out of the University and Library with literary magazines in their coat pockets. A court carriage stood before the Academy, the home of the plastic arts, which spreads its white wings between the Türkenstrasse and the Siegestor. And colorful groups of models, picturesque old men, women and children in Albanian costume, stood or lounged at the top of the balustrade.

Indolent, unhurried sauntering was the mode in all the long streets of the northern quarter. There life is lived for pleasanter ends than the driving greed of gain. Young artists with little round hats on the backs of their heads, flowing cravats and no canes—carefree bachelors who paid for their lodgings with color-sketches—were strolling up and down to let the clear blue morning play upon their mood, also to look at the little girls, the pretty, rather plump type, with the brunette bandeaux, the too large feet, and the unobjectionable morals. Every fifth house had studio windows blinking in the sun. Sometimes a fine piece of architecture stood out from a middle-class row, the work of some imaginative young architect; a wide front with shallow bays and decorations in a bizarre style very expressive and full of invention. Or the door to some monotonous façade would be framed in a bold improvisation of flowing lines and sunny colors, with bacchantes, naiads, and rosy-skinned nudes.

It was always a joy to linger before the windows of the cabinet-makers and the shops for modern articles *de luxe*. What a sense for luxurious nothings and amusing, significant line was displayed in the shape of everything! Little shops that sold picture-frames, sculptures, and antiques there were in endless number; in their windows you might see those busts of Florentine women of the Renaissance, so full of noble poise and poignant charm. And the owners of the smallest and meanest of these shops spoke of Mino da Fiesole and Donatello as though he had received the rights of reproduction from them personally.

But on the Odeonsplatz, in view of the mighty loggia with the spacious mosaic pavement before it, diagonally opposite to the Regent's palace, people were crowding round the large windows and glass show-cases of the big art-shop owned by M. Blüthenzweig. What a glorious display! There were reproductions of the masterpieces of all the galleries in the world, in costly decorated and tinted frames, the good taste of which was precious in its very simplicity. There were copies of modern paintings, works of a joyously sensuous fantasy, in which the antiques seemed born again in humorous and realistic guise; bronze nudes and fragile ornamental glassware; tall, thin earthenware vases with an iridescent glaze produced by a bath in metal steam; *éditions de luxe* which were triumphs of modern binding and presswork, containing the works of the most modish poets, set out with every possible advantage of sumptuous elegance. Cheek by jowl with these, the portraits of artists, musicians, philosophers, actors, writers, displayed to gratify the public taste for personalities.—In the first window, next the book-shop, a large picture stood on an easel, with a crowd of people in front of it, a fine sepia photograph in a wide old-gold frame, a very striking reproduction of the sensation at this year's great international exhibition, to which public attention is always invited by means of effective and artistic posters stuck up everywhere on hoardings among concert programs and clever advertisements of toilet preparations.

If you looked into the windows of the book-shop your eye met such titles as *Interior Decoration Since the Renaissance, The Renaissance in Modern Decorative Art, The Book as Work of Art, The Decorative Arts, Hunger for Art,* and many more. And you would remember that these thought-provoking pamphlets were sold and read by the thousand and that discussions on these subjects were the preoccupation of all the salons.

You might be lucky enough to meet in person one of the famous fair ones whom less fortunate folk know only through the medium of art; one of those rich and beautiful women whose Titian-blond coloring Nature's most sweet and cunning hand did *not* lay on, but whose diamond parures and beguiling charms had received immortality from the hand of some portrait-painter of genius and whose love-affairs were the talk of the town. These were the queens of the artist balls at carnival-time. They were a little painted, a little made up, full of haughty caprices, worthy of adoration, avid of praise. You might see a carriage rolling up the Ludwigstrasse, with such a great painter and his mistress inside. People would be pointing out the sight, standing still to gaze after the pair. Some of them would curtsy. A little more and the very policemen would stand at attention.

Art flourished, art swayed the destinies of the town, art stretched above it her rose-bound scepter and smiled. On every hand obsequious interest was displayed in her prosperity, on every hand she was served with industry and devotion. There was a downright cult of line, decoration, form, significance, beauty. Munich was radiant.

A youth was coming down the Schellingstrasse. With the bells of cyclists ringing about him he strode across the wooden pavement toward the broad façade of the Ludwigskirche. Looking at him it was as though a shadow passed across the sky, or cast over the spirit some memory of melancholy hours. Did he not love the sun which bathed the lovely city in its festal light? Why did he walk wrapped in his own thoughts, his eyes directed on the ground?

No one in that tolerant and variety-loving town would have taken offense at his wearing no hat; but why need the hood of his ample black cloak have been drawn over his head, shadowing his low, prominent, and peaked forehead, covering his ears and framing his haggard cheeks? What pangs of conscience, what scruples and self-tortures had so availed to hollow out these cheeks? It is frightful, on such a sunny day, to see care sitting in the hollows of the human face. His dark brows thickened at the narrow base of his hooked and prominent nose. His lips were unpleasantly full, his eyes brown and close-lying. When he lifted them, diagonal folds appeared on the peaked brow. His gaze expressed knowledge, limitation, and suffering. Seen in profile his face was strikingly like an old painting preserved at Florence in a narrow cloister cell whence once a frightful and shattering protest issued against life and her triumphs.

Hieronymus walked along the Schellingstrasse with a slow, firm stride, holding his wide cloak together with both hands from inside. Two little girls, two of those pretty, plump little creatures with the bandeaux, the big feet, and the unobjectionable morals, strolled toward him arm in arm, on pleasure bent. They poked each other and laughed, they bent double with laughter, they even broke into a run and ran away still laughing, at his hood and his face. But he paid them no heed. With bent head, looking neither to the right nor to the left, he crossed the Ludwigstrasse and mounted the church steps.

The great wings of the middle portal stood wide open. From somewhere within the consecrated twilight, cool, dank, incense-laden, there came a pale red glow. An old woman with inflamed eyes rose from a prayer-stool and slipped on crutches through the columns. Otherwise the church was empty.

Hieronymus sprinkled brow and breast at the stoup, bent the knee before the high altar, and then paused in the center nave. Here in the church his stature seemed to have grown. He stood upright and immovable; his head was flung up and his great hooked nose jutted domineeringly above the thick lips. His eyes no longer sought the ground, but looked straight and boldly into the distance, at the crucifix on the high altar. Thus he stood awhile, then retreating he bent the knee again and left the church.

He strode up the Ludwigstrasse, slowly, firmly, with bent head, in the center of the wide unpaved road, toward the mighty loggia with its statues. But arrived at the Odeonsplatz, he looked up, so that the folds came out on his peaked forehead, and checked his step, his attention being called to the crowd at the windows of the big art-shop of M. Blüthenzweig.

People moved from window to window, pointing out to each other the treasures displayed and exchanging views as they looked over one another's shoulders. Hieronymus mingled among them and did as they did, taking in all these things with his eyes, one by one.

He saw the reproductions of masterpieces from all the galleries in the world, the priceless frames so precious in their simplicity, the Renaissance sculpture, the bronze nudes, the exquisitely bound volumes, the iridescent vases, the portraits of artists, musicians, philosophers, actors, writers; he looked at everything and turned a moment of his scrutiny upon each object. Holding his mantle closely together with both hands from inside, he moved his hood-covered head in short turns from one thing to the next, gazing at each awhile with a dull, inimical, and remotely surprised air, lifting the dark brows which grew so thick at the base of the nose. At length he stood in front of the last window, which contained the startling picture. For awhile he looked over the shoulders of people before him and then in his turn reached a position directly in front of the window.

The large red-brown photograph in the choice old-gold frame stood on an easel in the center. It was a Madonna, but an utterly unconventional one, a work of entirely modern feeling. The figure of the Holy Mother was revealed as enchantingly feminine and beautiful. Her great smoldering eyes were rimmed with darkness, and her delicate and strangely smiling lips were half-parted. Her slender fingers held in a somewhat nervous grasp the hips of the Child, a nude boy of pronounced, almost primitive leanness. He was playing with her breast and glancing aside at the beholder with a wise look in his eyes.

Two other youths stood near Hieronymus, talking about the picture. They were two young men with books under their arms, which they had fetched from the Library or were taking thither. Humanistically educated people, that is, equipped with science and with art.

"The little chap is in luck, devil take me!" said one.

"He seems to be trying to make one envious," replied the other. "A bewildering female!"

"A female to drive a man crazy! Gives you funny ideas about the Immaculate Conception."

"No, she doesn't look exactly immaculate. Have you seen the original?"

"Of course; I was quite bowled over. She makes an even more aphrodisiac impression in color. Especially the eyes."

"The likeness is pretty plain."

"How so?"

"Don't you know the model? Of course he used his little dressmaker. It is almost a portrait, only with a lot more emphasis on the corruptible. The girl is more innocent."

"I hope so. Life would be altogether too much of a strain if there were many like this *mater amata*."

"The Pinakothek has bought it."

"Really? Well, well! They knew what they were about, anyhow. The treatment of the flesh and the flow of the linen garment are really first-class."

"Yes, an incredibly gifted chap."

"Do you know him?"

"A little. He will have a career, that is certain. He has been invited twice by the Prince Regent."

This last was said as they were taking leave of each other.

"Shall I see you this evening at the theater?" asked the first. "The Dramatic Club is giving Machiavelli's *Mandragola*."

"Oh, bravo! That will be great, of course. I had meant to go to the Variété, but I shall probably choose our stout Niccolò after all. Good-by."

They parted, going off to right and left. New people took their places and looked at the famous picture. But Hieronymus stood where he was, motionless, with his head thrust out; his hands clutched convulsively at the mantle as they held it together from inside. His brows were no longer lifted with that cool and unpleasantly surprised expression; they were drawn and darkened; his cheeks, half-shrouded in the black hood, seemed more sunken than ever and his thick lips had gone pale. Slowly his head dropped lower and lower, so that finally his eyes stared upward at the work of art, while the nostrils of his great nose dilated.

Thus he remained for perhaps a quarter of an hour. The crowd about him melted away, but he did not stir from the spot. At last he turned slowly on the balls of his feet and went hence.

But the picture of the Madonna went with him. Always and ever, whether in his hard and narrow little room or kneeling in the cool church, it stood before his outraged soul, with its smoldering, dark-rimmed eyes, its riddlingly smiling lips—stark and beautiful. And no prayer availed to exorcize it.

But the third night it happened that a command and summons from on high came to Hieronymus, to intercede and lift his voice against the frivolity, blasphemy, and arrogance of beauty. In vain like Moses he protested that he had not the gift of tongues. God's will remained unshaken; in a loud voice He demanded that the faint-hearted Hieronymus go forth to sacrifice amid the jeers of the foe.

And since God would have it so, he set forth one morning and wended his way to the great art-shop of M. Blüthenzweig. He wore his hood over his head and held his mantle together in front from inside with both hands as he went.

The air had grown heavy, the sky was livid and thunder threatened. Once more crowds were besieging the show-cases at the art-shop and especially the window where the photograph of the Madonna stood. Hieronymus cast one brief glance thither; then he pushed up the latch of the glass door hung with placards and art magazines. "As God wills," said he, and entered the shop.

A young girl was somewhere at a desk writing in a big book. She was a pretty brunette thing with bandeaux of hair and big feet. She came up to him and asked pleasantly what he would like.

"Thank you," said Hieronymus in a low voice and looked her earnestly in the face, with diagonal wrinkles in his peaked brow. "I would speak not to you but to the owner of this shop, Herr Blüthenzweig."

She hesitated a little, turned away, and took up her work once more. He stood there in the middle of the shop.

Instead of the single specimens in the show-windows there was here a riot and a heaping-up of luxury, a fullness of color, line, form, style, invention, good taste, and beauty. Hieronymus looked slowly round him, drawing his mantle close with both hands.

There were several people in the shop besides him. At one of the broad tables running across the room sat a man in a yellow suit, with a black goat's beard, looking at a portfolio of French drawings, over which he now and then emitted a bleating laugh. He was being waited on by an undernourished and vegetarian young man, who kept on dragging up fresh portfolios. Diagonally opposite the bleating man sat an elegant old dame, examining art embroideries with a pattern of fabulous flowers in pale tones standing together on tall perpendicular stalks. An attendant hovered about her too. A leisurely Englishman in a traveling cap, with his pipe in his mouth, sat at another table. Cold and smooth-shaven, of indefinite age, in his good English clothes, he sat examining bronzes brought to him by M. Blüthenzweig in person. He was holding up by the head the dainty figure of a nude young girl, immature and delicately articulated, her hands crossed in coquettish innocence upon her breast. He studied her thoroughly, turning her slowly about. M. Blüthenzweig, a man with a short, heavy brown beard and bright brown eyes of exactly the same color, moved in a semicircle round him, rubbing his hands, praising the statuette with all the terms his vocabulary possessed.

"A hundred and fifty marks, sir," he said in English. "Munich art— very charming, in fact. Simply full of charm, you know. Grace itself. Really extremely pretty, good, admirable, in fact." Then he thought of some more and went on: "Highly attractive, fascinating." Then he began again from the beginning.

His nose lay a little flat on his upper lip, so that he breathed constantly with a slight sniff into his mustache. Sometimes he did this as he approached a customer, stooping over as though he were smelling at him. When Hieronymus entered, M. Blüthenzweig had examined him cursorily in this way, then devoted himself again to his Englishman.

The elegant old dame made her selection and left the shop. A man entered. M. Blüthenzweig sniffed briefly at him as though to scent out his capacity to buy and left him to the young bookkeeper. The man purchased a faience bust of young Piero de' Medici, son of Lorenzo, and went out again. The Englishman began to depart. He had acquired the statuette of the young girl and left amid bowings from M. Blüthenzweig. Then the art-dealer turned to Hieronymous and came forward.

"You wanted something?" he said, without any particular courtesy.

Hieronymus held his cloak together with both hands and looked the other in the face almost without winking an eyelash. He parted his big lips slowly and said:

"I have come to you on account of the picture in the window there, the big photograph, the Madonna." His voice was thick and without modulation.

"Yes, quite right," said M. Blüthenzweig briskly and began rubbing his hands. "Seventy marks in the frame. It is unfadable—a first-class reproduction. Highly attractive and full of charm."

Hieronymus was silent. He nodded his head in the hood and shrank a little into himself as the dealer spoke. Then he drew himself up again and said:

"I would remark to you first of all that I am not in the position to purchase anything, nor have I the desire. I am sorry to have to disappoint your expectations. I regret if it upsets you. But in the first place I am poor and in the second I do not love the things you sell. No, I cannot buy anything."

"No? Well, then?" asked M. Blüthenzweig, sniffing a good deal. "Then may I ask—"

"I suppose," Hieronymus went on, "that being what you are you look down on me because I am not in a position to buy."

"Oh—er—not at all," said M. Blüthenzweig. "Not at all. Only—"

"And yet I beg you to hear me and give some consideration to my words."

"Consideration to your words. H'm—may I ask—"

"You may ask," said Hieronymus, "and I will answer you. I have come to beg you to remove that picture, the big photograph, the Madonna, out of your window and never display it again."

M. Blüthenzweig looked awhile dumbly into Hieronymus's face—as though he expected him to be abashed at the words he had just uttered. But as this did not happen he gave a violent sniff and spoke himself:

"Will you be so good as to tell me whether you are here in any official capacity which authorizes you to dictate to me, or what does bring you here?"

"Oh, no," replied Hieronymus, "I have neither office nor dignity from the state. I have no power on my side, sir. What brings me hither is my conscience alone."

M. Blüthenzweig, searching for words, snorted violently into his mustache. At length he said:

"Your conscience . . . well, you will kindly understand that I take not the faintest interest in your conscience." With which he turned round and moved quickly to his desk at the back of the shop, where he began to write. Both attendants laughed heartily. The pretty Fräulein giggled over her account-book. As for the yellow gentleman with the goat's beard, he was evidently a foreigner, for he gave no sign of comprehension but went on studying the French drawings and emitting from time to time his bleating laugh.

"Just get rid of the man for me," said M. Blüthenzweig shortly over his shoulder to his assistant. He went on writing. The poorly paid young vegetarian approached Hieronymus, smothering his laughter, and the other salesman came up too.

"May we be of service to you in any other way?" the first asked mildly. Hieronymus fixed him with his glazed and suffering eyes.

"No," he said, "you cannot. I beg you to take the Madonna picture out of the window, at once and forever."

"But—why?"

"It is the Holy Mother of God," said Hieronymus in a subdued voice.

"Quite. But you have heard that Herr Blüthenzweig is not inclined to accede to your request."

"We must bear in mind that it is the Holy Mother of God," said Hieronymus again and his head trembled on his neck.

"So we must. But should we not be allowed to exhibit any Madonnas—or paint any?"

"It is not that," said Hieronymus, almost whispering. He drew himself up and shook his head energetically several times. His peaked brow under the hood was entirely furrowed with long, deep cross-folds. "You know very well that it is vice itself that is painted there—naked sensuality. I was standing near two simple young people and overheard with my own ears that it led them astray upon the doctrine of the Immaculate Conception."

"Oh, permit me—that is not the point," said the young salesman, smiling. In his leisure hours he was writing a brochure on the modern movement in art and was well qualified to conduct a cultured conversation. "The picture is a work of art," he went on, "and one must measure it by the appropriate standards as such. It has been very highly praised on all hands. The state has purchased it."

"I know that the state has purchased it," said Hieronymus. "I also know that the artist has twice dined with the Prince Regent. It is common talk —and God knows how people interpret the fact that a man can become famous by such work as this. What does such a fact bear witness to? To the blindness of the world, a blindness inconceivable, if not indeed shamelessly hypocritical. This picture has its origin in sensual lust and is enjoyed in the same—is that true or not? Answer me! And you too answer me, Herr Blüthenzweig!"

A pause ensued. Hieronymus seemed in all seriousness to demand an answer to his question, looking by turns at the staring attendants and the round back M. Blüthenzweig turned upon him, with his own piercing and anguishing brown eyes. Silence reigned. Only the yellow man with the goat's beard, bending over the French drawings, broke it with his bleating laugh.

"It is true," Hieronymus went on in a hoarse voice that shook with his profound indignation. "You do not dare deny it. How then can honor be done to its creator, as though he had endowed mankind with a new ideal possession? How can one stand before it and surrender unthinkingly to the base enjoyment which it purveys, persuading oneself in all seriousness that one is yielding to a noble and elevated sentiment, highly creditable to the human race? Is this reckless ignorance or abandoned hypocrisy?

My understanding falters, it is completely at a loss when confronted by the absurd fact that a man can achieve renown on this earth by the stupid and shameless exploitation of the animal instincts. Beauty? What is beauty? What forces are they which use beauty as their tool today—and upon what does it work? No one can fail to know this, Herr Blüthenzweig. But who, understanding it clearly, can fail to feel disgust and pain? It is criminal to play upon the ignorance of the immature, the lewd, the brazen, and the unscrupulous by elevating beauty into an idol to be worshiped, to give it even more power over those who know not affliction and have no knowledge of redemption. You are unknown to me, and you look at me with black looks—yet answer me! Knowledge, I tell you, is the profoundest torture in the world; but it is the purgatory without whose purifying pangs no soul can reach salvation. It is not infantile, blasphemous shallowness that can save us, Herr Blüthenzweig; only knowledge can avail, knowledge in which the passions of our loathsome flesh die away and are quenched."

Silence.—The yellow man with the goat's beard gave a sudden little bleat.

"I think you really must go now," said the underpaid assistant mildly.

But Hieronymus made no move to do so. Drawn up in his hooded cape, he stood with blazing eyes in the center of the shop and his thick lips poured out condemnation in a voice that was harsh and rusty and clanking.

"Art, you cry; enjoyment, beauty! Enfold the world in beauty and endow all things with the noble grace of style!—Profligate, away! Do you think to wash over with lurid colors the misery of the world? Do you think with the sounds of feasting and music to drown out the voice of the tortured earth? Shameless one, you err! God lets not Himself be mocked, and your impudent deification of the glistering surface of things is an abomination in His eyes. You tell me that I blaspheme art. I say to you that you lie. I do not blaspheme art. Art is no conscienceless delusion, lending itself to reinforce the allurements of the fleshly. Art is the holy torch which turns its light upon all the frightful depths, all the shameful and woeful abysses of life; art is the godly fire laid to the world that, being redeemed by pity, it may flame up and dissolve altogether with its shames and torments.—Take it out, Herr Blüthenzweig, take away the work of that famous painter out of your window—you would do well to burn it with a hot fire and strew its ashes to the four winds—yes, to all the four winds—"

His harsh voice broke off. He had taken a violent backward step, snatched one arm from his black wrappings, and stretched it passionately forth, gesturing toward the window with a hand that shook as though palsied. And in this commanding attitude he paused. His great hooked nose seemed to jut more than ever, his dark brows were gathered so thick and high that folds crowded upon the peaked forehead shaded by the hood; a hectic flush mantled his hollow cheeks.

But at this point M. Blüthenzweig turned round. Perhaps he was outraged by the idea of burning his seventy-mark reproduction; perhaps Hieronymus's speech had completely exhausted his patience. In any case he was a picture of stern and righteous anger. He pointed with his pen to the door of the shop, gave several short, excited snorts into his mustache, struggled for words, and uttered with the maximum of energy those which he found:

"My fine fellow, if you don't get out at once I will have my packer help you—do you understand?"

"Oh, you cannot intimidate me, you cannot drive me away, you cannot silence my voice!" cried Hieronymus as he clutched his cloak over his chest with his fists and shook his head doughtily. "I know that I am single-handed and powerless, but yet I will not cease until you hear me, Herr Blüthenzweig! Take the picture out of your window and burn it even today! Ah, burn not it alone! Burn all these statues and busts, the sight of which plunges the beholder into sin! Burn these vases and ornaments, these shameless revivals of paganism, these elegantly bound volumes of erotic verse! Burn everything in your shop, Herr Blüthenzweig, for it is a filthiness in God's sight. Burn it, burn it!" he shrieked, beside himself, describing a wild, all-embracing circle with his arm. "The harvest is ripe for the reaper, the measure of the age's shamelessness is full—but I say unto you—"

"Krauthuber!" Herr Blüthenzweig raised his voice and shouted toward a door at the back of the shop. "Come in here at once!"

And in answer to the summons there appeared upon the scene a massive overpowering presence, a vast and awe-inspiring, swollen human bulk, whose limbs merged into each other like links of sausage—a gigantic son of the people, malt-nourished and immoderate, who weighed in, with puffings, bursting with energy, from the packing-room. His appearance in the upper reaches of his form was notable for a fringe of walrus beard; a hide apron fouled with paste covered his body from the waist down, and his yellow shirt-sleeves were rolled back from his heroic arms.

"Will you open the door for this gentleman, Krauthuber?" said M. Blüthenzweig; "and if he should not find the way to it, just help him into the street."

"Huh," said the man, looking from his enraged employer to Hieronymus and back with his little elephant eyes. It was a heavy monosyllable, suggesting reserve force restrained with difficulty. The floor shook with his tread as he went to the door and opened it.

Hieronymus had grown very pale. "Burn—" he shouted once more. He was about to go on when he felt himself turned round by an irresistible power, by a physical preponderance to which no resistance was even thinkable. Slowly and inexorably he was propelled toward the door.

"I am weak," he managed to ejaculate. "My flesh cannot bear the force . . . it cannot hold its ground, no . . . but what does that prove? Burn—"

He stopped. He found himself outside the art-shop. M. Blüthenzweig's giant packer had let him go with one final shove, which set him down on the stone threshold of the shop, supporting himself with one hand. Behind him the door closed with a rattle of glass.

He picked himself up. He stood erect, breathing heavily, and pulled his cloak together with one fist over his breast, letting the other hang down inside. His hollow cheeks had a gray pallor; the nostrils of his great hooked nose opened and closed; his ugly lips writhed in an expression of hatred and despair and his red-rimmed eyes wandered over the beautiful square like those of a man in a frenzy.

He did not see that people were looking at him with amusement and curiosity. For what he beheld upon the mosaic pavement before the great loggia were all the vanities of this world: the masked costumes of the artist balls, the decorations, vases and art objects, the nude statues, the female busts, the picturesque rebirths of the pagan age, the portraits of famous beauties by the hands of masters, the elegantly bound erotic verse, the art brochures—all these he saw heaped in a pyramid and going up in crackling flames amid loud exultations from the people enthralled by his own frightful words. A yellow background of cloud had drawn up over the Theatinerstrasse, and from it issued wild rumblings; but what he saw was a burning fiery sword, towering in sulphurous light above the joyous city.

"*Gladius Dei super terram* . . ." his thick lips whispered; and drawing himself still higher in his hooded cloak while the hand hanging down inside it twitched convulsively, he murmured, quaking: "*cito et velociter!*"

---

# THE STORY OF A PANIC

## E. M. Forster

*Born in 1879, E. M. Forster, essayist, critic, novelist, and short story writer, was educated at Tonbridge School and King's College, Cambridge, at which he was resident Honorary Fellow from 1946 until his death in 1970. At Cambridge he formed a close friendship with G. Lowes Dickinson, author and teacher, whose biography he later wrote. A Passage to India (1924), Forster's most famous novel, reveals his deep feelings for India, as well as his basic philosophic attitudes toward human rela-*

*tionships. His other writings, which deserve more recognition than they have up to now received, include his other novels*—Where Angels Fear to Tread (*1905*), The Longest Journey (*1907*), A Room with a View (*1908*), Howard's End (*1910*), *and* Maurice (*published posthumously in 1973*); *his essays*—Abinger Harvest (*1936*) *and* Two Cheers for Democracy (*1951*); *two biographies*—Goldsworthy Lowes Dickinson (*1934*) *and* Marianne Thornton (*1956*); *a nonfictional account of his experiences in India,* The Hill of Devi (*1953*); *and his short story collections*—The Celestial Omnibus and Other Stories (*1911*), The Eternal Moment and Other Stories (*1929*), *and* The Life to Come and Other Stories (*published posthumously in 1973*). *Forster's perceptive treatment of various technical elements of the novel is found in his* Aspects of the Novel (*1927*). *In his valuable study of Forster, Lionel Trilling, speaking of the short stories, points out that one of Forster's pervasive ideas, the need to resist "modern life", was to become one of D. H. Lawrence's themes. This idea is an important part of "The Story of a Panic." "The Pans of Forster's fantastic stories state," writes Trilling, "in various ways, this eternal lesson. Modern life . . . can kill the masculine power and tenderness; Pan inhabits the woods and fields which men have forsaken. . . . Inhabiting the woods and fields, Pan can bring about the liberation of an adolescent boy ('The Story of a Panic') or the salvation of a formerly facetious and insincere clergyman ('The Curate's Friend')."*

Eustace's career—if career it can be called—certainly dates from that afternoon in the chestnut woods above Ravello. I confess at once that I am a plain, simple man, with no pretensions to literary style. Still, I do flatter myself that I can tell a story without exaggerating, and I have therefore decided to give an unbiassed account of the extraordinary events of eight years ago.

Ravello is a delightful place with a delightful little hotel in which we met some charming people. There were the two Miss Robinsons, who had been there for six weeks with Eustace, their nephew, then a boy of about fourteen. Mr. Sandbach had also been there some time. He had held a curacy in the north of England, which he had been compelled to resign on account of ill-health, and while he was recruiting at Ravello he had taken in hand Eustace's education—which was then sadly deficient—and was endeavouring to fit him for one of our great public schools. Then there was Mr. Leyland, a would-be artist, and finally, there was the nice landlady, Signora Scafetti, and the nice English-speaking waiter, Emmanuele—though at the time of which I am speaking Emmanuele was away, visiting a sick father.

To this little circle, I, my wife, and my two daughters made, I venture to think, a not unwelcome addition. But though I liked most of the company well enough, there were two of them to whom I did not take at all. They were the artist, Leyland, and the Miss Robinsons' nephew, Eustace.

Leyland was simply conceited and odious, and, as those qualities will be amply illustrated in my narrative, I need not enlarge upon them here. But Eustace was something besides: he was indescribably repellent.

I am fond of boys as a rule, and was quite disposed to be friendly. I and my daughters offered to take him out—'No, walking was such a fag.' Then I asked him to come and bathe—'No, he could not swim.'

"Every English boy should be able to swim," I said, "I will teach you myself."

"There, Eustace dear," said Miss Robinson; "here is a chance for you."

But he said he was afraid of the water!—a boy afraid!—and of course I said no more.

I would not have minded so much if he had been a really studious boy, but he neither played hard nor worked hard. His favourite occupations were lounging on the terrace in an easy chair and loafing along the high road, with his feet shuffling up the dust and his shoulders stooping forward. Naturally enough, his features were pale, his chest contracted, and his muscles undeveloped. His aunts thought him delicate; what he really needed was discipline.

That memorable day we all arranged to go for a picnic up in the chestnut woods—all, that is, except Janet, who stopped behind to finish her water-colour of the Cathedral—not a very successful attempt, I am afraid.

I wander off into these irrelevant details, because in my mind I cannot separate them from an account of the day; and it is the same with the conversation during the picnic: all is imprinted on my brain together. After a couple of hours' ascent, we left the donkeys that had carried the Miss Robinsons and my wife, and all proceeded on foot to the head of the valley—Vallone Fontana Caroso is its proper name, I find.

I have visited a good deal of fine scenery before and since, but have found little that has pleased me more. The valley ended in a vast hollow, shaped like a cup, into which radiated ravines from the precipitous hills around. Both the valley and the ravines and the ribs of hill that divided the ravines were covered with leafy chestnut, so that the general appearance was that of a many-fingered green hand, palm upwards, which was clutching convulsively to keep us in its grasp. Far down the valley we could see Ravello and the sea, but that was the only sign of another world.

"Oh, what a perfectly lovely place," said my daughter Rose. "What a picture it would make!"

"Yes," said Mr. Sandbach. "Many a famous European gallery would be proud to have a landscape a tithe as beautiful as this upon its walls."

"On the contrary," said Leyland, "it would make a very poor picture. Indeed, it is not paintable at all."

"And why is that?" said Rose, with far more deference than he deserved.

"Look, in the first place," he replied, "how intolerably straight against the sky is the line of the hill. It would need breaking up and diversifying. And where we are standing the whole thing is out of perspective. Besides, all the colouring is monotonous and crude."

"I do not know anything about pictures," I put in, "and I do not pretend to know: but I know what is beautiful when I see it, and I am thoroughly content with this."

"Indeed, who could help being contented!" said the elder Miss Robinson; and Mr. Sandbach said the same.

"Ah!" said Leyland, "you all confuse the artistic view of Nature with the photographic."

Poor Rose had brought her camera with her, so I thought this positively rude. I did not wish any unpleasantness; so I merely turned away and assisted my wife and Miss Mary Robinson to put out the lunch—not a very nice lunch.

"Eustace, dear," said his aunt, "come and help us here."

He was in a particularly bad temper that morning. He had, as usual, not wanted to come, and his aunts had nearly allowed him to stop at the hotel to vex Janet. But I, with their permission, spoke to him rather sharply on the subject of exercise; and the result was that he had come, but was even more taciturn and moody than usual.

Obedience was not his strong point. He invariably questioned every command, and only executed it grumbling. I should always insist on prompt and cheerful obedience, if I had a son.

"I'm—coming—Aunt—Mary," he at last replied, and dawdled to cut a piece of wood to make a whistle, taking care not to arrive till we had finished.

"Well, well, sir!" said I, "you stroll in at the end and profit by our labours." He sighed, for he could not endure being chaffed. Miss Mary, very unwisely, insisted on giving him the wing of the chicken, in spite of all my attempts to prevent her. I remember that I had a moment's vexation when I thought that, instead of enjoying the sun, and the air, and the woods, we were all engaged in wrangling over the diet of a spoilt boy.

But, after lunch, he was a little less in evidence. He withdrew to a tree trunk, and began to loosen the bark from his whistle. I was thankful to see him employed, for once in a way. We reclined, and took a *dolce far niente*.

Those sweet chestnuts of the South are puny striplings compared with our robust Northerners. But they clothed the contours of the hills and valleys in a most pleasing way, their veil being only broken by two clearings, in one of which we were sitting.

And because these few trees were cut down, Leyland burst into a petty indictment of the proprietor.

"All the poetry is going from Nature," he cried, "her lakes and marshes are drained, her seas banked up, her forests cut down. Everywhere we see the vulgarity of desolation spreading."

I have had some experience of estates, and answered that cutting was very necessary for the health of the larger trees. Besides, it was unreasonable to expect the proprietor to derive no income from his lands.

"If you take the commercial side of landscape, you may feel pleasure in the owner's activity. But to me the mere thought that a tree is convertible into cash is disgusting."

"I see no reason," I observed politely, "to despise the gifts of Nature because they are of value."

It did not stop him. "It is no matter," he went on, "we are all hopelessly steeped in vulgarity. I do not except myself. It is through us, and to our shame, that the Nereids have left the waters and the Oreads the mountains, that the woods no longer give shelter to Pan."

"Pan!" cried Mr. Sandbach, his mellow voice filling the valley as if it had been a great green church, "Pan is dead. That is why the woods do not shelter him." And he began to tell the striking story of the mariners who were sailing near the coast at the time of the birth of Christ, and three times heard a loud voice saying: "The great God Pan is dead."

"Yes. The great God Pan is dead," said Leyland. And he abandoned himself to that mock misery in which artistic people are so fond of indulging. His cigar went out, and he had to ask me for a match.

"How very interesting," said Rose. "I do wish I knew some ancient history."

"It is not worth your notice," said Mr. Sandbach. "Eh, Eustace?"

Eustace was finishing his whistle. He looked up, with the irritable frown in which his aunts allowed him to indulge, and made no reply.

The conversation turned to various topics and then died out. It was a cloudless afternoon in May, and the pale green of the young chestnut leaves made a pretty contrast with the dark blue of the sky. We were all sitting at the edge of the small clearing for the sake of the view, and the shade of the chestnut saplings behind us was manifestly insufficient. All sounds died away—at least that is my account: Miss Robinson says that the clamour of the birds was the first sign of uneasiness that she discerned. All sounds died away, except that, far in the distance, I could hear two boughs of a great chestnut grinding together as the tree swayed. The grinds grew shorter and shorter, and finally that sound stopped also. As I looked over the green fingers of the valley, everything was absolutely motionless and still; and that feeling of suspense which one so often experiences when Nature is in repose, began to steal over me.

Suddenly, we were all electrified by the excruciating noise of Eustace's whistle. I never heard any instrument give forth so ear-splitting and discordant a sound.

"Eustace, dear," said Miss Mary Robinson, "you might have thought of your poor Aunt Julia's head."

Leyland who had apparently been asleep, sat up.

"It is astonishing how blind a boy is to anything that is elevating or beautiful," he observed. "I should not have thought he could have found the wherewithal out here to spoil our pleasure like this."

Then the terrible silence fell upon us again. I was now standing up and watching a catspaw of wind that was running down one of the ridges opposite, turning the light green to dark as it travelled. A fanciful feeling of foreboding came over me; so I turned away, to find to my amazement, that all the others were also on their feet, watching it too.

It is not possible to describe coherently what happened next: but I, for one, am not ashamed to confess that, though the fair blue sky was above me, and the green spring woods beneath me, and the kindest of friends around me, yet I became terribly frightened, more frightened than I ever wish to become again, frightened in a way I never have known either before or after. And in the eyes of the others, too, I saw blank, expressionless fear, while their mouths strove in vain to speak and their hands to gesticulate. Yet, all around us were prosperity, beauty, and peace, and all was motionless, save the catspaw of wind, now travelling up the ridge on which we stood.

Who moved first has never been settled. It is enough to say that in one second we were tearing away along the hillside. Leyland was in front, then Mr. Sandbach, then my wife. But I only saw for a brief moment; for I ran across the little clearing and through the woods and over the undergrowth and the rocks and down the dry torrent beds into the valley below. The sky might have been black as I ran, and the trees short grass, and the hillside a level road; for I saw nothing and heard nothing and felt nothing, since all the channels of sense and reason were blocked. It was not the spiritual fear that one has known at other times, but brutal overmastering physical fear, stopping up the ears, and dropping clouds before the eyes, and filling the mouth with foul tastes. And it was no ordinary humiliation that survived; for I had been afraid, not as a man, but as a beast.

## II

I cannot describe our finish any better than our start; for our fear passed away as it had come, without cause. Suddenly I was able to see, and hear, and cough, and clear my mouth. Looking back, I saw that the others were stopping too; and, in a short time, we were all together, though it was long before we could speak, and longer before we dared to.

No one was seriously injured. My poor wife had sprained her ankle, Leyland had torn one of his nails on a tree trunk, and I myself had scraped and damaged my ear. I never noticed it till I had stopped.

We were all silent, searching one another's faces. Suddenly Miss Mary Robinson gave a terrible shriek. "Oh, merciful heavens! where is Eustace?" And then she would have fallen, if Mr. Sandbach had not caught her.

"We must go back, we must go back at once," said my Rose, who was quite the most collected of the party. "But I hope—I feel he is safe."

Such was the cowardice of Leyland, that he objected. But, finding himself in a minority, and being afraid of being left alone, he gave in. Rose and I supported my poor wife, Mr. Sandbach and Miss Robinson helped Miss Mary, and we returned slowly and silently, taking forty minutes to ascend the path that we had descended in ten.

Our conversation was naturally disjointed, as no one wished to offer an opinion on what had happened. Rose was the most talkative: she startled us all by saying that she had very nearly stopped where she was.

"Do you mean to say that you weren't—that you didn't feel compelled to go?" said Mr. Sandbach.

"Oh, of course, I did feel frightened"—she was the first to use the word—"but I somehow felt that if I could stop on it would be quite different, that I shouldn't be frightened at all, so to speak." Rose never did express herself clearly: still, it is greatly to her credit that she, the youngest of us, should have held on so long at that terrible time.

"I should have stopped, I do believe," she continued, "if I had not seen mamma go."

Rose's experience comforted us a little about Eustace. But a feeling of terrible foreboding was on us all, as we painfully climbed the chestnut-covered slopes and neared the little clearing. When we reached it our tongues broke loose. There, at the further side, were the remains of our lunch, and close to them, lying motionless on his back, was Eustace.

With some presence of mind I at once cried out: "Hey, you young monkey! jump up!" But he made no reply, nor did he answer when his poor aunts spoke to him. And, to my unspeakable horror, I saw one of those green lizards dart out from under his shirt-cuff as we approached.

We stood watching him as he lay there so silently, and my ears began to tingle in expectation of the outbursts of lamentations and tears.

Miss Mary fell on her knees beside him and touched his hand, which was convulsively entwined in the long grass.

As she did so, he opened his eyes and smiled.

I have often seen that peculiar smile since, both on the possessor's face and on the photographs of him that are beginning to get into the illustrated papers. But, till then, Eustace had always worn a peevish, discontented frown; and we were all unused to this disquieting smile, which always seemed to be without adequate reason.

His aunts showered kisses on him, which he did not reciprocate, and then there was an awkward pause. Eustace seemed so natural and undisturbed; yet, if he had not had astonishing experiences himself, he ought to have been all the more astonished at our extraordinary behaviour. My wife, with ready tact, endeavoured to behave as if nothing had happened.

"Well, Mr. Eustace," she said, sitting down as she spoke, to ease her foot, "how have you been amusing yourself since we have been away?"

"Thank you, Mrs. Tytler, I have been very happy."

"And where have you been?"

"Here."

"And lying down all the time, you idle boy?"

"No, not all the time."

"What were you doing before?"

"Oh; standing or sitting."

"Stood and sat doing nothing! Don't you know the poem 'Satan finds some mischief still for—' "

"Oh, my dear madam, hush! hush!" Mr. Sandbach's voice broke in; and my wife, naturally mortified by the interruption, said no more and moved away. I was surprised to see Rose immediately take her place, and, with more freedom than she generally displayed, run her fingers through the boy's tousled hair.

"Eustace! Eustace!" she said, hurriedly, "tell me everything—every single thing."

Slowly he sat up—till then he had lain on his back.

"Oh Rose—," he whispered, and, my curiosity being aroused, I moved nearer to hear what he was going to say. As I did so, I caught sight of some goats' footmarks in the moist earth beneath the trees.

"Apparently you have had a visit from some goats," I observed. "I had no idea they fed up here."

Eustace laboriously got on to his feet and came to see; and when he saw the footmarks he lay down and rolled on them, as a dog rolls in dirt.

After that there was a grave silence, broken at length by the solemn speech of Mr. Sandbach.

"My dear friends," he said, "it is best to confess the truth bravely. I know that what I am going to say now is what you are all now feeling. The Evil One has been very near us in bodily form. Time may yet discover some injury that he has wrought among us. But, at present, for myself at all events, I wish to offer up thanks for a merciful deliverance."

With that he knelt down, and, as the others knelt, I knelt too, though I do not believe in the Devil being allowed to assail us in visible form, as I told Mr. Sandbach afterwards. Eustace came too, and knelt quietly enough between his aunts after they had beckoned to him. But when it was over he at once got up, and began hunting for something.

"Why! Someone has cut my whistle in two," he said. (I had seen Leyland with an open knife in his hand—a superstitious act which I could hardly approve.)

"Well, it doesn't matter," he continued.

"And why doesn't it matter?" said Mr. Sandbach, who has ever since tried to entrap Eustace into an account of that mysterious hour.

"Because I don't want it any more."

"Why?"

At that he smiled; and, as no one seemed to have anything more to say, I set off as fast as I could through the wood, and hauled up a donkey to carry my poor wife home. Nothing occurred in my absence, except that

Rose had again asked Eustace to tell her what had happened; and he, this time, had turned away his head, and had not answered her a single word.

As soon as I returned, we all set off. Eustace walked with difficulty, almost with pain, so that, when we reached the other donkeys, his aunts wished him to mount one of them and ride all the way home. I make it a rule never to interfere between relatives, but I put my foot down at this. As it turned out, I was perfectly right, for the healthy exercise, I suppose, began to thaw Eustace's sluggish blood and loosen his stiffened muscles. He stepped out manfully, for the first time in his life, holding his head up and taking deep draughts of air into his chest. I observed with satisfaction to Miss Mary Robinson, that Eustace was at last taking some pride in his personal appearance.

Mr. Sandbach sighed, and said that Eustace must be carefully watched, for we none of us understood him yet. Miss Mary Robinson being very much—over much, I think—guided by him, sighed too.

"Come, come, Miss Robinson," I said, "there's nothing wrong with Eustace. Our experiences are mysterious, not his. He was astonished at our sudden departure, that's why he was so strange when we returned. He's right enough—improved, if anything."

"And is the worship of athletics, the cult of insensate activity, to be counted as an improvement?" put in Leyland, fixing a large, sorrowful eye on Eustace, who had stopped to scramble on to a rock to pick some cyclamen. "The passionate desire to rend from Nature the few beauties that have been still left her—that is to be counted as an improvement too?"

It is mere waste of time to reply to such remarks, especially when they come from any unsuccessful artist, suffering from a damaged finger. I changed the conversation by asking what we should say at the hotel. After some discussion, it was agreed that we should say nothing, either there or in our letters home. Importunate truth-telling, which brings only bewilderment and discomfort to the hearers, is, in my opinion, a mistake; and, after a long discussion, I managed to make Mr. Sandbach acquiesce in my view.

Eustace did not share in our conversation. He was racing about, like a real boy, in the wood to the right. A strange feeling of shame prevented us from openly mentioning our fright to him. Indeed, it seemed almost reasonable to conclude that it had made but little impression on him. So it disconcerted us when he bounded back with an armful of flowering acanthus, calling out:

"Do you suppose Gennaro'll be there when we get back?"

Gennaro was the stop-gap waiter, a clumsy, impertinent fisher-lad, who had been had up from Minori in the absence of the nice English-speaking Emmanuele. It was to him that we owed our scrappy lunch; and I could not conceive why Eustace desired to see him, unless it was to make mock with him of our behaviour.

"Yes, of course he will be there," said Miss Robinson. "Why do you ask, dear?"

"Oh, thought I'd like to see him."

"And why?" snapped Mr. Sandbach.

"Because, because I do, I do; because, because I do." He danced away into the darkening wood to the rhythm of his words.

"This is very extraordinary," said Mr. Sandbach. "Did he like Gennaro before?"

"Gennaro has only been here two days," said Rose, "and I know that they haven't spoken to each other a dozen times."

Each time Eustace returned from the wood his spirits were higher. Once he came whooping down on us as a wild Indian, and another time he made believe to be a dog. The last time he came back with a poor dazed hare, too frightened to move, sitting on his arm. He was getting too uproarious, I thought; and we were all glad to leave the wood, and start upon the steep staircase path that leads down into Ravello. It was late and turning dark; and we made all the speed we could, Eustace scurrying in front of us like a goat.

Just where the staircase path debouches on the white high road, the next extraordinary incident of this extraordinary day occurred. Three old women were standing by the wayside. They, like ourselves, had come down from the woods, and they were resting their heavy bundles of fuel on the low parapet of the road. Eustace stopped in front of them, and, after a moment's deliberation, stepped forward and—kissed the left-hand one on the cheek!

"My good fellow!" exclaimed Mr. Sandbach, "are you quite crazy?"

Eustace said nothing, but offered the old woman some of his flowers, and then hurried on. I looked back; and the old woman's companions seemed as much astonished at the proceeding as we were. But she herself had put the flowers in her bosom, and was murmuring blessings.

This salutation of the old lady was the first example of Eustace's strange behaviour, and we were both surprised and alarmed. It was useless talking to him, for he either made silly replies, or else bounded away without replying at all.

He made no reference on the way home to Gennaro, and I hoped that that was forgotten. But when we came to the Piazza, in front of the Cathedral, he screamed out: "Gennaro! Gennaro!" at the top of his voice, and began running up the little alley that led to the hotel. Sure enough, there was Gennaro at the end of it, with his arms and legs sticking out of the nice little English-speaking waiter's dress suit, and a dirty fisherman's cap on his head—for, as the poor landlady truly said, however much she superintended his toilette, he always managed to introduce something incongruous into it before he had done.

Eustace sprang to meet him, and leapt right up into his arms, and put his own arms round his neck. And this in the presence, not only of us, but also of the landlady, the chambermaid, the facchino, and of two American ladies who were coming for a few days' visit to the little hotel.

I always make a point of behaving pleasantly to Italians, however little they may deserve it; but this habit of promiscuous intimacy was perfectly intolerable, and could only lead to familiarity and mortification for all. Taking Miss Robinson aside, I asked her permission to speak seriously to Eustace on the subject of intercourse with social inferiors. She granted it; but I determined to wait till the absurd boy had calmed down a little from the excitement of the day. Meanwhile, Gennaro, instead of attending to the wants of the two new ladies, carried Eustace into the house, as if it was the most natural thing in the world.

"Ho capito," I heard him say as he passed me. 'Ho capito' is the Italian for 'I have understood'; but, as Eustace had not spoken to him, I could not see the force of the remark. It served to increase our bewilderment, and, by the time we sat down at the dinner-table, our imaginations and our tongues were alike exhausted.

I omit from this account the various comments that were made, as few of them seem worthy of being recorded. But, for three or four hours, seven of us were pouring forth our bewilderment in a stream of appropriate and inappropriate exclamations. Some traced a connection between our behaviour in the afternoon and the behaviour of Eustace now. Others saw no connection at all. Mr. Sandbach still held to the possibility of infernal influences, and also said that he ought to have a doctor. Leyland only saw the development of "that unspeakable Philistine, the boy." Rose maintained, to my surprise, that everything was excusable; while I began to see that the young gentleman wanted a sound thrashing. The poor Miss Robinsons swayed helplessly about between these diverse opinions; inclining now to careful supervision, now to acquiescence, now to corporal chastisement, now to Eno's Fruit Salt.

Dinner passed off fairly well, though Eustace was terribly fidgety, Gennaro as usual dropping the knives and spoons, and hawking and clearing his throat. He only knew a few words of English, and we were all reduced to Italian for making known our wants. Eustace, who had picked up a little somehow, asked for some oranges. To my annoyance, Gennaro, in his answer made use of the second person singular—a form only used when addressing those who are both intimates and equals. Eustace had brought it on himself; but an impertinence of this kind was an affront to us all, and I was determined to speak, and to speak at once.

When I heard him clearing the table I went in, and, summoning up my Italian, or rather Neapolitan—the Southern dialects are execrable—I said, "Gennaro! I heard you address Signor Eustace with 'Tu.'"

"It is true."

"You are not right. You must use 'Lei' or 'Voi'—more polite forms. And remember that, though Signor Eustace is sometimes silly and foolish—this afternoon for example—yet you must always behave respectfully to him; for he is a young English gentleman, and you are a poor Italian fisher-boy."

I know that speech sounds terribly snobbish, but in Italian one can say things that one would never dream of saying in English. Besides, it is no good speaking delicately to persons of that class. Unless you put things plainly, they take a vicious pleasure in misunderstanding you.

An honest English fisherman would have landed me one in the eye in a minute for such a remark, but the wretched down-trodden Italians have no pride. Gennaro only sighed, and said: "It is true."

"Quite so," I said, and turned to go. To my indignation I heard him add: "But sometimes it is not important."

"What do you mean?" I shouted.

He came close up to me with horrid gesticulating fingers.

"Signor Tytler, I wish to say this. If Eustazio asks me to call him 'Voi,' I will call him 'Voi.' Otherwise, no."

With that he seized up a tray of dinner things, and fled from the room with them; and I heard two more wine-glasses go on the courtyard floor.

I was now fairly angry, and strode out to interview Eustace. But he had gone to bed, and the landlady, to whom I also wished to speak, was engaged. After more vague wonderings, obscurely expressed owing to the presence of Janet and the two American ladies, we all went to bed, too, after a harassing and most extraordinary day.

### III

But the day was nothing to the night.

I suppose I had slept for about four hours, when I woke suddenly thinking I heard a noise in the garden. And, immediately, before my eyes were open, cold terrible fear seized me—not fear of something that was happening, like the fear in the wood, but fear of something that might happen.

Our room was on the first floor, looking out on to the garden—or terrace, it was rather: a wedge-shaped block of ground covered with roses and vines, and intersected with little asphalt paths. It was bounded on the small side by the house; round the two long sides ran a wall, only three feet above the terrace level, but with a good twenty feet drop over it into the olive yards, for the ground fell very precipitously away.

Trembling all over I stole to the window. There, pattering up and down the asphalt paths, was something white. I was too much alarmed to see clearly; and in the uncertain light of the stars the thing took all manner of curious shapes. Now it was a great dog, now an enormous white bat, now a mass of quickly travelling cloud. It would bounce like a ball, or take short flights like a bird, or glide slowly like a wraith. It gave no sound—save the pattering sound of what, after all, must be human feet. And at last the obvious explanation forced itself upon my disordered mind; and I realized that Eustace had got out of bed, and that we were in for something more.

I hastily dressed myself, and went down into the dining-room which opened upon the terrace. The door was already unfastened. My terror had almost entirely passed away, but for quite five minutes I struggled with a curious cowardly feeling, which bade me not interfere with the poor strange boy, but leave him to his ghostly patterings, and merely watch him from the window, to see he took no harm.

But better impulses prevailed and, opening the door, I called out:

"Eustace! what on earth are you doing? Come in at once."

He stopped his antics, and said: "I hate my bedroom. I could not stop in it, it is too small."

"Come! come! I'm tired of affectation. You've never complained of it before."

"Besides I can't see anything—no flowers, no leaves, no sky: only a stone wall." The outlook of Eustace's room certainly was limited; but, as I told him, he had never complained of it before.

"Eustace, you talk like a child. Come in! Prompt obedience, if you please."

He did not move.

"Very well: I shall carry you in by force," I added, and made a few steps towards him. But I was soon convinced of the futility of pursuing a boy through a tangle of asphalt paths, and went in instead, to call Mr. Sandbach and Leyland to my aid.

When I returned with them he was worse than ever. He would not even answer us when we spoke, but began singing and chattering to himself in a most alarming way.

"It's a case for the doctor now," said Mr. Sandbach, gravely tapping his forehead.

He had stopped his running and was singing, first low, then loud—singing five-finger exercises, scales, hymn tunes, scraps of Wagner—anything that came into his head. His voice—a very untuneful voice—grew stronger and stronger, and he ended with a tremendous shout which boomed like a gun among the mountains, and awoke everyone who was still sleeping in the hotel. My poor wife and the two girls appeared at their respective windows, and the American ladies were heard violently ringing their bell.

"Eustace," we all cried, "stop! stop, dear boy, and come into the house."

He shook his head, and started off again—talking this time. Never have I listened to such an extraordinary speech. At any other time it would have been ludicrous, for here was a boy, with no sense of beauty and puerile command of words, attempting to tackle themes which the greatest poets have found almost beyond their power. Eustace Robinson, aged fourteen, was standing in his nightshirt saluting, praising, and blessing, the great forces and manifestations of Nature.

He spoke first of night and the stars and planets above his head, of the swarms of fire-flies below him, of the invisible sea below the fire-flies, of the great rocks covered with anemones and shells that were slumbering in the invisible sea. He spoke of the rivers and waterfalls, of the ripening bunches of grapes, of the smoking cone of Vesuvius and the hidden fire-channels that made the smoke, of the myriads of lizards who were lying curled up in the crannies of the sultry earth, of the showers of white rose leaves that were tangled in his hair. And then he spoke of the rain and the wind by which all things are changed, of the air through which all things live, and of the woods in which all things can be hidden.

Of course, it was all absurdly high faluting: yet I could have kicked Leyland for audibly observing that it was 'a diabolical caricature of all that was most holy and beautiful in life.'

"And then,"—Eustace was going on in the pitiable conversational doggerel which was his only mode of expression—"and then there are men, but I can't make them out so well." He knelt down by the parapet, and rested his head on his arms.

"Now's the time," whispered Leyland. I hate stealth, but we darted forward and endeavoured to catch hold of him from behind. He was away in a twinkling, but turned round at once to look at us. As far as I could see in the starlight, he was crying. Leyland rushed at him again, and we tried to corner him among the asphalt paths, but without the slightest approach to success.

We returned, breathless and discomfited, leaving him at his madness in the further corner of the terrace. But my Rose had an inspiration.

"Papa," she called from the window, "if you get Gennaro, he might be able to catch him for you."

I had no wish to ask a favour of Gennaro, but, as the landlady had by now appeared on the scene, I begged her to summon him from the charcoal-bin in which he slept, and make him try what he could do.

She soon returned, and was shortly followed by Gennaro, attired in a dress coat, without either waistcoat, shirt, or vest, and a ragged pair of what had been trousers, cut short above the knees for purposes of wading. The landlady, who had quite picked up English ways, rebuked him for the incongruous and even indecent appearance which he presented.

"I have a coat and I have trousers. What more do you desire?"

"Never mind, Signora Scafetti," I put in. "As there are no ladies here, it is not of the slightest consequence." Then, turning to Gennaro, I said: "The aunts of Signor Eustace wish you to fetch him into the house."

He did not answer.

"Do you hear me? He is not well. I order you to fetch him into the house."

"Fetch! fetch!" said Signora Scafetti, and shook him roughly by the arm.

"Eustazio is well where he is."

"Fetch! fetch!" Signora Scafetti screamed, and let loose a flood of Italian, most of which, I am glad to say, I could not follow. I glanced up nervously at the girls' window, but they hardly know as much as I do, and I am thankful to say that none of us caught one word of Gennaro's answer.

The two yelled and shouted at each other for quite ten minutes, at the end of which Gennaro rushed back to his charcoal-bin and Signora Scafetti burst into tears, as well she might, for she greatly valued her English guests.

"He says," she sobbed, "that Signor Eustace is well where he is, and that he will not fetch him. I can do no more."

But I could, for, in my stupid British way, I have got some insight into the Italian character. I followed Mr. Gennaro to his place of repose, and found him wriggling down on to a dirty sack.

"I wish you to fetch Signor Eustace to me," I began.

He hurled at me an unintelligible reply.

"If you fetch him, I will give you this." And out of my pocket I took a new ten lira note.

This time he did not answer.

"This note is equal to ten lire in silver," I continued, for I knew that the poor-class Italian is unable to conceive of a single large sum.

"I know it."

"That is, two hundred soldi."

"I do not desire them. Eustazio is my friend."

I put the note into my pocket.

"Besides, you would not give it me."

"I am an Englishman. The English always do what they promise."

"That is true." It is astonishing how the most dishonest of nations trust us. Indeed they often trust us more than we trust one another. Gennaro knelt up on his sack. It was too dark to see his face, but I could feel his warm garlicky breath coming out in gasps, and I knew that the eternal avarice of the South had laid hold upon him.

"I could not fetch Eustazio to the house. He might die there."

"You need not do that," I replied patiently. "You need only bring him to me; and I will stand outside in the garden." And to this, as if it were something quite different, the pitiable youth consented.

"But give me first the ten lire."

"No"—for I knew the kind of person with whom I had to deal. Once faithless, always faithless.

We returned to the terrace, and Gennaro, without a single word, pattered off towards the pattering that could be heard at the remoter end. Mr. Sandbach, Leyland, and myself moved away a little from the house, and stood in the shadow of the white climbing roses, practically invisible.

We heard "Eustazio" called, followed by absurd cries of pleasure from the poor boy. The pattering ceased, and we heard them talking. Their voices got nearer, and presently I could discern them through the creepers, the grotesque figure of the young man, and the slim little white-robed boy. Gennaro had his arm round Eustace's neck, and Eustace was talking away in his fluent, slip-shod Italian.

"I understand almost everything," I heard him say. "The trees, hills, stars, water, I can see all. But isn't it odd! I can't make out men a bit. Do you know what I mean?"

"Ho capito," said Gennaro gravely, and took his arm off Eustace's shoulder. But I made the new note crackle in my pocket; and he heard it. He stuck his hand out with a jerk; and the unsuspecting Eustace gripped it in his own.

"It is odd!" Eustace went on—they were quite close now—"It almost seems as if—as if—"

I darted out and caught hold of his arm, and Leyland got hold of the other arm, and Mr. Sandbach hung on to his feet. He gave shrill heart-piercing screams; and the white roses, which were falling early that year, descended in showers on him as we dragged him into the house.

As soon as we entered the house he stopped shrieking; but floods of tears silently burst forth, and spread over his upturned face.

"Not to my room," he pleaded. "It is so small."

His infinitely dolorous look filled me with strange pity, but what could I do? Besides, his window was the only one that had bars to it.

"Never mind, dear boy," said kind Mr. Sandbach. "I will bear you company till the morning."

At this his convulsive struggles began again. "Oh, please, not that. Anything but that. I will promise to lie still and not to cry more than I can help, if I am left alone."

So we laid him on the bed, and drew the sheets over him, and left him sobbing bitterly, and saying: "I nearly saw everything, and now I can see nothing at all."

We informed the Miss Robinsons of all that had happened, and returned to the dining-room, where we found Signora Scafetti and Gennaro whispering together. Mr. Sandbach got pen and paper, and began writing to the English doctor at Naples. I at once drew out the note, and flung it down on the table to Gennaro.

"Here is your pay," I said sternly, for I was thinking of the Thirty Pieces of Silver.

"Thank you very much, sir," said Gennaro, and grabbed it.

He was going off, when Leyland, whose interest and indifference were always equally misplaced, asked him what Eustace had meant by saying 'he could not make out men a bit.'

"I cannot say. Signor Eustazio" (I was glad to observe a little deference at last) "has a subtle brain. He understands many things."

"But I heard you say you understood," Leyland persisted.

"I understand, but I cannot explain. I am a poor Italian fisher-lad. Yet, listen: I will try." I saw to my alarm that his manner was changing, and tried to stop him. But he sat down on the edge of the table and started off, with some absolutely incoherent remarks.

"It is sad," he observed at last. "What has happened is very sad. But what can I do? I am poor. It is not I."

I turned away in contempt. Leyland went on asking questions. He wanted to know who it was that Eustace had in his mind when he spoke.

"That is easy to say," Gennaro gravely answered. "It is you, it is I. It is all in this house, and many outside it. If he wishes for mirth, we discomfort him. If he asks to be alone, we disturb him. He longed for a friend, and found none for fifteen years. Then he found me, and the first night I —I who have been in the woods and understood things too—betray him to you, and send him in to die. But what could I do?"

"Gently, gently," said I.

"Oh, assuredly he will die. He will lie in the small room all night, and in the morning he will be dead. That I know for certain."

"There, that will do," said Mr. Sandbach. "I shall be sitting with him."

"Filomena Giusti sat all night with Caterina, but Caterina was dead in the morning. They would not let her out, though I begged, and prayed, and cursed, and beat the door, and climbed the wall. They were ignorant fools, and thought I wished to carry her away. And in the morning she was dead."

"What is all this?" I asked Signora Scafetti.

"All kinds of stories will get about," she replied, "and he, least of anyone, has reason to repeat them."

"And I am alive now," he went on, "because I had neither parents nor relatives nor friends, so that, when the first night came, I could run through the woods, and climb the rocks, and plunge into the water, until I had accomplished my desire!"

We heard a cry from Eustace's room—a faint but steady sound, like the sound of wind in a distant wood heard by one standing in tranquillity.

"That," said Gennaro, "was the last noise of Caterina. I was hanging on to her window then, and it blew out past me."

And, lifting up his hand, in which my ten lira note was safely packed, he solemnly cursed Mr. Sandbach, and Leyland, and myself, and Fate, because Eustace was dying in the upstairs room. Such is the working of the Southern mind; and I verily believe that he would not have moved even then, had not Leyland, that unspeakable idiot, upset the lamp with his elbow. It was a patent self-extinguishing lamp, bought by Signora Scafetti, at my special request, to replace the dangerous thing that she was using. The result was, that it went out; and the mere physical change from light to darkness had more power over the ignorant animal nature of Gennaro than the most obvious dictates of logic and reason.

I felt, rather than saw, that he had left the room and shouted out to

Mr. Sandbach: "Have you got the key to Eustace's room in your pocket?" But Mr. Sandbach and Leyland were both on the floor, having mistaken each other for Gennaro, and some more precious time was wasted in finding a match. Mr. Sandbach had only just time to say that he had left the key in the door, in case the Miss Robinsons wished to pay Eustace a visit, when we heard a noise on the stairs, and there was Gennaro, carrying Eustace down.

We rushed out and blocked up the passage, and they lost heart and retreated to the upper landing.

"Now they are caught," cried Signora Scafetti. "There is no other way out."

We were cautiously ascending the staircase, when there was a terrific scream from my wife's room, followed by a heavy thud on the asphalt path. They had leapt out of her window.

I reached the terrace just in time to see Eustace jumping over the parapet of the garden wall. This time I knew for certain he would be killed. But he alighted in an olive tree, looking like a great white moth, and from the tree he slid on to the earth. And as soon as his bare feet touched the clods of earth he uttered a strange loud cry, such as I should not have thought the human voice could have produced, and disappeared among the trees below.

"He has understood and he is saved," cried Gennaro, who was still sitting on the asphalt path. "Now, instead of dying he will live!"

"And you, instead of keeping the ten lire, will give them up," I retorted, for at this theatrical remark I could contain myself no longer.

"The ten lire are mine," he hissed back, in a scarcely audible voice. He clasped his hand over his breast to protect his ill-gotten gains, and, as he did so, he swayed forward and fell upon his face on the path. He had not broken any limbs, and a leap like that would never have killed an Englishman, for the drop was not great. But those miserable Italians have no stamina. Something had gone wrong inside him, and he was dead.

The morning was still far off, but the morning breeze had begun, and more rose leaves fell on us as we carried him in. Signora Scafetti burst into screams at the sight of the dead body, and, far down the valley towards the sea, there still resounded the shouts and the laughter of the escaping boy.

# THE FORKS

## J. F. Powers

*Born in Jacksonville, Illinois, in 1917, J. F. Powers attended a parochial high school and, for a time, Northwestern University (Chicago). His first published story appeared in* Accent, *and since then he has continued to publish fiction, articles, and reviews. His first collection of stories,* Prince of Darkness and Other Stories *(1947), was critically acclaimed, as was* The Presence of Grace *(1956), a second collection. His fiction has appeared in the* O. Henry Prize Stories *and* Best American Short Stories; *he was awarded a Guggenheim Fellowship in 1948. His first novel,* Morte d'Urban *(1962), also favorably received, reflects the same concerns found in such short stories as "The Forks." His ironic portrayals of the clergy, mitigated by sympathy and understanding, written with much detail and authenticity, are the special marks of Powers's skill. His ability to express nuances and his gift of subtle humor are especially evident in the short story, a genre he has made his specialty.*

That summer when Father Eudex got back from saying Mass at the orphanage in the morning, he would park Monsignor's car, which was long and black and new like a politician's, and sit down in the cool of the porch to read his office. If Monsignor was not already standing in the door, he would immediately appear there, seeing that his car had safely returned, and inquire:

"Did you have any trouble with her?"

Father Eudex knew too well the question meant, Did you mistreat my car?

"No trouble, Monsignor."

"Good," Monsignor said, with imperfect faith in his curate, who was not a car owner. For a moment Monsignor stood framed in the screen door, fumbling his watch fob as for a full-length portrait, and then he was suddenly not there.

"Monsignor," Father Eudex said, rising nervously, "I've got a chance to pick up a car."

At the door Monsignor slid into his frame again. His face expressed what was for him intense interest.

"Yes? Go on."

"I don't want to have to use yours every morning."

"It's all right."

"And there are other times." Father Eudex decided not to be maudlin and mention sick calls, nor be entirely honest and admit he was tired of busses and bumming rides from parishioners. "And now I've got a chance to get one—cheap."

Monsignor, smiling, came alert at *cheap*.

"New?"

"No, I wouldn't say it's new."

Monsignor was openly suspicious now. "What kind?"

"It's a Ford."

"And not new?"

"Not new, Monsignor—but in good condition. It was owned by a retired farmer and had good care."

Monsignor sniffed. He *knew* cars. "V-Eight, Father?"

"No," Father Eudex confessed. "It's a Model A."

Monsignor chuckled as though this were indeed the damnedest thing he had ever heard.

"But in very good condition, Monsignor."

"You said that."

"Yes. And I could take it apart if anything went wrong. My uncle had one."

"No doubt." Monsignor uttered a laugh at Father Eudex's rural origins. Then he delivered the final word, long delayed out of amusement. "It wouldn't be prudent, Father. After all, this isn't a country parish. You know the class of people we get here."

Monsignor put on his Panama hat. Then, apparently mistaking the obstinacy in his curate's face for plain ignorance, he shed a little more light. "People watch a priest, Father. *Damnant quod non intelligunt*. It would never do. You'll have to watch your tendencies."

Monsignor's eyes tripped and fell hard on the morning paper lying on the swing where he had finished it.

"Another flattering piece about that crazy fellow. . . . There's a man who might have gone places if it weren't for his mouth! A bishop doesn't have to get mixed up in all that stuff!"

Monsignor, as Father Eudex knew, meant unions, strikes, race riots—all that stuff.

"A parishioner was saying to me only yesterday it's getting so you can't tell the Catholics from the Communists, with the priests as bad as any. Yes, and this fellow is the worst. He reminds me of that bishop a few years back—at least he called himself a bishop, a Protestant—that was advocating companionate marriages. It's not that bad, maybe, but if you listened to some of them you'd think that Catholicity and capitalism were incompatible!"

"The Holy Father——"

"The Holy Father's in Europe, Father. Mr. Memmers lives in this parish. I'm his priest. What can I tell him?"

"Is it Mr. Memmers of the First National, Monsignor?"

"It is, Father. And there's damned little cheer I can give a man like Memmers. Catholics, priests, and laity alike—yes, and princes of the Church, all talking atheistic communism!"

This was the substance of their conversation, always, the deadly routine in which Father Eudex played straight man. Each time it happened he seemed to participate, and though he should have known better he justified his participation by hoping that it would not happen again, or in quite the same way. But it did, it always did, the same way, and Monsignor, for all his alarums, had nothing to say really and meant one thing only, the thing he never said—that he dearly wanted to be, and was not, a bishop.

Father Eudex could imagine just what kind of bishop Monsignor would be. His reign would be a wise one, excessively so. His mind was made up on everything, excessively so. He would know how to avoid the snares set in the path of the just man, avoid them, too, in good taste and good conscience. He would not be trapped as so many good shepherds before him had been trapped, poor souls—caught in fair-seeming dilemmas of justice that were best left alone, like the first apple. It grieved him, he said, to think of those great hearts broken in silence and solitude. It was the worst kind of exile, alas! But just give him the chance and he would know what to do, what to say, and, more important, what not to do, not to say—neither yea nor nay for him. He had not gone to Rome for nothing. For him the dark forest of decisions would not exist; for him, thanks to hours spent in prayer and meditation, the forest would vanish as dry grass before fire, his fire. He knew the mask of evil already—birth control, indecent movies, salacious books—and would call these things by their right names and dare to deal with them for what they were, these new occasions for the old sins of the cities of the plains.

But in the meantime—oh, to have a particle of the faith that God had in humanity! Dear, trusting God forever trying them beyond their feeble powers, ordering terrible tests, fatal trials by nonsense (the crazy bishop). And keeping Monsignor steadily warming up on the side lines, ready to rush in, primed for the day that would perhaps never dawn.

At one time, so the talk went, there had been reason to think that Monsignor was headed for a bishopric. Now it was too late; Monsignor's intercessors were all dead; the cupboard was bare; he knew it at heart, and it galled him to see another man, this *crazy* man, given the opportunity, and making such a mess of it.

Father Eudex searched for and found a little salt for Monsignor's wound. "The word's going around he'll be the next archbishop," he said.

"I won't believe it," Monsignor countered hoarsely. He glanced at the newspaper on the swing and renewed his horror. "If that fellow's right, Father, I'm"—his voice cracked at the idea—"*wrong!*"

Father Eudex waited until Monsignor had started down the steps to the car before he said, "It could be."

"I'll be back for lunch, Father. I'm taking her for a little spin."

Monsignor stopped in admiration a few feet from the car—her. He was as helpless before her beauty as a boy with a birthday bicycle. He could not leave her alone. He had her out every morning and afternoon and evening. He was indiscriminate about picking people up for a ride in her. He kept her on a special diet—only the best of gas and oil and grease, with daily rubdowns. He would run her only on the smoothest roads and at so many miles an hour. That was to have stopped at the first five hundred, but only now, nearing the thousand mark, was he able to bring himself to increase her speed, and it seemed to hurt him more than it did her.

Now he was walking around behind her to inspect the tires. Apparently O.K. He gave the left rear fender an amorous chuck and eased into the front seat. Then they drove off, the car and he, to see the world, to explore each other further on the honeymoon.

Father Eudex watched the car slide into the traffic, and waited, on edge. The corner cop, fulfilling Father Eudex's fears, blew his whistle and waved his arms up in all four directions, bringing traffic to a standstill. Monsignor pulled expertly out of line and drove down Clover Boulevard in a one-car parade; all others stalled respectfully. The cop, as Monsignor passed, tipped his cap, showing a bald head. Monsignor, in the circumstances, could not acknowledge him, though he knew the man well—a parishioner. He was occupied with keeping his countenance kindly, grim, and exalted, that the cop's faith remain whole, for it was evidently inconceivable to him that Monsignor should ever venture abroad unless to bear the Holy Viaticum, always racing with death.

Father Eudex, eyes baleful but following the progress of the big black car, saw a hand dart out of the driver's window in a wave. Monsignor would combine a lot of business with pleasure that morning, creating what he called "good will for the Church"—all morning in the driver's seat toasting passers-by with a wave that was better than a blessing. How he loved waving to people!

Father Eudex overcame his inclination to sit and stew about things by going down the steps to meet the mailman. He got the usual handful for the Monsignor—advertisements and amazing offers, the unfailing crop of chaff from dealers in church goods, organs, collection schemes, insurance, and sacramental wines. There were two envelopes addressed to Father Eudex, one a mimeographed plea from a missionary society which he might or might not acknowledge with a contribution, depending upon what he thought of the cause—if it was really lost enough to justify a levy on his poverty—and the other a check for a hundred dollars.

The check came in an eggshell envelope with no explanation except a tiny card, "Compliments of the Rival Tractor Company," but even that was needless. All over town clergymen had known for days that the checks were on the way again. Some, rejoicing, could hardly wait. Father Eudex, however, was one of those who could.

With the passing of hard times and the coming of the fruitful war years, the Rival Company, which was a great one for public relations, had found the best solution to the excess-profits problem to be giving. Ministers and even rabbis shared in the annual jack pot, but Rival employees were largely Catholic and it was the checks to the priests that paid off. Again, some thought it was a wonderful idea, and others thought that Rival, plagued by strikes and justly so, had put their alms to work.

There was another eggshell envelope, Father Eudex saw, among the letters for Monsignor, and knew his check would be for two hundred, the premium for pastors.

Father Eudex left Monsignor's mail on the porch table by his cigars. His own he stuck in his back pocket, wanting to forget it, and went down the steps into the yard. Walking back and forth on the shady side of the rectory where the lilies of the valley grew and reading his office, he gradually drifted into the back yard, lured by a noise. He came upon Whalen, the janitor, pounding pegs into the ground.

Father Eudex closed the breviary on a finger. "What's it all about, Joe?"

Joe Whalen snatched a piece of paper from his shirt and handed it to Father Eudex. "He gave it to me this morning."

He—it was the word for Monsignor among them. A docile pronoun only, and yet when it meant the Monsignor it said, and concealed, nameless things.

The paper was a plan for a garden drawn up by the Monsignor in his fine hand. It called for a huge fleur-de-lis bounded by smaller crosses— and these Maltese—a fountain, a sundial, and a cloister walk running from the rectory to the garage. Later there would be birdhouses and a ten-foot wall of thick gray stones, acting as a moat against the eyes of the world. The whole scheme struck Father Eudex as expensive and, in this country, Presbyterian.

When Monsignor drew the plan, however, he must have been in his medieval mood. A spouting whale jostled with Neptune in the choppy waters of the fountain. North was indicated in the legend by a winged cherub huffing and puffing.

Father Eudex held the plan up against the sun to see the watermark. The stationery was new to him, heavy, simulated parchment, with the Church of the Holy Redeemer and Monsignor's name embossed, three initials, W. F. X., William Francis Xavier. With all those initials the man could pass for a radio station, a chancery wit had observed, or if his last name had not been Sweeney, Father Eudex added now, for high Anglican.

Father Eudex returned the plan to Whalen, feeling sorry for him and to an extent guilty before him—if only because he was a priest like Monsignor (now turned architect) whose dream of a monastery garden included the overworked janitor under the head of "labor."

Father Eudex asked Whalen to bring another shovel. Together, almost without words, they worked all morning spading up crosses, leaving the big fleur-de-lis to the last. Father Eudex removed his coat first, then his collar, and finally was down to his undershirt.

Toward noon Monsignor rolled into the driveway.

He stayed in the car, getting red in the face, recovering from the pleasure of seeing so much accomplished as he slowly recognized his curate in Whalen's helper. In a still, appalled voice he called across the lawn, "Father," and waited as for a beast that might or might not have sense enough to come.

Father Eudex dropped his shovel and went over to the car, shirtless.

Monsignor waited a moment before he spoke, as though annoyed by the everlasting necessity, where this person was concerned, to explain. "Father," he said quietly at last, "I wouldn't do any more of that—if I were you. Rather, in any event, I wouldn't."

"All right, Monsignor."

"To say the least, it's not prudent. If necessary"—he paused as Whalen came over to dig a cross within earshot—"I'll explain later. It's time for lunch now."

The car, black, beautiful, fierce with chromium, was quiet as Monsignor dismounted, knowing her master. Monsignor went around to the rear, felt a tire, and probed a nasty cinder in the tread.

"Look at that," he said, removing the cinder.

Father Eudex thought he saw the car lift a hoof, gaze around, and thank Monsignor with her headlights.

Monsignor proceeded at a precise pace to the back door of the rectory. There he held the screen open momentarily, as if remembering something or reluctant to enter before himself—such was his humility—but then called to Whalen with an intimacy that could never exist between them.

"Better knock off now, Joe."

Whalen turned in on himself. "*Joe*—is it!"

Father Eudex removed his clothes from the grass. His hands were all blisters, but in them he found a little absolution. He apologized to Joe for having to take the afternoon off. "I can't make it, Joe. Something turned up."

"Sure, Father."

Father Eudex could hear Joe telling his wife about it that night—yeah, the young one got in wrong with the old one again. Yeah, the old one, he don't believe in it, work, for them.

Father Eudex paused in the kitchen to remember he knew not what. It was in his head, asking to be let in, but he did not place it until he heard Monsignor in the next room complaining about the salad to the housekeeper. It was the voice of dear, dead Aunt Hazel, coming from the summer he was ten. He translated the past into the present: I can't come out and play this afternoon, Joe, on account of my monsignor won't let me.

In the dining room Father Eudex sat down at the table and said grace. He helped himself to a chop, creamed new potatoes, pickled beets, jelly, and bread. He liked jelly. Monsignor passed the butter.

"That's supposed to be a tutti-frutti salad," Monsignor said, grimacing at his. "But she used green olives."

Father Eudex said nothing.

"I said she used green olives."

"I like green olives all right."

"*I* like green olives, but *not* in tutti-frutti salad."

Father Eudex replied by eating a green olive, but he knew it could not end there.

"Father," Monsignor said in a new tone. "How would you like to go away and study for a year?"

"Don't think I'd care for it, Monsignor. I'm not the type."

"You're no canonist, you mean?"

"That's one thing."

"Yes. Well, there are other things it might not hurt you to know. To be quite frank with you, Father, I think you need broadening."

"I guess so," Father Eudex said thickly.

"And still, with your tendencies . . . and with the universities honeycombed with Communists. No, that would never do. I think I meant seasoning, not broadening."

"Oh."

"No offense?"

"No offense."

Who would have thought a little thing like an olive could lead to all this, Father Eudex mused—who but himself, that is, for his association with Monsignor had shown him that anything could lead to everything. Monsignor was a master at making points. Nothing had changed since the day Father Eudex walked into the rectory saying he was the new assistant. Monsignor had evaded Father Eudex's hand in greeting, and a few days later, after he began to get the range, he delivered a lecture on the whole subject of handshaking. It was Middle West to shake hands, or South West, or West in any case, and it was not done where he came from, and—why had he ever come from where he came from? Not to be reduced to shaking hands, you could bet! Handshaking was worse than foot washing and unlike that pious practice there was nothing to support it. And from handshaking Monsignor might go into a general discussion of Father Eudex's failings. He used the open forum method, but he was the only speaker and there was never time enough for questions from the audience. Monsignor seized his examples at random from life. He saw Father Eudex coming out of his bedroom in pajama bottoms only and so told him about the dressing gown, its purpose, something of its history. He advised Father Eudex to barber his armpits, for it was being done all over now. He let Father Eudex see his bottle of cologne, "Steeple," special for clergymen, and said he should not be afraid of it. He suggested that Father Eudex shave his face oftener, too. He loaned him his Rogers Peet catalogue, which had sketches of clerical blades togged out in the latest, and prayed that he would stop going around looking like a rabbinical student.

He found Father Eudex reading *The Catholic Worker* one day and had not trusted him since. Father Eudex's conception of the priesthood was evangelical in the worst sense, barbaric, gross, foreign to the mind of the Church, which was one of two terms he used as sticks to beat him with. The other was taste. The air of the rectory was often heavy with The Mind of the Church and Taste.

Another thing. Father Eudex could not conduct a civil conversation. Monsignor doubted that Father Eudex could even think to himself with anything like agreement. Certainly any discussion with Father Eudex ended inevitably in argument or sighing. Sighing! Why didn't people talk up if they had anything to say? No, they'd rather sigh! Father, don't ever, ever sigh at me again!

Finally, Monsignor did not like Father Eudex's table manners. This came to a head one night when Monsignor, seeing his curate's plate empty and all the silverware at his place unused except for a single knife, fork, and spoon, exploded altogether, saying it had been on his mind for weeks, and then descending into the vernacular he declared that Father Eudex did not know the forks—now perhaps he could understand that! Meals, unless Monsignor had guests or other things to struggle with, were always occasions of instruction for Father Eudex, and sometimes of chastisement.

And now he knew the worst—if Monsignor was thinking of recommending him for a year of study, in a Sulpician seminary probably, to learn the forks. So this was what it meant to be a priest. *Come, follow me. Going forth, teach ye all nations. Heal the sick, raise the dead, cleanse the lepers, cast out devils.* Teach the class of people we get here? Teach Mr. Memmers? Teach Communists? Teach Monsignors? And where were the poor? The lepers of old? The lepers were in their colonies with nuns to nurse them. The poor were in their holes and would not come out. Mr. Memmers was in his bank, without cheer. The Communists were in their universities, awaiting a sign. And he was at table with Monsignor, and it was enough for the disciple to be as his master, but the housekeeper had used green olives.

Monsignor inquired, "Did you get your check today?"

Father Eudex, looking up, considered. "I got *a* check," he said.

"From the Rival people, I mean?"

"Yes."

"Good. Well, I think you might apply it on the car you're wanting. A decent car. That's a worthy cause." Monsignor noticed that he was not taking it well. "Not that I mean to dictate what you shall do with your little windfall, Father. It's just that I don't like to see you mortifying yourself with a Model A—and disgracing the Church."

"Yes," Father Eudex said, suffering.

"Yes. I dare say you don't see the danger, just as you didn't a while ago when I found you making a spectacle of yourself with Whalen. You just don't see the danger because you just don't think. Not to dwell on it, but I seem to remember some overshoes."

The overshoes! Monsignor referred to them as to the Fall. Last winter Father Eudex had given his overshoes to a freezing picket. It had got back to Monsignor and—good Lord, a man could have his sympathies, but he had no right clad in the cloth to endanger the prestige of the Church by siding in these wretched squabbles. Monsignor said he hated to think of all the evil done by people doing good! Had Father Eudex ever heard of the Albigensian heresy, or didn't the seminary teach that any more?

Father Eudex declined dessert. It was strawberry mousse.

"Delicious," Monsignor said. "I think I'll let her stay."

At that moment Father Eudex decided that he had nothing to lose. He placed his knife next to his fork on the plate, adjusted them this way and that until they seemed to work a combination in his mind, to spring a lock which in turn enabled him to speak out.

"Monsignor," he said. "I think I ought to tell you I don't intend to make use of that money. In fact—to show you how my mind works—I have even considered endorsing the check to the strikers' relief fund."

"So," Monsignor said calmly—years in the confessional had prepared him for anything.

"I'll admit I don't know whether I can in justice. And even if I could I don't know that I would. I don't know why . . . I guess hush money, no matter what you do with it, is lousy."

Monsignor regarded him with piercing baby blue eyes. "You'd find it pretty hard to prove, Father, that *any* money *in se* is . . . what you say it is. I would quarrel further with the definition 'hush money.' It seems to me nothing if not rash that you would presume to impugn the motive of the Rival company in sending out these checks. You would seem to challenge the whole concept of good works—not that I am ignorant of the misuses to which money can be put." Monsignor, changing tack, tucked it all into a sigh. "Perhaps I'm just a simple soul, and it's enough for me to know personally some of the people in the Rival company and to know them good people. Many of them Catholic. . . ." A throb had crept into Monsignor's voice. He shut it off.

"I don't mean anything that subtle, Monsignor," Father Eudex said. "I'm just telling you, as my pastor, what I'm going to do with the check.

Or what I'm not going to do with it. I don't know what I'm going to do with it. Maybe send it back."

Monsignor rose from the table, slightly smiling. "Very well, Father. But there's always the poor."

Monsignor took leave of Father Eudex with a laugh. Father Eudex felt it was supposed to fool him into thinking that nothing he had said would be used against him. It showed, rather, that Monsignor was not winded, that he had broken wild curates before, plenty of them, and that he would ride again.

Father Eudex sought the shade of the porch. He tried to read his office, but was drowsy. He got up for a glass of water. The saints in Ireland used to stand up to their necks in cold water, but not for drowsiness. When he came back to the porch a woman was ringing the doorbell. She looked like a customer for rosary beads.

"Hello," he said.

"I'm Mrs. Klein, Father, and I was wondering if you could help me out."

Father Eudex straightened a porch chair for her. "Please sit down."

"It's a German name, Father. Klein was German descent," she said, and added with a silly grin, "It ain't what you think, Father."

"I beg your pardon."

"Klein. Some think it's a Jew name. But they stole it from Klein."

Father Eudex decided to come back to that later. "You were wondering if I could help you?"

"Yes, Father. It's personal."

"Is it matter for confession?"

"Oh no, Father." He had made her blush.

"Then go ahead."

Mrs. Klein peered into the honeysuckle vines on either side of the porch for alien ears.

"No one can hear you, Mrs. Klein."

"Father—I'm just a poor widow," she said, and continued as though Father Eudex had just slandered the man. "Klein was awful good to me, Father."

"I'm sure he was."

"So good . . . and he went and left me all he had." She had begun to cry a little.

Father Eudex nodded gently. She was after something, probably not money, always the best bet—either that or a drunk in the family—but this one was not Irish. Perhaps just sympathy.

"I come to get your advice, Father. Klein always said, 'If you got a problem, Freda, see the priest.'"

"Do you need money?"

"I got more than I can use from the bakery."

"You have a bakery?"

Mrs. Klein nodded down the street. "That's my bakery. It was Klein's. The Purity."

"I go by there all the time," Father Eudex said, abandoning himself to her. He must stop trying to shape the conversation and let her work it out.

"Will you give me your advice, Father?" He felt that she sensed his indifference and interpreted it as his way of rejecting her. She either had no idea how little sense she made or else supreme faith in him, as a priest, to see into her heart.

"Just what is it you're after, Mrs. Klein?"

"He left me all he had, Father, but it's just laying in the bank."

"And you want me to tell you what to do with it?"

"Yes, Father."

Father Eudex thought this might be interesting, certainly a change. He went back in his mind to the seminary and the class in which they had considered the problem of inheritances. Do we have any unfulfilled obligations? Are we sure? . . . Are there any impedimenta? . . .

"Do you have any dependents, Mrs. Klein—any children?"

"One boy, Father. I got him running the bakery. I pay him good—too much, Father."

"Is 'too much' a living wage?"

"Yes, Father. He ain't got a family."

"A living wage is not too much," Father Eudex handed down, sailing into the encyclical style without knowing it.

Mrs. Klein was smiling over having done something good without knowing precisely what it was.

"How old is your son?"

"He's thirty-six, Father."

"Not married?"

"No, Father, but he's got him a girl." She giggled, and Father Eudex, embarrassed, retied his shoe.

"But you don't care to make a will and leave this money to your son in the usual way?"

"I guess I'll have to . . . if I die." Mrs. Klein was suddenly crushed and haunted, but whether by death or charity, Father Eudex did not know.

"You don't have to, Mrs. Klein. There are many worthy causes. And the worthiest is the cause of the poor. My advice to you, if I understand your problem, is to give what you have to someone who needs it."

Mrs. Klein just stared at him.

"You could even leave it to the archdiocese," he said, completing the sentence to himself: but I don't recommend it in your case . . . with your tendencies. You look like an Indian giver to me.

But Mrs. Klein had got enough. "Huh!" she said, rising. "Well! You *are* a funny one!"

And then Father Eudex realized that she had come to him for a broker's tip. It was in the eyes. The hat. The dress. The shoes. "If you'd like to speak to the pastor," he said, "come back in the evening."

"You're a nice young man," Mrs. Klein said, rather bitter now and bent on getting away from him. "But I got to say this —you ain't much of a priest. And Klein said if I got a problem, see the priest—huh! You ain't much of a priest! What time's your boss come in?"

"In the evening," Father Eudex said. "Come any time in the evening." Mrs. Klein was already down the steps and making for the street.

"You might try Mr. Memmers at the First National," Father Eudex called, actually trying to help her, but she must have thought it was just some more of his nonsense and did not reply.

After Mrs. Klein had disappeared Father Eudex went to his room. In the hallway upstairs Monsignor's voice, coming from the depths of the clerical nap, halted him.

"Who was it?"

"A woman," Father Eudex said. "A woman seeking good counsel."

He waited a moment to be questioned, but Monsignor was not awake enough to see anything wrong with that, and there came only a sigh and a shifting of weight that told Father Eudex he was simply turning over in bed.

Father Eudex walked into the bathroom. He took the Rival check from his pocket. He tore it into little squares. He let them flutter into the toilet. He pulled the chain—hard.

He went to his room and stood looking out the window at nothing. He could hear the others already giving an account of their stewardship, but could not judge them. I bought baseball uniforms for the school. I bought the nuns a new washing machine. I purchased a Mass kit for a Chinese missionary. I bought a set of matched irons. Mine helped pay for keeping my mother in a rest home upstate. I gave mine to the poor.

And you, Father?

# Prejudice and Perception

## WILHELM

**Gabrielle Roy**

Gabrielle Roy, one of Canada's most distinguished writers, was born (1909) and educated in St. Boniface, Manitoba, a French-speaking community on the Canadian prairie. The youngest of eight children, she earned money by teaching in a rural school, went abroad for a short time, and then returned to Montreal in 1939. She had always been interested in the theatre and writing, and in 1945 published her first novel, Bonheur d'occasion (The Tin Flute, 1947), for which she was awarded a Governor-General's Award and Le Prix Femina in France. She now lives in Quebec City, but she and her husband, Marcel Carbotte, a doctor, travel extensively. Her other works include Alexandre Chenevert (1954, The Cashier, 1955), a novel; Rue Deschambault (1955, The Street of Riches, 1957), from which "Wilhelm" is taken; and La Route d'Altamont (The Road Past Altamont, 1966), a sequel of sorts to The Street of Riches. The separate stories in The Street of Riches are all linked by Christine, the youngest daughter of a large family, who, as can be seen from "Wilhelm," is also the narrator. Wilhelm, as the first sentence tells us, is Christine's first *suitor, and Gabrielle Roy, perhaps drawing upon her own memories, perceptively and with great sensitivity depicts the feelings and desires of her heroine. Speaking of her work, she once said: "I have tried to express something of the bewildering beauty of life, at once so sad, so poignant, at once so great, so utterly splendid." The reader can respond to "Wilhelm" on these terms.*

My first suitor came from Holland. He was called Wilhelm and his teeth were too regular; he was much older than I; he had a long, sad face . . . at least thus it was that others made me see him when they had taught me to consider his defects. As for me, at first I found his face thoughtful rather than long and peaked. I did not yet know that his teeth —so straight and even—were false. I thought I loved Wilhelm. Here was the first man who, through me, could be made happy or unhappy; here was a very serious matter.

I had met him at our friends' the O'Neills', who still lived not far from us in their large gabled house on Rue Desmeurons. Wilhelm was their boarder; for life is full of strange things: thus this big, sad man was a chemist in the employ of a small paint factory then operating in our city, and—as I have said—lodged with equally uprooted people, the O'Neills, formerly of County Cork in Ireland. A far journey to have come merely to behave, in the end, like everyone else—earn your living, try to make friends, learn our language, and then, in Wilhelm's case, love someone who was not for him. Do adventures often turn out so tritely? Obviously enough, though, in those days I did not think so.

Evenings at the O'Neills' were musical. Kathleen played "Mother Machree," while her mother, seated on a sofa, wiped her eyes, trying the while to avert our attention, to direct it away from herself, for she did not like people to believe her so deeply stirred by Irish songs. Despite the music, Elizabeth kept right on digging away at her arithmetic; she still was utterly indifferent to men. But Kathleen and I cared a great deal. We feared dreadfully to be left on the shelf; we feared we should fail to be loved and to love with a great and absolutely unique passion.

When Mrs. O'Neill requested it of me—"to relieve the atmosphere," as she put it—I played Paderewski's "Minuet"; then Wilhelm would have us listen to Massenet on a violin of choice quality. Afterward he would show me in an album scenes of his country, as well as his father's house and the home of his uncle, his father's partner. I think he was anxious to convey to me that his family was better off than you might think if you judged by him—I mean by his having had to quit his native land and come live in our small city. Yet he need have had no fear that I should form an opinion on the basis of silly social appearances; I wanted to judge people in strict accordance with their noble personal qualities. Wilhelm would explain to me how Ruisdael had really most faithfully rendered the full, sad sky of the Low Countries; and he asked me whether I thought I should like Holland enough one day to visit it. Yes, I replied; I should much like to see the canals and the tulip fields.

Then he had had sent to me from Holland a box of chocolates, each one of which was a small vial containing a liqueur.

But one evening he had the ill-starred notion of accompanying me back home, as far as our front door, though it was only two steps away and darkness had not wholly fallen. He was chivalrous: he insisted that a man should not let a woman go home all alone, even if that woman only yesterday had still been playing with hoops or walking on stilts.

Alas! The moment his back was turned, Maman asked me about my young man. "Who is that great beanstalk?"

I told her it was Wilhelm of Holland, and all the rest of it: the box of chocolates, the tulip fields, the stirring sky of Wilhelm's country, the windmills. . . . Now all that was fine and honorable! But why, despite what I thought of appearances, did I believe myself obliged also to speak of the uncle and the father, partners in a small business which . . . which . . . made a lot of money?

My mother at once forbade me to return to the O'Neills, so long, said she, as I had not got over the idea of Wilhelm.

But Wilhelm was clever. One or two days each week he finished work early; on those days he waited for me at the convent door. He took over my great bundle of books—Lord, what homework the Sisters piled on us in those days!—my music sheets, my metronome, and he carried all these burdens to the corner of our street. There he would lower upon me his large and sad blue eyes and say to me, "When you are bigger, I'll take you to the opera, to the theater. . . ."

I still had two years of the convent ahead of me; the opera, the theater seemed desperately far away. Wilhelm would tell me that he longed to see me in an evening gown; that then he would at last remove from its mothproof bag his dress clothes and that we should go in style to hear symphonic music.

My mother ultimately learned that Wilhelm had the effrontery to carry my books, and it annoyed her very much. She forbade me to see him.

"Still," said I to Maman, "I can hardly prevent his walking next to me along the pavement."

My mother cut through that problem. "If he takes the same sidewalk as you, mind you, cross right over to the other."

Now, she must have sent a message of rebuke to Wilhelm and told him, as she had me, precisely which sidewalk he should take, for I began seeing him only on the opposite side of the street, where he would stolidly await my passage. All the while I was going by, he held his hat in his hand. The other young girls must have been horribly envious of me; they laughed at Wilhelm's baring his head while I was passing. Yet I felt death in my soul at seeing Wilhelm so alone and exposed to ridicule.

He was an immigrant, and Papa had told me a hundred times that you could not have too much sympathy, too much consideration for the uprooted, who have surely suffered enough from their expatriation without our adding to it through scorn or disdain. Why then had Papa so completely changed his views, and why was he more set even than Maman against Wilhelm of Holland? True enough, no one at home, since Georgianna's marriage, looked favorably upon love. Perhaps because as a whole we had already had too much to suffer from it. But I—presumably —I had not yet suffered enough at its hands. . . .

And then, as I have said, Wilhelm was clever. Maman had forbidden him to speak to me on the street, but she had forgotten letters. Wilhelm had made great progress in English. He sent me very beautiful epistles which began with: "My own beloved child . . ." or else "Sweet little maid. . . ." Not to be outdone, I replied: "My own dearest heart. . . ." One day my mother found in my room a scrawl on which I had been practicing my handwriting and in which I expressed to Wilhelm a passion that neither time nor cruel obstacles could bend. . . . Had my mother glanced into the volume of Tennyson lying open upon my table, she would have recognized the whole passage in question, but she was far too angry to listen to reason. I was enjoined from writing to Wilhelm, from reading his letters, if, by a miracle, one of them succeeded in penetrating the defenses thrown up by Maman; I was even enjoined from thinking of him. I was allowed only to pray for him, if I insisted upon it.

Until then I had thought that love should be open and clear, cherished by all and making peace between beings. Yet what was happening? Maman was turned into something like a spy, busy with poking about in my wastebasket; and I then thought that she was certainly the last person in the world to understand me! So that was what love accomplished! And where was that fine frankness between Maman and me! Does there always arise a bad period between a mother and her daughter? Is it love that brings it on? . . . And what, what is love? One's neighbor? Or some person rich, beguiling?

During this interval Wilhelm, unable to do anything else for me, sent me many gifts; and at the time I knew nothing of them, for the moment they arrived, Maman would return them to him: music scores, tulip bulbs from Amsterdam, a small collar of Bruges lace, more liqueur-filled chocolates.

The only means left to us by which to communicate was the telephone. Maman had not thought of that. Obviously she could not think of everything; love is so crafty! Then, too, during her loving days the telephone did not exist, and this, I imagine, was why Maman forgot to ban it for me. Wilhelm often called our number. If it was not I who answered, he hung up gently. And many a time did Maman then protest, "What's going on? . . . I shall write the company a letter; I'm constantly being bothered for nothing. At the other end I can barely hear a sort of sighing sound." Naturally she could not foresee how far the tenacity of a Wilhelm would extend.

But when it was I who answered, Wilhelm was scarcely better off. There could be between us no real conversation without its exposing us to the discovery of our secret and consequent prohibition of the telephone. Moreover, we neither of us had any taste for ruses; Gervais employed them when he had on the wire the darling of his heart, to whom he spoke as though she were another schoolboy. But Wilhelm and I—without blaming Gervais, for love is love, and when it encounters obstacles, is even more worthy!—we strove to be noble in all things. Thus Wilhelm merely murmured to me, from afar, "Dear heart . . ." after which he remained silent. And I listened to his silence for a minute or two, blushing to the roots of my hair.

One day, though, he discovered an admirable way to make me understand his heart. As I was saying "Allo!" his voice begged me to hold the wire; then I made out something like the sound of a violin being tuned, then the opening bars of "Thaïs." Wilhelm played me the whole composition over the phone. Kathleen must have been accompanying him. I heard piano chords somewhere in the distance, and—I know not why—this put me out a trifle, perhaps at thinking that Kathleen was in on so lovely a secret. It was the first time, however, that Wilhelm put me out at all.

Our phone was attached to the wall at the end of a dark little hallway. At first no one was surprised at seeing me spend hours there, motionless and in the most complete silence. Only little by little did the people at home begin to notice that at the telephone I uttered no word. And from then on, when I went to listen to "Thaïs" the hall door would open slightly; someone hid there to spy on me, motioning the others to advance one by one and watch me. Gervais was the worst, and it was very mean on his part, for I had respected his secret. He manufactured reasons for making use of the hall; as he went by he tried to hear what I could be listening to. At first, however, I held the receiver firmly glued to my ear. Then I must already have begun to find "Thaïs" very long to hear through. One evening I allowed Gervais to listen for a moment to Wilhelm's music; perhaps I hoped that he would have enough enthusiasm to make me myself admire the composition. But Gervais choked with mirth; later on I saw him playing the fool in front of the others, at the far end of the living room, bowing an imaginary violin. Even Maman laughed a little, although she tried to remain angry. With a long, sad countenance which—I knew not how—he superimposed upon his own features, Gervais was giving a fairly good imitation of Wilhelm in caricature. I was a little tempted to laugh. For it is a fact that there is something quite comic in seeing a sad person play the violin.

When you consider it, it is astonishing that all of them together should not have thought much sooner of parting me from Wilhelm by the means they so successfully employed from that night forward.

All day long, when I went by, someone was whistling the melody of "Thaïs."

My brother grossly exaggerated the Dutchman's slightly solemn gait, his habit of keeping his eyes lifted aloft. They discovered in him the mien of a Protestant minister, dry—said they—and in the process of preparing a sermon. Maman added that the "Netherlander" had a face as thin as a knife blade. This was the way they now referred to him: the "Netherlander" or the "Hollander." My sister Odette—I should say Sister Edouard—who had been informed and was taking a hand in the matter, even though she had renounced the world, my pious Odette herself told me to forget the "foreigner" . . . that a foreigner is a foreigner. . . .

One evening as I listened to "Thaïs," I thought I must look silly, standing thus stock still, the receiver in my hand. I hung up before the end of the performance.

Thereafter, Wilhelm scarcely crossed my path again.

A year later, perhaps, we learned that he was returning to Holland.

My mother once more became the just and charitable pre-Wilhelm person I had loved so dearly. My father no longer harbored anything against Holland. Maman admitted that Mrs. O'Neill had told her concerning Wilhelm that he was the best man in the world, reliable, a worker, very gentle. . . . And Maman hoped that Wilhelm, in his own country, among his own people, would be loved . . . as, she said, he deserved to be.

---

# A GOOD MAN IS HARD TO FIND

## Flannery O'Connor

*Born in Savannah, Georgia, in 1925, Flannery O'Connor attended Georgia State College for Women and then the University of Iowa, from which she took her M.F.A. in creative writing in 1947. Although her active career covered only about twenty years (an incurable disease caused her death in 1964), Flannery O'Connor was able to distinguish herself as one of the masters of the short story. Although she wrote two novels that received critical acclaim,* Wise Blood *(1952) and* The Violent Bear It Away *(1960), she is mostly remembered for collections of her stories:* A Good Man Is Hard to Find and Other Stories *(1955) and* Everything That Rises Must Converge *(1965). Ms. O'Connor is another who is often thought of as a Southern writer. She lived the last thirteen years of her life with her mother in Milledgeville, Georgia, but her work cannot be categorized in regional terms. Her many awards for fiction, including several O. Henry awards and a grant from the National Academy of Arts and Letters, indicate the high critical praise she received from her fellow writers as well as critics. Many of the characters in her stories appear to be "grotesques" but are finally revealed through her art to have those human qualities that earn sympathy and even admiration. She had that vision that is the mark of a true artist, the vision that Walter Sullivan characterized as "clear and direct and as annoyingly precious as that of an Old Testament prophet or one of the more irascible Christian saints."*

The grandmother didn't want to go to Florida. She wanted to visit some of her connections in east Tennessee and she was seizing at every chance to change Bailey's mind. Bailey was the son she lived with, her only boy. He was sitting on the edge of his chair at the table, bent over the orange sports section of the *Journal*. "Now look here, Bailey," she said, "see here, read this," and she stood with one hand on her thin hip and the other rattling the newspaper at his bald head. "Here this fellow that calls himself The Misfit is aloose from the Federal Pen and headed toward Florida and you read here what it says he did to these people. Just you read it. I wouldn't take my children in any direction with a criminal like that aloose in it. I couldn't answer to my conscience if I did."

Bailey didn't look up from his reading so she wheeled around then and faced the children's mother; a young woman in slacks, whose face was as broad and innocent as a cabbage and was tied around with a green headkerchief that had two points on the top like rabbit's ears. She was sitting on the sofa, feeding the baby his apricots out of a jar. "The children have been to Florida before," the old lady said. "You all ought to take them somewhere else for a change so they would see different parts of the world and be broad. They never have been to east Tennessee."

The children's mother didn't seem to hear her, but the eight-year-old boy, John Wesley, a stocky child with glasses, said, "If you don't want to go to Florida, why dontcha stay at home?" He and the little girl, June Star, were reading the funny papers on the floor.

"She wouldn't stay at home to be queen for a day," June Star said without raising her yellow head.

"Yes, and what would you do if this fellow, The Misfit, caught you?" the grandmother asked.

"I'd smack his face," John Wesley said.

"She wouldn't stay at home for a million bucks," June Star said. "Afraid she'd miss something. She has to go everywhere we go."

"All right, Miss," the grandmother said. "Just remember that the next time you want me to curl your hair."

June Star said her hair was naturally curly.

The next morning the grandmother was the first one in the car, ready to go. She had her big black valise that looked like the head of a hippopotamus in one corner, and underneath it she was hiding a basket with Pitty Sing, the cat, in it. She didn't intend for the cat to be left alone in the house for three days because he would miss her too much and she was afraid he might brush against one of the gas burners and accidentally asphyxiate himself. Her son, Bailey, didn't like to arrive at a motel with a cat.

She sat in the middle of the back seat with John Wesley and June Star on either side of her. Bailey and the children's mother and the baby sat in the front and they left Atlanta at eight forty-five with the mileage on the car at 55890. The grandmother wrote this down because she thought it would be interesting to say how many miles they had been when they got back. It took them twenty minutes to reach the outskirts of the city.

The old lady settled herself comfortably, removing her white cotton gloves and putting them up with her purse on the shelf in front of the back window. The children's mother still had on slacks and still had her head tied up in a green kerchief, but the grandmother had on a navy blue straw sailor hat with a bunch of white violets on the brim and a navy blue dress with a small white dot in the print. Her collar and cuffs were white organdy trimmed with lace and at her neckline she had pinned a purple spray of cloth violets containing a sachet. In case of an accident, anyone seeing her dead on the highway would know at once that she was a lady.

She said she thought it was going to be a good day for driving, neither too hot nor too cold, and she cautioned Bailey that the speed limit was fifty-five miles an hour and that the patrolmen hid themselves behind billboards and small clumps of trees and sped out after you before you had a chance to slow down. She pointed out interesting details of the scenery: Stone Mountain; the blue granite that in some places came up to both sides of the highway; the brilliant red clay banks slightly streaked with purple; and the various crops that made rows of green lace-work on the ground. The trees were full of silver-white sunlights and the meanest of them sparkled. The children were reading comic magazines and their mother had gone back to sleep.

"Let's go through Georgia fast so we won't have to look at it much," John Wesley said.

"If I were a little boy," said the grandmother, "I wouldn't talk about my native state that way. Tennessee has the mountains and Georgia has the hills."

"Tennessee is just a hillbilly dumping ground," John Wesley said, "and Georgia is a lousy state too."

"You said it," June Star said.

"In my time," said the grandmother, folding her thin veined fingers, "children were more respectful of their native states and their parents and everything else. People did right then. Oh look at the cute little pickaninny!" she said and pointed to a Negro child standing in the door of a shack. "Wouldn't that make a picture, now?" she asked and they all turned and looked at the little Negro out of the back window. He waved.

"He didn't have any britches on," June Star said.

"He probably didn't have any," the grandmother explained. "Little niggers in the country don't have things like we do. If I could paint, I'd paint that picture," she said.

The children exchanged comic books.

The grandmother offered to hold the baby and the children's mother passed him over the front seat to her. She set him on her knee and bounced him and told him about the things they were passing. She rolled her eyes and screwed up her mouth and stuck her leathery thin face into his smooth bland one. Occasionally he gave her a faraway smile. They passed a large cotton field with five or six graves fenced in the middle of it, like a small island. "Look at the graveyard!" the grandmother said, pointing it out. "That was the old family burying ground. That belonged to the plantation."

"Where's the plantation?" John Wesley asked.

"Gone With the Wind," said the grandmother. "Ha. Ha."

When the children finished all the comic books they had brought, they opened the lunch and ate it. The grandmother ate a peanut butter sandwich and an olive and would not let the children throw the box and the paper napkins out the window. When there was nothing else to do they played a game by choosing a cloud and making the other two guess what shape it suggested. John Wesley took one the shape of a cow and June Star guessed a cow and John Wesley said, no, an automobile, and June Star said he didn't play fair, and they began to slap each other over the grandmother.

The grandmother said she would tell them a story if they would keep quiet. When she told a story, she rolled her eyes and waved her head and was very dramatic. She said once when she was a maiden lady she had been courted by a Mr. Edgar Atkins Teagarden from Jasper, Georgia. She said he was a very good-looking man and a gentleman and that he brought her a watermelon every Saturday afternoon with his initials cut in it, E.A.T. Well, one Saturday, she said, Mr. Teagarden brought the watermelon and there was nobody at home and he left it on the front porch and returned in his buggy to Jasper, but she never got the watermelon, she said, because a nigger boy ate it when he saw the initials, E.A.T.! This story tickled John Wesley's funny bone and he giggled and giggled but June Star didn't think it was any good. She said she wouldn't marry a man that just brought her a watermelon on Saturday. The grandmother said she would have done well to marry Mr. Teagarden because he was a gentleman and had bought Coca-Cola stock when it first came out and that he had died only a few years ago, a very wealthy man.

They stopped at The Tower for barbecued sandwiches. The Tower was a part-stucco and part-wood filling station and dance hall set in a clearing outside of Timothy. A fat man named Red Sammy Butts ran it and there were signs stuck here and there on the building and for miles up and down the highway saying, TRY RED SAMMY'S FAMOUS BARBECUE. NONE LIKE FAMOUS RED SAMMY'S! RED SAM! THE FAT BOY WITH THE HAPPY LAUGH. A VETERAN! RED SAMMY'S YOUR MAN!

Red Sammy was lying on the bare ground outside The Tower with his head under a truck while a gray monkey about a foot high, chained to a small chinaberry tree, chattered nearby. The monkey sprang back into the tree and got on the highest limb as soon as he saw the children jump out of the car and run toward him.

Inside, The Tower was a long dark room with a counter at one end and tables at the other and dancing space in the middle. They all sat down at a broad table next to the nickelodeon and Red Sam's wife, a tall burnt-brown woman with hair and eyes lighter than her skin, came and took their order. The children's mother put a dime in the machine and played "The Tennessee Waltz," and the grandmother said that tune always made her want to dance. She asked Bailey if he would like to dance but he only glared at her. He didn't have a naturally sunny disposition like she did and trips made him nervous. The grandmother's brown eyes were very bright. She swayed her head from side to side and pretended she was dancing in her chair. June Star said play something she could tap to so the children's mother put in another dime and played a fast number and June Star stepped out onto the dance floor and did her tap routine.

"Ain't she cute?" Red Sam's wife said, leaning over the counter. "Would you like to come be my little girl?"

"No, I certainly wouldn't," June Star said. "I wouldn't live in a broken-down place like this for a million bucks!" and she ran back to the table.

"Ain't she cute?" the woman repeated, stretching her mouth politely.

"Aren't you ashamed?" hissed the grandmother.

Red Sam came in and told his wife to quit lounging on the counter and hurry up with these people's order. His khaki trousers reached just to his hip bones and his stomach hung over them like a sack of meal swaying under his shirt. He came over and sat down at a table nearby and let out a combination sigh and yodel. "You can't win," he said. "You can't win," and he wiped his sweating red face off with a gray handkerchief. "These days you don't know who to trust," he said. "Ain't that the truth?"

"People are certainly not nice like they used to be," said the grandmother.

"Two fellers come in here last week," Red Sammy said, "driving a Chrysler. It was a old beat-up car but it was a good one and these boys looked all right to me. Said they worked at the mill and you know I let them fellers charge the gas they bought? Now why did I do that?"

"Because you're a good man!" the grandmother said at once.

"Yes'm, I suppose so," Red Sam said as if he were struck with this answer.

His wife brought the orders, carrying the five plates all at once without a tray, two in each hand and one balanced on her arm. "It isn't a soul in this green world of God's that you can trust," she said. "And I don't count nobody out of that, not nobody," she repeated, looking at Red Sammy.

"Did you read about that criminal, The Misfit, that's escaped?" asked the grandmother.

"I wouldn't be a bit surprised if he didn't attact this place right here," said the woman. "If he hears about it being here, I wouldn't be none surprised to see him. If he hears it's two cent in the cash register, I wouldn't be atall surprised if he. . . ."

"That'll do," Red Sam said. "Go bring these people their Co'Colas," and the woman went off to get the rest of the order.

"A good man is hard to find," Red Sammy said. "Everything is getting terrible. I remember the day you could go off and leave your screen door unlatched. Not no more."

He and the grandmother discussed better times. The old lady said that in her opinion Europe was entirely to blame for the way things were now. She said the way Europe acted you would think we were made of money and Red Sam said it was no use talking about it, she was exactly right. The children ran outside into the white sunlight and looked at the monkey in the lacy chinaberry tree. He was busy catching fleas on himself and biting each one carefully between his teeth as if it were a delicacy.

They drove off again into the hot afternoon. The grandmother took cat naps and woke up every few minutes with her own snoring. Outside of Toombsboro she woke up and recalled an old plantation that she had visited in this neighborhood once when she was a young lady. She said the house had six white columns across the front and that there was an avenue of oaks leading up to it and two little wooden trellis arbors on either side in front where you sat down with your suitor after a stroll in the garden. She recalled exactly which road to turn off to get to it. She knew that Bailey would not be willing to lose any time looking at an old house, but the more she talked about it, the more she wanted to see it once again and find out if the little twin arbors were still standing. "There was a secret panel in this house," she said craftily, not telling the truth but wishing that she were, "and the story went that all the family silver was hidden in it when Sherman came through but it was never found. . . ."

"Hey!" John Wesley said. "Let's go see it! We'll find it! We'll poke all the woodwork and find it! Who lives there? Where do you turn off at? Hey Pop, can't we turn off there?"

"We never have seen a house with a secret panel!" June Star shrieked. "Let's go to the house with the secret panel! Hey, Pop, can't we go see the house with the secret panel!"

"It's not far from here, I know," the grandmother said. "It wouldn't take over twenty minutes."

Bailey was looking straight ahead. His jaw was as rigid as a horseshoe. "No," he said.

The children began to yell and scream that they wanted to see the house with the secret panel. John Wesley kicked the back of the front seat and June Star hung over her mother's shoulder and whined desperately into her ear that they never had any fun even on their vacation, that they could never do what THEY wanted to do. The baby began to scream and John Wesley kicked the back of the seat so hard that his father could feel the blows in his kidney.

"All right!" he shouted and drew the car to a stop at the side of the road. "Will you all shut up? Will you all just shut up for one second? If you don't shut up, we won't go anywhere."

"It would be very educational for them," the grandmother murmured.

"All right," Bailey said, "but get this. This is the only time we're going to stop for anything like this. This is the one and only time."

"The dirt road that you have to turn down is about a mile back," the grandmother directed. "I marked it when we passed."

"A dirt road," Bailey groaned.

After they had turned around and were headed toward the dirt road, the grandmother recalled other points about the house, the beautiful glass over the front doorway and the candle lamp in the hall. John Wesley said that the secret panel was probably in the fireplace.

"You can't go inside this house," Bailey said. "You don't know who lives there."

"While you all talk to the people in front, I'll run around behind and get in a window," John Wesley suggested.

"We'll all stay in the car," his mother said.

They turned onto the dirt road and the car raced roughly along in a swirl of pink dust. The grandmother recalled the times when there were no paved roads and thirty miles was a day's journey. The dirt road was hilly and there were sudden washes in it and sharp curves on dangerous embankments. All at once they would be on a hill, looking down over the blue tops of trees for miles around, then the next minute, they would be in a red depression with the dust-coated trees looking down on them.

"This place had better turn up in a minute," Bailey said, "or I'm going to turn around."

The road looked as if no one had traveled on it in months.

"It's not much farther," the grandmother said and just as she said it, a horrible thought came to her. The thought was so embarrassing that she turned red in the face and her eyes dilated and her feet jumped up, upsetting her valise in the corner. The instant the valise moved, the newspaper top she had over the basket under it rose with a snarl and Pitty Sing, the cat, sprang onto Bailey's shoulder.

The children were thrown to the floor and their mother, clutching the baby, was thrown out the door onto the ground; the old lady was thrown into the front seat. The car turned over once and landed right-side-up in a gulch on the side of the road. Bailey remained in the driver's seat with the cat—gray-striped with a broad white face and an orange nose—clinging to his neck like a caterpillar.

As soon as the children saw they could move their arms and legs, they scrambled out of the car, shouting, "We've had an ACCIDENT!" The grandmother was curled up under the dashboard, hoping she was injured so that Bailey's wrath would not come down on her all at once. The horrible thought she had had before the accident was that the house she had remembered so vividly was not in Georgia but in Tennessee.

Bailey removed the cat from his neck with both hands and flung it out the window against the side of a pine tree. Then he got out of the car and started looking for the children's mother. She was sitting against the side of the red gutted ditch, holding the screaming baby, but she only had a cut down her face and a broken shoulder. "We've had an ACCIDENT!" the children screamed in a frenzy of delight.

"But nobody's killed," June Star said with disappointment as the grandmother limped out of the car, her hat still pinned to her head but the broken front brim standing up at a jaunty angle and the violet spray hanging off the side. They all sat down in the ditch, except the children, to recover from the shock. They were all shaking.

"Maybe a car will come along," said the children's mother hoarsely.

"I believe I have injured an organ," said the grandmother, pressing her side, but no one answered her. Bailey's teeth were clattering. He had on a yellow sport shirt with bright blue parrots designed in it and his face was as yellow as the shirt. The grandmother decided that she would not mention that the house was in Tennessee.

The road was about ten feet above and they could see only the tops of the trees on the other side of it. Behind the ditch they were sitting in there were more woods, tall and dark and deep. In a few minutes they saw a car some distance away on top of a hill, coming slowly as if the occupants were watching them. The grandmother stood up and waved both arms dramatically to attract their attention. The car continued to come on slowly, disappeared around a bend and appeared again, moving even slower, on top of the hill they had gone over. It was a big black battered hearselike automobile. There were three men in it.

It came to a stop just over them and for some minutes, the driver looked down with a steady expressionless gaze to where they were sitting, and didn't speak. Then he turned his head and muttered something to the other two and they got out. One was a fat boy in black trousers and a red sweat shirt with a silver stallion embossed on the front of it. He moved around on the right side of them and stood staring, his mouth partly open in a kind of loose grin. The other had on khaki pants and a blue striped coat and a gray hat pulled down very low, hiding most of his face. He came around slowly on the left side. Neither spoke.

The driver got out of the car and stood by the side of it, looking down at them. He was an older man than the other two. His hair was just beginning to gray and he wore silver-rimmed spectacles that gave him a scholarly look. He had a long creased face and didn't have on any shirt or undershirt. He had on blue jeans that were too tight for him and was holding a black hat and a gun. The two boys also had guns.

"We've had an ACCIDENT!" the children screamed.

The grandmother had the peculiar feeling that the bespectacled man was someone she knew. His face was as familiar to her as if she had known him all her life but she could not recall who he was. He moved away from the car and began to come down the embankment, placing his feet carefully so that he wouldn't slip. He had on tan and white shoes and no socks, and his ankles were red and thin. "Good afternoon," he said. "I see you all had you a little spill."

"We turned over twice!" said the grandmother.

"Oncet," he corrected. "We seen it happen. Try their car and see will it run, Hiram," he said quietly to the boy with the gray hat.

"What you got that gun for?" John Wesley asked. "Whatcha gonna do with that gun?"

"Lady," the man said to the children's mother, "would you mind calling them children to sit down by you? Children make me nervous. I want all you all to sit down right together there where you're at."

"What are you telling us what to do for?" June Star asked.

Behind them the line of woods gaped like a dark open mouth. "Come here," said their mother.

"Look here now," Bailey began suddenly, "we're in a predicament! We're in. . . ."

The grandmother shrieked. She scrambled to her feet and stood staring.

"You're The Misfit!" she said. "I recognized you at once!"

"Yes'm," the man said, smiling slightly as if he were pleased in spite of himself to be known, "but it would have been better for all of you, lady, if you hadn't of reckernized me."

Bailey turned his head sharply and said something to his mother that shocked even the children. The old lady began to cry and The Misfit reddened.

"Lady," he said, "don't you get upset. Sometimes a man says things he don't mean. I don't reckon he meant to talk to you thataway."

"You wouldn't shoot a lady, would you?" the grandmother said and removed a clean handkerchief from her cuff and began to slap at her eyes with it.

The Misfit pointed the toe of his shoe into the ground and made a little hole and then covered it up again. "I would hate to have to," he said.

"Listen," the grandmother almost screamed, "I know you're a good man. You don't look a bit like you have common blood. I know you must come from nice people!"

"Yes mam," he said, "finest people in the world." When he smiled he showed a row of strong white teeth. "God never made a finer woman than my mother and my daddy's heart was pure gold," he said. The boy with the red sweat shirt had come around behind them and was standing with his gun at his hip. The Misfit squatted down on the ground. "Watch them children, Bobby Lee," he said. "You know they make me nervous." He looked at the six of them huddled together in front of him and he seemed to be embarrassed as if he couldn't think of anything to say. "Ain't a cloud in the sky," he remarked, looking up at it. "Don't see no sun but don't see no cloud neither."

"Yes, it's a beautiful day," said the grandmother. "Listen," she said, "you shouldn't call yourself The Misfit because I know you're a good man at heart. I can just look at you and tell."

"Hush!" Bailey yelled. "Hush! Everybody shut up and let me handle this!" He was squatting in the position of a runner about to sprint forward but he didn't move.

"I pre-chate that, lady," The Misfit said and drew a little circle in the ground with the butt of his gun.

"It'll take a half a hour to fix this here car," Hiram called, looking over the raised hood of it.

"Well, first you and Bobby Lee get him and that little boy to step over yonder with you," The Misfit said, pointing to Bailey and John Wesley. "The boys want to ast you something," he said to Bailey. "Would you mind stepping back in them woods there with them?"

"Listen," Bailey began, "we're in a terrible predicament! Nobody realizes what this is," and his voice cracked. His eyes were as blue and intense as the parrots in his shirt and he remained perfectly still.

The grandmother reached up to adjust her hat brim as if she were going to the woods with him but it came off in her hand. She stood staring at it and after a second she let it fall on the ground. Hiram pulled Bailey up by the arm as if he were assisting an old man. John Wesley caught hold of his father's hand and Bobby Lee followed. They went off toward the woods and just as they reached the dark edge, Bailey turned and supporting himself against a gray naked pine trunk, he shouted, "I'll be back in a minute, Mamma, wait on me!"

"Come back this instant!" his mother shrilled but they all disappeared into the woods.

"Bailey Boy!" the grandmother called in a tragic voice but she found she was looking at The Misfit squatting on the ground in front of her. "I just know you're a good man," she said desperately. "You're not a bit common!"

"Nome, I ain't a good man," The Misfit said after a second as if he had considered her statement carefully, "but I ain't the worst in the world neither. My daddy said I was different breed of dog from my brothers and sisters. 'You know,' Daddy said, 'it's some that can live their whole life out without asking about it and it's others has to know why it is, and this boy is one of the latters. He's going to be into everything!'" He put on his black hat and looked up suddenly and then away deep into the woods as if he were embarrassed again. "I'm sorry I don't have on a shirt before you ladies," he said, hunching his shoulders slightly. "We buried our clothes that we had on when we escaped and we're just making do until we can get better. We borrowed these from some folks we met," he explained.

"That's perfectly all right," the grandmother said. "Maybe Bailey has an extra shirt in his suitcase."

"I'll look and see terrectly," The Misfit said.

"Where are they taking him?" the children's mother screamed.

"Daddy was a card himself," The Misfit said. "You couldn't put anything over on him. He never got in trouble with the Authorities though. Just had the knack of handling them."

"You could be honest too if you'd only try," said the grandmother. "Think how wonderful it would be to settle down and live a comfortable life and not have to think about somebody chasing you all the time."

The Misfit kept scratching in the ground with the butt of his gun as if he were thinking about it. "Yes'm, somebody is always after you," he murmured.

The grandmother noticed how thin his shoulder blades were just behind his hat because she was standing up looking down on him. "Do you ever pray?" she asked.

He shook his head. All she saw was the black hat wiggle between his shoulder blades. "Nome," he said.

There was a pistol shot from the woods, followed closely by another. Then silence. The old lady's head jerked around. She could hear the wind move through the tree tops like a long satisfied insuck of breath. "Bailey Boy!" she called.

"I was a gospel singer for a while," The Misfit said. "I been most everything. Been in the arm service, both land and sea, at home and abroad, been twict married, been an undertaker, been with the railroads, plowed Mother Earth, been in a tornado, seen a man burnt alive oncet," and he looked up at the children's mother and the little girl who were sitting close together, their faces white and their eyes glassy; "I even seen a woman flogged," he said.

"Pray, pray," the grandmother began, "pray, pray. . . ."

"I never was a bad boy that I remember of," The Misfit said in an almost dreamy voice, "but somewheres along the line I done something wrong and got sent to the penitentiary. I was buried alive," and he looked up and held her attention to him by a steady stare.

"That's when you should have started to pray," she said. "What did you do to get sent to the penitentiary that first time?"

"Turn to the right, it was a wall," The Misfit said, looking up again at the cloudless sky. "Turn to the left, it was a wall. Look up it was a ceiling, look down it was a floor. I forget what I done, lady. I set there and set there, trying to remember what it was I done and I ain't recalled it to this day. Oncet in a while, I would think it was coming to me, but it never come."

"Maybe they put you in by mistake," the old lady said vaguely.

"Nome," he said. "It wasn't no mistake. They had the papers on me."

"You must have stolen something," she said.

The Misfit sneered slightly. "Nobody had nothing I wanted," he said. "It was a head-doctor at the penitentiary said what I had done was kill my daddy but I known that for a lie. My daddy died in nineteen ought nineteen of the epidemic flu and I never had a thing to do with it. He was buried in the Mount Hopewell Baptist churchyard and you can go there and see for yourself."

"If you would pray," the old lady said, "Jesus would help you."

"That's right," The Misfit said.

"Well then, why don't you pray?" she asked trembling with delight suddenly.

"I don't want no hep," he said. "I'm doing all right by myself."

Bobby Lee and Hiram came ambling back from the woods. Bobby Lee was dragging a yellow shirt with bright blue parrots in it.

"Throw me that shirt, Bobby Lee," The Misfit said. The shirt came flying at him and landed on his shoulder and he put it on. The grandmother couldn't name what the shirt reminded her of. "No, lady," The Misfit said while he was buttoning it up, "I found out the crime don't matter. You can do one thing or you can do another, kill a man or take a tire off his car, because sooner or later you're going to forget what it was you done and just be punished for it."

The children's mother had begun to make heaving noises as if she couldn't get her breath. "Lady," he asked, "would you and that little girl like to step off yonder with Bobby Lee and Hiram and join your husband?"

"Yes, thank you," the mother said faintly. Her left arm dangled helplessly and she was holding the baby, who had gone to sleep, in the other. "Hep that lady up, Hiram," The Misfit said as she struggled to climb out of the ditch, "and Bobby Lee, you hold onto that little girl's hand."

"I don't want to hold hands with him," June Star said. "He reminds me of a pig."

The fat boy blushed and laughed and caught her by the arm and pulled her off into the woods after Hiram and her mother.

Alone with The Misfit, the grandmother found that she had lost her voice. There was not a cloud in the sky nor any sun. There was nothing around her but woods. She wanted to tell him that he must pray. She opened and closed her mouth several times before anything came out. Finally she found herself saying, "Jesus, Jesus," meaning, Jesus will help you, but the way she was saying it, it sounded as if she might be cursing.

"Yes'm," The Misfit said as if he agreed. "Jesus thrown everything off balance. It was the same case with Him as with me except He hadn't committed any crime and they could prove I had committed one because they had the papers on me. Of course," he said, "they never shown me my papers. That's why I sign myself now, I said long ago, you get you a signature and sign everything you do and keep a copy of it. Then you'll know what you done and you can hold up the crime to the punishment and see do they match and in the end you'll have something to prove you ain't been treated right. I call myself The Misfit," he said, "because I can't make what all I done wrong fit what all I gone through in punishment."

There was a piercing scream from the woods, followed closely by a pistol report. "Does it seem right to you, lady, that one is punished a heap and another ain't punished at all?"

"Jesus!" the old lady cried. "You've got good blood! I know you wouldn't shoot a lady! I know you come from nice people! Pray! Jesus, you ought not to shoot a lady. I'll give you all the money I've got!"

"Lady," The Misfit said, looking beyond her far into the woods, "there never was a body that give the undertaker a tip."

There were two more pistol reports and the grandmother raised her head like a parched old turkey hen crying for water and called, "Bailey Boy, Bailey Boy!" as if her heart would break.

"Jesus was the only One that ever raised the dead," The Misfit continued, "and He shouldn't have done it. He thrown everything off balance. If He did what He said, then it's nothing for you to do but throw away everything and follow Him, and if He didn't then it's nothing for you to do but enjoy the few minutes you got left the best way you can —by killing somebody or burning down his house or doing some other meanness to him. No pleasure but meanness," he said and his voice had become almost a snarl.

"Maybe He didn't raise the dead," the old lady mumbled, not knowing what she was saying and feeling so dizzy that she sank down in the ditch with her legs twisted under her.

"I wasn't there so I can't say He didn't," The Misfit said. "I wisht I had of been there," he said, hitting the ground with his fist. "It ain't right I wasn't there because if I had of been there I would of known. Listen lady," he said in a high voice, "if I had of been there I would of known and I wouldn't be like I am now." His voice seemed about to crack and the grandmother's head cleared for an instant. She saw the man's face twisted close to her own as if he were going to cry and she murmured, "Why, you're one of my babies. You're one of my own children!" She reached out and touched him on the shoulder. The Misfit sprang back as if a snake had bitten him and shot her three times through the chest. Then he put his gun down on the ground and took off his glasses and began to clean them.

Hiram and Bobby Lee returned from the woods and stood over the ditch, looking down at the grandmother who half sat and half lay in a puddle of blood with her legs crossed under her like a child's and her face smiling up at the cloudless sky.

Without his glasses, The Misfit's eyes were red-rimmed and pale and defenseless-looking. "Take her off and thow her where you thown the others," he said, picking up the cat that was rubbing itself against his leg.

"She was a talker, wasn't she?" Bobby Lee said, sliding down the ditch with a yodel.

"She would of been a good woman," The Misfit said, "if it had been somebody there to shoot her every minute of her life."

"Some fun!" Bobby Lee said.

"Shut up, Bobby Lee," The Misfit said. "It's no real pleasure in life."

---

# FLYING HOME

## Ralph Ellison

*Born in Oklahoma City in 1914, Ralph Ellison lived there until 1933, when he left to attend Tuskegee Institute. After three years at Tuskegee studying music he went to New York, and there he met and formed friendships with such writers as Richard Wright and Langston Hughes. His essays and stories began to appear in such publications as* The New Masses *and the* Negro Quarterly, *which Ellison himself edited for a time, but his first novel,* Invisible Man *(1952), established at once his reputation as a writer and as spokesman for blacks.* Invisible Man *received the National*

Book Award for that year and remains one of the most forceful artistic statements of our time. In 1964 Ellison's Shadow and Act, *a collection of essays and other writings,* appeared. Ellison has traveled and lectured extensively and has taught in a number of places, including the University of Chicago, Rutgers University, and New York University. In 1963 Tuskegee awarded him an honorary Ph.D. in Humane Letters. Robert A. Bone in The Negro Novel in America *(1958) and Ihab Hassan in* Radical Innocence: The Contemporary American Novel *(1962) provide some important insights into Ellison's work, and Benoit and Fabre in their* "A Bibliography of Ralph Ellison's Published Writings," Studies in Black Literature, *2 (Autumn 1971) list Ellison's other writings. Ellison himself, in one of his essays, helps the reader approach such stories as "Flying Home" and his novel* Invisible Man. *"There is value for the writer," he states, "in trying to give as thorough a report of social reality as possible. Only by doing so may we grasp and convey the cost of change. . . . Speaking from my own area of American culture, I feel that to embrace uncritically values which are extended to us by others is to reject the validity, even the sacredness, of our own experience. It is also to forget that the small share of reality which each of our diverse groups is able to snatch from the whirling chaos of history belongs not to the group alone, but to all of us." In this credo is found the source of Ellison's claim as a major writer: He writes not for any one group alone, but for all of us.*

When Todd came to, he saw two faces suspended above him in a sun so hot and blinding that he could not tell if they were black or white. He stirred, feeling a pain that burned as though his whole body had been laid open to the sun which glared into his eyes. For a moment an old fear of being touched by white hands seized him. Then the very sharpness of the pain began slowly to clear his head. Sounds came to him dimly. He done come to. Who are they? he thought. Naw he ain't, I coulda sworn he was white. Then he heard clearly:

"You hurt bad?"

Something within him uncoiled. It was a Negro sound.

"He's still out," he heard.

"Give 'im time. . . . Say, son, you hurt bad?"

Was he? There was that awful pain. He lay rigid, hearing their breathing and trying to weave a meaning between them and his being stretched painfully upon the ground. He watched them warily, his mind traveling back over a painful distance. Jagged scenes, swiftly unfolding as in a movie trailer, reeled through his mind, and he saw himself piloting a tail-spinning plane and landing and landing and falling from the cockpit and trying to stand. Then, as in a great silence, he remembered the sound of crunching bone, and now, looking up into the anxious faces of an old Negro man and a boy from where he lay in the same field, the memory sickened him and he wanted to remember no more.

"How you feel, son?"

Todd hesitated, as though to answer would be to admit an inacceptable weakness. Then, "It's my ankle," he said.

"Which one?"

"The left."

With a sense of remoteness he watched the old man bend and remove his boot, feeling the pressure ease.

"That any better?"

"A lot. Thank you."

He had the sensation of discussing someone else, that his concern was with some far more important thing, which for some reason escaped him.

"You done broke it bad," the old man said. "We have to get you to a doctor."

He felt that he had been thrown into a tailspin. He looked at his watch; how long had he been here? He knew there was but one important thing in the world, to get the plane back to the field before his officers were displeased.

"Help me up," he said. "Into the ship."

"But it's broke too bad. . . ."

"Give me your arm!"

"But, son . . ."

Clutching the old man's arm he pulled himself up, keeping his left leg clear, thinking, "I'd never make him understand," as the leather-smooth face came parallel with his own.

"Now, let's see."

He pushed the old man back, hearing a bird's insistent shrill. He swayed giddily. Blackness washed over him, like infinity.

"You best sit down."

"No, I'm O.K."

"But, son. You jus' gonna make it worse. . . ."

It was a fact that everything in him cried out to deny, even against the flaming pain in his ankle. He would have to try again.

"You mess with that ankle they have to cut your foot off," he heard.

Holding his breath, he started up again. It pained so badly that he had to bite his lips to keep from crying out and he allowed them to help him down with a pang of despair.

"It's best you take it easy. We gon' git you a doctor."

Of all the luck, he thought. Of all the rotten luck, now I have done it. The fumes of high-octane gasoline clung in the heat, taunting him.

"We kin ride him into town on old Ned," the boy said.

Ned? He turned, seeing the boy point toward an ox team browsing where the buried blade of a plow marked the end of a furrow. Thoughts of himself riding an ox through the town, past streets full of white faces, down the concrete runways of the airfield made swift images of humiliation in his mind. With a pang he remembered his girl's last letter. "Todd," she had written, "I don't need the papers to tell me you had the intelligence to fly. And I have always known you to be as brave as anyone else. The papers annoy me. Don't you be contented to prove over and over again that you're brave or skillful just because you're black, Todd. I think they keep beating that dead horse because they don't want to say why you boys are not yet fighting. I'm really disappointed, Todd. Anyone with brains can learn to fly, but then what? What about using it, and who will you use it for? I wish, dear, you'd write about this. I sometimes think they're playing a trick on us. It's very humiliating. . . ." He wiped cold sweat from his face, thinking, What does she know of humiliation? She's never been down South. Now the humiliation would come. When you must have them judge you, knowing that they never accept your mistakes as your own, but hold it against your whole race —that was humiliation. Yes, and humiliation was when you could never be simply yourself, when you were always a part of this old black ignorant man. Sure, he's all right. Nice and kind and helpful. But he's not you. Well, there's one humiliation I can spare myself.

"No," he said, "I have orders not to leave the ship. . . ."

"Aw," the old man said. Then turning to the boy, "Teddy, then you better hustle down to Mister Graves and get him to come. . . ."

"No, wait!" he protested before he was fully aware. Graves might be white. "Just have him get word to the field, please. They'll take care of the rest."

He saw the boy leave, running.

"How far does he have to go?"

"Might' nigh a mile."

He rested back, looking at the dusty face of his watch. But now they know something has happened, he thought. In the ship there was a perfectly good radio, but it was useless. The old fellow would never operate it. That buzzard knocked me back a hundred years, he thought. Irony danced within him like the gnats circling the old man's head. With all I've learned I'm dependent upon this "peasant's" sense of time and space. His leg throbbed. In the plane, instead of time being measured by the rhythms of pain and a kid's legs, the instruments would have told him at a glance. Twisting upon his elbows he saw where dust had powdered the plane's fuselage, feeling the lump form in his throat that was always there when he thought of flight. It's crouched there, he thought, like the abandoned shell of a locust. I'm naked without it. Not a machine, a suit of clothes you wear. And with a sudden embarrassment and wonder he whispered, "It's the only dignity I have. . . ."

He saw the old man watching, his torn overalls clinging limply to him in the heat. He felt a sharp need to tell the old man what he felt. But that would be meaningless. If I tried to explain why I need to fly back, he'd think I was simply afraid of white officers. But it's more than fear . . . a sense of anguish clung to him like the veil of sweat that hugged his face. He watched the old man, hearing him humming snatches of a tune as he admired the plane. He felt a furtive sense of resentment.

Such old men often came to the field to watch the pilots with childish eyes. At first it had made him proud; they had been a meaningful part of a new experience. But soon he realized they did not understand his accomplishments and they came to shame and embarrass him, like the distasteful praise of an idiot. A part of the meaning of flying had gone then, and he had not been able to regain it. If I were a prizefighter I would be more human, he thought. Not a monkey doing tricks, but a man. They were pleased simply that he was a Negro who could fly, and that was not enough. He felt cut off from them by age, by understanding, by sensibility, by technology and by his need to measure himself against the mirror of other men's appreciation. Somehow he felt betrayed, as he had when as a child he grew to discover that his father was dead. Now for him any real appreciation lay with his white officers; and with them he could never be sure. Between ignorant black men and condescending whites, his course of flight seemed mapped by the nature of things away from all needed and natural landmarks. Under some sealed orders, couched in ever more technical and mysterious terms, his path curved swiftly away from both the shame the old man symbolized and the cloudy terrain of white men's regard. Flying blind, he knew but one point of landing and there he would receive his wings. After that the enemy would appreciate his skill and he would assume his deepest meaning, he thought sadly, neither from those who condescended nor from those who praised without understanding, but from the enemy who would recognize his manhood and skill in terms of hate. . . .

He sighed, seeing the oxen making queer, prehistoric shadows against the dry brown earth.

"You just take it easy, son," the old man soothed. "That boy won't take long. Crazy as he is about airplanes."

"I can wait," he said.

"What kinda airplane you call this here'n?"

"An Advanced Trainer," he said, seeing the old man smile. His fingers were like gnarled dark wood against the metal as he touched the low-slung wing.

" 'Bout how fast can she fly?"

"Over two hundred an hour."

"Lawd! That's so fast I bet it don't seem like you moving!"

Holding himself rigid, Todd opened his flying suit. The shade had gone and he lay in a ball of fire.

"You mind if I take a look inside? I was always curious to see. . . ."

"Help yourself. Just don't touch anything."

He heard him climb upon the metal wing, grunting. Now the questions would start. Well, so you don't have to think to answer. . . .

He saw the old man looking over into the cockpit, his eyes bright as a child's.

"You must have to know a lot to work all these here things."

He was silent, seeing him step down and kneel beside him.

"Son, how come you want to fly way up there in the air?"

Because it's the most meaningful act in the world . . . because it makes me less like you, he thought.

But he said: "Because I like it, I guess. It's as good a way to fight and die as I know."

"Yeah? I guess you right," the old man said. "But how long you think before they gonna let you-all fight?"

He tensed. This was the question all Negroes asked, put with the same timid hopefulness and longing that always opened a greater void within him than that he had felt beneath the plane the first time he had flown. He felt light-headed. It came to him suddenly that there was something sinister about the conversation, that he was flying unwillingly into unsafe and uncharted regions. If he could only be insulting and tell this old man who was trying to help him to shut up!

"I bet you one thing . . ."

"Yes?"

"That you was plenty scared coming down."

He did not answer. Like a dog on a trail the old man seemed to smell out his fears and he felt anger bubble within him.

"You sho' scared me. When I seen you coming down in that thing with it a-rollin' and a-jumpin' like a pitchin' hoss, I thought sho' you was a goner. I almost had me a stroke!"

He saw the old man grinning. "Ever'thin's been happening round here this morning, come to think of it."

"Like what?" he asked.

"Well, first thing I know, here come two white fellers looking for Mister Rudolph, that's Mister Graves's cousin. That got me worked up right away. . . ."

"Why?"

"Why? 'Cause he done broke outta the crazy house, that's why. He liable to kill somebody," he said. "They oughta have him by now though. Then here you come. First I think it's one of them white boys. Then doggone if you don't fall outta there. Lawd, I'd done heard about you boys but I haven't never seen one o' you-all. Cain't tell you how it felt to see somebody what look like me in a airplane!"

The old man talked on, the sound streaming around Todd's thoughts like air flowing over the fuselage of a flying plane. You were a fool, he thought, remembering how before the spin the sun had blazed bright against the billboard signs beyond the town, and how a boy's blue kite had bloomed beneath him, tugging gently in the wind like a strange, odd-shaped flower. He had once flown such kites himself and tried to find the boy at the end of the invisible cord. But he had been flying too high and too fast. He had climbed steeply away in exultation. Too steeply, he thought. And one of the first rules you learn is that if the angle of thrust is too steep the plane goes into a spin. And then, instead of pulling out of it and going into a dive you let a buzzard panic you. A lousy buzzard!

"Son, what made all that blood on the glass?"

"A buzzard," he said, remembering how the blood and feathers had sprayed back against the hatch. It had been as though he had flown into a storm of blood and blackness.

"Well, I declare! They's lots of 'em around here. They after dead things. Don't eat nothing what's alive."

"A little bit more and he would have made a meal out of me," Todd said grimly.

"They bad luck all right. Teddy's got a name for 'em, calls 'em jimcrows," the old man laughed.

"It's a damned good name."

"They the damnedest birds. Once I seen a hoss all stretched out like he was sick, you know. So I hollers, 'Gid up from there, suh!' Just to make sho'. An' doggone, son, if I don't see two ole jimcrows come flying right up outta that hoss's insides! Yessuh! The sun was shinin' on 'em and they couldn't a been no greasier if they'd been eating barbecue."

Todd thought he would vomit, his stomach quivered.

"You made that up," he said.

"Nawsuh! Saw him just like I see you."

"Well, I'm glad it was you."

"You see lots a funny things down here, son."

"No, I'll let you see them," he said.

"By the way, the white folks round here don't like to see you boys up there in the sky. They ever bother you?"

"No."

"Well, they'd like to."

"Someone always wants to bother someone else," Todd said. "How do you know?"

"I just know."

"Well," he said defensively, "no one has bothered us."

Blood pounded in his ears as he looked away into space. He tensed, seeing a black spot in the sky, and strained to confirm what he could not clearly see.

"What does that look like to you?" he asked excitedly.

"Just another bad luck, son."

Then he saw the movement of wings with disappointment. It was gliding smoothly down, wings outspread, tail feathers gripping the air, down swiftly—gone behind the green screen of trees. It was like a bird he had imagined there, only the sloping branches of the pines remained, sharp against the pale stretch of sky. He lay barely breathing and stared at the point where it had disappeared, caught in a spell of loathing and admiration. Why did they make them so disgusting and yet teach them to fly so well? It's like when I was up in heaven, he heard, starting.

The old man was chuckling, rubbing his stubbled chin.

"What did you say?"

"Sho', I died and went to heaven . . . maybe by time I tell you about it they be done come after you."

"I hope so," he said wearily.

"You boys ever sit around and swap lies?"

"Not often. Is this going to be one?"

"Well, I ain't so sho', on account of it took place when I was dead." The old man paused, "That wasn't no lie 'bout the buzzards, though."

"All right," he said.

"Sho' you want to hear 'bout heaven?"

"Please," he answered, resting his head upon his arm.

"Well, I went to heaven and right away started to sproutin' me some wings. Six good ones, they was. Just like them the white angels had. I couldn't hardly believe it. I was so glad that I went off on some clouds by myself and tried 'em out. You know, 'cause I didn't want to make a fool outta myself the first thing. . . ."

It's an old tale, Todd thought. Told me years ago. Had forgotten. But at least it will keep him from talking about buzzards.

He closed his eyes, listening.

". . . First thing I done was to git up on a low cloud and jump off. And doggone, boy, if them wings didn't work! First I tried the right; then I tried the left; then I tried 'em both together. Then Lawd, I started to move on out among the folks. I let 'em see me. . . ."

He saw the old man gesturing flight with his arms, his face full of mock pride as he indicated an imaginary crowd, thinking, It'll be in the newspapers, as he heard, ". . . so I went and found me some colored angels—somehow I didn't believe I was an angel till I seen a real black one, ha, yes! Then I was sho'—but they tole me I better come down 'cause us colored folks had to wear a special kin' a harness when we flew. That was how come they wasn't flyin'. Oh yes, an' you had to be extra strong for a black man even, to fly with one of them harnesses. . . ."

This is a new turn, Todd thought, what's he driving at?

"So I said to myself, I ain't gonna be bothered with no harness! Oh naw! 'Cause if God let you sprout wings you oughta have sense enough not to let nobody make you wear something what gits in the way of flyin'. So I starts to flyin'. Heck, son," he chuckled, his eyes twinkling, "you know I had to let eve'ybody know that old Jefferson could fly good as anybody else. And I could too, fly smooth as a bird! I could even loop-the-loop—only I had to make sho' to keep my long white robe down roun' my ankles. . . ."

Todd felt uneasy. He wanted to laugh at the joke, but his body refused, as of an independent will. He felt as he had as a child when after he had chewed a sugar-coated pill which his mother had given him, she had laughed at his efforts to remove the terrible taste.

". . . Well," he heard, "I was doing all right 'til I got to speeding. Found out I could fan up a right strong breeze, I could fly so fast. I could do all kin'sa stunts too. I started flying up to the stars and divin' down and zooming roun' the moon. Man, I like to scare the devil outa some ole white angels. I was raisin' hell. Not that I meant any harm, son. But I was just feeling good. It was so good to know I was free at last. I accidentally knocked the tips offa some stars and they tell me I caused a storm and a coupla lynchings down here in Macon County—though I swear I believe them boys what said that was making up lies on me. . . ."

He's mocking me, Todd thought angrily. He thinks it's a joke. Grinning down at me . . . His throat was dry. He looked at his watch; why the hell didn't they come? Since they had to, why? One day I was flying down one of them heavenly streets. You got yourself into it, Todd thought. Like Jonah in the whale.

"Justa throwin' feathers in everybody's face. An' ole Saint Peter called me in. Said, 'Jefferson, tell me two things, what you doin' flyin' without a harness; an' how come you flyin' so fast?' So I tole him I was flyin' without a harness 'cause it got in my way, but I couldn'ta been flyin' so fast, 'cause I wasn't usin' but one wing. Saint Peter said, 'You wasn't flyin' with but one wing?' 'Yessuh,' I says, scared-like. So he says, 'Well, since you got sucha extra fine pair of wings you can leave off yo' harness awhile. But from now on none of that there one-wing flyin', 'cause you gittin' up too damn much speed!'"

And with one mouth full of bad teeth, you're making too damned much talk, thought Todd. Why don't I send him after the boy? His body ached from the hard ground and seeking to shift his position he twisted his ankle and hated himself for crying out.

"It gittin' worse?"

"I . . . I twisted it," he groaned.

"Try not to think about it, son. That's what I do."

He bit his lip, fighting pain with counter-pain as the voice resumed its rhythmical droning. Jefferson seemed caught in his own creation.

". . . After all that trouble I just floated roun' heaven in slow motion. But I forgot, like colored folks will do, and got to flyin' with one wing again. This time I was restin' my old broken arm and got to flyin' fast enough to shame the devil. I was comin' so fast, Lawd, I got myself called befo' ole Saint Peter again. He said, 'Jeff, didn't I warn you 'bout that speedin'?' 'Yessuh,' I says, 'but it was an accident.' He looked at me sad-like and shook his head and I knowed I was gone. He said, 'Jeff, you and that speedin' is a danger to the heavenly community. If I was to let you keep on flyin', heaven wouldn't be nothin' but uproar. Jeff, you got to go!' Son, I argued and pleaded with that old white man, but it didn't do a bit of good. They rushed me straight to them pearly gates and gimme a parachute and a map of the state of Alabama . . .'"

Todd heard him laughing so that he could hardly speak, making a screen between them upon which his humiliation glowed like fire.

"Maybe you'd better stop awhile," he said, his voice unreal.

"Ain't much more," Jefferson laughed. "When they gimme the parachute ole Saint Peter ask me if I wanted to say a few words before I went. I felt so bad I couldn't hardly look at him, specially with all them white angels standin' around. Then somebody laughed and made me mad. So I tole him, 'Well, you done took my wings. And you puttin' me out. You got charge of things so's I can't do nothin' about it. But you got to admit just this: While I was up here I was the flyinest sonofabitch what ever hit heaven!'"

At the burst of laughter Todd felt such an intense humiliation that only great violence would wash it away. The laughter which shook the old man like a boiling purge set up vibrations of guilt within him which not even the intricate machinery of the plane would have been adequate to transform and he heard himself screaming, "Why do you laugh at me this way?"

He hated himself at that moment, but he had lost control. He saw Jefferson's mouth fall open, "What—?"

"Answer me!"

His blood pounded as though it would surely burst his temples and he tried to reach the old man and fell, screaming, "Can I help it because they won't let us actually fly? Maybe we are a bunch of buzzards feeding on a dead horse, but we can hope to be eagles, can't we? Can't we?"

He fell back, exhausted, his ankle pounding. The saliva was like straw in his mouth. If he had the strength he would strangle this old man. This grinning, gray-headed clown who made him feel as he felt when watched by the white officers at the field. And yet this old man had neither power, prestige, rank nor technique. Nothing that could rid him of this terrible feeling. He watched him, seeing his face struggle to express a turmoil of feeling.

"What you mean, son? What you talking 'bout . . . ?"

"Go away. Go tell your tales to the white folks."

"But I didn't mean nothing like that. . . . I . . . I wasn't tryin' to hurt your feelings. . . ."

"Please. Get the hell away from me!"

"But I didn't, son. I didn't mean all them things a-tall."

Todd shook as with a chill, searching Jefferson's face for a trace of the mockery he had seen there. But now the face was somber and tired and old. He was confused. He could not be sure that there had ever been laughter there, that Jefferson had ever really laughed in his whole life. He saw Jefferson reach out to touch him and shrank away, wondering if anything except the pain, now causing his vision to waver, was real. Perhaps he had imagined it all.

"Don't let it get you down, son," the voice said pensively.

He heard Jefferson sigh wearily, as though he felt more than he could say. His anger ebbed, leaving only the pain.

"I'm sorry," he mumbled.

"You just wore out with pain, was all. . . ."

He saw him through a blur, smiling. And for a second he felt the embarrassed silence of understanding flutter between them.

"What you was doin' flyin' over this section, son? Wasn't you scared they might shoot you for a cow?"

Todd tensed. Was he being laughed at again? But before he could decide, the pain shook him and a part of him was lying calmly behind the screen of pain that had fallen between them, recalling the first time he had ever seen a plane. It was as though an endless series of hangars had been shaken ajar in the air base of his memory and from each, like a young wasp emerging from its cell, arose the memory of a plane.

The first time I ever saw a plane I was very small and planes were new in the world. I was four-and-a-half and the only plane that I had ever seen was a model suspended from the ceiling of the automobile exhibit at the State Fair. But I did not know that it was only a model. I did not know how large a real plane was, nor how expensive. To me it was a fascinating toy, complete in itself, which my mother said could only be owned by rich little white boys. I stood rigid with admiration, my head straining backwards as I watched the gray little plane describing arcs above the gleaming tops of the automobiles. And I vowed that, rich or poor, someday I would own such a toy. My mother had to drag me out of the exhibit and not even the merry-go-round, the Ferris wheel, or the racing horses could hold my attention for the rest of the Fair. I was too busy imitating the tiny drone of the plane with my lips, and imitating with my hands the motion, swift and circling, that it made in flight.

After that I no longer used the pieces of lumber that lay about our back yard to construct wagons and autos . . . now it was used for airplanes. I built biplanes, using pieces of board for wings, a small box for the fuselage, another piece of wood for the rudder. The trip to the Fair had brought something new into my small world. I asked my mother repeatedly when the Fair would come back again. I'd lie in the grass and watch the sky, and each fighting bird became a soaring plane. I would have been good a year just to have seen a plane again. I became a nuisance to everyone with my questions about airplanes. But planes were new to the old folks, too, and there was little that they could tell me. Only my uncle knew some of the answers. And better still, he could carve propellers from pieces of wood that would whirl rapidly in the wind, wobbling noisily upon oiled nails.

I wanted a plane more than I'd wanted anything; more than I wanted the red wagon with rubber tires, more than the train that ran on a track with its train of cars. I asked my mother over and over again:

"Mamma?"

"What do you want, boy?" she'd say.

"Mamma, will you get mad if I ask you?" I'd say.

"What do you want now? I ain't got time to be answering a lot of fool questions. What you want?"

"Mamma, when you gonna get me one . . . ?" I'd ask.

"Get you one what?" she'd say.

"You know, Mamma; what I been asking you. . . ."

"Boy," she'd say, "if you don't want a spanking you better come on an' tell me what you talking about so I can get on with my work."

"Aw, Mamma, you know. . . ."

"What I just tell you?" she'd say.

"I mean when you gonna buy me a airplane."

"Airplane! Boy, is you crazy? How many times I have to tell you to stop that foolishness. I done told you them things cost too much. I bet I'm gon' wham the living daylight out of you if you don't quit worrying me 'bout them things!"

But this did not stop me, and a few days later I'd try all over again.

Then one day a strange thing happened. It was spring and for some reason I had been hot and irritable all morning. It was a beautiful spring. I could feel it as I played barefoot in the backyard. Blossoms hung from the thorny black locust trees like clusters of fragrant white grapes. Butterflies flickered in the sunlight above the short new dew-wet grass. I had gone in the house for bread and butter and coming out I heard a steady unfamiliar drone. It was unlike anything I had ever heard before. I tried to place the sound. It was no use. It was a sensation like that I had when searching for my father's watch, heard ticking unseen in a room. It made me feel as though I had forgotten to perform some task that my mother had ordered . . . then I located it, overhead. In the sky, flying quite low and about a hundred yards off was a plane! It came so slowly that it seemed barely to move. My mouth hung wide; my bread and butter fell into the dirt. I wanted to jump up and down and cheer. And when the idea struck I trembled with excitement: "Some little white boy's plane's done flew away and all I got to do is stretch out my hands and it'll be mine!" It was a little plane like that at the Fair, flying no higher than the eaves of our roof. Seeing it come steadily forward I felt the world grow warm with promise. I opened the screen and climbed over it and clung there, waiting. I would catch the plane as it came over the swing down fast and run into the house before anyone could see me. Then no one could come to claim the plane. It droned nearer. Then when it hung like a silver cross in the blue directly above me I stretched out my hand and grabbed. It was like sticking my finger through a soap bubble. The plane flew on, as though I had simply blown my breath after it. I grabbed again, frantically, trying to catch the tail. My fingers clutched the air and disappointment surged tight and hard in my throat. Giving one last desperate grasp, I strained forward. My fingers ripped from the screen, I was falling. The ground burst hard against me. I drummed the earth with my heels and when my breath returned, I lay there bawling.

My mother rushed through the door.

"What's the matter, chile! What on earth is wrong with you?"

"It's gone! It's gone!"

"What gone?"

"The airplane . . ."

"Airplane?"

"Yessum, jus' like the one at the Fair. . . . I . . . I tried to stop it an' it kep' right on going. . . ."

"When, boy?"

"Just now," I cried, through my tears.

"Where it go, boy, what way?"

"Yonder, there . . ."

She scanned the sky, her arms akimbo and her checkered apron flapping in the wind as I pointed to the fading plane. Finally she looked down at me, slowly shaking her head.

"It's gone! It's gone!" I cried.

"Boy, is you a fool?" she said. "Don't you see that there's a real airplane 'stead of one of them toy ones?"

"Real . . . ?" I forgot to cry. "Real?"

"Yass, real. Don't you know that thing you reaching for is bigger'n a auto? You here trying to reach for it and I bet it's flying 'bout two hundred miles higher'n this roof." She was disgusted with me. "You come on in this house before somebody else sees what a fool you done turned out to be. You must think these here lil ole arms of you'n is mighty long. . . ."

I was carried into the house and undressed for bed and the doctor was called. I cried bitterly, as much from the disappointment of finding the plane so far beyond my reach as from the pain.

When the doctor came I heard my mother telling him about the plane and asking if anything was wrong with my mind. He explained that I had had a fever for several hours. But I was kept in bed for a week and I constantly saw the plane in my sleep, flying just beyond my fingertips, sailing so slowly that it seemed barely to move. And each time I'd reach out to grab it I'd miss and through each dream I'd hear my grandma warning:

> Young man, young man,
> Yo' arms too short
> To box with God. . . .

"Hey, son!"

At first he did not know where he was and looked at the old man pointing, with blurred eyes.

"Ain't that one of you-all's airplanes coming after you?"

As his vision cleared he saw a small black shape above a distant field, soaring through waves of heat. But he could not be sure and with the pain he feared that somehow a horrible recurring fantasy of being split in twain by the whirling blades of a propeller had come true.

"You think he sees us?" he heard.

"See? I hope so."

"He's coming like a bat outa hell!"

Straining, he heard the faint sound of a motor and hoped it would soon be over.

"How you feeling?"

"Like a nightmare," he said.

"Hey, he's done curved back the other way!"

"Maybe he saw us," he said. "Maybe he's gone to send out the ambulance and ground crew." And, he thought with despair, maybe he didn't even see us.

"Where did you send the boy?"

"Down to Mister Graves," Jefferson said. "Man what owns this land."

"Do you think he phoned?"

Jefferson looked at him quickly.

"Aw sho'. Dabney Graves is got a bad name on accounta them killings but he'll call though. . . ."

"What killings?"

"Them five fellers . . . ain't you heard?" he asked with surprise.

"No."

"Everybody knows 'bout Dabney Graves, especially the colored. He done killed enough of us."

Todd had the sensation of being caught in a white neighborhood after dark.

"What did they do?" he asked.

"Thought they was men," Jefferson said. "An' some he owed money, like he do me. . . ."

"But why do you stay here?"

"You black, son."

"I know, but . . ."

"You have to come by the white folks, too."

He turned away from Jefferson's eyes, at once consoled and accused. And I'll have to come by them soon, he thought with despair. Closing his eyes, he heard Jefferson's voice as the sun burned blood-red upon his lips.

"I got nowhere to go," Jefferson said, "an' they'd come after me if I did. But Dabney Graves is a funny fellow. He's all the time making jokes. He can be mean as hell, then he's liable to turn right around and back the colored against the white folks. I seen him do it. But me, I hates him for that more'n anything else. 'Cause just as soon as he gits tired helping a man he don't care what happens to him. He just leaves him stone cold. And then the other white folks is double hard on anybody he done helped. For him it's just a joke. He don't give a hilla beans for nobody—but hisself. . . ."

Todd listened to the thread of detachment in the old man's voice. It was as though he held his words arm's length before him to avoid their destructive meaning.

"He'd just as soon do you a favor and then turn right around and have you strung up. Me, I stays outa his way 'cause down here that's what you gotta do."

If my ankle would only ease for a while, he thought. The closer I spin toward the earth the blacker I become, flashed through his mind. Sweat ran into his eyes and he was sure that he would never see the plane if his head continued whirling. He tried to see Jefferson, what was it that Jefferson held in his hand? It was a little black man, another Jefferson! A little black Jefferson that shook with fits of belly-laughter while the other Jefferson looked on with detachment. Then Jefferson looked up from the thing in his hand and turned to speak, but Todd was far away, searching the sky for a plane in a hot dry land on a day and age he had long forgotten. He was going mysteriously with his mother through empty streets where black faces peered from behind drawn shades and someone was rapping at a window and he was looking back to see a hand and a frightened face frantically beckoning him from a cracked door and his mother was looking down the empty perspective of the street and shaking her head and hurrying him along and at first it was only a flash he saw and a motor was droning as through the sun-glare he saw it gleaming silver as it circled and he was seeing a burst like a puff of white smoke and hearing his mother yell, Come along, boy, I got no time for them fool airplanes, I got no time, and he saw it a second time, the plane flying high, and the burst appeared suddenly and fell slowly, billowing out and sparkling like fireworks and he was watching and being hurried along as the air filled with a flurry of white pinwheeling cards that caught in the wind and scattered over the rooftops and into the gutters and a woman was running and snatching a card and reading it and screaming and he darted into the shower, grabbing as in winter he grabbed for snowflakes and bounding away at his mother's, Come on here, boy! Come on, I say! and he was watching as she took the card away, seeing her face grow puzzled and turning taut as her voice quavered, "Niggers Stay From The Polls," and died to a moan of terror as he saw the eyeless sockets of a white hood staring at him from the card and above he saw the plane spiraling gracefully, agleam in the sun like a fiery sword. And seeing it soar he was caught, transfixed between a terrible horror and a horrible fascination.

The sun was not so high now, and Jefferson was calling and gradually he saw three figures moving across the curving roll of the field.

"Look like some doctors, all dressed in white," said Jefferson.

They're coming at last, Todd thought. And he felt such a release of tension within him that he thought he would faint. But no sooner did he close his eyes than he was seized and he was struggling with three white men who were forcing his arms into some kind of coat. It was too much for him, his arms were pinned to his sides and as the pain blazed in his eyes, he realized that it was a straitjacket. What filthy joke was this?

"That oughta hold him, Mister Graves," he heard.

His total energies seemed focused in his eyes as he searched their faces. That was Graves; the other two wore hospital uniforms. He was poised between two poles of fear and hate as he heard the one called Graves saying, "He looks kinda purty in that there suit, boys. I'm glad you dropped by."

"This boy ain't crazy, Mister Graves," one of the others said. "He needs a doctor, not us. Don't see how you led us way out here anyway. It might be a joke to you, but your cousin Rudolph liable to kill somebody. White folks or niggers, don't make no difference. . . ."

Todd saw the man turn red with anger. Graves looked down upon him, chuckling.

"This nigguh belongs in a straitjacket, too, boys. I knowed that the minit Jeff's kid said something 'bout a nigguh flyer. You all know you cain't let the nigguh git up that high without his going crazy. The nigguh brain ain't built right for high altitudes. . . ."

Todd watched the drawling red face, feeling that all the unnamed horror and obscenities that he had ever imagined stood materialized before him.

"Let's git outta here," one of the attendants said.

Todd saw the other reach toward him, realizing for the first time that he lay upon a stretcher as he yelled.

"Don't put your hands on me!"

They drew back, surprised.

"What's that you say, nigguh?" asked Graves.

He did not answer and thought that Graves's foot was aimed at his head. It landed on his chest and he could hardly breathe. He coughed helplessly, seeing Graves's lips stretch taut over his yellow teeth, and tried to shift his head. It was as though a half-dead fly was dragging slowly across his face and a bomb seemed to burst within him. Blasts of hot, hysterical laughter tore from his chest, causing his eyes to pop and he felt that the veins in his neck would surely burst. And then a part of him stood behind it all, watching the surprise in Graves's red face and his own hysteria. He thought he would never stop, he would laugh himself to death. It rang in his ears like Jefferson's laughter and he looked for him, centering his eyes desperately upon his face, as though somehow he had become his sole salvation in an insane world of outrage and humiliation. It brought a certain relief. He was suddenly aware that although his body was still contorted it was an echo that no longer rang in his ears. He heard Jefferson's voice with gratitude.

"Mister Graves, the Army done tole him not to leave his airplane."

"Nigguh, Army or no, you gittin' off my land! That airplane can stay 'cause it was paid for by taxpayers' money. But you gittin' off. An' dead or alive, it don't make no difference to me."

Todd was beyond it now, lost in a world of anguish.

"Jeff," Graves said, "you and Teddy come and grab holt. I want you to take this here black eagle over to that nigguh airfield and leave him."

Jefferson and the boy approached him silently. He looked away, realizing and doubting at once that only they could release him from his overpowering sense of isolation.

They bent for the stretcher. One of the attendants moved toward Teddy.

"Think you can manage it, boy?"

"I think I can, suh," Teddy said.

"Well, you better go behind then, and let yo' pa go ahead so's to keep that leg elevated."

He saw the white men walking ahead as Jefferson and the boy carried him along in silence. Then they were pausing and he felt a hand wiping his face; then he was moving again. And it was as though he had been lifted out of his isolation, back into the world of men. A new current of communication flowed between the man and boy and himself. They moved him gently. Far away he heard a mockingbird liquidly calling. He raised his eyes, seeing a buzzard poised unmoving in space. For a moment the whole afternoon seemed suspended and he waited for the horror to seize him again. Then like a song within his head he heard the boy's soft humming and saw the dark bird glide into the sun and glow like a bird of flaming gold.

---

# THE LOVES OF FRANKLIN AMBROSE

## Joyce Carol Oates

*Born in Lockport, New York, in 1938, Joyce Carol Oates, teacher, poet, critic, and writer of fiction, is one of the youngest and most prolific writers in this generation. Educated at the Universities of Wisconsin and Syracuse, she taught for a time at the*

*University of Detroit and is now at the University of Windsor, Canada, where she serves as fiction editor of the* University of Windsor Review. *Her works are many and varied, and she has been the recipient of many awards, including the National Book Award for Fiction in 1970 for her novel* Them *and several O. Henry awards for short stories. Among her works are the following:* A Garden of Earthly Delights (1967); Expensive People (1968); The Wheel of Love and Other Stories (1970); Love and Its Derangements (1970), *poems;* The Edge of Impossibility: Tragic Forms in Literature (1972), *criticism;* Marriages and Infidelities (1972), *a collection of short stories;* The Hostile Sun: The Poetry of D. H. Lawrence (1973), *criticism;* Angel Fire (1973), *poems; and* Do with Me What You Will (1973). *"The Loves of Franklin Ambrose," which appeared originally in* Playboy, *is typically Oatesian in its treatment of character and its presentation of events. In commenting on her fiction, Michael Wood pointed out that the life people lead in the fiction of Joyce Carol Oates is both drab and electric, full of melodrama and yet curiously dull. Mr. Wood goes on to indicate that what he perceives as her special talent is her ability to get "this complex perception across without excessive insistence on its significance, and without rigging her fiction too much for the purpose."*

A decade before the phrase "Black is beautiful" became popular, Franklin Ambrose knew that he was beautiful. But his beauty had nothing to do with being black. He was naturally handsome in a small, neat way; he cultivated a thin mustache and a very black, rugged, almost savage goatee; his shoes were so shiny that they looked varnished; he wore Pierre Cardin shirts of various peacock-gay colors, expensive silk-twill ties and ascots, and suits whose notched and peaked lapels expanded and narrowed according to fashion laws totally unknown to Frank's mundane, hard-working colleagues at the university. He took an obvious, healthy pride in physical appearances and was critical of his wife's clothes, which always seemed shapeless and dowdy. "Do you want to embarrass me?" he sometimes asked in exasperation.

But most of the time he was cheerful and very energetic. He hastened to put all white people at their ease, immediately, by emphasizing the scorn he felt for anything "black" (he hated that modish word; he preferred the more sanitary and middle-class "Negro"). In fact, he accepted a position at a small university in southern Canada, near Hamilton, because he suspected—correctly—that there would be few Negroes in the school. He had only one real rival—a popular professor of psychology who sported an Afro haircut and love beads; but Franklin put him down by saying, whenever the man's name was mentioned, "There's a real professional black." This made his white friends laugh appreciatively.

Franklin was not "black," but he was very professional. His degrees were all from Harvard and he had spent a year in England as a Fulbright Fellow; during that time, he had developed a faint, clipped English accent. At Harvard he had been very popular with Radcliffe girls, especially a kind of bright, intense Jewish girl who shared many of his interests in literature and music. But he wanted to marry another kind of girl—he didn't know why, exactly—he had his heart set on a Wellesley girl whose father was a judge in Boston, a sweet girl, not very intelligent but gifted with a pale, smooth, almost porcelain complexion. Their marriage was violently opposed by her family, but Franklin won, and in 1965 he accepted a position at Hilberry University and took his bride to a small city in southeastern Ontario: with great anticipation, a sense of drama, for he was the only Negro in the English department and the only Harvard man.

Frank became the department's most popular professor at once. And yet something began to happen in the second year: He felt a strange, aimless melancholy, his classroom successes came too easily, he noticed that he and Eunice, out together, no longer attracted the attention and the occasional outraged glares they had attracted in the past. No doubt about it, Eunice was becoming dowdy, her waist and hips thickening; she was not even very pretty. The only happiness in Frank's life was his twin sons, wonderfully light, almost fair little boys, with beautiful features—especially their dark, thickly lashed eyes. At times he stared at them as if unable to believe the miracle of their physical beauty. How had anything so wonderful happened to him?

As his wife's looks dwindled and Frank began to sink into the ordinary routine of teaching in an ordinary university—no overwrought, neurotic, brilliant Radcliffe girls to stir the adrenaline!—he felt at times a sense of panic. What, he was 28 years old? What, already he was 30? For his 32nd birthday he gifted himself with a white MG, though his family could obviously not fit in it. He bought an elegant, rather Beau Brummellish smoking jacket to wear in his study at home and a sueded-calfskin belted coat that drew all eyes to it as he strolled across the gray-lit campus. He began going with his students to The Cave, a popular pub, crowded and noisy and merry; the majority of his student friends were boys, who eagerly appreciated his wit and his friendliness—most of the other professors nervously avoided all personal contact with students—but a few were girls. They were all the same type, more or less: intellectual, casual, a little brazen, a little sloppy, and they seemed to appreciate Frank even more than the boys did.

A possibility dawned on Frank.

Yes, he was attracted to the girls as if to searing, caressing rays of light: their pale skins, their moving, twisting, smirking, giggling mouths, their tight, thigh-high skirts, their nervous writhing mannerisms when they came in for "conferences" to his office. They brushed their long hair out of their eyes and smiled at him. Frank would feel at such times an intoxication that forced him to lean forward, gazing at them, his own eyes bright and his flesh livened by their closeness. They complained to him about their families or their other professors or their boyfriends: "My boyfriend is, I don't know, he's so *dumb* compared with someone like you,

Dr. Ambrose. . . . I mean, he's so *dumb* when it comes to conversation that I just sort of blank out and think about, well, you, I guess. I mean I think about how funny you were in class or something and . . . well . . . I think about *you* when I'm with him, you know, when the two of us are . . . you know. . . . I feel real rotten about it, because it isn't fair, I guess, to him, because we're really sort of in love . . . and . . . and. . . ." And they would gaze at Frank with their eyes sometimes misting over. At such times he felt his heart beat with certainty: *Unmistakable!*

The girls were so sweet, with their kisses and their sudden, rationed tears, that Frank went about in a perpetual daze, more genial than ever before.

Being a gentleman, he made no more than the most subtle of allusions to his colleagues in the department, most of whom were prematurely weary, slowed down with families, balding, thickening, and yet still fired feebly with hopes of romance; they were temporarily freshened by stray rumors of secret liaisons, even though the liaisons never happened to them. They appreciated Frank, who was, after all, black (the word began to be used, cautiously, around 1969–1970), so trim and handsome and elegantly turned out, and they quipped that he was their liaison man with the students.

"Frank will bridge the generation gap for us," they said with wistful, encouraging smiles.

But then, in the late Sixties, an essay with the title "The Student as Nigger" became widely circulated; it was even published in the student newspaper. Frank was aghast. He couldn't believe it. Colleagues and students began talking quite familiarly, openly, of the oppression of students and "niggers"—often in Frank's presence, as if to demonstrate to him how liberal and understanding they were. *The word nigger! On everyone's lips!* Frank was furious, demoralized, befuddled; he would not explain his moods to his wife; he went out one evening by himself to a cocktail lounge far from the university, where he got drunk and had to be sent home in a taxicab. At such times, when he was very drunk, he had the confused idea that some white man—any white man at all—was trying to appropriate his twin boys. "They want to take my babies away, my babies," he would weep. "They want to take my babies because I'm black and my babies are white. . . ."

He knew he was not a nigger, and yet he wasn't sure that other people, glancing at him, knew. He recalled with horror the evening, at a faculty party, when the slightly drunken wife of a colleague had cornered him to ask whether he planned "to go back to the ghetto to help his people," seeing that he himself was so successful. That white bitch!

But his young girl students fawned over him, even pursued him, singly and in small packs. There was no doubt of his manhood with *them*. Their names were Cindy and Laurie and Sandy and Cheryl; they passed in and out of his arms with the rotation of the academic semesters, some of them wise and cynical with experience, others incredibly naïve and therefore dangerous; they were like figures in the most riotous, improbable of his adolescent dreams, somehow lacking substance, lacking souls, because of their very eagerness to oblige him. "But, Dr. Ambrose, you're a genius from Harvard and all that, I'm afraid to talk to you, I'm afraid you're giving me a grade when you just *look* at me!" One of the Cindys or Sandys whose bold stare had misled Frank nearly caused a scandal by confessing to her parents, who in turn called the university's president and several members of the board of trustees; but after a four-hour conference in the president's office, Franklin managed to be forgiven. He promised not to be "indiscreet" again.

That was in the winter of 1969. In the spring of that year, the appointments and promotions committee (called the hiring and firing committee) of the department interviewed applicants for the position of lecturer in English. Franklin was the youngest member of this powerful committee and he grilled candidates for the job seriously. He was not very impressed with a young Ph.D. from Yale nor with a young Indian student from Oxford; he was very impressed with a young woman named Molly Holt, who rushed in 15 minutes late for her interview, wearing a very short leather skirt and bright-gold boots.

Franklin stared at this girl. She was no more than five feet, one or two, and therefore shorter than he. She was very pretty, with a small, pixylike face, blonde hair snipped short and puffed out carelessly about her face, so young, so pretty, with impressive recommendations from the University of Chicago! It was hard to believe. Frank's interest in her grew as he glanced through her application and saw that she was a divorcee with a three-year-old son. She was answering questions pertly and brightly. Obviously an intelligent woman. Frank was careful to ask her questions that might lead her to admirable statements: "I am deeply committed to literature and to teaching, yes," she said. "And to the future, to the struggle for equality between men and women." Hastily, Frank asked her about her doctoral thesis, which she had just begun: "It's called *Crises of Sexual Identity in Trollope and Dickens*," she said. "It grew out of my fascination with the role of women in Victorian literature. Imagine, Charles Dickens created Edith Dombey!—and yet in his personal life he was such a bastard, a real male chauvinist pig—"

After this, it took Frank several hours and several meetings of the committee to hire Miss Holt: He had a lot of talking to do.

When she arrived in September, he drove her around in his neat little white sports car, helping her locate an apartment, helping her unpack books (she had a small mountain of books); he lent himself out as her escort at university functions for the first few weeks. Someone sent his wife an anonymous note that said, "Your husband is extremely attentive to a certain young lady professor," but Frank tore it up with such contempt and such finesse that his wife could not help but believe him, though she wept. Frank, in Molly Holt's company, was careful to be polite and witty and distant, never staring too boldly at her nor taking up her vivacious comments—she was always complimenting him on his clothes—as if he feared what might happen might happen too quickly. Molly herself dressed rather flamboyantly for a young lady with her rigorous academic background (before Chicago, she had gone to Bennington); she was always hurrying through the department's corridors in miniskirts and serapes and boots and then, as the fashions gradually changed, in pants and a blouse that clung tightly to her firm, intense little body. At department meetings she was a little arch; she sometimes interrupted people, even the head of the department, a small white-haired man named Barth. "We must all learn to be more *contemporary*," she urged.

Frank had lunch with her every day, hung around her office, drove her to her apartment in bad weather, talked her into joining him and his students at The Cave. But she was always anxious to get home, to relieve her baby sitter and to work on her classroom preparations; she was so serious! At times Frank's patient grin began to ache, waiting for her to get through with all this seriousness and talk of literature and "relevance." They sat crowded together in pub booths, arguing and complimenting each other; from time to time a sharp, almost searing glance flashed between them and Frank would feel a little dizzy with certainty. . . . But always she had to get home, always she was gathering up her big leather purse and striding away, and he would be left with his gaggle of students.

At home, he sat in his study, in his big black-leather chair, and thought about Molly. His wife's comfortable, bovine presence annoyed him; even his boys distracted him from his dreams of Molly. Sometimes he went out late at night, saying he needed cigarettes (he had begun smoking again, after meeting Molly, breaking his five-year period of abstinence); he telephoned Molly to ask how she was. She always said, "Very busy! My head is whirling, I have so much to do! But I love it." Frank could not decide if she were being deliberately coy. She really confused him. So he would ask if she needed any help, if she needed a mature, male viewpoint . . . he would be glad to drop in. . . .

But she always said, "No, thanks! It's very thoughtful of you, though."

As the winter deepened and the Ontario sky became perpetually smudged, pressing low upon the spirit, even Molly began to slow down. Frank noticed that her stride was not quite so energetic, and one of his colleagues commented zestfully: "It looks like Molly is coming in for a landing, like the rest of us." Frank took her out for coffee and asked her if anything was wrong. She wore an outfit that seemed to be made of green burlap, hanging dramatically about her and highlighting her small, serious face.

"Well, I've been working very hard this semester," she said slowly. "I have so many student compositions to correct. I'm way behind on my dissertation."

"Anything else?"

Molly hesitated. "Well, I'm having trouble with my ex-husband. He's trying to get out of the child-support payments. He is such a bastard, you wouldn't know. Or, yes, maybe you would know," she said, raising her eyes dramatically to Frank.

They were sitting in a small, grimy coffee shop; Frank dared public attention and patted her hand. It was a very small, delicate, pale hand, and the sight of his own dark hand on it pleased him, excited him. *Unmistakable!*

"Maybe I would know, yes," he said, wondering what he meant by this.

"You and I understand each other. We have so much in common, so much . . ." Molly said, her large brown eyes filling with tears. "Oh, sometimes I could scream, this whole university is filled with fossils who don't *understand,* they just don't *understand.*"

And then, as if she'd confessed too much, she hurried away to a class. Frank was left sitting there, stunned, wondering if he were falling in love.

Obviously, he had never been in love before.

She avoided him for several days after this; he asked her to lunch and their conversation was interrupted by the intrusion of the department's would-be poet, Ron Blazack; Frank called her one evening when his wife was at a meeting of the Faculty Wives' Association, told her he had something to say to her and talked her into letting him come over.

"All right," she said reluctantly, "but give me time to put Jimmy to bed . . . he hasn't been feeling well."

When he got there, he was a little disappointed at the way her apartment was furnished. "I'm trying to live within my means," she said dryly. She offered him a drink, though, and Frank smiled happily. He believed he could feel how dazzling his smile was.

"Let's talk," he said. "Are you happy here?"

"Yes. No. Not really," she said.

Such a pretty young woman, in spite of the circles of fatigue under her eyes! She wore black net stockings with a diamond design that made Frank lose track of the conversation now and then. She was complaining about her ex-husband and then about the heavy teaching load. "But, Frank, this job means more to me than anything right now. Thank God you people hired me! So many universities turned me down . . . I was getting desperate. My son has this allergy problem I told you about, and I don't have medical coverage for him, and I was really getting panicked. I think that some English departments wouldn't hire me because of my appearance, maybe, or my views on things," she said, looking Frank in the eye, as if he might not believe so bizarre a statement. Frank nodded slowly. "And of course there's the male chauvinism to fight. God, what a fight it's going to be! Centuries of discrimination and prejudice. Men have got to be re-educated if it destroys them."

She stared down at her polished nails and her several big, metallic rings. Frank wondered why she had referred to men as "them" in his presence, as if she weren't talking to a man. This was strange.

"Have men exploited you very much?" Frank asked.

"God, yes."

He got up and went to sit beside her. She laughed bitterly.

"Why don't you tell me about it?" he said in a gentle voice.

"Thank you, but I'm not a self-pitying woman. Thank you anyway," she said, drawing back from him. "But you know what it's like."

"What it's like?"

"To be discriminated against."

Frank stared at her.

"What's wrong?" she said.

Frank began to stammer. "Just what—what did you mean by that statement? Would you kindly explain that statement?"

"What statement?"

"That I—I'm supposed to know—supposed to know what it's like to be discriminated against—"

"Well, don't you?" Molly asked. "Being a black, you've been treated like dirt by the white male establishment—haven't you? Haven't they victimized you? Blacks and women are both—"

Frank could not believe his ears. He grabbed her arm.

"Well, we didn't get together tonight to talk about that kind of stuff," he said hotly; and as she tugged away from him, he felt his accent slipping, growing richer, thicker. "There's anything I hate, it's a woman who talks too much—"

"What? You're crazy!"

"*You're* crazy!" Frank yelled. A flame seemed to burn in his brain, he was so angry. "Look, you been givin' me the eye now for four months an' I been tailin' around after you as if I got nothin' better to do, when Jesus Christ, there are little girls waitin' in line—*I mean waitin' in line,* sister—so don't hand me none of this crap—"

Molly jumped to her feet. She yanked his pale-yellow ascot out of his shirt and up onto his face, so that he was blinded for a second.

"Get the hell out of here! Go home to your honkie wife!" she cried.

He went home, furious. He was never to speak to her again.

For weeks he went around muttering to himself, avoiding Molly in the hall, avoiding even his students. When a red-haired freshman dropped in to chat with him about the "erotic symbolism of T. S. Eliot," he did not trust his assessment of her sweet little smiles. No, he couldn't trust his judgment. Was the girl really smiling so deeply at him? Or was he being fooled again?

One day Frank put on his neatest, grayest suit, asked the head of the department, Dr. Barth, to call an emergency meeting of the appointments and promotions committee, and explained in a terse, quiet voice that his "special relationship" with the student body allowed him to know things that the rest of the department did not know.

When the meeting was convened, Frank spoke first. "The students have no respect for Miss Holt," he said sadly. "They laugh at her—evidently, she mispronounces words. She doesn't prepare her lectures. I've overheard her talking with students in the coffee shop and she actually gives them misinformation—it's just pathetic, unbelievable. I've put off telling you this, because the situation is so ugly. But it was on my strong recommendation that she was hired last year and it's my responsibility now to tell you what is going on."

"No complaints about her have come to me," Dr. Barth said slowly.

"The students are reluctant to talk to you, Dr. Barth," Frank said, "because you're—well, you're so obviously above their trivial problems, so they think. They come to me because there's—well, I suppose less of an age difference."

Dr. Barth nodded gravely. "Yes, I know I'm out of touch with this generation. I know. But about Miss Holt: There may be trouble dismissing her. She's going to be awarded a Ph.D. from Chicago, after all."

"No, she hasn't been working on her dissertation all year," Frank said. "I don't know what she's been doing. Actually, I wonder about her professional commitment."

The other members of the committee murmured agreement.

Frank went on solemnly. "It comes down to the preservation of our professional standards. We cannot afford," he said, looking from face to face, "in this time of disintegrating values, to have so casual and uncommitted a teacher in our department. Miss Holt is just not respected by her students. Evidently, she refers to the rest of us, in her classes, as *fossils*."

"Fossils?"

"I told you it was an ugly situation," Frank said softly.

Dr. Barth called a special meeting of the entire department for Monday morning. Molly came in late and Frank did no more than glance at her, nervously. She pulled out a chair at the far end of the big oval table everyone was seated around and the giddiness of her outfit—really, she had gone too far, wearing a loose-knit black tunic over violet-jersey pants to school!—seemed to show everyone how hopeless she was. Dr. Barth began the meeting in his usual grim, paternal voice, his hands clasped in front of him. He spoke of unpleasant reports, of an unfortunate situation, of the rigorous standards of this particular department, etc., etc. He was the only one who was looking at Molly, who in her turn was glancing around, curiously. Frank stared at his own manicured fingernails. His heart raced. Why, the old man sounded so sorry for her, was he going to change his mind? Maybe just reprimand her?

Dr. Barth said, "Because of special circumstances, the committee on appointments and promotions has been forced to suggest that the contract of Miss Holt not be renewed for next year. This decision was reached after many hours of anguish, after many, many hours of discussion. There are budget problems, also, which might involve our slightly reducing the salaries of other department members, unless the lectureship held by Miss Holt is terminated. But this should in no way, of course, influence your vote on the matter. Under the terms of our bylaws, I have therefore called this meeting of the department to request that you support the committee's recommendation and terminate Miss Holt's contract."

Molly was gaping at him.

"What?" she said faintly.

No one dared look at her. Many of the department members had been told by Dr. Barth of the reason for the meeting; the others stared at one another in disbelief.

Molly, sitting so pertly at the far end of the table, seemed suddenly to shrink.

"But why? What are the reasons? Can't I defend myself?"

"Under the terms of our university bylaws," Dr. Barth said gently, "no reasons for nonrenewal of contract need be stated. Only in the case of nonrenewal of a tenured faculty member need reasons be given."

"But I . . . I don't understand. . . ."

Frank glanced down at her. That small, pale face! That white bitch!

"If you would like to say anything, I'm sure we would all listen with sympathy," Dr. Barth said.

"I . . . I. . . ."

She fell silent.

After a minute or so, Dr. Barth said, "Then we really should get on with the vote. Some of us have eleven-o'clock classes we must teach."

Stiff white slips of paper were passed around for the vote.

Frank scribbled "Dismissal" on his ballot at once, folded it neatly in two and then in two again.

Next to him sat old Miss Snyder, a back number from the university's really mediocre years; with her billowing gray dresses and her stern, medieval nose, she had always disliked Molly Holt. No problem there. On Frank's left was the poet, Blazack, who kept shifting miserably in his seat. Around the large, highly polished table everyone sat in silence, staring down at their ballots. They seemed reluctant to vote. The only people who sat with their heads up were Frank and Dr. Barth and Molly, whose ballot lay before her, untouched.

"Really, we must hurry. It's a quarter to eleven," Dr. Barth said.

The ballots were collected by the departmental secretary and counted out. Frank could overhear the count: *For* dismissal. *Against* dismissal. He began to sweat, wondering if he might lose. What if . . . ? What if . . . ? What if that bitch had managed to win her way into the hearts of the other professors? What if she'd told them the same hard-luck story she had told him? What if they refused to believe him? His nostrils flared. In that case, he would quit. Would quit. Would quit with dignity. Yes, he would quit. He would not remain in this department if his professional integrity were doubted.

Dr. Barth announced the results: "The vote is sixteen to five for non-renewal of Miss Holt's contract."

Molly pushed her chair back clumsily and got to her feet. "But I . . . I still don't understand. . . ."

"I will be happy to talk with you and to make suggestions about where you might apply for a new position," Dr. Barth said at once. "In fact, we would all be happy to help you."

Molly snatched up her big leather purse and hurried out of the room.

Relief.

Frank lingered with some of the others, shaking his head gravely as they shook theirs. He had to admit he'd been taken in by her . . . he had to admit he'd made a mistake. . . . The whole ugly mess was his fault, he said.

"No, don't blame yourself, Frank," everyone said.

Dr. Barth patted his arm. "Frank, we belong to a profession with extremely rigorous standards. Personal feelings shouldn't enter into it at all. I'm sure Miss Holt will be happier in another university, with less demanding criteria of excellence."

But Frank found it difficult to be comforted. He felt really down. Instead of going out to The Cave with his students that afternoon, he went right home. His wife was frightened by his dour, peevish frown.

"You're not sick, Frank?"

No, not sick. He put on his smoking jacket and went to sit in his leather chair; he wanted to be alone. His wife opened his study door to ask, meekly, if he wanted dinner delayed. "Yes. Maybe an hour," he said. She then asked if the twins could come play with him for a few minutes—they'd been waiting for him to come home all day.

Frank considered this.

His eyes traveled up from his excellent shoes to his slim, checked trousers, to the casual richness of his navy-blue smoking jacket. He had knotted a white ascot quickly around his neck. He sensed his totality, his completion—a man who did not need anyone else, certainly not a woman. But he had lived through a certain emotional experience—there was no doubt in his mind that it had been an experience—and though he had triumphed, still he felt a little melancholy. It was a delicate, sensitive melancholy and the twins were so healthy and noisy that they might destroy it.

Finally, he said, "No, not right now. I want to be alone. I feel a little melancholy and I want to be alone."

# Parable and Allegory

## THE MINISTER'S BLACK VEIL

**Nathaniel Hawthorne**

*Born in Salem, Massachusetts, in 1804, Hawthorne was educated at Bowdoin College, where he became friends with Henry Wadsworth Longfellow and a future President of the United States, Franklin Pierce. After graduating from Bowdoin in 1825, Hawthorne spent the following twelve years in relative seclusion, a period usually regarded as his literary apprenticeship. His first novel,* Fanshawe *(1828), was a failure, and his first collection of short stories,* Twice-Told Tales *(1837), did not meet with much success. Only a few critics, Edgar Allan Poe among them, recognized the virtues that were to bring Hawthorne his eventual fame and reputation. After his marriage to Sophia Peabody in 1842, Hawthorne and his wife first settled in Concord and then in Salem, where he served as surveyor in the Custom House from 1846 to 1849. Although he lost this post in the next election, his literary fame and financial security were assured with the publication of* The Scarlet Letter *in 1850. Hawthorne later served for a time as consul at Liverpool (1850–1853), an appointment he owed to President Pierce; he died on May 18, 1864, at Plymouth, New Hampshire, while on a walking tour. His major works, besides those already mentioned, include the novels*

The House of Seven Gables (1851), The Blithedale Romance (1852), and The Marble Faun (1860); and two short story collections, Mosses from an Old Manse (1846) and The Snow-Image (1851). In reviewing Twice-Told Tales, in which "The Minister's Black Veil" appeared, Edgar Allan Poe, one of the pioneers in the short story, expressed pride as an American in the book: "We have very few American tales of real merit," he wrote. Commenting on those specific virtues of Hawthorne's writing that he felt noteworthy, virtues found in all Hawthorne's fiction—novels as well as the stories—Poe went on: "Mr. Hawthorne's distinctive trait is invention, creation, imagination, originality, a trait which, in the literature of fiction, is positively worth all the rest."

## A Parable

Another clergyman in New England, Mr. Joseph Moody, of York, Maine, who died about eighty years since, made himself remarkable by the same eccentricity that is here related of the Reverend Mr. Hooper. In his case, however, the symbol had a different import. In early life he had accidentally killed a beloved friend; and from that day till the hour of his own death, he hid his face from men.

The sexton stood in the porch of Milford meeting-house, pulling busily at the bell-rope. The old people of the village came stooping along the street. Children, with bright faces, tripped merrily beside their parents, or mimicked a graver gait, in the conscious dignity of their Sunday clothes. Spruce bachelors looked sidelong at the pretty maidens, and fancied that the Sabbath sunshine made them prettier than on week days. When the throng had mostly streamed into the porch, the sexton began to toll the bell, keeping his eye on the Reverend Mr. Hooper's door. The first glimpse of the clergyman's figure was the signal for the bell to cease its summons.

"But what has good Parson Hooper got upon his face?" cried the sexton in astonishment.

All within hearing immediately turned about, and beheld the semblance of Mr. Hooper, pacing slowly his meditative way towards the meeting-house. With one accord they started, expressing more wonder than if some strange minister were coming to dust the cushions of Mr. Hooper's pulpit.

"Are you sure it is our parson?" inquired Goodman Gray of the sexton.

"Of a certainty it is good Mr. Hooper," replied the sexton. "He was to have exchanged pulpits with Parson Shute, of Westbury; but Parson Shute sent to excuse himself yesterday, being to preach a funeral sermon."

The cause of so much amazement may appear sufficiently slight. Mr. Hooper, a gentlemanly person, of about thirty, though still a bachelor, was dressed with due clerical neatness, as if a careful wife had starched his band, and brushed the weekly dust from his Sunday's garb. There was but one thing remarkable in his appearance. Swathed about his forehead, and hanging down over his face, so low as to be shaken by his breath, Mr. Hooper had on a black veil. On a nearer view it seemed to consist of two folds of crape, which entirely concealed his features, except the mouth and chin, but probably did not intercept his sight, further than to give a darkened aspect to all living and inanimate things. With this gloomy shade before him, good Mr. Hooper walked onward, at a slow and quiet pace, stooping somewhat, and looking on the ground, as is customary with abstracted men, yet nodding kindly to those of his parishioners who still waited on the meeting-house steps. But so wonder-struck were they that his greeting hardly met with a return.

"I can't really feel as if good Mr. Hooper's face was behind that piece of crape," said the sexton.

"I don't like it," muttered an old woman, as she hobbled into the meeting-house. "He has changed himself into something awful, only by hiding his face."

"Our parson has gone mad!" cried Goodman Gray, following him across the threshold.

A rumor of some unaccountable phenomenon had preceded Mr. Hooper into the meeting-house, and set all the congregation astir. Few could refrain from twisting their heads towards the door; many stood upright, and turned directly about; while several little boys clambered upon the seats, and came down again with a terrible racket. There was a general bustle, a rustling of the women's gowns and shuffling of the men's feet, greatly at variance with that hushed repose which should attend the entrance of the minister. But Mr. Hooper appeared not to notice the perturbation of his people. He entered with an almost noiseless step, bent his head mildly to the pews on each side, and bowed as he passed his oldest parishioner, a white-haired great-grandsire, who occupied an armchair in the centre of the aisle. It was strange to observe how slowly this venerable man became conscious of something singular in the appearance of his pastor. He seemed not fully to partake of the prevailing wonder, till Mr. Hooper had ascended the stairs, and showed himself in the pulpit, face to face with his congregation, except for the black veil. That mysterious emblem was never once withdrawn. It shook with his measured breath, as he gave out the psalm; it threw its obscurity between him and the holy page, as he read the Scriptures; and while he prayed, the veil lay heavily on his uplifted countenance. Did he seek to hide it from the dread Being whom he was addressing?

Such was the effect of this simple piece of crape, that more than one woman of delicate nerves was forced to leave the meeting-house. Yet perhaps the pale-faced congregation was almost as fearful a sight to the minister, as his black veil to them.

Mr. Hooper had the reputation of a good preacher, but not an energetic one: he strove to win his people heavenward by mild, persuasive influences, rather than to drive them thither by the thunders of the Word.

The sermon which he now delivered was marked by the same characteristics of style and manner as the general series of his pulpit oratory. But there was something, either in the sentiment of the discourse itself, or in the imagination of the auditors, which made it greatly the most powerful effort that they had ever heard from their pastor's lips. It was tinged, rather more darkly than usual, with the gentle gloom of Mr. Hooper's temperament. The subject had reference to secret sin, and those sad mysteries which we hide from our nearest and dearest, and would fain conceal from our own consciousness, even forgetting that the Omniscient can detect them. A subtle power was breathed into his words. Each member of the congregation, the most innocent girl, and the man of hardened breast, felt as if the preacher had crept upon them, behind his awful veil, and discovered their hoarded iniquity of deed or thought. Many spread their clasped hands on their bosoms. There was nothing terrible in what Mr. Hooper said, at least, no violence; and yet, with every tremor of his melancholy voice, the hearers quaked. An unsought pathos came hand in hand with awe. So sensible were the audience of some unwonted attribute in their minister that they longed for a breath of wind to blow aside the veil, almost believing that a stranger's visage would be discovered, though the form, gesture, and voice were those of Mr. Hooper.

At the close of the services, the people hurried out with indecorous confusion, eager to communicate their pent-up amazement, and conscious of lighter spirits the moment they lost sight of the black veil. Some gathered in little circles, huddled closely together, with their mouths all whispering in the centre; some went homeward alone, wrapt in silent meditation; some talked loudly, and profaned the Sabbath day with ostentatious laughter. A few shook their sagacious heads, intimating that they could penetrate the mystery; while one or two affirmed that there was no mystery at all, but only that Mr. Hooper's eyes were so weakened by the midnight lamp, as to require a shade. After a brief interval, forth came good Mr. Hooper also, in the rear of his flock. Turning his veiled face from one group to another, he paid due reverence to the hoary heads, saluted the middle aged with kind dignity as their friend and spiritual guide, greeted the young with mingled authority and love, and laid his hands on the little children's heads to bless them. Such was always his custom on the Sabbath day. Strange and bewildered looks repaid him for his courtesy. None, as on former occasions, aspired to the honor of walking by their pastor's side. Old Squire Saunders, doubtless by an accidental lapse of memory, neglected to invite Mr. Hooper to his table, where the good clergyman had been wont to bless the food almost every Sunday since his settlement. He returned, therefore, to the parsonage, and, at the moment of closing the door, was observed to look back upon the people, all of whom had their eyes fixed upon the minister. A sad smile gleamed faintly from beneath the black veil, and flickered about his mouth, glimmering as he disappeared.

"How strange," said a lady, "that a simple black veil, such as any woman might wear on her bonnet, should become such a terrible thing on Mr. Hooper's face!"

"Something must surely be amiss with Mr. Hooper's intellects," observed her husband, the physician of the village. "But the strangest part of the affair is the effect of this vagary, even on a sober-minded man like myself. The black veil, though it covers only our pastor's face, throws its influence over his whole person, and makes him ghostlike from head to foot. Do you not feel it so?"

"Truly do I," replied the lady; "and I would not be alone with him for the world. I wonder he is not afraid to be alone with himself!"

"Men sometimes are so," said her husband.

The afternoon service was attended with similar circumstances. At its conclusion, the bell tolled for the funeral of a young lady. The relatives and friends were assembled in the house, and the more distant acquaintances stood about the door, speaking of the good qualities of the deceased, when their talk was interrupted by the appearance of Mr. Hooper, still covered with his black veil. It was now an appropriate emblem. The clergyman stepped into the room where the corpse was laid, and bent over the coffin, to take a last farewell of his deceased parishioner. As he stooped, the veil hung straight down from his forehead, so that, if her eyelids had not been closed forever, the dead maiden might have seen his face. Could Mr. Hooper be fearful of her glance, that he so hastily caught back the black veil? A person who watched the interview between the dead and living scrupled not to affirm, that, at the instant when the clergyman's features were disclosed, the corpse had slightly shuddered, rustling the shroud and muslin cap, though the countenance retained the composure of death. A superstitious old woman was the only witness of this prodigy. From the coffin Mr. Hooper passed into the chamber of the mourners, and thence to the head of the staircase, to make the funeral prayer. It was a tender and heart-dissolving prayer, full of sorrow, yet so imbued with celestial hopes, that the music of a heavenly harp, swept by the fingers of the dead, seemed faintly to be heard among the saddest accents of the minister. The people trembled, though they but darkly understood him when he prayed that they, and himself, and all of mortal race, might be ready, as he trusted this young maiden had been, for the dreadful hour that should snatch the veil from their faces. The bearers went heavily forth, and the mourners followed, saddening all the street, with the dead before them, and Mr. Hooper in his black veil behind.

"Why do you look back?" said one in the procession to his partner.

"I had a fancy," replied she, "that the minister and the maiden's spirit were walking hand in hand."

"And so had I, at the same moment," said the other.

That night, the handsomest couple in Milford village were to be joined in wedlock. Though reckoned a melancholy man, Mr. Hooper had a placid cheerfulness for such occasions, which often excited a sympathetic smile where livelier merriment would have been thrown away. There was no quality of his disposition which made him more beloved than this. The company at the wedding awaited his arrival with impatience, trusting that the strange awe, which had gathered over him throughout the day, would now be dispelled. But such was not the result. When Mr. Hooper came, the first thing that their eyes rested on was the same horrible black veil, which had added deeper gloom to the funeral, and could portend nothing but evil to the wedding. Such was its immediate effect on the guests that a cloud seemed to have rolled duskily from beneath the black crape, and dimmed the light of the candles. The bridal pair stood up before the minister. But the bride's cold fingers quivered in the tremulous hand of the bridegroom, and her deathlike paleness caused a whisper that the maiden who had been buried a few hours before was come from her grave to be married. If ever another wedding were so dismal, it was that famous one where they tolled the wedding knell. After performing the ceremony, Mr. Hooper raised a glass of wine to his lips, wishing happiness to the new-married couple in a strain of mild pleasantry that ought to have brightened the features of the guests, like a cheerful gleam from the hearth. At that instant, catching a glimpse of his figure in the looking-glass, the black veil involved his own spirit in the horror with which it overwhelmed all others. His frame shuddered, his lips grew white, he spilt the untasted wine upon the carpet, and rushed forth into the darkness. For the Earth, too, had on her Black Veil.

The next day, the whole village of Milford talked of little else than Parson Hooper's black veil. That, and the mystery concealed behind it, supplied a topic for discussion between acquaintances meeting in the street, and good women gossiping at their open windows. It was the first item of news that the tavern-keeper told to his guests. The children babbled of it on their way to school. One imitative little imp covered his face with an old black handkerchief, thereby so affrighting his playmates that panic seized himself, and he well-nigh lost his wits by his own waggery.

It was remarkable that of all the busybodies and impertinent people in the parish, not one ventured to put the plain question to Mr. Hooper, wherefore he did this thing. Hitherto, whenever there appeared the slightest call for such interference, he had never lacked advisers, nor shown himself averse to be guided by their judgment. If he erred at all, it was by so painful a degree of self-distrust, that even the mildest censure would lead him to consider an indifferent action as a crime. Yet, though so well acquainted with this amiable weakness, no individual among his parishioners chose to make the black veil a subject of friendly remonstrance. There was a feeling of dread, neither plainly confessed nor carefully concealed, which caused each to shift the responsibility upon another, till at length it was found expedient to send a deputation of the church, in order to deal with Mr. Hooper about the mystery before it should grow into a scandal. Never did an embassy so ill discharge its duties. The minister received them with friendly courtesy, but became silent, after they were seated, leaving to his visitors the whole burden of introducing their important business. The topic, it might be supposed, was obvious enough. There was the black veil swathed round Mr. Hooper's forehead, and concealing every feature above his placid mouth, on which, at times, they could perceive the glimmering of a melancholy smile. But that piece of crape, to their imagination, seemed to hang down before his heart, the symbol of a fearful secret between him and them. Were the veil but cast aside, they might speak freely of it, but not till then. Thus they sat a considerable time, speechless, confused, and shrinking uneasily from Mr. Hooper's eye, which they felt to be fixed upon them with an invisible glance. Finally, the deputies returned abashed to their constituents, pronouncing the matter too weighty to be handled, except by a council of the churches, if, indeed, it might not require a general synod.

But there was one person in the village unappalled by the awe with which the black veil had impressed all beside herself. When the deputies returned without an explanation, or even venturing to demand one, she, with the calm energy of her character, determined to chase away the strange cloud that appeared to be settling round Mr. Hooper, every moment more darkly than before. As his plighted wife, it should be her privilege to know what the black veil concealed. At the minister's first visit, therefore, she entered upon the subject with a direct simplicity, which made the task easier both for him and her. After he had seated himself, she fixed her eyes steadfastly upon the veil, but could discern nothing of the dreadful gloom that had so overawed the multitude: it was but a double fold of crape, hanging down from his forehead to his mouth, and slightly stirring with his breath.

"No," said she aloud, and smiling, "there is nothing terrible in this piece of crape, except that it hides a face which I am always glad to look upon. Come, good sir, let the sun shine from behind the cloud. First lay aside your black veil: then tell me why you put it on."

Mr. Hooper's smile glimmered faintly.

"There is an hour to come," said he, "when all of us shall cast aside our veils. Take it not amiss, beloved friend, if I wear this piece of crape till then."

"Your words are a mystery, too," returned the young lady. "Take away the veil from them, at least."

"Elizabeth, I will," said he, "so far as my vow may suffer me. Know, then, this veil is a type and a symbol, and I am bound to wear it ever, both in light and darkness, in solitude and before the gaze of multitudes, and as with strangers, so with my familiar friends. No mortal eye will see it withdrawn. This dismal shade must separate me from the world: even you, Elizabeth, can never come behind it!"

"What grievous affliction hath befallen you," she earnestly inquired, "that you should thus darken your eyes forever?"

"If it be a sign of mourning," replied Mr. Hooper, "I, perhaps, like most other mortals, have sorrows dark enough to be typified by a black veil."

"But what if the world will not believe that it is the type of an innocent sorrow?" urged Elizabeth. "Beloved and respected as you are, there may be whispers that you hide your face under the consciousness of secret sin. For the sake of your holy office, do away this scandal!"

The color rose into her cheeks as she intimated the nature of the rumors that were already abroad in the village. But Mr. Hooper's mildness did not forsake him. He even smiled again—that same sad smile, which always appeared like a faint glimmering of light, proceeding from the obscurity beneath the veil.

"If I hide my face for sorrow, there is cause enough," he merely replied; "and if I cover it for secret sin, what mortal might not do the same?"

And with this gentle, but unconquerable obstinacy did he resist all her entreaties. At length Elizabeth sat silent. For a few moments she appeared lost in thought, considering, probably, what new methods might be tried to withdraw her lover from so dark a fantasy, which, if it had no other meaning, was perhaps a symptom of mental disease. Though of a firmer character than his own, the tears rolled down her cheeks. But, in an instant, as it were, a new feeling took the place of sorrow: her eyes were fixed insensibly on the black veil, when, like a sudden twilight in the air, its terrors fell around her. She arose, and stood trembling before him.

"And do you feel it then, at last?" said he mournfully.

She made no reply, but covered her eyes with her hand, and turned to leave the room. He rushed forward and caught her arm.

"Have patience with me, Elizabeth!" cried he passionately. "Do not desert me, though this veil must be between us here on earth. Be mine, and hereafter there shall be no veil over my face, no darkness between our souls! It is but a mortal veil—it is not for eternity! O! you know not how lonely I am, and how frightened, to be alone behind my black veil. Do not leave me in this miserable obscurity forever!"

"Lift the veil but once, and look me in the face," said she.

"Never! It cannot be!" replied Mr. Hooper.

"Then farewell!" said Elizabeth.

She withdrew her arm from his grasp, and slowly departed, pausing at the door, to give one long, shuddering gaze, that seemed almost to penetrate the mystery of the black veil. But, even amid his grief, Mr. Hooper smiled to think that only a material emblem had separated him from happiness, though the horrors which it shadowed forth must be drawn darkly between the fondest of lovers.

From that time no attempts were made to remove Mr. Hooper's black veil, or, by a direct appeal, to discover the secret which it was supposed to hide. By persons who claimed a superiority to popular prejudice, it was reckoned merely an eccentric whim, such as often mingles with the sober actions of men otherwise rational, and tinges them all with its own semblance of insanity. But with the multitude, good Mr. Hooper was irreparably a bugbear. He could not walk the street with any peace of mind, so conscious was he that the gentle and timid would turn aside to avoid him, and that others would make it a point of hardihood to throw themselves in his way. The impertinence of the latter class compelled him to give up his customary walk at sunset to the burial ground; for when he leaned pensively over the gate, there would always be faces behind the gravestones, peeping at his black veil. A fable went the rounds that the stare of the dead people drove him thence. It grieved him, to the very depth of his kind heart, to observe how the children fled from his approach, breaking up their merriest sports, while his melancholy figure was yet afar off. Their instinctive dread caused him to feel more strongly than aught else, that a preternatural horror was interwoven with the threads of the black crape. In truth, his own antipathy to the veil was known to be so great, that he never willingly passed before a mirror, nor stooped to drink at a still fountain, lest, in its peaceful bosom, he should be affrighted by himself. This was what gave plausibility to the whispers, that Mr. Hooper's conscience tortured him for some great crime too horrible to be entirely concealed, or otherwise than so obscurely intimated. Thus, from beneath the black veil, there rolled a cloud into the sunshine, an ambiguity of sin or sorrow, which enveloped the poor minister, so that love or sympathy could never reach him. It was said that ghost and fiend consorted with him there. With self-shudderings and outward terrors, he walked continually in its shadow, groping darkly within his own soul, or gazing through a medium that saddened the whole world. Even the lawless wind, it was believed, respected his dreadful secret, and never blew aside the veil. But still good Mr. Hooper sadly smiled at the pale visages of the worldly throng as he passed by.

Among all its bad influences, the black veil had the one desirable effect of making its wearer a very efficient clergyman. By the aid of his mysterious emblem—for there was no other apparent cause—he became a man of awful power over souls that were in agony for sin. His converts always regarded him with a dread peculiar to themselves, affirming, though but figuratively, that, before he brought them to celestial light, they had been with him behind the black veil. Its gloom, indeed, enabled him to sympathize with all dark affections. Dying sinners cried aloud for Mr. Hooper, and would not yield their breath till he appeared; though ever, as he stooped to whisper consolation, they shuddered at the veiled face so near their own. Such were the terrors of the black veil, even when Death had bared his visage! Strangers came long distances to attend service at his church, with the mere idle purpose of gazing at his figure, because it was forbidden them to behold his face. But many were made to quake ere they departed! Once, during Governor Belcher's administration, Mr. Hooper was appointed to preach the election sermon. Covered with his black veil, he stood before the chief magistrate, the council, and the representatives, and wrought so deep an impression, that the legislative measures of that year were characterized by all the gloom and piety of our earliest ancestral sway.

In this manner Mr. Hooper spent a long life, irreproachable in outward act, yet shrouded in dismal suspicions; kind and loving, though unloved and dimly feared; a man apart from men, shunned in their health and joy, but ever summoned to their aid in mortal anguish. As years wore on, shedding their snows above his sable veil, he acquired a name throughout the New England churches, and they called him Father Hooper. Nearly all his parishioners who were of mature age when he was settled had been borne away by many a funeral: he had one congregation in the church, and a more crowded one in the churchyard; and having wrought so late into the evening, and done his work so well, it was now good Father Hooper's turn to rest.

Several persons were visible by the shaded candle-light, in the death chamber of the old clergyman. Natural connections he had none. But there was the decorously grave, though unmoved physician, seeking only to mitigate the last pangs of the patient whom he could not save. There were the deacons, and other eminently pious members of his church. There, also, was the Reverend Mr. Clark, of Westbury, a young and zealous divine, who had ridden in haste to pray by the bedside of the expiring minister. There was the nurse, no hired handmaiden of death, but one whose calm affection had endured thus long in secrecy, in solitude, amid the chill of age, and would not perish, even at the dying hour. Who, but Elizabeth! And there lay the hoary head of good Father Hooper upon the death pillow, with the black veil still swathed about his brow, and reaching down over his face, so that each more difficult gasp of his faint breath caused it to stir. All through life that piece of crape had hung between him and the world: it had separated him from cheerful brotherhood and woman's love, and kept him in that saddest of all prisons, his own heart: and still it lay upon his face, as if to deepen the gloom of his darksome chamber, and shade him from the sunshine of eternity.

For some time previous, his mind had been confused, wavering doubtfully between the past and the present, and hovering forward, as it were, at intervals, into the indistinctness of the world to come. There had been feverish turns, which tossed him from side to side, and wore away what little strength he had. But in his most convulsive struggles, and in the wildest vagaries of his intellect, when no other thought retained its sober influence, he still showed an awful solicitude lest the black veil should slip aside. Even if his bewildered soul could have forgotten, there was a faithful woman at his pillow, who, with averted eyes, would have covered that aged face, which she had last beheld in the comeliness of manhood. At length the death-stricken old man lay quietly in the torpor of mental and bodily exhaustion, with an imperceptible pulse, and breath that grew fainter and fainter, except when a long, deep, and irregular inspiration seemed to prelude the flight of his spirit.

The minister of Westbury approached the bedside.

"Venerable Father Hooper," said he, "the moment of your release is at hand. Are you ready for the lifting of the veil that shuts in time from eternity?"

Father Hooper at first replied merely by a feeble motion of his head: then, apprehensive, perhaps, that his meaning might be doubtful, he exerted himself to speak.

"Yea," said he, in faint accents, "my soul hath a patient weariness until that veil be lifted."

"And is it fitting," resumed the Reverend Mr. Clark, "that a man so given to prayer, of such a blameless example, holy in deed and thought, so far as mortal judgment may pronounce; is it fitting that a father in the church should leave a shadow on his memory, that may seem to blacken a life so pure? I pray you, my venerable brother, let not this thing be! Suffer us to be gladdened by your triumphant aspect as you go to your reward. Before the veil of eternity be lifted, let me cast aside the black veil from your face!"

And thus speaking, the Reverend Mr. Clark bent forward to reveal the mystery of so many years. But, exerting a sudden energy, that made all the beholders stand aghast, Father Hooper snatched both his hands from beneath the bedclothes, and pressed them strongly on the black veil, resolute to struggle, if the minister of Westbury would contend with a dying man.

"Never!" cried the veiled clergyman. "On earth, never!"

"Dark old man!" exclaimed the affrighted minister, "with what horrible crime upon your soul are you now passing to the judgment?"

Father Hooper's breath heaved; it rattled in his throat; but, with a mighty effort, grasping forward with his hands, he caught hold of life, and held it back till he should speak. He even raised himself in bed; and there he sat, shivering with the arms of death around him, while the black veil hung down, awful, at the last moment, in the gathered terrors of a lifetime. And yet the faint, sad smile, so often there, now seemed to glimmer from its obscurity, and linger on Father Hooper's lips.

"Why do you tremble at me alone?" cried he, turning his veiled face round the circle of pale spectators. "Tremble also at each other! Have men avoided me, and women shown no pity, and children screamed and fled, only for my black veil? What, but the mystery which it obscurely typifies, has made this piece of crape so awful? When the friend shows his inmost heart to his friend; the lover to his best beloved; when man does not vainly shrink from the eye of his Creator, loathsomely treasuring up the secret of his sin; then deem me a monster, for the symbol beneath which I have lived, and die! I look around me, and, lo! on every visage a Black Veil!"

While his auditors shrank from one another, in mutual affright, Father Hooper fell back upon his pillow, a veiled corpse, with a faint smile lingering on the lips. Still veiled, they laid him in his coffin, and a veiled corpse they bore him to the grave. The grass of many years has sprung up and withered on that grave, the burial stone is moss-grown, and good Mr. Hooper's face is dust; but awful is still the thought that it mouldered beneath the Black Veil.

---

# THE ROCKING-HORSE WINNER

## D. H. Lawrence

*A coal miner's son born in 1885 in the mining town of Eastwood, Nottinghamshire, D. H. Lawrence was a teacher in an elementary school for a time. After the publication of his first novel,* The White Peacock, *in 1911, Lawrence devoted the rest of his life to writing novels, essays, short stories, plays, and poetry. In 1914 Lawrence married Frieda von Richthofen, and because of her nationality he suffered in England during the war. Afterward he traveled to America, Australia, and Europe, spending some time in Italy because of his increasing ill health from tuberculosis. He died in France, near Nice, in 1930, one of the most respected writers of his generation. His works include* Sons and Lovers (1913), *an autobiographical novel;* Love Poems and Others (1913); The Prussian Officer and Other Stories (1914); The Rainbow (1915), *a novel;* Twilight in Italy (1916), *a travel book;* Amores (1916), *a book of poems;* New Poems (1918); Women in Love (1920), Aaron's Rod (1922), The Plumed Serpent (1926), Lady Chatterly's Lover (1928), *and* The Man Who Died (1931), *all novels. The furor over the publication of* Lady Chatterly's Lover, *condemned by many as an "obscene" book, obscured for some the solid reputation of Lawrence as stylist and craftsman, as a writer dedicated to what he regarded all his life as the high seriousness of his art. "The Rocking-Horse Winner" represents Lawrence at his best in terms of this craftsmanship and high seriousness; it is a convincing demonstration of Graham Hough's assertion that those who say "that Lawrence's best work is in his shorter pieces have much reason on their side." Hough explains: "Precisely because it is not in these shorter tales that the original exploration is done, they are often superior in artistic organisation to the long exploratory novels. . . . In sustained realisation, in formal completeness there is certainly nothing to better the best of his shorter tales."*

There was a woman who was beautiful, who started with all the advantages, yet she had no luck. She married for love, and the love turned to dust. She had bonny children, yet she felt they had been thrust upon her, and she could not love them. They looked at her coldly, as if they were finding fault with her. And hurriedly she felt she must cover up some fault in herself. Yet what it was that she must cover up she never knew. Nevertheless, when her children were present, she always felt the centre of her heart go hard. This troubled her, and in her manner she was all the more gentle and anxious for her children, as if she loved them very much. Only she herself knew that at the centre of her heart was a hard little place that could not feel love, no, not for anybody. Everybody else said of her: "She is such a good mother. She adores her children." Only she herself, and her children themselves, knew it was not so. They read it in each other's eyes.

There were a boy and two little girls. They lived in a pleasant house, with a garden, and they had discreet servants, and felt themselves superior to anyone in the neighbourhood.

Although they lived in style, they felt always an anxiety in the house. There was never enough money. The mother had a small income, and the father had a small income, but not nearly enough for the social position which they had to keep up. The father went in to town to some office. But though he had good prospects, these prospects never materialized. There was always the grinding sense of the shortage of money, though the style was always kept up.

At last the mother said: "I will see if *I* can't make something." But she did not know where to begin. She racked her brains, and tried this thing and the other, but could not find anything successful. The failure made deep lines come into her face. Her children were growing up, they would have to go to school. There must be more money, there must be more money. The father, who was always very handsome and expensive in his tastes, seemed as if he never *would* be able to do anything worth doing. And the mother, who had a great belief in herself, did not succeed any better, and her tastes were just as expensive.

And so the house came to be haunted by the unspoken phrase: *There must be more money! There must be more money!* The children could hear it all the time, though nobody said it aloud. They heard it at Christmas, when the expensive and splendid toys filled the nursery. Behind the shining modern rocking-horse, behind the smart doll's-house, a voice would start whispering: "There *must* be more money! There *must* be more money!" And the children would stop playing, to listen for a moment. They would look into each other's eyes, to see if they had all heard. And each one saw in the eyes of the other two that they too had heard. "There *must* be more money! There *must* be more money!"

It came whispering from the springs of the still-swaying rocking-horse, and even the horse, bending his wooden, champing head, heard it. The big doll, sitting so pink and smirking in her new pram, could hear it quite plainly, and seemed to be smirking all the more self-consciously because of it. The foolish puppy, too, that took the place of the teddy-bear, he was looking so extraordinarily foolish for no other reason but that he heard the secret whisper all over the house: "There *must* be more money!"

Yet nobody ever said it aloud. The whisper was everywhere, and therefore no one spoke it. Just as no one ever says: "We are breathing!" in spite of the fact that breath is coming and going all the time.

"Mother," said the boy Paul one day, "why don't we keep a car of our own? Why do we always use uncle's, or else a taxi?"

"Because we're the poor members of the family," said the mother.

"But why *are* we, mother?"

"Well—I suppose," she said slowly and bitterly, "it's because your father has no luck."

The boy was silent for some time.

"Is luck money, mother?" he asked rather timidly.

"No, Paul. Not quite. It's what causes you to have money."

"Oh!" said Paul vaguely. "I thought when Uncle Oscar said *filthy lucker*, it meant money."

"*Filthy* lucre does mean money," said the mother. "But it's lucre, not luck."

"Oh!" said the boy. "Then what *is* luck, mother?"

"It's what causes you to have money. If you're lucky you have money. That's why it's better to be born lucky than rich. If you're rich, you may lose your money. But if you're lucky, you will always get more money."

"Oh! Will you? And is father not lucky?"

"Very unlucky, I should say," she said bitterly.

The boy watched her with unsure eyes.

"Why?" he asked.

"I don't know. Nobody ever knows why one person is lucky and another unlucky."

"Don't they? Nobody at all? Does *nobody* know?"

"Perhaps God. But He never tells."

"He ought to, then. And aren't you lucky either, mother?"

"I can't be, if I married an unlucky husband."

"But by yourself, aren't you?"

"I used to think I was, before I married. Now I think I am very unlucky indeed."

"Why?"

"Well—never mind! Perhaps I'm not really," she said.

The child looked at her, to see if she meant it. But he saw, by the lines of her mouth, that she was only trying to hide something from him.

"Well, anyhow," he said stoutly, "I'm a lucky person."

"Why?" said his mother, with a sudden laugh.

He stared at her. He didn't even know why he had said it.

"God told me," he asserted, brazening it out.

"I hope He did, dear!" she said, again with a laugh, but rather bitter.

"He did, mother!"

"Excellent!" said the mother, using one of her husband's exclamations.

The boy saw she did not believe him; or rather, that she paid no attention to his assertion. This angered him somewhat, and made him want to compel her attention.

He went off by himself, vaguely, in a childish way, seeking for the clue to "luck." Absorbed, taking no heed of other people, he went about with a sort of stealth, seeking inwardly for luck. He wanted luck, he wanted it, he wanted it. When the two girls were playing dolls in the nursery, he would sit on his big rocking-horse, charging madly into space, with a frenzy that made the little girls peer at him uneasily. Wildly the horse careered, the waving dark hair of the boy tossed, his eyes had a strange glare in them. The little girls dared not speak to him.

When he had ridden to the end of his mad little journey, he climbed down and stood in front of his rocking-horse, staring fixedly into its lowered face. Its red mouth was slightly open, its big eye was wide and glassy-bright.

"Now!" he would silently command the snorting steed. "Now, take me to where there is luck! Now take me!"

And he would slash the horse on the neck with the little whip he had asked Uncle Oscar for. He *knew* the horse could take him to where there was luck, if only he forced it. So he would mount again, and start on his furious ride, hoping at last to get there. He knew he could get there.

"You'll break your horse, Paul!" said the nurse.

"He's always riding like that! I wish he'd leave off!" said his elder sister Joan.

But he only glared down on them in silence. Nurse gave him up. She could make nothing of him. Anyhow he was growing beyond her.

One day his mother and his Uncle Oscar came in when he was on one of his furious rides. He did not speak to them.

"Hallo, you young jockey! Riding a winner?" said his uncle.

"Aren't you growing too big for a rocking-horse? You're not a very little boy any longer, you know," said his mother.

But Paul only gave a blue glare from his big, rather close-set eyes. He would speak to nobody when he was in full tilt. His mother watched him with an anxious expression on her face.

At last he suddenly stopped forcing his horse into the mechanical gallop, and slid down.

"Well, I got there!" he announced fiercely, his blue eyes still flaring, and his sturdy long legs straddling apart.

"Where did you get to?" asked his mother.

"Where I wanted to go," he flared back at her.

"That's right, son!" said Uncle Oscar. "Don't you stop till you get there. What's the horse's name?"

"He doesn't have a name," said the boy.

"Gets on without all right?" asked the uncle.

"Well, he has different names. He was called Sansovino last week."

"Sansovino, eh? Won the Ascot. How did you know his name?"

"He always talks about horse-races with Bassett," said Joan.

The uncle was delighted to find that his small nephew was posted with all the racing news. Bassett, the young gardener, who had been wounded in the left foot in the war and had got his present job through Oscar Cresswell, whose batman he had been, was a perfect blade of the "turf." He lived in the racing events, and the small boy lived with him.

Oscar Cresswell got it all from Bassett.

"Master Paul comes and asks me, so I can't do more than tell him, sir," said Bassett, his face terribly serious, as if he were speaking of religious matters.

"And does he never put anything on a horse he fancies?"

"Well—I don't want to give him away—he's a young sport, a fine sport, sir. Would you mind asking him himself? He sort of takes a pleasure in it, and perhaps he'd feel I was giving him away, sir, if you don't mind."

Bassett was serious as a church.

The uncle went back to his nephew and took him off for a ride in the car.

"Say, Paul, old man, do you ever put anything on a horse?" the uncle asked.

The boy watched the handsome man closely.

"Why, do you think I oughtn't to?" he parried.

"Not a bit of it! I thought perhaps you might give me a tip for the Lincoln."

The car sped on into the country, going down to Uncle Oscar's place in Hampshire.

"Honour bright?" said the nephew.

"Honour bright, son!" said the uncle.

"Well, then, Daffodil."

"Daffodil! I doubt it, sonny. What about Mirza?"

"I only know the winner," said the boy. "That's Daffodil."

"Daffodil, eh?"

There was a pause. Daffodil was an obscure horse comparatively.

"Uncle!"

"Yes, son?"

"You won't let it go any further, will you? I promised Bassett."

"Bassett be damned, old man! What's he got to do with it?"

"We're partners. We've been partners from the first. Uncle, he lent me my first five shillings, which I lost. I promised him, honour bright, it was only between me and him; only you gave me that ten-shilling note I started winning with, so I thought you were lucky. You won't let it go any further, will you?"

The boy gazed at his uncle from those big, hot, blue eyes, set rather close together. The uncle stirred and laughed uneasily.

"Right you are, son! I'll keep your tip private. Daffodil, eh? How much are you putting on him?"

"All except twenty pounds," said the boy. "I keep that in reserve."

The uncle thought it a good joke.

"You keep twenty pounds in reserve, do you, you young romancer? What are you betting, then?"

"I'm betting three hundred," said the boy gravely. "But it's between you and me, Uncle Oscar! Honour bright?"

The uncle burst into a roar of laughter.

"It's between you and me all right, you young Nat Gould," he said, laughing. "But where's your three hundred?"

"Bassett keeps it for me. We're partners."

"You are, are you! And what is Bassett putting on Daffodil?"

"He won't go quite as high as I do, I expect. Perhaps he'll go a hundred and fifty."

"What, pennies?" laughed the uncle.

"Pounds," said the child, with a surprised look at his uncle. "Bassett keeps a bigger reserve than I do."

Between wonder and amusement Uncle Oscar was silent. He pursued the matter no further, but he determined to take his nephew with him to the Lincoln races.

"Now, son," he said, "I'm putting twenty on Mirza, and I'll put five for you on any horse you fancy. What's your pick?"

"Daffodil, uncle."

"No, not the fiver on Daffodil!"

"I should if it was my own fiver," said the child.

"Good! Good! Right you are! A fiver for me and a fiver for you on Daffodil."

The child had never been to a race-meeting before, and his eyes were blue fire. He pursed his mouth tight, and watched. A Frenchman just in front had put his money on Lancelot. Wild with excitement, he flayed his arms up and down, yelling *"Lancelot! Lancelot!"* in his French accent.

Daffodil came in first, Lancelot second, Mirza third. The child, flushed and with eyes blazing, was curiously serene. His uncle brought him four five-pound notes, four to one.

"What am I to do with these?" he cried, waving them before the boy's eyes.

"I suppose we'll talk to Bassett," said the boy. "I expect I have fifteen hundred now; and twenty in reserve; and this twenty."

His uncle studied him for some moments.

"Look here, son!" he said. "You're not serious about Bassett and that fifteen hundred, are you?"

"Yes, I am. But it's between you and me, uncle. Honour bright!"

"Honour bright all right, son! But I must talk to Bassett."

"If you'd like to be a partner, uncle, with Bassett and me, we could all be partners. Only, you'd have to promise, honour bright, uncle, not to let it go beyond us three. Bassett and I are lucky, and you must be lucky, because it was your ten shillings I started winning with. . . ."

Uncle Oscar took both Bassett and Paul into Richmond Park for an afternoon, and there they talked.

"It's like this, you see, sir," Bassett said. "Master Paul would get me talking about racing events, spinning yarns, you know, sir. And he was always keen on knowing if I'd made or if I'd lost. It's about a year since, now, that I put five shilling on Blush of Dawn for him—and we lost. Then the luck turned, with that ten shillings he had from you, that we put on Singhalese. And since that time, it's been pretty steady, all things considering. What do you say, Master Paul?"

"We're all right when we're sure," said Paul. "It's when we're not quite sure that we go down."

"Oh, but we're careful then," said Bassett.

"But when are you *sure?*" smiled Uncle Oscar.

"It's Master Paul, sir," said Bassett, in a secret, religious voice. "It's as if he had it from heaven. Like Daffodil, now, for the Lincoln. That was as sure as eggs."

"Did you put anything on Daffodil?" asked Oscar Cresswell.

"Yes, sir. I made my bit."

"And my nephew?"

Bassett was obstinately silent, looking at Paul.

"I made twelve hundred, didn't I, Bassett? I told uncle I was putting three hundred on Daffodil."

"That's right," said Bassett, nodding.

"But where's the money?" asked the uncle.

"I keep it safe locked up, sir. Master Paul he can have it any minute he likes to ask for it."

"What, fifteen hundred pounds?"

"And twenty! And *forty*, that is, with the twenty he made on the course."

"It's amazing!" said the uncle.

"If Master Paul offers you to be partners, sir, I would, if I were you; if you'll excuse me," said Bassett.

Oscar Cresswell thought about it.

"I'll see the money," he said.

They drove home again, and sure enough, Bassett came round to the garden-house with fifteen hundred pounds in notes. The twenty pounds reserve was left with Joe Glee, in the Turf Commission deposit.

"You see, it's all right, uncle, when I'm *sure!* Then we go strong, for all we're worth. Don't we, Bassett?"

"We do that, Master Paul."

"And when are you sure?" said the uncle, laughing.

"Oh, well, sometimes I'm *absolutely* sure, like about Daffodil," said the boy; "and sometimes I have an idea; and sometimes I haven't even an idea, have I, Bassett? Then we're careful, because we mostly go down."

"You do, do you! And when you're sure, like about Daffodil, what makes you sure, sonny?"

"Oh, well, I don't know," said the boy uneasily. "I'm sure, you know, uncle; that's all."

"It's as if he had it from heaven, sir," Bassett reiterated.

"I should say so!" said the uncle.

But he became a partner. And when the Leger was coming on, Paul was "sure" about Lively Spark, which was a quite inconsiderable horse. The boy insisted on putting a thousand on the horse, Bassett went for five hundred, and Oscar Cresswell two hundred. Lively Spark came in first, and the betting had been ten to one against him. Paul had made ten thousand.

"You see," he said, "I was absolutely sure of him."

Even Oscar Cresswell had cleared two thousand.

"Look here, son," he said, "this sort of thing makes me nervous."

"It needn't, uncle! Perhaps I shan't be sure again for a long time."

"But what are you going to do with your money?" asked the uncle.

"Of course," said the boy, "I started it for mother. She said she had no luck, because father is unlucky, so I thought if *I* was lucky, it might stop whispering."

"What might stop whispering?"

"Our house. I *hate* our house for whispering."

"What does it whisper?"

"Why—why"—the boy fidgeted—"why, I don't know. But it's always short of money, you know, uncle."

"I know it, son, I know it."

"You know people send mother writs, don't you uncle?"

"I'm afraid I do," said the uncle.

"And then the house whispers, like people laughing at you behind your back. It's awful, that is! I thought if I was lucky . . ."

"You might stop it," added the uncle.

The boy watched him with big blue eyes, that had an uncanny cold fire in them, and he said never a word.

"Well, then!" said the uncle. "What are we doing?"

"I shouldn't like mother to know I was lucky," said the boy.

"Why not, son?"

"She'd stop me."

"I don't think she would."

"Oh!"—and the boy writhed in an odd way—"I *don't* want her to know, uncle."

"All right, son! We'll manage it without her knowing."

They managed it very easily. Paul, at the other's suggestion, handed over five thousand pounds to his uncle, who deposited it with the family lawyer, who was then to inform Paul's mother that a relative had put five thousand pounds into his hands, which sum was to be paid out a thousand pounds at a time, on the mother's birthday, for the next five years.

"So she'll have a birthday present of a thousand pounds for five successive years," said Uncle Oscar. "I hope it won't make it all the harder for her later."

Paul's mother had her birthday in November. The house had been "whispering" worse than ever lately, and, even in spite of his luck, Paul could not bear up against it. He was very anxious to see the effect of the birthday letter, telling his mother about the thousand pounds.

When there were no visitors, Paul now took his meal with his parents, as he was beyond the nursery control. His mother went into town nearly every day. She had discovered that she had an odd knack of sketching furs and dress materials, so she worked secretly in the studio of a friend who was the chief "artist" for the leading drapers. She drew the figures of ladies in furs and ladies in silk and sequins for the newspaper advertisements. This young woman artist earned several thousand pounds a year, but Paul's mother only made several hundreds, and she was again dissatisfied. She so wanted to be first in something, and she did not succeed, even in making sketches for drapery advertisements.

She was down to breakfast on the morning of her birthday. Paul watched her face as she read her letters. He knew the lawyer's letter. As his mother read it, her face hardened and became more expressionless. Then a cold, determined look came on her mouth. She hid the letter under the pile of others, and said not a word about it.

"Didn't you have anything nice in the post for your birthday, mother?" said Paul.

"Quite moderately nice," she said, her voice cold and absent.

She went away to town without saying more.

But in the afternoon Uncle Oscar appeared. He said Paul's mother had had a long interview with the lawyer, asking if the whole five thousand could not be advanced at once, as she was in debt.

"What do you think, uncle?" said the boy.

"I leave it to you, son."

"Oh, let her have it, then! We can get some more with the other," said the boy.

"A bird in the hand is worth two in the bush, laddie!" said Uncle Oscar.

"But I'm sure to *know* for the Grand National; or the Lincolnshire; or else the Derby. I'm sure to know for *one* of them," said Paul.

So Uncle Oscar signed the agreement, and Paul's mother touched the whole five thousand. Then something very curious happened. The voices in the house suddenly went mad, like a chorus of frogs on a spring evening. There were certain new furnishings, and Paul had a tutor. He was *really* going to Eton, his father's school, in the following autumn. There were flowers in the winter, and a blossoming of the luxury Paul's mother had been used to. And yet the voices in the house, behind the sprays of mimosa and almond blossom, and from under the piles of iridescent cushions, simply trilled and screamed in a sort of ecstasy: "There *must* be more money! Oh-h-h; there *must* be more money. Oh, now, now-w! Now-w-w—there *must* be more money!—more than ever! More than ever!"

It frightened Paul terribly. He studied away at his Latin and Greek with his tutors. But his intense hours were spent with Bassett. The Grand National had gone by: he had not "known," and had lost a hundred pounds. Summer was at hand. He was in agony for the Lincoln. But even for the Lincoln he didn't "know," and he lost fifty pounds. He became wild-eyed and strange, as if something were going to explode in him.

"Let it alone, son! Don't you bother about it!" urged Uncle Oscar. But it was as if the boy couldn't really hear what his uncle was saying.

"I've got to know for the Derby! I've got to know for the Derby!" the child reiterated, his big blue eyes blazing with a sort of madness.

His mother noticed how overwrought he was.

"You'd better go to the seaside. Wouldn't you like to go now to the seaside, instead of waiting? I think you'd better," she said, looking down at him anxiously, her heart curiously heavy because of him.

But the child lifted his uncanny blue eyes.

"I couldn't possibly go before the Derby, mother!" he said. "I couldn't possibly!"

"Why not?" she said, her voice becoming heavy when she was opposed. "Why not? You can still go from the seaside to see the Derby with your Uncle Oscar, if that's what you wish. No need for you to wait here. Besides, I think you care too much about these races. It's a bad sign. My family has been a gambling family, and you won't know till you grow up how much damage it has done. But it has done damage. I shall have to send Bassett away, and ask Uncle Oscar not to talk racing to you, unless you promise to be reasonable about it; go away to the seaside and forget it. You're all nerves!"

"I'll do what you like, mother, so long as you don't send me away till after the Derby," the boy said.

"Send you away from where? Just from this house?"

"Yes," he said, gazing at her.

"Why, you curious child, what makes you care about this house so much, suddenly? I never knew you loved it."

He gazed at her without speaking. He had a secret within a secret, something he had not divulged, even to Bassett or to his Uncle Oscar.

But his mother, after standing undecided and a little bit sullen for some moments, said:

"Very well, then! Don't go to the seaside till after the Derby, if you don't wish it. But promise me you won't let your nerves go to pieces. Promise you won't think so much about horse-racing and *events,* as you call them!"

"Oh, no," said the boy casually. "I won't think much about them, mother. You needn't worry. I wouldn't worry, mother, if I were you."

"If you were me and I were you," said his mother, "I wonder what we *should* do!"

"But you know you needn't worry, mother, don't you?" the boy repeated.

"I should be awfully glad to know it," she said wearily.

"Oh, well, you *can,* you know. I mean you ought to know you needn't worry," he insisted.

"Ought I? Then I'll see about it," she said.

Paul's secret of secrets was his wooden horse, that which had no name. Since he was emancipated from a nurse and a nursery-governess, he had had his rocking-horse removed to his own bedroom at the top of the house.

"Surely, you're too big for a rocking-horse!" his mother had remonstrated.

"Well, you see, mother, till I can have a *real* horse, I like to have *some* sort of animal about," had been his quaint answer.

"Do you feel he keeps you company?" she laughed.

"Oh, yes! He's very good, he always keeps me company, when I'm there," said Paul.

So the horse, rather shabby, stood in an arrested prance in the boy's bedroom.

The Derby was drawing near, and the boy grew more and more tense. He hardly heard what was spoken to him, he was very frail, and his eyes were really uncanny. His mother had sudden strange seizures of uneasiness about him. Sometimes, for half-an-hour, she would feel a sudden anxiety about him that was almost anguish. She wanted to rush to him at once, and know he was safe.

Two nights before the Derby, she was at a big party in town, when one of her rushes of anxiety about her boy, her first-born, gripped her heart till she could hardly speak. She fought with the feeling, might and main, for she believed in common-sense. But it was too strong. She had to leave the dance and go downstairs to telephone to the country. The children's nursery-governess was terribly surprised and startled at being rung up in the night.

"Are the children all right, Miss Wilmot?"

"Oh, yes, they are quite all right."

"Master Paul? Is he all right?"

"He went to bed as right as a trivet. Shall I run up and look at him?"

"No," said Paul's mother reluctantly. "No! Don't trouble. It's all right.

Don't sit up. We shall be home fairly soon." She did not want her son's privacy intruded upon.

"Very good," said the governess.

It was about one o'clock when Paul's mother and father drove up to their house. All was still. Paul's mother went to her room and slipped off her white fur cloak. She had told her maid not wait up for her. She heard her husband downstairs, mixing a whisky-and-soda.

And then, because of the strange anxiety at her heart, she stole upstairs to her son's room. Noiselessly she went along the upper corridor. Was there a faint noise? What was it?

She stood, with arrested muscles, outside his door, listening. There was a strange, heavy, and yet not loud noise. Her heart stood still. It was a soundless noise, yet rushing and powerful. Something huge, in violent, hushed motion. What was it? What in God's name was it? She ought to know. She felt that she knew the noise. She knew what it was.

Yet she could not place it. She couldn't say what it was. And on and on it went, like a madness.

Softly, frozen with anxiety and fear, she turned the door-handle.

The room was dark. Yet in the space near the window, she heard and saw something plunging to and fro. She gazed in fear and amazement.

Then suddenly she switched on the light, and saw her son, in his green pyjamas, madly surging on the rocking-horse. The blaze of light suddenly lit him up, as he urged the wooden horse, and lit her up, as she stood, blonde, in her dress of pale green and crystal, in the doorway.

"Paul!" she cried. "Whatever are you doing?"

"It's Malabar!" he screamed, in a powerful, strange voice. "It's Malabar!"

His eyes blazed at her for one strange and senseless second, as he ceased urging his wooden horse. Then he fell with a crash to the ground, and she, all her tormented motherhood flooding upon her, rushed to gather him up.

But he was unconscious, and unconscious he remained, with some brain-fever. He talked and tossed, and his mother sat stonily by his side.

"Malabar! It's Malabar! Bassett, Bassett, I *know*! It's Malabar!"

So the child cried, trying to get up and urge the rocking-horse that gave him his inspiration.

"What does he mean by Malabar?" asked the heart-frozen mother.

"I don't know," said the father stonily.

"What does he mean by Malabar?" she asked her brother Oscar.

"It's one of the horses running for the Derby," was the answer.

And, in spite of himself, Oscar Cresswell spoke to Bassett, and himself put a thousand on Malabar: at fourteen to one.

The third day of the illness was critical: they were waiting for a change. The boy, with his rather long, curly hair, was tossing ceaselessly on the pillow. He neither slept nor regained consciousness, and his eyes were like blue stones. His mother sat, feeling her heart had gone, turned actually into a stone.

In the evening, Oscar Cresswell did not come, but Bassett sent a message, saying could he come up for one moment, just one moment? Paul's mother was very angry at the intrusion, but on second thought she agreed. The boy was the same. Perhaps Bassett might bring him to consciousness.

The gardener, a shortish fellow with a little brown moustache, and sharp little brown eyes, tip-toed into the room, touched his imaginary cap to Paul's mother, and stole to the bedside, staring with glittering, smallish eyes, at the tossing, dying child.

"Master Paul!" he whispered. "Master Paul! Malabar came in first all right, a clean win. I did as you told me. You've made over seventy thousand pounds, you have; you've got over eighty thousand. Malabar came in all right, Master Paul."

"Malabar! Malabar! Did I say Malabar, mother? Did I say Malabar? Do you think I'm lucky, mother? I knew Malabar, didn't I? Over eighty thousand pounds. I call that lucky, don't you, mother? Over eighty thousand pounds! I knew, didn't I know I knew? Malabar came in all right. If I ride my horse till I'm sure, then I tell you, Bassett, you can go as high as you like. Did you go for all you were worth, Bassett?"

"I went a thousand on it, Master Paul."

"I never told you, mother, that if I can ride my horse, and *get there*, then I'm absolutely sure—oh, absolutely! Mother, did I ever tell you? I *am* lucky!"

"No, you never did," said the mother.

But the boy died in the night.

And even as he lay dead, his mother heard her brother's voice saying to her: "My God, Hester, you're eighty-odd thousand to the good, and a poor devil of a son to the bad. But, poor devil, poor devil, he's best gone out of a life where he rides his rocking-horse to find a winner."

---

# MARGINS

## Donald Barthelme

Donald Barthelme, born in Philadelphia in 1931, worked as a reporter, then as a museum director. His first collection of stories was Come Back, Dr. Caligari (1964). Since then he has published a novel, Snow White (1967), and Unspeakable Practices, Unnatural Acts (1968), City Life (1970), and Sadness (1972), all collections of stories. He has also published The Slightly Irregular Fire Engine (1972), which won the 1972 National Book Award for children's books, and Guilty Pleasures (1974), a collection of pieces that he labels "nonfiction." Barthelme, an admirer of Vladimir Nabokov, Samuel Beckett, and John Ashbery, authors whose techniques are reflected in his own work, has said: "I try to avoid saying anything directly and just hope that something emerges from what has been written."

Edward was explaining to Carl about margins. "The *width* of the margin shows culture, aestheticism and a sense of values or the lack of them," he said. "A very wide left margin shows an impractical person of culture and refinement with a deep appreciation for the best in art and music. Whereas," Edward said, quoting his handwriting analysis book. "whereas, narrow left margins show the opposite. No left margin at all shows a practical nature, a wholesome economy and a general lack of good taste in the arts. A very wide *right* margin shows a person afraid to face reality, oversensitive to the future and generally a poor mixer."

"I don't believe in it," Carl said.

"Now," Edward continued, "with reference to your sign there, you have an *all-around wide margin* which shows a person of extremely delicate sensibilities, with love of color and form, one who holds aloof from the multitude and lives in his own dream world of beauty and good taste."

"Are you sure you got that right?"

"I'm communicating with you," Edward said, "across a vast gulf of ignorance and darkness."

"*I* brought the darkness, is that the idea?" Carl asked.

"You brought the darkness, you black mother," Edward said. "Funky, man."

"Edward," Carl said, "for God's sake."

"Why did you write all that jazz on your sign, Carl? Why? It's not true, is it? Is it?"

"It's kind of true," Carl said. He looked down at his brown sandwich boards, which said: *I Was Put In Jail in Selby County Alabama For Five Years For Stealing A Dollar and A Half Which I Did Not Do. While I Was In Jail My Brother was Killed & My Mother Ran Away When I Was Little. In Jail I Began Preaching & I Preach to People Wherever I Can Bearing the Witness of Eschatological Love I Have Filled Out Papers for Jobs But Nobody Will Give Me a Job Because I Have Been In Jail & The Whole Scene Is Very Dreary, Pepsi Cola. I Need Your Offerings to Get Food. Patent Applied For & Deliver Us From Evil.* "It's true," Carl said, "with a kind of *merde-y* inner truth which shines forth as the objective correlative of what actually did happen, back home."

"Now, look at the way you made that 'm' and that 'n' there," Edward said. "The tops are pointed rather than rounded. That indicates aggressiveness and energy. The fact that they're also pointed rather than rounded at the bottom indicates a sarcastic, stubborn and irritable nature. See what I mean?"

"If you say so," Carl said.

"Your capitals are very small," Edward said, "indicating humility."

"My mother would be pleased," Carl said, "if she knew."

"On the other hand, the excessive size of the loops in your 'y' and your 'g' display exaggeration and egoism."

"That's always been one of my problems," Carl answered.

"What's your whole name?" Edward asked, leaning against a building. They were on Fourteenth Street, near Broadway.

"Carl Maria von Weber," Carl said.

"Are you a drug addict?"

"Edward," Carl said, "you *are* a swinger."

"Are you a Muslim?"

Carl felt his long hair. "Have you read *The Mystery of Being*, by Gabriel Marcel? I really liked that one. I thought that one was fine."

"No, c'mon Carl, answer the question," Edward insisted. "There's got to be frankness and honesty between the races. Are you one?"

"I think an accommodation can be reached and the government is doing all it can at the moment," Carl said. "I think there's something to be said on all sides of the question. This is not such a good place to hustle, you know that? I haven't got but two offerings all morning."

"People like people who look neat," Edward said. "You look kind of crummy, if you don't mind my saying so."

"You really think it's too long?" Carl asked, feeling his hair again.

"Do you think I'm a pretty color?" Edward asked. "Are you envious?"

"No," Carl said. "Not envious."

"See? Exaggeration and egoism. Just like I said."

"You're kind of boring, Edward. To tell the truth."

Edward thought about this for a moment. Then he said: "But I'm white."

"It's the color of choice," Carl said. "I'm tired of talking about color, though. Let's talk about values or something."

"Carl, I'm a fool," Edward said suddenly.

"Yes," Carl said.

"But I'm a *white* fool," Edward said. "That's what's so lovely about me."

"You *are* lovely, Edward," Carl said. "It's true. You have a nice look. Your aspect is good."

"Oh, hell," Edward said despondently. "You're very well-spoken," he said. "I noticed that."

"The reason for that is," Carl said, "I read. Did you read *The Cannibal* by John Hawkes? I thought that was a hell of a book."

"Get a haircut, Carl," Edward said. "Get a new suit. Maybe one of those new Italian suits with the tight coats. You could be upwardly mobile, you know, if you just put your back into it."

"Why are you worried, Edward? Why does my situation distress you? Why don't you just walk away and talk to somebody else?"

"You bother me," Edward confessed. "I keep trying to penetrate your inner reality, to find out what it is. Isn't that curious?"

"John Hawkes also wrote *The Beetle Leg* and a couple of other books whose titles escape me at the moment," Carl said. "I think he's one of the best of our younger American writers."

"Carl," Edward said, "*what is* your inner reality? Blurt it out, baby."

"It's mine," Carl said quietly. He gazed down at his shoes, which resembled a pair of large dead brownish birds.

"Are you sure you didn't steal that dollar and a half mentioned on your sign?"

"Edward, I *told* you I didn't steal that dollar and a half." Carl stamped up and down in his sandwich boards. "It sure is *cold* here on Fourteenth Street."

"That's your imagination, Carl," Edward said. "This street isn't any colder than Fifth, or Lex. Your feeling that it's colder here probably just arises from your marginal status as a despised person in our society."

"Probably," Carl said. There was a look on his face. "You know I went to the government, and asked them to give me a job in the Marine Band, and they wouldn't do it?"

"Do you blow good, man? Where's your axe?"

"They wouldn't *give* me that cotton-pickin' job," Carl said. "What do you think of that?"

"This eschatological love," Edward said, "what kind of love is that?"

"That is later love," Carl said. "That's what I call it, anyhow. That's love on the other side of the Jordan. The term refers to a set of conditions which . . . It's kind of a story we black people tell to ourselves to make ourselves happy."

"Oh me," Edward said. "Ignorance and darkness."

"Edward," Carl said, "you don't *like* me."

"I do too like you, Carl," Edward said. "Where do you steal your books, mostly?"

"Mostly in drugstores," Carl said. "I find them good because mostly they're long and narrow and the clerks tend to stay near the prescription counters at the back of the store, whereas the books are usually in those revolving racks near the front of the store. It's normally pretty easy to slip a couple in your overcoat pocket, if you're wearing an overcoat."

"But . . ."

"Yes," Carl said, "I know what you're thinking. If I'll steal books I'll steal other things. But stealing books is metaphysically different from stealing money. Villon has something pretty good to say on the subject I believe."

"Is that in 'If I Were King'?"

"Besides," Carl added, "haven't *you* ever stolen anything? At some point in your life?"

"My life," Edward said. "Why do you remind me of it?"

"Edward, you're not satisfied with your life! I thought white lives were *nice!*" Carl said, surprised. "I love that word 'nice.' It makes me so happy."

"Listen Carl," Edward said, "why don't you just concentrate on improving your handwriting."

"My character, you mean."

"No," Edward said, "don't bother improving your character. Just improve your handwriting. Make larger capitals. Make smaller loops in your 'y' and your 'g'. Watch your word-spacing so as not to display disorientation. Watch your margins."

"It's an idea. But isn't that kind of a superficial approach to the problem?"

"Be careful about the spaces between the lines," Edward went on. "Spacing of lines shows clearness of thought. Pay attention to your finals. There are twenty-two different kinds of finals and each one tells a lot about a person. I'll lend you the book. Good handwriting is the key to advancement, or if not *the* key, at least *a* key. You could be the first man of your race to be Vice-President."

"That's something to shoot for, all right."

"Would you like me to go get the book?"

"I don't think so," Carl said, "no thanks. It's not that I don't have any faith in your solution. What I *would* like is to take a leak. Would you mind holding my sandwich boards for a minute?"

"Not at all," Edward said, and in a moment had slipped Carl's sandwich boards over his own slight shoulders. "Boy, they're kind of heavy, aren't they?"

"They cut you a bit," Carl said with a malicious smile. "I'll just go into this men's store here."

When Carl returned the two men slapped each other sharply in the face with the back of the hand, that beautiful part of the hand where the knuckles grow.

# The Human Condition

## GYM PERIOD

**Rainer Maria Rilke**

Born in Prague in 1875, Rilke suffered an unhappy childhood, including five years (1886–1891) in military schools. He attended the Universities of Prague, Munich, and Berlin, publishing his first volume of poems, Life and Songs, in 1894. He gained critical recognition, however, with his collection of short stories, Stories of God (1900), and The Book of Pictures (1902), a book of poetry. For a time he was secretary to the sculptor Rodin and in 1903 published a book on the artist. He served in World War I in Austria and died in 1926, after much suffering, of myeloid leukemia. His other works include New Poems (1907–1908), Duino Elegies (1923), and Sonnets to Orpheus (1923), poetry; and an autobiographical novel, The Notebook of Malte Laurids Brigge (1910), also called The Journal of My Other Self. In speaking of Rilke's poetry, Arthur Gregor has written that he "used language with increased directness, discovering an internal life in words to convey his innermost vision and his acclaim of existence." "Gym Period" is not poetry, to be sure, but Gregor's words are still appropriate; the theme of the story is clearly an affirmation of the human spirit.

TRANSLATOR: Carl Niemeyer

The Military School of St. Severin. The gymnasium. The class in their white cotton shirts stand in two rows under the big gas lights. The gym teacher, a young officer with a hard, swarthy face and contemptuous eyes, has given the order for exercises and is dividing the class into sections. "First section, horizontal bars; second section, parallel bars; third section, horses; fourth section, pole climbing. Fall out!" And the boys in their light, resined shoes scatter quickly. A few remain standing in the middle of the floor, hesitating and reluctant. They are the fourth section, the poor gymnasts, who do not enjoy playing on the equipment and are already tired after their twenty knee-bends, as well as somewhat bewildered and out of breath.

But one, Karl Gruber, ordinarily the very first on such occasions, already stands near the poles set up in a dimly lit corner of the gymnasium just beside the lockers where the coats of the boys' uniforms now hang. He has seized the nearest pole and with unusual strength pulls it shaking out to the spot designated for practice. Gruber does not even let go. He jumps and grabs a hold rather high up. His legs, involuntarily wound around the pole in a position for climbing such as he never achieved before, cling to the shaft. He waits for the rest of the class and seems to be considering with peculiar pleasure the astonished anger of the little Polish sergeant, who calls to him to come down. But Gruber does not obey, and Jastersky, the blond sergeant, finally shouts, "Very well. Either you come down, Gruber, or you climb the rest of the way up. Otherwise I shall report you to the lieutenant in charge."

And then Gruber begins to climb, at first frenziedly, pulling up his legs a little, his eyes raised, estimating with some alarm the incalculable section of the pole still to come. Then his movements grow slower; and as though he were relishing every fresh hold as something new and delightful, he pulls himself higher than anyone usually goes. He pays no attention to the excitement of the exasperated sergeant, but climbs and climbs, his eyes staring upward, as though he had discovered an outlet in the gymnasium roof and were straining to reach it. The eyes of his whole section follow him. And in the other sections too some notice is taken of the climber who had hardly ever been able to climb even the first third of the way without getting a cough, a red face, and a bloodshot eye.

"Bravo, Gruber!" someone calls over from the first section. Many look up then, and for a while the gym is quiet.

But at this very moment when all eyes are upon him, Gruber, high up under the roof, gestures as though to shake them off; and when he obviously does not succeed, he rivets all their glances on the iron hook above him and swishes down the slippery pole, so that everyone is still looking up, whereas he, dizzy and hot, already stands below and gazes with strangely lusterless eyes at his burning palms.

Then one or another of the boys around him asks what got into him.

"Do you want to make the first section?" Gruber laughs and seems about to reply, but he thinks better of it and lowers his eyes.

And then, when the noisy tumult has begun again, he retires quietly to his locker, sits down, looks about uneasily, and after two panting breaths laughs again and tries to say something. But already he is unobserved.

Only Jerome, also in the fourth section, notices that he is bent over like someone deciphering a letter in bad light again inspecting his hands. He walks over to him presently and asks, "Did you hurt yourself?"

Gruber starts. "What?" he asks in his habitual slobbering voice.

"Let's have a look." Jerome takes his hand and turns it toward the light. A little skin is scraped from the palm. "Say, I've got something to fix it," says Jerome, who always gets sticking-plaster sent from home. "Come to my room when we get out." But it is as though Gruber did not hear. He stares straight ahead into the gym as though he were seeing something indefinable, perhaps something not in the gym, perhaps outside against the window even though it is late on a dark autumn afternoon.

At this moment, the sergeant shouts in his haughty way, "Gruber!" Gruber remains as before. Only his outstretched feet slide gracelessly forward on the slippery floor. "Gruber!" roars the sergeant, and his voice breaks. Then he waits a while, and says in a quick gruff tone without looking at the boy, "Report after class. I shall see that you. . . ." And the class continues.

"Gruber," says Jerome and bends over his friend, who is leaning back farther and farther in his locker, "it was your turn to climb on the rope. Go ahead, try it. If you don't, Jastersky will fix up some kind of a story against you. You know how he is."

Gruber nods. But instead of getting up, he abruptly shuts his eyes and slips forward while Jerome is talking. As if borne by a wave, he slides slowly and silently, farther and farther—slides from his seat, and Jerome doesn't realize what is happening till Gruber's head bangs hard against the wooden seat and then droops forward. "Gruber!" he calls hoarsely. At first no one notices. Jerome stands helpless, his arms at his sides, and calls "Gruber! Gruber!" He doesn't even think to pull him up.

Then he is given a push. Someone says, "Dumbbell!" Someone else shoves him aside, and he watches them lift the motionless boy to carry him off somewhere, probably into the next room. The lieutenant in charge hurries in. In a harsh, loud voice he issues curt orders. The commands cut short the buzzing chatter. Silence. Only here and there is there any movement: swinging on the bars, gentle leaps, a belated laugh from someone who doesn't know what it's all about.

Then rapid questions. "What? What? Who? Gruber? Where?" And still more questions. Then aloud someone says, "Fainted."

And red-faced Jastersky, the sergeant, runs back of the lieutenant in charge and cries in his disagreeable voice, trembling with rage, "He's faking, lieutenant, he's faking." The lieutenant pays no attention. He looks straight ahead, gnaws his mustache so that his strong chin juts out sharper and firmer, and gives an occasional brief order. He and four pupils carrying Gruber disappear into the room.

At once, the four pupils return. A servant runs through the gym. The four get a good deal of attention and are plied with questions. "How does he look? What's the matter with him? Has he come to yet?" None of the four really knows anything. And then the lieutenant in charge calls to them that the class may continue and gives the command to Goldstein, the sergeant-major. So the exercises begin again, on the parallel and horizontal bars; and the little boys of the third section straddle the tall horse with their bowed legs.

Yet the activity is not as before. It is as though everyone were listening. Swinging on the parallel bars abruptly stops, and only small feats are performed on the horizontal bar. The voices are less confused, and the hum is fainter, as though all were uttering just one word, "Ssss. Ssss." In the meantime sly little Krix is listening at the door. The sergeant of the second section chases him away, lifting his hand to slap his bottom. Krix leaps back, catlike, his eyes bright and cunning. He has learned enough. And after a while, when no one is watching, he tells Pavlovich, "The regimental doctor's come."

Now Pavlovich's behavior is notorious. As boldly as though he were obeying an order, he goes about the gym from one section to another, saying loudly, "The regimental doctor's in there." And even the noncoms appear to be interested in the news. Glances toward the door become more and more frequent, the exercises slower and slower. A small boy with black eyes remains crouching on the horse and stares open-mouthed at the door. The strongest boys in the first class exert themselves a little, struggle against it, whirl their legs.

Pombert, the strong Tyrolean, bends his arm and contemplates his muscles, which stand out taut and strong under his shirt. His supple young limbs even make a few more turns on the bars, and suddenly the lively movement of his body is the only one in the whole gym. It is a great dazzling circle, somehow ominous in the midst of great stillness. Abruptly the little fellow brings himself to a stop, drops involuntarily to his knees, and makes a face as though he despised them all. But even his dull little eyes rest finally on the door.

Now the singing of the gasjets and the ticking of the wall clock are audible. And then the dismissal bell rattles. Today its tone is strange and peculiar. And it stops suddenly, incomplete, interrupting itself when its message is only half spoken. Sergeant-major Goldstein, however, knows his duty. He calls, "Fall in!" No one hears. No one can recall the meaning these words once had. Once? When? "Fall in!" croaks the sergeant-major angrily, and now the other noncoms cry in succession, "Fall in!" And also many of the pupils say, as if to themselves or in their sleep, "Fall in! Fall in!" But actually, all of them know there is still something to wait for.

And at this very moment the door is opening. For a second nothing happens; then Wehl, the lieutenant in charge, walks out, and his eyes are big and wrathful and his pace is decided. He marches as though he were on parade and says hoarsely, "Fall in!" With astonishing speed ranks are formed. Then no one moves. It is as though a field marshal were present. And now the command, "Attention!" A pause, and then dry and harsh, "Your friend Gruber has just died. Heart attack. Forward, march!" A pause.

And only after a little while, the voice of the pupil on duty, small and weak, "Company, column left! March!" Slow and unready, the group turns to the door. Jerome is the last. No one looks back. From the corridor chill, damp air blows against the boys. One of them suggests that it smells of carbolic acid. Pombert makes a vulgar joke about the smell. No one laughs. Suddenly Jerome feels somebody grab his arm, as though for assault. Krix is hanging on to him. "I saw him," he whispers breathlessly, and squeezes Jerome's arm while an inner laughter convulses him. He can hardly go on. "He's stark naked and caved in and all stretched out. And he's got a seal on the soles of his feet. . . ."

And then he giggles shrilly, as though someone had tickled him, giggles and bites down through Jerome's sleeve.

---

# CHRISTMAS SONG

## Langston Hughes

*Born in Joplin, Missouri, in 1902, Langston Hughes spent his early years in various places in the Middle West. After graduation from high school in Cleveland, he spent two years in Mexico with his father. He attended Columbia University, but left after a year and traveled to Europe and Africa as a seaman. He later attended Lincoln University on a scholarship and was graduated in 1929. Hughes had written his famous poem "The Negro Speaks of Rivers" shortly after his graduation from high school and it had gained him some attention, but the success of his literary career was assured with his winning the first prize for poetry from* Opportunity *magazine in 1925 and the Witter Bynner poetry award the following year. His first book of poetry,* The Weary Blues, *was published the same year and identified him with the Harlem Renaissance group. He published a second volume of poetry,* Fine Clothes to the Jew, *the following year, and in 1930 published his first novel,* Not Without Laughter. *Until his death in 1967, Hughes wrote prolifically in all genres; his works include poetry, prose, essays, drama, and collections and anthologies of all kinds. Among his many works are the following:* The Big Sea (*1940*) *and* I Wonder as I Wander (*1956*), *two autobiographical pieces;* Shakespeare in Harlem (*1942*) *and* The Panther and the Lash (*1967*), *poetry;* Tambourines to Glory (*1958*), *a novel;* The Way of White Folks (*1934*), The Best of Simple (*1961*), *in which "Christmas Song" appears, and* Something in Common (*1963*), *short stories and anecdotes; and an* African Treasury (*1960*) *and* The Best Short Stories by Negro Writers (*1967*), *anthologies. A good introduction to Hughes and his work is* Black Troubador: Langston Hughes (*1970*), *by Charlemae Rollins. Perhaps Hughes's best-known character is Jessie B. Simple, who has been called the black Everyman. Certainly "Christmas Song" has those qualities that make Simple so memorable: innocence, wit, and "simple" wisdom. "I am interested primarily in life, not in 'local color,' " Hughes once wrote, and "Christmas Song" is proof of his having achieved his goal.*

"Just like a Negro," said Simple, "I have waited till Christmas Eve to finish my shopping."

"You are walking rather fast," I said. "Be careful, don't slip on the ice. The way it's snowing, you can't always see it underneath the snow."

"Why do you reckon they don't clean off the sidewalks in Harlem nice like they do downtown?"

"Why do *you* reckon?" I asked. "But don't tell me! I don't wish to discuss race tonight, certainly not out here in the street, as cold as it is."

"Paddy's is right there in the next block," said Simple, heading steadily that way. "I am going down to 125th Street to get two rattles, one for Carlyle's baby, Third Floor Front, and one for that other cute little old baby downstairs in the Second Floor Rear. Also I aims to get a box of hard candy for my next-door neighbor that ain't got no teeth, poor Miss Amy, so she can suck it. And a green rubber bone for Trixie. Also some kind of game for Joyce to take her godchild from me during the holidays."

"It's eight o'clock already, fellow. If you've got all that to do, you'd better hurry before the stores close."

"I am hurrying. Joyce sent me out to get some sparklers for the tree. Her and her big old fat landlady and some of the other roomers in their house is putting up a Christmas tree down in the living room, and you are invited to come by and help trim it, else watch them trimming. Do you want to go?"

"When?"

"Long about midnight P.M., I'd say. Joyce is taking a nap now. When she wakes up she's promised to make some good old Christmas eggnog —if I promise not to spike it too strong. You might as well dip your cup in our bowl. Meanwhile, let's grab a quick beer here before I get on to the store. Come on inside. Man, I'm excited! I got another present for Joyce."

"What?"

"I'm not going to tell you until after Christmas. It's a surprise. But whilst I am drinking, look at this which I writ yesterday."

### XMAS

I forgot to send
A card to Jennie—
But the truth about cousins is
There's too many.

I also forgot
My Uncle Joe,
But I believe I'll let
That old rascal go.

I done bought
Four boxes now.
I can't afford
No more, nohow.

So Merry Xmas,
Everybody!
Cards or no cards,
Here's HOWDY!

"That's for my Christmas card," said Simple. "Come on, let's go."

"Not bad. Even if it will be a little late, be sure you send me one," I said as we went out into the snow.

"Man, you know I can't afford to have no cards printed up. It's just jive. I likes to compose with a pencil sometimes. Truth is, come Christmas, I has feelings right up in my throat that if I was a composer, I would write me a song also, which I would sing myself. It would be a song about that black Wise Man who went to see the Baby in the Manger. I would put into it such another music as you never heard. It would be a baritone song."

"There are many songs about the Three Wise Men," I said. "Why would you single out the black one?"

"Because I am black," said Simple, "so my song would be about the black Wise Man."

"If you could write such a song, what would it say?"

"Just what the Bible says—that he saw a star, he came from the East, and he went with the other Wise Mens to Bethlehem in Judea, and bowed down before the Child in the Manger, and put his presents down there in the straw for that Baby—and it were the greatest Baby in the world, for it were Christ! That is what my song would say."

"You don't speak of the Bible very often," I said, "but when you do, you speak like a man who knew it as a child."

"My Aunt Lucy read the Bible to me all the time when I were knee high to a duck. I never will forget it. So if I wrote a Christmas song, I would write one right out of the Bible. But it would not be so much what words I would put in it as what my music would say—because I would also make up the music myself. Music explains things better than words and everybody in all kind of languages could understand it then. My music would say everything my words couldn't put over, because there wouldn't be many words anyhow.

"The words in my song would just say a black man saw a star and followed it till he came to a stable and put his presents down. But the music would say he also laid his heart down, too—which would be my heart. It would be *my* song I would be making up. But I would make it like as if I was there myself two thousand years ago, and *I* seen the star, and *I* followed it till I come to that Child. And when I riz up from bending over that Baby in the Manger I were strong and not afraid. The end of my song would be, *Be not afraid.* That would be the end of my song."

"It sounds like a good song," I said.

"It would be the kind of song everybody could sing, old folks and young folks. And when they sing it, some folks would laugh. It would be a happy song. Other folks would cry because—well, I don't know," Simple stopped quite still for a moment in the falling snow. "I don't know, but something about that black man and that little small Child—something about them two peoples—folks would cry."

---

# THE SOJOURNER

## Carson McCullers

*Born in Columbus, Georgia, in 1917, Carson McCullers went to New York at the age of seventeen to attend Columbia University and study at the Julliard School of Music. Although considered a Southern writer by most critics, she lived in the East most of her life until her death in 1967. Despite a severe paralytic stroke in 1946 that left her a semi-invalid from that time on, Ms. McCullers continued to write, and the quantity and variety of her work are impressive. Her first novel,* The Heart Is a Lonely Hunter, *published in 1940, was an instant success. The next year* Reflections in a Golden Eye, *a short novel, was published, and* The Member of the Wedding *appeared in 1946. Other works are* The Ballad of the Sad Cafe (1951) *in which "The Sojourner" appeared; a dramatic version of* The Member of the Wedding (1950), *which won the New York Drama Critics' Award for that year;* The Square Root of Wonderful (1958), *another play;* Clock Without Hands (1961), *a novel; and* Sweet as a

Pickle and Clean as a Pig (1964), *a collection of poems for children. Although Carson McCullers is often thought of as a regional writer, "The Sojourner" and many of her other writings demonstrate clearly that she is a writer whose work transcends narrow boundaries of place or time; her interest is in human actions and feelings, particularly such basic ones as fear, hatred, love, and joy.*

The twilight border between sleep and waking was a Roman one this morning: splashing fountains and arched, narrow streets, the golden lavish city of blossoms and age-soft stone. Sometimes in this semi-consciousness he sojourned again in Paris, or war German rubble, or Swiss skiing and a snow hotel. Sometimes, also, in a fallow Georgia field at hunting dawn. Rome it was this morning in the yearless region of dreams.

John Ferris awoke in a room in a New York hotel. He had the feeling that something unpleasant was awaiting him—what it was, he did not know. The feeling, submerged by matinal necessities, lingered even after he had dressed and gone downstairs. It was a cloudless autumn day and the pale sunlight sliced between the pastel skyscrapers. Ferris went into the next-door drugstore and sat at the end booth next to the window glass that overlooked the sidewalk. He ordered an American breakfast with scrambled eggs and sausage.

Ferris had come from Paris to his father's funeral which had taken place the week before in his home town in Georgia. The shock of death had made him aware of youth already passed. His hair was receding and the veins in his now naked temples were pulsing and prominent and his body was spare except for an incipient belly bulge. Ferris had loved his father and the bond between them had once been extraordinarily close—but the years had somehow unraveled this filial devotion; the death, expected for a long time, had left him with an unforseen dismay. He had stayed as long as possible to be near his mother and brothers at home. His plane for Paris was to leave the next morning.

Ferris pulled out his address book to verify a number. He turned the pages with growing attentiveness. Names and addresses from New York, the capitals of Europe, a few faint ones from his home state in the South. Faded, printed names, sprawled drunken ones. Betty Wills: a random love, married now. Charlie Williams: wounded in the Hürtgen Forest, unheard of since. Grand old Williams—did he live or die? Don Walker: a B.T.O. in television, getting rich. Henry Green: hit the skids after the war, in a sanitarium now, they say. Cozie Hall: he had heard that she was dead. Heedless, laughing Cozie—it was strange to think that she too, silly girl, could die. As Ferris closed the address book, he suffered a sense of hazard, transience, almost of fear.

It was then that his body jerked suddenly. He was staring out of the window when there, on the sidewalk, passing by, was his ex-wife. Elizabeth passed quite close to him, walking slowly. He could not understand the wild quiver of his heart, nor the following sense of recklessness and grace that lingered after she was gone.

Quickly Ferris paid his check and rushed out to the sidewalk. Elizabeth stood on the corner waiting to cross Fifth Avenue. He hurried toward her meaning to speak, but the lights changed and she crossed the street before he reached her. Ferris followed. On the other side he could easily have overtaken her, but he found himself lagging unaccountably. Her fair brown hair was plainly rolled, and as he watched her Ferris recalled that once his father had remarked that Elizabeth had a 'beautiful carriage.' She turned at the next corner and Ferris followed, although by now his intention to overtake her had disappeared. Ferris questioned the bodily disturbance that the sight of Elizabeth aroused in him, the dampness of his hands, the hard heartstrokes.

It was eight years since Ferris had last seen his ex-wife. He knew that long ago she had married again. And there were children. During recent years he had seldom thought of her. But at first, after the divorce, the loss had almost destroyed him. Then after the anodyne of time, he had loved again, and then again. Jeannine, she was now. Certainly his love for his ex-wife was long since past. So why the unhinged body, the shaken mind? He knew only that his clouded heart was oddly dissonant with the sunny, candid autumn day. Ferris wheeled suddenly and, walking with long strides, almost running, hurried back to the hotel.

Ferris poured himself a drink, although it was not yet eleven o'clock. He sprawled out in an armchair like a man exhausted, nursing his glass of bourbon and water. He had a full day ahead of him as he was leaving by plane the next morning for Paris. He checked over his obligations: take luggage to Air France, lunch with his boss, buy shoes and an overcoat. And something—wasn't there something else? Ferris finished his drink and opened the telephone directory.

His decision to call his ex-wife was impulsive. The number was under Bailey, the husband's name, and he called before he had much time for self-debate. He and Elizabeth had exchanged cards at Christmastime, and Ferris had sent a carving set when he received the announcement of her wedding. There was no reason *not* to call. But as he waited, listening to the ring at the other end, misgiving fretted him.

Elizabeth answered; her familiar voice was a fresh shock to him. Twice he had to repeat his name, but when he was identified, she sounded glad. He explained he was only in town for that day. They had a theater engagement, she said—but she wondered if he would come by for an early dinner. Ferris said he would be delighted.

As he went from one engagement to another, he was still bothered at odd moments by the feeling that something necessary was forgotten. Ferris bathed and changed in the late afternoon, often thinking about Jeannine: he would be with her the following night. "Jeannine," he would say, "I happened to run into my ex-wife when I was in New York. Had dinner with her. And her husband, of course. It was strange seeing her after all these years."

Elizabeth lived in the East Fifties, and as Ferris taxied uptown he glimpsed at intersections the lingering sunset, but by the time he reached his destination it was already autumn dark. The place was a building with a marquee and a doorman, and the apartment was on the seventh floor.

"Come in, Mr. Ferris."

Braced for Elizabeth or even the unimagined husband, Ferris was astonished by the freckled red-haired child; he had known of the children, but his mind had failed somehow to acknowledge them. Surprise made him step back awkwardly.

"This is our apartment," the child said politely. "Aren't you Mr. Ferris? I'm Billy. Come in."

In the living room beyond the hall, the husband provided another surprise; he too had not been acknowledged emotionally. Bailey was a lumbering red-haired man with a deliberate manner. He rose and extended a welcoming hand.

"I'm Bill Bailey. Glad to see you. Elizabeth will be in, in a minute. She's finishing dressing."

The last words struck a gliding series of vibrations, memories of the other years. Fair Elizabeth, rosy and naked before her bath. Half-dressed before the mirror of her dressing table, brushing her fine, chestnut hair. Sweet, casual intimacy, the soft-fleshed loveliness indisputably possessed. Ferris shrank from the unbidden memories and compelled himself to meet Bill Bailey's gaze.

"Billy, will you please bring that tray of drinks from the kitchen table?"

The child obeyed promptly, and when he was gone Ferris remarked conversationally, "Fine boy you have there."

"We think so."

Flat silence until the child returned with a tray of glasses and a cocktail shaker of martinis. With the priming drinks they pumped up conversation: Russia, they spoke of, and the New York rain-making, and the apartment situation in Manhattan and Paris.

"Mr. Ferris is flying all the way across the ocean tomorrow," Bailey said to the little boy who was perched on the arm of his chair, quiet and well behaved. "I bet you would like to be a stowaway in his suitcase."

Billy pushed back his limp bangs. "I want to fly in an airplane and be a newspaperman like Mr. Ferris." He added with sudden assurance, "That's what I would like to do when I am big."

Bailey said, "I thought you wanted to be a doctor."

"I do!" said Billy. "I would like to be both. I want to be a atom-bomb scientist too."

Elizabeth came in carrying in her arms a baby girl.

"Oh, John!" she said. She settled the baby in the father's lap. "It's grand to see you. I'm awfully glad you could come."

The little girl sat demurely on Bailey's knees. She wore a pale pink crepe de Chine frock, smocked around the yoke with rose, and a matching silk hair ribbon tying back her pale soft curls. Her skin was summer tanned and her brown eyes flecked with gold and laughing. When she reached up and fingered her father's horn-rimmed glasses, he took them off and let her look through them a moment. "How's my old Candy?"

Elizabeth was very beautiful, more beautiful perhaps than he had ever realized. Her straight clean hair was shining. Her face was softer, glowing and serene. It was a madonna loveliness, dependent on the family ambiance.

"You've hardly changed at all," Elizabeth said, "but it has been a long time."

"Eight years." His hand touched his thinning hair self-consciously while further amenities were exchanged.

Ferris felt himself suddenly a spectator—an interloper among these Baileys. Why had he come? He suffered. His own life seemed so solitary, a fragile column supporting nothing amidst the wreckage of the years. He felt he could not bear much longer to stay in the family room.

He glanced at his watch. "You're going to the theater?"

"It's a shame," Elizabeth said, "but we've had this engagement for more than a month. But surely, John, you'll be staying home one of these days before long. You're not going to be an expatriate, are you?"

"Expatriate," Ferris repeated. "I don't much like the word."

"What's a better word?" she asked.

He thought for a moment. "Sojourner might do."

Ferris glanced again at his watch, and again Elizabeth apologized. "If only we had known ahead of time—"

"I just had this day in town. I came home unexpectedly. You see, Papa died last week."

"Papa Ferris is dead?"

"Yes, at Johns-Hopkins. He had been sick there nearly a year. The funeral was down home in Georgia."

"Oh, I'm so sorry, John. Papa Ferris was always one of my favorite people."

The little boy moved from behind the chair so that he could look into his mother's face. He asked, "Who is dead?"

Ferris was oblivious to apprehension; he was thinking of his father's death. He saw again the outstretched body on the quilted silk within the coffin. The corpse flesh was bizarrely rouged and the familiar hands lay massive and joined above a spread of funeral roses. The memory closed and Ferris awakened to Elizabeth's calm voice.

"Mr. Ferris's father, Billy. A really grand person. Somebody you didn't know."

"But why did you call him *Papa* Ferris?"

Bailey and Elizabeth exchanged a trapped look. It was Bailey who answered the questioning child. "A long time ago," he said, "your mother and Mr. Ferris were once married. Before you were born—a long time ago."

"Mr. Ferris?"

The little boy stared at Ferris, amazed and unbelieving. And Ferris's eyes, as he returned the gaze, were somehow unbelieving too. Was it indeed true that at one time he had called this stranger, Elizabeth, Little Butterduck during nights of love, that they had lived together, shared perhaps a thousand days and nights and—finally—endured in the misery of sudden solitude the fiber by fiber (jealousy, alcohol and money quarrels) destruction of the fabric of married love.

Bailey said to the children, "It's somebody's suppertime. Come on now."

"But Daddy! Mama and Mr. Ferris—I—"

Billy's everlasting eyes—perplexed and with a glimmer of hostility—reminded Ferris of the gaze of another child. It was the young son of Jeannine—a boy of seven with a shadowed little face and knobby knees whom Ferris avoided and usually forgot.

"Quick march!" Bailey gently turned Billy toward the door. "Say good night now, son."

"Good night, Mr. Ferris." He added resentfully, "I thought I was staying up for the cake."

"You can come in afterward for the cake," Elizabeth said. "Run along now with Daddy for your supper."

Ferris and Elizabeth were alone. The weight of the situation descended on those first moments of silence. Ferris asked permission to pour himself another drink and Elizabeth set the cocktail shaker on the table at his side. He looked at the grand piano and noticed the music on the rack.

"Do you still play as beautifully as you used to?"

"I still enjoy it."

"Please play, Elizabeth."

Elizabeth arose immediately. Her readiness to perform when asked had always been one of her amiabilities; she never hung back, apologized. Now as she approached the piano there was the added readiness of relief.

She began with a Bach prelude and fugue. The prelude was as gaily iridescent as a prism in a morning room. The first voice of the fugue, an announcement pure and solitary, was repeated intermingling with a second voice, and again repeated within an elaborated frame, the multiple music, horizontal and serene, flowed with unhurried majesty. The principal melody was woven with two other voices, embellished with countless ingenuities—now dominant, again submerged, it had the sublimity of a single thing that does not fear surrender to the whole. Toward the end, the density of the material gathered for the last enriched insistence on the dominant first motif and with a chorded final statement the fugue ended. Ferris rested his head on the chair back and closed his eyes. In the following silence a clear, high voice came from the room down the hall.

"Daddy, how *could* Mama and Mr. Ferris—" A door was closed.

The piano began again—what was this music? Unplaced, familiar, the limpid melody had lain a long while dormant in his heart. Now it spoke to him of another time, another place—it was the music Elizabeth used to play. The delicate air summoned a wilderness of memory. Ferris was lost in the riot of past longings, conflicts, ambivalent desires. Strange that the music, catalyst for this tumultuous anarchy, was so serene and clear. The singing melody was broken off by the appearance of the maid.

"Miz Bailey, dinner is out on the table now."

Even after Ferris was seated at the table between his host and hostess, the unfinished music still overcast his mood. He was a little drunk.

"*L'improvisation de la vie humaine,*" he said. "There's nothing that makes you so aware of the improvisation of human existence as a song unfinished. Or an old address book."

"Address book?" repeated Bailey. Then he stopped, noncommittal and polite.

"You're still the same old boy, Johnny," Elizabeth said with a trace of the old tenderness.

It was a Southern dinner that evening, and the dishes were his old favorites. They had fried chicken and corn pudding and rich, glazed candied sweet potatoes. During the meal Elizabeth kept alive a conversation when the silences were overlong. And it came about that Ferris was led to speak of Jeannine.

"I first knew Jeannine last autumn—about this time of the year—in Italy. She's a singer and she had an engagement in Rome. I expect we will be married soon."

The words seemed so true, inevitable, that Ferris did not at first acknowledge to himself the lie. He and Jeannine had never in that year spoken of marriage. And indeed, she was still married—to a White Russian money-changer in Paris from whom she had been separated for five years. But it was too late to correct the lie. Already Elizabeth was saying: "This really makes me glad to know. Congratulations, Johnny."

He tried to make amends with truth. "The Roman autumn is so beautiful. Balmy and blossoming." He added, "Jeannine has a little boy of six. A curious trilingual little fellow. We go to the Tuileries sometimes."

A lie again. He had taken the boy once to the gardens. The sallow foreign child in shorts that bared his spindly legs had sailed his boat in the concrete pond and ridden the pony. The child had wanted to go in to the puppet show. But there was not time, for Ferris had an engagement at the Scribe Hotel. He had promised they would go to the guignol another afternoon. Only once had he taken Valentin to the Tuileries.

There was a stir. The maid brought in a white-frosted cake with pink candles. The children entered in their night clothes. Ferris still did not understand.

"Happy birthday, John," Elizabeth said. "Blow out the candles."

Ferris recognized his birthday date. The candles blew out lingeringly and there was the smell of burning wax. Ferris was thirty-eight years old. The veins in his temples darkened and pulsed visibly.

"It's time you started for the theater."

Ferris thanked Elizabeth for the birthday dinner and said the appropriate good-byes. The whole family saw him to the door.

A high, thin moon shone above the jagged, dark skyscrapers. The streets were windy, cold. Ferris hurried to Third Avenue and hailed a cab. He gazed at the nocturnal city with the deliberate attentiveness of departure and perhaps farewell. He was alone. He longed for flighttime and the coming journey.

The next day he looked down on the city from the air, burnished in sunlight, toylike, precise. Then America was left behind and there was only the Atlantic and the distant European shore. The ocean was milky pale and placid beneath the clouds. Ferris dozed most of the day. Toward dark he was thinking of Elizabeth and the visit of the previous evening. He thought of Elizabeth among her family with longing, gentle envy and inexplicable regret. He sought the melody, the unfinished air, that had so moved him. The cadence, some unrelated tones, were all that remained; the melody itself evaded him. He had found instead the first voice of the fugue that Elizabeth had played—it came to him, inverted mockingly and in a minor key. Suspended above the ocean the anxieties of transience and solitude no longer troubled him and he thought of his father's death with equanimity. During the dinner hour the plane reached the shore of France.

At midnight Ferris was in a taxi crossing Paris. It was a clouded night and mist wreathed the lights of the Place de la Concorde. The midnight bistros gleamed on the wet pavements. As always after a transocean flight the change of continents was too sudden. New York at morning, this midnight Paris. Ferris glimpsed the disorder of his life: the succession of cities, of transitory loves; and time, the sinister glissando of the years, time always.

"*Vite! Vite!*" he called in terror. "*Dépêchez-vous.*"

Valentin opened the door to him. The little boy wore pajamas and an outgrown red robe. His grey eyes were shadowed and, as Ferris passed into the flat, they flickered momentarily.

*"J'attends Maman."*

Jeannine was singing in a night club. She would not be home before another hour. Valentin returned to a drawing, squatting with his crayons over the paper on the floor. Ferris looked down at the drawing—it was a banjo player with notes and wavy lines inside a comic-strip balloon.

"We will go again to the Tuileries."

The child looked up and Ferris drew him closer to his knees. The melody, the unfinished music that Elizabeth had played, came to him suddenly. Unsought, the load of memory jettisoned—this time bringing only recognition and sudden joy.

"Monsieur Jean," the child said, "did you see him?"

Confused, Ferris thought only of another child—the freckled, family-loved boy. "See who, Valentin?"

"Your dead papa in Georgia." The child added, "Was he okay?"

Ferris spoke with rapid urgency: "We will go often to the Tuileries. Ride the pony and we will go into the guignol. We will see the puppet show and never be in a hurry any more."

"Monsieur Jean," Valentin said. "The guignol is now closed."

Again, the terror the acknowledgment of wasted years and death. Valentin, responsive and confident, still nestled in his arms. His cheek touched the soft cheek and felt the brush of the delicate eyelashes. With inner desperation he pressed the child close—as though an emotion as protean as his love could dominate the pulse of time.

---

# A WORN PATH

## Eudora Welty

*Born in 1909 in Jackson, Mississippi, educated at Mississippi State College for Women, the University of Wisconsin, and Columbia University, Eudora Welty, like so many other writers, received her first recognition for her contributions to "little" magazines. Her first successful collection of short stories was* A Curtain of Green *(1941), in which "A Worn Path" appears; other collections of short stories are* The Wide Net *(1943),* The Golden Apples *(1949), and* The Bride of Innisfallen *(1955). Her novels include* The Robber Bridegroom *(1942),* The Ponder Heart *(1954), and her latest,* The Optimist's Daughter *(1973). Other awards include a Guggenheim Fellowship in 1942; honorary consultant to the Library of Congress, 1958–1961; and the William Dean Howells medal. One of Eudora Welty's most perceptive critics, Ruth Vande Kieft, author of* Eudora Welty, *a critical study of Ms. Welty's works, provides a clue to understanding and appreciating "A Worn Path" and the other stories of* this most elusive and allusive author. "Miss Welty's stories," she writes, "are largely concerned with the mysteries of the inner life. She explains that to her the interior world is 'endlessly new, mysterious, and alluring'; and 'relationship is a pervading and changing mystery; it is not words that make it so in life, but words have to make it so in a story. Brutal or lovely, the mystery waits for people wherever they go, whatever extreme they run to.'" Ms. Vande Kieft concludes: "The term 'mystery' has here to do with the enigma of man's being—his relationship to the universe; what is secret, concealed, inviolable in any human being, resulting in distance or separation between human beings; the puzzles and difficulties we have about our own feelings, our meaning and our identity."

It was December—a bright frozen day in the early morning. Far out in the country there was an old Negro woman with her head tied in a red rag, coming along a path through the pinewoods. Her name was Phoenix Jackson. She was very old and small and she walked slowly in the dark pine shadows, moving a little from side to side in her steps, with the balanced heaviness and lightness of a pendulum in a grandfather clock. She carried a thin, small cane made from an umbrella, and with this she kept tapping the frozen earth in front of her. This made a grave and persistent noise in the still air, that seemed meditative like the chirping of a solitary little bird.

She wore a dark striped dress reaching down to her shoe tops, and an equally long apron of bleached sugar sacks, with a full pocket: all neat and tidy, but every time she took a step she might have fallen over her shoelaces, which dragged from her unlaced shoes. She looked straight ahead. Her eyes were blue with age. Her skin had a pattern all its own of numberless branching wrinkles and as though a whole little tree stood in the middle of her forehead, but a golden color ran underneath, and the two knobs of her cheeks were illumined by a yellow burning under the dark. Under the red rag her hair came down on her neck in the frailest of ringlets, still black, and with an odor like copper.

Now and then there was a quivering in the thicket. Old Phoenix said, "Out of my way, all you foxes, owls, beetles, jack rabbits, coons and wild animals! . . . Keep out from under these feet, little bobwhites. . . . Keep the big wild hogs out of my path. Don't let none of those come running my direction. I got a long way." Under her small black-freckled hand her cane, limber as a buggy whip, would switch at the brush as if to rouse up any hiding things.

On she went. The woods were deep and still. The sun made the pine needles almost too bright to look at, up where the wind rocked. The cones dropped as light as feathers. Down in the hollow was the mourning dove—it was not too late for him.

The path ran up a hill. "Seem like there is chains about my feet, time I get this far," she said, in the voice of argument old people keep to use with themselves. "Something always take a hold of me on this hill—pleads I should stay."

After she got to the top she turned and gave a full, severe look behind her where she had come. "Up through pines," she said at length. "Now down through oaks."

Her eyes opened their widest, and she started down gently. But before she got to the bottom of the hill a bush caught her dress.

Her fingers were busy and intent, but her skirts were full and long, so that before she could pull them free in one place they were caught in another. It was not possible to allow the dress to tear. "I in the thorny bush," she said. "Thorns, you doing your appointed work. Never want to let folks pass, no sir. Old eyes thought you was a pretty little *green* bush."

Finally, trembling all over, she stood free, and after a moment dared to stoop for her cane.

"Sun so high!" she cried, leaning back and looking, while the thick tears went over her eyes. "The time getting all gone here."

At the foot of this hill was a place where a log was laid across the creek.

"Now comes the trial," said Phoenix.

Putting her right foot out, she mounted the log and shut her eyes. Lifting her skirt, leveling her cane fiercely before her, like a festival figure in some parade, she began to march across. Then she opened her eyes and she was safe on the other side.

"I wasn't as old as I thought," she said.

But she sat down to rest. She spread her skirts on the bank around her and folded her hands over her knees. Up above her was a tree in a pearly cloud of mistletoe. She did not dare to close her eyes, and when a little boy brought her a plate with a slice of marble-cake on it she spoke to him. "That would be acceptable," she said. But when she went to take it there was just her own hand in the air.

So she left that tree, and had to go through a barbed-wire fence. There she had to creep and crawl, spreading her knees and stretching her fingers like a baby trying to climb the steps. But she talked loudly to herself: she could not let her dress be torn now, so late in the day, and she could not pay for having her arm or her leg sawed off if she got caught fast where she was.

At last she was safe through the fence and risen up out in the clearing. Big dead trees, like black men with one arm, were standing in the purple stalks of the withered cotton field. There sat a buzzard.

"Who you watching?"

In the furrow she made her way along.

"Glad this not the season for bulls," she said, looking sideways, "and the good Lord made his snakes to curl up and sleep in the winter. A pleasure I don't see no two-headed snake coming around that tree, where it come once. It took a while to get by him, back in the summer."

She passed through the old cotton and went into a field of dead corn. It whispered and shook and was taller than her head. "Through the maze now," she said, for there was no path.

Then there was something tall, black, and skinny there, moving before her.

At first she took it for a man. It could have been a man dancing in the field. But she stood still and listened, and it did not make a sound. It was as silent as a ghost.

"Ghost," she said sharply, "who be you the ghost of? For I have heard of nary death close by."

But there was no answer—only the ragged dancing in the wind.

She shut her eyes, reached out her hand, and touched a sleeve. She found a coat and inside that an emptiness, cold as ice.

"You scarecrow," she said. Her face lighted. "I ought to be shut up for good," she said with laughter. "My senses is gone. I too old. I the oldest people I ever know. Dance, old scarecrow," she said, "while I dancing with you."

She kicked her foot over the furrow, and with mouth drawn down, shook her head once or twice in a little strutting way. Some husks blew down and whirled in streamers about her skirts.

Then she went on, parting her way from side to side with the cane, through the whispering field. At last she came to the end, to a wagon track where the silver grass blew between the red ruts. The quail were walking around like pullets, seeming all dainty and unseen.

"Walk pretty," she said. "This the easy place. This the easy going."

She followed the track, swaying through the quiet bare fields, through the little strings of trees silver in their dead leaves, past cabins silver from weather, with the doors and windows boarded shut, all like old women under a spell sitting there. "I walking in their sleep," she said, nodding her head vigorously.

In a ravine she went where a spring was silently flowing through a hollow log. Old Phoenix bent and drank. "Sweet-gum makes the water sweet," she said, and drank more. "Nobody know who made this well, for it was here when I was born."

The track crossed a swampy part where the moss hung as white as lace from every limb. "Sleep on, alligators, and blow your bubbles." Then the track went into the road.

Deep, deep the road went down between the high green-colored banks. Overhead the live-oaks met, and it was as dark as a cave.

A black dog with a lolling tongue came up out of the weeds by the ditch. She was meditating, and not ready, and when he came at her she only hit him a little with her cane. Over she went in the ditch, like a little puff of milkweed.

Down there, her senses drifted away. A dream visited her, and she reached her hand up, but nothing reached down and gave her a pull. So she lay there and presently went to talking. "Old woman," she said to herself, "that black dog come up out of the weeds to stall your off, and now there he sitting on his fine tail, smiling at you."

A white man finally came along and found her—a hunter, a young man, with his dog on a chain.

"Well, Granny!" he laughed. "What are you doing there?"

"Lying on my back like a June-bug waiting to be turned over, mister," she said, reaching up her hand.

He lifted her up, gave her a swing in the air, and set her down. "Anything broken, Granny?"

"No sir, them old dead weeds is springy enough," said Phoenix, when she had got her breath. "I thank you for your trouble."

"Where do you live, Granny?" he asked, while the two dogs were growling at each other.

"Away back yonder, sir, behind the ridge. You can't even see it from here."

"On your way home?"

"No sir, I going to town."

"Why, that's too far! That's as far as I walk when I come out myself, and I get something for my trouble." He patted the stuffed bag he carried, and there hung down a little closed claw. It was one of the bobwhites, with its beak hooked bitterly to show it was dead. "Now you go on home, Granny!"

"I bound to go to town, mister," said Phoenix. "The time come around."

He gave another laugh, filling the whole landscape. "I know you old colored people! Wouldn't miss going to town to see Santa Claus!"

But something held old Phoenix very still. The deep lines in her face went into a fierce and different radiation. Without warning, she had seen with her own eyes a flashing nickel fall out of the man's pocket onto the ground.

"How old are you, Granny?" he was saying.

"There is no telling, mister," she said, "no telling."

Then she gave a little cry and clapped her hands and said, "Git on away from here, dog! Look! Look at that dog!" She laughed as if in admiration. "He ain't scared of nobody. He a big black dog." She whispered, "Sic him!"

"Watch me get rid of that cur," said the man. "Sic him, Pete! Sic him!"

Phoenix heard the dogs fighting, and heard the man running and throwing sticks. She even heard a gunshot. But she was slowly bending forward by that time, further and further forward, the lids stretched down over her eyes, as if she were doing this in her sleep. Her chin was lowered almost to her knees. The yellow palm of her hand came out from the fold of her apron. Her fingers slid down and along the ground under the piece of money with the grace and care they would have in lifting an egg from under a setting hen. Then she slowly straightened up, she stood erect, and the nickel was in her apron pocket. A bird flew by. Her lips moved. "God watching me the whole time. I come to stealing."

The man came back, and his own dog panted about them. "Well, I scared him off that time," he said, and then he laughed and lifted his gun and pointed it at Phoenix.

She stood straight and faced him.

"Doesn't the gun scare you?" he said, still pointing it.

"No, sir. I seen plenty go off closer by, in my day, and for less than what I done," she said, holding utterly still.

He smiled, and shouldered the gun. "Well, Granny," he said, "you must be a hundred years old, and scared of nothing. I'd give you a dime if I had any money with me. But you take my advice and stay home, and nothing will happen to you."

"I bound to go on my way, mister," said Phoenix. She inclined her head in the red rag. Then they went in different directions, but she could hear the gun shooting again and again over the hill.

She walked on. The shadows hung from the oak trees to the road like curtains. Then she smelled wood-smoke, and smelled the river, and she saw a steeple and the cabins on their steep steps. Dozens of little black children whirled around her. There ahead was Natchez shining. Bells were ringing. She walked on.

In the paved city it was Christmas time. There were red and green electric lights strung and crisscrossed everywhere, and all turned on in the daytime. Old Phoenix would have been lost if she had not distrusted her eyesight and depended on her feet to know where to take her.

She paused quietly on the sidewalk where people were passing by. A lady came along in the crowd, carrying an armful of red-, green- and silver-wrapped presents; she gave off perfume like the red roses in hot summer, and Phoenix stopped her.

"Please, missy, will you lace up my shoe?" She held up her foot.

"What do you want, Grandma?"

"See my shoe," said Phoenix. "Do all right for out in the country, but wouldn't look right to go in a big building."

"Stand still then, Grandma," said the lady. She put her packages down on the sidewalk beside her and laced and tied both shoes tightly.

"Can't lace 'em with a cane," said Phoenix. "Thank you, missy. I doesn't mind asking a nice lady to tie up my shoe, when I gets out on the street."

Moving slowly and from side to side, she went into the big building, and into a tower of steps, where she walked up and around and around until her feet knew to stop.

She entered a door, and there she saw nailed up on the wall the document that had been stamped with the gold seal and framed in the gold frame, which matched the dream that was hung up in her head.

"Here I be," she said. There was a fixed and ceremonial stiffness over her body.

"A charity case, I suppose," said an attendant who sat at the desk before her.

But Phoenix only looked above her head. There was sweat on her face, the wrinkles in her skin shone like a bright net.

"Speak up, Grandma," the woman said. "What's your name? We must have your history, you know. Have you been here before? What seems to be the trouble with you?"

Old Phoenix only gave a twitch to her face as if a fly were bothering her.

"Are you deaf?" cried the attendant.

But then the nurse came in.

"Oh, that's just old Aunt Phoenix," she said. "She doesn't come for herself—she has a little grandson. She makes these trips just as regular as clockwork. She lives away back off the Old Natchez Trace." She bent down. "Well, Aunt Phoenix, why don't you just take a seat? We won't keep you standing after your long trip." She pointed.

The old woman sat down, bolt upright in the chair.

"Now, how is the boy?" asked the nurse.

Old Phoenix did not speak.

"I said, how is the boy?"

But Phoenix only waited and stared straight ahead, her face very solemn and withdrawn into rigidity.

"Is his throat any better?" asked the nurse. "Aunt Phoenix, don't you hear me? Is your grandson's throat any better since the last time you came for the medicine?"

With her hands on her knees, the old woman waited, silent, erect and motionless, just as if she were in armor.

"You mustn't take up our time this way, Aunt Phoenix," the nurse said. "Tell us quickly about your grandson, and get it over. He isn't dead, is he?"

At last there came a flicker and then a flame of comprehension across her face, and she spoke.

"My grandson. It was my memory had left me. There I sat and forgot why I made my long trip."

"Forgot?" The nurse frowned. "After you came so far?"

Then Phoenix was like an old woman begging a dignified forgiveness for waking up frightened in the night. "I never did go to school, I was too old at the Surrender," she said in a soft voice. "I'm an old woman without an education. It was my memory fail me. My little grandson, he is just the same, and I forgot it in the coming."

"Throat never heals, does it?" said the nurse, speaking in a loud, sure voice to Old Phoenix. By now she had a card with something written on it, a little list. "Yes. Swallowed lye. When was it?—January—two-three years ago—"

Phoenix spoke unasked now. "No, missy, he not dead, he just the same. Every little while his throat begin to close up again, and he not able to swallow. He not get his breath. He not able to help himself. So the time come around, and I go on another trip for the soothing medicine."

"All right. The doctor said as long as you came to get it, you could have it," said the nurse. "But it's an obstinate case."

"My little grandson, he sit up there in the house all wrapped up, waiting by himself," Phoenix went on. "We is the only two left in the world. He suffer and it don't seem to put him back at all. He got a sweet look. He going to last. He wear a little patch quilt and peep out holding his mouth open like a little bird. I remembers so plain now. I not going to forget him again, no, the whole enduring time. I could tell him from all the others in creation."

"All right." The nurse was trying to hush her now. She brought her a bottle of medicine. "Charity," she said, making a check mark in a book.

Old Phoenix held the bottle close to her eyes, and then carefully put it into her pocket.

"I thank you," she said.

"It's Christmas time, Grandma," said the attendant. "Could I give you a few pennies out of my purse?"

"Five pennies is a nickel," said Phoenix stiffly.

"Here's a nickel," said the attendant.

Phoenix rose carefully and held out her hand. She received the nickel and then fished the other nickel out of her pocket and laid it beside the new one. She stared at her palm closely, with her head on one side.

Then she gave a tap with her cane on the floor.

"This is what come to me to do," she said. "I going to the store and buy my child a little windmill they sells, made out of paper. He going to find it hard to believe there such a thing in the world. I'll march myself back where he waiting, holding it straight up in this hand."

She lifted her free hand, gave a little nod, turned around, and walked out of the doctor's office. Then her slow step began on the stairs, going down.

# comments and criticism

# Introduction

The following essays are critical statements that offer insight into and direction and guidance for greater understanding of either the technical aspects of the genre or the stories themselves. The pieces by Booth and Ellison deal chiefly with the craft of fiction, one speaking as artist, the other as critic. What emerges from the Ellison interview is Ellison's sense of himself as a craftsman and his concept of the nature of his art; he sees fiction as communication provided through form and through "the systems of values, the beliefs and customs and sense of the past, and that hope for the future which have evolved through the history of the republic." Booth, writing as critic and, in one sense, historian, is looking on, in contrast to Ellison, from the outside; and his close and detailed study of narrative devices in fiction is an example of a lucid and authoritative analysis. Booth's critical ability is especially evident in his avoidance of simplistic statements and his definitive examples of the techniques he is discussing and examining. One can readily understand why John Crowe Ransom, the distinguished critic and author, was prompted to write of *The Rhetoric of Fiction,* from which "Types of Narration" is taken: "I do not imagine that there is another critic in the field . . . who can handle the complex of methods so easily and yet so subtly." Ease and subtlety are indeed distinctive virtues of Booth's criticism.

The other four essays concentrate on individual stories. Each is an example of how a reader can "enter" a story so that he can arrive at deeper understanding of its significance and come to a fuller appreciation of the way art and thematic statement are brought together by the author. By calling attention to the artistic design of the story and by stressing those devices that Eudora Welty employs to underline the "total meaning," Neil Isaacs is carrying out the critic's role as mediator between author and reader, a role especially needful in the case of an author as complex and as allusive as Eudora Welty. His critical examination of the manner in which the author utilizes the Christian nature-myth and a "miniature nature-myth" of her own devising increases the reader's reward and pleasure from "A Worn Path." Blyden Jackson's comments on Richard Wright also add to the reader's understanding and appreciation of "Big Boy Leaves Home." Jackson's long interest in black literature and his detailed knowledge of Wright make his account of the genesis of Wright's story and his critical comments on the theme both perceptive and convincing, especially in his analysis of what some have seen as Wright's "conscious intent" and what Jackson sees as the ultimate significance of the "inherent form and content" of "Big Boy Leaves Home."

The two essays on Hardy's "The Three Strangers," besides offering two possible entries into the story, illustrate how critics can disagree with grace and reasonableness. O'Connor's essay is an explication of the various levels on which a story may operate; it is also a useful explanation of the way an author uses various technical devices in the process of creating a work of art. Roberts' critical disagreement is directly concerned with the problem of how a story may be approached. In his refutation of O'Connor's "forced" reading, Roberts stresses Hardy's use of a well-known legend and emphasizes the background and atmosphere of Hardy country; instead of a "refutation," however, Roberts in fact complements O'Connor's approach to the story.

# TYPES OF NARRATION

## Wayne Booth

We have seen that the author cannot choose to avoid rhetoric; he can choose only the kind of rhetoric he will employ. He cannot choose whether or not to affect his readers' evaluations by his choice of narrative manner; he can only choose whether to do it well or poorly. As dramatists have always known, even the purest of dramas is not purely dramatic in the sense of being entirely presented, entirely shown as taking place in the moment. There are always what Dryden called "relations" to be taken care of, and try as the author may to ignore the troublesome fact, "some parts of the action are more fit to be represented, some to be related."[1] But related by whom? The dramatist must decide, and the

---

[1] *An Essay of Dramatic Poesy* (1668). Though this quotation comes from Lisideius, in his defense of French drama, and not from Neander, who seems to speak more nearly for Dryden, the position is taken for granted in Neander's reply; the only dispute is over *which* parts are more fit to be represented.

novelist's case is different only in that the choices open to him are more numerous.

If we think through the many narrative devices in the fiction we know, we soon come to a sense of the embarrassing inadequacy of our traditional classification of "point of view" into three or four kinds, variables only of the "person" and the degree of omniscience. If we name over three or four of the great narrators—say Cervantes' Cid Hamete Benengeli, Tristram Shandy, the "I" of *Middlemarch,* and Strether, through whose vision most of *The Ambassadors* comes to us, we realize that to describe any of them with terms like "first-person" and "omniscient" tells us nothing about how they differ from each other, or why they succeed while others described in the same terms fail.[2] It should be worth our while, then, to attempt a richer tabulation of the forms the author's voice can take. . . .

Perhaps the most overworked distinction is that of person. To say that a story is told in the first or the third person[3] will tell us nothing of importance unless we become more precise and describe how the particular qualities of the narrators relate to specific effects. It is true that choice of the first person is sometimes unduly limiting; if the "I" has inadequate access to necessary information, the author may be led into improbabilities. And there are other effects that may dictate a choice in some cases. But we can hardly expect to find useful criteria in a distinction that throws all fiction into two, or at most three, heaps. In this pile we see *Henry Esmond,* "A Cask of Amontillado," *Gulliver's Travels,* and *Tristram Shandy.* In that, we have *Vanity Fair, Tom Jones, The Ambassadors,* and *Brave New World.* But in *Vanity Fair* and *Tom Jones* the commentary is in the first person, often resembling more the intimate effect of *Tristram Shandy* than that of many third-person works. And again, the effect of *The Ambassadors* is much closer to that of the great first-person novels, since Strether in large part "narrates" his own story, even though he is always referred to in the third person.

Further evidence that this distinction is less important than has often

---

[2] There is no point in listing any of the conventional classifications here in order to reject them. They range from the simplest and least useful, in a clever popular essay by C. E. Montague (" 'Sez 'e' or 'Thinks 'e,' " *A Writer's Notes on His Trade* [London, 1930; Pelican ed., 1952], pp. 34–35) to the valuable study by Norman Friedman ("Point of View," *PMLA,* LXX [December, 1955], 1160–84).

[3] Efforts to use the second person have never been very successful, but it is astonishing how little real difference even this choice makes. When I am told, at the beginning of a book, "You have put your left foot. . . . You slide through the narrow opening. . . . Your eyes are only half open . . . ," the radical unnaturalness is, it is true, distracting for a time. But in reading Michel Butor's *La Modification* (Paris, 1957), from which this opening comes, it is surprising how quickly one is absorbed into the illusory "present" of the story, identifying one's vision with the "vous" almost as fully as with the "I" and "he" in other stories.

been claimed is seen in the fact that all of the following functional distinctions apply to both first- and third-person narration alike.

Perhaps the most important differences in narrative effect depend on whether the narrator is dramatized in his own right and on whether his beliefs and characteristics are shared by the author.

The *implied author* (the author's "second self")—Even the novel in which no narrator is dramatized creates an implicit picture of an author who stands behind the scenes, whether as stage manager, as puppeteer, or as an indifferent God, silently paring his fingernails. This implied author is always distinct from the "real man"—whatever we may take him to be—who creates a superior version of himself, a "second self," as he creates his work.[4]

In so far as a novel does not refer directly to this author, there will be no distinction between him and the implied, undramatized narrator; in Hemingway's "The Killers," for example, there is no narrator other than the implicit second self that Hemingway creates as he writes.

*Undramatized narrators*—Stories are usually not so rigorously impersonal as "The Killers"; most tales are presented as passing through the consciousness of a teller, whether an "I" or a "he." Even in drama much of what we are given is narrated by someone, and we are often as much interested in the effect on the narrator's own mind and heart as we are in learning what *else* the author has to tell us. When Horatio tells of his first encounter with the ghost in *Hamlet*, his own character, though never mentioned, is important to us as we listen. In fiction, as soon as we encounter an "I," we are conscious of an experiencing mind whose views of the experience will come between us and the event. When there is no such "I," as in "The Killers," the inexperienced reader may make the mistake of thinking that the story comes to him unmediated. But no such mistake can be made from the moment that the author explicitly places a narrator into the tale, even if he is given no personal characteristics whatever.

*Dramatized narrators*—In a sense even the most reticent narrator has been dramatized as soon as he refers to himself as "I," or, like Flaubert, tells us that "we" were in the classroom when Charles Bovary entered. But many novels dramatize their narrators with great fullness, making them into characters who are as vivid as those they tell us about (*Tristram Shandy, Remembrance of Things Past, Heart of Darkness, Dr. Faustus*). In such works the narrator is often radically different from the implied author who creates him. The range of human types that have been dramatized as narrators is almost as great as the range of other fictional characters—one must say "almost" because there are some

---

[4] A fine account of the subtleties that underlie the seemingly simple relations between real authors and the selves they create as they write can be found in "Makers and Persons," by Patrick Cruttwell, *Hudson Review*, XII (Winter, 1959–60), 487–507.

characters who are not fully qualified to narrate or "reflect" a story (Faulkner can use the idiot for *part* of his novel only because the other three parts exist to set off and clarify the idiot's jumble).

We should remind ourselves that many dramatized narrators are never explicitly labeled as narrators at all. In a sense, every speech, every gesture, narrates; most works contain disguised narrators who are used to tell the audience what it needs to know, while seeming merely to act out their roles.

Though disguised narrators of this kind are seldom labeled so explicitly as God in Job, they often speak with an authority as sure as God's. Messengers returning to tell what the oracle said, wives trying to convince their husbands that the business deal is unethical, old family retainers expostulating with wayward scions—these often have more effect on us than on their official auditors; the king goes ahead with his obstinate search, the husband carries out his deal, the hell-bound youth goes on toward hell as if nothing had been said, but we know what we know —and as surely as if the author himself or his official narrator had told us. "She's laughing at you to your face, brother," Cleante says to Orgon in *Tartuffe,* "and frankly, without meaning to anger you, I must say she's quite right. Has there ever been the like of such a whim? . . . You must be mad, brother, I swear." [5] And in tragedy there is usually a chorus, a friend, or even a forthright villain, to speak truth in contrast to the tragic mistakes of the hero.

The most important unacknowledged narrators in modern fiction are the third-person "centers of consciousness" through whom authors have filtered their narratives. Whether such "reflectors," as James sometimes called them, are highly polished mirrors reflecting complex mental experience, or the rather turbid, sense-bound "camera eyes" of much fiction since James, they fill precisely the function of avowed narrators— though they *can* add intensities of their own.

> Gabriel had not gone to the door with the others. He was in a dark part of the hall gazing up the staircase. A woman was standing near the top of the first flight, in the shadow also. He could not see her face but he could see the terracotta and salmon-pink panels of her skirt which the shadow made appear black and white. It was his wife. She was leaning on the banisters, listening to something. . . . He asked himself what is a woman standing on the stairs in the shadow, listening to distant music, a symbol of [Joyce's "The Dead"].

The very real advantages of this method, for some purposes, have provided a dominant theme in modern criticism. Indeed, so long as our attention is on such qualities as naturalness and vividness, the advantages seem overwhelming. Only as we break out of the fashionable assumption that all good fiction tries for the same kind of vivid illusion in the same

---

[5] From an unpublished translation by Marcel Gutwirth.

way are we forced to recognize disadvantages. The third-person reflector is only one mode among many, suitable for some effects but cumbersome and even harmful when other effects are desired.

Among dramatized narrators there are mere observers (the "I" of *Tom Jones, The Egoist, Troilus and Criseyde*), and there are narrator-agents, who produce some measurable effect on the course of events (ranging from the minor involvement of Nick in *The Great Gatsby,* through the extensive give-and-take of Marlow in *Heart of Darkness*,[6] to the central role of Tristram Shandy, Moll Flanders, Huckleberry Finn, and—in the third person—Paul Morel in *Sons and Lovers*). Clearly, any rules we might discover about observers may not apply to narrator-agents, yet the distinction is seldom made in talk about point of view (chap. xii).

All narrators and observers, whether first or third person, can relay their tales to us primarily as scene ("The Killers," *The Awkward Age*, the works of Ivy Compton-Burnett and Henry Green), primarily as summary or what Lubbock called "picture" (Addison's almost completely non-scenic tales in *The Spectator*), or, most commonly, as a combination of the two.

Like Aristotle's distinction between dramatic and narrative manners, the somewhat different modern distinction between showing and telling does cover the ground. But the trouble is that it pays for broad coverage with gross imprecision. Narrators of all shapes and shades must either report dialogue alone or support it with "stage directions" and description of setting. But when we think of the radically different effect of a scene reported by Huck Finn and a scene reported by Poe's Montresor, we see that the quality of being "scenic" suggests very little about literary effect. And compare the delightful summary of twelve years given in two pages of *Tom Jones* (Book III, chap. i) with the tedious showing of even ten minutes of uncurtailed conversation in the hands of a Sartre when he allows his passion for "durational realism" to dictate a scene when summary is called for. The contrast between scene and summary, between showing and telling, is likely to be of little use until we specify the kind of narrator who is providing the scene or the summary.

Narrators who allow themselves to tell as well as show vary greatly depending on the amount and kind of commentary allowed in addition

---

[6] For a careful interpretation of the development and functions of Marlow in Conrad's works, see W. Y. Tindall, "Apology for Marlow," in *From Jane Austen to Joseph Conrad*, ed. Robert C. Rathburn and Martin Steinmann, Jr. (Minneapolis, Minn., 1958), pp. 274–85. Though Marlow is often himself a victim of Conrad's ironies, he is generally a reliable reflector of the clarities and ambiguities of the implied author. A much fuller treatment, and a remarkable work for an undergraduate, is James L. Guetti, Jr., *The Rhetoric of Joseph Conrad* ("Amherst College Honors Thesis," No. 2 [Amherst, Mass., 1960]).

to a direct relating of events in scene and summary. Such commentary can, of course, range over any aspect of human experience, and it can be related to the main business in innumerable ways and degrees. To treat it as a single device is to ignore important differences between commentary that is merely ornamental, commentary that serves a rhetorical purpose but is not part of the dramatic structure, and commentary that is integral to the dramatic structure, as in *Tristram Shandy*.

Cutting across the distinction between observers and narrator-agents of all these kinds is the distinction between *self-conscious narrators*, aware of themselves as writers (*Tom Jones, Tristram Shandy, Barchester Towers, The Catcher in the Rye, Remembrance of Things Past, Dr. Faustus*), and narrators or observers who rarely if ever discuss their writing chores (*Huckleberry Finn*) or who seem unaware that they are writing, thinking, speaking, or "reflecting" a literary work (Camus' *The Stranger*, Lardner's "Haircut," Bellow's *The Victim*).

Whether or not they are involved in the action as agents or as sufferers, narrators and third-person reflectors differ markedly according to the degree and kind of distance that separates them from the author, the reader, and the other characters of the story. In any reading experience there is an implied dialogue among author, narrator, the other characters, and the reader. Each of the four can range, in relation to each of the others, from identification to complete opposition, on any axis of value, moral, intellectual, aesthetic, and even physical. (Does the reader who stammers react to the stammering of H. C. Earwicker as I do? Surely not.) The elements usually discussed under "aesthetic distance" enter in of course; distance in time and space, differences of social class or conventions of speech or dress—these and many others serve to control our sense that we are dealing with an aesthetic object, just as the paper moons and other unrealistic stage effects of some modern drama have had an "alienation" effect. But we must not confuse these with the equally important effects of personal beliefs and qualities, in author, reader, narrator, and all others in the cast of characters.

1. The *narrator* may be more or less distant from the *implied author*. The distance may be moral (Jason vs. Faulkner, the barber vs. Lardner, the narrator vs. Fielding in *Jonathan Wild*). It may be intellectual (Twain and Huck Finn, Sterne and Tristram Shandy on the influence of noses, Richardson and Clarissa). It may be physical or temporal: most authors are distant from even the most knowing narrator in that they presumably know how "everything turns out in the end." And so on.

2. The *narrator* also may be more or less distant from the *characters* in the story he tells. He may differ morally, intellectually, and temporally (the mature narrator and his younger self in *Great Expectations* or *Redburn*); morally and intellectually (Fowler the narrator and Pyle the

American in Greene's *The Quiet American,* both departing radically from the author's norms but in different directions); morally and emotionally (Maupassant's "The Necklace," and Huxley's "Nuns at Luncheon," in which the narrators affect less emotional involvement than Maupassant and Huxley clearly expect from the reader); and thus on through every possible trait.

3. The *narrator* may be more or less distant from the *reader's* own norms; for example, physically and emotionally (Kafka's *The Metamorphosis*); morally and emotionally (Pinkie in *Brighton Rock,* the miser in Mauriac's *Knot of Vipers,* and the many other moral degenerates that modern fiction has managed to make into convincing human beings).

With the repudiation of omniscient narration, and in the face of inherent limitations in dramatized reliable narrators, it is hardly surprising that modern authors have experimented with unreliable narrators whose characteristics change in the course of the works they narrate. Ever since Shakespeare taught the modern world what the Greeks had overlooked in neglecting character change (compare *Macbeth* and *Lear* with *Oedipus*), stories of character development or degeneration have become more and more popular. But it was not until authors had discovered the full uses of the third-person reflector that they could effectively show a narrator changing *as he narrates.* The mature Pip, in *Great Expectations,* is presented as a generous man whose heart is where the reader's is supposed to be; he watches his young self move away from the reader, as it were, and then back again. But the third-person reflector can be shown, technically in the past tense but in effect present before our eyes, moving toward or away from values that the reader holds dear. Authors in the twentieth century have proceeded almost as if determined to work out all of the possible plot forms based on such shifts: start far and end near; start near, move far, and end near; start far and move farther; and so on. Perhaps the most characteristic, however, have been the astonishing achievements in the first of these, taking extremely unsympathetic characters like Faulkner's Mink Snopes and transforming them, both through character change and technical manipulation, into characters of dignity and power. We badly need thoroughgoing studies of the various plot forms that have resulted from this kind of shifting distance.

4. The *implied author* may be more or less distant from the *reader.* The distance may be intellectual (the implied author of *Tristram Shandy,* not of course to be identified with Tristram, more interested in and knowing more about recondite classical lore than any of his readers), moral (the works of Sade), or aesthetic. From the author's viewpoint, a successful reading of his book must eliminate all distance between the essential norms of his implied author and the norms of the postulated reader. Often enough, there is very little fundamental distance to begin with; Jane Austen does not have to convince us that pride and prejudice

are undesirable. A bad book, on the other hand, is often most clearly recognizable because the implied author asks that we judge according to norms that we cannot accept.

5. The *implied author* (carrying the reader with him) may be more or less distant from *other characters*. Again, the distance can be on any axis of value. Some successful authors keep most of their characters very far "away" in every respect (Ivy Compton-Burnett), and they may work very deliberately, as William Empson says of T. F. Powys, to maintain an artificiality that will keep their characters "at a great distance from the author."[7] Others present a wider range from far to near, on a variety of axes. Jane Austen, for example, presents a broad range of moral judgment (from the almost complete approval of Jane Fairfax in *Emma* to the contempt for Wickham in *Pride and Prejudice*), of wisdom (from Knightley to Miss Bates or Mrs. Bennet), of taste, of tact, of sensibility.

It is obvious that on each of these scales my examples do not begin to cover the possibilities. What we call "involvement" or "sympathy" or "identification," is usually made up of many reactions to author, narrators, observers, and other characters. And narrators may differ from their authors or readers in various kinds of involvement or detachment, ranging from deep personal concern (Nick in *The Great Gatsby,* MacKellar in *The Master of Ballantrae,* Zeitblom in *Dr. Faustus*) to a bland or mildly amused or merely curious detachment (Waugh's *Decline and Fall*).

For practical criticism probably the most important of these kinds of distance is that between the fallible or unreliable narrator and the implied author who carries the reader with him in judging the narrator. If the reason for discussing point of view is to find how it relates to literary effects, then surely the moral and intellectual qualities of the narrator are more important to our judgment than whether he is referred to as "I" or "he," or whether he is privileged or limited. If he is discovered to be untrustworthy, then the total effect of the work he relays to us is transformed.

Our terminology for this kind of distance in narrators is almost hopelessly inadequate. For lack of better terms, I have called a narrator *reliable* when he speaks for or acts in accordance with the norms of the work (which is to say, the implied author's norms), *unreliable* when he does not. It is true that most of the great reliable narrators indulge in large amounts of incidental irony, and they are thus "unreliable" in the sense of being potentially deceptive. But difficult irony is not sufficient to make a narrator unreliable. Nor is unreliability ordinarily a matter of lying, although deliberately deceptive narrators have been a major re-

---

[7] *Some Versions of Pastoral* (London, 1935), p. 7. For an excellent discussion of Powys' deliberate artificiality, see Martin Steinmann's "The Symbolism of T. F. Powys," *Critique,* I (Summer, 1957), 49–63.

source of some modern novelists (Camus' *The Fall*, Calder Willingham's *Natural Child*, etc.).[8] It is most often a matter of what James calls *inconscience*; the narrator is mistaken, or he believes himself to have qualities which the author denies him. Or, as in *Huckleberry Finn*, the narrator claims to be naturally wicked while the author silently praises his virtues behind his back.

Unreliable narrators thus differ markedly depending on how far and in what direction they depart from their author's norms; the older term "tone," like the currently fashionable terms "irony" and "distance," covers many effects that we should distinguish. Some narrators, like Barry Lyndon, are placed as far "away" from author and reader as possible, in respect to every virtue except a kind of interesting vitality. Some, like Fleda Vetch, the reflector in James's *The Spoils of Poynton*, come close to representing the author's ideal of taste, judgment, and moral sense. All of them make stronger demands on the reader's powers of inference than do reliable narrators.

Both reliable and unreliable narrators can be unsupported or uncorrected by other narrators (Gully Jimson in *The Horse's Mouth*, Henderson in Bellow's *Henderson the Rain King*) or supported or corrected (*The Master of Ballantrae*, *The Sound and the Fury*). Sometimes it is almost impossible to infer whether or to what degree a narrator is fallible; sometimes explicit corroborating or conflicting testimony makes the inference easy. Support or correction differs radically, it should be noted, depending on whether it is provided from within the action, so that the narrator-agent might benefit from it in sticking to the right line or in changing his own views (Faulkner's *Intruder in the Dust*), or is simply provided externally, to help the reader correct or reinforce his own views as against the narrator's (Graham Greene's *The Power and the Glory*). Obviously, the effects of isolation will be extremely different in the two cases.

Observers and narrator-agents, whether self-conscious or not, reliable or not, commenting or silent, isolated or supported, can be either privileged to know what could not be learned by strictly natural means or

---

[8] Alexander E. Jones in a recent essay argued convincingly for a "straight" reading of *The Turn of the Screw*, offering as one reason that "the basic convention of first-person fiction is necessarily a confidence in the narrator. . . . Unless James has violated the basic rules of his craft, the governess cannot be a pathological liar" (*PMLA*, LXXIV [March, 1959], 122). Whatever may have been true in James's time, it is clear that in modern fiction there is no longer any such convention. The only convention that can be relied on, as I show in chapter eleven, is that if a narrator presents himself as speaking or writing to the reader, he really is doing so. The content of what he says *may* turn out to be dream (Schwartz's "In Dreams Begin Responsibilities"), or falsehood (Jean Cayrol's *Les corps étrangers*), or it may not "turn out" at all—that is, it may be left indeterminately between dream, falsehood, fantasy, and reality (Unamuno's *Mist*, Beckett's *Comment c'est*).

limited to realistic vision and inference. Complete privilege is what we usually call omniscience. But there are many kinds of privilege, and very few "omniscient" narrators are allowed to know or show as much as their authors know.

We need a good study of the varieties of privilege and limitation and their function. Some limitations are only temporary, or even playful, like the ignorance Fielding sometimes imposes on his "I," as when he doubts his own powers of narration and invokes the Muses for aid (*Tom Jones*, Book XIII, chap. i). Some are more nearly permanent but subject to momentary relaxation, like the generally limited, humanly realistic Ishmael in *Moby Dick*, who can yet break through his human limitations when the story requires ("'He waxes brave, but nevertheless obeys; most careful bravery that!' murmured Ahab"—with no one present to report to the narrator). And some are confined to what their literal condition would allow them to know (first person, Huck Finn; third person, Miranda and Laura in Katherine Anne Porter's stories).

The most important single privilege is that of obtaining an inside view of another character, because of the rhetorical power that such a privilege conveys upon a narrator. There is a curious ambiguity in the term "omniscience." Many modern works that we usually classify as narrated dramatically, with everything relayed to us through the limited views of the characters, postulate fully as much omniscience in the silent author as Fielding claims for himself. Our roving visitation into the minds of sixteen characters in Faulkner's *As I Lay Dying*, seeing nothing but what those minds contain, may seem in one sense not to depend on an omniscient author. But this method is omniscience with teeth in it: the implied author demands our absolute faith in his powers of divination. We must never for a moment doubt that he knows everything about each of these sixteen minds or that he has chosen correctly how much to show of each. In short, impersonal narration is really no escape from omniscience—the true author is as "unnaturally" all-knowing as he ever was. If evident artificiality were a fault—which it is not—modern narration would be as faulty as Trollope's.

Another way of suggesting the same ambiguity is to look closely at the concept of "dramatic" storytelling. The author can present his characters in a dramatic situation without in the least presenting them in what we normally think of as a dramatic manner. When Joseph Andrews, who has been stripped and beaten by thieves, is overtaken by a stage-coach, Fielding presents the scene in what by some modern standards must seem an inconsistent and undramatic mode. "The poor wretch, who lay motionless a long time, just began to recover his senses as a stage-coach came by. The postilion, hearing a man's groans, stopped his horses, and told the coachman, he was certain there was a dead man lying in the ditch. . . . A lady, who heard what the postilion said, and likewise heard the groan, called eagerly to the coachman to stop and see what was the matter. Upon which he bid the postilion alight, and look into the ditch. He did so, and returned, 'That there was a man sitting upright, as naked as ever he was born.'" There follows a splendid description, hardly meriting the name of scene, in which are recorded the selfish reactions of each passenger. A young lawyer points out that they might be legally liable if they refuse to take Joseph up. "These words had a sensible effect on the coachman, who was well acquainted with the person who spoke them; and the old gentleman above mentioned, thinking the naked man would afford him frequent opportunities of showing his wit to the lady, offered to join with the company in giving a mug of beer for his fare; till, partly alarmed by the threats of the one, and partly by the promises of the other, and being perhaps a little moved with compassion at the poor creature's condition, who stood bleeding and shivering with the cold, he at length agreed." Once Joseph is in the coach, the same kind of indirect reporting of the "scene" continues, with frequent excursions, however superficial, into the minds and hearts of the assembly of fools and knaves, and occasional guesses when complete knowledge seems inadvisable. If to be dramatic is to show characters dramatically engaged with each other, motive clashing with motive, the outcome depending upon the resolution of motives, then this scene is dramatic. But if it is to give the impression that the story is taking place by itself, with the characters existing in a dramatic relationship vis-à-vis the spectator, unmediated by a narrator and decipherable only through inferential matching of word to word and word to deed, then this is a relatively undramatic scene.

On the other hand, an author can present a character in this latter kind of dramatic relationship with the reader without involving that character in any internal drama at all. Many lyric poems are dramatic in this sense and undramatic in any other. "That is no country for old men—" Who says? Yeats, or his "mask," says. To whom? To us. How do we know that it is Yeats and not some character as remote from him as Caliban is remote from Browning in "Caliban upon Setebos"? We infer it as the dramatized statement unfolds; the need for the inference is what makes the lyric dramatic in this sense. Caliban, in short, is dramatic in two senses; he is in a dramatic situation with other characters, and he is in a dramatic situation over against us. Yeats's poem is dramatic in only one sense.

The ambiguities of the word dramatic are even more complicated in fiction that attempts to dramatize states of consciousness directly. Is *A Portrait of the Artist as a Young Man* dramatic? In some respects, yes. We are not told about Stephen. He is placed on the stage before us, acting out his destiny with only disguised helps or comments from his author. But it is not his actions that are dramatized directly, not his speech that we hear unmediated. What is dramatized is his mental record of everything that happens. We see his consciousness at work on the world. Sometimes what it records is itself dramatic, as when Stephen observes himself in a scene with other characters. But the report itself, the internal record, is dramatic in the second sense only. The report we are given of what goes on in Stephen's mind is a monologue uninvolved in any modifying dramatic context. And it is an infallible report, even less subject to critical doubts than the typical Elizabethan soliloquy. We accept, by convention, the claim that what is reported as going on in Stephen's mind really goes on there, or in other words, that Joyce knows how Stephen's mind works. "The equation of the page of his scribbler began to spread out a widening tail, eyed and starred like a peacock's; and, when the eyes and stars of its indices had been eliminated, began slowly to fold itself together again. The indices appearing and disappearing were eyes opening and closing; the eyes opening and closing were stars. . . ." Who says so? Not Stephen, but the omniscient, infallible author. The report is direct, and it is clearly unmodified by any "dramatic" context—that is, unlike a speech in a dramatic scene, it does not lead us to suspect that the thoughts have been in any way aimed at an effect. We are thus in a dramatic relation with Stephen only in a limited sense—the sense in which a lyric poem is dramatic.[9]

Finally, narrators who provide inside views differ in the depth and the axis of their plunge. Boccaccio can give inside views, but they are extremely shallow. Jane Austen goes relatively deep morally, but scarcely skims the surface psychologically. All authors of stream-of-consciousness narration presumably attempt to go deep psychologically, but some of them deliberately remain shallow in the moral dimension.[10] We should remind ourselves that any sustained inside view, of whatever depth, temporarily turns the character whose mind is shown into a narrator; inside views are thus subject to variations in all of the qualities we have described above, and most importantly in the degree of unreliability. Generally speaking, the deeper our plunge, the more unreliability we will accept without loss of sympathy.

[9] I am aware that my terminology here contrasts with Joyce's own use of the triad, *lyric, epic,* and *dramatic. Portrait* is dramatic in Joyce's sense, but in that sense only.

[10] Discussion of the many devices covered by the loose term "stream-of-consciousness" has generally concentrated on their service to psychological realism, avoiding the moral effect of different degrees of depth. Even unfriendly critics—Mauriac in *Le romancier et ses personnages* (Paris, 1933), for example—have generally pointed to their amorphousness, their lack of clear control and their obvious artifice, not to their moral implications. Too often, both attack and defense have assumed that there is a single device which can be assessed as good or bad, once and for all, for such-and-such general reasons. Melvin Friedman (*Stream of Consciousness* [New Haven, Conn., 1955]) concludes that it is "almost axiomatic that no further work of the first order can be done within this tradition," since the method depended on a "certain literary mentality which died out with Joyce, Virginia Woolf, and the early Faulkner" (p. 261). But the works he treats make use of dozens of varieties of stream-of-consciousness, some of which are now an established part of the novelist's repertory. Most of them are likely to find new uses in the future.

Narration is an art, not a science, but this does not mean that we are necessarily doomed to fail when we attempt to formulate principles about it. There are systematic elements in every art, and criticism of fiction can never avoid the responsibility of trying to explain technical successes and failures by reference to general principles. But we must always ask where the general principles are to be found.

It is not surprising to hear practicing novelists report that they have never had any help from critics about point of view. In dealing with point of view the novelist must always deal with the individual work: which particular character shall tell this particular story, or part of a story, with what precise degree of reliability, privilege, freedom to comment, and so on. Shall he be given dramatic vividness? Even if the novelist has decided on a narrator who will fit one of the critic's classifications—"omniscient," "first person," "limited omniscient," "objective," "roving," "effaced," or whatever—his troubles have just begun. He simply cannot find answers to his immediate, precise, practical problems by referring to statements such as that the "omniscient is the most flexible method," or that "the objective is the most rapid or vivid." Even the soundest of generalizations at this level will be of little use to him in his page-by-page progress through his novel.

As Henry James's detailed records show, the novelist discovers his narrative technique as he tries to achieve for his readers the potentialities of his developing idea. The majority of his choices are consequently choices of degree, not kind. To decide that your narrator shall not be omniscient decides practically nothing. The hard question is: Just how *inconscient* shall he be? Again, to decide on first-person narration settles only a part of one's problem, perhaps the easiest part. What kind of first person? How fully characterized? How much aware of himself as narrator? How reliable? How much confined to realistic inference; how far privileged to go beyond realism? At what points shall he speak truth and at what points utter no judgment or even utter falsehood? These questions can be answered only by reference to the potentialities and necessities of particular works, not by reference to fiction in general, or the novel, or rules about point of view.

There are no doubt *kinds* of effect to which the author can refer; for example, if he wants to make a scene more amusing, poignant, vivid, or ambiguous, or if he wants to make a character more sympathetic or more convincing, such-and-such practices may be indicated. But we can understand why in his search for help in his decisions, the novelist should find the practice of his peers more helpful than the abstract rules of the textbooks: the sensitive author who reads the great novels finds in them a storehouse of precise examples, of how *this* effect, as distinct from all other possible effects, was heightened by the proper narrative choice. In dealing with the types of narration, the critic must always limp behind, referring constantly to the varied practice which alone can correct his temptations to overgeneralize. In place of our modern "fourth unity," in place of abstract rules about consistency and objectivity in the use of point of view, we need more painstaking, specific accounts of how great tales are told.

---

# A COMPLETION OF PERSONALITY

**Ralph Ellison**

INTERVIEWER: John Hersey

HERSEY: About motive—what gives you the psychic energy to take on a massive work and keep at it for a very long time?
ELLISON: I guess it is the writing itself. I am terribly stubborn, and once I get engaged in that kind of project, I just have to keep going until I finally make something out of it. I don't know what the something is going to be, but the process is one through which I make a good part of my own experience meaningful. I don't mean in any easy autobiographical sense, but the matter of drawing actual experience, thought, and emotion together in a way that creates an artifact through which I can reach other people. Maybe that's vanity; I don't know. Still I believe that fiction does help create value, and I regard this as a very serious—I almost said "sacred"—function of the writer.

Psychic energy? I don't know, I think of myself as kind of lazy. And yet, I do find that working slowly, which is the only way I seem able to work—although I write fast much of the time—the problem is one of being able to receive from my work that sense of tension, that sense of high purpose being realized, that keeps me going. This is a crazy area that I don't understand—none of the Freudian explanations seem adequate.
HERSEY: As to the short range, you used a phrase last night that interested me. You said you wanted to keep the early morning free "in case the night before had generated something that could be put to good use." What did you mean by that?
ELLISON: I never know quite what has gone on in my subconscious in the night, I dream vividly, and all kinds of things happen; by morning they have fallen below the threshold again. But I like to feel that whatever takes place becomes active in some way in what I do at the typewriter.

In other words, I believe that a human being's life is of a whole, and that he lives the full twenty-four hours. And if he is a writer or an artist, what happens during the night feeds back, in some way, into what he does consciously during the day—that is, when he is doing that which is self-achieving, so to speak. Part of the pleasure of writing, as well as the pain, is involved in pouring into that thing which is being created all of what he cannot understand and cannot say and cannot deal with, or cannot even admit, in any other way. The artifact is a completion of personality.

HERSEY: Do you experience anything like daydreaming or dreaming when you are writing? Do you feel that the writing process may involve a somewhat altered state of consciousness in itself?

ELLISON: I think a writer learns to be as conscious about his craft as he can possibly be—not because this will make him absolutely lucid about what he does, but because it prepares the stage for structuring his daydreaming and allows him to draw upon the various irrational elements involved in writing. You know that when you begin to structure literary forms you are going to have to play variations on your themes, and you are going to have to make everything vivid, so that the reader can see and hear and feel and smell, and, if you're lucky, even taste. All that is on a conscious level and very, very important. But then, once you get going, strange things occur. There are things in *Invisible Man*, for instance, that I can't *imagine* my having consciously planned. They materialized as I worked consciously at other things. Take three of the speeches: the speech made at the eviction, the funeral address in Mount Morris Park, and the one that Barbee made in chapel. Now, I realized consciously, or I *discovered* as I wrote, that I was playing variations on what Otto Rank identified as the myth of the birth and death of the hero. So in the re-writing that conscious knowledge, that insight, made it possible to come back and add elements to the design which I had written myself into under the passion of telling a story.

What should also be said in this connection is that somewhere—it doesn't have to be right in the front of the mind, of the consciousness—writers, like other artists, are involved in a process of comparative culture. I looked at the copy of *The Lower Depths* on the table there this morning, and I remembered how much of Gorki I had read, and how I was always—not putting his characters into blackface, but finding equivalents for the experience he depicted; the equivalents for turns of phrase, for parables and proverbs, which existed within the various backgrounds which I knew. And I think that something of that goes on when a conscious writer goes about creating a fiction. It's part of his workshop, his possession of the culture of the form in which he works.

HERSEY: You once said that it took you a long time to learn how to adapt myth and ritual into your work. Faulkner speaks of a "lumber room of the unconscious," where old things are kept. How do you get at the sources of these things deep down in your mind?

ELLISON: I think I get at them through sheer work, converting incidents into patterns—and also by simply continuing at a thing when I don't seem to be getting anywhere. For instance, I wrote a scene in which Hickman is thinking about the difficulty of communicating with someone as constituting a "wall"; he thinks this as he is drifting off to sleep. Well, later in my work I suddenly realized that the damn wall had turned up again in another form. And that's when that voice in my unconscious finally said, "Hey, *this* is what you've been getting at." And looking back, I saw that I had worked up a little pattern of these walls. What the unconscious mind does is to put all manner of things into juxtaposition. The conscious mind has to provide the logical structure of narrative and incident through which these unconscious patterns can be allowed to radiate by throwing them into artful juxtaposition on the page.

HERSEY: Do you, as some writers do, have a sense of standing in a magic circle when you write?

ELLISON: To the extent that unexpected things occur, that characters say things, or see things which, for all my attempts to be conscious and to work out of what I call a conceptual outline, are suddenly just *there*. That *is* magical, because such things seem to emerge out of the empty air. And yet, you know that somehow the dreams, emotions, ironies, and hidden implications of your material often find ways of making themselves manifest. You work to make them reveal themselves.

HERSEY: Do you, when you are writing, sometimes find yourself so totally engaged by a character that you are carried away outside yourself by *his* feelings—are literally beside yourself?

ELLISON: I find myself carried away and emotionally moved, sometimes quite unexpectedly, and my tendency is to distrust it, feeling that perhaps I'm being sentimental, being caught in a situation which I am not adequately transforming into art. So I put it aside and wait awhile, maybe months, and then go back, and if it still works after I've examined it as well as I can, as objectively as I can, I then perhaps read it to Fanny, and if she doesn't indicate that it's slobbering sentimentality, in bad taste, or just poorly achieved—then I leave it in.

HERSEY: Would you say that, by and large, when you have had these surges of feeling the writing does hold up in the long run?

ELLISON: Sometimes it does, sometimes it doesn't. I won't be able to say about this book until it has been read by enough objective readers. I won't be able to judge until then because it has some crazy developments.

I found myself writing a scene in which Hickman and Wilhite, his deacon, go into a strange house in Washington, and find a bunch of people in the hallway who are very upset because the police won't tell them what has happened in the apartment of one of their neighbors. Then one of the women goes hysterical and pretty soon she's outraging the crowd by talking about the most personal matters as she addresses herself to a bewildered Wilhite and Hickman. Not only was I shocked to discover myself writing this unplanned scene, but I still have questions about how it functions. Yet, for all its wild, tragicomic emotion—there it is! Now when your material takes over like that you are really being pushed. Thus, when this woman started confessing, she forced *me* to think about Hickman's role as minister on a different level; I mean on the theological level; which was something I hadn't planned, since I wasn't writing an essay but a novel. Finally, Hickman came to my aid by recognizing that the woman had been unfolding a distorted and highly personalized dream-version of the immaculate birth. To me she sounded merely irrational and comic, but Hickman, being a minister, forced himself to look beneath her raving, even though she is without question a most unacceptable surrogate for the Virgin. After that, I was forced to realize that this crazy development was really tied in with the central situation of the novel: that of an old man searching throughout the years for a little boy who ran away. So I guess it sprang from that magic circle you referred to, from that amorphous level which lies somewhere between the emotions and the intellect, between the consciousness and the unconscious which supports our creative powers but which we cannot control.

HERSEY: I have wondered about the ways in which your musical experience has fed into your writing.

ELLISON: My sense of form, my basic sense of artistic form, is musical. As a boy I tried to write songs, marches, exercises in symphonic form, really before I received any training, and then I studied it. I listened constantly to music, trying to learn the processes of developing a theme, of expanding and contracting and turning it inside out, of making bridges, and working with techniques of musical continuity, and so on. I think that basically my instinctive approach to writing is through *sound*. A change of mood and mode comes to me in terms of sound. That's one part of it, in the sense of composing the architecture of a fiction.

On the other hand, one of the things I work for is to make a line of prose *sound* right, or for a bit of dialogue to fall on the page in the way I hear it, aurally, in my mind. The same goes for the sound and intonation of a character's voice. When I am writing of characters who speak in the Negro idiom, in the vernacular, it is still a real problem for me to make their accents fall in the proper place in the visual line.

HERSEY: Which comes first for you in writing, hearing or seeing?

ELLISON: I might conceive of a thing aurally, but to realize it you have got to make it vivid. The two things must operate together. What is the old phrase—"the planned dislocation of the senses"? That *is* the condition of fiction, I think. Here is where sound becomes sight and sight becomes sound, and where sign becomes symbol and symbol becomes sign; where fact and idea must not just be hanging there but must become a functioning part of the total design, involving itself in the reader as idea as well as drama. You do this by providing the reader with as much detail as is possible in terms of the visual *and* the aural, *and* the rhythmic—to allow him to involve himself, to attach himself, and then begin to collaborate in the creation of the fictional spell. Because you simply cannot put it all there on the page, you can only evoke it—or evoke what is already there, implicitly, in the reader's head: his sense of life.

HERSEY: You mentioned "making bridges" a minute ago. I remember that you once said that your anxiety about transitions greatly prolonged the writing of *Invisible Man*.

ELLISON: Yes, that has continued to be something of a problem. I try to tell myself that it is irrational, but it is what happens when you're making something, and you know that you are *making* something rather than simply relating an anecdote that actually happened. But at the same time you have to strike a balance between that which you can imply and that which you must make explicit, so that the reader can follow you. One source of this anxiety comes, I think, from my sense of the variations in American backgrounds—especially as imposed by the racial situation. I can't always be certain that what I write is going to be understood. Now, this doesn't mean that I am writing for whites, but that I realize that as an American writer I have a problem of communicating across our various social divisions, whether of race, class, education, region, or religion—and much of this holds true even within my own racial group. It's dangerous to take things for granted.

This reminds me of something that happened out at a northwestern university. A young white professor said to me, "Mr. Ellison, how does it feel to be able to go to places where most Negroes can't go?" Before I could think to be polite I answered, "What you mean is: 'How does it feel to be able to go places where most *white* men can't go?'" He was shocked and turned red, and I was embarrassed; nevertheless, it was a teaching situation so I told him the truth. I wanted him to understand that individuality is still operative beyond the racial structuring of American society. And that, conversely, there are many areas of black society that are closed to *me* while open to certain whites. Friendship and shared interests make the difference.

When you are writing fiction out of your individual sense of American life it's difficult to know what to take for granted. For instance, I don't know whether I can simply refer to an element of decor and communicate the social values it stands for, because so much depends upon the way a reader makes associations. I am more confident in such matters than I was when writing *Invisible Man,* but for such an allusion—say, to a certain type of chair or vase or painting—to function, the reader must not be allowed to limit his understanding of what is implied simply because the experience you are presenting is, in its immediate sense, that of blacks. So the writer must be aware that the reality of race conceals a complex of manners and culture. Because such matters influence the shaping of fictional form and govern, to a large extent, the writer's sense of proportion, and determine what he feels obligated to render as well as what he feels he can simply imply.

I had to learn, for instance, that in dramatic scenes, if you got the reader going along with your own rhythm, you could omit any number of explanations. You could leave great gaps, because in his sense of urgency the reader would say, "Hell, don't waste time telling me how many steps he walked to get there, I want to know what he *did* once he got there!" An ellipsis was possible and the reader would fill the gap.

Still, I have uncertainty about some of the things I'm doing, and especially when I'm using more than one main voice, and with a time scheme that is much more fragmented than in *Invisible Man.* There I was using a more tidy dramatic form. This novel is dramatic within its incidents, but it moves back and forth in time. In such a case I guess an act of faith is necessary, a faith that if what you are writing is of social and artistic importance and its diverse parts are presented vividly in the light of its overall conception, and if you *render* the story rather than just tell it, then the reader will go along. That's a lot of 'ifs,' but if you can involve him in the process his reading becomes a pleasurable act of discovery.

HERSEY: Do you have in mind an image of some actualized reader to whom you are communicating as you write?

ELLISON: There is no *specific* person there, but there is a sort of ideal reader, or informed persona, who has some immediate sense of the material that I'm working with. Beyond that there is my sense of the rhetorical levers within American society, and these attach to all kinds of experiences and values. I don't want to be a behaviorist here, but I'm referring to the systems of values, the beliefs and customs and sense of the past, and that hope for the future which have evolved through the history of the republic. These do provide a medium of communication.

For instance, the old underdog pattern. It turns up in many guises, and it allows the writer to communicate with the public over and beyond whatever the immediate issues of his fiction happen to be. That is, deep down we believe in the underdog, even though we give him hell; and this provides a rhetoric through which the writer can communicate with a reader beyond any questions of their disagreements over class values, race, or anything else. But the writer must be aware that that is what is there. On the other hand, I do not think he can manipulate his readers too directly; it must be an oblique process, if for no other reason than that to do it too directly throws you into propaganda, as against that brooding, questioning stance that is necessary for fiction.

HERSEY: How much is anger a motive force for novelists of all kinds? Does the artist start with anger more than with other emotions?

ELLISON: I don't think that he necessarily starts with anger. Indeed, anger can get in the way, as it does for a fighter. If the writer starts with anger, then if he is truly writing he immediately translates it through his craft into consciousness, and thus into understanding, into insight, perception. Perhaps, that's where the morality of fiction lies. You see a situation which outrages you, but as you write about the characters who embody that which outrages, your sense of craft and the moral role of your craft demands that you depict those characters in the breadth of their humanity. You try to give them the density of the human rather than the narrow intensity of the demonic. That means that you try to delineate them as men and women who possess feelings and ideals, no matter how much you reject their feelings and ideals. Anyway, I find this happening in my own work; it humanizes *me*. So the main motive is not to express raw anger, but to present—as sentimental as it might sound—the wonder of life, in the fullness of which all these outrageous things occur.

HERSEY: Have you felt some defiance of death as a writer—in the sense that what you are making may possibly circumvent death?

ELLISON: No, I dare not. (*He laughs*) No, you just write for your own time, while trying to write in terms of the density of experience, knowing perfectly well that life repeats itself. Even in this rapidly changing United States it repeats itself. The mystery is that while repeating itself it always manages slightly to change its mask. To be able to grasp a little of that change within continuity and to communicate it across all these divisions of background and individual experience seems enough for me. If you're lucky, of course, if you splice into one of the deeper currents of life, then you have a chance of your work lasting a little bit longer.

# Critical Essays and Appraisals

## RICHARD WRIGHT IN A MOMENT OF TRUTH

**Blyden Jackson**

Many people, if not most, perhaps never associate Richard Wright with the state of Mississippi, which is another way of saying that they do not associate him with the South. He was, however, a Mississippian, a Southerner, and to call him that is not merely to demand due recognition for the statistics of his birth and residence during his plastic years, but also to recognize a fact of the utmost importance in understanding the growth and peculiarities of his artistic imagination. Richard Wright still remains best-known as the author of the novel *Native Son*. Four years before *Native Son*, however, he had published a novella which he called "Big Boy Leaves Home." It is of this earlier and relatively unnoticed novella that I wish to evangelize.

"Big Boy Leaves Home" [1] is a story which proceeds from beginning to

---

[1] "Big Boy Leaves Home" in Richard Wright, *Uncle Tom's Children* (New York, 1949).

end as a simple, straight-line narrative. Mechanically, at least, it is assembled like a play, detachable into five episodes, each as clearly discrete as a scene in a formal drama, and each along the time-scheme of the novella, placed somewhat later than its immediate predecessor, until the action, at the point which in a theater would ring down the final curtain, conveys Big Boy, the story's titular protagonist, northward toward Chicago, secreted in the covered back of a truck.

The first episode breathes something of the atmosphere of a rural Eden. On a clear, warm day in Mississippi four self-indulgent Negro boys are discovered in a wood on the outskirts of the little town in which they and their families reside. The boys are Big Boy and his constant companions Lester, Buck, and Bobo. It becomes quickly obvious that Big Boy is the natural leader of the four and the constant recipient of hero-worship from the other three. It becomes equally obvious that the four should not be where they are, for it is a school day and they are decidedly of school age. They are, then, young rebels giving full vent to some of their rebellious tendencies. And yet it does not appear that they are criminally inclined. They are, rather, healthy and high-spirited cousins-german of Huck Finn, with a proper ambivalence of attitude toward the queer world of adults and a proper interest in enjoying their youth while they still have it to enjoy. They are not, it must be confessed, altogether nice by the standards of a Little Lord Fauntleroy. Their language, for example, runs to words not used in polite child-rearing circles. Their sense of fun expresses itself too often in the sadistic exploitation of some defenseless victim's physical discomfiture. They know, too, about sex, and not through programs of sex education. Even so, they cannot be classed as juvenile delinquents. Nothing about them stamps them as young practitioners of vice and violence. But just as undeniably they cannot be classed as adults. To recognize this is of the utmost importance in a reading of their story. They like to try to act like grownups. What normal adolescents do not? Nevertheless, as adults, they are actually only innocents, actually only ingénues uninitiated into most of what are often called the facts of life. To be classed as adults, they have still seen far too little of the scattered and extensive middens of corruption which tend to separate in a most decisive manner prototypical adulthood from even the latest phase of non-adulthood. Their innocence does not make them as pure as the driven snow. But it does permit them still to think and act like irresponsible children. And it is as irresponsible children out for a children's lark, that they suddenly, and capriciously, decide to quit their wood—one is strongly tempted to say their enchanted forest—and go swimming, trespassing on the land and the pond of Ol Man Harvey, a white man noted for his lack of love for Negroes and, not incidentally, noted especially to them for his aversion to their swimming in his pond.

The second episode takes them, consequently, from their open wood to Ol Man Harvey's pond. For a golden moment it is as if they had not left the wood, as if they are still, as it were, in the innocent world of their enchanted youth. They swim, appropriately for innocents, in the nude. They have, at least temporarily, abandoned swimming and are sunning themselves, still in the nude, on the beach of Ol Man Harvey's pond when they look up and find, fixedly regarding them from a spot on the pond's opposite bank, a white woman whom they do not know and who does not know them. Abruptly their story has changed worlds. It has crossed a line. The woman watching them clearly is already virtually on the verge of hysteria. They try to prevent an apparently all too impending disaster, to assure the strange white woman, who looms between them and their clothes, that all they want is to get those clothes and depart the pond in peace. But this woman is not part of the world of the beginning of their story. She belongs to the world controlled and interpreted by adults. In that world, at least when "Big Boy Leaves Home" was written, all Negro males, even young and with their clothes on, were potential rapists. And so this woman screams, and screams again, for someone named Jim, and Jim himself, a white man from her world, comes apace, with a rifle in his hands. He asks no questions and pauses not at all to profit from a single bit of rational analysis. Instead, he fires and kills two of the potential rapists, Buck and Lester, instantly. But Bobo and Big Boy, in a manner of speaking, have better luck. They survive the white man's initial barrage. Swiftly a moment of violent confusion ensues, and then ends, with the white man's rifle somehow in Big Boy's hands. Unable, as he sees it, under the circumstances to resort to any other method of deterrence, Big Boy shoots to death the white man and he and Bobo, with their clothes and the now expendable garments of Buck and Lester, vanish in the direction of town.

The third episode changes the setting from a white adult world to a black. Big Boy has managed to make his way home to his own house. Presumably, so has Bobo. At Big Boy's house his parents and his sister now are told about the terrible thing which has happened at the pond. Hastily they summon, for advice and counsel, a handful of the respected elders of their local black community. The elders summoned decide that Big Boy perforce must hide himself for the evening and the night in one of a set of pits dug for kilns on the side of a hill overlooking a main highway known as Bullard's Road. Word is to be sent to Bobo to join Big Boy in hiding there. At six in the morning Will Sanders, a son of one of the counseling elders will pick the two boys up. By a fortuitous coincidence Will is already scheduled, just after the approaching dawn, to drive a load of goods to Chicago for his employers, a trucking company.

In the fourth episode Big Boy does reach the prescribed hill safely and does conceal himself deep within a chosen pit. He is waiting now for Bobo. Darkness comes, but no Bobo. What does, however, arrive at last, direfully impinging itself upon Big Boy's consciousness, is a mob that gathers on a hill directly across the road from the one in which he is concealed and from which he can hardly fail to see, as from a seat within the mezzanine of a theater or concert hall, virtually any atrocity that the mob may intend to perpetrate. And the mob does perpetrate a major atrocity. It has captured Bobo and it brings him to its hill. As Big Boy watches, helpless to intervene or withdraw, it proceeds there, on its hill, to tar and feather Bobo, and to burn him at the stake. Then, as a rain begins to fall, the mob, its baser appetites assuaged, melts away in small groups into the night.

The fifth, and final episode is muted and brief. Morning comes, and with it, unobtrusively parked on Bullard's Road, Will Sanders' truck, into which, collected from his night-long perch, Big Boy is safely stowed and thus spirited away to Chicago, famished and thirsty, and bereft forever of the kind of innocence which had still been largely his before the incident at Ol Man Harvey's pond.

"Big Boy Leaves Home" was accepted for publication in the spring of 1936. It seems to have been actually written down in the summer and fall of 1935. It seems also to have a discernible pre-history to which I wish now to allude, for reasons that I trust will appear as I proceed.

Richard Wright fled the South in 1927, two months after his nineteenth birthday. He came directly to Chicago, where by 1932, led by his enthusiastic attachment to a John Reed Club, he had become a Communist. His Communist affiliation brought him eventually into association with a fellow Communist who, like himself, was a Negro born and bred at a considerable distance below the Mason and Dixon Line. Wright speaks of this black fellow-Communist, under the almost certain alias of Ben Ross, in Wright's version of his own experience of communism, which he originally contributed, under the title, "I Tried to Be a Communist," to the *Atlantic Monthly* in 1944. This so-called Ross, who had a Jewish wife, the mother, by him, of a young son, interested Wright deeply. Wright saw Ross as "a man struggling blindly between two societies," and felt that if he "could get . . . Ross's story, . . . he could make known some of the difficulties in the adjustment of a folk people to an urban environment."[2] Therefore, he persuaded Ross, in effect, to sit for a pen portrait. On occasion he interviewed Ross for hours in Ross's home. Meanwhile, however, the Communist command in Chicago had become cognizant of Wright's interest in Ross and had begun to view this interest with mounting concern. Once aware of the Party's apprehensions, Ross ceased to speak freely to Wright either of his life or of himself. This inhibition of Ross's responsiveness sabotaged Wright's original hopes. Through Ross, moreover, Wright had met some of Ross's friends and, expanding on his original plan, had conceived the notion now of doing, with Ross and Ross's friends all in mind, a series of biographical sketches. Now, however, not

[2] "Richard Wright," in Richard Crossman, ed., *The God That Failed* (New York, 1949), p. 115. Wright's "I Tried to Be a Communist" appeared in the *Atlantic Monthly* CLXXXIV (August, 1944), 61–70.

only Ross but all of Ross's friends as well had become afraid to talk to Wright as Wright had once had ample reason to suppose they might. Wright consequently altered his intentions. In virtually Wright's own words, after he saw that he could do nothing to counteract the effect of the Party's powerful influence, he merely sat and listened to Ross and his friends tell tales of Southern Negro experience, noting them down in his mind, and no longer daring to ask questions for fear his informants would become alarmed. In spite of his informants' reticence, he became drenched in the details of their lives. He gave up the idea of writing biographical sketches and settled finally upon writing a series of short stories, using the material he had got from Ross and his friends, building upon it and inventing from it. Thus he wove a tale of a group of black boys trespassing upon the property of a white man and the lynching that followed. The story was published eventually under the title of "Big Boy Leaves Home." [3]

Corroboration of Wright's direct testimony in "I Tried to Be a Communist," and some further suggestions concerning the genesis of "Big Boy Leaves Home," are supplied in Constance Webb's recent biography of Wright.[4] This biography, it is of some significance here to note, bears the character of an official life. Indeed, in the book's "Introduction" Miss Webb so defines the nature of what she has done in no uncertain terms. In this "Introduction," that is to say, she first makes specific allusion to her personal friendship with Wright and his family which began, she tells us, when Wright was at work on *Black Boy* in the earlier 1940s and lasted until his death. She then cites the many materials, such as notes, letters, telegrams, manuscripts, and ideas for new books which, from the time of her decision in 1945 to compose a study of him and his work, and in full knowledge of her plans, Wright delivered to her over a period of fifteen years. She also refers to her many long hours of conversations with Wright in New York City, on Long Island, and in Paris; to her continuing relations with Wright's wife after Wright's untimely death; to the assistance provided her by Wright's brother, Alan, Wright's close boyhood friend, Joe C. Brown, and Wright's literary agent, Paul R. Reynolds, Jr.; to the aid given her by an impressive number of Wright's fellow authors and others of Wright's acquaintances who were in a position to speak of Wright with some authority; and, finally in this present context, to the access granted her by Wright and his family to hundreds of letters from Wright to Wright's editor, Edward C. Aswell.

With these credentials, which are not to be summarily dismissed, Miss Webb positively identifies the pseudonymous Ben Ross as one David Poindexter, a black member of the Communist Party, who had been born in southwest Tennessee in 1903 and had come North when he was seventeen. The family attributed by Miss Webb to Poindexter is the same as

[3] *Ibid.*, pp. 119–20.
[4] Constance Webb, *Richard Wright* (New York, 1968).

that attributed by Wright to Ross. In all the other details which she stipulates, moreover, including Poindexter's status as the original of Big Boy, Miss Webb assimilates Poindexter to the person whom Wright, conceivably in order not to expose a friend and benefactor to possible jeopardy, named as Ross in "I Tried to Be a Communist." But when she reports directly on the genesis of "Big Boy Leaves Home," [5] Miss Webb does not parrot what Wright had once said about his determination, if he could, to use Poindexter, or Ross, as an instrument by means of which he could make known some of the difficulties attendant upon the adjustment of a folk people to an urban environment. In this context, as a matter of fact, she makes a statement which would seem to contradict Wright's own about the folk. She says, instead and unequivocally, that in his first series of short stories, *Uncle Tom's Children* (the series of which "Big Boy Leaves Home" became a part), Wright set himself a conscious problem, the explication of the quality of will the Negro must possess to live and die in a country which denies him his humanity.[6] Furthermore, applying her statement to "Big Boy Leaves Home" specifically, she asserts, within her analysis of that story, that "Big Boy Leaves Home" represents this quality of will as being "only that of the most elemental level—the ability to endure," [7] for, she finally adds, the lesson to be extracted from Big Boy's experience is the dependence of his survival "upon the communal nature of the black community which planned, aided, and organized an escape." [8]

When she says that Wright, in creating "Big Boy Leaves Home" and the other stories in *Uncle Tom's Children*, "set himself a conscious problem," the significant word is *conscious*. She has left no doubt, as already indicated here earlier, of her conception of her relationship with Wright. He made of her, according to her implication it is clear, an *alter ego* privy to virtually all of himself that he could communicate to her or anyone. Furthermore, although the word *conscious* does not appear in her declaration that Big Boy's story was planned to demonstrate how his community rallied round him to ensure the preservation of his life, it seems unmistakably clear that here she speaks, too, as a medium who is reporting not only what was in Wright's mind, but also what she would contend he knew was there. Here, then, is testimony, much of it of a hearsay nature indeed, but nevertheless purporting, in its general trend, to have the value of evidence which Wright himself could not have failed to give had he ever had to speak about the intended function of "Big Boy" under solemn oath in a court of law. It reveals, to repeat for emphasis, that Wright had chosen a definite thing to do when he wrote "Big Boy Leaves Home," and that he was not confused as to the nature of that thing. It

[5] *Ibid.*, p. 125.
[6] *Ibid.*, p. 157.
[7] *Ibid.*, p. 159.
[8] *Ibid.*, p. 159.

seems to argue also Wright's own belief that he had substantially achieved his conscious intent.

Writers, however, sometimes belie their own intentions. Sometimes, moreover, what they actually do may well seem better than what they thought they had intended. No one, I think, would argue seriously for a reading of "Big Boy Leaves Home" as an account of an adjustment by an agrarian folk to an urban setting, deeply though Wright once indicated that he was interested in Ross-Poindexter and drenched though he once was in Ross-Poindexter's life and history. If then, however, "Big Boy Leaves Home" is to be read primarily as a parable about the quality of will necessary for the Negro to solve the major problem which he faces in his American environment, and if the message of such a parable centers in an account of the manner in which one Negro community expressed the quality of its will through its capacity to save some of its own, then neither the form nor the content of the parable is aesthetically impressive. "Big Boy Leaves Home" becomes then only an exercise in the depiction of a failure. Its focal point, if not its climax, must then be found to be in its third episode, for in this episode the representatives of the Negro community do gather, in Big Boy's home. The preacher, Elder Peters, is there, and Brother Jenkins and Brother Sanders, with Big Boy's parents and his sister. They commune with each other. But with what results? Big Boy's father can only berate Big Boy on the folly of his disobedience to his mother's injunction to go to school. The women in the house can only watch the men gathered there in virtually unbroken silence. No one can respond affirmatively to the distressed father's plea for financial aid. The sister has done some service in bringing to the house the three outside counsellors. The mother gives Big Boy simple food to take with him when he leaves. Still, it is chance alone and Big Boy's own animal excellences which pave the way for his escape from certain death. No effective aid reaches Bobo. No account is taken of provisions to safeguard Big Boy's family, who, as Big Boy later overhears in his kiln, are burned out of their modest dwelling. The most that can be said when all is done is that Big Boy did elude his would-be slayers and that a fellow Negro, who happened to be going in that direction anyhow, drove him North.

But to read "Big Boy Leaves Home," whatever Wright's original conscious aims, in accord with the form dictated for it by its own development, and to sense its content shaping itself to match that form and its function emerging as the strong, inevitable concomitant of both, is to witness what well may be one of the three or four finest moments in Negro fiction. Of this inherent form and content it is now high time to speak.

It will be remembered that Big Boy's story is shaped into five episodes, five scenes conducting a flow of action and related meaning from a point of attack to a conclusion which should round out and justify the whole. This form, at least in its handling here, is flexible as well as fluid. It permits variations of pitch and tone and atmosphere which all contribute to the story's total impact. At the beginning the pitch is moderate. The tone and atmosphere are genial, almost sweet. The function of the content is expository. The identity of the protagonist is established and the condition of all four of the boys made known. And beyond all this a theme is adumbrated. For these boys are scholars out of school. They have interrupted their vocation for a holiday of their own making. Still, the fact is clear. They are young, much untaught, and at an impressionable age. To learn, to grow, in other words, in one way or another, is their *métier*. It is hard to see how they should live through any single day without acquiring some new knowledge. In what they are reside the germs of what this tale must be. Then comes the first progression, bringing with itself a proper set of changes. At the swimming hole the white world intrudes. The mood of the first episode is shattered by the killings. In a swirl of strident sound and emotions at high pitch and harshly tuned, with corresponding action that is equally cacophonous, a motif of pain and mystery, the ugliness of racistic custom is introduced. Then comes an interlude with a reduction in pitch and a moderation of tone, but without a return to the relative serenity of the introduction, as Big Boy spends a moment with his own kind in his father's house. But this interlude is also prelude, and a fitting one, to the big scene of the story. This big scene, as the logic of the story would demand, is the lynching on the hill, the spectacle of Bobo coated with hot tar and white feathers, burning in the night. This, as we shall see in terms of content, is the moment of truth in the story. It is also the very peak of the wave of form, when pitch and tone and atmosphere all coalesce at their highest points. The story cannot end at such a level of crescendo and fortissimo. It does not; it declines to the low key of its final episode when Big Boy, all passion spent, drifts off to slumber on the bed of the truck that bears him away to the North. But let us return to the lynching on the hill.

I have said that for this story it is the moment of truth. And it is. It is the moment when Wright, whether wittingly or not, gathers up the essence of that which he is struggling to express and stores it all into one symbol and its attendant setting. For the spectacle of Bobo aflame at the stake does constitute a symbol. It is a symbol, moreover, the phallic connotations of which cannot be denied. Indeed, the particularity of its detail —the shape of its mass, its coating of tar, the whiteness of the feathers attached to its surface or floating out into the surrounding air—are almost all too grossly and gruesomely verisimilar for genteel contemplation. Whether Wright so intended it or not, the lynching of Bobo is symbolically a rite of castration. It is the ultimate indignity that can be inflicted upon an individual. Such an indignity strips from a man his manhood, removes from him the last vestige of his power and the last resort of his self-respect. In the lynching of Bobo, thus, all lynchings are explained, and all race prejudice. Both are truly in essence acts of castration. It is not for nothing that the grinning darky, hat in hand and bowing low, his backside exposed as if for a kick in the buttocks, seems so much a eunuch. He has accepted in his heart the final abasement, the complete surrender of his will, and so of his citadel of self, to anyone with a white skin. He has capitulated to the most arrogant demand which one human creature can make upon another. This, then, is the true anatomy of racism. It makes no difference where or how it prefers its claims, whether in an apology for its own being so adroitly composed as the novel *So Red the Rose* or in the blatant conduct of the old-style sheeted Ku Klux Klan. What racism demands is that every white man should be permitted to reserve the right to visit, with impunity, upon any Negro whatever, any outrage of that Negro's personality the white man chooses to impose. This, then, is the symbolism of Bobo's burning body on the hill. But around that symbolism clusters another set of facts put into another pregnant image. For, as Bobo burning illustrates the essence of one indispensable aspect of racism, the mob illustrates another. It is an efficient mob, a homogeneous grouping. Yet no one has really organized it. It has no officers and no carefully compiled manual of behavior. Still it operates like a watchmaker universe. Its members know what they are supposed to do, and they do it, as if they were performing the steps of a ritual dance —which of course they are. For that is the real secret of the people gathered around Bobo on his Golgotha. They are responding not only to xenophobia and to an obscene lust for power. They are responding also to an urge equally as neanderthal as its origins. They are acting tribally, even as every lodge brother, black or white or yellow or red, who ever gave a secret handshake and every Babbitt who ever applauded a toastmaster's feeble attempts at jollity at the luncheon of his service club.

To belong, to conform, and thus to avoid the existentialist nightmare of exercising the prerogative of individual freedom of choice; to be able to contribute all of one's own release of foible and malice to custom that must be followed for the good of the community; to accept the myth that at some time in the misty past a voice, as it were, from some local Sinai spoke to the elders of the tribe and told them how certain things must be done and what prescribed rites must be followed to avert the anger of the god; thus to be exempted from a sense of guilt at one's own evil; thus to hallow the meanest of the herd instincts; thus to institutionalize mediocrity's hatred of the indomitable spirit and its envy of strength and beauty; this is the pathos, and yet an important part of the explanation, of the capacity to endure of the tribe. This is also as much a part of racism as its lust for power. The castration and the tribalism complement each other. Without either, racism would not be at all exactly what it is. To perceive them, to really take them in, is, as Henry James might say, to see and know what is there. And it is part of the excellence of form in this story that Big Boy does see them, that by the story's own handling of its arrangements he is put in such a position that he cannot do otherwise.

For, as this story so manages the sense of form which shapes its episodes to place its big scene right, it regulates concurrently another element of form, its control of its own point of view, to the end that at the proper point in the narrative's development the impression it conveys of who is doing the seeing will be as right as the prominence and the substance of what is to be seen.

Thus at the beginning of the story we are aware of, and share, to some extent, in the consciousness of all the boys. But this is Big Boy's story. It is really he whose loss of innocence, as it were, and compulsory education under special circumstances embody all that this story has to say. And so, increasingly, as the story moves from the open country to the lynching on the hill, Big Boy's consciousness becomes the sole point of view. Yet this constriction and this concentration are really the ultimate outgrowth of a rather delicate continuous maneuver of adjustment. Throughout the bulk of his story Wright's handling of his point of view is as dramatic as his separation of his matter into scenes. We watch the characters perform. We hear them talk. From outside their consciousnesses we infer their thoughts and feelings. Yet we identify increasingly with Big Boy, if for no other reason than that we see nothing which he cannot see and hear nothing which he cannot hear. But after Big Boy bids adieu to his parents and their friends and, successfully negotiating his sprint through hostile territory to Bullard's Road, comes to bay at last crouched deep within his kiln, we become more and more intensely one with him. We wonder with him why Bobo has not come, share with him his reverie as he relives the events of his day, mourn with him for Buck and Lester, regret with him that he did not bring with him his father's shotgun, and finally, in fantasy, imagine with him that he is blasting away with that shotgun as he withstands a mob. As white men searching for the Negro "bastards" drift down his hill we share, too, his fear, and finally, as the lynch mob gathers, our senses become, like his, preternaturally acute, to watch with him in anguish and extreme distress the torture and destruction of the last of his close boyhood friends. Thus the heightening and the concentration of the point of view join with the elevation of the episode and the power of the symbolism and the imagery to speak in blended voices acting in mighty concert of the inner nature of racism and to trace its roots deep down into the past of human psychology and custom.

It is not a quality of the Negro will which this story explicates, nor is it anything to do with folk adjustment in a city. Far from either. It is, rather, the psychology, and the anthropology, of American racism. It is a lesson given to Big Boy and through him to the world at large. It is a lesson, moreover, which rounds off beautifully both the form and substance of "Big Boy Leaves Home." For the plot of this story represents a progress, not a conflict. Its succession of vignettes combine to form a curious kind of sentimental journey in which Big Boy does leave home; does lose, that is, his relative state of innocence; and does experience an illumination, an exercise in education, that provides him with a terrible, but richly freighted, insight into the adult world.

It has been rather customary not to think of Richard Wright as a Southern writer, except, of course, by the accident of birth. I cannot share that view. A writer belongs, I would argue, in the final analysis, to the country where his artistic imagination is most at home. Wright clearly supposed that this country, for him, was not the South, just as he supposed that in "Big Boy Leaves Home," in spite of the resemblances between Ol Man Harvey's pond and the pond in Jackson, Mississippi, around which Wright had played in his own youth, he was writing about Ross-Poindexter and, in a philosophic vein, either about a folk people seeking a new adjustment in a setting alien to their past or struggling for self-gratifying survival against a powerful outer world hostile to their hopes. Indeed, in one of the major episodes of *Black Boy*, his own account of his youth and early manhood, Wright tells of his last encounter with his father, an encounter that occurred after twenty-five years of absolute separation between the two, as well as, also, after Wright had published *Native Son*. He meets his father on a Mississippi hillside. He tries to talk to him and then he says, "I realized that, though ties of blood made us kin, though I could see a shadow of my face in his face, though there was an echo of my voice in his voice, we were forever strangers, speaking a different language, living on vastly different planes of reality." On one level of interpretation Wright here does speak true. Between him and his father time and experience had fixed an impenetrable gulf. But the possibly implied symbolism of the confrontation is false. Deep at the core of his own being, whether as a person or as an artist, Wright always remained his own Big Boy who never did leave home, and it was always true that the closer he could get to the homeland of his youth, which was also the homeland of his creative skill, the happier he was in the fiction he was able to produce.

Wright's last considerable essay into fiction was his final novel, *The Long Dream*. In startling ways it reproduces all the significant elements of "Big Boy Leaves Home." Its setting is a Mississippi town and, incidentally one which, for all of his obvious intentions to have it otherwise, he does not update from the Mississippi which he quitted as a youth. Its protagonist is a Negro boy as exceptional among his peers as Big Boy is among his. Moreover, this boy too is in the process of growing up, for *The Long Dream*, like "Big Boy Leaves Home," is an initiation story. Fire figures prominently in the drama of *The Long Dream*. Indeed, fire repeatedly plays a mythopoeic role in Wright's important fiction, as in the furnace of *Native Son* or the collision of electrically driven monsters in the subway wreck of *The Outsider*. The Negro elders of "Big Boy Leaves Home" reappear in the protagonist's father, the doctor, the madam, the mistress, and the father's helper of *The Long Dream*. They are no more potent in the latter work than in the former. They have neither the grace nor the glory of the father in "Fire and Cloud" or the mother in "Bright and Morning Star." The strange white woman who precipitates catastrophe for the protagonist of "Big Boy Leaves Home" precipitates catastrophe also for the protagonist in *The Long Dream*. And, as at the end of "Big Boy Leaves Home," Big Boy is headed for another life in another world, so at the end of *The Long Dream* its protagonist is on a plane *en route* to Paris. The real difference, indeed, between "Big Boy Leaves Home" and *The Long Dream* is in the relative quality of the art of each. James Baldwin, whose attitudes toward Richard Wright are much too complex for quick definition, once referred, with complimentary intent, to Wright as a "Mississippi pickaninny." In so doing Baldwin directly was comparing Wright with the Existentialists amongst whom Wright, in his later life, found himself consorting in Paris, and was thus paying genuine respect to a capacity in Wright to see life as it actually is and not according to some evanescent theory, which Baldwin thought he could divine in Wright, but not in Sartre and his disciples—and which, additionally, Baldwin, in pensive mood, attributed to the lessons Wright had learned during Wright's rough-and-tumble existence as a boy and precocious adolescent in the Delta South. I think the phrase is apt, especially since it is clear that through it Baldwin intended no racial slur. For Wright was a child of his own youth. Out of that youth he derived not only his practical sense of hard reality but also the home country for his artistic imagination. Thus in much more than the mere statistics of his place of birth is he a Southern writer. When he follows his home country North, as he does in the first two books of *Native Son*, he is still on his native ground. When he tries to return to it, as in *The Long Dream*, seeing it through other eyes than truly his own, he has deserted the one source of his greatest strength. He has become, that is, in all too sad a consequence, his own Big Boy away from home.

---

# LIFE FOR PHOENIX

## Neil Isaacs

The first four sentences of "A Worn Path" [1] contain simple declarative statements using the simple past of the verb "to be": "It was Decem-

[1] References are to Eudora Welty, *A Curtain of Green*, Garden City, N.Y. (Doubleday, Doran and Company), 1943.

ber . . . ," ". . . there was an old Negro woman . . . ," "Her name was Phoenix Jackson," "She was very old and small. . . ." The note of simplicity thus struck is the keynote of Eudora Welty's artistic design in the story. For it is a simple story (a common reaction is "simply beautiful"). But it is also a story which employs many of the devices which can make of the modern short story an intricate and densely complex form. It uses them, however, in such a way that it demonstrates how a single meaning may be enriched through the use of various techniques. Thus, instead of various levels of meaning, we have here a single meaning reinforced on several levels of perception. Moreover, there is no muddying of levels and techniques; they are neatly arranged, straightforwardly presented, and simply perceived.

The plot-line follows Phoenix Jackson, who is graphically described in the second paragraph, on her long walk into Natchez where she has to get medicine for her grandson. The trek is especially difficult because of her age, and in the process of struggling on she forgets the reason for the struggle. At the end she has remembered, received the medicine, and decided to buy the child a Christmas present with the ten cents she has acquired during the day.

What makes this a story? It barely appears to fulfill even Sidney Cox's generous criterion of "turning a corner or at least a hair." [2] But it does belong to a specific story-teller's genre familiar from Homer to Fielding to Kerouac—"road" literature. This form provides a ready-made plot pattern with some inherent weaknesses. The story concerns the struggle to achieve a goal, the completion of the journey; and the story's beginning, middle, and end are the same as those of the road. The primary weakness of this structure is its susceptibility to too much middle.

A traditional concept of road literature, whether the mythical journey of the sun across the heavens or a boy's trip down the Mississippi or any other variation, is its implicit equation with life: the road of life, life's journey, ups and downs, the straight and narrow, and a host of other clichés reflect the universality of this primitive metaphor. "A Worn Path" makes explicit, beginning with the very title, Eudora Welty's acceptance of the traditional equation as a basic aspect of the story. In fact, the whole meaning of "A Worn Path" will rely on an immediate recognition of the equation—the worn path equals the path of life—which is probably why it is so explicit. But we needn't start with a concept which is metaphorical or perhaps primitively allegorical. It will probably be best for us to begin with the other literal elements in the story: they will lead us back to the sub- or supra-literal eventually anyway.

An important part of the setting is the time element, that is, the specific time of the year. We learn immediately that it is "a bright frozen day" in December, and there are several subsequent, direct statements

[2] Familiar words to a generation of students at Dartmouth College.

which mark it more precisely as Christmas time. The hunter talks about Santa Claus and the attendant at the hospital says that "It's Christmas time," echoing what the author has said earlier. There are several other references and images forming a pattern to underline the idea of Christmas time, such as "Up above her was a tree in a pearly cloud of *mistletoe*." [Italics in this paragraph all mine.] Notice especially the elaborate color pattern of red, green, and silver, the traditional colors of Christmas. It begins with Phoenix's head "in a *red* rag, coming along a path through the pinewoods" (which are green as well as Christmas trees). Later she sees "a wagon track, where the *silver grass* blew between the *red* ruts" and "little strings of trees *silver* in their dead leaves" (reddish brown?). This pattern comes to a climax in the description of the city and the lady's packages, which also serves to make explicit its purpose, return it to the literal: "There were red and green electric lights strung and crisscrossed everywhere. . . . . . . an armful of red-, green-, and silver-wrapped presents."

From the plot-line alone the idea of Christmas doesn't seem to be more than incidental, but it is obvious from the persistent references that Christmas is going to play an important part in the total effect of the story. Besides the direct statements already mentioned, there proliferates around the pattern throughout the story a dense cluster of allusions to and suggestions of the Christmas myth at large and to the *meanings* of Christmas in particular. For instance, as Phoenix rests under a tree, she has a vision of a little boy offering her a slice of marble-cake on a little plate, and she says, "That would be acceptable." The allusion here is to Communion and Church ritual. Later, when a bird flies by, Phoenix says, "God watching me the whole time." Then there are references to the Eden story (the ordering of the species, the snake in summer to be avoided), to the parting of the Red Sea (Phoenix walking through the field of corn), to a sequence of temptations, to the River Jordan and the City of Heaven (when Phoenix gets to the river, sees the city shining, and hears the bells ringing; then there is the angel who waits on her, tying her shoes), to the Christ-child in the manger (Phoenix describing her grandson as "all wrapped up" in "a little patch quilt . . . like a little bird" with "a sweet look"). In addition, the whole story is suggestive of a religious pilgrimage, while the conclusion implies that the return trip will be like the journey of the Magi, with Phoenix following a star (the marvelous windmill) to bring a gift to the child (medicine, also windmill). Moreover, there's the hunter who is, in part, a Santa Claus figure himself (he carries a big sack over his shoulder, he is always laughing, he brings Phoenix a gift of a nickel).

The richness of all this avocation of a Christianity-Christmas frame of reference heightens the specific points about the meanings of Christmas. The Christmas spirit, of course, is the Christian ethic in its simplest terms: giving, doing for others, charity. This concept is made explicit when the nurse says of Phoenix, "She doesn't come for herself." But it had already been presented in a brilliant piece of ironic juxtaposition [Italics mine]:

> She entered a door, and there she saw *nailed up on the wall* the document that had been stamped with the *gold seal* and framed in the *gold frame* which *matched the dream that was hung up in her head.*
> "Here I be," she said. There was a *fixed and ceremonial stiffness* over her body.
> "A *charity* case, I suppose," said an attendant. . . .

Amid the Christmas season and the dense Christmas imagery, Phoenix, with an abiding intuitive faith, arrives at the shrine of her pilgrimage, beholds a symbolic crucifixion, presents herself as a celebrant in the faith, and is recognized as an embodiment of the message of the faith. This entire scene, however, with its gold trimming and the attitude of the attendant, is turned ironically to suggest greed, corruption, cynicism —the very opposite of the word used, charity. Yet the episode, which is Phoenix's final and most severe trial, also results in her final emergence as a redeemer and might be called her Calvary.

Perhaps a better way to get at the meaning of Christmas and the meaning of "A Worn Path" is to talk about life and death. In a sense, the meaning of Christmas and that of Easter are the same—a celebration of life out of death. (Notice that Phoenix refers to herself as a *June* bug and that the woman with the packages "gave off perfume like the *red roses in hot summer.*") [Italics mine.] Christ is born in the death of the year and in a neat dead nature-society situation in order to rejuvenate life itself, naturally and spiritually. He dies in order that the life of others may be saved. He is reborn out of death, and so are nature, love, and the spirit of man. All this is the potent Christian explanation of the central irony of human existence, that life means death and death is life. One might state the meaning of "A Worn Path" in similar terms, where Phoenix endures a long, agonizing dying in order to redeem her grandson's life. So the medicine, which the nurse calls charity as she makes a check in her book, is a symbol of love and life. The windmill represents the same duality, but lighter sides of both aspects. If the path is the path of life, then its end is death and the purpose of that death is new life.

It would be misleading, however, to suggest that the story is merely a paralleling of the Christian nature-myth. It is, rather, a miniature nature-myth of its own which uses elements of many traditions. The most obvious example is the name Phoenix from the mythological Egyptian bird, symbol of immortality and resurrection, which dies so that a new Phoenix may emerge from its ashes. There is a reference to the Daedalus labyrinth myth when Phoenix walks through the corn field and Miss Welty puns: "'Through the maze now,' she said, for there was no path." That ambivalent figure of the hunter comes into play here as both a death figure (killer, bag full of slain quail) and a life figure (unconscious giver of life with the nickel, banisher of Cerberus-like black dog who is attacking Phoenix), but in any case a folk-legend figure who can fill "the whole landscape" with his laugh. And there are several references to the course of the sun across the sky which gives a new dimension to the life-road equation; e.g., "Sun so high! . . . The time getting all gone here."

The most impressive extra-Christian elements are the patterns that identify Phoenix as a creature of nature herself and as a ritual magic figure. Thus, Phoenix makes a sound "like the chirping of a solitary little bird," her hair has "an odor like copper," and at one point "with [her] mouth drawn down, [she] shook her head once or twice in a little strutting way." Even more remarkable is the "fixed and ceremonial stiffness" of her body, which moves "like a festival figure in some parade." The cane she carries, made from an umbrella, is tapped on the ground like a magic wand, and she uses it to "switch at the brush as if to rouse up any hiding things." At the same time she utters little spells:

> Out of my way, all you foxes, owls, beetles, jack rabbits, coons, and wild animals! . . . Keep out from under these feet, little bob-whites. . . . Keep the big wild hogs out of my path. Don't let none of those come running my direction. . . . Ghost, . . . who be you the ghost of? . . . Sweetgum makes the water sweet. . . . Nobody know who made this well for it was here when I was born. . . . Sleep on, alligators, and blow your bubbles.

Other suggestions of magic appear in the whirling of cornhusks in streamers about her skirts, when she parts "her way from side to side with the cane, through the whispering field," when the quail seem "unseen," and when the cabins are "all like old women under a spell sitting there." Finally, ironically, when Phoenix swings at the black dog, she goes over "in the ditch, like a little puff of milk-weed."

More or less remote, more or less direct, all these allusions are used for the same effect as are the references to Christianity, to reinforce a statement of the meaning of life. This brings us back to the basic life-road equation of the story, and there are numerous indications that the path is life and that the end of the road is death and renewal of life. These suggestions are of three types; statements which relate the road, the trip, or Phoenix to time: Phoenix walks "with the balanced heaviness and lightness of a pendulum in a grandfather clock"; she tells the hunter, "I bound to go. . . . The time come around"; and the nurse says "She makes these trips just as regular as clockwork." Second (the most frequent type), there are descriptions of the road or episodes along the way which are suggestive of life, usually in a simple metaphorical way: "I got a long way" (ambiguously referring to past and future); "I in the thorny bush"; "Up through pines. . . . Now down through oaks"; "This the easy place. This the easy going." Third, there are direct references to death, age, and life: Phoenix says to a buzzard, "Who you watching?" and to a scarecrow, "Who be you the ghost of? For I have heard of nary death close by"; then she performs a little dance of death with the scarecrow after she says, "My senses is gone. I too old. I the oldest people I ever know."

This brings us full circle in an examination of the design of the story, and it should be possible now to say something about the total meaning of "A Worn Path." The path is the path of life, and the story is an attempt to probe the meaning of life in its simplest, most elementary terms. Through the story we arrive at a definition of life, albeit a teleological one. When the hunter tells Phoenix to "take my advice and stay home, and nothing will happen to you," the irony is obvious and so is the metaphor: don't live and you can't die. When Phoenix forgets why she has made the arduous trek to Natchez,[3] we understand that it is only a rare person who knows the meaning of his life, that living does not imply knowing. When Phoenix describes the Christ-like child waiting for her and says, "I not going to forget him again, no, the whole enduring time. I could tell him from all the others in creation," we understand several things about it: her life is almost over, she sees clearly the meaning of life, she has an abiding faith in that meaning, and she will share with her grandson this great revelation just as together they embody its significance. And when Phoenix's "slow step began on the stairs, going down," as she starts back to bring the boy the medicine and the windmill, we see a composite symbol of life itself, dying so that life may continue. Life is a journey toward death, because one must die in order that life may go on.

---

# COSMIC IRONY IN HARDY'S "THE THREE STRANGERS"

## William Van O'Connor

In order to analyze a work of literature we need critical terms and concepts. In talking about "The Three Strangers" I am going to use only a few: intention, theme, plot, focus-of-narration, cosmic irony, atmos-

---

[3] P. 283: "It was my memory had left me. . . . I forgot it in the coming."

phere, and tone. Used by over-ingenious readers, critical terminology can lead to unnecessary complications. Judiciously used, it can be helpful.

In reading a story we must look for the writer's *intention;* or, to put it another way, we must ask what it is he is trying to say. You may feel that asking such a question is making a lot out of a simple problem, that a story says what it says, and that is all there is to it. But this isn't all there is to it. Different readers tend to see different things in a story, and to make different interpretations of it.

Presumably a man writes to tell us something that he believes. He has insights into the nature of the universe or human conduct, and he feels compelled to state them, to body them forth in the form of poems, short stories, or novels. But let us stay with the short story. If a story is worthwhile it makes a revelation; it tells us, dramatizes for us, something the author feels to be true about human conduct.

Let me tell you right off what I think Hardy's "The Three Strangers" says, and then attempt to justify my interpretation. I believe the story exists on two levels: the level of exciting plot, and the level of a view of the human situation.

First, the level of exciting plot. We see a man join a country baptismal party at a cottage called Higher Crowstairs. He sits in the chimney corner and joins in the fun. Shortly, another man enters, and gradually we learn he is a hangman, on his way to Casterbridge to hang a man who was condemned for a theft. Then another man comes to the door. He looks at the group inside, especially at the hangman, he becomes frightened, and runs away. A cannon booms in the distance, signifying that a prisoner has escaped. The hangman asks if a constable is present, and one of the men identifies himself as the constable. In some confusion, all of the men take off into the darkness in pursuit of the man they believe to be the escaped criminal. The baby cries and the women go upstairs to attend to it, leaving the room empty. Very soon the man who had been sitting at the fireside returns and begins to wolf down food and drink. He is joined by the hangman. Both of them give reasons for abandoning the chase. Then they leave. The scene shifts to the outdoors, and we see the constable and others confronting the man they were chasing. He allows himself to be captured and they return with him to the house. Two of the officers from the Casterbridge jail are there, and one of them says this is not the right man. His description of the escaped criminal is a description of the man in the chimney corner. We then learn that the man caught by the constable is his brother. He says when he had seen his brother and the hangman he had become terrified and run away. He is released. Next day the search is renewed, but the escaped prisoner is not found, indeed is never found. Speculation says he has gone overseas or lost himself in a populous city. The neighborhood is sympathetic with him because of his coolness in escaping and because his sentence was disproportionate to his crime. (He and his family had been starving, and he had stolen a sheep in open defiance of its owner.) Then we are told that all this happened a good while ago; the shepherd and his wife are both dead, and the baby who had been baptized is now an old lady. And we are told that the story of the three strangers is well known throughout the countryside.

What do we have on this level of exciting action? We have confusion of identity, the chase, and suspense. All of these are common elements in adventure stories. There are also comic touches of various sorts. The story can be read on this level, for its excitement and humor. Presumably Hardy wanted to write an exciting story, and he succeeded. But what does the story mean? What was Hardy's *intention*? Put another way, what is the *theme* of "The Three Strangers"?

I think the story means something like this: life is short, the law is sometimes grossly unjust, human beings are comic and pathetic, capable of affection, admiring of courage and skill. Hardy's intention in the story is to tell us that human strivings occur against a backdrop of cosmic mystery.

How did I arrive at this interpretation? Generally speaking, from internal evidence in the story and evidence from Hardy's other work. By internal evidence I mean such matters as the tone of the narrator's "voice" and the focus-of-narration. Hardy's poems and other stories frequently employ the view of the cosmic ironist. Writers tend to have a persistent view of things throughout their poetry or fiction, and knowing their work as a whole one can often get a clue to the meaning of any individual part of their work. Let me cite a poem of Hardy's, "Nature's Questioning," before I return to the question of "internal evidence."

> When I look forth at dawning, pool
>   Field, flock, and lonely tree,
>   All seem to gaze at me
> Like chastened children sitting silent in
>   a school;
>
> Their faces dulled, constrained, and
>   worn,
>   As though the master's ways
>   Through the long teaching days
> Had cowed them til their early zest was
>   overborne.
>
> Upon them stirs in lippings mere
>   (As if once clear in call,
>   But now scarce breathed at all)—
> "We wonder, ever wonder, why we find
>   us here!
>
> "Has some Vast Imbecility,
>   Mighty to build and blend,

> But important to tend,
> Framed us in jest, and let us now to
>     hazardry?
>
> "Or come we of an Automaton
>     Unconscious of our pains? . . .
>     Or are we live remains
> Of Godhead dying downwards, brain
>     and eye now gone?
>
> "Or is it that some high Plan betides,
> As yet not understood,
>     Of Evil stormed by Good,
> We the forlorn Hope over which
>     Achievement strides?"
>
> Thus things around. No answer I . . .
>     Meanwhile the winds, and rains,
>     And Earth's old glooms and pains
> Are still the same, and Life and Death
>     are neighbors nigh.[1]

What does the poem say? It says the poet cannot see any intelligence in the universe, although it may be there. He does not know what the riddle of the universe is. He does know the earth has winds and rains, that human beings suffer, and that life is always shadowed by death. This is not so very different from what he says in "The Three Strangers."

Hardy is commonly said to be an ironic writer, and of course he is. More specifically, he is a cosmic ironist. By cosmic irony I mean seeing human affairs not as they appear to human participants but from great distances of time and space. A human struggle viewed close up has intensity; viewed from a great distance the struggle will seem rather pointless, for time and space cause any human concern to dwindle into insignificance. There is also a strong element of pathos in this, especially because, as Hardy implies in his poem, on the one hand we feel ourselves and our affairs to be very important (possibly involved with divinity) and on the other hand we feel that the hugeness of the universe and the vastness of eternity say our self-concern is presumptuous.

Thus far I have used several critical terms: intention, theme, plot, focus-of-narration, and cosmic irony. I want to introduce the figure of the narrator or the question of the focus of narration. The narrator is not introduced and we do not visualize him. He is impersonal. The language of the story, however, is his, just as the interpretation of the action is his. The tone, a mixture of comedy and pathos, is his. The perspective in which the story is told is his. The action is viewed from a

---

[1] From *Collected Poems*. Reprinted by permission of the Macmillan Company.

distance. Undoubtedly this distance is a key factor, for it contributes to the irony.

Consider the opening paragraphs:

> Among the few features of agricultural England which retain an appearance but little modified by the lapse of centuries may be reckoned the high, grassy and furzy downs, coombs, or ewe-leases, as they are indifferently called, that fill a large area of certain counties in the south and southwest. If any mark of human occupation is met hereon, it usually takes the form of the solitary cottage of some shepherd.
>
> Fifty years ago such a lonely cottage stood on such a down, and may possibly be standing there now. In spite of its loneliness, however, the spot, by actual measurement, was not more than five miles from a county-town. Yet that affected it little. Five miles of irregular upland, during the long inimical seasons, with their sleets, snow, rains, and mists, afford withdrawing space enough to isolate a Timon or a Nebuchadnezzar; much less, in fair weather, to please that less repellent tribe, the poets, philosophers, artists, and others who "conceive and meditate of pleasant things."

The land is desolate, inimical to human life. Nothing much has changed with the centuries. But the generations pass quickly and their habitations, too, last only a short span. Two points are made that will be repeated throughout the story: Nature is harsh, and Time passes on indifferently. And consider the closing paragraph:

> The grass has long been green on the graves of Shepherd Fennel and his frugal wife; the guests who made up the christening party have mainly followed their entertainers to the tomb; the baby in whose honor they all had met is a matron in the sere and yellow leaf. But the arrival of the three strangers at the shepherd's that night, and the details connected therewith, is a story as well-known as ever in the country about Higher Crowstairs.

Here too Time has conquered or will soon conquer. All the excitement of the story, the escape of a condemned man, has turned to legend. The countryside presumably is the same as ever; only the generation has changed. The opening and closing paragraphs frame the story, inviting the reader to see the action as something that is now a part of history and legend.

Nature and Time function in the story almost as if they were characters. The rain smites the cottage roof and beats against the cabbages in the garden and against the beehives. The land is rocky and the gullies are precipitate. The pleasures of the people living at Higher Crowstairs are the small, marginal pleasures of those who live in a barren region. We learn that Higher Crowstairs was not built against a hedge ("some starved fragment of ancient hedge is usually taken advantage of in the erection of these forlorn dwellings"), but out in the open. And the narrator says why: "The only reason for its precise situation seemed to be the crossing of two footpaths at right angles hard by, which may have crossed there and thus for a good five hundred years." Time and history seem to echo through the story, even in the language itself: "The level rainstorm smote walls, slopes and hedges like the clothyard shafts of Senlac and Crecy." The battle of Senlac was in 1066 and Crecy was in 1346—and of course references to such ancient battles seem to make the land itself timeless, contrasting with the transiency of the lives of the characters in the story. The edge of the cup used for drinking mead had been worn "by the rub of whole generations of thirsty lips that had gone the way of all flesh."

Consider also that we see the characters as though from a distance, their distance from us in time and their distance in the sense that they seem to be not so much individuals as figures typifying human emotions. We are never shown complicated intellectual or philosophical speculations. The point of the story does not depend on the thinking or decision of any one or more of the characters. We see the characters from the outside, almost as though they were in a play or a ballet. We learn their names but we do not get to know them intimately. This is our introduction to the group gathered for the party:

> Nineteen persons were gathered there. Of these, five women, wearing gowns of various bright hues, sat in chairs along the wall; girls, shy and not shy, filled the window-bench; four men, including Charles Jake the hedge carpenter. Elijah New the parish-clerk, and John Pitcher, a neighboring dairyman, the shepherd's father-in-law, lolled in the settle; a young man and maid, who were blushing over tentative pour-parlers on a life-companionship, sat beneath the corner cupboard; and an elderly engaged man of fifty or upward moved restlessly about from spots where his betrothed was not to the spot where she was.

We do not learn much more about the central characters. Shepherd Fennel is hospitable and his wife is stingy. The hangman likes his grog and is thick-skinned. The condemned man is resourceful and courageous. The constable is inept. Perhaps one might say the characters are identifiable not by the nature of their thoughts but by the nature of their emotions. One and all they seem to be a part of the long human procession.

An air of irrationality pervades the story. The fireplace is described thus: "On the hearth, in front of a backbrand to give substance, blazed a fire of thorns that cracked 'like the laughter of a fool.'" This is another description: "And so the dance whizzed on with cumulative fury, the performers moving in their planet-like courses, direct and retrograde, from apogee to perigee, till the hand of the well-kicked clock at the bottom of the room had traveled over the circumference of an hour." The first passage suggests that there is something madly comical about human activities, and the second that human lives are driven, like the planets, by mysterious forces.

Irony is everywhere. The hangman drinks from a cup bearing this inscription:

> There is No Fun
> Until i Cum.

There is irony in the song that asks God's mercy on the soul of a man unjustly condemned to death. And there is irony in the hangman's confronting the condemned but not knowing who he is, and in the general mistaking of the third stranger for the condemned man.

With few exceptions, the characters are unintentionally comic. Shepherdess Fennel plans the sort of party that will keep the guests entertained but not make them ravenously hungry or thirsty—but the dancing gets out of hand and she is unable to prevent a run on her larder. There is something almost wild about the movements of the young fiddler—"his fingers were so small and short as to necessitate a constant shifting for the high notes, from which he scrambled back to the first position with sounds of unmixed purity of tone." The engaged man of fifty is incongruous, and, as the constable, he is like one of the low characters in Shakespeare, impressed with the dignity of the law but not having himself the poise and authority necessary to enforce it with dignity.

> The engaged man of fifty stepped quavering out from the wall, his betrothed beginning to sob on the back of the chair.
> "You are a sworn constable?"
> "I be, Sir."
> "Then pursue the criminal at once, with assistance, and bring him back here. He can't have gone far."
> "I will, Sir, I will—when I've got my staff. I'll go home and get it, and come sharp here, and start in a body."
> "Staff!—never mind your staff; the man'll be gone!"
> "But I can't do nothing without my staff—can I, William and John, and Charles Jake? No; for there's the king's royal crown painted on en in yaller and gold, and the lion and the unicorn. . . ."

And on he goes. Finally persuaded that the pursuit should be immediate, the constable leads the men out onto the dangerous terrain. When he finds the man he believes to be the condemned man, he says,

> "Your money or your life!"
> "No, no," whispered John Pitcher. " 'Tisn't our side ought to say that. That's the doctrine of vagabonds like him, and we be on the side of the law."
> "Well, well," replied the constable, impatiently; "I must say something, mustn't I? and if you had all the weight o' this undertaking upon your mind, perhaps you'd say the wrong thing, too!—Prisoner at the bar, surrender in the name of the Father—the Crown, I mane!"

What is the intention of Hardy's irony? Presumably it is a way of saying that so much incongruity and irrationality are comic and pathetic, especially when viewed, as they are in "The Three Strangers," against the backdrop of a universe no one understands.

Hardy is often discussed as a writer who makes much of *atmosphere*, and perhaps I should make a comment about atmosphere in "The Three Strangers." Atmosphere can be a misleading term because it means more than the description of a physical setting. In "The Three Strangers," atmosphere is not merely the lonely cottage and the rugged landscape, it is the author's dramatized view of the lives of his characters. The atmosphere expresses his ironic view of the human situation, and his sympathy. For clearly "The Three Strangers" is not a bitter or cynical story. If a single word had to be used to clarify its tone the word would be *pathos*. Atmosphere helps generate the tone of the story. And as I have suggested, the chief clue to understanding this tone is cosmic irony.

At the beginning I said that usually a writer has a subject matter and themes that continue to engage him. If we read Dickens or Henry James or William Faulkner we come to recognize what the Dickens "world" is like, or the James "world," or the Faulkner "world." The same is true of Hardy. Let us take a look at "Channel Firing," one of his most famous poems:

> That night your great guns, unawares,
> Shook all our coffins as we lay,
> And broke the chancel window-squares,
> We thought it was the Judgement-day
>
> And sat upright. While drearisome
> Arose the howl of wakened hounds:
> The mouse let fall the altar-crumb,
> The worms drew back into their
>   mounds,
>
> The glebe cow drolled. Till God called,
>   "No;
> It's gunnery practice out at sea
> Just as before you went below;
> The world is as it used to be:
>
> "All nations striving strong to make
> Red war yet redder. Mad as hatters
> They do no more for Christes sake
> Than you who are helpless in such matters.
>
> "That this is not the judgement-hour
> For some of them's a blessed thing,

> For if it were they'd have to scour
> Hell's floor for so much threatening ....
>
> "Ha, ha. It will be warmer when
> I blow the trumpet (if indeed
> I ever do; for you are men,
> And rest eternal sorely need)."
>
> So down we lay again. "I wonder,
> Will the world ever saner be,"
> Said one, "than when He sent us under
> In our indifferent century!"
>
> And many a skeleton shook his head.
> "Instead of preaching forty year,"
> My neighbor Parson Thirdly said,
> "I wish I had stuck to pipes and beer."
>
> Again the guns disturbed the hour,
> Roaring their readiness to avenge,
> As far inland as Stourton Tower,
> And Camelot, and starlit Stonehenge.

In this poem Hardy posits a deity, but notice that he is whimsical. God laughs in saying the guns booming at sea should not be mistaken for judgment day. He adds there may never be a judgment day. The poem implies that the world never changes. The hounds howl, the mice nibble and the cow drools—and men fight. The poem was written in 1914 but things were no different during the Roman occupation of England or during the days of King Arthur. The war of 1914 is viewed against the long backdrop of history and against an indifferent cosmos. "Channel Firing" is another instance of cosmic irony.

Cosmic irony is everywhere in Hardy's fiction and poetry. As a matter of fact, it was rather common in nineteenth century literature. Undoubtedly there were many reasons why it was common. For one thing, the doctrine of evolution implied that man was a chance phenomenon in the universe, a product of what Darwin called "natural selection." To be a chance phenomenon and to have evolved from a lower species was humbling, and inevitably writers began to see the human being not only in terms of his own instinctive estimate of his importance but in relation to his part in the history of the universe.

Since Hardy makes so much of cosmic irony perhaps we should ask ourselves whether or not it is a good or a bad thing to see our preoccupations constantly in such a way. Obviously this way of looking at ourselves can be a corrective for self-centeredness. The quality of deadly earnestness that sometimes gets into our lives will seem foolish and excessive so viewed. However, there may also be a danger in cosmic irony. It may be true that the universe is indifferent to us, and certainly our lives are brief, as Hardy insists. On the other hand, if what happens to us is not important, then nothing is important. Our lives are lived in a social context, with civilization as the immediate backdrop. Self-preservation and our need of a sense of significance require that we take our affairs seriously. But at whatever point our self-centeredness tends to become excessive we can afford to take the longer view, to remember that our affairs can be viewed against the backdrop of history and of eternity. Hardy's "The Three Strangers" is an example of cosmic irony. As a story it does not investigate or evaluate the view of the cosmic ironist, but anyone reading the story should want to raise the question for himself.

In conclusion, I should ask whether or not "The Three Strangers" is a successful story. The term "successful" is relative. On the level of plot it holds the reader's interest. On several occasions "The Three Strangers" has been dramatized, as a stage play and for television. It is well paced, it has suspense and is generally exciting. It also has humor. But what about the level of meaning, of theme? Any plot, comic or otherwise, could be treated in a similar way, from a similar perspective of time and space, and be made to take on the same meaning. There is no inevitable connection between the action or plot and meaning. The meaning the story is made to carry seems superimposed and therefore is arbitrary. To this extent, "The Three Strangers" is not wholly successful.

---

# LEGEND AND SYMBOL IN HARDY'S "THE THREE STRANGERS"

## James L. Roberts

In a recent article, William Van O'Connor maintained that "Writers tend to have a persistent view of things throughout their poetry or fiction, and knowing their work as a whole one can often get a clue to the meaning of any individual part of their work."[1] Using this approach, O'Connor forced Hardy's "The Three Strangers" into the established pattern of cosmic irony—"seeing human affairs not as they appear to human participants but from great distances of time and space. A human struggle viewed close up has intensity; viewed from a great distance the struggle will seem rather pointless, for time and space cause any human concern to dwindle into insignificance."[2] Several aspects of the story, however, do not easily fit this pattern; Albert Guerard's belief that "Hardy's novels,

[1] O'Connor, "Cosmic Irony in Hardy's 'The Three Strangers,'" *The English Journal*, XLVII (May, 1958), 249.
[2] O'Connor, p. 250.

read in sequence, are by no means uniformly gloomy"[3] may be a more accurate approach to "The Three Strangers."

The story of the condemned man, Timothy Summers, is widespread "in the country about Higher Crowstairs." In fact, Hardy presents the story as a well-known legend, an integral part of the lives of the people. Though the cosmic irony theory suggests that men's actions will seem pointless when viewed from a great distance, Hardy indicates the condemned man's struggle has an intensity and meaning that have not "dwindled into insignificance," even after fifty years. If the story had been forgotten or if the legend had involved a pessimistic view of life, then one could interpret the entire narrative in terms of cosmic irony. However, neither of these were the case. The simple story evolved into a legend and then, due to Hardy's craft, into art.

To understand the meaning of the legend, it is necessary to understand the values of the people among whom it grew. Throughout the story, Hardy emphasized that the lives and values of the people are dependent upon the country and climate around Higher Crowstairs. Since the time of "Senlac and Crecy," these people have been involved in an eternal struggle with the country and its long inimical seasons. This struggle with the elements has affected their lives which, in turn, have been imbued with an elemental quality—a quality of stubborn endurance that relies upon a firm grasp of the fundamentals of life. The values the people look for are courage, resourcefulness, shrewdness, and composure. Timothy Summers possessed these qualities, and his every act became meaningful to the people.

His original act—taking a sheep to feed his family—captured their sympathy. To hang such a man is perversion of justice; to escape from such a punishment is a sign of courage and resourcefulness. His subsequent encounter with the hangman showed his shrewdness and composure, and his ultimate escape indicates the victory of the simple man over the injustice of the law. Therefore, through his adventures, the condemned man became a representative of the simple man's triumph over injustice and a legendary symbol of those values or qualities necessary for preservation in the country around Higher Crowstairs. That these meanings are inherent in the condemned man's actions is immediately demonstrable through the manner in which the shepherds protected him from the law, and ultimately, through their retelling of his story until it became legend.

These values account for the story of the condemned man being made into legend. In transposing the legend into art, Hardy universalizes its meaning by the use of symbols. In his imaginative recreation of the legend, Hardy used Christian symbols so as to correlate the legend of the condemned man with the Christian legend. This correlation thereby emphasizes the inherent values in the condemned man's story, and by the use of this analogy, a further level of significance is added to the latter legend.

[3] Guerard, *Thomas Hardy*, p. 2.

The symbols are well integrated into the story and do not demand attention for a full appreciation of the story. However, the frequent use of symbol and the repeated use of the mystical number "three" can hardly be viewed as accidental. There are three strangers, three stanzas of the hangman's song, and three knocks upon the door which is opened to the third stranger during the third stanza of the song. The action takes place at the PASTORAL dwelling of some SHEPHERDS who are celebrating a CHRISTENING. Their house, in which a fire of thorns burns brightly, is located at the CROSS of the roads. A condemned man, victim of an injustice, appears at the cross of the roads, approaches the house, kneels and drinks a "copious draught" of water, and knocks. (In the dramatized version, *The Three Wayfarers*, the man is thirty years old.) The door is readily opened, and he is offered all the comforts of home—a pipe, the choice seat by the fire, and the family's communal cup with the engraving:

> There is No Fun
> Until i Cum.

The second stranger arrives—a man in cinder grey—but his presence is resented. He is described in terms befitting the Devil (Guerard believes that "Hardy introduced an at least metaphorical Devil into three of his stories,"[4]) and the hangman's profession makes him a foil to the condemned man. When the hangman arrives at the christening, it is the condemned man who offers the communal cup to the hangman, who, in turn, quaffs it down and blatantly calls for more. After he reveals his profession in the third verse, the simple shepherds formed a circle around the hangman whom they "seemed to take for the Prince of Darkness himself." Such an open conflict enhances the values already inherent in the legend, especially when the conflict is seen as one between these two opposing forces and the persecuted innocent comes out the victor.

There seems, therefore, to be a rather clear analogy to the Christian myth, but we should in no way view the condemned man as a Christ figure. Rather, by using this analogy to an established legend, Hardy was able to emphasize the legendary characteristics of his story and the basic values inherent in his legend. Furthermore, by making the comparison to an already established legend, Hardy establishes the condemned man's encounter with the hangman as a struggle of great import.

In conclusion, Hardy was concerned with the creation of a legend, the values of that legend and its continuation, and the meaning of the legend viewed from a distance of fifty years. Rather than being a story about cosmic irony, "The Three Strangers" illustrates by the use of legend and symbol that the endeavors of certain human beings have an innate importance—an importance that increases rather than diminishes with time.

---

[4] Guerard, p. 3.

# A GLOSSARY OF USEFUL TERMS

*Action* The events that take place in a story. These may be either external (those events that are narrated or dramatized) or internal (the thoughts of one or several characters).

*Allegory* A genre in which characters, events, and, at times, setting represent either other characters, events, and settings, or abstract or moral qualities. *Pilgrim's Progress* and *Gulliver's Travels* are allegorical works.

*Allusion* An indirect reference to a character, event, idea, or place. An allusion often enriches the meaning or strengthens the significance of a story or a word.

*Ambiguity* The use of a word or phrase in such a way that it has a number of possible meanings. When the ambiguity is not deliberate, the result is a weakening of the effectiveness of the word or phrase. When the ambiguity is deliberate, the result may be positive, increasing the impact of the word or phrase and consequently, the entire story.

*Antagonist* The character or force that represents the opposition to the *protagonist,* for which term see below.

*Anticlimax* A sudden drop from the important to the trivial or commonplace. In a story something becomes anticlimactic when it occurs after the climax or major resolution has taken place. See also *climax*.

*Atmosphere* The prevailing mood or the feeling aroused by the different elements in a story or novel. See also *tone* and *mood*.

*Character* A character is a person in a story or novel. There are many ways to identify characters, each being dependent on the extent to which the author has identified them for us. A *flat* character is one who has little or no variety; he may be described as one dimensional. A *stereotype* is a character who has been used so often in fiction that he is recognized immediately and his traits are predictable. He may be, for instance, the strong, silent sheriff of the typical Western movie or story. A *round* character is the opposite of either a flat or stereotype one; he is a complex personality and cannot be "typed." He is, in short, very much like most human beings, a mixture of good and bad, conventional and unconventional. For an illuminating discussion of "flat" and "round" character, see E. M. Forster's *Aspects of the Novel*.

*Cliché* A term that is outworn, trite, overused; as a result of continued use, it has lost all freshness and effectiveness. Examples of trite expressions or clichés are "strong as an ox," "pretty as a picture," and "as American as apple pie." Situations and plots may also be regarded as clichés. Typical is the one in which the rich, spoiled young man learns to value love and loyalty over money only after a series of reversals and defeats.

*Climax* The culminating event or idea in a sequence or series of events or ideas; the point in a story where the fortunes of the hero or protagonist take a turn for better or worse. See also *anticlimax*.

*Closed form* A term to denote a story or a novel with a clearly defined resolution or *denouement,* for which term see below. Unlike an "open-ended" story, one with a "closed-ending" leaves very few questions in the reader's mind. There is a sense of "closure," of all loose ends being tied up, of all problems being solved. "The Minister's Black Veil," for instance, is a good example of a story with a strong sense of "closure." See also *open form* and *structure*.

*Conflict* Conflict is essential to any story or novel, for it is the narration or dramatization of conflict and its eventual resolution that create suspense and interest. Conflict may involve two opposing characters or ideas or a character and his environment. It may be external or internal, the latter usually involving the thoughts or ideas of a single character. Most often the conflict is between the *protagonist* and his *antagonist(s)*.

*Connotation* The meanings suggested by or associated with a word, rather than the literal or denotative meaning. The word "snake," for instance, has a denotative meaning, but it suggests far more. See also *denotation*.

*Denotation* The literal or exact meaning of a word or term, as opposed to the suggested or connotative meanings. Scientific writing is usually thought of as being mostly denotative, while poetry, fiction, and drama depend greatly on the connotative values given to words and phrases. See also *connotation*.

*Denouement* The final unraveling or resolution of the plot; the falling action after the climax.

*Determinism* An extreme form of *naturalism*, for which term see below. The main element of determinism is the belief that circumstances or chance or environment determines a person's fate. See also *realism* and *expressionism*.

*Deus ex machina* In Latin, literally, "god from a machine." In ancient Greek and Roman drama a deity was often brought in by stage machinery to intervene in the action. Consequently, the phrase refers to any device, character, event, or information brought in unexpectedly to resolve a conflict or situation. The sudden discovery that a character is not really a peasant but is of royal blood is an example of such a resolution.

*Dialogue* The conversation or exchange of words between or among characters in a story, novel, or play. Very often the dialogue will be the means by which the author reveals an important part of the plot or demonstrates some facet of character.

*Diction* The choice or selection of words by the author.

*Didactic* That intended to improve or instruct the reader. The superior novel or story accomplishes this instruction or improvement not by overt preaching, but by the careful arrangement on the part of the author of the various elements of the story to emphasize his thematic intent. In "The Forks," for instance, the author is attempting to instruct the reader as to the nature of "religious" faith, and he does this chiefly through characterization, symbolism, and thematic emphasis.

*Empathy* The identification of one's own feeling or personality with that of another person, often a character in fiction or drama. The ability to empathize with a character may result in a better understanding of him and his plight. Not to be confused with *sympathy*, for which term see later.

*Episode* A division of the plot, or a separate incident, usually narrated, rather than dramatized, and complete in itself. Not to be confused with *scene*, for which term see below. An episodic plot is one in which the episodes have no causal connection and simply follow one another in chronological sequence.

*Exposition* The information concerning such elements as plot, character, and previous events that enables the reader to understand clearly and appreciate fully the development and eventual climax and resolution of the story, novel, or play. Exposition that is "natural" and does not seem gratuitously provided is a mark of a mature and skilled author.

*Expressionism* A late nineteenth and early twentieth-century movement in the arts, especially in drama, which attempted, chiefly by means of symbols, to give objective expression to inner feelings and emotions. Directly opposed to *realism* and *naturalism,* for which terms see below, expressionism relies mainly on distortion and other nonrealistic means to portray the inner life of the characters. Expressionistic fiction, for instance, makes great use of dream sequences and hallucinatory experiences.

*Figurative language* Language which is nonliteral or nondenotative, and contains many figures of speech, such as metaphor, simile, and personification, and employs much *imagery,* for which term see below. Figurative language seeks not simply to convey information, but also to evoke responses. See also *connotation* and *denotation.*

*Flashback* An interruption in the continuity of a story, novel, or play by the dramatization or narration of an earlier episode or scene. A story which begins with a dying man recalling his early years might have a series of flashbacks. See also *in medias res.*

*Foil* A character who is directly contrasted with another, either by behavior, appearance, or attitude toward life, or by all or a combination of these. To be most effective, a foil should illuminate the reader's conception of the character against whom he is set. Also he should be not *flat,* but a character in his own right. Laertes, for example, is often cited as the foil of Hamlet.

*Foreshadowing* A hint to the reader concerning a future action or development. When used skillfully, foreshadowing creates suspense; when used unskillfully, it merely reveals, prematurely, what the reader should not know until much later and thus lessens the impact of the story.

*Form* The ordering of all the elements of a work of art (poem, novel, play, picture) into an integrated, interrelated whole. Form should not be confused with *structure,* for which term see below, which usually refers to the more formal or mechanical arrangements of the parts of the work. Thus, *form* might be seen as the soul of a work; *structure,* the body.

*Genre* In French, literally, a kind or type; thus, in critical terminology a particular type or class, such as drama, poetry, fiction.

*Imagery* Often a collective term for figures of speech, it is also used as a broad designation for images— that is, any use of *figurative language* to suggest visual pictures. Very often an author will use a consistent thread of imagery to unify the story or to illuminate the theme. In Hamlet, for example, the imagery of disease is a pervasive one, while in Hardy's "The Three Strangers" religious imagery predominates. See also *connotation* and *denotation.*

*In medias res* (Latin) In the middle of things; a term used in the criticism of fiction to describe narratives that open in the middle of events, rather than at the beginning of them. See also *flashback*.

*Irony* Distinctions are often made between irony of statement, situational irony, and dramatic irony. *Irony of statement* refers to a sarcastic or humorous manner of discourse in which what is literally said is meant to express its opposite. For example, tone of voice may reveal that "You are a bright boy" is to be interpreted as "You are not very bright." *Situational irony* involves a situation, event, or pairing in which the main elements are emotionally or rationally incompatible because of contrast, conflict, or surprise. *Gulliver's Travels* makes extensive use of situational irony. In *dramatic irony* the audience is made aware of something a character or participant does not know.

*Mood* The emotional effect or feeling that the story evokes in the reader; not to be confused with *tone*, for which term see below. See also *atmosphere*.

*Motif* A recurrent image, idea, or incident, the constant repetition of which supports the meaning or theme. Various references to music, for instance, form a motif in "Sonny's Blues," while the word "blue" in "The Blue Hotel" is repeated often enough for the reader to sense Crane's deliberate use of the word in order to support the thematic intent of the story.

*Motivation* The presentation of the actions of characters as plausible by providing, directly or indirectly, convincing psychological causation for their actions.

*Naturalism* An emphatic form of *realism* reflecting the influence nineteenth-century biological and social sciences had upon literary method. Emile Zola's *Le Roman Expérimental* (1875) provided the movement with its manifesto. Affected by the ideas of Darwin and Marx, among others, naturalism has been described as realism plus a deterministic philosophy. The following qualities are often found in naturalism, although many naturalistic works will lack one or more of them:

1. A detached scientific objectivity. The strict naturalist presents his material without authorial comment and without passing moral judgments.

2. Freedom of choice regarding subject matter. Freedom to include the commonplace, the sensational, the sordid, and the unpleasant.

3. Freedom of method. Rejection of plot as artificial and "unnatural." The presentation of a "slice of life," in all its detail, in order to demonstrate the effect of heredity and environment as the forces molding the fate of the characters.

4. Social purpose. Conflicts often involve characters not only as individuals but also as representatives of social groups. Sympathetic depiction of underprivileged social groups, such as in Zola's *Germinal* or Hauptmann's *The Weavers,* often gives naturalistic works a social as well as an aesthetic objective. See also *determinism, expressionism,* and *realism.*

*Open form* A term used synonymously with "open ended" to denote a story or a novel whose ending does not present a final resolution or *denouement*, for which term see above. In an open-ended story, the reader is left with many questions unanswered, but, since this same situation applies in life itself, the reader is not left with a sense of frustration or dissatisfaction. The open form depends for its effectiveness on the author's skillful presentation and development of the various elements rather than on an ending that "ties up" all loose ends. See also *closed form* and *structure*.

*Parable* A short fictitious story that illustrates a moral attitude or a religious principle. See also *allegory*.

*Persona* Commonly, a character in a drama, novel, or story. Also used in the psychological and critical sense for a mask, or the character or personality assumed by the author to present, in disguise, his private voice and attitudes.

*Plot* The scheme or pattern of the events, incidents, or situations of a story. Plot is not a mere succession of events, but an organized series linked by causal relationships.

*Point of view* Sometimes called the angle of narration, point of view has a specific meaning in the technique of fiction; it refers to the angle from which the story is told. The most common angles are first person and third person. In the first person point of view, the story is told by one of the characters. A tale told in the third person is presented by someone outside the story. If the writer chooses the first person point of view, he may employ the protagonist or leading character, or one or more of the minor characters. If he chooses the third person point of view, he may write as the "omniscient" author, revealing not only the words, actions, and appearances but also the mental activities (thoughts, emotions, desires, and even the subconscious tendencies) of his characters in their various situations. Or the writer can present his material in the third person "limited," confining the narrative to the experience of a reflector character who reveals only what he knows of the characters and their action in the narrative. A more complex angle of vision is the "multiple" point of view in which the circumstances of a single situation are seen through the eyes of more than one narrator.

*Protagonist* Originally, the actor who played the chief part in a Greek drama. In fiction, the leading character or the center of interest in a given narrative. See also *antagonist*.

*Realism* Writing which attempts to present life as it is, including the commonplace, the average, and the unpleasant. It differs from naturalism in that it employs more selection in the choice of material and more organization in its presentation. See also *determinism, expressionism,* and *naturalism*.

*Scene* A scene is that part of the plot that is dramatized rather than narrated; the characters act and talk. Not to be confused with *episode*, for which term see above.

*Setting* The physical location in which the actions of a story take place. This does not always necessitate the elaborate use of description; the setting of a story may be wholly concrete although a specific geographical location is not revealed. (See "Margins.") Setting may assume a relatively important place in the effect of a story. (See "Sonny's Blues.") It can be presented obliquely and impressionistically. In order to achieve a special effect, the author can employ setting to convey a certain *tone*. (See "The Story of a Panic.")

*Stream of consciousness* A method of writing in which the author objectifies the inward thoughts, feelings, and sensations of the characters in order to supplement or replace dialogue and narrated action. The term was coined by William James in *Principles of Psychology* (1890) to describe the flux of mental imagery as it ranges from consciousness to unconsciousness. Writers who use this method—James Joyce and Virginia Woolf, for example—frequently employ *interior monologue* to reveal the minds and personalities of their characters. The method involves a flowing association of ideas and images, frequently without punctuation, logical transitions, or conventional syntax, to demonstrate the fluid and ceaseless activity of the mind.

*Structure* The mechanical arrangement of the parts of a work of art, not to be confused with *form,* for which term see above.

*Style* The author's *style,* or *mode of expression,* is the linguistic aspect of the narrative and involves language in a wide sense—diction, rhythm, figurative language, sound, and sentence patterns. Style should suit, or grow out of, the theme and plot of a piece of fiction and be a part of its total meaning.

*Symbol* Something which stands for or is emblematic of something else. A concrete object or an image used to represent another object, emotion, or abstract idea.

*Sympathy* A mutual liking or understanding based on a similarity of emotions or other qualities. Not to be confused with *empathy,* for which term see earlier.

*Theme* The central idea elaborated in a story. [There may also be minor themes.]

*Tone* The author's attitude toward his material as it can be inferred from his work. Not to be confused with *atmosphere* or *mood,* for which terms see above. The author's tone may be light, serious, ironic, compassionate, sympathetic, or unsympathetic.

*Verisimilitude* Likeness to truth and actuality produced by multiplying recognizable details and familiar situations, and by employing normal motivation to achieve credibility.

Baldwin, James, 10
Barthelme, Donald, 330
*Big Boy Leaves Home*, 56
*Blue Hotel, The*, 99
Boll, Heinrich, 87
Booth, Wayne, 362
Borges, Jorge Luis, 95

Cather, Willa, 3
*Christmas Song*, 339
*Clean, Well-Lighted Place, A*, 51
*Completion of Personality, A*, 375
*Cosmic Irony in Hardy's "The Three Strangers,"* 398
Crane, Stephen, 99

Ellison, Ralph, 280, 375

*Flying Home*, 280
*Forks, The*, 250
Forster, E. M., 232

*Gladius Dei*, 221
*Good Man Is Hard to Find, A*, 267
*Gym Period*, 335

Hardy, Thomas, 203
Hawthorne, Nathaniel, 307
*He*, 36
Hemingway, Ernest, 51
*Hue and Cry*, 152
Hughes, Langston, 339

Isaacs, Neil, 393

Jackson, Blyden, 382
James, Henry, 190
Joyce, James, 185

Lawrence, D. H., 318
*Legend and Symbol in Hardy's "The Three Strangers,"* 407
*Life for Phoenix*, 393
*Loves of Franklin Ambrose, The*, 296

McCullers, Carson, 342
McPherson, James Alan, 152
*Magic Barrel, The*, 138
Malamud, Bernard, 138
Mann, Thomas, 221
*Man with the Knives, The*, 87
*Margins*, 330
*Minister's Black Veil, The*, 307
Moore, Brian, 122

*Next Door*, 44

Oates, Joyce Carol, 296
O'Connor, Flannery, 267

Porter, Katherine Anne, 36
Powers, J. F., 250

*Richard Wright in a Moment of Truth*, 382
Rilke, Ranier Maria, 335
Roberts, James L., 407
*Rocking-Horse Winner, The*, 318
Roy, Gabrielle, 262

*Shape of the Sword, The*, 95
*Sojourner, The*, 342
*Sonny's Blues*, 10
*Story of a Panic, The*, 232

*Three Strangers, The*, 203
*Tree of Knowledge, The*, 190
*Types of Narration*, 362

*Uncle T*, 122

Van O'Connor, William, 398
Vonnegut, Kurt, Jr., 44

*Wagner Matinee, A*, 3
Welty, Eudora, 350
*Wilhelm*, 262
*Worn Path, A*, 350
Wright, Richard, 56

# an index of authors and titles

ABOUT THE AUTHOR

MICHAEL TIMKO is Chairman of the Department of English at Queens College of the City University of New York. He received his M.A. at the University of Missouri and his Ph.D. at the University of Wisconsin. A specialist in Victorian literature, he is the author of *Innocent Victorian: The Satiric Poetry of Arthur Hugh Clough* (1966). He has also edited *Hoopdriver's Holiday,* a play by H. G. Wells (1964), and, with Clinton F. Oliver, *Thirty-Eight Short Stories* (1968).

### A NOTE ON THE TYPE

The text of this book is set in Caledonia, a Linotype face designed by W. A. Dwiggins. It belongs to the family of printing types called "modern face" by printers—a term used to mark the change in style of type-letters that occurred about 1800. Caledonia borders on the general design of Scotch Modern, but is more freely drawn than that letter.

The book was composed by Colonial Press Inc., Clinton, Mass. Printed and bound by Halliday Lithograph Corp., West Hanover, Mass.